SCARRED *Hearts*

THE COMPLETE DUET

SCARRED *Hearts*

THE COMPLETE DUET

HOLLY CASTE

Scarred Hearts
Paperback Edition

Love N. Books Press
An Imprint of Wolfpack Publishing
1707 E. Diana Street
Tampa, FL 33610

www.lovenbookspress.com

Scarred Hearts was originally self published in 2022 by Holly Caste.

Edited by My Brother's Editor

Paperback ISBN 979-8-89567-657-8
Ebook ISBN 979-8-89567-656-1
LCCN 2026938450

To the man who inspired the character Mateo
and
To those who see a reflection of themselves in Ellie—
the voiceless,
the confused,
the desperately seeking love from an external source because they're so ashamed to love the messy part of themselves.

This one is for us.

Author's Note

Scarred Hearts is not for everyone. This is not a typical romance novel, and a big portion of this story centers around healing. One of the intentions behind this book is to explore the complexities, frustrations, and lingering effects of emotional abuse.

These characters are flawed, and all of them will most likely piss you off at one point or another.

The journey is raw and turbulent, but the fulfilling destination is worth the ride.

TRIGGER WARNINGS:

Explicit language, sex scenes, emotional abuse, mental health struggles, self-harm, assault, grief, addiction, suicidal ideation, medical concerns/hospitalization, alcohol and marijuana use.

SCARRED *Hearts*

THE COMPLETE DUET

Year One

CHAPTER ONE

Ellie

AUGUST

It's been two years since I last cut myself.

I'm pissed that I even started.

I hate these scars.

Hunter mindlessly runs his hand down my arm, his fingertips brushing over the faded white lines on my left wrist, causing me to internally cringe. He doesn't notice my moment of tension. His mind is focused elsewhere.

Pressing his lips to my neck, he then whispers, "I love you, Ellie."

I hate myself.

Well, most of myself.

I often feel as though I'm nothing but broken pieces strewn together by threads of anxiety and desperation. "I love you too," I say back to Hunter as he continues to pepper me with kisses.

He has me seated on my desk—my new dorm desk—with my legs parted so he can stand between them. I know what he's doing. He's attempting to distract me from my thoughts.

If only it were that simple.

But as Hunter's lips roam around my throat, my erratic pulse pounding through my veins, I can't quiet the trepidation screaming at me. I don't deal with change well. Even if it seems like a positive change, all I do is wait for the next shoe to drop, knowing that something bad will happen.

I can feel Hunter getting hard at the same time his touch becomes more tender, but my brain is in an endless flurry of thoughts.

My eyes dart around the room. My side is bare and bland, with stacks of unopened boxes haphazardly scattered about. I haven't met my roommate yet, but judging by her section, I assume she moved all of her belongings in. Bright colors and bold patterns ooze their way into my untouched side.

"I know you're nervous about moving in and starting college," Hunter says against my skin.

Nervous? No.

More than nervous. I'm anxious.

There's a difference for me.

I go to correct him, but he speaks before I can. "But this is going to be a fresh start for you. For us. We need this, angel."

A fresh start does sound nice.

Hunter begins leaning his weight against my rigid body. "Just relax."

"I—" Before I can get the word *can't* out, his lips are molding to mine.

Convincing myself to ease up, little by little, I soften in his hold. My arms wrap around his neck, and his hands sneak under my shirt, inching their way upward until he connects with my bra.

"Hey!" The door swings open, and we break apart. "Oh shit. Am I interrupting something?" a girl, who I assume is my roommate, asks. Flustered, I hop off my desk and shake my head in response. "Are you sure? Because I can come back later."

"No, you're fine," I say, slightly out of breath.

The girl moves further into our dorm room. "I'm Bree. I live here too. Are you Elena?"

"That's me." I run my fingers through my hair to smooth it out. "You can call me Ellie."

There's a beat of awkward silence as Bree glances over at Hunter.

"And I'm Ellie's boyfriend, Hunter," he announces, politely shaking her hand. After the exchange of pleasantries, he focuses back on me. "I'm going to run down and get the last of your boxes from the car."

"Want help?"

"Not a chance, angel." He gives me a small peck on my forehead before leaving Bree and me alone. Having her walk in on Hunter and me making out was probably not the best first impression.

With a faint blush spotting my cheeks, I return to unpacking.

Bree hangs up a bronze-colored strand of phases of the moon above her headboard, unbothered by our first encounter. "What's your sun sign?"

"Um…Scorpio," I answer, taking out a wrinkled pair of leggings from one of my boxes.

"That's so amazing, because I'm a Leo, and I need a water sign to balance out all my fire!" She flutters her way over to me. "Do you want help unpacking?"

"Sure." My lips pull upward at her kindness.

Bree looks exactly how I would imagine someone to look if one of the first questions out of their mouth was asking about my zodiac sign. She has wild, dark, curly hair that's messily flowing past her shoulders and stunning hazel eyes. She has a septum piercing and random tattoos sprinkled on her body. She moves too fast for me to figure out what type of designs her tattoos are. I think the one inside her arm is a Chinese food container. Or is it a slice of bread?

"What about over here?" Bree inquires, snapping me out of deciphering the art drawn on her. She's holding a quote board in her hands, and my face heats up with embarrassment. Mom bought a corkboard and decked it out in cliché quotes like, "Reach for the moon. Even if you miss, you'll land among the stars." I have no idea why she made it, but I would've felt like an asshole if I didn't bring it, so I reluctantly packed it.

"Do you want to hang this up over your desk?" Bree is being way too kind about my cringe-worthy corkboard.

"No, that's okay. I don't think I'm going to hang that up anywhere."

She shrugs and tosses it to the side.

My attention swings to the doorway where Hunter reemerges with two boxes stacked on top of each other. I dart over to help him.

"When's your birthday?" Bree asks Hunter as he makes his way into the room.

"Uh…November eighth. Why?"

"Double Scorpios in a relationship. That must be intense!" Bree giggles as she pulls out my clothing.

Hunter looks at me, confused, and I smile, shaking my head because I have no clue what she's talking about. She might as well be speaking a foreign language to me when talking about astrology.

Hunter goes on to make polite conversation with Bree. He has the ability to be very charming and make anyone comfortable when he wants to, which is one of the reasons he won me over.

As they continue to chat, I admire Hunter's dirty-blond hair and captivating, bright blue eyes.

"How long have the two of you been together?" Bree asks.

"A little over two years," Hunter replies, grinning as he glances my way.

"We went to high school together, but Hunter's a year older, so he started college last year," I chime in.

"Was that tough?"

"Yeah, I guess you could say that." I look over at Hunter to get a read on him. His stance is relaxed, and his lips are still curled in a small smile, so I continue. "This past school year was a little challenging. While he was here at the University of Connecticut, I spent my senior year of high school hours away from him in our hometown right outside of Boston. The distance was hard on us, but I like to think we're a stronger couple now because of it." Happiness coats my last few words.

"I'm sure you guys are glad to be back in school together. I started dating my girlfriend, Amber, a few months ago." Bree begins to tell me her life story as she continues to shuffle through my belongings. Her immediate comfort around me, as if we've been friends forever, puts me at ease. "We met at a crystal shop called Go Sage Yourself. It's in California. Oh, that's where I'm from. I forgot to mention that." She chuckles. "But anyway, Amber's going to college in New York to study filmmaking."

"What's your major, Bree?" Hunter asks as he checks out her side of the room. The walls are covered in drawings, rainbow flags, and pictures of her and who I imagine is Amber.

"Fine arts."

"I see," he states as his focus lands on her *Smash the Patriarchy* drawing. He turns to me and rolls his eyes without Bree noticing.

"What about you, Ellie? What's your major?" Bree asks.

"Undecided. I don't have my heart on a specific major. I'm taking a wide range of classes this year to see if it leads me to anything."

"Not settling. I like that."

"You'll figure it out," Hunter says as he comes from behind, wrapping his arms around me.

"Eventually." I allow myself a few seconds to settle into his hold. He can be so comforting when he wants to be. He's like this most of the time, and today I could use an extra amount of love, so I give myself a moment to meld into his compassion.

"Oh my god! What's *this*?" Bree exclaims as she pulls out my high school uniform.

Immediately jumping out of Hunter's embrace, I grab the hideous maroon and gray plaid skirt from Bree's hands. "How did that get in there?" I turn to Hunter, who's hysterically laughing.

"I threw it in there as a joke," he says.

"Is this some kinky shit that I shouldn't be touching?" Bree asks, chuckling, joining in with Hunter.

"No," I try to clarify. "It's our old uniform. We went to Catholic high school." I shove it into the back of a drawer.

Hunter rubs my back, but this time, my spine becomes rigid. "I'm sorry. I was just having a little fun with you."

"It's fine."

Thankfully, his phone rings, and the focus goes off me and onto his quick call. There are a few *all rights* and *yeahs* until he says, "Be there in ten," and hangs up. "They need my help moving furniture at the frat, and then I have to go pick up stuff for tonight," Hunter says to me.

"What's tonight?" Bree interjects.

"Party at my frat house. First one of the year. It's going to be a big one. You coming?" Hunter asks both of us.

"I'm not sure," I say before Bree can answer. "I wanted to spend the day settling in and looking for a job."

"A job? You worked your ass off all summer. You don't need a job."

Did I work over the summer? Yes. Did I work my ass off? No. I worked a few days a week at the local bookshop. Working a little bit this semester isn't going to kill me. I like knowing there's extra cushion to fall back on. I don't come from a trust fund family like Hunter does. Although I'll never bring that point up to him.

"Come on, Ellie," he pleads. "None of my brothers believe you exist because you didn't visit me at all last year. Please come to the party tonight."

Biting the inside of my cheek, the slight guilt trip he's giving me is enough to make me cave.

I suppose I could always search for a job another day.

Not wanting to start the school year off with friction between us, I force myself to perk up. "Fine. I guess it's time for your invisible girlfriend to make an appearance," I playfully respond.

"Good." Hunter grins.

"Hmm..." Bree says. "The Greek system really isn't my thing, but parties are. I'll keep an open mind and join."

"All right. Cool." Hunter turns to me. "Now, what do you need help with before I leave?"

I stare at my mountain of boxes, wishing they could unpack themselves. "Um..." My head dizzies with overwhelm. "I don't think I need help with anything."

"Don't worry, I'm here if she needs help." Bree flashes Hunter a smile.

But there's a beat of hesitation before he offers one back. I can't get a clear read on which emotion just flickered in his eyes because he's quick to mask it.

"I'll call you when I'm done," he says to me before giving me a kiss. "I love you, angel."

"I love you too."

CHAPTER TWO

Ellie

After an hour, Bree and I stand next to each other, admiring our dorm room. "I think it looks great!" she states, proudly putting her hands on her hips.

"I agree!"

"The vibe our room is giving is just so cool. It's artsy, hippie aesthetic on my side and clean, indie aesthetic on yours."

I laugh. "I had no idea what to call my style, but that works."

"Oh yeah. You're totally clean, indie girl vibes. I mean, look at your perfectly curated record collection." She gestures to a shelf hanging above my desk.

"That's not even half of it."

My gaze dances over the colorful, thin spines of my records, strumming my heart with their charm.

Music is my lifeline and helps me process everything.

Music has always been my way to drown out the world. I never understood why it isn't considered a type of love language. It should be. When a person shares their favorite songs with someone, it's like they share a part of their story. When I struggle to express myself, I find my voice through the humming of instruments and the poetic lyrics. I can find chapters of my story in the soft whispers of a cello or the distorted screams of guitar riffs.

"And," Bree continues, snapping me out of my thoughts. "Those paintings over there are *so* indie aesthetic. Once they're hung up, your side will be finished, and our room will be complete." Bree gestures to the two canvases on my bed, which are the last things on my to-do list, but I need Hunter's assistance hanging them up. I send him a text to let him know I'll need his assistance as Bree admires them. One is a picture of the Eiffel Tower, and the other is of Monet's garden. "Have you ever been to France?"

"I wish," I state, slipping my phone into my back pocket. "I've been unhealthily obsessed with France ever since I was a little girl. I dreamed of going since I first read the book *Madeline*."

"Oh, I remember those books! The girl at the boarding school who wore a chic beret everywhere, right?"

"Yep," I say, chuckling. "When I was little, I would pretend to be her, living in a boarding school in Paris. I'd imagine myself escaping my house and running through the Parisian streets, carefree and full of wonder." I let myself linger in the memory for a beat, but then my smile fades as I realize why I'd fantasize about that in the first place.

I needed an escape. A place where my mind could go and feel safe, since my real childhood was clouded by bouts of crying or explosive fights almost every night.

My parents, both deeply depressed and deeply angry, found comfort in alcohol.

They hid it pretty well. *Functional* alcoholics. The kind where, to the outside world, we seemed like your average, everyday white-picket fence family. But the walls of our house hid their secret, and I kept quiet too.

"Some girls in our hallway wanted to head to the dining hall for lunch. Wanna join?" Bree asks.

"I'm actually a little tired, so I'm going to hang here. I'll go next time." My social battery is draining, as is my energy from moving in, so I sit down on my mattress. It's a little stiff as I wiggle around, trying to get comfortable.

"Okay. I'll be back in a little bit. See you later, roomie!" With an extra bounce in her step, she saunters away.

Bree's joyful energy is infectious, and a resounding sense of gratitude flutters in my chest, glad that the universe paired me with Bree. I've heard of some college roommate horror stories and had been worried I'd experience something similar.

Adjusting myself on my bed, I suddenly get jabbed in the back of my hip. "Ouch." I glance over my shoulder to see my two canvases poking me.

Picking up the one with the Eiffel Tower detailed on the coarse material, my fingers skim over the bumpy texture of the painting. I try to admire the gentle brushstrokes, but my stomach sinks with a sudden feeling of impending doom.

As long as I can remember, my dream was to run away to France. But I could never *actually* do that. I'm only two hours from home and had multiple anxiety attacks over moving away.

Not to mention, I've been feeling an overwhelming sense of guilt and fear of leaving Mom alone.

I thought that after Dad died, she would get better. She didn't.

I feel like a shit daughter because I wasn't able to help Dad, and now I'm not able to help Mom either. I'm angry at both of them. I don't want to be, but I am. If it were anyone else in the world, I'd have immense empathy for them, but for some reason, I can't find it for my parents.

Maybe bitterness is easier than forgiveness.

The logical side of my brain knows that addiction is a horrible disease, but the child inside of me wishes my parents had found help for their illness and is resentful toward them for never doing so.

My internal screams, crying out for a savior, were deafening to me, but no one else heard them.

No one else ever noticed.

Until Hunter.

He was the only one who saw me at a time when I wished I were invisible. When I would hope and pray to disappear from this planet, Hunter spotted my shrinking presence and brought life back into my bones.

He lit me up in ways I've never experienced.

My first date, my first kiss...my second chance at life.

Closing my eyes, I suck in a deep breath, hoping it'll quell the anxiety brewing inside me. Worry takes hold of my ribcage, tightening around my lungs little by little.

I do my best to breathe.

Think of something good. Something happy. Anything.

Think of Hunter.

My hands won't stop fidgeting. I've never been on a date before, but I thought once the movie started, my nerves would calm down. I was wrong.

Glancing over at Hunter, I see him watching me. "This movie sucks," he whispers. I stifle a laugh, nodding. Honestly, I haven't been paying attention enough to even realize. "Come on," he says. "Let's get out of here." I follow his lead, and we exit the theater.

We end up walking around the huge parking lot and crossing over to a strip mall, talking and getting to know each other. I'm trying so hard to relax and come across a lot cooler than I am. Hunter tells me about his family and how they recently went to Europe. I couldn't tell you what they did in Europe because I'm too nervous to actually absorb what he's saying, but I do remember him saying something about having a brother.

"What about you? Any siblings?" Hunter asks.

"No. It's just me."

"I always wondered what it'd be like to be an only child."

"It has its pros and cons," I tell him, explaining my likes and dislikes.

Then, I somehow open up about losing Dad. I've never gone into detail about what actually happened, but somehow Hunter made me feel comfortable enough to do so.

"I'm so sorry, Ellie." He reaches out and holds my hand in his.

"It's okay."

Silence falls over us.

Great, I just made this super awkward. Who the hell talks about their dead dad on a first date?

Hunter clears his throat. "I had a sister."

My eyes bounce up to look at his, waiting for him to continue.

"Kayla. She passed away when she was three. I was seven."

"Oh my god," I gasp, bringing my free hand to my heart. There are so many questions on the tip of my tongue, I don't know which one to spit out first.

"I don't like talking about it," he says before I can speak. "I just…" He lifts up one of his shoulders. "I just wanted to let you know."

I nod, and Hunter's body relaxes.

We continue our walk, talking about more lighthearted topics, never letting go of each other's hands. It starts to drizzle, and we turn back around so that we can get back to the movie theater parking lot. We laugh as we get rained on, and for the first time in a long time, a sense of joy courses through me. I didn't think things like this actually happened in real life, and if they did, I definitely didn't think they would happen to me.

The rain gets heavier, and Hunter guides us under an awning in front of a store. We're both out of breath and drenched. I'm sure whatever little makeup I had on is now dripping down my face, and I bet my hair is a knotted, wet mess.

Hunter smiles as he observes me soaked from head to toe. "You're a lot different than I thought you'd be," he says.

My heart beats a little faster. "How so?"

Hunter takes a step closer to me, and I draw in a sharp inhale. "I don't know. But I like it." He hesitates for a moment, then places his hand on my cheek and bends down to kiss me.

Oh my god. My heart rate skyrockets so high that it might explode. This is my first kiss. Well, my first real kiss. Nate in second grade doesn't count.

Hunter slowly pulls away. I'm left wanting more, but I'm frozen.

We let the moment linger as the rain continues to pour. I'm in my own little movie, excited for what scenes are coming next.

"Let's go Huskies!" A loud cheer filtering through my window jolts me out of my past.

Rising to take a peek at what's going on, I look outside and spot dozens of college kids mingling and celebrating being back with their friends. Strangers' laughter and chatter fill my room. My empty room.

The realization that if I truly want to try enjoying life here, I probably shouldn't isolate myself makes my shoulders tense. But I let out a long sigh and force myself to venture out of my dorm.

Walking down the stairs and into the lobby of my dorm, there's a guy stapling flyers to a bulletin board, and I pause to check if there are any job opportunities.

"Are you a freshman?" he asks with a welcoming voice.

"Yeah." I smile. "I just moved in."

"Cool. I'm Vince, and I work for res life, so if you ever need help with anything, you can stop by my office." He points to a door down the hall. "And I put flyers up here all the time, so if nothing catches your eye now, be sure to check back."

I nod. "Thanks." Once he leaves, my focus immediately lands on a posting for a babysitting job, but as I continue to read, I begin to deflate. It's over ten miles away, and without a car or license, there's no way that's happening. I browse the rest of the flyers but have no luck finding anything else. I leave, making a mental note to check back in a couple of days, like Vince suggested.

Opening the doors to go outside, the sun beams down on the vast campus. I haven't gotten a chance to admire the impressive estate. The campus seems to go on for miles, towering brick buildings with ivy snaking up the sides blending into one another.

I wander around, admiring the gigantic oak trees haphazardly rooted into the ground on the Great Lawn. College students sit under their shade, eating and talking. I come across a tree different from all the others. It's significantly narrower and shorter with distorted, twisted limbs and low-hanging leaves.

Following the lead of the other students, I park myself by the tree. Leaning my back against the trunk, I adjust myself so the bark isn't poking my back, then let my head rest against it.

I people-watch, observing how everyone is engulfed in their own little worlds, all of them with bright smiles and happiness animating their conversations.

My teeth find the inside of my cheek, making little bites into the soft tissue.

My anxiety followed me out of my dorm. Maybe getting some fresh air was a bad idea.

Maybe moving to UConn was a bad idea. Maybe this is too big of a change for me.

My whole life, I've always stayed within the limits of what I've known. Even if it hasn't always been the healthiest choice, it's what felt normal. Although my version of normal is always entangled with turmoil.

Dysfunction is sewn into my DNA, impossible for me to break free from it.

Mom and I aren't close, but I'm constantly torn between wanting to run from her and feeling compelled to be by her side. I keep my distance from her as much as possible, except for when she needs me. Other than that, I drown myself in school or Hunter. I want nothing to do with her, but at the same time, I feel bad for not being there. I'm in a constant state of confusion.

Always.

For once in my life, I'd like to be confident in the choices I make.

Today is not that day.

I loudly let out a puff of air, frustrated with myself.

"You okay?" a deep voice on the opposite side of the tree asks me.

My body jumps, not realizing someone else was here.

I peer around the tree trunk to tell the person that I'm fine, but the second my eyes meet his, I forget how to speak. All of the words in the world vanish from my brain, and I can't form a single sound.

His vibrant brown eyes penetrate my wholesome green ones. He's familiar to me, but not. I can't describe it. I've never seen him before, but there's something about him that I just know.

Say something, Ellie.

"Yeah, sorry," I manage to get out.

"You're apologizing for breathing?"

"I-I don't know."

He chuckles and moves himself closer to me so that we don't have to break our necks looking at each other. He extends his arm toward me, his tattoos catching my attention. Black and gray roses cover most of his skin, and vines with thorns reach down to his hand. "You want a smoke?" He goes to pass me an unlit cigarette. "You seem a little tense."

"No thanks. I don't smoke."

"Yeah, me neither." He retracts his arm and twirls the cigarette between his fingers. "I quit."

"Then why do you have that?"

"I've been debating smoking it for the past half hour."

"How come?"

I know I should probably mind my business, but there's something about him that is luring me in. There's an edge to him, like he's seen a lot in his seemingly short lifetime. He looks like he's strong enough to rip someone's head off with his bare hands. He's covered in tattoos, some peeking out of his shirt and making their way to the base of his neck.

"Stressed," he says.

"What are you stressed about?" I find myself shifting closer to him.

His attention moves from the cigarette toward me. My stomach flips as his gaze flickers over my body. "You ask a lot of questions."

"I was just curious. Sorry."

"You don't need to apologize." He offers me a thoughtful grin as his shaggy, dark hair moves slightly in the breeze. "Family shit," he says with his full lips.

"What?"

"My family is stressing me out," he clarifies.

"Oh. I can relate to that."

"Is that why you were just groaning?" he asks with a playful lilt in his voice.

"I wasn't groaning!" I giggle, and his entire face lights up.

"You got a cute laugh."

I tuck a strand of my golden hair behind my ear. "Thanks."

"What's your name?"

"Elena. No, Ellie."

"Which one is it?" His voice hums with amusement.

"Ellie. Call me Ellie."

"I'm Mateo."

Mateo. I like that name.

"So, Ellie, what were you *definitely not* groaning about?"

My lips turn upward as I pluck a blade of grass out of the earth. "Life. It's complicated." I point a finger at him. "And for the record, I wasn't groaning. I was loudly exhaling."

My comment makes him chuckle. "Fair enough," he says. "What's causing your life to be so complicated?"

"You're asking a lot of questions for someone who just called me out for doing the same thing," I tease.

I watch as his cheeks rise, and his eyes crinkle at the corners as he smiles. "You're right."

"But thanks anyway. I'm fine."

Mateo tilts his head to the side, observing me. His facial expression lets me know that he doesn't fully believe me, but he doesn't push for more information. Not that I would give it to him. There's no way I'm baring my soul to a complete stranger.

As he continues to study me, a tingling sensation runs down my spine. Butterflies flutter in my stomach as our gazes lock, neither of us peeling our attention away from one another.

My mouth is suddenly dry, and I wet my lips, Mateo's eyes following the movement of my tongue.

My body naturally inches closer, but the jarring noise of my ringtone halts me from getting too close. Immediately pulling back, I take my phone out of my pocket. My breath catches in my throat when I see Hunter's name on the screen, spearing me straight in the heart. I can't believe he disappeared from my mind while I was fawning over this random guy.

"It's my boyfriend," I tell Mateo, so he knows I'm off-limits.

There's a short pause. "You gonna answer it?" he asks.

Shit. I was staring at him.

I fumble with my phone and answer. "Hey, Hunter."

"Hey, angel. I finished at my frat house, and I'm on my way back to you so I can hang up your pictures."

"Oh, that's okay. It doesn't need to get done urgently—"

"I'll be there in ten. I love you."

A small sigh escapes me. "Okay. I love you too." We hang up, and I sense Mateo's attention on me.

"Part of the complication?" Mateo asks, motioning his chin toward my phone.

"What?" My brow furrows. "No. Not at all."

He doesn't respond. Instead, he goes back to weaving the cigarette between his long fingers.

"Um…I need to…"

"Go?" Mateo finishes my sentence.

"Yeah." I rise and brush off my jean shorts.

"Okay."

"Maybe I'll see you again sometime." I smile.

"Maybe." He gives me a wink and puts the cigarette back in his pocket.

Well, *that* was the sexiest thing ever. Who would've thought a tiny wink would make my entire body heat up?

Get it together, Ellie. You have Hunter, who you're insanely in love with. He loves you so much, and he'll probably parade you all around his fraternity brothers tonight.

As an attempt to rid the pang of guilt expanding in my chest for flirting with a stranger, I focus on Hunter and how wonderful he makes me feel.

I head back to my dorm, my hands fidgeting as I think about Hunter.

CHAPTER THREE

Mateo

I can't put my finger on where I've seen her before, but I swear I know the girl in front of me.

Sitting under one of the trees on the Great Lawn, I look into her sage-colored eyes, and my veins heat up in a way they never have before.

She tells me her name is Ellie, but it doesn't ring a bell.

There's a strange familiarity about her energy, though. Like my soul already knows who she is, but my mind hasn't the faintest clue.

I give her a wink, slipping my cigarette into my pocket, and watch her walk away. The sway of her hips stirs my insides, and I let my gaze linger over her hourglass figure.

"Checking out the fresh meat?" Jasmine asks, entering my line of sight as she sits across from me on the grass. Putting her freshly dyed, burgundy-colored hair into a ponytail, she checks out Ellie with me. "She's cute."

"Yeah."

"Too innocent, though."

Smirking, I know what's going through her mind. Jasmine and I have been fuck buddies since I started at UConn. It's never been anything serious, and neither of us wants it to be. It's the best arrangement for both of us since neither of us bothers with relationships.

"Anyway, speaking of our lack of innocence," Jas continues. "You free to come over tonight?"

"Can't. I have a gig," I state, thankful my musical skills are good enough to occasionally get some extra cash.

"All right. Well, if you're bored afterward, let me know." She takes a hit of her vape, but sudden shock strikes her. "Shit. I forgot you quit. Sorry."

"I quit the real thing. You can keep your shitty vapes," I tease, and she chuckles. I don't bother letting her know I have a cigarette in my pocket and almost caved a few minutes ago.

I'm not quite sure what triggered the itch to break my streak, but I woke up with my mind fixated on my past, my family—mostly Dad—and went down a rabbit hole. I'm glad that girl Ellie interrupted my opportunity to light up.

"What are you doing on campus?" Jas asks. "Shouldn't you be soaking up the last days of summer at your apartment?"

"I had a meeting with my advisor to make sure I'm up to date with all my credits so I can graduate on time."

"And are you?"

"Pretty much. I just need to retake this one class I fucked up in during my freshman year. Aside from that, I'm on track."

Entering my senior year of college feels a little too real for me. Maybe that's why I wanted to quell my jitters with a cigarette. I've come a long way since being the shit kid I used to be, but as I inch my way closer to having a career, I'm becoming more aware of the need to let that kid inside of me go and meet myself as a full-blown adult.

I know the man I want to evolve into—the polar opposite of Dad.

I'm just not sure if I'm capable of transforming into that person.

CHAPTER FOUR

Ellie

Bree skims my record collection while I swipe mascara on my lashes. "Can never go wrong with some Rolling Stones," she says, putting the vinyl on my record player that's stationed next to me.

"Agreed."

As the notable drum beat to "Sympathy For The Devil" plays, I do my best to tame the anxiety in my chest, which has me feeling like I just came back from a jog. To say I'm a little less excited about Hunter's frat party than Bree is would be an understatement.

HUNTER

can't wait to see you soon

Smiling, I text him back. I find myself being able to take longer inhales, his message acting as a place of shelter for my anxiety.

When we started dating, I wasn't planning on telling him any of my shameful secrets, especially not about my history of self-harm or Mom's addiction. But I was struggling with panic attacks, and he eventually caught on that something was wrong.

Luckily, Hunter let me lean on him. I shared everything with him, even showing him the marks on my wrist that were offering temporary relief.

Aside from me being aware that they're there every second of every day, the scars have faded and aren't as noticeable unless you look closely, which no one does, aside from Hunter. I had wanted to get a tattoo to cover up the area when I turned eighteen, but Hunter thinks tattoos are trashy. I'll just have to hope they become less visible over the years.

"I'm almost ready," Bree states. She's wearing an oversized purple tank top so that her black bralette peeks through the armholes and neckline. Her outfit is complete with acid-wash jean shorts and black pumps, which goes against any fashion rule I've ever heard of, but Bree makes it work.

I glance down at my plain white T-shirt and jeans and can't help feeling underdressed while Bree looks like a rock star. "I think I'm going to wear something else," I say, shuffling through my dresser.

"You're more than welcome to try on anything of mine if you want," she offers.

"Really?"

"Of course. Let me see what I have." Bree finishes her makeup and goes to her closet, flitting clothes on the rack back and forth. "Here." She pulls out a black lace shirt and passes it toward me. It's two layers. The first is a low-cut, satin spaghetti strap, while the second is a lace overlay that goes up to the neck and cuts off at the arms.

It's a little sexier than what I would normally wear, but the thought of borrowing Bree's confidence for the night is enticing. I could definitely use the boost, considering this is my first college party. I take the shirt from her, and she squeals with excitement.

I swear I'm in an alternate universe as we exit the Uber and walk up to Hunter's frat. The gigantic gray house with huge Greek letters hanging on the siding is littered with liquor bottles and empty cups. The front lawn is filled with people acting obnoxiously. Athletic-looking boys are shotgunning beers, while primed girls are cheering them on. We enter the loud, smoky house and push our way through the drunk and sweaty bodies. My nose wrinkles at the overpowering scent of skunk.

"I met this guy, Liam, earlier, and he told me that he's playing with the band tonight," Bree says.

"There's a band here?" I shout over the noise. "What the hell kind of party is this?"

She chuckles. "I know, right. Apparently, the frats at UConn go big." We meander farther into the house, taking it all in. "Do you care if I head to the backyard to check out the band?"

"Go for it. I'll catch up with you later."

"Okay, I'll be in the back," she says, sauntering off to the yard as if she owns the place.

The bottoms of my shoes stick to some type of liquid on the floor, and I'm quick to stand literally anywhere else. Nervousness pricks me as I scour the living room for Hunter, and all I see are the endless faces of strangers. But as I make my way into the kitchen, I spot him laughing with a bunch of guys. He catches sight of me, and excitement radiates off him.

As he moves toward me, his eyes travel down my body, and I notice as his expression abruptly changes.

My stomach twists.

"Hey," he says before giving me a kiss.

"Hi," I say with a smile plastered on my face.

"What's with the shirt?"

"I thought I'd try something a little different. Bree let me borrow it."

His attention fixates on where the neckline dips down. "A little slutty, no?"

His pointed word makes my defenses rise. The shirt is sexy. However, I would in no way call my outfit slutty. "Seriously?" I glare at him.

There's no way he's going to start with this shit now, is there?

Hunter's quick to change his tune. He brushes his soft lips on my cheek and whispers in my ear, "I'm sorry, angel. You look so beautiful, I just don't want any assholes hitting on you." He gives me another kiss. "I love you," he continues. "Let's try to have some fun."

"I love you too." I accept his apology. I don't want to end up fighting tonight.

"Hey, Hunter! Is that her?" a voice yells from across the kitchen.

"Come meet my brothers." He grabs my hand and takes me toward them.

Three guys gripping on to red Solo cups greet me with wide smiles on their faces. "This is Ellie," Hunter introduces us. "Ellie, this is Derek, Mike, and Rhett." He points to each of them.

Derek speaks up first. "Not gonna lie. I thought he made you up. Hunter talked about you nonstop last year, but I thought he was bullshitting us."

I chuckle. "No, I'm real. I just couldn't make it out here." Guilt begins to bubble, so I swiftly keep the conversation going. "But I'm glad to hear he was talking about me. All good things, I hope?"

"Oh yeah, all good things." Rhett gives a sly smirk to Hunter.

I tilt my head and look up at Hunter to see if he'll fill me in, but he doesn't.

"You want a drink?" Rhett passes me a cup without giving me the opportunity to answer.

"No." Hunter intercepts the cup and hands it back to Rhett. "She doesn't drink."

Hunter knows my resentment toward alcohol. I hate the constant reminder of how my dad died and how it's slowly taking over Mom's body too.

Hunter's hand glides down my wrist, skimming over my scars, and threads his fingers between mine. He always knows when to offer me support. He even agreed not to go crazy drinking and partying when he left for college last year. I'm assuming that still stands for this year.

"That's cool," Mike slurs. "I stopped smoking weed for like a month last month because I felt like I was getting stupider."

"Yeah, now look how smart you are," Derek teases.

"Shut the fuck up." Mike nudges him, and the two of them leave to fill up their cups.

"So, Ellie…" Rhett moves in closer to me, and Hunter tightens his grip on my hand.

Hunter's jealousy can cause trouble for him, so I try to ease his concerns by leaning into him. "Yes?" I ask Rhett.

"I know that *you're* taken." Rhett glances up at Hunter with a mischievous glimmer in his eyes. "But do you happen to have any single friends who are here tonight?"

"No. Sorry. I'm here with my roommate, Bree, but she's spoken for." I glance out of the kitchen window and see her taking shots with a group of strangers, acting like they've known each other for decades.

"Got it." Rhett nods. "Well, if anything changes, I'm always available." He grins, staring at my cleavage before he walks away.

As soon as Rhett is out of earshot, I spin into Hunter, but before I can say anything, he starts. "I fucking hate him. That's why I don't like your fucking shirt, because of dickheads like him." His jaw clenches as he stares in the direction of where Rhett walked off.

"Hunter…" I try to break his fixation on Rhett. I've always been able to ground him if we make eye contact. "Hunter, look at me." I put my hand on his chin and turn his head to focus on me. "I'm only interested in you. Always. This is our first college party together. You can't lose it every time you *think* a guy is attracted to me, which they aren't. You'll never end up graduating, and I really don't feel like marrying someone who's unemployed," I joke, hoping to lighten his mood.

"Yeah. I guess."

The topic of marriage isn't new for us. We've talked about it plenty of times and have everything planned out. We'll get engaged after I graduate and get married two years later. Hunter wants to buy a house right away with a loan from his parents, but I don't mind living in an apartment and saving up for a house with our own money. That's one thing we still don't meet eye to eye on just yet.

"Looks like Bree wants you to go out there with her." Hunter gestures toward the window, and I see Bree waving at me to come outside. He smiles. "Go join your weird roommate. I'll be there in a few."

"You sure?"

"Yeah. I have to help Mike with something."

He gives me a peck before we part ways. Once I'm outside, I spot Bree dancing to the lively music coming from the band. "Come dance!" she yells and pulls me onto the lawn.

"I don't dance," I say, hoping she hears me over the music. She doesn't. As she freely moves her body to the music, I uncomfortably shift on my heels.

"Do you like drummers?" she shouts.

"What?"

"Because the drummer seems to like you." She motions her head at the band.

I turn to figure out what the hell she's talking about, and when I do, a familiar tingling sensation blasts through my bloodstream.

Mateo.

He's playing the drums. Oh god, of course he's a musician.

I drink him in, unable to look away. His sleeveless shirt shows off his strong muscles, and the tatted arms, and he's wearing a backward hat, which I didn't even know was an instant turn-on for me until right now.

He catches me staring at him and gives me a wink.

Oh my god.

"Oh my god! He totally just winked at you!" Bree squeals, taking me out of my hypnotic trance. I take her arm and pull her away from the music.

"Shh! You can't say that." I scan the yard for Hunter.

"Why are you so uptight? You're in your prime, and you look hella sexy." She grabs another shot from somewhere and runs back onto the faux dance floor.

I can't see Mateo again. I've only crossed paths with him twice, and he's doing crazy things to my mind and body. I need to get myself inside.

Rushing back into the house, I see Hunter laughing with a brunette who's using one hand to hold her drink and the other to…stroke his arm? What's going on here?

Hunter spots me and pulls away, leaving the girl's hand hanging midair, disappointment crossing her face. Satisfaction rises in me until he directs me back to the brunette.

"Ellie, this is Delilah." He motions back and forth between us. "Delilah, this is Ellie."

Her composure shifts, and she's no longer laughing.

"Hey," she says.

"Hi," I respond, matching her aloof energy.

Hunter puts his hand around my waist. "I'm glad you guys finally get to meet. Delilah is in one of the sororities here, and I'm always telling her about you." He draws me closer to him, subsiding my paranoia. Hunter is clearly giving her signals that he's taken, which is making her upset. I can't blame her. Hunter is such a catch, but he's my catch.

"Well, I'm going to leave you two to it and get a refill." Delilah gestures to her cup and steps toward the keg.

Once she's gone, Hunter spins me around to look at him. He grins, taking my hand in his. "I want to show you my room."

I knew this moment was coming.

Without hesitation, he leads me through a sea of drunken college students and toward his bedroom. As we stroll up the stairs, Rhett is walking down. He stops and looks at both of us, chuckling and vigorously patting Hunter on the back. Hunter smirks back at him. We continue the trek up the stairs and down the hallway to the corner room.

Hunter opens the door. "Here it is," he says as we enter. As soon as the door closes, it becomes quiet, and I can finally hear myself think, aside from a brief moment where someone yells that the band is taking a ten-minute break.

Hunter's room is larger than I thought it would be. The walls are painted a white-yellowish color that I know he didn't pick out, and hung on them are a few shelves with pictures of us. His desk is pretty bare aside from his laptop and chargers, and his dresser contains multiple bottles of cologne on top.

Hunter sits on his bed and pulls me next to him. I let out a little giggle, but I'm quickly silenced as he presses his mouth against mine. He eagerly threads his hands through my hair, causing strands to get caught in my earrings. Quickly taking them off, I toss them onto his nightstand. Before I can move again, Hunter trails his mouth downward, kissing my neck.

"You look so hot," he tells me, my muscles relaxing at his contact.

Hunter effortlessly peels Bree's shirt off me and leads our bodies so that I'm lying down, and he's hovering over me.

"Hunter," I murmur, trying to slow down his quick movements.

"Yeah?" he says as he sucks my neck and thrusts his hands under my bra.

"There's a party going on."

"So?" He sucks harder on my neck, and I let out a small moan.

"Don't give me a hickey." My voice sounds so soft, I don't even know if he heard me.

Feeling my body under his is familiar, as he taunts me by kissing my neck and collarbone. The way his mouth caresses me, I fall under his spell.

And he knows it.

With each touch of his lips, my body melts farther into the bed. One of his hands grazes over my stomach, traveling down to my jeans. The moment he goes to unbutton them, my mind reenters the room. "No, not now."

He ignores me and slips his hand into my panties, sucking even harder on my neck.

"Hunter," I say to get him to stop, but he doesn't. Instead, he moves his mouth around my neck, roughly drawing in my skin. "Hunter, stop!" I push him off. "That's going to leave a mark!" I put my hand on my throat.

"And?"

"And I don't want to go to my first day of classes with hickeys all over me."

"You want to dress like a slut, you might as well act the part."

I stand up, anger igniting in my veins. "Are you kidding me? You're calling me a slut because of the shirt I chose to wear?"

"No, I'm calling you a slut because you come to my house and flaunt your body in front of all my brothers."

I grab Bree's shirt and throw it back on while Hunter continues.

"You *want* to get their attention. You're a fucking tease."

"I'm not a tease."

"I don't know, Ellie, you've been teasing me for a pretty long time. How much longer do you think this shit is going to go on for?"

"It's not 'this shit.' It's our virginity!"

"Can you keep your voice down? I don't want anyone hearing you shout that."

My mind jumps to earlier in the night with Rhett implying that he's heard stories about me, and then again when he encouraged him as we walked up the stairs. Things start clicking. "What did you tell them about me?"

"Tell who? What are you talking about?"

"Your 'brothers.'" I use air quotes because it's annoying how this group of humans is now a part of his family. "You made up stories, didn't you?"

He blinks rapidly and opens his mouth to speak, but nothing comes out. His lack of response makes the blood drain from my face as my brain spins a web of lewd stories he told about me.

"You made up sex stories about me, didn't you?"

"I-I..." He scrambles for words.

"You're an asshole," I say before racing out of his room.

"Ellie!" he shouts as I run down the stairs.

Pushing through people, I dash out the door and onto the front lawn. It's still filled with obnoxious people, only now they're even more drunk and rowdy. The street is lined with parked cars, and I walk toward the curb as I take my phone out and click on the Uber app.

I can't believe Hunter has been telling all of these random guys lies about our sex life. I didn't expect him to tell them he was a virgin, but I also didn't expect him to tell crude fantasies about me as if they were actually happening.

I wrap my arms around my body, suddenly feeling very exposed.

In reality, we've done everything except sex. I don't know why I've been putting it off for so long. I know that we love each other, and there have been countless times where we've had the opportunity to, but for some reason, I always stop it just before. I've felt slightly pressured into other things, and sex is the one thing that I'm not willing to do until I feel one hundred percent ready.

My eyes begin to water. *Do not cry, Elena. Don't you dare cry.* I hold my breath, hoping the tears will disappear, but my embarrassment is making it hard to hold them back. *Dammit.* They roll down my cheeks, the salty moisture hitting my lips. Sniffling, I try to swallow them down.

"Ellie?"

Turning, I spot Mateo standing next to a car with a concerned look etched onto his face.

I quickly wipe my cheeks. "Hey."

"Are you okay?"

"Yeah, I'm good."

"You sure?" He ambles over. "Because you seem like you're *definitely not* crying." His lips turn slightly upward. If I weren't so upset, I'd grin along with him at this new inside joke we have.

"I'm fine, I'm just..." I try to think of any excuse as to why I'd be crying right now, but I've got nothing.

"You need a ride somewhere?"

More than anything, I want him to take me back to my dorm, but Hunter would be irate if he knew another man was driving me. I don't have it in me to get into a fight about that too.

"It's really no big deal. I don't mind." Mateo's standing directly in front of me now, his dark eyes peering into mine. His stature is much taller and broader than Hunter's, so much so that if I wanted to kiss him, I'd need to go on my tippy toes.

"Elena, what the fuck?" Hunter's voice booms from across the lawn.

My head whips around. I know he notices how close Mateo is to me, and that's only making him stride toward us faster.

I rush to meet Hunter halfway before he can get to Mateo. I don't want this to end in some type of conflict between them, and judging by the tension that's building in Hunter's shoulders as he stomps forward, he's itching for a fight.

"Two seconds after you leave my bedroom, you're out here with some guy?" he says in the most condescending tone that I can tell was meant to make the situation sound worse than it actually is.

"Hunter, I don't want to do this right now. I just want to go back to campus," I try to say firmly, but my voice cracks, betraying me.

"Cut the fucking dramatics, Ellie."

His comment makes me snap. A blast of adrenaline explodes inside me, making me lose my composure. "I'm not being dramatic. You're such an asshole!" I shout at him, getting in his face.

Hunter moves in closer, his posture growing intimidating as he feeds off my emotions. "Get back upstairs, Elena," he says through gritted teeth.

"No. Leave me alone." I attempt to turn away from him, but he puts his hands on my shoulders, stopping me. Balling my hands into fists, I bang against his chest, experiencing both relief and regret with each strike I take.

Truthfully, moments like these are part of our norm. Our fights are intense, which in some sick way turns us on and leads our make-ups to be just as extreme.

One of us will fold soon.

This is part of our dance.

"Let me explain. You're jumping to conclusions, just like you always do." Hunter's hands still prevent me from turning away.

"I don't want to hear it, Hunter." I push him with all my might, but I'm not strong enough to get him off me. Hunter snickers at my attempt to shove him.

"Stop! Stop laughing at me!" More tears drip down, and I grow defeated. I'm suddenly cognizant that there are people around, and my head hangs in humiliation, hoping no one is paying attention to us. "I just want to go back. I don't want to be here anymore." My tone softens.

Hunter sighs, recognizing that my energy has shifted. "Can we go back upstairs and finish our conversation…please?" As I catch my breath and consider if I should go back in with him, I notice his gaze looking past me. "I got her. Thanks," he says.

I turn and see Mateo leaning up against a car, glaring at Hunter. I completely forgot that he was there, and now I'm even more humiliated by the scene we just caused.

"I said she's good now. You can go," Hunter barks.

"I heard you, but I'm not leaving until I hear *Ellie* say she's good," Mateo states in the calmest, yet most commanding voice ever. "I don't like the way you treat her, so until I hear her say she's fine being alone with you, I'm not going anywhere."

My eyes widen. I am *definitely* living in an alternate universe right now. There's no way those words just came out of his mouth.

"Excuse me?" Hunter pushes past me, moving toward Mateo.

"Do you need me to repeat it?" Mateo eggs him on, smirking.

Grabbing hold of Hunter's arm, I yank him toward me. "Hunter! Hunter, stop!" He keeps barreling forward. Fear frays my nerve endings as the image of how ugly this could get plagues my mind. My heart rises to my throat, pounding with panic.

Anxiety builds and builds and builds until I can't take it anymore. I grow desperate. "I'll go back upstairs with you!"

My words flip a switch, and Hunter's attention is back on me.

He smirks as I inflate his ego. "Yeah, let's finish what we were doing in my room." He wraps his arms around my waist and sticks his fingers under my shirt so he can reconnect with my skin. I know exactly what he's doing, but I would rather have another person think I sleep around than have Hunter get into another fight. I want to look over my shoulder to give Mateo some type of nonverbal communication that I'm okay, but I don't.

Without a word, we head back inside and up toward Hunter's bedroom. At the top of the stairs are Rhett and Delilah. "Yeah, man, round two!" Rhett cheers us on as Delilah rolls her eyes. Hunter doesn't acknowledge either one of them and pulls me along the hallway, entering his room again.

"We need to talk," Hunter says as he closes the door behind him.

"Yeah. We do," I respond, crossing my arms.

"Who was that guy?"

"You're joking, right? I find out that you're making up sex stories about me to all your buddies, and you have the nerve to start pinning something on *me* because some random person offered to drive me back to campus?"

"Ellie, I'm just trying to keep you safe. That guy could've been anyone." Concern paints his features as he sits down on his bed.

Both of us regulate our breathing as we come down from our quick uproar. I stand over him as he continues talking.

"There are some really fucked-up men out there. I'm sorry I freaked. I just want to protect you."

"Are you sorry for anything else?" I snap.

Hunter glances at the floor and then back to my eyes, letting out a sigh. "I know what I did was messed up. I'll tell my brothers the truth, I swear." He reaches for my hand, tugging me closer. "I was just so upset you didn't come here at all last year, and they were swapping stories, so I joined in occasionally."

Yet again, my guilt tries to surface. I truly do feel bad for not coming here last year, but I was so consumed with taking care of Mom and trying to stay afloat in school.

Before I can make a rebuttal, Hunter continues, "And I know that doesn't make it right, and I don't want to make you feel any worse than you already do. I really am sorry, angel." I look into his blue eyes, feeling out if this apology is genuine. We get into fights so often, and the word *sorry* gets thrown around more times than I can count. "I know I've done some shitty things in the past, but I never intended to hurt you. You know that. I'm never going to hurt you like your dad or your mom has," he declares.

The mention of my parents sends a deep ache into my heart.

Hunter and I have been through so much together. He didn't have to stick around as long as he has, but he did, and he chose to stay with me even through all of my drama.

We don't have the healthiest relationship, but for some reason, we can't separate from each other, no matter how many times we've tried. The highs and lows are our natural state. There's a deep connection between us that seems impossible to sever.

"I love you," he says, grasping my face with one of his hands.

"I love you too."

CHAPTER FIVE

Ellie

Before leaving for my first day of classes, I give myself a once-over in the mirror. I groan when I notice the hickeys from Saturday night are still visible. I put concealer on them, then toss the makeup into my bag, making a mental note to refresh it every couple of hours.

The day moves quickly, even though my first two classes, Psychology Basics and English Lit, were a lot to digest. My head spins from all this new information and the amount of work that I need to complete this semester.

My pace picks up as I pass by several large buildings, making my way to my philosophy class, which is all the way across campus.

My phone vibrates in my bag, and I fish it out, seeing a text from Hunter.

HUNTER

Hope your first day is awesome. I love you

ME

So far, so good. I love you too

By the time I make it to my classroom, it's practically filled. There are only a few seats left in the back corner.

After sitting down, I scan the room to see if there's anyone I recognize from earlier in the day, but no one looks familiar, except for one person at the front of the class, surrounded by others who look exactly like her. Delilah. Her flawless brunette hair swishes back and forth as she talks to other girls who also have flawless, voluminous hair. They're laughing about something she's showing them on her phone. A spark of jealousy rises in my chest before I can stop it. I know Hunter made it clear to her that he and I are together, but something feels off.

"Hey."

My head turns to see who interrupted my envious thoughts. Shaggy, dark hair invades my vision, and excitement bursts through my core, shooting down my limbs when I realize it's Mateo taking the seat next to me.

As he makes himself comfortable, I study him more closely. While I admire the detailed ink all over his body, something else catches my attention. He has a big scar starting under the sleeve of his T-shirt, twisting down and stopping just before his elbow crease.

"Looks like you guys had an okay night after all," Mateo says, nodding at my neck.

Fuck. I forgot to check on my hickeys to see if I needed to retouch the makeup. My hand flies up to cover my throat, and Mateo chuckles at my poor attempt to hide my markings. I hate when Hunter gives me these. I swear it's his way of marking his territory.

"Meaning. Purpose. Truth," the professor says with a flourish, pulling everyone's attention to him. "That is what we will be searching for this entire semester, and if you're lucky enough, maybe even next semester when you take another one of my classes." The class lightly chuckles. "Welcome. I'm Professor Boland," he says. "I like to do some things the old-fashioned way—paper." He holds up the class roster. "I'm passing around the attendance sheet. Put your initials next to your name."

Professor Boland is a balding, middle-aged man in a tweed blazer and khaki pants. He's stocky and already appears to have a big enough personality to fill up the entire campus.

The attendance sheet floats around the room as he continues to speak. "I'm also handing out the syllabus, but please save your questions until the very end."

A girl in front of me spins around and hands me the attendance sheet. I find my name, Elena Connor, and put an EC next to it. I glance at Mateo, who is paying attention to where I was signing, and casually pass him the paper. I peek at where he signs. Mateo Rivera.

After Mateo passes the paper to another student, I sense his attention on me. Adjusting myself slightly, my pulse picks up as I watch his gaze lock on my hips and roam upward. He takes his time, noticing every curve, then pauses for a moment at my neck and continues his journey until his captivating eyes meet mine. He gives me a wink, not even trying to hide that he was undressing me in his head.

I swear the temperature in the room just rose twenty degrees.

"Here!" The girl in the seat in front of me shakes a stack of papers at Mateo and me, breaking our connection.

"For the final..." Professor Boland continues his explanation of the course. "You're going to partner up with someone and write a paper comparing and contrasting your views on morals, reality, and existence. What is their truth? What do they believe the meaning of life is? How does it equate to your views? Can your two views peacefully coexist even if they differ? Ask and uncover."

Professor Boland pauses, surveying the room for our reaction, and then continues, "I suggest you find a classmate soon. There is a list of questions on the back of the syllabus. These are not easy questions. They require a lot of thought and processing. So I'd recommend you learn about one another on a surface level first, before asking any hard hitters like, 'Is humanity as we know it doomed?'" Laughter briefly fills the room, and then he goes on to discuss our assignments.

Anxiety climbs up my body, spiraling my thoughts. Partnering up with someone to identify the meaning of life causes an ache to pulsate in my skull.

For the rest of the class, I'm in a daze. I'm sure Professor Boland said some brilliant things and answered what seemed to be an endless amount of questions regarding the syllabus. Mateo's focus went off me ever since the annoying girl interrupted him checking me out. He's been scrolling through his phone, texting on and off.

"That's all for today, folks." Professor Boland ends class. "If you'd like to talk to me privately after class, I have about twelve minutes before my wife calls me asking what time she should expect me home." Almost immediately, everyone begins to talk. Some rush up to the professor holding the syllabus, others are picking out their partners, and some complain about the amount of work they have to do.

Mateo and I stand at the same time and leave the classroom together. "So when do you want to meet?" he asks.

"I'm sorry?"

"Boland said we should start by getting to know each other first," he states.

It finally clicks. "Oh, you want to be together?"

He smiles at the accidental offer. I shake my head. "I meant you want to be partners…for the final."

"Yeah, I do." Mateo adds, "If that's cool with you."

"Yeah, definitely." The words tumble out of my mouth, and I realize a second later that this is going to cause an issue with Hunter.

"Mateo, let's go!" a voice from a distance calls for him. A girl with her dark hair in a high ponytail impatiently taps her foot, hurrying him up. She must be his girlfriend. This might actually work out to be completely fine. I can tell Hunter that Mateo's with someone else and that he is in no way interested in me.

Mateo signals with a nod of his head at the girl waving to him at the front of the building, then turns back to me. "Let me see your phone," he says, and I do what he asks, handing my phone over.

Mateo snickers at the background picture of Hunter and me in Cape Cod in July and starts typing. Giving me back my phone, he says, "I texted myself so we have each other's number. I'll reach out to you, and we can set up a date."

"You mean just a getting-to-know-you type of thing…for our final."

He subtly wets his lips. "Yeah."

"All right, lover boy. Speed it up. I got places to go!" the girl shouts at him. I'm surprised how casual both of them are being. Maybe she isn't his girlfriend? I'm just going to assume she is because it'll make it easier when I tell Hunter.

Mateo types something into his phone, and a second later, mine vibrates in my hand. "See you later," he says, walking backward to join his girlfriend.

I open my phone to read his message:

You're definitely not smiling right now.

My lips twitch, but I press them together to stifle it and delete the text.

"How was your first day of college?" Hunter asks as he sits on my bed.

"Amazing. I love all of my classes so far." I fill him in, watching him light up at my enthusiasm, and decide to leave out the project with Mateo for now. Hunter and I are both happy with how our days went, and I don't want to screw that up by mentioning Mateo and having it blow up in my face.

We continue catching each other up, and he lets me in on his plans for the rest of the week, the highlight being his frat having another big party scheduled for Saturday.

Hunter's phone buzzes in his hand, and a text pops up on the screen. "It's Derek. We're going to grab some pizza. You want to come?"

"No, it's okay. I think I'm going to get started on reading about Freud. I want to make sure I get an A on my first paper."

He smiles. "Okay, nerd."

The door swings open. "What a day." Bree rests one hand on the doorknob, jutting her hip out and thrusting her hand in the air like she just finished a performance. "Hey, roomie. Hey, boy toy." The sight would've been comical if it weren't for Hunter's subtle grimace. It doesn't seem like he's a fan of Bree. I don't know why. She exudes cheerfulness, something I find contagious.

"Ellie's going to have to fill me in tonight. I was just leaving." Hunter turns to me. "I'll text you later, angel." He kisses me and walks out the door.

"I fucking love college!" Bree exclaims.

She tells me about her art classes and her unique assignments and projects, then asks me if I have any big projects like she does. I hesitate, and she gives me a strange look.

"What's wrong?" Bree goes into defense mode, jumping to her feet. "You don't have one of those sleazy professors who's making you do some unethical, fucked-up shit, do you? Because I will march right into the university president's office and—"

"No, no, no!" I motion for her to sit. "It's nothing like that."

"Okay. So what is it?"

"I have an assignment in my philosophy class where we're supposed to explore these questions with a partner." I lift up my syllabus. "They're about life, morals, love, humanity…"

"Okay?"

"My partner is Mateo."

"Who's Mateo?"

"Remember when we were at Hunter's party, and the guy in the band winked at me?"

Bree's jaw drops. "The sexy drummer?"

"Yep."

"Oh my god! This is going to get interesting."

"No! It can't get interesting. It can't get anything. We're just going to do this paper, and that's it."

"Uh-huh, sure," she says, snorting.

I cover my mouth to hold back my laughter, but I'm failing miserably. "Stop!"

"You *so* like him!"

"No one else can tell, right?"

She shakes her head. "No, I'm just really good at reading people's energy. And I don't think Hunter can tell if that's what you're really asking. But you may want to fuck him a little bit more so that he doesn't catch on, just to be sure," she jokes. My face drops even though I try to play along with her, but my attempt is poorly executed. Bree immediately catches on. She *is* good at reading people. "Wait, you're a virgin? You've never had sex before? Like…ever?"

"I mean, we've done everything else except."

"That's actually really cool. There are so many people hooking up with randos, it's rare to find someone who's going old school and waiting for marriage."

"Oh, I'm not waiting for marriage."

"Then what are you waiting for?"

I pause. What *am* I waiting for? My brows knit together as I try to come up with a response, but I'm as confused as Bree. "Honestly, I don't know. I just feel like I'll know when the time is right, and that hasn't happened yet. I always stop him right before."

"It's gotta be the right vibe."

"Exactly."

"So what does Hunter think about it? You've been together for over two years, right?"

"He's willing to wait as long as I am."

"But he's not a virgin."

"No, he is."

Bree slants her head to the side. "Huh."

"What?"

"He just doesn't strike me as the virgin type. But when I look at you, that kind of makes sense," she teases.

"Hey!" I toss a pillow at her.

I can't help but wonder what Bree meant by her comment about Hunter. Before I can ask her to elaborate, she's going on about how badly she misses her girlfriend, Amber, and how she's going to New York to visit her in two weeks.

The rest of our night is consumed by crappy reality TV shows, ramen noodles, and comparing celebrity crushes. Oh, and a little bit of reading up on Freud.

CHAPTER SIX

Ellie

SEPTEMBER

The next few days go by fast. It's already Thursday evening, and Hunter and I are taking a stroll around town a few blocks from campus. We would've met here straight from my last class, but we decided to take his car so we could do a Target run and pick up some last-minute items for my dorm room.

Things between us have been going great this past week. No dramatic outbursts and nothing intense happened. Just calmness. I love simple moments like this.

Hunter shows me around the quaint town, Mahogany Ridge. We dip in and out of tiny, locally owned shops, but he's been looking forward to showing me one place in particular called the Cozy Nook.

When we open the door, I gape at how charming this bookshop is. It's much larger than the one I used to work at. The display tables by the front door house books by local independent authors, while the brick walls have photography from nearby artists hanging on them. Vintage rugs cover the hardwood floors, and there are several oversized chairs with side tables stacked with books next to them. There's a metal spiral staircase leading upstairs to a loft area where a fuzzy teal couch sits between a few bookshelves. Jazz music softly plays as the aroma of coffee beans spreads throughout the room.

"Wow," I state.

"I knew you'd love this place."

I nod, mesmerized by this shop, wishing I could live here instead of my actual home. Hunter chuckles and rubs his thumb over the back of my hand.

"Why don't you go wander around a bit? I want to check some stuff out too," he suggests.

We part ways, and I watch him head toward the crime section while I bounce between romance and fantasy.

As I make my way into an aisle, I notice that the wall across from me has a large glass window. Next to it is a hollowed-out archway allowing patrons to move between the bookstore and the shop next door, which happens to be a coffee shop. *That explains the smell.*

I start to travel in that direction, but my phone buzzing in my pocket distracts me. I check it, and as soon as I see it's Mateo, my heart beats faster. I haven't heard from him all week and, to be quite honest, I was somewhat relieved because I had a feeling my body would react this way.

MATEO

Sorry I haven't texted you, I've been working a lot.
You free tomorrow?

I glance around, making sure Hunter isn't nearby.

My fingers hover over the screen when voices in the aisle next to me catch my attention.

"There's too much to get done in one day," a woman says.

"It's just been a hectic few weeks. It'll go back to normal soon," a man responds.

"No, it won't. We're getting more and more inventory."

The man huffs and says something inaudible.

"You're being stubborn." The woman keeps speaking. "Hire someone for a couple of hours a week, and it'll be a lot easier for us to handle."

I let out a small gasp. This would be perfect for me. I only need a few hours to keep myself afloat. It's a quick walk from my dorm, *and* I already have the experience.

Mustering up confidence, forcing myself to step out of my comfort zone now, I round the corner into the mystery aisle, where the two people are talking.

"Hi." I clear my throat so I don't sound too mousy. "I didn't mean to eavesdrop, but I heard you're looking to hire someone, and I used to work at the local bookshop in my hometown, so I—"

The woman's eyes widen. "Yes!"

"No." The man shoots her a look of annoyance.

She pushes past him and extends her hand for me to shake. "I'm Sandy, one of the managers here. It's nice to meet you."

"Nice to meet you too. I'm Ellie."

"This is Edgar." Sandy motions to the large man with tan skin and salt-and-pepper hair. "He's the owner of both the bookstore and coffee shop.

He could definitely use another employee here." She glances up at him, grinning, and he sighs.

Edgar focuses on me. "How long did you work at the bookshop?"

"About a year. I can give you my manager's number for a reference."

He shakes his head. "You know how to work a cash register?"

I nod, and he rubs his hand over the scruff on his jaw. He goes on to ask me a series of questions, quizzing my knowledge of literature, customer service skills, and processing inventory. I answer all of them to the best of my ability, ignoring the fact that I'm breaking out into a nervous sweat.

He squints his eyes. "Fine. We'll do a trial run."

Sandy claps her hands as I thank Edgar, shocked that he'd hire me on the spot.

"Hey." Hunter sidles up next to me.

"Hey." I move to face him. "I just got a job working here!"

His posture straightens. "Oh." I hold my breath, concerned with his reaction, but when his lips turn upward into a large smile, I breathe easy. "Congrats." He loops his arm around my waist. "When do you start?"

I look over at Edgar. "Tomorrow. Four to seven," Edgar states before focusing on a stack of books in front of him, dismissing me.

"Nice." Hunter tugs me closer. "Let's get some celebratory drinks."

To most, that usually means alcohol. To us, that means caffeine.

We make our way through the archway and into the coffee shop. Funky art made out of recycled metal hangs on the brightly painted walls, and mismatched, comfy furniture occupies the room. There's a small stage by the front window with a stool and a mic set up, ready for someone to perform.

A petite barista with purple hair and a lip piercing takes our order—an iced vanilla latte for me and an Americano for Hunter. She goes to make our drinks, and when it's time to add vanilla to mine, there's nothing coming out of the pump. She tries to grab another bottle of vanilla flavoring on the top shelf, but she's too short to reach.

"It's okay. Don't worry about it," I say, watching her struggle for my unnecessary sweetener.

"No, it's fine. I'll just get my manager to grab it for me," she states. "Mateo!" she yells in the direction of the back, toward another room. "Can you grab something off the top shelf for me?"

Mateo? There's no way that it's my Mateo. Jeez, just listen to me. I didn't mean my *Mateo.*

"I got you, Lynn.," I hear his deep voice echoing from the back room.

Oh god. That's definitely him.

Mateo goes toward Lynn, the barista. "Which one?" Just the brief sight of his broad back and the sound of his strong vibrato make the butterflies dance around my stomach. Thankfully, Hunter's texting someone on his phone, so he doesn't realize Mateo's here.

"Vanilla. For her." Lynn points to me.

I suck in a breath as Mateo turns to see who Lynn is pointing at. He looks at me and smiles, but it quickly fades as soon as he realizes who I'm with. He spins back around to grab the big bottle of vanilla and hands it to Lynn so she can continue making our drinks.

Mateo comes to the counter. *He's not actually going to try to talk to me, is he?*

"Hey."

Yep, he is.

Hunter's head snaps out of his phone. "Fucking great," Hunter mutters loud enough for us to hear.

"Hey," I automatically respond to Mateo without thinking of Hunter's reaction.

"What are you doing? Don't talk to him," Hunter demands. Blood rushes to my cheeks out of both embarrassment and anger. I hate it when he tries to control me.

Lynn passes our drinks to Mateo as she moves to the register. "That'll be eight dollars."

"No, that's all right. It's on the house," Mateo says to all of us.

Hunter digs a ten-dollar bill out of his wallet, ignoring Mateo's comment. "Keep the change. I'm sure you need anything you can get."

My jaw drops. "Hunter!"

"What? Making a living from selling coffee can't be that lucrative. I'm just trying to help him scrape by so he can live a decent life."

"Stop it," I say through gritted teeth.

Mateo slams our drinks onto the counter, throwing daggers at Hunter with his eyes. Then he softens his gaze and focuses on me. "Now that I know your drink order, I'll bring it with me to philosophy next week."

Hunter's body stills, and I can sense his temper rising. He's pissed that in all our conversations about class, I just so happened to leave out that Mateo and I are taking one together. On top of that, we are also doing a semester-long project where we share our deepest thoughts about the purpose of life. And thanks to my new job, we'll now be working in close proximity to one another.

I don't look at Hunter. Instead, I'm staring directly back at Mateo, my eyes pleading with him not to divulge any information about our assignment. I really hope he's not as big a jerk as Hunter is. If the situation were reversed, Hunter would definitely throw it in his face, creating an outright brawl in the middle of the coffee shop.

Mateo picks up on my plea and eases his stance. "Relax. I was just fucking with you," he says to Hunter before walking back into the room where he came from.

Quickly grabbing our drinks, I dart out the door with Hunter tailing me. We hurry toward the municipal parking lot, completely silent. My stomach cramps anticipating his reaction. I open my mouth to try to explain that this isn't a big deal, but the second I do, Hunter takes his drink from me and throws it against a nearby garbage can. Coffee goes flying, the cup and lid crashing onto the ground.

Hunter keeps walking, getting into his car as I pick up his trash and toss it into the can.

His car pulls out of the parking spot and comes to a skidding stop next to me. The window rolls down, and Hunter furiously commands, "Get in."

CHAPTER SEVEN

Ellie

My heart bangs against my ribs.

Hunter's car screeches out of the lot as he makes sharp turns toward the street. He drives down the road and flies past the entrance to the campus.

"Where are we going?" I ask.

He doesn't answer. Instead, he blows a few red lights, abruptly turning onto the highway.

"Where are we going?" I repeat in a more demanding tone. He's silent and avoids making eye contact with me. I watch the speedometer race up to eighty miles per hour.

"Can we please talk?" I try to calmly ask him while struggling to steady my breathing.

"No," Hunter says.

He weaves in and out of cars, cutting people off and causing them to slam on their brakes.

This is escalating so quickly.

"You're going to cause an accident." My voice trembles. He doesn't care, so I try a different approach. "Can you look at me?"

Nothing.

We rapidly move past dozens of cars. Bad memories, horrible memories flood my mind. My chest is turning into a giant knot. It's becoming harder to breathe. "Hunter, please!" I beg him to slow down, but he ignores me.

He hits ninety.

Cars blast their horns.

"Hunter! Talk to me!"

"Why the fuck wouldn't you tell me he was in your class, Elena?" he yells, seething with rage.

"I don't know! I'm sorry!"

"Is that why you took the job? So you could suck him off in the break room?"

"What? No. I didn't even know he worked there."

"Bullshit!"

"I didn't!"

The tendons in his hand flex as his hold on the wheel tightens. He presses down on the gas even harder.

The sound of my heartbeat thrashes in my ears. "Slow down. Please!"

"Nope. We're going over a hundred." He laughs in my face as he speeds up to a hundred ten.

"Please! Just stop!"

I don't know what else to do to get him to slow down, so I choose to unbuckle my seat belt. Maybe that will snap him back to reality. Maybe he'll immediately calm down with the realization that he could easily kill me.

"You're going to cause an accident!" My vision blurs as I choke on my words. "You're going to kill us!"

Hunter doesn't flinch as the car hits one hundred twenty.

Memories keep flashing before me. I close my eyes, but I can't escape them.

I'm trapped.

Trapped in my mind.

Trapped in this car.

Trapped with Hunter.

My lungs constrict so tight that my chest burns.

I can't take full breaths.

Only short, shallow pants.

My hands shake uncontrollably.

I put my seat belt back on and accept my fate.

I can't breathe. All the air has been sucked out of the car. "Please," I manage to whisper. "Please."

My eyes are screwed shut for what feels like days.

I don't know how long it's been, but the car feels like it's coming to a more reasonable speed. But I'm scared that if I look at the speedometer, it'll still be high.

I feel us slowing down and slightly turning to get off the highway.

More oxygen fills up my lungs. My breathing is returning back to normal.

We stop.

When my eyes open, the red glow of a traffic light casts down onto my face. We're in a town I've never seen before. It looks a little run-down and definitely not as affluent as the area we were just in.

"Ellie, I'm…" Hunter tries to speak.

I hold up my hand, not looking at him. "Don't."

We drive in silence back to campus.

As we pull into the parking lot of my dorm, Hunter blurts out, "I think we need to take a break."

Fury saturates every inch of my body, causing me to rattle with rage. "You nearly kill me because you're mad that I'm in class with some guy—something I had zero control over—and *you* have the nerve to tell *me* that we need a break?" I give him a second to respond, but he doesn't, making me angrier. "If there's anyone who should be saying we need a break, it should be me! Fuck you!"

I try to get out of the car, but he grabs my arm, jerking me back in. "No, wait." His emotions completely switch on me. "Let's talk."

"No. I tried that earlier, and you couldn't snap out of your rage."

"You know I have jealousy issues, Ellie."

"Then work on them!"

"I've been trying to, but it's pretty fucking hard when I find out my girlfriend has been hiding shit from me. Do you know what that does to me? You know how I get when you make me jealous."

"I didn't *make* you jealous!" I yank my arm out of his grip. "We're taking a break, just like you want." I get out of the car, slamming the door behind me.

Moving into the lobby of my dorm, I storm over to the staircase. Before I can reach the first step, something stops me dead in my tracks—a flyer stapled to the bulletin board, a picture of the Eiffel Tower with the words "Enlighten Yourself in the City of Lights" typed above it. Early submission for a summer abroad program in France, studying philosophy.

Fuck it. I'm applying.

I snatch the flyer down and dash up to my room, immediately reaching for my laptop.

Hunter thinks he can control every move I make? Let's see him try to do that when I'm all the way in fucking France.

Opening up the online application, I furiously type away, fluffing up all the knowledge I have on the topic and falsely claiming my love for philosophy.

Once I hit the submit button, I let out a big exhale and throw myself down on my bed. I come down from my defiant high and stare up at my pictures of France, wishing I were there right now, just like I'd do when I was younger.

I doubt I'll get selected for the abroad program, but it felt good doing something of my own volition. Even if I were accepted, I wouldn't realistically be able to go unless I got a scholarship. Working at a bookstore won't pay for a getaway to France.

My phone rings, and Hunter's name flashes on the screen. There's no way I'm talking to him. I let it go to voicemail, then I decide to text Mateo.

ME

Tomorrow works, let me know when and where

Maybe I'm not quite done with my defiant streak.

I know I'm just being spiteful. I know that this is going to cause even more problems between Hunter and me. I know I should text Mateo saying that he should look for a different partner, but I don't.

MATEO

Meet me at the coffee shop at 7

The butterflies are back, and a smile flickers across my face. Clearly, my body wants me to be with him—as a partner for our class project, of course. I shouldn't even worry about this causing an issue with Hunter. We're taking a break from each other. We've taken breaks before. It's actually quite normal for us. We get into some big fight, take a break for a few days, and then plead for the other's forgiveness and adore one another until the next big fight happens.

Is that normal for couples? Probably not, but we love each other, and this is what's normal for *our* love. Hunter just needs to understand that he can't control every single interaction I have with people.

This meeting with Mateo is for school, and that's it. Nothing more.

CHAPTER EIGHT

Ellie

"And the damaged books go in this pile." Sandy shows me a plastic bin in the storage room of the bookstore. We've been in here for most of my shift while Edgar works in the front. She's taught me how to log and scan inventory into their computer system and how to process return items.

"Let's get you to the register so I can show you a little of that before your shift ends," she says, tying her platinum-blonde hair up into a ponytail. I glance at the clock on the wall and nervously nibble on my bottom lip as the time gets closer to seven.

We make our way to the front of the store for the first time since the beginning of my shift. Sandy goes over the ins and outs of the register, and I try to pay attention, but my eyes have a mind of their own and keep looking through the large window across from me, into the coffee shop.

Mateo is behind the counter, moving back and forth, prepping orders. Three college girls walk toward him and make it obvious in the way they're checking him out. Mateo stops what he's doing and saunters over to them, making conversation. Judging by his body language, he's clearly flirting, and the girls reciprocate. One of them passes their phone to him, and he types in what I imagine to be his number.

Something that feels an awful lot like envy prickles under my skin.

Sandy keeps talking to me, but I can't stop staring at the potential hookup that's happening in front of me. When the girls finally leave, Mateo goes back to making drinks. He looks over in the direction of the bookstore and does a double-take when he spots me behind the register. I dart my focus back to Sandy.

"Then you void it out by pressing this button." Sandy shows me, and I nod along, pretending to have listened to all of her instructions. "I'm going to go work in the back. You only have a few minutes left, so you should be fine up here, but if you need anything, you can ask Edgar."

"No, she can't," he shouts from somewhere in the store.

Sandy laughs. "He's playing with you. Yes, you can." She starts to leave. "I'll see you for your next shift in a couple of days."

"Sounds good. Thanks for everything." I wave to her before she gets sucked back into the storage room.

Time moves insanely slowly, but as soon as it hits seven, I search for Edgar. "Um…Edgar?"

"Yeah?" His voice comes from above as he cleans the loft area.

"It's seven. I'm going to head out."

"See you later."

Before I get into the coffee shop, I run my fingers through my hair, flattening any flyaways, then tug at my olive-colored shirt, letting a little cleavage show. *No, don't do that. That's too much.* I pull my shirt back up. *Now it looks too high.* I pull it down a small amount. *I'm allowed to show some cleavage. They're my boobs, for goodness' sake.*

After a much too long debate with myself on how much skin I should show, I make my way through the archway toward Mateo. He notices me and comes from behind the counter. I can't help but notice how handsome he looks wearing black jeans and a black T-shirt, which tightly hugs his arms.

"You're working at the bookstore?" Mateo asks.

"Yep."

"Good to know," he says with a smirk. "Go sit down. I'll grab your drink." He gestures toward a table in the back.

I make myself comfortable at the table he set aside for us. The tabletop is a mosaic pieced together with colorful chunks of glass. As I admire the unique art, Mateo breaks my gaze by putting down two cups and taking the seat across from me.

"Thank you."

"No problem."

Nerves jump around in my belly. I'm not sure what I should do or say, so I shift my brain into school mode, pulling out my phone. "I have the list of questions we need to ask each other. I thought that maybe we could talk about a few of them—"

"Whoa, whoa, whoa," he interjects, leaning back in his chair. "We're not here to go over those questions."

"Then what are we here for?"

"Boland said that we should get to know each other. You know, keep it casual, no big scary questions. Not yet."

My heart flutters at his words. "Oh, okay." *Keep it casual. Casual.* "So… where are you from?"

He raises his left eyebrow. "You mean where am I from, as in where did I grow up, or why am I not white?"

"Oh my god. I'm so sorry, that was poorly worded."

Mateo chuckles. "I'm just fucking with you. I grew up in Queens, New York." He tries to stifle his grin before saying, "And I'm Puerto Rican."

"I'm sorry. I didn't mean for that to come off as insensitive. I can be really awkward when I'm nervous."

"Why are you nervous, Ellie?" He's no longer trying to hide his smile.

"I didn't mean that…" I try to backtrack.

Mateo ignores my obvious embarrassment and tries to make me feel more at ease. "Where are you from?"

"I grew up a half hour outside of Boston…and aside from my first name, I'm one hundred percent Irish," I say, trying to make light of the situation.

"That explains those green eyes." Looping a strand of hair behind my ear, I coyly glance down at the pretty table. "That shirt really makes them pop out," he states.

I jerk my attention back to him, unsure of what he's referring to by *them*.

"Your eyes," he clarifies. "The shirt brings out the color of your eyes." His gaze drops down to my shirt, and I get the feeling that he isn't referring to just my eyes anymore, but I don't mind.

I guess I decided on the perfect amount of cleavage.

For the first time in my entire life, I start to feel sexy. An overwhelming feeling of confidence washes over me, and I flip my hair away from my chest so he can see more of my…

shirt. "Thanks," I say with a coquettish smile.

We spend the next half hour getting to know each other. We cover food, music, and TV shows. I try to explain the appeal of reality TV, but Mateo doesn't buy it.

"It just makes annoying, rich people famous, which makes them more annoying and more rich," he complains. However, he did approve of my taste in music and was shocked when I told him that more than half of the music on my phone is metal. He didn't believe me, so I proved it to him by showing him the songs on my phone.

"I didn't peg you as the type of girl who listens to this kind of music." Mateo's voice brightens with intrigue.

"Oh? And what type of girl did you peg me as?"

"You got the whole girl-next-door thing going on." He waves his hand up and down in front of me.

I roll my eyes. "There's more to me than just that."

"All right." He puts his elbows on the table and leans in closer. "Tell me something more."

"Like what?"

"Let's start with something simple. What's your goal after you graduate?"

"That's not a simple question. I don't have a major yet." My gaze shifts to my nearly gone latte. "I'm not sure what I want to do for the rest of my life, but I do know that whatever it is, I want to make a difference." Realization that I might've gotten too vulnerable hits me, so I immediately perk up and focus on him. "What about you? What's your goal after school?"

"Social worker."

"Really?" I take him in, surprised by his comment.

"Yep, the plan is to go to grad school next year, get my social work degree, and then move back to Queens to work with the kids in my community."

"Grad school next year? You're a senior?"

"Yep."

"Then why are you taking a freshman class?"

Mateo rubs the back of his neck. "I might've fucked around my first semester here and need to make up some credits."

"You *might've*?"

He chuckles. "Yeah, but I got my shit together pretty quick. My advisor said that I should get into grad school no problem as long as I get straight As this semester."

"I guess this final paper is really important to you, then."

His dark, inviting eyes fixate on mine. "It sure is." My body heats up, and I can't take my attention off him. Thankfully, Mateo breaks the silence. "You want a refill?" He gestures down at my mug. "I mean, if you want to stay a little bit longer."

"Sure." I grin, enjoying our time together.

He calls over Lynn and politely asks her for another round. It is so nice to be with someone who is genuinely polite to people, unlike Hunter, whose kindness changes at the drop of a hat. Just the thought of him makes me sink into my chair.

"What's wrong?" Mateo asks. "It's okay if you don't want to stay. You don't have to."

"No, I want to," I assure him. "And besides, I don't have anywhere else to go." I try making a joke, but it comes out as more of a self-pitying statement.

"I'm sorry for yesterday. I didn't mean to put you in a difficult spot. I just wanted to mess with him. I didn't realize I was doing that at your expense until after." His empathetic gaze lets me know that he's telling the truth. There's no second-guessing the motive behind his apology.

"It's okay." I reciprocate his honesty.

"Can I ask you something?"

"Go for it."

"Why are you with him?"

I hesitate. I wasn't expecting that question. Not after all of our lighthearted conversation about which topping tastes best on pizza. My saying pineapple almost made him spit out his drink.

I open my mouth to defend Hunter, but then realize, "I'm not...right now."

"Oh. Okay."

"Here you go!" Lynn drops off our drinks at the table. "And I'm sorry to interrupt, but there's someone here wanting to book you for his party next month," she says to Mateo.

"Thanks, I'll be right there," he says to Lynn. "I'll be back in a second. Don't go anywhere," he tells me, placing his hand on top of mine before getting up.

He touched me.

It was the smallest physical contact in the world, but I'm pretty sure I forgot how to breathe.

As my brain remembers how to do the whole inhale-exhale thing, I watch Mateo talk to a college student. He looks familiar. He must be in one of my classes. Mateo pulls out his phone and types something into it, nodding his head. I can't hear their conversation, but I do catch them saying "man" a few times and then exchanging goodbyes.

"Sorry about that," Mateo says as he sits back down at our table. "He wanted to book the band I play in. It's me and a few guys from town. We get hired all the time to play for college parties."

That's how I know that guy. It was Derek, one of Hunter's frat brothers.

"That's awesome," I state.

He shrugs. "It's nothing serious, but it's a fun way to make some cash. Helps make ends meet."

"I wish I could play something, but I failed miserably at the recorder, so I can only assume it'd be downhill from there," I joke.

Mateo laughs. "No, you just need to find your instrument. It's all about finding the right fit."

"Maybe. Or maybe I've been doomed from the start."

"I don't believe that," he says, his voice getting soft, tugging at the center of my chest.

Everyone else seems to disappear, and for a split second, it feels like it's just the two of us. That is, until my phone lights up with an incoming call, bringing me back to reality. The moment I see "Mom" flashing across my screen, knots form in my stomach.

I hope she's not drunk dialing me. She hasn't called me since I started college, but I have been texting her to make sure she's okay. This could be epically embarrassing if I answer in front of Mateo.

"I'm so sorry. I need to take this," I tell Mateo, and abruptly walk outside.

"Mom?" I say into the phone. "Is everything okay?"

"Hi, Ellie," Mom says, her volume low.

"What's going on?"

"Nothing. I just miss you and wanted to hear your voice."

I can't tell what kind of state she's in. She's not slurring her words, but she's also not putting on her facade that life's wonderful and great.

"Oh." I let out a sigh. "I miss you too, Mom."

I don't think that's the truth, though.

It's been quite nice not to feel as if I'm in constant turbulence, aside from being with Hunter. Mom always confuses me. She says nice things like she misses the sound of my voice, but then denies any heartache she's ever caused me.

We only talk for a few more minutes. She sounds so sad, and I can't help but think that it's all my fault. Here I am away from her, happy to finally breathe some fresh air. Meanwhile, I've left her alone to fend for herself.

After we hang up, I slide my phone into my pocket and allow the guilt to seep into my pores. I should move back home. I never should've left her to begin with. She has no one to take care of her. I'm so selfish for going away to school. I should've just gone to community college instead. She needs me. What's wrong with me? Why did I leave Mom?

Tightness in my chest begins to creep in. I shut my eyes and focus on my breathing.

Inhale. Exhale.

Inhale. Exhale.

"Everything okay?" Mateo asks, breaking me out of my meditative state. "Sorry. I didn't mean to scare you. I just wanted to check if you were all right. You've been out here for a while."

Have I? How long was I focusing on my breathing? Why is my face wet? Was I crying?

"I'm not the best mind reader, but I'm assuming something's wrong." He lifts his thumb to my cheek and wipes away a tear. My breath stutters as the sensation of his fingertips causes sparks to go off inside me. Mateo jerks his hand back, seeming alarmed by his choice in breaking a boundary, and frankly, so am I. Sticking his hands in his pockets, he clears his throat.

"I'm fine." I shake off any signs of distress. "It's complicated. Stories for another time."

He nods his head. "I get it. I got a lot of stories too."

I smile, relieved that he's not pressing me to tell him about my family history. I don't like talking about my parents to anyone.

"Want a ride back to campus?"

I fixate my gaze on his gentle eyes. "Sure."

Mateo drives us back to campus in his battered gold Toyota. The interior has well-loved leather seats and a pungent pine car freshener swinging off his rearview mirror.

"I didn't know anyone still sold these things anymore." I point to the pine tree air freshener.

He snorts. "Drumming is a sweaty job. It was either that or let my car smell like ass." I chuckle at his crass comment. "Which building is yours?" Mateo asks as we pull into campus.

"Durham Hall." I point to the brick building, tucked into the corner and surrounded by trees.

Mateo pulls up to the building and parks his car. I go to thank him for the ride, but before I can, he shuts off his car and unbuckles his seat belt.

"What are you doing?" I ask.

"What type of gentleman would I be if I didn't walk you to your door?" he says, as if I uphold every man to gentleman status. His words make me laugh as we step out of his car.

"If I knew you were coming over, I would've cleaned," I warn him, trying to remember the state of my room before I left.

"Are you inviting me inside?" he asks as we walk up the stairs.

"Oh, well, I guess since you're walking me here, you might as well come in."

"I'd love to," he says, his voice getting even deeper.

I hope he's not getting the wrong impression. We've definitely been flirting, but I don't think I was hinting for him to come and get it.

Oh my god. I just invited him into my room.

Oh my god. He thinks we're going to hook up.

I stop short in front of my door. "I'm not going to have sex with you," I blurt out.

"What?"

"I know I said you could come in, but that wasn't an invitation for us to sleep together."

"Ellie, five minutes ago, you were crying. Do you really think I was coming up here to fuck you?"

I open my mouth to say something, but nothing comes out.

Mateo's cheeks rise, amusement stamped across his face. "You need help opening the door?"

I narrow my eyes at him. "No, I got it."

When the door opens, Bree is sitting on her bed in an oversized tee and a pair of cotton shorts. Crap. I should've let her know that I was bringing someone back. That's what good roommates do. Bree moves her attention from the TV screen to us. Her face dances with excitement at the sight of Mateo standing behind me.

"Hey, Bree. I'm sorry I didn't let you know ahead of time…"

"No worries at all." She moves the Chinese food container off her lap and stands up, completely unfazed by her appearance. "Hi, sexy drummer. I'm Bree. It's so nice to meet you."

Mateo laughs and turns to me. "I didn't realize I had a nickname." He looks back at Bree. "Nice to meet you, Bree. I'm Mateo."

"Come on in. Make yourself at home," she says. "You folks are in luck. I ordered enough Chinese food to feed the entire campus. You want some?"

Mateo shrugs and looks at me to gauge my reaction to the question.

My stomach growls from the scent of fried rice. "Sure. Why not?"

"Dig in," Bree exclaims.

Grabbing dumplings and fried rice, I sit on my mattress while Mateo seats himself at my desk chair.

"Whoa," he says, his brows lifting in surprise when he notes my records. "Your collection is sick."

"Yeah, Ellie is a music buff," Bree states.

Mateo nods, checking out the band names on the spines. His cheeks rise, admiring every one. "Which one's your favorite?" he asks me.

"Depends on my mood."

"Put one on," Bree suggests. "We can listen while we eat and then watch some TV."

Mateo puts on a record by Bleachers, and my curiosity stirs, wondering what made him choose it.

As the music plays, our evening is spent eating delicious food and then eventually watching horrible reality shows. Mateo's commentary throughout the episodes has Bree and me in hysterics, and we try to convince him that these shows are actually entertaining.

There's a sense of ease, like Mateo just naturally fits into my new world.

Without realizing it, I begin to yawn.

"Am I keeping you up too late?" Mateo grins at me.

I check the clock on my desk, and somehow, it's already after midnight.

"No, I'm fine." I yawn again. "But I might put my pj's on and lie down while we watch the next episode."

"Okay, I'll step out."

"It's fine. Just turn around." I don't know why, but I trust him enough to not be a perv. Just in case, I look at Bree. "Make sure he's not peeking."

"I'm on it." Bree fake glares at Mateo as he lets out a chuckle and turns around. Going to grab my pajamas from my drawer, I notice the only clean pair of pants I have are very baggy, with an ugly plaid pattern. I open up a different drawer and find my old black yoga pants. These are definitely better than the plaid.

I slip into the form-fitting pants, put on a white tank top, and throw my hair up in a messy bun.

"Okay," I tell Mateo as I finish putting my hair up.

Mateo spins around, and his eyes go to my body, traveling up and down, hugging every inch with his gaze—but I don't mind it. In fact, I like it. I *really* like it. He takes his bottom lip between his teeth as if to stop himself from saying the thoughts that are popping into his head.

Climbing into my bed as he continues to sit in the chair next to me, I look over at Bree, who's struggling so hard not to call us out. "Hit play, Bree." I try to fight back my smile as I talk.

I doze in and out as the TV show plays. I hear Bree and Mateo talking and laughing, but I can't make out what they're saying because I'm too tired. Suddenly, I feel the gentlest touch on my arm. My eyes flutter open, and I see Mateo's dark, kind eyes.

"I'm gonna head out so you can sleep," he whispers. I nod and fall back into my sweet slumber.

CHAPTER NINE

Ellie

Mateo hands me a coffee cup as he sits down next to me in our philosophy class. "Told you I'd bring you your favorite drink." He winks, and my heart beats a little faster.

Professor Boland starts the class with existential questions and goes on to lecture about Aristotle and Plato. I take as many notes as I can, while Mateo sits next to me with nothing on his desk.

My phone next to my laptop starts flashing Hunter's name. I click Ignore.

A few seconds later, I get a text.

HUNTER

Can we talk?

ME

No.

HUNTER

Ellie, I'm sorry, what I did in the car was fucked up. Just give me 5 minutes to talk to you

I try to focus on the lecture.

HUNTER

Please angel, I love you so much, you deserve so much better than how I've been treating you. Let me make it up to you

I continue to ignore him.

HUNTER

I'll come to your dorm when you're done with class. What time does it end?

Don't answer, Elena.

HUNTER

You know I'm going to show up there either way.
You might as well tell me the time.

I roll my eyes and cave.

ME

5.

HUNTER

See you then, angel

Putting my phone down, I glance over to see Mateo staring at me. Judging by the expression on his face, I'm pretty sure he read the entire conversation. I don't want to jump to conclusions, but he's giving me a what-the-fuck-is-wrong-with-you, he's-an-asshole, we-were-flirting-all-Friday-night, I-guess-that-means-nothing look.

"It's complicated," I whisper.

He nods and focuses his attention back on Professor Boland.

When class is over, we start walking in the same direction. Mateo hasn't acknowledged me since he gave me a half-assed nod. I don't know if I should just leave him alone or call him out. I do neither and choose to beat around the bush.

"When are you free to meet again so we can go over some questions?"

"Mateo!" The same girl from last week is at the exit, calling his name. I completely forgot about her. Annoyance knits my brows together. He has a girlfriend and shouldn't be so weird about me making up with Hunter.

Mateo glances at his girlfriend and then back at me. "Um…I'm not sure yet. I'll text you." He pivots and goes to leave.

I'm not sure why he's being so standoffish, but I can't spend my time thinking about that. I have to prepare for this conversation with Hunter.

I swiftly walk back to my dorm. Class ended a little early, so I have some time to collect myself. However, when I open my door, Hunter is already here, sitting on my bed.

"How did you get in?"

"Bree let me in a few minutes ago. I asked her if she could give us some privacy so we can talk." Hunter's head is down, and his demeanor is calm—a little too calm.

I put my stuff down on my desk. "Okay. So talk."

"Do you want to sit next to me?"

"No, I don't. What do you want to talk about?"

"How are you doing?" his voice is laced with gentleness.

"Fantastic. Anything else you want to say?"

His jaw tics, taking a deep inhale. My shoulders tense, and I take a step back. He notices my movements and reaches for my hand, bringing me nearer. He exhales as if pacified by the contact of my skin. "I need you to know that I'm sorry for how I acted the other day."

"I've heard."

"I'm fucked up, Elena. I don't know what's wrong with me. You make me unable to control myself sometimes. I love you *so much*. The thought of losing you literally makes me insane. I know I don't deserve you, but I can't live without you. You know that."

My mind flashes to January when we had broken up for what we said was going to be the last time. We had an epic blowout, complete with waterworks and destroyed furniture. We didn't talk for three weeks until one day he called me up, hysterical, telling me he was extremely depressed and didn't have anyone else he could talk to. I biked to his house and stayed by his side all night until he eventually fell asleep on my lap. The next morning, we decided that we're more toxic apart from each other than with each other.

We agreed on forever. Until now.

"Please, just give me one more chance," he begs as his beautiful blue eyes become glassy. "You don't have to give me an answer now. Just tell me you'll think about it, okay?"

I chew the inside of my cheek.

I don't want him to get back into that dark, scary place. And I love him so much. We've been through countless battles together, and I'm not going to let one stupid car ride bring us down.

"Okay," I say, the strength in my voice leaving. "I'll think about it."

"That's all I'm asking."

Hunter rises, and we hold each other's gaze while the energy between us cyclones a myriad of mixed emotions. We wait for the other to say something, but it never comes.

He cups my face with his hand and leans in, giving me a kiss on the forehead, then leaves.

I stand alone, processing our conversation.

We're not together, but not apart.

We're floating in limbo.

Hunter keeps his distance for the remainder of the week, occasionally texting throughout the day to say that he misses me or to see how I am doing. It's Friday, and Bree left for New York to spend the weekend with her girlfriend, Amber, and since I'm not on the schedule to work, I have the dorm to myself with zero plans.

Getting some fresh air, I go for a relaxing stroll around town. Walking past the Cozy Nook, I attempt to inconspicuously peer into the window of the coffee shop. Lynn's awesome purple hair moves back and forth as she chats with customers. A part of me wants to go inside to get my favorite drink and see if Mateo is in there. Another part of me is afraid that if I go in there, he won't be working, or worse, he'll be in there but act standoffish toward me, like he did in class. We didn't even cross paths while I was at work this week.

He said he'd text me, but I haven't heard from him at all.

Irritation begins to build. This is for class. He should be able to put his feelings aside so that we can get a good grade on our paper. Mateo is acting so childish about this. He has a girlfriend. He shouldn't even care if I'm back with Hunter.

My teeth grind together, and I sense confrontational Ellie making her way to center stage.

He's pissing me off.

On impulse, I push open the door. Lynn spins to see who's in the doorway and spots me. "Mateo!" she shouts toward the back with a huge grin.

I clam up, and any gusto I had is washed away. "Oh, no. I'm not here for him," I say as Mateo walks to the counter. "I'm not here for you."

"Okay?" His brow furrows.

"Okay."

"Do you want a drink?"

"Sure." I try not to make things more awkward than they already are.

"Have a seat, and I'll make it for you." He busies himself with the coffee machine as I glance over to where we sat last week and see another couple there. I find a small table against the wall and patiently wait.

"Here you are." Lynn comes to my table and hands me my latte.

"Thanks," I say, glancing past her shoulder to see if Mateo is anywhere to be found.

"Do you want me to pretend I need something so you can see him again?" She catches onto my musings, and before I can respond, she walks away.

Within a few minutes, Mateo plops down at my table. "Lynn is very pushy, and if I didn't come over here, she would nag me about it for the rest of eternity."

"I don't need you to sit with me because of her. I'm perfectly fine on my own."

Mateo rests his back on the chair and candidly asks, "Why did you meet up with him?"

"Why did you look at my phone?"

"Are you back with him?"

"Why does it matter?"

Something about our exchange draws a smile to my face, which Mateo reciprocates.

"Because if you're not, I'd invite you over later."

"What about your girlfriend?"

"I don't have a girlfriend."

"No? Then who's the girl who's always waiting for you after class?"

"That's my cousin, Michelle."

"Oh," I respond, stunting our fast-paced rhythm.

Mateo chuckles and then explains, "I drive her to her job in the next town over every Monday. That's why she's always rushing me. Her dad, my uncle, owns this place." He motions to the coffee shop and bookstore. "I'm one of the managers here and work a few days a week."

"Edgar is your uncle?"

"Yep."

"Oh."

After a few moments of silence, Mateo switches back to our original conversation. "So…you free tonight?"

I pause and sit back in my seat. "Possibly."

"I'm having a few people over at my place later if you want to come over."

"What time?"

"Any time after ten."

"I might be able to stop by." I take a sip of my drink.

"I'll text you my address." He gives me a wink and goes back to work.

CHAPTER TEN

Mateo

Michelle describes the house we rent as lived-in, which sounds nicer than, "It looks like people in their early-twenties who party too much crash here." Either way, our split-level home is worn in, to say the least. Our secondhand couches have rips and tears in the fabric, and the cushions have lost their firmness, sinking in the middle. Chipped paint and scuff marks are scattered on the walls, none of us remembering how they got there, but none of us are bothered enough by them to do any repainting.

Michelle and I each have separate bedrooms upstairs, and on the first floor, Nick and Rosa share one room. They're in grad school and might as well be married at this point because they've been together forever.

Our backyard is small, with a patch of grass and a concrete patio, but it's spacious enough to have people hang out there during our parties. Like tonight, when a bunch of Michelle's friends dance around to the loud music coming from a speaker. She insisted this party was for me, but I knew she just wanted an excuse to get rowdy.

"Jasmine coming over tonight?" Nick asks, grabbing a bottle of Patrón from one of our kitchen cabinets. The hinges squeak as the door struggles to stay intact when he closes it.

"Nah," I respond, glancing around at the other cabinets, noticing most of their doors are on their last leg. "I didn't tell her about the party."

"Why not?"

"I just wanted a low-key night. All of this is Michelle's doing," I say, gesturing around to the clusters of people in our home.

"Yeah, Michelle hasn't quite learned what low-key means," he says, laughing.

"Not in the slightest." I chuckle along with him, knowing that as much as Michelle can be a thorn in my side, we're cousins who care about one another. "At least I convinced my sisters not to come. Otherwise, I'd have no chance of chilling for my birthday."

Four older sisters. I'm the baby of the family, surrounded by women.

As much as I love them, living in Connecticut is a nice reprieve from them. They all live in Queens. Three of them have kids, while Stephanie, my sister who's closest in age to me, is living her single life. Steph was going to come tonight, but she got invited to a concert, so she chose the better option.

"So you got no one coming over for your supposed birthday party?" Nick asks.

"I invited this girl, Ellie." My lips twitch. "We'll see if she shows, though."

The strum of my heart picks up the pace.

There's something about Ellie that entices me. Aside from her gorgeous looks, there's an air of perplexity about her. Someone could quickly overlook her soft smile and gentle voice, but pausing to take her in, there's more. There's depth behind her eyes, hidden layers behind her words. I picked up on it the day I met her.

And I've been intrigued ever since.

A commotion coming from the guys hanging on the front stoop brings my focus out of my thoughts and onto the noise. Making my way over to them, I overhear one of Michelle's sleazy friends talking to someone.

"You lost, baby?" he says in a teasing tone.

Looking out the storm door, I spot Ellie getting closer to my house, and possessiveness instantly roars inside me.

Before she has a chance to answer, I swing open the door and step onto the stoop. "Back off. She's with me," I snap at him. "And if you ever make her or any of my guests feel uncomfortable, you'll be kicked out and never invited back." Without waiting for his response, I reach for Ellie and guide her inside.

My hand lands on the small of her back.

It's a small physical connection that I've done countless times with countless women, but never in my life have I felt my palm tingle with magnetism like it is right now with Ellie. And when Michelle erratically bursts into the living room, startling Ellie, my hand lights up even more as she leans into my touch.

I have the two officially meet, and after Michelle gives her a once-over, she disappears, going back to whatever it is she was doing. Leading Ellie past our smoke-stained walls and into our kitchen, I have her meet Nick and Rosa before they go into the backyard.

"Can I get you something to drink?" I ask Ellie as I take a beer out of my fridge.

"No thanks. I'm okay." She glances around the room, observing the others as she nervously shifts her weight from foot to foot.

"We have more than just beer. We have tequila, vodka, rum. I think we even have some of that girly spiked seltzer shit."

"It's okay. I don't drink."

"Oh. Okay." I put my beer back in the fridge.

"You don't have to do that."

"Nah, it's fine. I don't need it." I give her a reassuring smile, assuming there's a story behind her not wanting to drink. I want to respect her reasoning, whether she wants to share it with me or not, and don't want to get wasted with her if she's not into it.

Someone cranks the speaker outside, pulling Ellie's attention to the backyard. I watch her stare out the window, witnessing a group of people dance on the concrete patio. Her eyes light up with something that looks an awful lot like temptation, and my veins heat up, imagining what it'd be like to have her body close to mine if we were out there.

"Wanna dance?" I ask.

Her attention moves back to me, shock widening her eyelids. "No way. I don't dance."

Leaning my back against the kitchen counter, I can't help but shamelessly check her out. "You just move your feet and twirl your hips around." My eyes go to my hips, then back up to her face. "It's easy."

"Trust me. No one wants to see my hip action."

"I beg to differ."

A spark of electricity hits me, wondering if the rest of my body would tingle the same way my palm did if I were to touch more than just her lower back. But the rosiness painting her cheeks lets me know I'm moving a bit too quickly for her liking.

"We can head upstairs to my room and go over some questions for class instead, if you want," I suggest, easing our way into the night.

"Okay." She fidgets with the hem of her shirt as she follows me upstairs.

I don't have any expectations for tonight, but the fact that she's willing to hang out in my bedroom shoots excitement down my spine.

Entering, I move past my dark wooden furniture that's pushed up against my green walls and witness Ellie's jaw drop when she takes note of the center of my bedroom, which is encompassed by a multitude of my instruments—drums, guitars, a keyboard, and my amps.

"You play more than just the drums," Ellie states. A genuine smile lights up her features, and my heart skips a beat when I notice her dimple on her left cheek.

"What makes you think that?"

Ignoring my sarcasm, she looks in wonder at my collection. "I wish I could play something."

"I can teach you sometime if you want." My mouth moves faster than my brain can process. Confusion throws me off for a beat, unsure why I'd offer to teach her.

"I'd like that."

Getting back on track, I sit on my bed and pat the empty space next to me. She starts to move closer but hesitates, not sure if she should.

"Don't worry. I don't bite that hard."

"I hope you don't bite at all," she says, choosing to sit on the bed, but the farthest spot possible.

"Not into that?"

"No!" Her voice rises in pitch, causing me to chuckle.

There's a slight moment of silence, and I decide to break the ice. "You want to pick a question to discuss or have sex first?" I tease, reminiscent of her comment when she invited me into her dorm room.

Her breath catches in her throat, and she coughs out a laugh. "Oh my god!"

"I'm kidding! I'm kidding!" I say, reaching for her hands. Time freezes for a split second the instant I make contact with her. My body stirs in an unfamiliar way, as if there's a new surge of energy inside me, waiting to be let free.

"You better be. I definitely didn't envision my first time with a bunch of people standing right outside the room."

Time immediately resumes, and I drop her hands as if they burned me. "Your *what*?"

Ellie's face reddens, realizing what she had just admitted. "Like, my first time outside of my own bed," she tries to backpedal.

"No. That's not what you said."

My eyes locked with hers. A million racing thoughts bombard me. Jasmine had Ellie figured out the first day I met her. She is way too innocent. She shouldn't be with me, or anyone who has a tarnished past like mine. But my brain suddenly flips, realizing that this means she's never slept with her douchebag ex-boyfriend. She definitely shouldn't be with someone like him.

A fierce protectiveness radiates out of the depths of my soul.

The more I stare into her sage-colored eyes, the more transfixed I become. Shades of green are swirled with innocence, but not in totality. There are flickers of defiance and emotional complexity fraying the edges of purity.

"So…" Ellie breaks the silence. "Now that I've officially made things super awkward, I think I'm going to head out." She starts to stand, and on impulse, I gently take hold of her wrist, getting her to pause.

But I don't know why.

There's zero chance we're hooking up, and neither of us has it in us to play the charade of wanting to answer philosophy questions.

But I like spending time with her. I like the way she makes me feel. It's different from anything I've ever experienced.

And I don't want her to leave.

CHAPTER ELEVEN

Ellie

Fire heats up my cheeks, and as I stand, ready to dart out of Mateo's room, he gently takes hold of me, getting me to pause.

I glance down at where his fingers landed, his callused skin wrapping around the shameful scars on my wrist.

My pulse spikes.

Not because he's touching me, but out of fear that he might see me.

The real me.

The scarred, broken, unstable girl and not the one who puts on a happy face for the rest of the world.

"Don't leave," Mateo says, letting go of me. "You weren't planning on doing anything with me anyway, so what does it matter, right?"

I mull over his comment, letting my heart rate steady. "I guess it doesn't matter." I sit back down, only this time in closer proximity to him. "I just get uncomfortable whenever someone finds out."

He shakes his head. "It's nothing to be ashamed about."

"I mean, I've done everything else except sex," I start to nervously ramble off my thoughts. "And it's not for Hunter's lack of trying. We had the opportunity to do it a thousand times, but I just..." I bite my tongue, realizing I'm sharing way too much and need to flip the focus off me. "Are you a virgin?" I instantly cringe at the first question that popped into my head and out of my mouth.

Mateo impulsively laughs, then quickly composes himself. "No."

Nodding, I pick at my nails as we sit in silence until my curiosity gets the best of me. "How old were you?"

"You sure you want to get this personal?"

"I'm sorry if that came out rude. You don't have to share anything you don't want to."

"I don't mind sharing it." Mateo shifts closer to me, and my breathing gets heavier. "I just didn't know if you wanted to go there." The rasp in his voice strikes the center of my core.

My attention flickers to his lips, then back to his soulful eyes. My voice is just above a whisper as I say, "I want to go there."

Just then, someone bangs on the door, jolting us out of our conversation.

"Let's go, lover boy. Time for your birthday cake!" Michelle shouts.

Mateo groans. "Ugh. Fuck."

"It's your birthday?"

"Maybe." He stands and pulls me up to join him. "They're never gonna leave us alone if I don't go down for cake."

We walk downstairs for cake and end up staying there for the rest of the evening, neither of us bringing up the conversation we had in his bedroom.

We hang out in the living room, and I get to know more about Mateo and his housemates, Nick and Rosa. By the time two in the morning rolls around, my energy starts to dwindle. I definitely need to work on being a night owl now that I'm in college.

"You look tired. You okay to drive?" Mateo asks.

"I don't drive. I took an Uber."

His face drops. "I didn't know that. I would've picked you up if I knew you were going to pay someone to drive you here."

"It's okay. I don't mind."

"Let me drive you back at least."

"No, seriously, don't worry about it." I try to stop myself from yawning, but it doesn't work.

Mateo puts his arm around my shoulders, grinning. "Come on. We'll head out now."

Mateo follows me to my room, creating space between us as he leans against the wall next to my door while I unlock it. Out of respect or fear, I'm not sure, but I find it funny how cautious he's being now that he's learned this new information about me. "Are you going to come in?" I ask.

"Do you want me to?"

I roll my eyes. "Just come in."

Mateo enters, shutting the door behind him. "Where's Bree?"

"She's in New York visiting her girlfriend for the weekend. I have the room all to myself."

"Nice," he says, standing in the middle of my room with his hands shoved in his pockets.

"You can sit, you know." I gesture toward my bed.

"Oh." He takes one of his hands from his pocket and tugs on the collar of his shirt. "Okay."

I watch as he makes himself comfortable on my bed. "Close your eyes. I'm going to change."

"You don't have Bree here to check on me to make sure I'm not peeking," Mateo teases as he covers his face.

"Well, I guess I'm just going to have to trust you," I say as I slip into yoga pants and a pink tank top. "Okay, you're good," I inform him as I put my hair up into a bun.

He turns to look at me and examines my body once again. His openness sends a thrill through me. I like the way he looks at me.

I want more of it.

Hunter's image pops into my head, but I push it away as I join Mateo on my bed. "Thanks for driving me back."

"Anytime."

I know Mateo should probably leave, but I don't want him to. "Pick a number, one through ten."

"Eight," Mateo says without missing a beat.

Leaning over toward my desk, I shuffle through my papers. I can feel the back of my shirt rise up, so I yank it down. I hear Mateo chuckle to himself as I take out the question sheet from philosophy class. My eyes glance down at number eight. *What is love?* Nope, not asking him that question tonight. I look at the one right above it, "Will the world ever know peace?"

He scoffs. "With how our country is, probably not. What about you? Do you think the world will ever know peace?"

I shrug. "I'd like to think that and hope the world will evolve for the better, but who knows." His eyes are glued to me, taking in what I said, but I don't feel finished. I don't know why, but I allow my vulnerability to poke through as I continue, "I want to transform into the best version of myself and pass my morals down to my children, who I hope pass them down to theirs. Hopefully, my small amount of kindness will have some sort of positive ripple effect on the world." A rush of heat rises to my face, self-conscious that I've exposed some of my personal thoughts.

Mateo doesn't comment. Instead, he gets more comfortable on my bed, lying on his side with one of his arms holding up his head. He's close enough for me to notice a small scar on his right temple and the details of the large scar on his upper arm. My pulse quickens. I've never been this close to anyone on a bed before, aside from Hunter.

"Can I ask you something?"

"You can ask me anything," he says.

"How did you get your scar?" I motion to his arm.

"A knife."

I stare at him, waiting for him to divulge more, but he doesn't. "Is that how you got this one too?" I ask, touching the small scar on his face. The nerve endings in my fingertips sizzle at the contact. For a brief moment, I get lost in the connection, and my hand lingers a little too long on his skin.

"No, that one I got when I was little. I was in my kitchen, and I tripped over—"

"You're going to give me an entire story about tripping over something, but you're not going to give me any details about getting knifed?"

Mateo grins. "I didn't know if you wanted me to go into detail about that. You didn't have any follow-up questions."

"Yes, I want the details!" I slink down so that I'm no longer sitting. I lie on my side, mirroring his position. We're now extremely close, the heat from his body roasting up mine.

Mateo deeply inhales before speaking. "I was at a party, and some guy kept mouthing off about one of my sisters. I had enough, so I went after him. He had a knife on him, and that's how I got this." He moves his arm to better expose his wound.

"Jeez." His eyes watch as my fingers run over the long, scarred line on his arm.

I snap my hand back.

I need to stop touching him. I shouldn't be touching him.

"Yeah, I got myself into a lot of trouble when I was younger," Mateo states.

"What kind of trouble?"

"Stealing, drinking, drugs, fights. I was the token problem child of the family."

I gaze at him, wanting to know so many things about this seemingly composed man with a rebellious past. "Why?"

"I was an angry kid."

"How come?"

He presses his lips together into a line, debating whether or not to tell me. "I guess it kind of started with my dad." Mateo clears his throat. "He was abusive to all of us—my mom, sisters, me. He beat the shit out of us. I would try to fight back no matter who he was hitting, but that usually didn't pan out so well. He left when I was eleven, and I started hanging out with the wrong people. I did a lot of fucked-up shit." He pauses and studies my reaction. I nod my head for him to continue, and he seems relieved by my encouragement.

"My school convinced my mom to send me to a residential placement during my junior year of high school, so I was sent away, which turned out to be the best thing for me. The people there helped me get my life together. They even helped me get into college—helped me with my application, scholarships, financial aid...everything." He stops for a brief second, but then keeps revealing more. "That's why I want to be a social worker. I want to help kids who are as fucked up as I once was and get them back on track."

His honesty warms the center of my chest. My perception of him has definitely changed, but in an even better way. "You're a really great person, Mateo."

"So are you."

"You don't know me that well. I could be a serial killer."

He smiles for a second, but then grows serious. "No one outside of my family knows about any of that."

The warmth in my chest radiates down the rest of me, bursting out of the tips of my toes. "So...you just told me one of your secrets?" He nods in response, and I say the only thing I can think of. "Why?"

Intensity swirls around his dark irises. "I don't know." His gaze fixates on my lips, and he seems like he has to force himself to look back up at my eyes. "Your turn to tell me something."

Sensing my walls knocking down by the minute, I try to decipher just how vulnerable to get with him. Endless stories flood my mind, and my attention bounces around my room, eventually landing on the pictures hanging on my wall. "I've been fascinated with France since I was a little kid," I say, gesturing to the image of the Eiffel Tower.

He keeps his focus trained on me. "How come?"

Exhaling a shaky breath, I prepare to share a very fragile part of myself. "There were these books I used to read when I was little, about a girl who lives in a boarding school in Paris. I would read them over and over again and pretend that I was her. I hung up pictures of France on my wall and would stare at them all day and imagine that I could escape there, away from my parents, having an entirely new life. It became my safe place and still is, I guess. It sounds stupid, but I ended up falling in love with a place I've never been to. My only dream in life since I could remember has been to go there."

Mateo's gentle eyes wander over my face, studying me. "You'll make it to France one day, Ellie," he states as if he's making a promise he swears to keep.

Comfortable quietness falls between us as our gazes lock. Little by little, our bodies naturally drift even closer. "Ellie, I need to apologize," he says before we get *too* close.

"For what?"

"For coming on too strong. I read everything wrong. I thought—"

"It's okay."

I like that he came on strong.

I like this new feeling pummeling through me.

I like that we're lying next to each other, close enough to connect, but only choosing to do so with our words.

He shifts the conversation to trivial things. My arm gets tired from holding my head up, so I allow myself to rest on my pillow. I should tell him to go, but I don't want to. I enjoy his company, his presence, his energy.

"Ellie?"

My eyes flutter open, and Mateo's dark-brown hair fills my vision. We must've fallen asleep talking last night. I roll over, wondering who startled me awake.

There's a loud knock on my door. "Elena?"

Oh my god. It's Hunter.

Jumping out of bed, my sudden movements wake Mateo. My heart rattles against my rib cage, my entire body trembling.

"What—" Mateo starts to speak, but I slam my hand over his mouth.

"Hunter is right outside," I whisper. "Please get in the closet. Please."

He looks at me like I'm insane, but I cannot have Hunter knowing Mateo slept over, in my bed, no less.

"Please," I beg, fear permeating from my pores.

He rolls his eyes, grabs his shoes, and goes into my closet.

"Elena, are you okay?" Hunter asks through the door.

"One sec. I'm just waking up," I say as I close the shuttered door to my closet.

Anxiety thrashes around in my gut. Taking a deep breath, I compose myself, then open the door. Hunter's standing there with a bouquet of flowers, his blue puppy-dog eyes pleading for forgiveness.

"Hey, angel. I got you these," Hunter says as he passes me the flowers.

"These are beautiful. Thank you," I respond sincerely and take them out of his hands, placing them on my desk. He reads that as an invitation to enter.

"I'm surprised you're still sleeping. It's almost one."

"Is it? I stayed up really late watching TV."

Hunter zeros in on me, grasping my hand. He gets straight to the point. "Are you ready for our break to be over?"

My heart is pounding so loud I swear he can hear it. I need to get him out of my room, but I'm not sure how to respond. "Um..."

He pulls me closer, and one of his hands reaches for my face. "I've missed you so much." His lips claim mine.

This is awkward. So awkward. But if I act weird, he'll suspect something, so I kiss him back. His fingers skim the top of my pants, eager to get inside. I flinch, breaking free, but he grabs hold of my hips.

Hunter moves his mouth to my neck while his hands shimmy my pants down, exposing part of my thong. I try to wiggle free, but he's so much stronger than I am. I *really* hope Mateo is being the gentleman he says he is and closing his eyes right now.

"Hunter." My voice strains as my breath trembles.

Panic twists around my lungs.

He shoves his hand down the front of my pants before I can refuse and begins to circle my clit. I reflexively let out a small moan. *Oh my god. This cannot be happening right now.*

"Hunter."

He's not quitting. I rapidly inhale and exhale as my pants sink lower when his fingers enter me. My shuddering hands grip on to his blond hair, jerking his head away from my throat so we can make eye contact. "Hunter, I just got out of bed. I need to pee and shower."

He stops. "Okay. Go do what you have to do. I'll wait for you."

Of course, it wouldn't be that easy. I say the one thing I know will get him off my back for a little bit. "Why don't I get ready for the day, and I'll meet you over at the house later?"

His features brighten. "You're going to come to the house later?"

"Yeah," I respond, as if that was my plan all along.

"We're having a party."

"I figured. It's Saturday. I catch on quick," I say, adjusting my pants so they're resting properly on my hips.

"So does this mean that we're back together?"

"I don't know. I'm confused." I walk toward the door, hoping he will follow my lead. He does.

"Confused about what? I thought you were just pissed at me for the car thing."

"I was…am. I don't know. I just need more time to think."

Hunter's jaw tics, but he keeps his cool. "Okay. I'll see you at the house later." He gives me a peck and walks out the door.

I close the door behind him, making sure it's locked. Resting my forehead against it, I let out a huge exhale. When I turn around to open the closet for Mateo, he's already standing on the outside.

"I'm gonna go," Mateo says, putting on his shoes.

"I'm sorry." My voice shakes.

"Don't be." He finishes tying his sneaker and stands up. "I'll back off."

"What do you mean?"

"Obviously, I'm one of the reasons why you're feeling confused, and I don't want to do that to you."

"I-I'm sorry."

"You don't need to apologize for everything, Ellie," Mateo says, moving to the door. "I'll see you around."

CHAPTER TWELVE

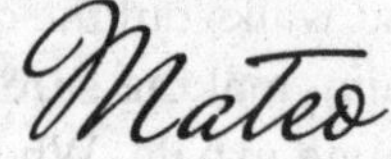

I wish I could've yanked my eyes out of my skull.

It was like a train wreck. I couldn't look away as much as I hated it.

Jealousy crawls up my back as I dart out of Ellie's room, down the stairs, and out of Durham Hall.

The moment the soles of my shoes hit the blacktop of the parking lot, I text Jasmine.

ME

wanna come over? I'll be home in 10

JAS

I'm down

I attempt to rid myself of envy while driving back to my apartment, but my mind won't stop replaying the scene I witnessed play out in front of me while I hid in a fucking closet.

My pulse whirls with bitterness.

The thought of Hunter's lips on Ellie's skin and his fingers touching her pussy unlocks a vicious response from under my ribcage.

The angry pounding of my heart follows me from my car and into my bedroom while I wait for Jasmine on my mattress.

I don't even know why I care. Never in my fucking life have I ever been jealous if a girl has a boyfriend. In fact, I'd get a sense of relief because that meant she didn't want to get into a relationship with me.

"Hey," Jasmine says, entering my room and thankfully interrupting my thoughts.

She's exactly what I need right now—a distraction.

"Hey," I respond, pulling my shirt over my head.

Neither of us bothers with small talk as we strip down and get to business.

Maybe that's what's bothering me. Ellie and I spent the night having deep conversations, learning more about each other and our perceptions of life. I've never done that with another person before.

Not even with Jasmine. She's sucked my dick how many fucking times? And we still don't talk about anything with substance. Our topics include classes, sex, and parties. That's it, and that's how I've kept it with every one of my hookups.

Glancing down, I gingerly thread my fingers through Jasmine's hair as her head bobs up and down. Closing my eyes, I let my imagination wander, thinking about how incredible it would feel to have Ellie's lips wrapped around me. Her soft, golden strands knotting around my fingertips, but not before I spent all the time in the world touching her, getting her off, having her moan for me in a way that's a million times stronger than the one I heard earlier.

Jasmine abruptly stops, and my eyelids fling open. "You're being too gentle," she says with a smirk. "Fuck my mouth, Mateo." She dips back down, and I fist her hair, tugging at the strands and roughly moving her head at the pace I want.

But even as she's trying to get me off, my mind keeps drifting back to Ellie.

How her small frame felt cradled against me. The little dimple in her left cheek that pops up when she *really* smiles. The way we both felt safe sharing about ourselves.

My body tenses.

Just as I'm about to come in Jasmine's mouth, the realization hits me.

Fuck. I like Ellie.

CHAPTER THIRTEEN

Ellie

I made it through my second frat party unscathed, although I must admit I'm not really a fan of a shit ton of people piling into a house and getting hammered. It's not fun for me. I don't think I'll ever let loose and act like a normal college kid.

Not to mention, Delilah killed any opportunity of me enjoying myself by giving me death glares the entire time. Thank God we sit far enough away from each other in philosophy class that I don't have to deal with her.

My stomach has been in worried knots all day, anticipating going to philosophy and seeing Mateo.

I'm so nervous that I forgot my laptop in my room. My feet move as fast as possible back to my dorm to grab my things before class starts. Mateo hasn't texted at all since being held captive in my closet. I guess he's doing what he said he would and is backing off. I wonder if he'll even talk to me in class.

I make it to my room with just enough time to go back across campus for class if I hurry fast enough. As I reach for my laptop on my desk, my phone rings. It's an unknown number from Massachusetts. Normally, I wouldn't answer, but the panging sensation in my gut is telling me to take the call.

"Hello?" I ask whoever is on the other line.

"Hi, Elena."

A lump grows in my throat. I'd recognize that frail voice anywhere. "Mom? Is everything okay?" I haven't been checking in as often. I should've been texting her more.

"Do you have a minute to talk?"

"Yeah, what's going on?" I pace the length of my room.

Mom lets out a shaky sigh. "I'm in rehab."

Gasping, relief swims through my veins. I've been begging Mom to go to rehab for years. "Rehab!"

"Yes. It…it's court-ordered."

"Court-ordered?" I freeze.

"I was arrested two days ago," she tells me, her voice so timid it's almost inaudible.

"*Arrested?* For what!"

There's a very long pause. "Driving under the influence and possession."

I'm momentarily paralyzed. I see red as rage encompasses every cell in my body. "Possession of *what*?"

"Pills."

My heart dives into my stomach and drowns there. I've tried to take care of her for years, only for her to pick up a new habit.

"Pills?" Memories of her constantly needing to go to the doctor for her back pain are filtering in. I was so stupid to assume those appointments were legit.

I tried so hard to fix her.

Years spent taking care of her for nothing.

My nights consumed with cleaning up vomit and broken bottles. My days walking around her on eggshells. Covering for her when people would ask how she was doing. Staying home to help her instead of going to school events like a normal teenager. Soaking up the verbal offenses she throws at me when she's trashed. Falling for her lies every single time she swore when she was sober that last night was the last time.

"My attorney got them to lower the sentence. The judge revoked my license and sent me to rehab until mid-December." She waits for my response, but I'm speechless. "I'm so sorry, Ellie." Her voice breaks, and I know she's crying, but I don't have the capacity to care right now.

"No, you're not."

"Of course I am, Elena. I never wanted this life for you."

Years of resentment boil over, finally pushing me to my breaking point. "Don't you dare do that."

"Do what?"

"Sit in rehab and pretend that you're sorry. You don't give a shit about me."

"That's not true—"

"I don't want to hear it." My hands shake with anger, an outburst of things I've always wanted to say exploding from my mouth. "You're a grown woman who's always depended on her daughter to clean up her mess. I'm done with it. I don't want to deal with your shit anymore. I'm glad you got arrested."

I hang up before she can say another word, but in an instant, I'm chained down with regret for speaking to her that way.

Heat swells in my body, causing me to break out in a sweat.

I can't control my emotions that are avalanching.

The walls are closing in.

I'm trapped.

The pain building inside of me is overwhelming.

Too overwhelming.

I dig my nails into my arm and drag them down to my wrist. The urge to cut myself is intensifying. I haven't had this temptation in years.

My chest constricts.

My vision is spotty.

Breathe, Ellie.

Out of habit, my fingers reach for my phone to call Hunter.

Hunter tenderly holds me in my bed. "Maybe I can see if anyone in my family can pull some strings and get her out early." Implying that his family can pay someone off.

"No way. I'm not getting your family involved." The thought of anyone knowing about this makes me nauseous, and the idea of Hunter's family getting tangled in this web makes me feel even worse. "How could she do this? After everything we've been through." Tears continue to fall down, even though it's been hours since my phone call with Mom.

Hunter squeezes me. "I love you, angel," he says into my hair. "Even if no one else does, I always will. You know that, right?"

The realization of that stings, but I'm thankful that there's someone to love me. I told him everything, even admitting to wanting to cut myself.

I'm a fucking mess, and he loves me despite that.

"I love you too."

He kisses my forehead. "You should get some rest."

"Don't leave me." I cling to his shirt.

"There's no way in hell I'm leaving you. I'll stay here all night if you want me to."

I nod into his chest. "Please."

Hunter delicately pulls me closer, as if he's scared that if he moves too fast, he'll shatter me. He comforts me the way I always longed to be comforted as a helpless little girl.

"You're the most incredible person I've ever known," he says as he weaves his fingers through my golden strands. "You deserve so much more than this."

He then picks up my left wrist and rubs his thumb over my scars. I wince at the thought of me having that urge.

"I'll give you everything you deserve, Ellie. Whatever you want and need, I'll be the one to give it to you." He smiles. "We can go on dates every day. I'll get you a house by the water. How many kids do you want? Seven? Twelve?"

I chuckle, and his smile grows wider.

"Nineteen?"

I laugh a little louder.

"We'll go to France every summer. All twenty-one of us."

"If we're having nineteen kids, then you and I are going to France alone." I manage to joke along.

"That sounds even better."

He nuzzles into me, and I glance up at the pictures hanging on my wall. The thought of running away to France sounds better and better. I never told Hunter about my rash decision to apply to the abroad program, but I haven't even heard back from them. It was silly of me to even entertain the idea that I'd be fine on my own. Look at me. One call from Mom and I broke into pieces. How on earth did I think I'd survive on my own?

CHAPTER FOURTEEN

Ellie

OCTOBER

The entire week goes by in a daze. I go through the motions, not really wanting to think about anything else aside from school and work. I want to avoid thinking about Mom for as long as possible. Hunter and I are back together, but that's no surprise after the way he's been supporting me.

Before leaving for class on Monday morning, I glance at myself in the mirror. I look like I just rolled out of bed—a messy bun, an oversized purple sweatshirt, and old leggings. Dark circles imprint under my eyes, making it seem like I haven't slept in weeks. At least my appearance matches most of the other students since it's midterms and everyone's studying like mad.

I'm on autopilot the entire day and somehow end up in philosophy class. I doze off at my desk before Professor Boland even enters the room.

"You okay?"

I turn to see Mateo sitting next to me. I managed to successfully avoid seeing him at the Cozy Nook due to spending my short shifts in the stockroom. The thought of Mateo knowing that Hunter and I are back together has been tugging at my heartstrings.

"Yeah," I lie.

"Why weren't you in class last week?"

"I was sick."

He doesn't respond. Instead, he just stares, seeing right through me. No follow-up questions. Admittedly, I'm disappointed. In a small and selfish way, I wanted him to show that he cares, even though I don't deserve it. It's a bitter pill to swallow.

It's already Friday, the day we are supposed to enroll for next semester's classes. Hunter is with me in my room, helping me choose. He suggests that since we both need a math credit, we take the class together. I take a look at my classes, and it excites me for the first time in weeks—Algebra 1, Developmental Psychology, French, World History, and Critical Thinking in Philosophy.

"Come here," Hunter says, and I realize he's lounging on my bed and no longer sitting next to me. "I can tell you have a lot on your mind. Let's talk."

I cuddle up next to him. "I don't feel like talking. Help me get my mind off things."

Hunter has been amazing the past two weeks, patient and understanding. This isn't new for us. When I'm completely taken over by the emotional rollercoaster that is Mom, he lets me lean on him to get by.

"Next Saturday is Halloween," he says, trying to distract my swirling thoughts.

"Does that mean you're having a party?" I ask, even though I know the answer.

"It sure does. I think it could be good for you to get out. You know, a change of pace, socializing, actually looking presentable," he teases.

"Rude." I nudge him.

"I'm kidding. But I do think you should come."

"Maybe."

Hunter's pants start buzzing with an incoming text. I pat them, reaching for the pocket, but he gets there before me and takes out his phone. I see Delilah's name pop up, but Hunter turns the phone, and I can't read her message.

"Delilah's texting you?"

"Yeah, she just wanted to know about the party."

I move away from him and stand up. "You know she likes you, right?"

Hunter sits up and places his phone next to him. "What?"

"Don't play stupid. She obviously has a thing for you."

He gives me a dismissive laugh. "Ellie, I have no idea what you're talking about."

"Is there something going on between the two of you?"

"Are you kidding me? I've been dealing with your issues for weeks, and you're accusing me of cheating on you?"

"I didn't accuse you of anything. I just genuinely want to know if there's anything going on."

"You're paranoid."

The comment causes my muscles to get rigid. "Don't call me that," I snap.

"Elena." His tone softens, and he takes my hand. "You know how much I love you, right? You know I would never cheat on you."

I glance at the floor, letting my guard down due to his gentleness. He has been so incredible through all of this. I should've kept my mouth shut about Delilah.

He feathers kisses on my hand. "Angel," he says. "I'm saying this out of pure love and concern."

My eyes flicker to his, and my brow furrows, unsure of what he's concerned about.

Hunter continues, "I think you should go back on your medicine."

"What?" I yank my hand from his grip.

"You've been anxious, depressed, paranoid..."

"I get it," I say, trying to interrupt him, my guard instantly flying back up.

"Having panic attacks."

"The last time I had a panic attack was in your car because you decided to drive like a fucking maniac and almost kill us," I bite out, which isn't entirely true because I've had a few others since, but he wasn't there.

"Ellie, I barely went over eighty."

"Barely went over eighty? You literally laughed in my face, telling me that we were hitting over a hundred."

"I didn't *actually* go over a hundred." His voice is unnervingly calm. It's as if he's talking to a crazy person who's seconds away from exploding.

"Yes, you did! I watched you hit a hundred twenty!"

"I think you need to call your doctor. You even told me you were thinking of cutting yourself again."

"I told you because I wanted to be open and honest with you. I didn't think you'd throw it back in my face. I told you because I needed your support!"

"And you have my support. It's just that sometimes you're so fragile, I get scared. You need a lot of help, Elena."

"No, I don't!"

"Yes, you do. Just look at your family. Of course you're going to need professional help going through all of that shit."

"Stop it!"

"Elena, you're screaming when I'm just trying to have a normal conversation."

He's making me feel fucking crazy.

Pacing the room, I put my hands up to my head. I know I saw the speedometer, and it said one hundred twenty. I know I've been a little emotional lately, but it's because I have a lot of shit to worry about. I went off my medicine over the summer, and I've been doing okay until recently. Sure, I thought of hurting myself, but I didn't go through with it. And yeah, I might've had a few panic attacks, but I was able to calm myself down. I'm doing pretty well, all things considered.

"You should call your doctor tomorrow," he says in such a sweet tone that it feels like he's mocking me.

"Don't do that!" I shout.

"Do what?"

"Twist my thoughts and feelings. I had a few rough weeks, but I'm doing fine!"

"It's okay if you're on medicine, Ellie. It's nothing to be ashamed about. Some people just aren't as capable or strong enough to go through this type of stuff—"

Anger blasts through my veins. "Don't call me weak!" I snatch his phone and throw it across the room, smashing it into pieces.

Hunter jumps up, towering over me, and yells in my face. "What is wrong with you, fucking psycho?" He shoulders me out of the way and goes over to his broken phone.

The room spins.

I need to get out of here.

I grab my phone and sweatshirt and run into the hallway. Bree is there, but I barrel past her. Bursting through the doors of Durham Hall, the cool, brisk air hits my face.

I don't know where I'm going. I just need to get away.

My AirPods are sitting on my desk, so I play my music on my phone through the speaker, as loud as I can, praying it can drown out my thoughts. Angry, screaming music is now contaminating the beautiful, picturesque campus.

But the music doesn't help. My mind is still whirling.

Was he really only going eighty? Did I make up the one hundred twenty? I could've sworn that I saw him go over a hundred. Maybe it wasn't exactly one hundred twenty, but I'm pretty sure it was at least a hundred. And why does he think I need to go back on medicine? Because I'm upset over Mom? It's fine, I'll get over it eventually. Although I did think about cutting myself. Maybe that is a sign that I'm not okay. But I didn't cut myself, so that's a good thing, right? Am I depressed, like he said? He said I haven't been looking presentable. I think that's a sign of depression. I know difficulty sleeping is a sign too. Maybe I should go back on the medicine. I just hate the thought of him belittling me for needing to depend on them. I guess I'm not strong, just like he said. I'm weak. I'm a "fucking psycho," as he so graciously called me.

I am nothing more than this endless cycle.

I'm trapped.

It never ends.

It's never going to fucking end.

"Ellie?"

"What?" I say through gritted teeth, and spin around to see who called my name.

It's Mateo. I'm in front of the coffee shop? How did I get here? I walked into town without even realizing it. Maybe I am a psycho.

"What are you listening to?" He chuckles.

"Oh." I turn off the screams and heavy guitars coming from my phone. "Sorry."

"Are you okay?"

I immediately burst into tears.

Oh my god, I am crazy. Why am I so emotional? What is wrong with me?

"Ellie? What's going on?" Mateo reaches out, putting his hand on my arm. "Do you want to go somewhere to talk?"

CHAPTER FIFTEEN

Ellie

Mateo hands me a glass of water as I sit on his bed. He waits for me to take a sip and then places the glass on his desk. "Do you mind if I sit next to you?" he asks.

"Not at all," I say. He joins me on his bed, and I instantly begin talking. There's something about his energy that invites me to open up to him. I don't tell him about Hunter, but I do share what happened with Mom.

"I can't believe she got arrested." I let my thoughts fall out of my mouth. Mateo stays quiet while I continue to speak. "I've taken care of her for years, and the second I'm not there, this happens. I knew I should've never left her."

"Your dad's not in the picture?" Mateo asks, picking up that I haven't mentioned him.

"No, he's dead."

"Oh shit. I had no idea."

"It's fine. It happened five years ago. I kind of moved past it."

"I don't know if loss is anything that you can move past."

"What do you mean?"

"I feel like loss is always going to be a part of someone, no matter how much time has passed."

"So I'm basically going to be grieving forever," I say. The concept has me snorting with disbelief.

"You're always going to carry that part with you, but it's not always going to feel as heavy."

"What about you?" I ask. "Have you ever lost someone?"

He nods. "Yeah, my grandparents and a few friends."

"I'm sorry." I hate that generic response for when someone tells you someone they loved died. "I can't imagine losing any of my friends. That must be horrible."

"Definitely wasn't some of my favorite moments."

We sit in stillness. The silence isn't uncomfortable, though. Instead, it invites my thoughts to wander deeper. "What do you think the purpose of all of this is?"

"Of what?"

"Life. What's the purpose?" I ask, even though it's rhetorical. "Why do we get placed into a little bubble that we have no say over, and spend our time alive either fighting against it or giving in to it?" Mateo is quiet, but I can tell he's thinking over what I just said. After several moments of quietness, I keep talking, "What do you think happens when we die?"

"What do you believe happens?"

I ponder for a moment. I'm not really sure. The only concept of the afterlife I'm aware of is what I have been taught in private school. I never questioned it enough to not believe it.

"I guess…" I try to think of how to intelligently string together my words. "I guess that there's a heaven somewhere up there, and that's where we go when we're dead." The simplicity of what I said makes me sound like a kindergartener. "It sounds childish and stupid, I know. But it gives me some type of comfort knowing that my dad is floating around heaven somewhere, I guess."

"That's not stupid."

As I stare into his dark eyes, I feel my guard lowering, trusting him more and more. "Your turn to answer the question," I say with sass, acknowledging his avoidance.

He smiles. "My idea of what happens is different from what you think, and what my family thinks, for that matter. I believe in reincarnation."

"So we just keep regenerating over and over again?"

"Sort of."

"Tell me more." I'm familiar with the basic concept, but I'm genuinely curious to know his thoughts on all of this. I've never had this type of conversation with someone before.

"Well." Mateo shifts himself fully onto the bed. "There's this concept that we travel through lifetimes with a group of souls, and before each lifetime, our souls choose what they want to learn here on earth, and we agree to help one another. And we keep choosing to reincarnate with them, learning new things until our souls feel fulfilled."

"I never heard of anything like that," I whisper in awe. "That's really beautiful."

He shrugs. "I guess we're covering some of the questions for class."

"At least all of this will count toward something."

"I hope it does," he says, his voice dropping in pitch.

The sound of his thick tone hits me with a spark of desire. I focus on his lips, and my body buzzes with temptation. But it's quickly erased when the image of Hunter slams into my brain.

"Who taught you how to play?" I motion toward his instruments as a way to escape my lustful thoughts.

"I taught myself." He turns his head toward his guitar. "One of my uncles gave me an acoustic guitar right after my dad left, and whatever time I didn't spend being a shithead, I spent teaching myself how to play. It became a form of therapy for me."

"What about the drums?"

"There was a music room at my placement, and that's where I learned how to play. I ended up liking the drums better than anything else because I was able to hit something." He laughs. "I worked so many hours saving up for everything." He proudly admires his musical collection.

"Can you play something for me?"

"Oh. I don't really like playing in front of people."

"What are you talking about? You play in your band all the time."

"Yeah, but playing in a band during a party is different than playing something one-on-one in my bedroom."

This is the first time that he isn't overflowing with confidence. I don't want to push him since he's clearly uncomfortable. "Okay."

Mateo sighs. "Fine, something quick." He gets up and grabs his acoustic guitar.

The corners of my mouth lift upward as he sits on a stool and begins methodically moving his fingers over the strings. The warm, rich sound captivates me as it vibrates through my bones.

I pay attention to the song he chooses. I don't know it, but I know he's sharing a part of his story with me.

His playing pulls me into a trance. As he continues to reveal pieces of himself, I witness all the small details—his veins exposed in his arms and hands, his lips pressing together in a thin line as he focuses only on the guitar, his big fingers expertly moving around the guitar frets.

After about a minute, Mateo stops and looks up at me with an unsure expression on his face.

"Wow," I whisper, floored by his talent.

"Yeah, that one usually wins over the ladies." He puts his guitar back on its stand and comes back to sit next to me on his bed.

"Oh, does it?" I ask in a lighthearted way, but if I'm being honest, I want to know.

He grins. "Sometimes."

"How many ladies have there been?"

"In terms of..."

"In terms of girlfriends."

"Zero."

"Zero?"

"I've never had a girlfriend."

"But I thought..." I stop talking, hoping that he will offer up more information.

"I've had a fair amount of girls...who...we would..." He struggles to find polite wording.

"Fuck?"

Mateo chuckles. "Yeah."

"So you like to play the field." I try to disguise my disappointment, despite the fact that I have a boyfriend.

"I used to, but I realized very recently that it wasn't making me happy. I want more."

I can't tell if he is telling me all of this as a friend or because he wants more with *me*. Either way, I love how candidly he speaks to me. He's so vulnerable, even when he plays guitar.

I can't stop staring at him. Heat rises throughout my body, igniting a tingly sensation. My gaze is drawn to his full lips. They look so soft and inviting.

Before my brain can register what I'm doing, my body leans in to kiss him.

"Ellie..." Mateo swiftly backs away.

My cheeks burn bright red as I fling myself off his bed. "I'm sorry. I didn't mean that." I rush to his door.

"Ellie, wait." He gets off the bed and moves to me before I can run away. "It's not that I don't want to kiss you."

"It's okay, Mateo. You don't have to say anything to make me feel better." I try to make my way to the door, but he stands in front of it.

"I'm not saying any of this to make you feel better. Trust me, I want to do more than just kiss you." His eyes flicker down my body and back up to my eyes.

Oh god, Mateo. Don't do that. The more you look at me like that, the more I want to let you rip all my clothes off.

"I just don't want to make shit worse for you."

I clamp my eyes shut, my lungs deflating. I can't believe I almost cheated. "I should go."

"I'll drive you back."

I nod, and we exit his room.

When we pull into the campus parking lot, he shuts off his car. I immediately stop him before he can take his seat belt off.

"That's probably not a good idea," I say. His brows draw in, puzzled, and I continue to explain. "Hunter might be nearby, and he's already pissed at me."

"For what?"

"I threw his phone against the wall and broke it," I say as if I were rattling off a mundane fact.

His forehead crinkles. "You broke his phone? Why?"

I cover my face with my hands. "Because he knows how to push my buttons and make me crazy." Mateo begins to laugh, and I quickly take my hands off my face and glare at him. "What are you laughing at?"

"You're a little feisty. I like it." He gives me a wink.

I fight back a smile. "Okay, I think that's enough for the night." I get out of the car, closing the door. The car window is open, and I lean against the frame. "Mateo?"

"Yeah?"

"Thanks."

CHAPTER SIXTEEN

Ellie

I'm assuming Hunter bought a new phone since he's been texting me as if nothing happened. He told me about his weekend and his plans for the Halloween party. I followed suit and avoided bringing up my meltdown. I'll just pretend like nothing's wrong and be thankful for his constant forgiveness toward me. He told me that he wouldn't be able to see me until the party because he has a big assignment due. I don't mind the extra time apart. I need it.

I haven't spoken to Mom either. I need some time apart from her too.

As Professor Boland lectures, I peek over at Mateo. Aside from stealing a few glances at each other at work, I didn't hear from him all weekend, though I was expecting that. I've learned that Mateo likes to give me my space while he takes his.

"How are you?" Mateo whispers.

"I'm okay," I say back in a hushed tone.

He nods and continues listening to the professor.

After some time has passed, he leans in closer. "Are you going to the Halloween party at his house?" I know exactly who he is referring to when he says *his*.

"I think so." I feel obligated to go after how I treated Hunter and how easily he chose to forgive me. Mateo sits back in his chair and doesn't say anything else for the remainder of the class.

Once class is over, Mateo repeats his question. "You're going to the party?"

"Yeah, why?"

"I'm going to be there with my band. Will that be weird? Should I find someone to cover me?"

"No, it's fine." Although I'm surprised they hired him back. Hunter must not realize Mateo is a part of the band. Otherwise, he'd never let that fly.

"Are you sure? Because I don't have to—"

"Mateo, I swear it's fine." There's no way I'm having him miss out on an opportunity to help pay his bills because of my brief lapse in judgment. I'll be able to keep my lips to myself.

We walk out of the classroom together, and Michelle is already calling his name. She sees me and offers a quick hello from across the building.

"Let me know if you change your mind, okay?" Mateo says to me. I smile and nod at his thoughtfulness before he goes to meet up with Michelle.

"Are you sure you're okay with going to the Halloween party tonight?" Bree asks me again.

"For the millionth time, yes," I joke with her. "What's with you? Why do you think I wouldn't want to go?"

Bree changes into her barely there witch costume. "I don't know. I just thought you and Hunter were fighting. That's all."

My brow furrows. "What makes you think that?"

"He hasn't been around much." She takes a beat, then says, "And I might've heard the two of you arguing last week."

"Oh."

"I know we saw each other in the hallway when you ran out of the room, but I was actually out there for a couple of minutes. I didn't mean to eavesdrop, but I was in Bianca's room and heard yelling."

I have no clue who Bianca is, but I let her finish talking.

"I stepped out into the hallway because I recognized your voice. I heard things escalating and was coming in here to see if you were okay, and that's when you left." Bree steps closer to me, and her voice softens. "Listen, I know you love Hunter, but maybe he isn't the best guy for you."

"What?"

"He seems kind of—"

"Bree, I don't mean for this to sound rude, but you don't know half the shit I dragged Hunter through. And he stayed. He loves me, and I love him. We might bring out the worst in each other sometimes, but that's how our relationship is. We have crazy highs and lows. It works for us. It *is* us."

"Okay. I was just looking out for you. I'm here if you ever need anything." She tries to ease the situation.

"Thanks," I say, trying to keep my cool.

The moment lingers a bit, then she continues to get ready. "I'm sorry if I overstepped, Ellie."

"It's okay." I shrug, rummaging through my wardrobe, trying to find something to wear.

After some time, Bree speaks again. "I heard this party is infamous," she says in her normal, peppy tone, breaking the tension between us.

"Infamous?"

"That's the rumor. This house goes big for 'ween!" She laughs at her own joke, which causes me to laugh. "What are you going as?"

"I still have no clue."

"Take a look through my closet and see if you can throw something together."

I take her up on her offer and sift through her clothes, trying to piece articles together to make an outfit. After a while, I still can't find anything that comes across as a costume.

"Wait! I know!" Bree runs over to my dresser and searches through my neatly folded clothes.

"What are you doing?"

"It's in here somewhere." She closes a drawer and opens up another one, reaching all the way in the back. "Aha!" She whips out my plaid skirt for high school. "Sexy schoolgirl!" she exclaims.

I immediately shake my head. "No way!"

"Come on. Just try." She takes out my white tank top and heads to her dresser, pulling out her black bralette. "Here, put this on too."

Hesitantly, I change my clothes and look at myself in the mirror. The top half of me looks okay—a little scandalous, but it is Halloween. However, the bottom half of me looks atrocious. The maroon and gray skirt hits an inch above my knee, and I'm having flashbacks to girls getting written up if it was any shorter than that.

"Hmm…" Bree says as if she's agreeing with my thoughts.

"It's hideous."

"It has potential." Bree looks at the skirt like she's solving a math equation. "Oh, I know." She hurries to her desk and quickly returns with a handful of safety pins. "Hold still," she tells me as she begins to pin my skirt up. A couple of minutes and a few finger pricks later…

"All done!"

We look at her costume alteration in the mirror. The once long, ugly skirt is now sitting mid-thigh with heightened sex appeal. This is definitely out of my element, but I'm willing to let myself wear something a little risqué for the holiday. Plus, Hunter obviously wanted me to wear the skirt. Otherwise, he wouldn't have packed it.

"One more thing," Bree says to me, turning me toward her. She shimmies my shirt down, so more of my boobs and bralette pop out.

I start laughing and swat her hand away.

Bree's phone goes off, notifying us that our Uber has arrived. She tosses me a pair of her slimmest heels, and I slip into them before we leave.

When we get there, the frat house is jam-packed. Bree didn't exaggerate when she said this Halloween party was infamous, judging by all the detailed costumes and how crammed it is. Bree and I part ways as I search for Hunter and she goes to mingle.

A cloud of recurring smoke hovers in the house as I move around groups of people, searching for a familiar face. When I see Delilah, she gives me an evil scowl and struts off with her friends. I spot Derek and Mike, and they both give me a look of approval in regard to my costume, making me internally cringe.

"Do you know where Hunter is?" I ask Derek. Derek calls over Hunter, and Hunter pushes past at least thirty people to get to me. As soon as he sees my outfit, his face contorts.

"What the fuck are you wearing?" Hunter says loud enough for everyone around us to hear.

My stomach drops. "It's just a costume."

"You look like a fucking whore. You know that, right?"

My body concaves in as people whip their heads around to see what I'm wearing. Hunter takes my arm in a tight grip and leads me toward a corner to talk semiprivately.

"This is the shit I'm talking about, Ellie. This isn't normal for you."

"It's just a costume," I repeat.

"Are you trying to get me to fight someone? Is that what you want? You want me to get expelled? Because you *know* you're going to get hit on wearing that, and you *know* that I'm going to have to beat the shit out of them."

"No, of course not. I just wanted to wear this. I don't know what the big deal is."

He scoffs at me in disgust. "You know what? Do whatever the hell you want. I should've dumped your crazy ass last week."

His words pack a punch, the pain provoking my anger. "Can you not make me feel like shit for wearing a costume on Halloween?" My hands flail as I talk. "And can you stop calling me fucking crazy!" As I move my arms around, someone places a red Solo cup in my hand.

I pause, staring at it.

"Don't drink that," Hunter orders.

His demand stirs my defiance, and I clutch the cup tighter. He keeps toying with me. One week, he's the best boyfriend ever, and the next, he's berating me.

On impulse, I gulp down the drink, wincing. It tastes horrible. I've never had a drop of alcohol before. I have no idea why anyone would become addicted to this crap. It burns the whole way down.

"You're going to end up just like your mother."

"Leave my mom out of this," I grit out, my jaw tightly clenched.

"Or worse, you're going to end up dead like your dad."

"Get the fuck away from me."

"Fine, have it your way, but I'm not cleaning up your mess this time." He throws his hands up and storms off.

I'm left alone in a crowd of people.

I'm hurt, lonely, and angry. Mostly just angry, and with my anger comes spite. I grab a bottle of liquor that's sitting on the counter and begin to fill up my cup.

"Whoa, you're gonna need a mixer with all of that."

I glance over my shoulder and see Rhett. He seems as sleazy as hell, but I'm sure he knows how to make a good drink. "Okay," I say, toying with the hem of my skirt. "You want to make me a drink?"

Rhett looks me up and down, but I don't get butterflies like when Mateo does it. Rhett's actions are lewd and raise red flags up everywhere. "I sure do." He pours various things into the cup with a cunning smirk on his face. "Here you go." He hands me the drink, and I quickly swallow the entire cup.

"Holy shit." Rhett laughs. "You want another?"

"I would love another one." I twirl the ends of my hair around my fingers. I don't give a fuck that I'm openly flirting with him.

Rhett makes me a similar drink. "If you're feeling a little woozy, you can always lie down in my bed for a bit." There is a glimmer in his eye as he hands me my drink and points toward a door.

"I'm sure I can." I pat his shoulder and head out to the backyard.

Bree is already a few shots in and dancing with some of her friends. I look over and see the band playing.

Mateo.

I got so swept up in the nonsense with Hunter that I ended up forgetting Mateo would be here. I hope he doesn't judge me for drinking tonight, or for dressing like this.

Bree sees me standing with a red cup in my hand and runs—well, *attempts* to run over to me.

"Oh my god. Are you drinking?" she squeals. I never told her about my parents. In the past, I just told her I didn't like the taste of alcohol, which I now know is true, so I can continue saying that in the future.

"I guess so," I say.

"Your man's checking you out." Bree nods toward Mateo. I turn and see him staring at my legs while drumming. Lust sparks in his eyes, causing my insides to heat up.

My mouth becomes dry, and I take another sip from my cup to quench *one* of my thirsts. It doesn't taste as bad as it initially had. It's actually quite yummy. I drink the rest, and my muscles loosen up as I continue to watch Mateo.

I lost track of time.

And drinks.

And Bree.

Mateo's band is taking a break, and I want to find him so I can tell him how hot he looks.

Stumbling inside, I spot him by the fridge, grabbing a water bottle. "Hi!"

Whoa, that came out squeaky, even for me.

Mateo grins. "Hey," he says after scanning the room.

"You looked…played…really good."

"Are you drunk?"

"How do I know if I'm drunk if I've never drank before?" I start giggling.

"You should really have someone help you out. Where's Bree?"

"I lost her!"

"Great. And Hunter?"

I shrug. "Last time I saw him…he yelled…"

"And how long ago was that?"

"Before you."

Mateo exhales and drops his head with a smile. "You should go lie down."

"Rhett said I could in his bed." I try to remember which room is his. I think he pointed to the door next to the bathroom. Or was it the brown door?

"Yeah, that's not gonna happen," Mateo says, an authoritative tone encasing his words. My attention snaps back to him.

That was fucking hot.

"Almost did, though." I bite my bottom lip with the sick desire to make Mateo more jealous.

"I'm gonna choose to ignore what you just said. Do you want me to find Hunter?"

I stare at Mateo's lips. I want more than anything to feel them on me. All over my body.

"Ellie." Mateo draws me out of my dirty thoughts about him. He takes a step back as if he knows what was going on in my mind.

I coyly smile and take a step closer to him so that we're the same distance as we just were.

He shakes his head. "No, you're drunk."

"Stop calling me names!"

My comment throws him off. "I'm not calling you names. I just don't want you to do something that you'll regret once you're sober."

I think he says more words, but I get distracted by his sexy body. His broad shoulders and tattooed arms are so nice to look at. I wonder what kind of tattoos are under his shirt.

"Do you?" he interrupts my thoughts again.

I glance up at his face. "What?"

He lets out a defeated chuckle. "Do you want me to drive you back to your dorm?"

"Yes, but tell Bree, please?"

"Okay. I'll find her. Please stay right here."

CHAPTER SEVENTEEN

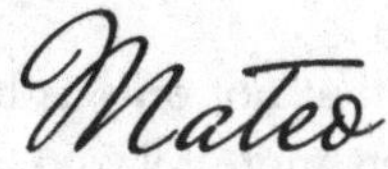

Pulling my car to the side of the road for the second time, Ellie flings the door open and hangs her head out. I'm quick to grab hold of her hair before she starts puking again.

When she's done, she settles back in the passenger seat, out of breath with beads of sweat rolling down her face.

"Do you normally puke this much when you're drunk?"

"I never drank before," Ellie slurs.

"You never drank before?" I ask, unable to conceal my concern. She shakes her head. "How much did you have to drink?"

"I don't know. I had a few shots, and Rhett made me some drinks."

My muscles tense. I don't know who's worse, Hunter or Rhett.

Ellie lolls her head to the side, her eyes getting heavy. She's too far gone and definitely shouldn't be alone if this is the first time she's drunk.

"Do you want me to hang out with you in your dorm?" I ask, realizing that Bree said she's crashing at a friend's place when I told her I was driving Ellie back.

"No. If he comes over and finds you in my room, he'll lose his shit."

She doesn't need to tell me who she's talking about when she says *he*. Before I can respond, I'm on hair duty, holding it back for her as she empties her stomach for a third time.

"Do you want to crash at my place, and I'll take care of you?"

She nods, sitting upright as she wipes her mouth with the back of her hand. "Please."

After Ellie washes her face and has free rein of a spare toothbrush and an unopened bottle of mouthwash, she stumbles into my room. Her body sways to the left, and she crashes into my dresser.

"Oops!" Ellie says, giggling. She kicks off her heels, then lifts her tank top up to her nose, causing her face to scrunch in disgust. "My shirt smells like throw up." She attempts to take it off but struggles and starts to fall.

"Whoa," I say, rushing to her side so she doesn't face-plant.

"Can you help me get a new shirt?" Her eyes move in and out of focus as she tries to look at me.

Glancing down, I notice that not only is her shirt covered but also her skirt. "Y-yeah." Her body gets more relaxed, and I lean her up against my dresser so she can rest her bodyweight on it.

Moving with extreme precision, my fingertips carefully roll up the fabric of her shirt. My heart pounds as I make sure not to touch her skin, wanting to make sure I don't come off as disrespectful in any way. When the fabric reaches her bra, I stare up at the ceiling as I lift the shirt up, pulling it over her arms and head.

"This too," Ellie says, yanking at her skirt.

My line of sight drops, but I keep it trained on the zipper on the side of her hip. I tug it a few times, but nothing's happening.

"Zipper's stuck," I tell her. After a few more tries, I decide to kneel down in front of her, seeing if I can unjam the sliver of fabric that's caught.

A playful chuckle comes from Ellie. "You can stay down there longer if you'd like." Her comment makes me pause. *There's no way she's insinuating what I think she is, right*? "I bet you'd be really good at eating me out."

My gaze flies upward, staring at a plastered Ellie who's hazed over by lust. Blood rushes to my lower half, but I ignore it.

"I think I'm horny," she announces, causing me to laugh.

"I'd say so." With one last pull of the zipper, I'm able to get it down, and her skirt falls to the floor. I'm quick to look away so I don't see something she wouldn't want me to once she's sober. Standing up, I reach into one of my drawers and grab the first shirt I can find. I drape my black tee over her body, and it nearly swallows her whole.

Shuffling Ellie toward my mattress, I cringe when I spot the tussled bedsheets, remembering that just a few hours before I left for the party, I fucked Jasmine in my bed.

"Let me just change the sheets quick—" I start to say, but Ellie plops down on my bed, sprawling out as if it were her own. I can't help but smile at the sight of her.

She seems to fall asleep immediately, so I shut the lights off and get out of my shirt and jeans. Taking one of my pillows, I drop it on the floor and try to make myself a comfortable bed for the night.

"What are you doing?" Ellie mutters, half asleep. She picks up her head to look at me, golden strands of hair covering her line of vision.

"Gonna lie down on the floor. Go back to sleep."

"No." She reaches for me, her fingers encircling my forearm, making my insides light up. "I'm gonna feel like a bitch if you sleep on the floor. Sleep in your bed."

"I don't know if that's a good idea, Ellie."

"We already technically slept in a bed together. You passed out in my bed, remember?"

"Yeah, but…" My voice trails off.

"Okay, fine. I'll sleep on the floor." She attempts to get up but falls back onto the bed, her grip on me tightening as she pulls me with her. She lets out a puff of air, defeated. "Just sleep here with me, Mateo."

I smile. "Okay."

Within a few moments, Ellie is nestled under the covers and sound asleep. But I've never been more awake. My gaze flickers over her and catches on uneven scars on her left wrist. Skimming my thumb over them, an ache in my chest arises. She shifts slightly, and I draw my hand away so I don't wake her.

I try to steady my breathing as my thoughts whirl in my head.

After realizing I was catching feelings for Ellie, I tried my best to keep my distance and keep myself distracted. But it's fucking impossible to do either right now.

I don't know why she keeps going back to that asshole frat boy. She can do a thousand times better. I'm not sure if that even means me, but if she were to give me the opportunity, then I'd try to be the best boyfriend for her.

I nearly give myself a heart attack, stunned by my own thoughts. The idea of being in a relationship with someone has never been something I wanted, but there's something about Ellie that feels *right*.

My mind drifts a few weeks back when we were talking about the afterlife, which who the fuck does that with a girl? I don't think I've told anyone about my beliefs before, but with Ellie, it seemed so natural to talk about.

Who knows? Maybe I'm so captivated by her because our souls know each other.

Maybe we've done this once or twice before, in different lives.

CHAPTER EIGHTEEN

Ellie

NOVEMBER

Unfamiliar voices come from the hallway. Someone shifts next to me, startling me awake. Fluttering my eyes open, I stare up at the ceiling. I don't recognize it. The realization that I'm not in my room springs me into panic, and I focus on the person lying next to me, smiling.

Relief uncoils the knot that was forming in my chest.

"How are you feeling?" Mateo asks.

"Okay," I respond, even though it's too soon to know if that's true.

"You had a rough night."

"Did I? I don't remember anything. How did I even end up here?"

"When you were puking on the side of the road, I asked if you wanted to stay over so I could take care of you. And as much as I wanted to drop you off at your dorm and ditch your drunk ass, I couldn't let you be alone on your first time getting wasted."

"We didn't do anything, did we?"

"No. Although you were a little forward."

"Oh god. What did I say?"

"I don't think you want to know." He holds back a laugh. "You have a bit of a dirty mouth on you when you're drunk."

"Please tell me that's not true!"

"I'm kidding. You only said you wanted to kiss me, which who could blame you for that?"

I shield my face with my hands and realize that I'm not wearing my costume. Glancing down, I notice I'm in an oversized black shirt. "Um… whose clothes am I wearing?"

I'm not sure I want to know the answer.

"Mine."

Yep, definitely didn't want to know the answer.

"Why?" My hand covers my mouth out of sheer concern.

"You threw up all over yourself, and I wasn't going to let you sleep in your vomit. Don't worry. I didn't look at…anything."

My stomach bubbles, and I groan. "I'm never drinking again."

"The famous day-after words."

Standing up, I gather my belongings. "I'm sorry."

Mateo follows my lead and gets out of bed. "For what?"

My breath sticks in my throat when I notice he's only wearing his boxers. Curiosity gets the best of me, and I can't help but stare at his body.

How on earth did I sleep next to this man all night and not know it?

My eyes are glued to him, paying attention to the art inked into his skin. There's very little space left untouched, but a few specific tattoos grab my attention. Words that I think are in Latin are written in script across his chest. A large dead tree covers his side and appears to wrap around his back. Instead of shading in the trunk and branches to look like wood, they are filled in with bars of music. My gaze shifts downward to a sparrow near his hip bone, the end of its wing dipping just below the waistband of his boxers. Boxers that cling to him. I sense his eyes on me. I peer up at him through my lashes and see him grinning.

My phone suddenly vibrates, ripping my focus away from Mateo and onto the pounding in my head.

Oh my god, that is the loudest sound in the world.

I search for my phone, rubbing my temples. Mateo points to his desk, and I see Hunter's name popping up on my screen. My stomach contorts, and bile shoots up my esophagus.

Darting over to the garbage can, I immediately start puking. Mateo is by my side in a heartbeat, holding up my hair.

When my stomach finally finishes emptying itself, I sit on the floor and look up at Mateo, who's looking back at me with empathy pouring from his eyes. "I'm sorry," I tell him again.

"For what?" he repeats.

"This. Dragging you into my drama. You don't deserve it."

"Well, I don't think you deserve it either."

I scoff at his image of me.

"You don't believe that you deserve better, and that's the problem." He stops for a beat, but then lets out his thoughts. "The guy is a dick, Ellie." My shoulders tense, and I glare at him. "I'm just saying that if he actually treated his girl right, you wouldn't be here right now."

I ignore his comment and talk to myself out loud. "He's going to be so pissed at me."

"How come?"

"Because of last night. How I dressed and acted. Not to mention coming back to your place and sleeping in your bed with you."

"He doesn't have to know about the last part."

I let out a big sigh. "I should probably go back to campus and get myself ready to see him."

Mateo helps me off the floor. I look down at what I'm wearing. There's no way I'm walking through my dorm wearing only this. "Do you have pants I can borrow?"

"Hold on." He steps out into the hallway and begins speaking in Spanish. A few minutes later, he comes back with a pair of sweatpants in his hands. "Here." He tosses them to me.

"Whose are these?"

"Michelle's."

"Does she mind?"

"She owes me. You're fine."

I slip on Michelle's pants, trying not to glance over at Mateo as he gets dressed.

When we get to campus, Mateo walks me upstairs as he normally does.

"I'll wash your shirt and give it back to you tomorrow," I tell Mateo.

"Don't worry about it."

My brows draw in. "Well, you need your shirt back."

"I like that you have it," he confesses with a spark lighting up his expression.

"I really shouldn't have a guy's shirt when he's not *my* guy."

"You shouldn't, but you do." He winks.

Butterflies flutter around my fragile stomach. "I think you need to go before I get myself into more trouble."

He fights back a chuckle. "I'll see you in class on Monday."

Hunter has called me five times. I watch my phone as he calls for the sixth. Guilt encompasses every fiber of my being. He's going to be livid when he finds out that Mateo took care of me last night. I can't blame him. If the situation were reversed, and I found out Hunter had some girl sleep in his bed with him, I would be fuming. I need to make things right by him. I'm a better person than this, and Hunter deserves me at my best, not my worst.

I call Hunter back. He sounds winded. "Ellie?"

"Yeah, what's wrong?" I grow troubled at the sound of his voice trembling. My feet are planted on the floor, ready to run to wherever he needs me.

"Nothing. I was so worried that something was wrong with *you*. I had no idea where you went last night, and then when you didn't answer your phone, I got scared."

A weight drops in my gut. He's spending his day concerned about me, yet here I am wearing another man's shirt. I have to come clean. "Can I come over?"

I take a few deep breaths to calm myself down, but my hands still shake as I knock on the front door of the frat house.

Rhett opens it, looking hungover as ever. "Hey, Ellie. He's in his room." In the house, it looks like an after-party war zone with piles of trash and clothes littering the floor. I stride up the stairs toward Hunter's room. Swallowing down my nervousness, I enter.

Hunter's lying on his bed in his boxers, and as soon as he sees me, he sits up. "Hey."

"Hi," I say, picking at my nails.

"Come sit. I want to talk to you."

"I want to talk to you too." I rush next to him.

"Do you want to go first?"

"No, you go." I'm secretly hoping that what he has to say is worse so I don't feel as bad.

Hunter's presence is soft and gentle, which makes it easier to breathe. He takes one of my hands in his. "I know that you have a lot going on with your mom's arrest."

The reminder weighs my body down. I really wish he didn't bring her up. I've been avoiding thinking about her at all costs, and I especially don't want that pushed into my brain at this very moment.

"I'm trying to be as supportive as possible, and I know sometimes I suck at that, and I know that I haven't always been the best to you, but…" His shoulders drop in defeat. "But you haven't always been the best to me."

I might puke again.

Hunter continues, "I tried having a calm conversation with you last week, and you flipped out, screaming, cursing, and even broke my phone—"

"I know, and I'm *so* sorry! I'm going to give you the money for the new one. Just tell me how much."

"Ellie." Hunter pushes my hair behind my ear. "I would never ask you for money. You know I wouldn't do that, no matter how much money in damage you caused." My mind jumps to our fights over the years. I've thrown a lot of items when I was mad, but none of them were expensive. It was usually a remote or an occasional picture frame.

"What I'm trying to say is…" His voice grows delicate, his blue eyes pooling with water. "You've really been hurting me lately." He looks directly at me, piercing me straight in the heart. "When you showed up here last night wearing that, it felt like you were *purposefully* hurting me, and then you started drinking on top of everything. I couldn't stand to see you like that. I don't want to see you go down the same path as your parents. I want a better life for you. You deserve better. Don't you agree?"

My mind spins. His words mirror Mateo's from earlier, but they only make things more confusing. Is Hunter trying to give me a better life, and I keep sabotaging it because I don't believe I deserve better?

"What even happened to you last night? Where did you go?" Hunter asks.

"Um…" My eyes drift off him as I prepare to tell him the truth. "Mateo took care of me." I glance back at him.

Hunter's face drops, and his body turns to steel. "Mateo? Who's Mateo?" He puts the pieces together and jumps to his feet. "What do you mean, he took care of you? He was with you all night?"

"I…no. He just helped me get back to my dorm." My leg bounces up and down. He knows I'm lying. I know he knows.

"Here I am freaking out that you're on some self-destructive binge, turning into your parents, and I find out that you let another man bring you home. You're fucking disgusting, Elena."

Tears well up as my remorse strangles me. "I'm sorry, I—"

"Did you cheat on me?"

"No!"

"I swear to god, if I find out you cheated on me, Elena." He clenches his fist and winds up his arm, punching a hole into the drywall right next to where I'm sitting.

Yelping, I dart to the opposite side of the bed.

He snaps his head around, startled by the sudden movement. His eyes connect with mine, and I watch as the rage leaves his body. He's always able to come back down when he makes eye contact with me. I'm the only one who can do that for him.

He swipes his hands over his face and sits next to me. "Sorry." He lets out a puff of air. "I love you, Elena, and I know I'm not always the greatest boyfriend, but that doesn't justify me being treated like this. You should've never gone home with another guy."

"I know. I feel awful. I am so sorry, Hunter."

He's quiet.

I don't know how to make this better. "I love you, Hunter," I whisper.

"I need to know you really love me."

I gently clutch his reddened hand. "Of course I do, Hunter."

"I need you to prove to me that you love me."

"Okay. How?"

He gives me a look, and it takes me a second before it registers. "Oh. You want to have sex?"

He nods. "We've been together for over two years, and I've been having doubts about you truly loving me. How else am I supposed to really know?"

He's right. I haven't been showing him that I love him at all. If this is what he needs to know how I really feel about him, then I will.

"Okay."

One of his eyebrows arches. "You will?"

"But I have my period, so next week." *That was a lie. Why did I just lie about that?*

"Okay." He parts a crooked smile. "My birthday gift."

Shit.

CHAPTER NINETEEN

Ellie

The comfy, oversized chairs are so tempting. I wish I could grab one of these books and curl myself up in one, but I'm pretty sure Edgar would fire me if I did that. So instead, I stroll past the chairs and organize one of the bookshelves.

Hunter tried to convince me to quit because he didn't want me around Mateo. I told him how much I needed this job and how the money I save is going to help Mom, since she hasn't been making an income while in rehab. We have some of Dad's life insurance still put away, but we only use that as emergency money. So I'll give her whatever extra I have to help her get by. Hunter and I settled on a compromise of me working fewer hours. Relationships are all about compromise. At least that's what I've always heard.

The strumming of fingers at the checkout counter snaps me out of my thoughts. I poke my head out from around the shelf and see Mateo using the countertop as his personal drum. I'd find the action cute if I hadn't been avoiding him all week. I kept our conversation in class minimal. I don't want my feelings for him to mess with my head.

"Need something?" I ask, advancing to the register.

Mateo's head whips up. "Hey."

"Hi."

There's a long pause.

"Uh…" Mateo tugs at his shirt. "Are you free this weekend?" My eyebrow arches. "To go over questions for the final," he adds.

"Oh," I say with a breath of relief. "I can't this weekend. I'm busy."

Busy losing my virginity, and I really don't want to see you beforehand.

"What about before class next week?"

I nod. I'm obviously going to have to meet up with him a few more times to pass my final. "Sure. I can meet at three."

"Mateo!" Edgar stands in the loft area, looking down at us. "If you knew shit about books, I would've hired you to work here. Get your ass back where it belongs." He points to the coffee shop.

Mateo says something to him in Spanish, and the two bicker back and forth until Edgar gives up and goes back to whatever he was doing.

Mateo shifts his focus back to me. "I'll come to your dorm on Monday." He gives me a smile, and I watch him walk through the hollowed-out archway.

Several hours go by, and I successfully make it to the end of my shift without talking to Mateo again. As I trek back to my dorm, my thoughts remain on Hunter. The temperature drastically dropped, and the wind lashes around me. Although my feet keep moving me forward, the cold air stinging my cheeks keeps my mind stuck in the past.

My cheeks are frozen from riding my bike in the frigid January weather, but I knew I had to come over as soon as I heard Hunter's voice on the phone. In all the time we've been together, I've never heard him in such distress. I don't know what's going on aside from him saying he's in a really bad headspace. I know what that's like and would never wish that on anyone. We've been broken up for a few weeks and haven't spoken to each other in a while until tonight, when he called me up hysterical. I've seen him shed a few tears before, but never to this extent.

We sit on his bedroom floor as he cries next to me. We've been here for a long time. Not much has been said, but I'm trying my best to be here for him.

"I don't know why I'm like this, Ellie," Hunter says, shielding his face with his hands.

"Like what?" My question hovers just above a whisper.

"I'm so fucked up, Ellie. I can't help it. It's just who I am." I scoot closer to him as he continues to talk. "Sometimes I wish I could go be with Kayla."

Kayla? My stomach plunges to the floor. His sister, who passed away. He wants to be with her, meaning he wants to…

"Hunter." My voice cracks. "Hunter, do you mean that?"

He doesn't answer. The longer he's quiet, the tighter fear coils around my bones.

After minutes of stillness, he sniffles and tries to compose himself. "Did you like it when you used to cut yourself?"

I blink, caught off guard by the question. "What?"

"The pain. Did you like it?"

"I…" I contemplate what he's asking. I've never thought of it like that. "I guess a part of me did, yeah."

He nods and then looks at me, his blue eyes more vibrant from shedding so many tears. "I like pain too. I just find different ways to feel it."

His words strike me.

We're silent for even longer, sitting in our pain, partially suffering and partially getting high. It's a toxic combination, but we both crave it.

"We're both pretty fucked up," I say, offering a small smile.

Hunter threads his fingers in between mine. "You're the only one who gets me."

"And you're the only one who gets me."

"You know how much you mean to me, right? You know how much I love you?" I open my mouth to speak, but he interjects, "You mean everything to me, Ellie." Hunter's grasp on my hand strengthens. "I don't deserve you. You're like a goddamn angel compared to me."

"Don't say that." I continue to grow uncomfortable with how he's speaking.

"It's true." His eyes plead with me to understand what he's trying to convey. "You're too good for me, and I keep messing it up. I don't know what's wrong with me, but I swear I'll do better. I fucking swear. For you. For us."

The sincerity in his voice makes me teary-eyed. We are kindred spirits with tortured souls. We don't know why we keep doing this to ourselves and to each other, but it's the only way we know how.

"I can't live without you, Elena. I don't want to live without you."

What does he mean, he doesn't want to live without me? The way he's talking is scaring me.

"I need you." His voice comes out hushed.

His vulnerability makes me cave. I kiss his salty lips, and we give in to our unhealthy dependence on each other and the thrill of our pain.

CHAPTER TWENTY

Ellie

The rest of my week is riddled with anxiety. I don't know why I lied to Hunter about having my period. I should've just gotten it over with so I wouldn't have spent all week overthinking. But I did, and then I somehow talked myself into standing in front of the door to Hunter's frat house.

"Hi, angel," Hunter greets me with a huge grin on his face. We make our way upstairs, and I catch him eyeing up my plum-colored dress and black sweater.

When I enter Hunter's room, the flickering of dozens of candles and the sweet scent of flowers catch me by surprise, and I let out a little gasp. "Hunter, I love it."

He comes from behind and wraps his arms around me. "I wanted to make it special for you," he says in a low voice before kissing my neck.

Before I can blink, he's taking off my sweater, unzipping my dress, and I'm standing here in my black bra and thong. He takes his clothes off, down to his blue boxers, and guides me to his bed.

Hunter lays me down, then pulls off my underwear and unhooks my bra. My breathing gets heavier. My hands tremble.

"You're so beautiful," Hunter whispers as he sucks on my neck and moves down to my nipples. I begin to let out little sighs. He pauses for a moment to take off his boxers and then continues marking up my skin. I don't stop him. He starts to circle my clit, and I try to relax into the bed, but my body is too tense, and my brain won't shut off.

"I can't wait for this, Ellie," Hunter says as his hands roam over me. "I've wanted all of you for so long, and now I finally have you."

My heart races, but not like how it does when I see Mateo.

It's similar to how I feel before a panic attack.

Hunter reaches toward his nightstand and grabs a condom. He quickly puts it on and positions himself over me. My legs involuntarily cross themselves.

"What are you doing?" he asks.

"I-I don't know." It's getting harder to breathe.

"Open your legs."

I shuffle out from under him. "No…I…"

A frustrated look crosses Hunter's face. "Are you being serious right now?"

I manage to get off the bed and start putting on my clothes. "I'm sorry. I can't do this right now."

"Why not?"

"It just doesn't feel right." I struggle to zip my dress up all the way, but I eventually get it.

"So you don't love me."

"No, I do! It just doesn't feel like the right time for me."

"No, you don't. I ask you to show how much you truly love me, and you can't because you don't."

My voice trembles. "Please don't say that. I—"

"Get out," he demands.

"What?"

"I said…Get. Out."

I stand frozen.

Is he actually kicking me out for not having sex with him?

After he doesn't falter, I grab my things and rush out of the house.

A whirlwind of emotions brews beneath my ribcage, and my vision blurs. I stop in the driveway to catch my breath.

"He told you?" Rhett leans against a car as his thumbs tap on his phone.

I wipe my eyes. "I'm sorry, I didn't hear you. What did you say?"

"He told you about Delilah?"

A shock wave of anger strikes through me. I have no idea what Rhett means by this, but I'm going to find out.

"Yeah, he did."

He shakes his head. "I'm sorry. That was such a dick move. I told him to stop hooking up with her because I had a feeling you two would get back together sooner or later."

I fucking knew it.

My tears suddenly stop.

My face feels like it's on fucking fire.

I don't think I've ever been this angry in my entire life, not even toward Mom. My body moves right back into the house, and I stomp my way up to Hunter's room, swinging open his door.

"Did you have sex with Delilah?"

"What?"

"I'm giving you one fucking opportunity to tell me the truth. Did you have sex with Delilah?" I stalk over to him, getting in his face.

Hunter doesn't answer.

"When?" I demand.

"When we were taking some time apart," he says.

"Give me a date."

"I didn't mark it on my calendar, Ellie."

"Month."

He presses his lips together and then says, "January."

My eyes are about to pop out of my head. My hands shake with pure fury. "You've been fucking her since January?"

"We stopped when you and I got back together and then started again a few weeks ago when you and I were off." He doesn't look at me.

My body acts before my mind can tell it to stop, and my hand makes contact with his face, smacking him so hard that a red outline of my hand blossoms across his cheek. My hand hurts, but the satisfaction is immense. "We're officially over."

CHAPTER TWENTY-ONE

Ellie

Someone taps their knuckles against my door, waking me up.

"Bree, can you…" I look across the room and don't see her. I huff as I toss my blankets aside and get out of bed.

There's another knock.

"I'm coming," I groan, annoyed at this impatient person. Opening the door to Mateo's concerned face, I'm instantly self-conscious of my appearance. I probably look horrendous. My pajamas are extremely unflattering, and I can only imagine that I have mascara smeared under my eyes. Not to mention my hair is probably knotted from tossing and turning all night.

"Are you okay?"

"Fantastic," I say and walk away from the door to let him enter. I plop down on my bed. "What are you doing here?"

"We said last week that we'd meet today."

"Yeah, at three."

His head tilts, puzzled. "It is three."

I grab my phone to check the time. "Holy shit. I slept the entire day?"

"I guess so?"

"I can't believe I slept through my first two classes."

"What's going on?"

Pinching the bridge of my nose, I consider telling him everything, but I choose not to and just say, "Hunter."

"Got it."

"We broke up," I tell him. He doesn't say anything, but I can tell by the look in his eyes that he doesn't fully believe my statement. "For real this time," I try to convince him.

"I'm sorry." Mateo changes his tune. "Actually, no. I'm not sorry you guys broke up, but I'm sorry for whatever he did to hurt you."

"How do you know that he did something to me? Maybe I'm the one who did something really bad to end it."

"You're not like that."

"You don't know me that well."

"I know you enough." His voice is thick and smooth.

Just like that, warmth spreads through my chest. My eyes flutter to his inviting lips. It would feel so good to kiss him right now.

"Let's order you some food." He snaps his focus to his phone. "What do you want? Pizza? Tacos?"

I shake my head. "We should really do the questions, and then I need to get ready for class."

"We're not going to class."

"What? Why?"

"We're gonna skip, eat some food, and watch your shitty TV shows that I hate."

"We can't skip. I missed a few weeks ago, and you really can't skip because you need to get into grad school."

"I haven't missed any classes yet, and we're allowed to miss two before our grade gets docked. If it makes you feel better, we'll go over some questions, and I'll do my best impression of Boland." He smiles, and I can't help but chuckle.

"Deal."

"Wait, *she's* the oldest? I thought the other one was the older sister," Mateo comments on the reality show we're watching.

"No, she's the middle sister." I try educating him about this family for the tenth time.

The door opens, and Bree's eyebrows shoot up in amusement at the sight of Mateo and me sitting on my bed. "Well, hello, you two."

"Hey, Bree. You want a slice of pizza?" Mateo offers.

"Why not?" She throws her bag on her bed and comes over to us. "What did I miss?" She motions her head toward the TV.

"You're just in time. One of the sisters is mad at the other one about something stupid," Mateo says.

"Naturally," Bree says, grabbing a slice. "What are you guys doing here anyway? Don't you have your philosophy class?"

"We're skipping," he tells her before I can.

Her jaw opens. "*You're* skipping, Ellie?"

I nod, not able to explain because my mouth is full of pizza.

"Just for today. Ellie needs some downtime to chill." Mateo turns to me. "What comes next after we finish with this awful show? Painting our nails?"

"If you're lucky." I nudge him.

"What's going on? Why are you in need of some downtime?" Bree asks me.

Mateo shoots an apologetic wince, and I give him a look, telling him it's fine.

"Hunter and I broke up."

"That explains the comfort food and skipping class." She slants her head to the side. "I'm sorry, Ellie."

"It's okay. I don't want to talk about it. I just want to distract myself."

"I'm the queen of distractions!" she proclaims.

For the rest of the evening, she and Mateo attempt to do just that, and I'm partially able to get my mind off Hunter. The three of us spend the entire time talking about silly things. After a while of debating what we would bring along with us on a deserted island, Bree excuses herself to the bathroom, and Mateo and I are alone again.

"When can I see you next?" he asks.

I take a moment to think and answer honestly. "I think I need to take some time to process everything."

"Okay. You let me know when you're ready."

My arms wrap around him, giving him a hug, but I quickly pull away before my body starts acting with a mind of its own. "I will."

CHAPTER TWENTY-TWO

Mateo

I have a nice setup in the back office of the Cozy Nook. With multiple tabs open on my computer, I flip back and forth from finishing up an assignment for my human development class to updating the inventory for the coffee shop. To the left of me, there's a piece of paper hanging on the wall that says, *"Te amo, Tío Mateo,"* with a little drawing of a guitar from my nephew, Christian.

"I think everyone's doing their own thing for Thanksgiving," my sister, Stephanie, says as I put her on speakerphone so I can type at the same time.

"All right. I'll probably hang out in Connecticut then." Thanksgiving isn't a deal breaker in my family. Christmas, however, is another story.

"How's school going? Still on top of everything?"

I smile. No matter how much I've grown or how much time has passed, my sisters always feel the need to make sure I'm not backsliding. "Nope. I dropped out."

"Not funny, Mateo."

"It's a little bit funny," I say, assuming she's giving me an eye roll on the other end of the phone.

"Yeah, yeah."

Out of all my sisters, I'm closest with Steph, although we've had our fair share of ups and downs. Things weren't always amicable between us. Just thinking about how chill things are now versus what they were like in the past has my mind flashing to a time when we were younger.

The taste of copper fills my mouth, and my knuckles burn from being split open, but I still look better than the other guy. And he would've looked even worse if my sister, Steph, didn't break up the fight.

"What the fuck is going on with you, Mateo?" Steph shouts as I lean against a brick wall, examining my hand. We're several blocks from home, and my friends and I ran into some shitheads on the street, which ended up in a brawl between parked cars and lampposts.

"Nothing. I'm fine," I state, wondering how she was able to spot me in the chaos. But as soon as she did, her piercing voice somehow scattered everyone—including my friends.

"You haven't been home in days."

"And?"

"And? You're fifteen years old. You can't just up and leave."

I shrug. "Just doing what my role model taught me."

Steph's defenses drop, and even though it's dark, it's easy to read the worry on her face. "You can't act like this forever because of Dad."

"Watch me." I push off the wall and start to walk away from her.

"You have to come home eventually."

"No, I don't."

"The school's gonna get involved for you being truant," she says to my back.

"Okay."

"Or worse, you're gonna get arrested if you keep acting like an asshole."

"Whatever, Steph." I don't bother looking over my shoulder to see if she's behind me because I hear her footsteps stop.

Fading into the city blocks, I wander around aimlessly. The adrenaline from the fight has worn off, and an overwhelming sensation of bitter loneliness infiltrates my bones.

I hate that Steph saw me. Not because she caught me doing something bad, but because I knew it probably scared the shit out of her. As much as she's pissing me off right now, I don't want to scare her. I don't want her to be scared of me like she was toward Dad.

Passing a row of restaurants, I peer into the windows, observing the strangers. A couple sits at a small table by the glass. They're holding each other's hands and gazing into each other's eyes as if they're the best damn thing in the world.

Resentfulness twists my features, the sting of isolation hurting more than my bloody lip and hand. Steph wants me home, but I know no one else does. Mom and my other sisters look at me with utter disappointment, and I hate feeling like a fucking failure.

So I'll hang out by myself and sometimes with my friends until one day it catches up with me.

My attention flickers over to the couple one last time, envious that I'll never have that kind of experience, and I hopelessly walk down the path that Dad paved for me.

"Mateo…" Lynn's voice summons me to the front counter, bringing me back into the present.

"Someone needs my help up front. I'll talk to you later," I say to Steph.

"See you at Christmas?"

"Of course."

"Good."

We say a quick goodbye, and I hang up before moving toward Lynn. When I go to the front, I spot a guy setting up his keyboard on the small stage. It's open mic night, and the artsy college crowd comes piling in for an evening of self-expression.

"What's up, Lynn?" I ask, wiping down a small spill on the countertop.

"Someone's here to see you," she says, with a twinkle in her eye. She gestures behind the small crowd by the stage, and the moment I spot Ellie, my heart jumps.

She asked for time and space, so I respected that. I've been hoping for a text from her, but seeing her here is even better.

She doesn't see me yet, so I make her a vanilla latte and pour it into a to-go cup for her, unsure of how long she's planning on hanging out here. Rounding the counter, I appear in her line of vision, and her cheeks rise.

"Hey," I say, outstretching my arms for a hug. I revel in the few seconds I get to hold her, noticing how cold she feels in my embrace. "God, you're freezing. Here, this should warm you up." I hand her the latte.

"Thanks." She takes a sip, coyly smiling at me.

The guy with the keyboard starts playing, the first note he hits being out of key. The sound makes me grimace. "Come with me." I take Ellie's hand, guiding her around the counter and to a back office.

Ellie's gaze travels around the small space, noting the computer, a rolling chair, and a stool. Her eyes land on wads of cash that are rubber-banded and stacked on top of each other with a calculator next to them, and she pauses, hovering in the doorway.

"I feel like I shouldn't be back here. Won't you get in trouble?"

I shrug. "I don't care."

"Well, I do. You need this job. I don't want you to get fired because of me." She starts to back out of the room, but I reach for her hand once more.

"I won't. My uncle owns the place, remember?" I move her closer to me, and out of instinct, I tuck her hair behind her ear as if I've done it hundreds of times. Her breath catches, and I'm not really sure if I should make a move or not, so I kill the moment by saying, "Come sit down." I roll the wheelie chair over to her while I sit on the stool.

I watch her glance around, her attention landing on the drawing hanging up on the wall. "Who made you that?" she asks, grinning.

"One of my nephews."

"Do you have a big family?"

"Oh, yeah. Three out of four of my sisters have kids."

Her face lights up. "That's awesome. Clearly, they love you." She points to the picture.

My hand clasps the back of my neck, and I rub my tense muscles. "For the most part," I say, chuckling.

"So..." Ellie shifts the energy. "Is this where you take all the ladies?" she asks, half kidding, half out of curiosity.

"Only the ones who don't put out," I joke.

She purses her lips. "And how many would that be?"

"Just you."

"I don't know if that makes me feel better or worse."

"It should make you feel better. I never cared about someone enough to bring them back here and potentially get fired."

"You told me you wouldn't get fired if I was in here!" Ellie leaps up, ready to run out of the room, but I halt her before she can get too far.

"I was just playing around," I assure her, threading my fingers in between hers. "I promise neither of us is going to get in trouble."

Relief settles around her shoulders. There's a moment of stillness between us, and then, as if there's a magnetic pull yanking us together, both of us step closer.

I study her sage green eyes as they eagerly stare back at me with anticipation. Her breathing gets heavier, as does mine, and she parts her lips ever so slightly.

A war breaks out in my mind, unsure if I should kiss her or not. Carefully, my fingertips brush over her jawline, and a surge of excitement courses through me as I slowly dip my head toward hers and—

"Mateo!" Lynn's voice echoes through the back room, destroying the moment. Ellie and I create space between us, and I sigh out in frustration. "Sorry, Mateo," Lynn appears at the doorway. "I didn't mean to interrupt, but there's a huge line forming, and I need some help."

"You got it." I nod and then look over at Ellie. "Can I see you another day?"

"Sure. When are you free?"

"How's Sunday night?"

Ellie hesitates for a beat, but then says, "Yeah, that works."

"My place?"

A smile draws across Ellie's face. "Okay."

"I'll pick you up around eight." I give her one of my infamous winks and then drift out of the office, walking backward. "See you Sunday."

CHAPTER TWENTY-THREE

Ellie

When I agreed to see Mateo on Sunday, I left out the part about it being my birthday. I don't need any big celebration or extra attention. I just want a fun, calm night, and I know Mateo can deliver that, even if it wasn't my birthday.

A sudden knock on my door makes me jump, and I open it, surprised to see Mateo on the other side. He picks up on my expression. "Everything okay?"

"Yeah, I just thought you'd text me when you were here, and I'd meet you outside." I smooth my palm over my olive button-up shirt and grab my jacket.

"That wouldn't be very gentlemanly." Mateo grins and then shamelessly undresses me with his eyes. I'm about to tease him about how doing *that* isn't gentlemanly, but my buzzing phone steals my attention.

It's Mom calling. She hasn't tried reaching out to me since she told me about her arrest. I'm not sure if she's calling for my birthday or if it's just a coincidence. Either way, I'm not answering. I don't want her ruining my night with Mateo.

My phone goes into my back pocket. "Ready?"

"Whenever you are."

We get into his car, and Latin music plays from the speakers. "Sorry." He goes to turn the music off.

"No, keep it on. I like it."

"You do?"

"Yeah. I mean, I don't know what they're saying, but I like the music. You can tell a lot about a person by the songs they listen to."

"Oh? And what can you tell about me?"

"Hmm." I listen to the flirty strums of the guitar and the breathy vocalist. It's obviously a song about falling for someone. "That you have a sensitive side."

"*I* have a sensitive side?"

"Yep."

"This is just a random song on the radio. I didn't turn it on."

"True," I agree with him. He starts to put his car in reverse, but I interrupt him. "Do you know this song?"

"Yes."

"Do you like it?"

Mateo narrows his eyes. "Maybe."

"Yep. You're a mush."

"How did I upgrade from sensitive to mush in a matter of seconds?"

"Because you're being shy about having a sensitive side, which makes you a mush."

He chuckles and goes on to claim that he is neither sensitive nor a mush. We debate this all the way to his place and up to his bedroom.

I received two more birthday calls on our drive here, one from my aunt and one from my cousin, but I ignored both of them. My phone rings again, and I click ignore before placing it on Mateo's desk.

"You're popular tonight." Mateo pauses. "It's not…"

I assume he's asking if it's Hunter. "No, thankfully." In fact, Hunter hasn't reached out for my birthday at all—not that I necessarily want him to, but I was expecting him to.

"Our paper's due in a few weeks," Mateo reminds me as I get comfortable on his mattress.

"I was actually looking at the questions last night, and we only have a couple left. I think we covered most of the topics in our normal conversations."

"Man, we talk about some heavy shit, don't we?" He smiles, joining me on his bed.

"Maybe we should lighten it up and go back to talking about reality TV."

"No, I like that we talk about real stuff."

"Me too. It's like we're being intimate without actually being intimate." Warmth instantly floods my cheeks.

"Emotionally intimate," he suggests.

I nod, fixating on the soulful brown eyes I have come to admire so much. Mateo takes his long fingers and gently moves my hair away from my face.

"I like that we're intimate in that type of way," he says. I swear his voice just dropped an octave. The heat rises in my body as he slowly traces my jawline, drawing my chin up closer to him. My heart is beating so fast,

I'm breathing like I ran a marathon. His dark eyes stare at my lips as I part them, waiting for him to kiss me.

"Mateo," I whisper, pleading with him to do something already.

He lets the smallest smile slip as he leans in and his soft, full lips gently meet mine.

In a millisecond, he has awakened every cell in my body.

I instinctively wrap my arms around his neck and delicately run my fingers through his thick hair. His tongue lightly grazes mine. The way he kisses me is unlike anything I've ever experienced—teasing and giving at the same time, making me desperate for more.

Mateo slowly guides us farther onto his bed so that we're lying down. He slides his fingers down my neck and onto the buttons of my shirt, as if tempted to pop them open. Instead, he places his hand under my shirt, caressing my waist. Heat sizzles off his fingertips as they follow the natural curve of my body. I can tell he's restraining himself, and I know I'm doing the same.

My body is trying to convince my mind to let Mateo take me here and now, but my mind wins the battle. As much as I craved this, I know I'm still heartbroken over Hunter, and I like Mateo too much to use him. I slow down our kisses, and he gathers that I want to stop. Our chests are rising and falling quickly, and he studies my face to see what I'm thinking.

"I don't know if this is a good idea," I say. "I don't want to hurt you."

Mateo pulls away, confused. "Hurt me?"

I shift my body so I'm on my side. "Yeah, I'm still not…" My voice trails off because I don't know how to say what I'm about to.

"Over him?"

"Yeah, I guess. I just have so much going on emotionally and mentally. I don't want to jump into anything and mess it up."

Mateo nods, being respectful of my request. He starts to say something, but my fucking phone goes off again, determined to ruin the atmosphere.

"Are you sure you don't need to get that? It's been ringing nonstop." Mateo reaches over to his desk and grabs my phone. It stops ringing, and the notification screen pops up. Mateo's jaw drops open. He must've seen the texts. "It's your birthday?"

"Yeah."

"Why didn't you tell me?"

"You didn't tell me about yours."

"You were at my party."

I roll my eyes. "I don't like my birthday."

"Why?"

"It was just never my thing." I try to distract him by pulling him closer to me and playing with his hair. My gaze goes back and forth from his eyes to his lips.

"You think you're gonna get me to make out with you so that I can ignore the fact that it's your birthday?"

"Yep," I say, giggling.

"Not gonna happen, but I'll make out with you anyway." Mateo leans in closer and kisses me with more force than before. His hand slides under my shirt, gripping my waist again with his callused fingers. He moves his lips to my neck, taunting me with his tongue. *Wow, he's good at this.* I let out a sigh, and he immediately stops. "Sorry, I got carried away." Mateo doesn't appear sorry, but neither do I.

"Let's go," he says, standing up.

"Go where?"

"Dessert. I'm taking you out for your birthday."

"You don't have to do that for me."

"I'm also doing it for me, because I'm gonna go crazy from not touching you while you sit on my bed with that sexy shirt on."

I glance at my button-down. I don't think it's sexy, but I'll roll with it. "Okay, but this is *not* a date."

"Whoever said this was a date? Just two friends celebrating a birthday," Mateo says. "Come on." He pulls me up from the bed and places a kiss on my cheek.

Yep, I'm officially screwed.

Mateo takes me to a little '50s-themed restaurant outside of town. It's decked out in old-fashioned decor with newspaper clippings of what the town used to look like framed on the walls. We slide into the red vinyl booth, and our waiter hands us the menus.

"They have the best ice cream here, any flavor you can think of," Mateo tells me with childlike excitement.

I scan the extensive list of ice cream flavors and discover that Mateo wasn't kidding. They really do have any flavor anyone could imagine.

"Do you know what you're going to get?" Mateo asks after a few minutes of reading the long list.

"Um..." I'm overwhelmed by the number of options. "Maybe just vanilla?" I look at him, and his face drops.

"Out of all those flavors, you're gonna choose vanilla?"

"There are too many options!"

"Why don't you live it up a little for your birthday?"

I check out the flavors once more. "Cookie butter does sound delicious."

"It is."

The waiter takes down our order, letting us know it will be out momentarily.

"So..." Mateo rests his arms on the table. "What was your best birthday ever?"

His question stumps me. "I honestly don't know."

"What about your sixteenth? Did you have a big party?"

I scoff. "No, definitely not." I think some more. "Maybe my fifteenth."

"Tell me about it."

"My friends surprised me by showing up at a restaurant, and then after dinner, we all went to a movie." I shrug. "Nothing wild or scandalous."

"You don't need to do anything wild or scandalous for it to be your best birthday."

"I guess." Even though I imagine his fifteenth birthday was nothing similar to mine.

The waiter comes over with our ice cream, which is overflowing in the bowl. One scoop must equate to three at this place. I take a bite of my cookie butter ice cream, letting the sweetness linger in my mouth. It really is the best I've ever had.

"Tell me about your friends," Mateo inquires before he takes a spoonful of ice cream.

"I had a few close ones in high school, but since graduation, everyone went their own way." I take another scoop. Honestly, I'm not in touch with most of them because Hunter would always complain when I would prioritize spending time with them over him. He was always sacrificing time away from his friends, so he thought I should do the same. It seemed reasonable at the time, but I ended up pushing everyone away without realizing it.

"Did you talk to any of them today?"

"Most of them texted me. One of them called me earlier, but I haven't talked to them yet."

"You should," Mateo tells me. The kindness of his response, encouraging me to continue my friendships, brings a lightness to my body. Meanwhile, the whole reason why I fell out of touch with them is because of Hunter's jealousy.

My phone vibrates on the table with Hunter's name flashing, and I hit ignore.

Hunter calls again, and my finger presses the ignore button once more.

"Sorry," I tell Mateo.

"Not your fault."

My shoulders drop as Hunter calls for a third time. "I'm just going to block him."

Mateo extends his hand toward my phone. "Want to have a little fun first?" he asks with a vindictive smile.

Spitefulness swells under my skin. This could be a fun way to get back at Hunter. Smirking, I hand Mateo my phone.

"Hello?" Mateo says into the phone.

Hunter's voice booms through the earpiece. "Who the fuck is this?"

"Don't worry about it. You need something?"

"Yeah. Ellie."

"Oh, she's a little busy right now. She'll have to call you back after. But don't worry, man, she's in good hands." Mateo hangs up the phone, and both of us start laughing. I take my phone back and hit the block button.

My phone vibrates again, and I almost jump at the thought that it could be Hunter. "Mom" pops up, causing my stomach to automatically tighten. I know I should answer, but I don't—not because of how I feel toward her, but because of how I feel toward myself. I'm so ashamed of how I treated her last time we spoke. I feel like the shittiest daughter, and having a reminder of that on my birthday is not something I want to deal with.

Mateo watches me as I set my phone aside. He looks at me with a gentle expression and changes the mood back to how it was, making me laugh and blush in no time.

As we walk up the steps to my dorm room, I turn to Mateo. "You know, this birthday might top my fifteenth."

We walk close enough that the backs of our hands brush against one another, but neither of us takes the initiative to interlock them. When we get into my hallway, my gaze moves forward, and I freeze. Mateo's eyes follow mine, and his posture straightens.

"Elena." Hunter is in front of my room.

Shit.

"What are you doing here?" I ask as calmly as possible as I walk up to him, placing myself between both men.

"What are you doing with him?" Hunter ignores my question, looking past me and at Mateo. I try to answer, but Hunter starts talking again. "I should've known you'd start whoring around as soon as you could."

"Excuse me?" Mateo strides past me and right up to Hunter.

My heart pounds faster as I wedge myself back in between them. "It's my birthday. Can both of you not do this, please?"

Mateo listens and takes a step back with his jaw clenched.

"I'm not leaving until we talk," Hunter says.

Of course, he's not going to leave.

I look over at Mateo, and I know that he'll respect what I say. He's the easier bomb to detonate. "Thank you for everything tonight. I'll see you in class tomorrow?"

He gives a stiff nod and then glares at Hunter, who's sneering at him. I rush to open my door, and Hunter marches in behind me. Thankfully, Bree isn't here.

"What the fuck was that?" I snap at him.

"I should ask you the same, Ellie."

I massage my temples. "Why are you here? What do you want?"

"Are you fucking him?"

"What?"

"You heard me."

"First off, think about who you're asking that question to. Secondly, you and I are not together, so what does it matter?"

Hunter's tone softens. "Just because we're not together doesn't mean I stopped caring about you or loving you. I want to make sure you're safe. I don't trust him."

Hearing him tell me that he loves me sends an ache to my chest. "You don't even know him! And you can't come in here telling me that you still love me!" My voice cracks.

Hunter comes closer to comfort me, even though he is the one who caused the pain. He gently tilts my chin up to look at him.

"Of course I still love you, Elena." His whisper sends a chill down my spine.

"Stop saying that to me."

"I will always love you. We need each other. I know that I messed up, but you and I both know that we're going to end up back together."

I shake my head and look at the ground. He bends down to try to catch my gaze.

"Come on, angel. You know that I love you. I love all the fucked-up parts of you. Do you really think that any other guy could love you with all of your issues?" His voice is tender and compassionate, but his words are harsh, confusing the thoughts and emotions swimming around my head until they're a tangled mess. "Just think about it. I've been with you through everything, and I always will. The panic attacks, your mom, the cutting, the breakdowns—no other guy is going to love that about you, or hell, even stay long enough to put up with it."

I move out of his grip. He may be right, but his comment still burns. "Please leave."

"I'm the only one who's going to be with you through all of it. You know that, Ellie."

"Please leave," I repeat, wrapping my arms around myself.

"I'll leave. But first, tell me that you know."

My brow furrows. "Know what?"

"That I'm the only one who's ever going to love everything about you."

"Hunter—"

"I won't leave until you tell me."

I stay silent. We stare each other down, and just when I think I won this round, he makes himself comfortable sitting on top of my desk. I know he won't leave unless I say it. If I say it, it makes it that much more real. The silence fills the room as he waits for me to admit to him what we both know to be true.

I sense myself shrinking. After minutes of letting his powerful energy dominate mine, I give in.

"I know," I whisper, looking away from him.

Hunter waits a few seconds and then plants his feet on the floor. "Happy birthday, angel." I refuse to acknowledge him, but I hear the door shut as he leaves.

CHAPTER TWENTY-FOUR

Ellie

Thankfully, I had an entire week without any commotion. I unblocked Hunter out of sheer curiosity to see if he would reach out after our conversation in my room, but I haven't gotten a single text from him. And aside from briefly talking in class, Mateo hasn't reached out either. I'm sure the standoff with Hunter was enough drama for him.

Sitting down in my philosophy class, Mateo gives me a soft smile as a greeting. Professor Boland walks into the classroom and begins speaking, "We only have three classes left, and then your final is due." Mateo and I glance at each other at the same time.

I wonder if our connection will come to an end after we write the paper and finish this class. The entire reason we've been so intertwined is because of this paper. As soon as he gets an A on the assignment, he won't stick around. He'll go on to the next girl and continue playing the field.

"What are you doing for Thanksgiving?" Mateo whispers as the professor lectures.

"Hanging out in my room. Nothing special," I answer with a shrug.

"You're not going to see any family?"

I shake my head. It's not an easy choice, but I decided not to visit Mom. The idea of spending Thanksgiving at Mom's rehab for two visiting hours makes my stomach cramp. We don't do much for holidays anyway, so it's not a big deal if we're not together.

"Will Bree be there?"

"No, she's going back home to California on Wednesday," I tell him.

"I could stop by on Thanksgiving if you want," he says, adding, "We can finish the last of the questions."

"Sure," I say. Though beneath my ribcage, I wish he wanted to come over for something more than just our paper.

Wednesday evening approaches, and my boredom is killing me. Bree left early in the morning, so I've spent most of the day doing schoolwork and organizing. Now, there's nothing left for me to do.

I try to do relaxing things, like painting my nails and applying a face mask, but I kept smudging the nail polish, and the face mask burned after a couple of seconds. What I really want to do is ask Mateo to come over. We could go over the last of the questions tonight and maybe order in some food and hang out as friends. That way, he can spend his Thanksgiving with his family and not trudge over to do schoolwork.

Taking the plunge, I decide to text him.

ME

Want to come over?

I pick at my cuticles while waiting for his response, hoping he doesn't reject me.

MATEO

Be there in 15

The butterflies are back. I run over to the mirror to see how I look. I'm in my black yoga pants and an old, stained T-shirt. The pants are okay, but I should probably change my shirt. I hurry around my room, throw on a plain pink shirt, and run a comb through my hair.

Before I know it, fifteen minutes have passed, and he's knocking on my door.

"Hey," Mateo says, looking better than ever. He's dressed more casually than I've ever seen him, wearing a sweatshirt and sweatpants. His smile lights up the entire building, and his shaggy, dark hair is somehow a perfect mess.

"Hi," I say as my breath stutters.

Mateo enters, and I close the door behind him. As he walks past me, I notice his head slightly turns back, checking me out. He takes off his sweatshirt and places it on my chair. My body temperature rises when I see that he's wearing a white undershirt, showcasing his muscles and tattoos. It should be illegal for someone to look this sexy in workout clothes.

"Is Bree gone?" Mateo asks.

"Yeah, she left this morning."

"Good." He subtly wets his lips.

"I-I don't know why I asked you to come over here." I trip over my words.

"Oh?"

"Well, I mean, we were supposed to meet tomorrow to go over questions, but I figured we could meet today because I'm really bored." My fingers play with the end of my shirt.

"Okay," he says and plants himself on my bed. "But how about we just hang out for a bit, and later on we can do some work?" He takes my hand and draws me closer so I'm standing right in front of him.

"I don't know if that's a good idea." I'm starting to inhale faster.

"It doesn't matter if it's a good idea or not. It all depends on if you *want* to or not." Mateo's hands gradually move to the back of my thighs, causing my breath to hitch. I swear my legs are turning into jelly as he lightly massages them. My body wants to give in to him, but my mind won't stop replaying Hunter's words that another person will never be capable of loving me and all my baggage. I really like Mateo, and I don't want either of us to end up hurt.

"I don't want you to be my rebound," I say, as if I've ever had a rebound before.

"I don't want to be your rebound either. I want to be your boyfriend."

"My *boyfriend*?"

"Yes."

"But you don't have girlfriends."

Mateo grins. "Not yet."

This is seriously throwing me for a loop. I thought he just wanted to get an A in class. In no way did I think he'd want me to be his girlfriend, let alone his *first* girlfriend. He deserves someone better than me to be his girlfriend. I'll make his life a living nightmare and cause so much unnecessary chaos.

"I thought…I thought…" Words aren't coming to my mouth quickly enough.

"Thought what?"

"I thought you just wanted to work on the paper together. I didn't know you liked me."

Mateo's brows shoot up, stunned. "You didn't know I liked you?"

"I mean, I knew that you liked me a little because we kissed, but I didn't know that you liked me enough to be your girlfriend."

"Well," he starts to explain, his hands still not moving from my thighs. "I didn't know either until a few weeks ago. I never felt this way about someone before, and I thought about it—a lot—and I think we'd be good together."

I peer deep into his dark eyes. This poor guy has no clue what he is in for. I'd scare him away after one screaming match.

"I can't have a boyfriend right now," I tell him to save him from me.

He looks at me with the kindest expression. "Okay." He draws his hands away from my legs. But…I don't want him to.

"Why did you do that?"

"Do what?"

"Stop touching me."

His lips curl upward. "You want me to touch you?"

There is a slight pause, and I consider what I'm about to do. My chest rises and falls in quick succession as my heart hammers in my chest. My hormones have officially taken over. I nod in response, and my hands grab his face to kiss him. He kisses me back with more intensity, like he has been waiting a long time to do this. His large hands make their way up from behind me, up my thighs, and to my back, making me go haywire.

Mateo pauses our mouths for a second to guide me onto the bed and pulls his shirt over his head. I'm not sure what exactly is going to happen, but I'm comfortable going as far as my mind will let me. He gently lifts up my shirt and takes it off. He kisses my stomach, and tingles shoot up and down my body from his mouth touching my skin.

He goes to unhook my bra, and I freeze, instantly aware of the fact that no one else has seen me naked aside from Hunter.

"Want me to stop?"

Do I? Never in a million years did I think I'd be doing something like this with anyone other than Hunter, especially if the person wasn't even my boyfriend. But there's something about Mateo that is so alluring, yet safe.

Mateo moves away after a few seconds of my not responding. I instinctively grab his arm, halting him. "Don't stop."

A smile slowly grows on his face. Mateo continues to unhook my bra, his fingers brushing over me as he slips it off. He kisses my neck and brings his mouth down to lick my nipples. I let out little sighs as his tongue explores me, all the way to where my pants are hugging my hips.

Mateo looks up at me for nonverbal approval, and I give him a coy smile. He bites down on his lip and gently tugs my pants off. I'm down to my white lace thong.

"So sexy," he says in an incredibly deep voice. He wraps his fingers around the sides of my panties and delicately drags them down.

I am completely naked.

Mateo drinks me in. The way he looks at me makes me feel something I've never felt before, like I am liberated through my vulnerability. My heart slams against my bones as my breath comes out in uneven pants. His rough fingertips dance around my inner thighs. I breathe heavier, wanting his hands to touch more of me.

He glances up at me, again reading my face to get my permission. His thumb grazes over my clit, making me writhe under his touch.

Mateo lets one of his long fingers carefully enter me, and I immediately let out a moan I had been holding in.

"Fuck, you're already so wet."

He continues moving in and out of me, the slow, pleasing motion becoming torturous. I want more.

"Can I use another finger?" The strain in his tone implies this pace is becoming torturous for him too.

"Yes," I say between my short breaths.

A second finger enters me, and Mateo doesn't take his eyes off me as he moves at a quicker pace. My hips naturally move with the rhythm he set. "There you go, baby. Just like that," he says in his sexiest voice ever.

His seductive words make me moan even louder. I reach for his shirt on the bed, putting it in my mouth to stifle my sounds.

Mateo stops and lies next to me, on his side. He takes his shirt from me and throws it. "I want to hear you," he demands as he starts circling my clit.

My body is overflowing with pleasure. I watch him as he becomes enthralled by making me squirm.

Oh my god, he is incredible at this.

Watching him watch me turns me on even more. His eyes travel up my body and lock with mine. "You like how my fingers feel on your clit, baby?"

I moan at the same time, feeling a slight blush color my cheeks.

"That's what I thought."

I don't want him to stop. Mateo's hands are inviting me to newfound freedom. My head lifts slightly off the pillow, and he slides his free hand underneath, clasping the back of my neck.

Gripping on to my sheets with my eyes screwed shut, I allow myself to be taken over by him. My legs shake and my back arches.

"Come for me, Ellie," Mateo whispers in my ear, and my moans grow louder and stronger.

My entire body shudders. His touch has given me a new taste of ecstasy as I let myself finish.

Out of breath, I lie still, reveling in this amazing experience. Mateo gives me little kisses on my body. "You like when I talk like that," he says as a fact.

"I do. But it's not very gentlemanly," I tease.

"I never said I was a gentleman in bed." He presses his lips onto mine, and I almost come undone again. My hands travel down his body, pulling off his pants and boxers. He seems surprised by my eagerness, but doesn't say anything and helps me get them off. I want to make him feel the same way he made me feel—or at least something close.

Mateo lies on his back, and I kneel above his thighs, straddling him. As I grip his length and move my hand up and down, his large hands grasp on to my thighs.

"You look so fucking sexy on top of me." His breathing becomes heavy.

My hand continues the up and down motion as I watch him bite down on his lip and stare at me. My movements continue for a little bit longer, and his undeniable pleasure from me is making me more confident. If I moved a few inches up, he would be inside me right now.

"What are you smiling at?" Mateo asks as he pants.

"Nothing."

"Tell me." His hands squeeze my thighs, demanding an answer.

"I was thinking…that if I moved up a little bit…I would have you inside me."

"Fuck, Ellie." His nails dig into me as his legs tense up. He closes his eyes and spills onto my hand.

After a few seconds of letting him indulge in his satisfaction, I hop off him and wipe my hand with a tissue. As I climb back into bed with him, I pull the covers over us.

"Why are you doing that?" he asks, still catching his breath.

"Doing what?"

"Covering up," he says as his big arm wraps around my body. Our bare bodies connecting under the blankets makes me want to go at it again.

"I don't know. I feel weird. I don't want you to look at me."

"But I just saw you."

"Yeah, but that was when we were hooking up, and now we're not, so I don't want you to start looking and comparing me."

He pushes himself up on his forearm. "Compare you to who?"

"Mateo." I pause. "I know you've been with a bunch of other girls. Most of them were probably sexier and prettier."

His jaw drops, and he appears hurt. "I would *never* compare you to any of those girls." I roll my eyes at his response. "I'm serious. Do you think I chased any of them around like I did with you for months? They don't mean anything to me."

"You chased me?"

"Where have you been since August?" he jokes. "There's no competition, baby. You win all the categories."

"But I'm not as experienced as they are."

"All the better." He kisses my forehead.

Mateo pulls me closer to him, and I rake my fingernails up and down his skin. We spend what seems like hours slowly grazing our hands over each other's bodies, wanting to learn every crevice through touch. It's a calming and enchanting sensation.

I could lie naked in this bed with him all day and night.

"I'm still not ready for a boyfriend," I remind him.

"I know. I'll wait until you're ready, if that's what you want." He waits for me to protest, but I don't. "And in the meantime, we can keep doing this." He chuckles.

"I don't know how long it's going to take me to get my shit together."

"I don't want to be with anyone else, Ellie. And until I hear you tell me that you don't want to be with me, I'll keep waiting."

I smile. I do want to be with him, but I don't know if it's possible for him to ever accept me as I am.

CHAPTER TWENTY-FIVE

Ellie

"What should we order for dinner?" Mateo asks while looking at Grubhub on his phone.

"I'm not that hungry. Maybe just pizza?" I suggest.

"It's Thanksgiving. It would be wrong if we didn't stuff our faces."

Mateo slept over, and as much as I wanted to go further with him, we didn't. We spent our night watching a bad movie and working on our final. We only have one question to go over, the one that I think both of us have been avoiding. *What is love?*

"How about Chinese, Italian, and Mexican?" he asks to get my opinion, but I can tell he's already ordering it.

"That's way too much food for the two of us."

He shrugs. "We'll have leftovers for the next few days."

"Wait, what about your family?" It dawns on me that he doesn't need to be spending the day with me in my dorm room. A confused look crosses his face as his brows draw in. "Don't you want to spend the holiday with them?" I ask.

"Nope."

"Why not?"

"We don't really do much for Thanksgiving. I'd rather spend the day with you."

"Oh, okay."

My phone does a little dance across my desk.

"Can you see who it is?" I ask. It's probably Bree with a Thanksgiving message. She was sending turkey memes all yesterday.

"Your mom." He hands me my phone. I take it from him as guilt immediately pounds through my heart. "Have you spoken to her since…"

"No."

"Maybe you should."

I scrunch my face. "Why?"

"I don't know. See how she's doing. If the conversation goes badly, you can always just hang up."

My stomach twists, knowing I have to get this over with eventually. I take a deep breath and answer the phone. "Hi, Mom."

"Elena?" Her voice resonates with surprise.

"Yeah."

"I-I didn't think you'd answer. How are you?"

"I'm fine, I guess." I gnaw at my cuticles. "How are you doing?"

"I'm doing well. I'm enjoying the program here. It's hard, but I'm hoping this will get me on track." She sounds strong, which gives me the slightest bit of hope.

"Me too."

"I was speaking to your Aunt Margaret today, and she mentioned me traveling down to Florida to visit with her." She lets out a lifeless chuckle. "You know, after I get out of rehab. But, I'm not sure if I'll take her up on the offer. Maybe one day."

"It might do you some good to be in a different place for a while."

"You're right. And I wouldn't consider rehab much of a vacation." She attempts to be playful and lighten the mood. "I finish in a few weeks, and then I'll be back home. Are you coming home for winter break?"

"Yeah." Not that I have another option. However, if one presented itself, I might just be tempted to take it.

She lets out a sigh of relief. "I'm looking forward to seeing you, Ellie."

"Yeah, me too."

We share a few more minutes of stiff conversation and then hang up. I catch Mateo's eyes on me, assessing how the call went. "That didn't sound too horrible," he states.

"Yeah." I shrug. "She gets out of rehab in a couple of weeks, so I'll see her during the winter break."

"She's coming to pick you up?"

"Yeah." I lie.

I don't know why I lied. Mateo probably wouldn't care if I told him her license got revoked. I didn't even realize what I said until after it came out of my mouth. I'm so used to acting like everything is fine and covering for people's mistakes, it's second nature now.

We end up putting a sheet on my floor and laying out all the Thanksgiving food, having a faux picnic. Mateo ordered mounds of food, which we barely touched half of.

"I'm so full," I tell him as I finish off my egg roll.

"Me too," Mateo says.

"What should we do for the rest of the night? It's still pretty early."

"I can think of a few things." He wiggles his eyebrows.

"You're so smooth," I tease him. "But seriously, do you want to finish the last of these questions so we can be done with this?"

"Okay, pull out the list." Mateo sits up straight, waiting to be interviewed.

"I don't need to get the list. There's only one left."

"Did you memorize the questions?"

"Don't make fun!"

He laughs. "Okay, okay. What's the last question?"

I press my lips together and take a beat before saying, "What is love?"

"Oh." Mateo glances up, giving the question some consideration. He shrugs. "I don't know. We should probably start cleaning up." Mateo suddenly starts putting the food away.

His abrupt switch leaves me with mental whiplash, but I follow his lead, unsure how to respond. After a few minutes of cleaning in silence, the bedsheet is in my hamper, and the food is packed away in containers.

"Are you leaving soon?" I ask.

"Do you want me to leave?"

"Well, I was assuming since we cleaned up…"

"That wasn't my question," he states. I don't reply, so he asks again. "Do you want me to leave?"

"No, but—"

"Then I'll stay."

A smile pulls at my lips. "Okay."

I suddenly realize I've been in the same clothes since yesterday. He has an excuse. He unexpectedly slept over. I, on the other hand, have all my clothes here and haven't changed.

Oh god, I hope I don't smell. What if he thinks I'm one of those people who don't shower regularly?

"I'm going to shower," I blurt out.

Way to keep it cool.

"You got an extra towel?" Mateo asks, and my eyebrows raise at his question. "I meant for me to shower separately."

"Oh, yeah. I'll get you one." I go to my dresser and find one for him.

"Thanks," he says as his large hands grip the purple towel.

I hesitate and think about getting undressed in front of him, but I choose not to. "Turn around," I instruct with a twirl of my finger. He rolls his eyes and reluctantly gives me my privacy so I can take off my clothes and wrap a towel around myself. "You're good," I say, gathering my shower caddy.

Mateo turns back around and fixates on my toweled body. I let out a chuckle as I scoot out of the room.

When I reenter after my shower, Mateo isn't there. I shift through clean pajamas to find something to wear before he walks in. They're all unflattering. I'm going to need to buy sexier ones if we're going to start sleeping over at each other's places. My hands graze over Mateo's black shirt from a couple of weeks ago.

Mateo enters, his hair darker and wet, his skin and tattoos glistening from the shower. He has my towel tied around his waist, and I can't help but stare at this practically naked man entering my bedroom. He notices that I'm holding his shirt in my hands, and he lifts an eyebrow, slowly striding toward me. I already know what's on his mind, and he can tell what's on mine. "You gonna put that on after?"

"Maybe." The word comes out like a dare, thick with need.

Mateo takes his thumb, carefully brushing it against my cheek and down my face, past my neck.

My pulse quickens under his fingertips as they begin to outline my collarbones, goose bumps forming in their wake. He then slides one finger between my chest and the top of the towel, gliding it back and forth to tease me. Mateo's gaze connects with mine, and he watches me as my attention starts to wander down his body, landing on the towel.

"Get on the bed." His soft demand has sparks running through my veins. My heart races as I do as he says. He assertively, yet gently, shifts my body to where he wants me. "Can we do something a little different than yesterday?" he asks as he rips off both of our towels in a millisecond.

"O-okay," I say, not completely sure what he means.

"If you want me to stop, just tell me."

"Okay," I repeat, thankful for his words. I go to grab him to switch things up from last time, but he immediately pins my arm to the bed.

"No. You first," he says and begins pressing his lips to my body. His mouth, tongue, and teeth lightly make their way from my neck to my chest and then to my stomach. He kisses next to my hip bone, and I let out a sigh. My reaction brings a smile to his face, and he continues to skate his lips over my skin, making his way down.

Oh, *this* is what he means by different from yesterday. Excitement buzzes through my bloodstream as I open my legs wider.

"That's it, baby. Spread your legs for me." Mateo loops his arms around each of my thighs, and his skillful tongue makes contact with my clit. The way he moves his mouth is different from what I'm used to, but is un-fucking-believable.

I can barely control myself, pressing my lips hard against each other to muffle my sounds.

He stops for a brief second. "Don't hold back." Then goes back to rapidly moving his tongue.

I release my mouth, letting stronger moans escape. My hands grip my blankets as my back bows off the bed. "Mateo!" I call out his name. The corners of his mouth turn upward, which would've been a full-blown smile if his mouth weren't so busy.

I watch as he continues to pleasure me.

The sight of Mateo between my legs makes them tremble, and he clutches me stronger, holding me in place. Our eyes lock, and I can see the hunger swirling behind his. It's intense and shameless and claiming.

And I'm not afraid of it for a second.

His fingers press into my thighs as he watches me unravel. The tension inside me builds and builds and builds until it hits the maximum. I toss my head back, repeatedly moaning his name as I reach my orgasm, while Mateo's tongue lingers to bask in his accomplishment.

After a few seconds, he lies next to me, tracing my body with his fingertips. I'm left panting and craving him to make me come again.

"Wow," is the only word I can manage to say.

Mateo laughs. "Enjoyed yourself?"

I nod with a wide grin, still catching my breath.

"Good." He kisses the column of my neck, which riles me up again. I want to reciprocate, but I'm not sure if I'm quite ready to do it the same way. My eyebrows furrow as I overanalyze what I should do.

"Something wrong?"

"No," I say as I go to kiss him.

He pulls away from me. "Elena." He catches me off guard by calling me by my real name. He's only ever called me by Ellie, or now *baby*. "What's wrong?"

"I don't know what I should do."

"In terms of..."

"To you."

He shakes his head and chuckles.

"Don't laugh at me," I say, my defensiveness on the tip of my tongue.

"I'm sorry, baby. Just do whatever you're comfortable with. It doesn't have to be anything if you don't want to."

I sarcastically reply, "You would be okay if I didn't do anything?"

"I mean, I'd have to go take another shower, but yeah." He smirks.

"You're not expecting *anything* after you just did that for me?"

"Not if you're not comfortable."

I can't believe how gentle and patient he's being with me. I've been waiting so long for someone to treat me with his kindness.

I kiss him hard and push him over so that he's lying on his back and I'm on top of his body. He kisses me back as I hover over him, once again inches away from him entering me.

I slide my arm down in between us and stroke him, swallowing his low moans with my kisses. He breathes heavier as his hands frantically grip every part of me.

Mateo pulls away for a brief second to get a glance at what he can see of my body. "You're so beautiful, Ellie," he says between sharp inhales.

I press my lips against him so he can stop complimenting me and continue moving my hand up and down in a rhythmic motion. After several moments, I can tell he's getting closer by how quickly his chest is moving. "Come for me, Mateo," I whisper in his ear, just like he did to me last night.

"Jesus, Elle." He comes all over my hands.

No one calls me Elle, but I like it.

"Your sweet voice saying that. Fuck." He closes his eyes and tries to regulate his breathing. I chuckle. I was hoping that those words would elicit some type of response like this.

Again, we spend our time afterward wrapped in each other's embrace, skin on skin under the covers. Mateo's eyes are heavy, and he slowly closes them. I watch as his lips open ever so slightly to let air in and out. For whatever reason, the scar on his temple is more prominent now. I lightly place my fingertip on it and then journey down his face, feeling his prickly stubble and then his soft lips. His eyes flutter open.

"Sorry. I didn't mean to wake you," I whisper.

"Sorry. I didn't mean to fall asleep."

Mateo takes my hand and threads his fingers in between mine. I can tell he's feeling a similar sense of vulnerability to what I am. "Why did you avoid answering the question?" I ask.

"What question? I was sleeping. What did you ask?"

"No, earlier. The one from class," I state. He doesn't reply, so I remind him of the question. "'What is love?'"

"Oh." He inhales and then sighs out his breath. "I'm not sure." He's fully awake now, ready to converse. "I mean…I love my mom and my sisters, and my nieces and nephews, but they're family."

"So love is an obligation to you?"

"No. I don't love my dad."

"Okay." I take a second and explore further, not for the paper, but for my own personal benefit. "Have you ever been *in* love?"

His focus goes right to my eyes, our gazes so fixated that I can't look away. "No."

"Oh." I continue my exploration. "What do you think it means to be in love?"

"You mean, is it just a chemical reaction, or is it more?"

"Yeah, exactly."

"Definitely more." There is a brief moment of stillness, and then Mateo continues to speak in a tender tone. "You know, when I was talking to you about how our souls are here to learn lessons from certain people?"

I nod, and he props himself up a bit. "I think being in love is a part of that. Some souls come together to hurt each other, and other souls come together to love each other. Both cause us to learn and grow." There's a fluttery sensation building in my chest. "What about you? What does love mean to you?"

"Hmm." I scrunch my mouth to the side as I take time to think. "I think that you are more obligated to love your family because they're yours. And I think when you love outside of your family, it's completely out of your control."

"So a chemical thing?"

"Maybe." My mouth turns into a small smile. "Or maybe more."

"How many people outside of your family have you ever loved?"

"Just one."

My muscles tense. The thought of Hunter while I'm lying in bed naked with Mateo causes unease to twist around my belly. He nods, knowing exactly who I'm talking about.

"I feel like he's always going to have some hold over me." All of a sudden, tears that I've bottled up start bubbling to the surface. A few stray tears drip down my face and onto the pillow, and I shift my gaze off Mateo.

He rubs his thumb over my cheek. "I've never been in love before," he says. "But I heard it can hurt like a bitch."

I chuckle at his attempt to break the uncomfortable moment. This is so humiliating. "This is probably the worst experience you've ever had with a girl after messing around," I joke, blinking my tears away.

"In bed with the most gorgeous woman, talking about love hardly constitutes my worst experience," he states, causing me to roll my eyes at his spin on the situation. His tone picks up, "You know what they say is the best way to get over someone…"

"What?"

"Getting under someone." He kisses my neck. "So whenever you're ready for some revenge sex, I'm your guy," he teases.

"I want you to be more than just my revenge sex guy," I say, laughing.

His head pops up from my neck. "Are you telling me you're ready to be my girlfriend? I knew I was good, but I didn't think I would win you over that quickly."

"Shut up." I move to stand and put on his black T-shirt. "And no, I'm not ready." I stick my tongue out at him, and he chuckles.

CHAPTER TWENTY-SIX

Ellie

DECEMBER

I'm sitting in my normal seat in philosophy, waiting for Mateo to appear. Sadly, this is our last class together. We're not taking any of the same ones next semester.

"Hey, baby." Mateo hands me my latte and sits down. I stare at him blankly at the use of the pet name in public. "What? I can only call you baby in bed?" he teases, and a few people turn around to look at us.

"Mateo!" I swat his arm.

"Sorry," he says, chuckling. "That was louder than I intended."

He's lucky I like him, and that I think the way he lights up when he laughs is cute.

"Today is our very last class," Professor Boland's voice booms the way it always does. "We are going to reflect on our time together. What have you learned and discovered about yourselves and others? I hope that you were able to see things from a new perspective. Whether or not you take any more of my classes, I urge you to continue to explore and search for more meaning throughout your daily lives."

Professor Boland continues his inspiring lecture, and as he speaks, my heart beats a little faster. I want to do all the things he is suggesting. I want to explore, travel, ask questions, uncover, and find new meaning in the world around me. I want my beliefs challenged, only to bring me to a higher level of understanding. I want to experience the world with fresh eyes every day. I want more for my life, and for the very first time, I think it's possible for me to achieve more.

"Mateo!" Michelle's voice resonates throughout the hallway after class.

He ignores her and talks to me. "I have a lot of shit to do this week for finals."

"Yeah, me too."

"But I'll be working on Friday if you and Bree wanna stop by and have a little break," he suggests.

"I'd love that, and I'm sure Bree would too," I say, trying to keep it casual.

"Hey, Ellie," Michelle shouts in a sing-song voice, and I wave back.

Her tone surprises me, and I turn to Mateo. "Did you tell her about us?"

Mateo furrows his brow. "No. No, she just…"

My jaw opens. "You told her?"

"Not about the private shit. She asked where I was for two days, and I told her, with you." He tries to play it off cool, and his eyes wander around the hallway, avoiding looking at me.

My face lights up as I gape at him in shock. I can't believe Mateo is talking about me to the people in his life.

"Shut up. Otherwise, I'll rescind my offer of you visiting me at work," he teases before gently placing a kiss on my cheek. His sweet gesture sends a zing of pleasure through me. "See you later," he says, and I watch him walk away.

My last week of classes is officially finished, and I'm in full-blown finals mode. The whole campus is taken over by frazzled, worn-down college students. It's no longer the place for playing catch on the Great Lawn or socializing over smoothies. Instead, people move frantically from building to building, avoiding the cold weather and hunkering down to study and write papers.

"I've literally repeated the same thought five times but with different verbiage," Bree complains as she sits on her bed typing on her laptop.

"Welcome to academia," I sarcastically reply.

"How much do you have left?"

"Almost done with my psych paper. We can take a break as soon as you finish your art history paper," I say, reminding her of our agreement to encourage each other to complete one paper by Friday night.

She groans. "I hate college."

I finish editing my psychology final and upload it for my professor. It's a little strange that I'm excited to send off my paper, but I'm proud of myself for all that I accomplished this semester—in terms of school, at least. As for my personal life, I haven't accomplished much of anything, so there's nothing to be proud of.

"Fuck this shit. Let's go get coffee and see your man." Bree flings her computer onto her mattress and jumps to her feet.

"Bree, we're supposed to be motivating each other. I'd be failing as your friend if I let you off the hook…and he's not my man."

"Ellie, I'm falling asleep. I need some caffeine."

"Half an hour, and then you have to come back and finish your paper," I instruct her as if I'm bargaining with a child about their chores.

"Fine," she agrees and goes to put her jacket and shoes on.

Thankfully, Edgar gave me time off to focus on my finals, but I'd be lying if I said I didn't miss going to work, mainly because of a certain someone that I occasionally get to gawk at.

When we walk into the coffee shop, the fragrant scent greets us as we make our way farther inside. The crowd isn't as big as it usually is, but there's still a good amount of people considering it's finals week.

"Hey, Ellie. Your usual?" Lynn asks when she sees me.

"Yes, please," I tell Lynn. "What do you want?" I ask Bree.

"I need a minute to look at the menu. Go find your man."

"He's not my man!" I hip bump Bree as Mateo walks out from the back.

"Hey." Mateo's eyes lock onto mine. "If you guys want to sit, I'll be over in a few." He motions with his head toward the back table with the mosaic top.

"Okay."

Bree whispers, "I'm going to stay here and flirt with the cute barista while she makes our drinks."

"What about Amber?"

"I love Amber with all my heart and soul, but sometimes I just need to flirt a little."

I chuckle and make my way to our table. Taking off my winter jacket, I wrap it around the chair as Mateo approaches. "How are your finals going?"

"Pretty good, actually. I'm not as wound up as I thought I'd be," I respond.

Mateo's eyebrows shoot up, and he presses his lips together.

"Not because of that!"

"You know, if you find yourself getting a little wound up and need some type of release, I'm always eager to help." Mischief plays on his lips as they tip upward.

"Mateo!"

"You're the one who brought it up."

"No, I didn't. I…well, I guess I kind of did." I start chuckling. "But only because of the face you made." He laughs with me, then leans over to give me a kiss.

At that exact moment, a group of frat boys strolls in, and I recognize all of them. Derek, Mike, Rhett, and, of course, Hunter.

"Shit."

"What?" Mateo's eyes follow my gaze, and he lets out a puff of air.

What the hell is Hunter doing here? He knows that Mateo works here.

My brain automatically leaps to the worst-case scenario.

Is that why he came with his group of friends? Is he going to try to jump him?

The group goes to the counter where Bree and Lynn are. Rhett eyes up Bree from behind and taps Derek to check her out as well. Mike's staring at the menu, oblivious to everything. But Hunter's eyes are right on mine, and then on Mateo as he creates space between us.

My heart plummets into my stomach, fearful of what might happen. I grab Mateo's hand. "Please don't fight him."

"What? Why would I fight him?" Mateo seems puzzled, but I know how this type of thing works. I've seen Hunter do it before. "It's fine, Elle, I don't give a shit about them." He gets up, and I instinctively rise to my feet. Lynn notices, which causes Bree to turn around and catch on to what's happening, which then causes Rhett, Derek, and eventually Mike, to look over at Mateo and me. This domino effect happens in a split second, but I notice it all and then stare back at Hunter.

There's a good amount of customers scattered throughout, so this isn't a complete standoff, but everyone engaged is waiting for the other to break the ice.

It's Rhett. He comes up to me like we've been lifelong friends. "Damn, Ellie, I haven't seen you in a while," he says, giving me a hug. I don't want him to touch me, but at the same time, I'm thankful for his quick embrace.

"Hey." I shift my weight back and forth.

Mateo stands next to me, looming over Derek and Mike, who also come over to say hello. I'm assuming Hunter didn't tell them anything about Mateo and me. Otherwise, they wouldn't be this welcoming.

"Hey, man," Derek says to Mateo, and they do their bro fist-pound thing that college boys tend to do. Rhett and Mike follow Derek's lead once they realize that it's Mateo. It took them long enough. They've only been hiring his band to play at their parties since forever.

Rhett turns to me and talks with his back to Hunter, so he won't hear. "I heard you're single now. If you ever want to hang out sometime, I can make you more of those killer drinks."

Mateo immediately steps closer to me, his body language informing Rhett to back off. Hunter moves toward us after taking note of Mateo.

Rhett gapes. "Oh, man! You two?" He moves his finger back and forth between Mateo and me.

Hunter's now planted behind Rhett. "Told you she was easy," he states, and they all laugh at my expense.

"You wouldn't know." Mateo smirks at Hunter.

Hunter's face drops for a millisecond as he looks at me, hurt that I divulged personal information about him to Mateo. A small twinge of guilt creeps up, but I swallow it down.

"There is *way* too much testosterone in this corner. Break it up, people!" Bree shoves her way in between all of us and places our drinks on the table. "Let's go. Move it." Her hands shoo everyone away, including Mateo.

"I like a demanding girl," Rhett says to Bree as he walks away.

"So does my girlfriend," Bree snaps, then ignores their existence as she sits down at the table.

My attention darts around the room. I don't see Mateo anywhere. He must be in the back office. Anxiety claims my thoughts, weaving its way in and out of my bloodstream, and I'm scared that once I leave, there's going to be some sort of brawl. I need to talk to Mateo before Bree's and my half-hour break is up.

"I'll be right back. I'm going to go to the office," I tell Bree.

"The office?" She tilts her head.

"Yeah, that's where Mateo is. He took me back there once before."

"Of course he did." Bree takes a sip of her tea.

"Not the time…but I'll fill you in later."

I slink away into the office, knocking before I enter.

"Hey." I move farther into the room, shutting the door. "I'm sorry."

"For what?" he asks.

"That they're here."

"That's not your fault. I don't care."

My hands fidget with the sleeves of my shirt. "I'm worried about them being here."

"How come?"

"I don't know." Awful thoughts of all the possibilities that could happen swirl around in my mind. "I just don't want anything to happen now that the other guys know we're together."

"But we're not together." Mateo smiles.

"You know what I mean. They obviously know something's going on."

"So what if they do?"

"I don't want them to hurt you."

"Why are you so concerned about me getting hurt?" Amusement dances across his face.

"What if they wait for you to close and try to jump you? There are four of them and only one of you." My mind goes to a time when Hunter was bragging to me about jumping someone before he and I started dating. It makes me nauseous. I don't like violence of any kind, including verbal. It rattles my core. Probably from all the threats thrown around and the arguments my parents used to get into when they were wasted.

"Nothing I haven't handled before." Mateo shrugs. "Besides, if he wasn't a bitch, he'd fight me one-on-one, which I would have no problem with."

"Excuse me?"

"What? I'm just saying that if the opportunity arises…" He turns his palms up, as if to gesture, *Oh well.*

"No," I snap. "The two of you are not doing this. I'm not going to have either of you drag me through this."

Mateo walks up to me, startled by my reaction. "Hey." His voice is calming. "I'm not going to drag you through anything." He gently puts his hands on my arms.

"Mateo, promise me you won't fight him."

"I don't like fighting, Elle."

"That's not a promise."

Mateo bites his lip, but this time it isn't from desire or lust. It's out of frustration. He releases his mouth and exhales. "I can't promise that I won't fight back if Hunter fucks with me, but I *will* promise that I won't start a fight with him."

I silently look into his brown eyes, trying to feel out if he's being honest. He hasn't given me a reason not to trust him so far.

"Okay." My shoulders soften.

"Go enjoy your drink before you get me fired for having you back here."

"You said you wouldn't get f—"

"Kidding!" Mateo leans in and gives me a kiss. His large arms wrap around my small frame, and he runs his hands up and down my body. I cup his face in my hands so that I can get even closer to him. My mind imagines all the dirty things we could do in his office. I want to do them eventually, but not now when there are people right outside.

I suddenly back up. "Maybe now's not the best time. There might be an audience waiting for me."

"Let me go out there first," Mateo offers. He steps out of the room, looks around for a few moments, and then turns to me. "They're gone, baby," he assures me.

Instantly relieved, I scoot past him and into the café. Mateo gives me a wink and goes back into his office.

CHAPTER TWENTY-SEVEN

Ellie

I've been staring at my computer screen since Saturday morning and only managed to write "Intro to Philosophy Final." It's now Sunday evening, and my paper is due tomorrow. Mateo and I spent the entire semester together, exploring each other inside and out, yet I have no clue what to write for this paper. I decide to text him to see if he's having a similar dilemma.

ME

How's your paper coming along?

MATEO

Done. You?

ME

You're done? I haven't even started yet!

MATEO

Want me to come over there to help you?

ME

No, thank you though

MATEO

Want me to come over there to distract you?

ME

No…but maybe once I'm done with finals

MATEO

I'm ready whenever you are

My face reddens as I smile at the message.

"What are you smiling about?" Bree looks up from her laptop.

"Nothing."

"Okay." She chuckles, and it's clear she knows exactly who I'm texting.

I focus back on my computer. Maybe if I start my paper off with a quote, that'll help get the ball rolling. Remembering the cringey quote board Mom had made me to hang up in my dorm, I begin rummaging through my drawers and closet, hoping to find it, and hope that once I do, there will be a line or two from there that can inspire me.

"What are you doing?" Bree asks.

"Looking for that ugly quote board my mom made me," I tell her as I fumble through the junk at the bottom of my closet.

"The one from the day you moved in?"

"That's the one."

"I think I remember you throwing it under your bed in embarrassment."

"Thank you!" I move to my bed, reach underneath, and pull out the quote board. It had some shoes lying on top of it, so some of the pieces of paper are crinkled. I read the ones Mom picked out for me and wonder if she ever thought any of these words could inspire her too.

My mind drifts, thinking of her at my age. Did she have dreams? Did she want more for her life, or did she accept it as it was? Am I doing the same—accepting the road I'm headed on and not even trying to reach for more? Will I end up just like her?

I look at the different quotes until I find one that strikes me.

You are the music while the music lasts. —T. S. Eliot.

It figures she would pick this quote. To many, this would simply mean that the song we listen to lives in us as we listen, but not to Mom. No. She, of course, would have to go with the morbid shit. She's referring to life and death. Our song only plays as long as we do.

Then, it's over.

Life is a song composed of high and low notes. I usually only let people hear the high notes, hiding the low ones from the world.

I wonder what Mateo's song sounds like. Would it start off delicate and soft or loud and abrasive? Would he let me listen to the stripped version with just the soft backing instruments?

Can our songs harmoniously intertwine, as if our souls already know which part to play?

How can Mateo think so deeply about souls, grief, humanity, and love when I've just accepted the information that was given to me and never questioned it or expanded on my own beliefs? Why are Mateo and I so different and yet so connected? How do our differences peacefully coexist? Can this harmony exist for the rest of humanity? Can we all live out our lives, teaching and learning from one another so that our souls evolve, like Mateo says? Whose soul am I supposed to be growing with in this lifetime? Who is supposed to hear my song?

Suddenly, I'm writing my paper. It has more questions than answers to the initial questions Professor Boland assigned, but I think that is the point. I remember every word that Mateo said for each question. Carefully, I compare and contrast Mateo's views with mine, all the while exploring more points and expressing my new inquiries.

It's three in the morning, I've reviewed the paper twice, and I personally think it's the best thing I've ever written. I upload it for Professor Boland and text Mateo to let him know that I'm done.

The next morning, I stretch before getting out of bed and seeing Bree off for winter break.

"Have an amazing break, roomie." Bree hugs me.

"You too." I squeeze her back.

She grabs the last of her things as I stand by the door. I still have one more paper to write before I mentally check out of school.

As she wraps herself in a thick scarf, a notification pops up on my laptop. I rub my eyes before going to check out who sent me an email this early in the day. Nerves fly through me when I see it's from Professor Boland. *Shit, please don't tell me I failed the final.*

Bree's hand is on the handle of her suitcase, but my anxiety won't let me peel myself away from my computer. I click open the email, nearly falling over in shock.

Ms. Connor,

On behalf of the School of Liberal Arts, we are pleased to inform you that you have been selected for the philosophy summer abroad program in France. Attached is the application regarding scholarships, as well as the timeline of the program and how many credits will be applied to your degree.

Congratulations,
Professor Boland
Philosophy Department Chair

"Oh my god!"

Bree runs over. "What?"

"I got into the abroad program," I say in utter disbelief.

"What abroad program?"

"I applied to study in France over the summer on a whim. I just got the email confirming I got in."

"No fucking way!" She bounces up and down. "This is so awesome, Ellie!"

"I can't believe this. I didn't think I would get chosen."

"I'm so, so happy for you!" Bree grins at me and then notices that I'm not as hyped as she is. "You're happy, right?"

"Yes!" I say. "But also not sure if I'm going to take it."

Bree's brows draw in. "Why wouldn't you?"

"It's just a lot for me to process right now. I need to think this over."

Bree's Uber notifies her that they're here, and she gives me one more hug before leaving for the airport. "You don't need to decide right now, Ellie, but think about it. This could be so amazing for you."

"I will."

She exits, and I spin back around to my computer.

Oh my god!

CHAPTER TWENTY-EIGHT

Mateo

Hope ignites in my veins after receiving the best email of my life. I've been accepted into grad school. Sparks of elation shoot off inside me. I feel like I'm floating and exploding all at once.

As soon as I read the email, I didn't even think. I just automatically drove to campus so I can tell Elle in person.

ELLE

Just submitted my last final! I'm officially done with my first semester!

Smiling at my phone screen, I'm grateful for the perfect timing as I walk into Durham Hall to surprise her. Even before receiving my good news, I planned on dropping in. I haven't seen her in a couple of days, and I'm assuming she'll be headed home soon, so I want to spend time with her before she leaves for winter break.

My knuckles tap against her door. "One sec," Elle says, and I can hear her moving things around in her room. When she opens the door, she hides her body behind it, poking out her head. A flash of delight appears on her face. "What are you doing here?" she asks.

"I haven't seen you in a while and wanted to stop by."

Happiness dances around her sage eyes. "Come in."

Letting me enter, my attention immediately lands on her silky bare legs, admiring how she looks in my T-shirt and nothing else. "What are you wearing?" I tease, my lustful thoughts taking over my mind.

"I just got out of the shower and threw something on when I heard the knock." She crosses her arms over herself, and something about her bashfulness turns me on even more.

I shake my head, peeling her arms away. "You don't need to play shy with me." Dipping my head down, my mouth finds her neck at the same time I lift the shirt up slightly so I can get my hands underneath. My fingers skim over her goose bumps, and when I realize she's not wearing any panties, I take a sharp inhale as I grip on to her hips. "God, you're so sexy."

A twist of self-consciousness makes her wiggle out of my hold, and I respect her need for space, letting go of her. "No, I'm not."

"Yeah, you are. If I had the time, I'd stay here all day and make sure you're—"

"Make sure I'm what?" Elle playfully provokes, waiting for some crude comment to pop out of my mouth.

"Pleasantly satisfied." I grin, and she laughs at my choice of words.

She moves over to her dresser and pulls out a pair of pants. "So you're not here for long?"

"No. I have work, but I wanted to stop by and see you before my shift."

"You work a lot."

"Bills."

"Right."

"Plus, I've been working more than usual to get Christmas gifts for my nieces and nephews."

"I'm so jealous you have a big family. I always pictured what Christmas would be like with a bunch of kids running around."

"It can be pretty fun," I state, thankful that I'm in a better state of mind where I can enjoy the holiday with my family. "When do you head home?"

"Tomorrow."

"So you're free tonight?"

"Yep."

"Good," I say, leaning against her desk, acting nonchalant even though I can hardly contain my excitement. "Because I received some really good news, and I was thinking maybe we can hang out after my shift and celebrate."

Elle gasps, her entire being lighting up. "Celebrate?" She sucks in a deep breath, hopeful that what she's assuming is the correct answer.

My lips part into a huge smile. "I got into grad school."

"Oh my god!" Elle shrieks. She pounces on me, wrapping her arms and legs around my body in a tight hug as I hold her.

I chuckle, reveling in the peppering of kisses she places all over me. "I wanted you to be the first person I told."

"I'm so, so proud of you, Mateo. This is amazing!" Her excitement and pride seep into my bloodstream, intoxicating me. "We *need* to celebrate!" she proclaims, jumping back down to the ground. "Where do you want to go? We're going out tonight."

"I want to take you out on a date," I blurt out.

Hesitancy tenses her shoulders. "A date?"

"Yes. If you want to."

A twinge of nervousness simmers inside me, trying to get a read on what she's thinking and if she'll say yes. Finally, ease loosens her muscles, and she smiles.

"I do," Elle states, quickly adding, "but this doesn't mean you're my boyfriend."

"I know. It's just one date."

I've been on cloud nine all day. I knew I'd get into grad school, yet it still feels surreal. It feels like a whole new reality is forming right before my eyes, including when I gaze at Elle as she sits across from me.

The scent of fresh bread swirls around us as we sit in a dimly lit booth in an Italian restaurant. "You look beautiful," I say.

"Thanks." Elle adjusts the strap of her plum-colored dress, and my attention catches the way the fabric hugs her skin.

The waiter places lasagna in front of Elle and chicken parmesan in front of me. She takes a bite of her pasta dish and gets me back on track to what we were talking about before I was complimenting her. "You were telling me about the moment you realized you wanted to be a social worker."

"Right," I say, finishing my bite of chicken. "It was when I was lying in my bedroom at my placement. I was thinking of all the shit I'd been through, and if it wasn't for my social worker, Mr. Kevin, I wouldn't have been able to move past any of it. And then I started thinking about the future and what the fuck I wanted to do with my life, and then it clicked. I wanted to be like Mr. Kevin."

Her head cocks to the side as she stares at me in admiration. "It sounds like Mr. Kevin must've been great at his job to get you to that point."

"Definitely." Taking a sip of soda, I make a mental note to text him later. He's one of the main reasons why I am where I am today. "I was such a little shit too." I start chuckling as memories from when I was a teenager pop into my head.

"What did you used to do?"

"I got myself involved in a lot of fights with the other kids." I smirk. "I hated going to my sessions with Mr. Kevin and would always give him a hard time. Oh, and there was this one time when I tried to sneak drugs into the program, and that caused a whole big thing."

"What type of drugs did you used to do?"

"A bunch of different shit. I didn't really like it, though. I just did it because I thought I was a badass, and I liked to cause trouble. It's something that's definitely staying in the past. You never have to worry about that."

"What about drinking?"

"Why are you interrogating me on our date?" I joke.

A blush rises to her cheeks, and she takes a sip of her soda. "I'm sorry. I'm just genuinely curious about your past."

"I used to drink a lot, but I got myself under control. It's not something you have to worry about either."

"I'm not worried about that. I haven't seen you drunk in all these months."

"You've seen me drunk. You just didn't know it."

"What? When?" Her expression morphs into shock, surprised that she wasn't aware.

I take a bite of my chicken, and when I'm done chewing, I respond. "The first party you went to at Hunter's frat house. I was completely wasted."

"That explains it."

"Explains what?"

"You were practically undressing me with your eyes."

"I do that all the time."

"Yeah, but this was before you knew me. I was just some random girl dancing."

"You weren't dancing," I correct her.

My comment makes her pause for a moment. "How do you remember that?"

"I don't know. I just remember you." I continue eating and notice the way Elle's eyes twinkle at the coy flattery. "Do you remember anything about your first time being drunk?" I ask, trying to fight back my laughter because I already know the answer.

"Very little," Elle says. Glancing down at my plate, my lips curl upward as my mind gets wrapped up in thinking about how she looked in that costume. "What's that smile for?"

"Thinking about that night."

"Why? What happened?" Concern inches its way into her voice.

"Nothing," I reassure her. "I was just thinking of you in that outfit… and how you ended up in my bed instead of Hunter's."

"But nothing happened."

"You're right. But now that we're *friendlier* with each other, I wouldn't be opposed to you wearing something similar just for me."

Elle's lips twitch, and she tries to stop them from grinning, but it doesn't work. Heat turns her faint blush from earlier into a deeper shade of red. I chuckle as she casually takes another bite of her dinner, pretending to ignore that what I just said turned her on.

Walking hand in hand in the parking lot, we stroll toward my car. The only light comes from a few lampposts and a small sliver of the moon hanging in the sky.

Looking down at the ground, an unfamiliar twinge of nervousness tumbles around my insides. "Did you have a nice dinner?"

"It was lovely," Elle states.

"I don't know what to do next," I admit. "I didn't think this far ahead. I've never taken a girl out on a real date before."

"You've never been on a date?"

"Not like this."

"So…I'm your first?"

My lips twitch. "I guess so."

When we reach my car, I open the door for Elle, but she pauses, gazing up at me. The way the moonlight touches her face makes her look even more breathtaking than I thought possible. My pulse strums loudly throughout my insides.

Stepping in closer, my large frame shadows over Elle's. My hand cups her cheek, becoming pacified by her soft skin. Thoughts whirl around my head, basking in her beauty, surprised that celebrating my success with her feels natural, and yearning to kiss her and never stop.

I gently draw my fingers down Elle's jaw and then her chin, luring her in. The moment our lips connect, I'm left feeling breathless.

Her arms wrap around my neck as she twists my hair between her fingers. She pushes her hips against mine, causing a wave of desire to ripple through me. She embraces me tightly, and I give it right back to her. Desperation and neediness unleash with every kiss, and I try to tame my excitement.

"I have an idea on what we can do next," Elle whispers into my mouth as her hands run down my chest and stomach, idling over the button of my jeans.

Yeah, there's no point in trying to mask my excitement.

Bringing my lips to Elle's ear, my stubble tickles her cheek. I elicit goose bumps when I tell her, "Get in the car."

CHAPTER TWENTY-NINE

Ellie

We kiss our way up the stairs and stumble into Mateo's bedroom. Our lips break away for mere seconds as we attempt to rip each other's clothes off. I get out of my dress as Mateo throws his shirt across the room and steps out of his pants.

My hands reach for his face and slowly trail down his neck, across the images inked on his body, and down to his stomach. His muscles clench, and his breath quickens.

I gain a sense of power, and I like it.

An enticing feeling rushes through me.

Something feels different.

Something has shifted.

This is new for me. I want him, but more than just lustfully. I want all of him. I want to know about his past, his pain, his future, his dreams—everything. I want his body, his heart, his mind, his soul.

Reaching the elastic of Mateo's boxers, I decide to do something similar to what he has done to me. Taking one finger, I place it between his skin and the elastic band, slowly dragging it back and forth. He sinks his teeth into his bottom lip, and the desire flashing across his face tells me he wants me to keep going. I can tell by the outline of his boxers that he's hard, and I want to tease him even more.

Slowly, I slide his boxers down and get on my knees in front of him. "Baby," Mateo sighs and pleads at the same time.

I look up at him with innocent eyes, knowing exactly what I'm doing. "Yes?"

"God, you're so sexy."

I continue to tease him, placing my hands on his thighs and softly kissing the innermost part, getting closer and closer to where he actually wants me to be.

Then I stop and slowly come to a stand.

Mateo's face drops. "What are you doing?"

"Teasing you." I press my lips together to keep from grinning.

"Oh, hell no!" He picks me up over his shoulder and tosses me onto the bed as I laugh. "I can play that game too."

Excitement sparks my nerve endings as I splay myself out for him.

Wasting no time, Mateo gets on top of me. His tongue grazes my collarbone as his expert fingers unclasp my bra. He leisurely works his way down, sucking at my nipples, delighting in my little moans. He kisses and licks his way to my hip bones, creating more of a fire inside me.

Mateo shimmies my panties down and pushes my legs open. His mouth meets the inside of my thighs. He sucks hard on my skin, which is sure to leave a mark. I've never had a hickey on my inner thigh, but the thought of Mateo marking his territory there heats up my veins in a way they never have before.

"Mateo," I whine.

"Yes?" Mateo looks up at me with a sinister smile.

"Please," I beg, my hands clinging to the sheets, awaiting his magical touch.

"What do you want me to do?" He puts his mouth back on my inner thigh.

"Anything you want."

I can feel his mouth turn upward against me. "Don't say that, baby."

"I'm serious," I say, panting with need. "You can do whatever you want with my body." I mean it too. It's not just me being swept away in the moment. It's the feeling of complete safety with him, knowing that he'll only go as far as I feel comfortable, and if I don't, then I know he'll stop.

"Fuck, Elle. I'm gonna come just from hearing you talk."

Mateo presses his tongue on my clit, offering me immediate relief, and I let out a giant sigh. His fingers soon join his tongue, and together they work in harmony, making my insides spin with euphoria.

The way he moves his fingers in and out of me is faster and harder than ever before. My body writhes from the overwhelming sense of pleasure. I reach my hand down and grip his hair. He groans against me, the vibration of his sound causing my legs to shudder. He then curls his fingers and sucks at the same time.

I fucking lose it.

Tightly shutting my eyes, I let myself become immersed, shouting his name loud enough for the entire block to hear.

As I catch my breath and come down from my high, Mateo brings his body to lie next to me. Without hesitation, I pounce on him.

I need to make him feel intoxicated by me, like how I get when he touches me. I immediately wrap my lips around his length and begin sucking, moving my head up and down.

"Fuck," Mateo moans.

I twirl my tongue around him and suck even harder. He's breathing faster and faster. "Elle," he calls out my name. I love hearing him say my name like that. *Say it again, Mateo.* I move faster. He takes his hand and places it on the back of my head.

Suddenly, my entire body tenses.

My chest constricts.

My mind flashes to a time with Hunter.

I can't breathe.

I fling myself off him.

"Are you okay?" Mateo shoots up.

I get off the bed and search for clothes. "Yeah, I just need to stop."

"What's wrong?"

With shaky hands, I grab his shirt, throwing it over my body. "Nothing," I say, out of breath. "I just need to stop."

"I'm sorry. If you didn't want to, that's fine."

"No, no, it's okay." I run out of his room and into the bathroom. Shutting the door, I drop to the floor.

My heart races.

This is so embarrassing. There is no way in hell Mateo is going to come near me again.

Tears spill over, knowing that I fucked things up with Mateo.

How does Hunter still work his way into my mind? Why do the bad memories need to make an appearance? Is it worth it to tell Mateo what happened? Maybe Mateo will understand once I tell him. Or maybe it'll make things worse, and Mateo will realize that I'm a lot more fucked up than he originally thought.

"Elle?" Mateo's voice startles me. "Can I come in?"

Honestly, whatever string of possibilities there was for him and me to be in a relationship is over now, so seeing me cry on the bathroom floor isn't going to be a deal breaker at this point. "Yeah," I answer, defeated.

Mateo sees me on the floor and takes a seat next to me. "Are you okay?"

"I'm fine."

"Elena, if I pressured you in any way—"

"You didn't at all. Trust me, this is just another annoying Ellie moment and has nothing to do with you."

"It's not annoying. I just want to know what happened. I'm kind of clueless here."

"It's embarrassing. I don't want to tell you." Then it dawns on me. "Probably not as embarrassing as this, but still."

Mateo nods. "Okay. If you ever change your mind, you can always tell me." He takes his thumb and brushes away my tears for what feels like the millionth time since meeting him.

"Thank you." I study him through my glassy vision. "You're so sweet, Mateo. You're always coming in to save me."

"I don't want to save you," he states. The bluntness of his response stings, and I want to move away from him, but before I can, he continues. "You're not broken, Elle. You just think you are." He takes my hand in his. "You're going to save yourself, and I'll be right next to you while you do. For as long as you want."

CHAPTER THIRTY

Ellie

A tiny drop of blood appears at the edge of my fingernail where I've been anxiously picking my cuticles for the entirety of the bus ride home. My thoughts have been spinning between the epic embarrassment from my time with Mateo last night to the uncertainty of not knowing which version of Mom I'll be coming home to.

At the bus station, I grab an Uber and try not to focus on the twists and turns of unease that are rolling around in my stomach. We drive past Hunter's block, where I'm sure he's already home from school, and I do my best not to let thoughts of him add to my increasing nervousness. Before I know it, I'm standing in front of my two-story house with ivory-colored siding. From the exterior, it looks like a relatively normal house—inviting, even. But I hesitate to go inside, unsure of what awaits me. It takes me a few seconds to realize I've been skimming my thumb over my scarred wrist.

After forcing a few deep breaths, I unlock the door and push it open. The house looks relatively the same—beige walls with pictures of our family from my early days hung up. It's as if this house is frozen in time from when we were considered a "happy" family.

"Hey, Mom."

"Ellie!" Mom rushes to me, attempting to give me a hug but gets intercepted by my duffel. A waft of vanilla-scented shampoo tickles my nose when a few of her golden strands of hair brush against me. "I'm so happy you're here."

The absence of alcohol lingering on her breath eases me into the house as I cautiously pad farther inside. A tiny, Charlie Brown-esque Christmas tree sits on our coffee table. My spirits lift, knowing that she put in an attempt to decorate.

It's a small gesture. Very small. But at least it's *something*.

"Let's get you something to eat, and you can tell me all about college," she says, walking into the kitchen as if chatting about life over a home-cooked meal is our norm.

"College is going well," I answer, carefully scanning the room to see if there are any empties. Glancing at Mom, I notice that she seems put together, aside from the bags under her eyes and frail frame. But I don't fully buy into her peppiness, knowing that there's always melancholia hidden beneath.

"What did you say you were majoring in again?" Mom asks, pulling out an old mixing bowl from the back of one of our cabinets.

My body deflates. "I'm undecided."

"Oh, that's right." She opens the fridge and instantly slams the heel of her palm against her head. "Eggs. I forgot to pick up eggs." She looks over her shoulder, a feeble attempt at a smile on her face. "You wouldn't know a recipe for eggless French toast, would you?"

I shake my head. "Don't worry about it, Mom. I'm not even hungry right now."

"But I wanted to make you something nice when you got home," she whines, pouting like a child.

"It's fine. I'll find something for us to eat and cook it. Let me just put my bag down in my room first."

Mom lets out an easily defeated sigh. "Okay." Disappointment tugs down at her features, letting her cheery mask slip.

Walking up our set of stairs, the floorboards creak under my feet until I reach my bedroom. I'm greeted by my familiar lavender walls, but bypass the large picture of the Eiffel Tower, my bookshelf, and the rest of my record collection, instantly splaying out on my comforter and staring up at the ceiling.

Placing my hands on my belly, I take some deep breaths, hoping that'll be enough to tame my growing anxiety.

After much time has passed, I bring myself back down into the kitchen and end up heating up frozen Jimmy Dean sandwiches for us.

"That was delicious. Thank you," Mom says.

"You're welcome," I reply, taking her plate to the sink. I'll gladly scrub the dishes if it means I'll get a break from our surface conversation with forced smiles.

"So have you thought about getting a job while you're at school?" she asks.

Warm water splashes against my hands. I focus on the rising temperature pouring onto my skin because the burn from that hurts less than if I were to focus on her question. "I have a job," I state.

"Oh."

She doesn't know me. It's partly my fault because I don't come right out with the information, but she also doesn't care to know unless she's pressured into conversing with me.

"How much are you making?" she asks, bypassing the questions about where I'm working or if I'm enjoying it.

I flinch as the water gets hotter, but I let my hands soak in the soapy, scalding water and watch as it washes over my wrists, biting against my scars. "I'm not making that much money."

"Oh. Well, that's okay. I don't want it to interfere too much with school."

I nod, continuously scrubbing the plates clean. A long, drawn-out silence fills the space between us. When my skin can no longer take the fiery water, I shut the faucet off and move on to drying. When I turn to look at Mom, she's preoccupied with a pile of mail, opening up bills that are most likely past due.

We haven't spoken about her arrest, or rehab, or what her plan is moving forward. We rarely have meaningful conversations with any substance, but I figure I might as well try while I'm here. "How have you been doing after…you know…everything?"

Mom avoids eye contact. "It's over now. I'd rather not think about it."

What a surprise. "Okay."

The next day is Christmas Eve.

Mom and I have been keeping to ourselves the majority of the day, but by the time evening rolls around, I can hear her shifting things in the living room.

Padding down the stairs, I spot Mom placing a few gifts next to the feeble Christmas tree on the coffee table.

"I got you a few gifts," Mom says, sensing me in the room. "I figured we can open them before dinner."

"Tonight? Why not tomorrow, on actual Christmas?"

"I'm leaving to visit Aunt Margaret tomorrow morning."

"Wait, what?" My head spins. "You're leaving to go to Aunt Margaret's? In Florida?"

"Yes, I told you. She and I got to talking, and we thought it would be a good idea for me to get a change of scenery, after, you know, everything." She waves her hand in the air, as if to shoo away the brief mention of her blunder. "I assumed you'd be fine with that since you usually spend most of the holidays with Hunter and his family."

I force my voice not to shake as I speak. "Oh. Yeah, that's fine."

I haven't told her about my breakup with Hunter or about Mateo's existence. I don't want to get into it now. I don't want to be probed with questions, and I definitely don't want her to suggest I go down to Florida with her. I'd rather be alone than stuck with Mom in a state thousands of miles away.

"Flights are much cheaper on Christmas than if I were to leave earlier," she states.

"When are you coming back?"

"I'm not sure yet." She moves into the kitchen, starting to make us dinner as if she's suddenly vying for a Mother of the Year award. "Since I work remotely, I'm planning on bringing my laptop with me and staying down there until Aunt Margaret gets sick of me. Or until I get sick of her." She laughs.

"Okay." I try not to let the resounding loneliness sink in. At least not right now, in front of her.

After dinner, we sit in our living room, and Mom pushes presents my way with a huge smile on her face.

Surprisingly, she got me several gifts: clothes and gift cards. I had no clue what to get her, so she ended up with a bunch of UConn memorabilia.

"This teddy bear is adorable," she says, taking the stuffed animal wearing a UConn shirt out of the bag.

"Sorry, they didn't have much to pick from."

"It's perfect." She nuzzles the bear.

A beam of hope lights up in the crevasses of my wounded heart. I can put aside my lingering isolation to notice that, yes, Mom is far from perfect, but she's trying more than she's ever had before.

I've never seen her this composed. Maybe the rehab worked. Maybe she's turning over a new leaf.

"I think this trip to Florida will be really good for you, Mom."

"I think so too." She collects the wrapping paper from the floor. "The taxi is picking me up early. I need to run to the pharmacy before heading to the airport."

"Wake me up before you leave." Taking the wrapping paper from her, I throw it in the garbage. As I shift the can, I hear clanking coming from behind it.

No fucking way.

My arm reaches behind the trash can and connects with a bottle of vodka. My heart drops into my gut. "What's this?" I hold my arm up, showcasing the bottle.

She takes a quick glance at what I'm referring to, then brings her attention back to straightening up the living room. "It's old."

"It can't be that old if you haven't thrown it out yet," I snap.

"I drink a little before bed to help me sleep. It's nothing to worry about, Elena."

My emotions do a startling flip from just a few minutes ago. Anger surges through my veins, riling me up. My face gets hot with fury. *She can't be serious right now.*

"Nothing to worry about?"

"Yes. There's nothing to worry—"

"You got *arrested* for driving under the influence," I shout. "You had to go to court-ordered rehab!"

"I'm aware of that." She comes over to me.

My body shakes with rage. "You thought you could trick me into thinking you're a reformed person by being nice and buying me gifts?"

"I'm not tricking you into anything!" Mom gets shrill. "You're my daughter. I care about you so much—"

"Don't stand here and say that to me!"

"Say what? That I care about my only child? Of course I care."

"You don't fucking care about me!" Wrath thrashes against my bones, and I throw the vodka bottle against the kitchen wall, shattering it into pieces.

There is a moment of stillness.

I sense Mom's eyes on me, but I can't stand to look back at her.

Darting into my bedroom, I lock the door behind me. She shouts at me, but I'm able to tune it out like I normally do. If I were feeling anything other than pure fury, I'd probably be crying. My body instinctively crawls under my white comforter, and I clamp my eyes shut.

I don't want to be here.

I don't want to do this anymore.

I'm so tired of this.

I just want to run away, start over, and forget everything.

I want a new life. I need something other than this.

Lavender walls are the first thing I see when my eyes flutter open. It's dark in my room.

I rub my eyes, unsure of how long I fell asleep for. Tapping the screen of my phone, I see that it's only nine p.m., even though it feels like the middle of the night.

Creaking my bedroom door open, I tiptoe down the staircase. Shards of glass are still scattered on the kitchen floor, with the stench of vodka seeping through the entire house. I peer into the living room and see Mom passed out on the couch, a half-empty bottle of liquor next to her.

Resting my back on the living room wall, my body slinks down to the floor. I close my eyes, and I'm instantly brought back. I can hear the haunting echoes of my childhood bouncing off the walls. My parents screaming, cursing, threatening each other. I can see myself as a hysterical child, not knowing who these people are. They couldn't possibly be my parents. They're not the same people who are kind to me in the morning. This doesn't make any sense.

My eyes open and fixate on my reality.

"Don't you ever get tired of this?" I whisper, knowing she's asleep and can't hear me. "When will it be enough?" Words that I've wanted to say since I was a kid are making my eyes brim with tears. "Why won't you change? Why won't you at least try? For me. For us." I wipe my face. "I'm so fucked up, Mom. I don't know how to let myself be happy. I don't know how to be anything more than this."

Tears endlessly drip down my face.

I stare at her a bit longer.

She looks cold.

There's a stray blanket on the chair that I drape over her to keep her warm for the night. "Merry Christmas, Mom."

Moving back to my room, I bypass the glass on the floor, knowing I'll be cleaning it up in the morning. I curl up in my bed, and as I go to put some music on my phone, it lights up with an incoming FaceTime call from Mateo.

My pulse instantly races. I quickly wipe my cheeks and comb my fingers through my hair, hoping that I look somewhat okay.

Painting a smile on my face, I answer.

CHAPTER THIRTY-ONE

Mateo

Mom's place has been flooded with people all day. I've barely had a second to myself. Finally, stepping into my former bedroom, I'm able to have some alone time and a few minutes of quiet. Although my old bed is still here and a few posters are hanging up, it looks more like a playroom for my nieces and nephews, with their toy chest overflowing onto the floor. They've been clinging to my side ever since I got here this morning. But as much as I love spending time with them, I could use a quick break.

Glancing at my dresser, I spot the Christmas gifts I picked up for Elle. I hadn't planned on getting her anything, but during my last-minute shopping last night, I saw some things that reminded me of her and couldn't resist. Fishing my phone from my pocket, I finally have a moment to talk to Elle. I'm still clueless about what happened between us the other night and how abruptly things shifted, but I don't want to pressure her to talk about it. However, at the very least, I want to check in and see how she is.

Foregoing all the texting nonsense, I go straight for a FaceTime call.

After a few rings, Elle answers. "Hey," she says in a soft voice. Her room is dark. I can barely make out her face.

"Hey. Merry Christmas Eve."

She chuckles. "Merry Christmas Eve. Having a nice time with your family?"

I open my mouth to speak, but an explosion of laughter and cheering coming from behind the door interjects.

"Sounds like everyone's having fun," Elle says.

"Yeah, it's a good time. How are things with you and your mom?"

"Okay." Her pitch gets higher as if the word narrowly made it out of her mouth.

My senses prickle, knowing something is off. "I can hardly see you. Put a light on." I hear some shuffling on her end, and after a couple of seconds, a warm glow lights up her face. I immediately study her features. Her eyes look heavy and tired, and overall, she appears drained. "Are you having a nice time with your mom?" I ask again.

She nods, her smile looking forced.

"Elena."

Her eyes turn glassy the moment her smile drops. She bites on her bottom lip, trying to keep her composure.

"What's wrong?"

"Nothing," she whispers, desperately trying to curl her frown upward. But she can't hold it together much longer, as tears begin to drip down her face.

"Tell me," I say in a gentle plea.

She wipes her cheeks with the sleeve of her shirt. "My mom and I got into a fight, and I also found out that she's leaving to visit my aunt in Florida tomorrow morning."

"Tomorrow?"

"Yeah."

"On Christmas?"

"Yep."

I blink rapidly in disbelief. "So what are you going to do tomorrow?"

Elle blows out a puff of air and rests the back of her head against a light purple wall. "I don't know." Her eyes avert off her phone, scanning her surroundings. "I have some cleaning to do…"

"No," I blurt out. My heart pounds fast, each beat thumping with contempt toward Elle's mom and the urgent desire to be Elle's safeguard. "I'll come pick you up tomorrow morning and bring you back here. You'll celebrate Christmas with me and my family."

"Mateo, you're hours away from me."

"So?"

"You'll be spending half the day in your car."

"And the other half I'll be spending with you." Our eyes lock through the screen. The thought of getting to spend the holidays with her lights me up with excitement. "Elle, I *want* to spend Christmas with you, whether it's in your house, at my mom's, or in my car stuck in shitty traffic."

Her features brighten, and ever so slowly, her lips tug up into a smile. "Are you sure?"

"Positive."

After taking some time to figure out the logistics, we hang up, and I reenter the Christmas chaos with my family. The overpowering scent of garlic mixed with the aroma of the slow-roasting pork makes my stomach growl as I make my way to the kitchen.

Mom has a pretty big apartment compared to the others in Queens. Yet, with a decent amount of space, it still seems crowded with the amount of guests. Family and family friends fill the space, the conversations a blend of Spanish and English, while the kids run around hyped up on way too much sugar. I take a peek at Mom, who's diligently prepping the main dish, pernil, at the counter. She likes her space when she cooks, so I know better than to linger over her shoulder too long.

"Where'd you disappear to?" Steph asks me, grabbing a handful of veggies from the fridge to make a big salad. She balances an extra tomato on top of everything, and it wobbles side to side.

"Phone call," I say, taking the tomato and following her to the table. A few of my cousins are seated, but they're absorbed in their own conversation that they hardly notice us. Steph grabs two cutting boards, one for me and one for her, and we begin chopping up vegetables. "I'm gonna pick up my friend tomorrow morning, and we'll be back by dinner." Thankfully, Christmas Day is more chill than Christmas Eve, so there won't be as much mayhem when Elle gets here.

"It's gonna take you that long to pick up your friend?" Steph says as if I gave her a bullshit story that she can see right through. Her knife makes a rapid clanking against the thick block of wood. "If you're gonna dip to go hang out with people, just be up front and don't make up a stupid story, Mateo."

"I'm not. I'm going to pick up my friend, and then we're heading back here."

"Where the hell does your friend live that it's gonna take you that long?"

"Massachusetts."

She pauses, looking up at me with her brows knitting together. "Massachusetts?"

"Long story."

"All right." She shrugs and goes back to chopping. "I hope he likes *arroz con grandules* because we're gonna have a shit ton of rice left over. Mom's cooking is enough to feed the whole block."

Smiling, I don't correct Steph when she assumes the friend I'm bringing isn't a woman. I know my sisters will be asking questions all fucking night if I do, so I let it be. I'll cross that bridge tomorrow.

"Yeah, rice is good." Focusing back on the tomato, anticipation builds in my chest.

I've never brought a woman to meet my family before, and even though Elle will stick out like a sore thumb, I know they'll love her.

CHAPTER THIRTY-TWO

Ellie

Mom didn't wake me up before leaving. Instead, she left a note.

There's a stinging in my chest while I scour the kitchen floor for the remaining slivers of glass from the bottle I threw last night, but I try to ignore it and focus on Mateo coming to pick me up soon.

A tiny shard slices a precise line along the pad of my thumb. Even though it's a small cut, a droplet of crimson swells at the surface.

Running my finger under cold water, my doorbell rings. "Coming," I say, moving toward the front door. When I peel it open, my stomach twists when I spot familiar dirty-blond hair.

"Hunter?"

"Are you okay?" Hunter asks.

"Yeah, why?"

"I went to the pharmacy earlier and ran into your mom. She said she's going to Florida for a few months and that you're celebrating Christmas with me?"

Heat rushes to my face. "I…I…"

Think of an excuse, Elena!

"I didn't know what to say, but I covered for you the best I could," he says, inviting himself inside as he pushes past me. His nose immediately wrinkles. "What's that smell?"

"Vodka."

His head tilts, and he looks down at me with pity. "What's going on?"

I go back to the kitchen, finishing up cleaning the pieces of glass. "Nothing. I accidentally broke a bottle. My mom's going to Florida. That's all the updates." Crouching down, I collect small shards in my palm.

Hunter sees what I'm doing and checks around him. He spots a piece and tosses it in the garbage. "What happened?"

"I really don't want to get into it."

"Okay. Well, go get ready, and I'll do a sweep of the floor, and then we can head out."

Emptying the contents of my hand into the garbage, I stare at Hunter, knowing he's not going to like my response. "I'm not going with you, Hunter."

"Listen, I know you hate me right now, but at least come hang out with my family. Don't spend Christmas alone.

"I'm not spending Christmas alone. I'm going to a friend's house."

Hunter studies me, his features tensing. "Which friend?"

"Just a friend."

His eyes widen. "You're going with that lowlife?"

"Oh my god, stop it. You don't even know him."

"*You* barely know him. You can't go to some random guy's house for Christmas. His family is probably—"

"Probably what?" I wait for something horrific to come out of his mouth, but he swallows his words. I pinch the bridge of my nose. "What is the point of all this, Hunter? You see that I'm upset over something with my mom, so you think that means it's a good time to try to win me over?"

Hunter's shoulders slouch, his eyebrows furrowing in concern. "No. Not at all. I'm sorry if it came across that way." He comes closer and gently brushes a strand of hair away from my face. "I'm just trying to look out for you."

I scoff. "Look out for me?"

"Yeah." Pity permeates from his eyes. "I care about you."

If I hear someone tell me that they care about me one more time, I'm going to lose my shit. "I can't deal with this right now. I need you to leave." The heels of my palms push against him, moving toward the front door, but he becomes rigid before I fully kick him out.

Hunter silently stands in the doorway, not budging.

My muscles strain against his stone-like chest. "Leave!" I shout.

His jaw clenches. Annoyance flashes over his face, but he backs down, not saying a word or glancing back at me as he exits. Even though I won this time, it still feels like I'm losing.

Suddenly, my heart rate picks up.

My feet pace the hardwood floor as my attention flickers over to the garbage can filled with pieces of glass.

My mind races.

My chest tightens.

My head feels like it's on fire. I can't slow down all the thoughts that come flooding in.

I hate that Hunter came here on top of everything else. He always makes my mind spin. He has a power over me that I can't escape. I can't escape any of this.

I want out.

I want to fucking claw my way out, but I have no idea how. Is this what my life is going to be? Am I destined to be the miserable woman on the couch, drinking herself to sleep every night?

I can't catch my breath. It's as if a giant hand is squeezing my lungs tighter and tighter.

Gasping for air, I can't get my weak legs to move toward the couch.

I flop onto the floor.

I'm dizzy.

If I can just take one long breath, I'll be good.

Just one. Long. Breath.

"Elle?"

Moments later, I'm looking into Mateo's dark eyes. He's holding my hands and having me take extended inhales and exhales until I feel the vise around my chest ease up.

"You're here," I whisper.

"I got on the road early," Mateo states, still holding on to me.

I take a few more deep inhales. "Sorry for this."

"You don't need to apologize for a panic attack." Concern encases Mateo's voice.

"That was embarrassing."

"It doesn't have to be," he says as I continue to steady my breathing. "Do you know what started it?"

My gaze shifts to the floor. "A million thoughts. It probably won't make any sense."

"Just say whatever's in your head, and I'll put the pieces together."

I glance up at the compassionate man in front of me. Something about what he said makes my heart swell. "I feel like I'm trapped. Trapped on a roller coaster that I don't want to be on, but also too scared to get off of." My throat clogs with emotion. "I feel like I'm trapped by these walls. I don't want to be here anymore, Mateo." My voice breaks.

"Then let's get you out of here."

We drive for a while, not talking too much. The music fills the empty gaps, relaxing me.

"Can I ask you something?" Mateo peeks over at me, then back to the road as we head to New York. "You don't have to answer if you don't want to."

"Go for it."

"Do you get panic attacks a lot?"

Oh. I wasn't expecting that question. "Um…yeah, sometimes." My fingers instinctively graze over my scars. "I used to be on medication for it," I admit.

"You're not anymore?"

"No, I wanted to try to get off all my medication and see how I'd be on my own."

"All?"

Fuck. "I'm not crazy, I swear."

"I don't think people who take medicine are crazy. It's normal, and I definitely don't think *you're* crazy. In fact, I really like you talking about this kind of stuff."

"You do?"

"Yeah, you can be so closed off sometimes. I like knowing what's going on inside your head."

"Trust me, you don't want to know what it's like in here." I tap on my head. "It's a hot mess tangled with overthinking and hypervigilance."

Mateo looks over at me, his soulful eyes absorbing my defenselessness. "Tell me more."

"Why? So you can use me as practice for your future clients?" I joke.

"Obviously," he teases back.

Bare trees blur together as I stare out the window. "What do you want to know?"

"Have you ever been to therapy?"

"I've had more therapists, school social workers, and shrinks than I can count. I've been labeled with all types of diagnoses—anxiety, depression, PTSD. I'm pretty sure there were a few others thrown in there that I'm forgetting."

"What do you have PTSD from? If you don't mind me asking."

"They diagnosed me after my dad died, but who knows if it's accurate. Sometimes I feel like they just picked a random diagnosis from their book."

"How did he pass?"

A lump forms in my throat. A balloon filled with emotion, expanding in the narrow opening, dangerously close to popping.

I've only ever told Mateo that my dad wasn't alive. I never went into detail about what happened.

"Car accident. He was driving drunk. I wasn't in the car or anything, though."

My mouth instantly dries up. It's like sandpaper scratching my insides as I struggle to get the rest of the words out.

I swallow before telling him more. "I stayed late after school one day, and my dad was supposed to pick me up. When I got tired of waiting for him, I started walking home. That's when I saw his car wrapped around a telephone pole with ambulances and police cars blocking him off." I rattle off the incident as fast as possible. "My psychiatrist said that I had PTSD from the shock of the whole thing and seeing him in the hospital on life support for a week."

"I'm so sorry, Elena," he whispers. Then he connects the dots. "Is that why you don't drive?"

"Yep. I tried once, but I could barely sit behind the wheel for more than a few seconds without losing it." I attempt to shift the conversation to more of a playful energy. "So I guess I'm more fucked up than you thought I was."

Mateo smiles ever so slightly, confirming the statement, and without realizing it, confirming Hunter's thoughts about me too.

"You don't ever talk about your dad," he points out.

"You don't ever talk about yours."

"Because my dad's a dick."

"That doesn't mean you shouldn't talk about him, though."

"Touché." He presses his lips together, then says, "I'll trade you. You tell me about your dad, and I'll tell you about mine."

"Only if you go first."

Mateo shifts in his seat. "My dad always had a temper and became more and more violent. Shit just kept escalating and getting out of control. A huge part of me was happy when he left, but another part of me…" He stops himself.

"Another part of you, what?"

He pushes the back of his head against his headrest. "This is going to sound so fucked up." He pauses. I watch as his chest fills with air and then deflates. "A part of me was sad. No, more than sad. I was hurt. He up and left us like we were nothing to him."

The sorrow woven into his voice makes me wonder if the *was* is more of an *is*.

I reach for Mateo's free hand placed on his lap to comfort him, and he seems surprised by my action. He clears his throat. "Your turn."

I stare out the windshield, figuring out where to start. "At times, my dad could be great. He was the life of the party, but no one else saw who he truly was once the party was over. He wore a mask for the rest of the world to see. My mom and I were the only ones who knew who he really was—miserable and broken." A knot twists in my chest. "I still feel horrible for not being able to help him. Not being enough for him to stop drinking."

"That's not how addiction works."

"I know it's not, but that's how it feels sometimes. Like maybe if he loved me enough, he'd quit or at least try to get some help. It sounds selfish, but I can't stop these thoughts that are on constant repeat in the back of my mind. *I was never a good enough reason for him to change. I was never a good enough reason for him to live.*" My chin quivers, but I refuse to cry over this yet again. "And that's what I'm left with for the rest of my life. Feeling like I was and am never good enough."

And at the same time, feeling too much for anyone to love.

Both of our pains echo throughout the car. Mateo gives my hand a gentle squeeze as I focus my attention back to him, taking him in, wondering what he's thinking about as he looks at the road ahead of us.

CHAPTER THIRTY-THREE

Mateo

Elle is settled in the passenger seat of my car as we drive to New York to see my family. I shifted our conversation to lighter things, not wanting to be the cause of another panic attack.

"Are you sure your family is okay with me coming for Christmas?" Elle asks.

"They don't know you're coming," I state.

"What?"

"They would've given me so much shit if I told them I'm bringing you, so I'd rather just have the two of us show up. I wanted to avoid the nonstop questions until after Christmas."

"Mateo! I can't show up at your home unannounced! They need to put out an extra place setting and make extra food."

I rest my hand over hers to get them to calm down, while my other hand is fixed on the steering wheel. Glancing over, I give her a reassuring smile. "They have so many people coming over, one more won't matter. And we don't have place settings. Plus, I told them I was going to pick up a friend, but I didn't say who."

"Okay," she says in an unconvincing tone. "At least Edgar and Michelle will be there, so I'll know a couple of people."

"No, they do their own thing for Christmas."

"Great," Elle mumbles. I can practically feel the anxiety emanating out of her pores the closer we get to Mom's.

"Would it make you feel better if I gave you a rundown on everyone and what you're walking into?"

"Please."

So for the rest of our drive, I spend time talking about my family. I fill Elle in on my nieces and nephews and tell her I don't have a favorite, but if I did, it would be my five-year-old nephew, Christian.

"That kid is too cute for his own damn good," I say, and Elle laughs.

"What's your mom's name?"

"Camilla."

"And your sisters?"

"Angela, Valentina, Isabel, and Stephanie. I'm the baby out of all my siblings."

Elle shifts in her seat, leaning closer to me. "That must've been fun growing up."

"Yeah, I don't know if *fun* is the word I'd use to describe it."

She chuckles along with me. "Tell me about them."

Turning off the exit ramp, getting closer to home, I give her a quick rundown on my sisters. I let her know that Angela is the oldest, and sometimes I joke that she's like a second mom. Then, there's Valentina, who is seven years older than me. I let Elle know that she's the quiet one of the group and won't grill her with a ton of questions. Isabel, or "the pain in the ass" as I refer to her as, is three years older than me. She likes to start drama and always finds herself somewhere in the middle. She was fucking awful while she was pregnant, and although her baby is almost one, she still hasn't stopped being a hormonal bitch. Lastly, there's Steph. She's a year and a half older than me and the sibling I'm closest with.

Parallel parking along a row of apartment buildings, I turn the steering wheel quickly, asking Elle, "You ready?"

"I think so?"

"It'll be chill. It's no big deal."

I'm pretty sure I said those words for my own reassurance. I didn't feel nervous about bringing Elle to meet my family until right this very second. Warmth brims around the collar of my shirt. I hope my family doesn't make a thing out of this. I didn't want Elle to be alone for Christmas, so I invited her to be with me. That's it. It's no big deal.

Elle sidles up next to me, holding a box of chocolates. I told her she didn't need to bring anything, but she insisted on buying some type of dessert when we stopped at a rest stop earlier.

My heart hammers faster than usual as we walk up to the door. When it opens, there's a staircase directly in front of us, and another door to the left, which is wide open, exposing my mom's living room with a large Christmas tree filled with handmade ornaments.

Before I can fully enter, my nieces and nephews spot me. "*Tío* Mateo!" They shriek with joy, as if we didn't just see each other.

I can't help but beam, and I make sure to give them each a bear-sized hug,

"You're finally back," Steph says as I make my way further inside. Her line of sight moves off me as she notices Elle trailing behind me. Amusement is stamped across Steph's face. Her eyes are wide with disbelief. "Who's this?"

Reaching for Elle's hand, I bring her to my side. "This is Ellie," I state. "Elle, this is Steph."

"Hi," Elle says. "It's nice to meet you. I've heard a lot about you."

Stephanie's jaw drops. She looks down at my hand intertwined with Elle's and then back up at me. "Holy shit," she says with a giant grin. Her voice is loud enough that it caught others' attention, and now my fucking family is staring at Elle.

Remaining calm and collected, I ignore everyone's eyes on us. "Let me take your coat," I say to Elle, and she shuffles out of it, her cheeks becoming rosy.

"Mom, Mateo and his *friend* are here," Steph calls out.

Mom might be petite, but even through the cluster of people crowding the space, I can spot her. Shock appears on her face as her attention flickers from me to Elle, walking over to us.

"Hey, Mom. This is Ellie."

"I'm so sorry to show up unannounced. I brought you some chocolates," Elle blurts out. She extends her hand to shake, but Mom ignores it and goes right in for a hug.

"It's great to meet you, Ellie. I'm Camilla." She welcomes her. "I'm so happy Mateo brought you here. Come in." She guides Elle into the kitchen as if this is something she's done time and time again.

Steph mouths, *What the fuck,* still in utter disbelief from me bringing a girl home.

Once Elle is several feet away, I respond to Steph in a hushed tone. "Don't make a thing out of it."

"Is she your girlfriend?"

"I said don't make a thing out of this, Stephanie."

She lets out a small gasp. "Oh my god, she's your girlfriend!"

"She's not my girlfriend, but you're going to ruin my chances of changing that if she thinks my family is fucking weird, so chill."

Steph clamps her mouth shut, but she's unable to conceal the delight dancing in her eyes.

And as I gaze over at Elle, grinning ear to ear as she meets different members of my family, I don't think I'm able to conceal my joy either.

CHAPTER THIRTY-FOUR

Ellie

Mateo's childhood home is very different from how I envisioned it. It's spacious, with freshly painted walls, perfectly intact leather couches, and a long dining table draped with a Christmas tablecloth. It's nothing like his apartment by school.

"You hungry? We have plenty of food." Camilla gestures for me to take a seat.

"Yes, thank you."

"Angela!" she calls over to Mateo's sister and directs her to make me a plate of food. Angela beams as she passes the plate of food to Camilla, who places it in front of me. I don't know what type of dish this is, but my stomach growls as the scent of peppers and seasonings fills my nostrils. I instantly start eating the colorful dish prepared for me and compliment Camilla on her fantastic cooking. Camilla and Angela sit down, and I fill them in on the basics about myself while Mateo plays with his nieces and nephews in the living room. I learn that Camilla is a toxicologist, and Angela is a teacher at a nearby private school. Stephanie eagerly drifts over, introducing their other sister, Valentina, and they both join us at the table.

Smiling, I glance over at Mateo, who's got his hands full with his nieces and nephews as they climb all over him as if he belonged at a playground.

"I hope we didn't hold you guys up by getting here late in the day," I say to the table. "Do you guys do gifts after dinner? You don't have to wait for me to finish."

"We did gifts last night," Camilla states.

"You do gifts on Christmas Eve?"

"Yep, with the family, and then Santa comes Christmas morning," Stephanie informs me. "Christmas Eve is bigger for us than Christmas Day."

"One, two, three…go!" Mateo shouts, getting the kids to do some type of race so he can get a moment of respite.

A woman with a perfect ballerina bun balanced on the top of her head walks out from the hallway with a baby in her arms. The children run past her, giggling and shouting. "Whoa! Slow down!" she snaps at them before coming over to the dining table. The moment she notices me, her eyes press into mine.

"Who's this?" she addresses the room while staring me down.

"Ellie. She's with me." Mateo's deep voice cuts through the tension as he emerges. "Elle, this is Isabel and Luis," he tells me.

Isabel scrunches her face. "She's with *you*?"

"Yeah," Mateo says as he reaches for Luis. "Now give me my nephew." I watch as Mateo takes Luis and kisses him on his chunky baby cheeks.

I swear my ovaries just kicked me.

Isabel crosses over to her sisters, speaking to them in Spanish, and then directs her attention to me. "So, Ellie…" Isabel hovers over the table, looking down at me. "Why are you here?"

"Don't be a bitch, Isabel. I invited her," Mateo intervenes.

"I'm not being a bitch. I'm just trying to figure out why she wants to be here."

"Isabel, leave Mateo and Ellie alone," Camilla interrupts the conversation, and Isabel shuts up, but not without delivering an intimidating glare.

"Don't worry about her. That's just the way she's always been," Stephanie says, rolling her eyes.

The evening moves on, and Mateo introduces me to his extended family, each person pleasantly surprised that I'm here. One of Mateo's nephews, Christian, tugs on Mateo's shirt to get his attention.

"Is she your girlfriend?" Christian asks, glancing over at me.

"Something like that," Mateo says. He gives me a wink, and my stomach jumps. Christian presses up on his tippy toes, signaling Mateo to bend closer to him. He then whispers something in Mateo's ear, and Mateo whispers back. Christian giggles and runs off to play with the others.

"What was that about?" I ask.

"Secret boy stuff." He smirks.

At the end of the night, my body melts into one of the leather couches next to Mateo. His mom and sisters join us in the living room, each with tired eyes but with a glimmer of fulfillment. They're all treating me as part of their family. Even Isabel lightened up around me.

"Thank you again for letting me be here," I say to all of them, but specifically looking at Camilla.

Angela speaks before anyone else can. "I never thought I'd see the day where Mateo would bring a girl home." The women chuckle with one another, but Mateo stays quiet.

"We have plenty of embarrassing stories about him if you ever want to know," Valentina baits me.

I perk up in my seat. "Yes, please!"

"No! She doesn't need to know any of that shit," Mateo protests.

"Come on. We've been waiting years to tell someone about your love of Cinderella," Isabel teases him, and laughter fills the room.

"Cinderella?" I join in on the teasing.

"Okay, I think it's time we get ready for bed." Mateo stands up. "I'm going to get your overnight bag from my car," he says before escaping. Camilla yawns, agreeing that she needs some sleep, leaving Mateo's sisters and me in the living room. The energy shifts. It's the first time I'm alone with the four of them.

"You know, this is the first time Mateo has brought a girl to meet the family," Isabel tells me.

"He's never brought a girl home?" I ask, my brows pulling together in confusion.

Isabel scoffs. "I didn't say he never brought a girl home. I said he never brought a girl home to *meet his family*." Angela says something in Spanish, and Isabel and Valentina start laughing.

An uneasy sensation bubbles in my gut, and a twinge of jealousy mixes in, even though I have no right to be envious. However, I can't help but wonder just how many girls he's brought into his bedroom.

"Ignore them. They're just gossiping," Stephanie tells me in hopes of comforting me, but it really just confirms my thoughts.

Mateo reenters with my bag in his hand. "Come on. Let's go to my room." He motions his head toward the hallway. I follow him as his sisters continue their conversation.

In his bedroom, I get a glimpse of what younger Mateo was like. The room is sizable, with oak furniture and green walls. It's clear that it's a space for the kids, with their toy bin spilling over, but there are still a few band posters taped up near Mateo's queen-size bed.

As Mateo places my duffel on his mattress, all I can think of is how many girls have been in this bed with him. He sits down and looks at me.

"Something wrong?" he asks. I shake my head and move toward my bag to get my pajamas.

"What did they say to you?" Mateo asks me another question.

"Nothing." I feign indifference, changing into my pj's.

"Elena, tell me what's wrong."

I chew the inside of my cheek as I consider telling Mateo about my immature jealousy.

"It's just that..." I smooth my pajama shirt against my body. "I can't help but think about all the girls that have been in here with you. And now my mind is spiraling, wondering about all the girls who've been in your bed back at school."

He takes a deep inhale. "Did my sisters start some shit?"

"No, they only said that you've had girls over, but I'm the only one to meet your family."

"Exactly. I've had a bunch of girls over, but you're the only one I cared about enough to actually want to get to know my family." His response doesn't quite make me feel better, but he still continues, "Forget about all the other girls. They don't mean anything to me."

"How many *other girls* have there been?"

Mateo reaches out and clasps my hips, bringing me closer to him. "Elle, it doesn't matter how many girls I've been with. None of them meant anything to me. You're the only one I've ever cared about in this way." His eyes hold an infinite amount of compassion and honesty. "And," he continues. "I've never had a girl sleep over before. Here or at my place."

"What? They don't spend the night?"

Mateo shakes his head. "Nope." He smiles at me. "You're my first."

I chuckle at his choice of words, then continue to get ready for bed. Mateo goes to do the same but abruptly freezes.

"I'm an idiot," he states. "I've had your gift sitting here the whole time and forgot to give it to you." He motions to a little metallic gift bag on his dresser.

My face drops. "I didn't know we were exchanging gifts."

"It's just two small things." Mateo brings the bag over to me. "If they're too much or you hate them, you can give them back. I promise."

"Oh god, Mateo. I feel awful. I crashed your Christmas, and I didn't get you a single thing."

"You didn't crash it. I invited you, and I don't want you to get me anything."

"I don't deserve this."

"You don't even know what it is. It could suck."

Giving him a playful scowl, I take the gift bag from him. My fingers move around the white tissue paper and take out a record to add to my collection. My being lights up, smiling from ear to ear.

"You probably never heard of Straylight Run before," Mateo states. "They're a band from New York. They were popular in the early two thousands. They're kinda indie-emo. I figured you might like them."

Gazing at him, I beam with adoration. "What's your favorite song?"

"I have two favorites: 'The Tension and Terror' and 'Existentialism on Prom Night.'"

"I can't wait to listen to them."

He takes the record, placing it on his dresser, and says, "There's one more gift."

Fishing around in the bag, my fingers connect with a thin chain. I pull it out and look at the gorgeous necklace. The long silver chain drops down to a small, oval charm with a stunning green crystal in the center.

"I saw it, and it reminded me of you." Mateo shifts on his heels. "The green. You know, because it's the same color as your eyes." He clears his throat as I admire the necklace. "You hate it," he states.

"I love it. It's perfect."

"You don't have to say that, I can return—"

My mouth lands on his before he can finish his sentence. My hands embrace his face as our lips meld together and tongues intertwine. Mateo's thumbs sneak their way under my shirt so that he's delicately touching my skin.

Breaking our kiss ever so slightly, I ask, "Can you put the necklace on me?"

"Now? We're going to bed."

"I don't care." Handing him my beautiful gift, I spin around and lift up my hair.

Mateo brings the crystal to the front of me, clasping the chain around my neck. Goose bumps rise at the feel of his fingers softly lingering on my skin.

Turning back around, I stare up at him, my pulse humming with delight. "Thank you." Pressing up on my toes, I kiss him. Only this time it's less hurried and more indulgent.

His lips leisurely claim mine, as if he's taking his time to enjoy how I feel and taste. Delicately, his large hands clutch onto my body, and he begins drawing us over to his bed.

My pace picks up.

We haven't been intimate since I freaked out over a blow job. A big part of me—no, a massive part of me—assumed he wouldn't be interested in me that way anymore. But as he sits down on his mattress and I straddle him, I can tell by his hardness pushing through his gym shorts that my anxiety didn't completely turn him off.

The shakiness in my breath intensifies.

This is my chance for a do-over. This is my chance to show him I'm normal and not some anxious-ridden girl. This is…

Mateo breaks our kiss. "You're in your head."

"What?"

"I can tell you're in your head." His index finger gently taps against my temple. "Don't be. I had zero expectations of hooking up, not even this."

"Oh." My body tenses, as if creating its own shield of armor so his answer to my upcoming question doesn't hurt as much. "So you don't want to hook up?"

"I *definitely* want to hook up. Trust me. Every way and everywhere you'll let me." Mateo's reassuring smirk sends ease throughout me. "But I don't want to unless you're one hundred percent into it. And right now, I can tell that you're in your head…and that's okay." He gives me a peck on the lips. "Let's get some sleep. I'm fucking exhausted."

Scooting off Mateo, I watch with growing infatuation as he pulls back his comforter and makes room for me in his bed.

Patting the empty space next to him, he says, "Come cuddle me."

I chuckle. "When was the last time you asked someone to cuddle you?"

"Never. So you better not miss out on this opportunity."

A sense of peace uncoils my nerves, and I slink down next to him so we can both hold each other.

CHAPTER THIRTY-FIVE

Ellie

The next day, after eating a hearty lunch that Camilla whipped up, we decided we should head back to Connecticut. Mateo has to get back to working at the Cozy Nook, and I want to be sure that I don't overstay my welcome.

Zipping up my small duffel, I realize I have everything except for my phone charger. Checking around Mateo's room, it's nowhere in sight. "I must've put it in the living room," I say to myself. Stepping out into the hallway, Stephanie's voice catches my attention as I walk past her room.

Her door is only open a sliver, so I know I'm out of view when I pause next to it when I hear her ask, "So how long do I have to wait for you to tell me what the deal is between you and Ellie?"

"There's nothing to tell," Mateo responds.

My heart flutters.

I know I shouldn't eavesdrop, but my feet can't seem to move.

"Then she's just some random hookup you decided to invite to Christmas?"

"It's not like that."

"So Ellie *is* more than just a hookup."

"Just drop it, Steph," Mateo says, aggravation rising between his words.

"Did you get her something for Christmas?" Steph presses him, and when he doesn't respond, she keeps going. "Oh my god, you did! You bought her a gift *and* had her come to meet the family."

"I said, drop it."

"Mateo, I've never seen you like this."

"Shut up."

"Are you in love with her?"

"Stephanie, stop," he snaps. "I'm not in love with Ellie. I don't fall in love, and I never will. I'm just with her. That's it."

I'm just with her. That's it.

That's it?

An aching pain strikes my chest, severing it in half.

It's as if my heart has been ripped out of my chest and repeatedly stomped on. My muscles go limp, and dizziness spins around my skull.

Why do I care if he loves me or not? Why am I reacting this way?

"Mateo!" Camilla beckons for him from another room, causing me to jolt away from the door so he doesn't see me eavesdropping.

My heart races as I scurry into the living room. "I think he's on his way," I say to Camila as I mindlessly search for my charger.

Mateo appears seconds later, smiling when his attention lands on me. I force my lips to tip up, although sadness pricks my eyes. Quickly, I blink away any evidence of tears, even though it feels as if I'm being ripped to shreds.

What's wrong with me? Why am I so upset over this?

Once Mateo addresses Camilla, he comes over to me. "You good, baby?" he asks in a hushed tone.

"Yeah." I clear my throat. "Just looking for my charger."

"No, I meant…your eyes looked a little glassy."

"Oh, yeah. I just had a little tickle in my throat, and my eyes started to water."

"Do you need a drink?"

"Nope, I'm fine."

"Okay." He reaches past me, bending down to unplug something from the outlet. "Here's your charger."

"Oh. Thanks."

My lips press into a smile, all the while my insides painfully ache.

I pretend to busy myself, and Mateo goes back to talking with his mom. As I admire him, my emotions burn a hole through the center of my chest, and I can't help but wonder why it hurts so much to hear that he's not in love with me. I feel something with him that I've never felt in my entire life, not even when things were good with Hunter. I thought Mateo felt the same thing, but I guess I was wrong.

My heart stirs with longing, and that's when it hits me.

Oh my god.

Am I *in love with* him?

Mateo glances over at me. "Are you ready to head out soon?"

All I can do is nod because if I open my mouth, I might burst into tears. I try to act normal as I retrieve my duffel, but Mateo's voice declaring he doesn't love me and never will is echoing nonstop in my brain.

Of course, I'd find myself in this situation. Of course, I'd fall for a guy who never wants to be in love.

Even if Mateo and I start a real relationship, we'd probably crash and burn, and I'll be left even more brokenhearted.

On cue, my phone goes off in my pocket, and the moment I take it out, I see Hunter's name on the screen.

HUNTER

I miss you, angel

It's like he has a radar on me, knowing when I feel like trash, so he can swoop in and say something nice so he can suck me back into his orbit.

Ignoring the message, I quickly click the lock button so my screen goes black.

I make my rounds, saying thank you and goodbye to Mateo's family. Camilla is the last one I go to before leaving. Her hands embrace my face, and I look into her eyes. There is so much going on behind them. They hold years of stories, pain, memories, and joy.

"I'm so happy you came here, Ellie. You make my son very happy." She gives me a tight hug, and then we make our way to the car and head up to Connecticut.

"You've been pretty quiet," Mateo states as we slowly inch our way through traffic.

"Sorry. I'm just zoning out, thinking about stupid stuff." I wave it off as if I'm not overanalyzing my feelings for him.

"Thinking about why the hell you agreed to spend Christmas with my family?" he jokes.

"No, not at all! They're incredible."

"They're all right."

"And your home is really lovely," I state.

"Thanks." He's quiet for a few seconds, but then glances over at me. "You didn't think I grew up in that type of setting, did you?"

"I-I just figured after everything you told me…I expected…I don't know."

"Don't get me wrong, *I'm* broke as fuck. Working at a coffee shop isn't that lucrative." He half laughs. "But my family isn't. My mom worked her ass off so we could live comfortably."

"I'm sorry I assumed that you…you…" *Wow, I'm such an asshole.*

"Grew up on the streets?" He fills in the gaps. "I hung out on the streets and caused hell for my mom because I turned out to be everything she wanted me to avoid becoming. I spent years being a shitty person because I was pissed at my dad, but in the long run, all the trouble I caused hurt me. Not him."

"You're not a shitty person, Mateo. You had a tough time when you were younger, but you're more than that."

He interlaces his fingers between mine, bringing my hand up to his lips so he can kiss the back of it. "My family loved meeting you," he states, no longer wanting to linger in the past.

"Did your mom or any of your sisters ask you who I was…like if I was your just your friend or something?" I ask, letting my curiosity get a hold of me.

"They did."

"What did you tell them?"

"That you're someone important to me, and I'm doing things differently with you than I have with any other woman."

"What do you mean?"

Mateo chortles, bewilderment flickering across his face. "Elle, have I been unclear about what I'm hoping for with you? Because I thought I made it very obvious that I want to be in a relationship."

I grin at his statement. But hesitancy guards my heart, questioning if it's worth getting into a relationship with him, knowing full well that he's never going to love me. He's just going to be with me, *and that's it.*

"Well?" he presses.

"I don't know," I say, hiding my smile as I gaze out the window.

"Okay then, for the millionth time, I'm going to be here until you either tell me to fuck off or tell me you're ready to be my girlfriend."

I start laughing because he's right. He has made it extremely clear. He joins in my laughter, beaming. The red glow from the row of brake lights in front of us makes his smile look extra bright.

He keeps my hand in his the whole ride as we talk and flirt the entire time. Logic and emotions duel it out in the background of my mind, but I try not to pay attention to the doubts and insecurities screaming at me.

When we finally pull into UConn, quietness falls over us. The university resembles a ghost town. The security guard almost didn't let us in, but thankfully, after showing our IDs and explaining to him that I have nowhere to go, he let us.

Parking in front of my dorm, both of us hesitate to get out. Not a soul is around. The lampposts only slightly light up the empty walkway, while the rest of the campus looks like it's cloaked in dark shadows.

Mateo speaks. "It looks kind of…"

"Creepy?"

"Yeah."

"Can I…" I bite my tongue.

"Can you what?"

Taking a few seconds, I muster up enough courage to ask, "Can I…stay with you for the rest of break? Or would that be weird?"

Happiness dances across Mateo's face. "Of course you can."

I smile at him, relieved. "Thank you."

"You want to grab anything while we're here?"

"I might as well. All the clothes in my duffel bag are dirty."

Mateo shuts his car off, and the two of us make our way to my room. The cold wind whistles through the bare trees, and when we reach the building, the hallways are pitch black. Mateo flips a switch to turn on the overhead lights so we can see as we walk to my room.

Taking off my puffy winter jacket, I toss it on my desk chair, and Mateo does the same with his. I go toward my closet while he goes to my dresser and shifts through my clothes to help me pack for the rest of our time together. My eyebrow arches as I watch him pull out my yoga pants.

"I'm just helping you pack," he says.

"And you just so happened to pick out those?"

"Yeah, I did." Mateo struts over with a familiar flicker of hunger in his eyes. I don't even give him time to do his normal seductive start before I kiss him.

Mateo's tongue dances around mine, and his hands tightly grip on to my hips. The more we meld together, the more my soul becomes freed.

His lips feel so right. Everything about him feels right—his words, his touch, his heart.

Everything.

My veins light up with something I've never truly felt before, and as the puzzle pieces connect, my heart nearly jumps out of my chest as it dawns on me.

There's no denying what I now realize.

I am falling in love with him.

I don't care if he doesn't feel the same. I don't care if this is only for a fleeting moment in time. I want to give in to this feeling and allow myself to be happy, even if the ending won't be the same.

Mateo pulls the bottom of my shirt up over my head. My hands move to his pants, hurrying to take them off. "Sit down," I demand. Mateo listens with a smile plastered on his face. I drop to my knees and tug at his boxers.

"Wait," he stops me.

"What?"

"I don't want you to do this if you don't want to," he says, reminiscent of what happened last time I tried.

"If I didn't want to, I wouldn't be down here," I say, trying to yank off his boxers, but he won't let me. So instead, I begin palming him over his boxers.

He inhales sharply. "Baby."

"Yes?"

"I don't know if this is a good idea." He doesn't sound like he actually believes what he's saying.

"Please?" I whine and look up at him with pleading eyes.

Mateo groans. "Don't do that."

"Do what?" I ask with faux innocence.

"Don't get on your knees and beg to blow me. I'm not gonna be able to resist you."

"Then don't."

Mateo bites down on his lip, looking at my position in front of him, his breathing already becoming more labored. He takes a moment to observe me and then gives in to my simple seduction. "Are you sure?"

"Yes. Just don't touch my head."

As soon as he allows me to pull off his boxers, I immediately take as much of him as I can in my mouth and start sucking. Mateo lets out a sigh as I move up and down. I can hear his heavy breaths with each movement I make. My tongue swirls around his length, and he holds on to my arms. "Elle," he softly calls out my name as his nails dig into me.

I keep making the same motions, and he moans behind his tightly closed lips. My hair falls into my face, and I try to tuck it behind my ears. "Can I hold up your hair?" he asks, panting. I nod the best way I can without stopping. Mateo very tenderly takes my hair in one of his large hands. "Fuck, baby. I can watch you like this all day."

If I were able to fully grin, I would, but instead, I focus on pleasuring him. I want him to feel the ecstasy that I feel when he goes down on me.

I want him to relish in my every movement.

I want him to light up with lust and know I'm the reason why.

Mateo's legs tense. "I'm gonna come, baby," he says, panting. I suck even harder. "Lift your head up. I'm gonna come." I shake my head and keep going. He lets out a moan as he releases into my mouth.

Warm spurts of cum fill me up. I swallow everything he gives me, sucking him until there's nothing left.

Slowly pulling away, I wipe the corner of my mouth with my thumb. Mateo stares at me, dumbfounded, and I giggle as I start to stand. "You're distracting me from packing," I say, throwing my shirt back on.

Mateo catches his breath, his eyes following me as I move away from him. My focus shifts back to my original reason for coming into my room. I put the clothes that he picked out into my bag and find a few other things to bring with me.

Glancing over at Mateo, he's still in the same position that I left him in, his gaze still glued to me. "What's with you?" I chuckle as I ask the question.

"That was amazing."

I roll my eyes. "Oh my god, stop."

"No, seriously. I was not expecting that."

"Oh?" I put my hands on my hips. "And what kind of blow job were you expecting?"

Mateo laughs. "I don't fucking know, but not that. That was incredible."

"Good. Now get your clothes back on. I'm almost finished getting my things together."

"I like you a little bossy," Mateo says as he pulls up his boxers and pants.

Sparks fly through me, and I continue to pack, wondering what the rest of winter break will be like.

It's a month-long staycation at his apartment. The possibilities are endless.

CHAPTER THIRTY-SIX

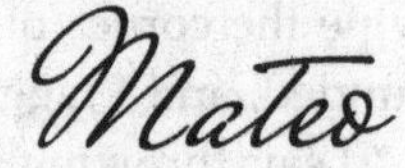

ANGELA

Ellie is so sweet!

ISABEL

you gonna tell us wtf is going on with the two of you?

STEPH

nope. He didn't tell me shit. Butttt he did buy Ellie a Christmas present sooo that has to mean something

VALENTINA

did our brother switch places with someone else? Because I never thought I'd see the day he brought a girl home lol

I immediately regret unmuting the group chat with my sisters.

ME

fuck all of you

good night

Muting the chat once more, I toss my phone next to me on the couch. Having Elle stay here has felt natural, like our lives fall perfectly in sync. We don't overcrowd one another, while at the same time enjoying each other's company.

My focus goes back onto Elle, who's trying on one of Michelle's dresses for tonight's New Year's Eve party. Michelle's the biggest party animal of us all, and she invited Elle and me to her friend's apartment for the night.

"How's this?" Elle asks.

Warmth floods down my body as I admire her. The black dress is tight, tighter than anything she usually wears, and the neckline dips low. The crystal necklace I got her for Christmas sits right above her breasts, drawing my attention to them.

"It's too slutty," Elle says, spinning around to change.

"What? No." I leap up, stopping her.

"I'm gonna try on something else."

"Why?"

"Because it's too much. You didn't say anything, so you obviously don't like it."

"I didn't say anything because I was too distracted by how hot you look."

Her lips twitch. "Really?"

"Fuck, yes." My eyes linger on her body again. Dirty scenes of me fucking her in this dress every way imaginable filter into my mind.

"But is it okay if I wear it out?"

My brows knit together. "Are you asking my permission?"

"I…" She timidly tucks her hair behind her ears. "Yeah, I guess."

"Don't." Something about that makes me feel grimy, and I try to shake it off. "Wear whatever you want, baby." Leaning over, I give her a peck on the lips.

Elle glances up at me, hesitancy forming behind her eyes. "You sure?"

"Positive."

"Okay." She smiles.

As she walks off, continuing to get ready, I catch her mindlessly grazing her thumb over her scarred wrist. I don't think she even realizes.

I know it's not the time or place to ask about her scars, but I can't help but wonder if there's a correlation to what made her touch them. I know Hunter is a dick, but did she actually have to ask his permission to wear certain clothes? Was she cutting herself because of him?

Anger swarms my veins, my face getting hot.

I don't know the details of their relationship, but I know it wasn't a good one, and that Hunter wounded Elle to the point of her being anxious about wearing a fucking dress.

My molars grind together as my heart thumps with rage. Had this been a few years ago, back when I was the old me, I would've kicked the shit out of him already. But I can't let my emotions impulsively guide me into trouble, especially since my career goal is getting closer and closer. If I were to fight Hunter, I could easily get an assault charge, and that could impact my chances of becoming a social worker.

Besides, I already have enough going against me from my juvenile charges.

"I'm ready." Elle's voice rips me from my thoughts.

The moment my attention lands on her, my body and mind are at ease. The tension melts away as she beams up at me with thick, mascara-coated lashes and loose curls coiling her golden hair.

I've always had the intention of treating her right, because that's a given and what she deserves. But in this moment, I realize just how important it is for her to have someone lifting her up. Hunter decimated her self-confidence, hoping to leave her a shattered mess. But I'm now making it my mission to stand by her side as she rebuilds herself, little by little.

CHAPTER THIRTY-SEVEN

Ellie

We enter Michelle's friend's apartment for the New Year's Eve party. I assumed it wouldn't be as crowded, considering we're on winter break, but I was wrong. It's packed. A smoky haze floats over the swarm of people as the loud music thuds in my chest.

"You're here!" Michelle runs up to Mateo and me. I've never seen her this enthusiastic. She goes to hug me, and the scent of alcohol lingers on her breath. She must be a friendly drunk.

"Hey, Michelle," I say, hugging her back.

"Let me take your coat," she yells over the pop music. I take off my big, puffy coat, which wasn't large enough to keep me warm in this skimpy dress. "Damn, Ellie! You look hot!" Michelle yells, and a few people turn to look.

"Yeah, she does," Mateo agrees, looping his hands around my waist.

"Thanks." I glance down at what I'm wearing. "And thank you for letting me raid your closet."

"Of course! I'm going to put your coat in my friend's room and then grab you a drink. Meet me downstairs," Michelle instructs before running off.

Mateo and I walk farther into the house and make our way through the sloppily drunk partygoers. We end up in the basement, where there are a few couches pushed against the wall, with people dancing in the center of the room. The lights are dimmed and groups of people are carelessly flirting with their bodies to the music.

"Here you go." Michelle hands me a red cup before I can even tell her if I want it or not. "You want some?" she asks Mateo.

Mateo shakes his head. "Driving."

"Suit yourself," Michelle says with a shrug and scampers off to dance.

Mateo takes my hand, leading me to an open spot on the couch. He sits close to me and glides the pad of his fingers up and down my crossed leg. "Are you gonna drink?" he asks.

I hesitate for a moment. "I think so."

"Go for it," he says, adding, "But I'm cutting you off if you get anywhere close to vomiting."

I chuckle. "Deal," I say before downing what Michelle gave me, cringing at how strong it tastes.

I think I'm three drinks in—or maybe it's two? Either way, I'm feeling carefree and bubbly. There have been several people who have come to sit next to Mateo and me on the couch, and I've befriended all of them. A familiar guy sits down next to us, and I stare at his face, trying to recall where I've seen him before.

"Hey, Ellie," he says to me. "Hey, man," he says to Mateo.

"Hi," Mateo replies with a curt nod.

Why is Mateo being short? Why does this person know my name?

It finally clicks. He's Hunter's frat brother. "Oh my god! Derek!" I shriek as if he's my best friend who I haven't seen in decades.

Both Mateo and Derek chuckle at my delayed reaction. "Sorry, I had a lot of these." I hold up my cup and laugh. Derek starts to say something, but Michelle interrupts.

"I'm stealing your girl," Michelle tells Mateo and takes my hand, pulling me up off the couch.

"Oh, I don't dance."

"Yes, you do!" she pushes me into the middle of the floor, surrounded by sweaty, intoxicated bodies.

I look over at Mateo, and he leans back on the couch with a wide grin. Normally, I would feel self-conscious, but the alcohol running through my veins frees me from my anxious thoughts. My body lets loose and moves rhythmically to the music. Tossing my hair around, I roll my hips while people glide up next to me, and we move around one another. I watch Mateo size me up, taking his bottom lip between his teeth. When his eyes meet mine, I give him a little wink, like he always does to me, and he can't help but laugh. He adjusts his position and is now sitting forward, leaning over his thighs. The alcohol violently stirs up my hormones. My tongue grazes my bottom lip, ready to devour Mateo.

He looks so hot. I want him. Right now.

Stumbling over, I almost fall right on top of him. His hands clasp on to my hips.

"How you feeling, baby?" he asks with a tickle of amusement.

"So good. I'm gonna get another drink," I slur.

"Last one. You're already wasted."

I giggle at what he says. It's not particularly funny, but for some reason, I can't stop giggling. When I'm done with my laughing fit, I fixate on his big lips and start roughly kissing him. His tongue engages mine, and the heat between my thighs increases.

I step away. "One more drink and then you're mine," I say before I run off to find more of my confidence serum. I'm going to need all that I can get if I'm going to sleep with Mateo. I don't want my mind interrupting my first time, telling me that I'm not as good as all the other girls he's had sex with.

I find the liquor and fill my cup.

Things are becoming fuzzy.

It's like I'm half here and half not.

Everything's becoming choppy.

"Five, four, three, two, one! Happy New Year!" everyone cheers.

Mateo places his hands on my face and gracefully kisses me. "Happy New Year, baby." Everyone is cheering and shouting, but my only focus is on him.

I lick Mateo's neck as he drives.

"We need to get you to bed," Mateo says, chuckling.

"We need to get *us* to bed," I correct him. "I'm serious." I string my words together. "I want to have sex with you."

He lets out a loud sigh. "Sit back in your seat."

"Mateo, let's have sex."

"Not tonight, baby."

"Why not?"

"Because you're drunk. I'm not doing that."

"Please?" I whine. "I want you to. I just want you to fuck me. You don't want to fuck me?"

Judging by the expression on Mateo's face, it looks like I'm torturing him. "I want to so badly, baby. But I don't want your—*our*—first time together to be like this, and I especially don't want it to be just fucking."

My head spins.

I'm so dizzy.

"Eat me out then," I demand.

His jaw drops. "You are so horny when you're drunk!"

"The least you can do is eat me out."

"Not tonight, baby."

"Please?" I play with his hair. "You do this thing with your tongue that feels so fucking good. I've never felt that before." He fights back a smile at the compliment, and I zone in on his ego. "You like that, don't you? You like it when I tell you that you're better." Mateo can no longer hold back his grin, and he can't deny the bulge forming in his jeans. I rub my hand over his pants, and he jolts in surprise.

My fingers reach for his zipper.

"Holy shit, Elle!"

"Drink some water," Mateo tells me as I lie in his bed. I tilt my head up ever so slightly to take a sip from the water bottle and then place my head back on his pillow. I'm freezing. I curl up next to Mateo's large body and nuzzle into his chest. His broad arms cover me, and he pulls me closer to him.

"Tell me something," I say to him with my eyes closed.

"What kind of something?" Mateo asks.

"Anything."

There is silence, and I start to drift off to sleep.

Mateo whispers something to me, but I can't make out what he says. I'm too tired.

CHAPTER THIRTY-EIGHT

Ellie

JANUARY

My vibrating phone startles my bones awake. Groaning at the sound, I do my best to ignore it and clamp the pillow over my ears. This hangover from last night's New Year's Eve party has my skull pounding.

A few seconds go by, and it vibrates again. I still have my eyes closed, concerned that if I open them, the room will start spinning. My phone stops, and I try to fall back asleep.

Not even a minute later, my phone vibrates again.

If this isn't some type of emergency, I'm going to be pissed.

"Hello?" I answer without checking to see who it is, drowsiness scratching my vocal cords.

"Where the hell are you?" Hunter's booming voice immediately springs me to a sitting position, fully alert.

"Hunter?"

"Where are you?"

I look next to me, but Mateo isn't in the bed. I don't see him anywhere in the room. *Where did he go?* The blankets slip down off my chest, cool air hitting my skin. Glancing down, I realize I'm not wearing anything. *Why am I naked*? I suck in a breath. I really hope I didn't sleep with him for my first time while I was wasted.

"Hello? Ellie?" Hunter's irritation grows.

"I'm fine," I say, avoiding his question.

"What's going on? Are you safe?"

"Yes, of course I'm safe. Why?"

"Do you know how fucking scared I've been?"

"Scared about what?"

"Oh, I don't know, maybe because last night you were completely shit-faced at a party and left with some ex-con."

How does he know that I was at a party? And drinking? And with Mateo? I don't answer because I'm too busy trying to connect the dots from what happened last night. *Did I drunk dial Hunter?*

"This isn't like you, Elena," Hunter says. "I'm really fucking worried about you."

I hold my head up with my hand to ease the throbbing pain pulsating through it. "What? Why?"

"You're putting yourself in these risky situations with that guy."

"Mateo is—"

"Ellie, I know you always try to see the best in people, and I love that about you. But he's not a good guy. There's a lot of talk about him."

"You don't know what you're talking about."

"No, *you* don't. You're acting like an idiot!" he yells.

"Don't call me up and start insulting me!"

"You were completely plastered and decided to go home with a fucking criminal. He could've fucking assaulted you, Ellie!" Hunter shouts. My blood turns cold, instantly aware of the fact that I have no clothes on.

But I know Mateo wouldn't do that. Hunter would have a point if it were any other man aside from Mateo.

"I know that you want to trust him and think he's this great person," Hunter continues. "But you've only known him for a few months. You've known me for years, and I need you to believe me when I say that he's not good for you. He's dangerous."

I don't respond. I recognize that I haven't known Mateo as long as I have Hunter, but I feel like I've known Mateo my entire life. My head spins. Hunter's words are skewing my perception.

"Where are you?" Hunter asks me again.

I keep quiet. I don't want him to picture me in Mateo's bed.

"I'm coming there," he states.

"No! Please don't!"

"Elena, you're too fucked up to realize what this guy is doing to you. He's manipulating you. He probably took advantage of you last night, and you have no memory of it. I have to come there and get you."

"Hunter, do not come here," I say through gritted teeth. "If you come here, I will never speak to you again. Do you understand?"

There is a long pause, and Hunter finally lets out a defeated sigh. "If I don't come there, will you promise to text me every day to let me know you're okay?"

I consider the consequences if I don't agree to his seemingly easy offer.

If this is the only way to keep him from coming to Mateo's, then I'll accept. "Fine."

"I'm serious, Elena. If I don't get a text by the end of every night, I'm driving there and taking you back home with me. Do you promise me?"

"Yes."

"And if you don't feel safe, call me immediately."

"Okay."

"Okay…I love you, angel." Hunter waits for me to say something back, but I don't. "Text me tonight. Bye." He hangs up.

Trying my best to cover myself with the comforter, I attempt to recall last night's events. I really don't think anything happened. *But then why am I naked?* I probably shouldn't have gotten so drunk. Hunter was right about that. He called Mateo a criminal and said that people talk about him. *Could I have been wrong about Mateo this entire time?*

"You're up early." Mateo enters the room with a towel wrapped around his waist.

With these new seeds planted in my head, I begin to look at him differently. I fixate on the giant scar on his upper arm. *Was the story he told me about how he got it true?*

"Where did you get that scar?" I ask him.

Mateo tilts his head, puzzled. "I told you, a knife."

"Yeah, but was there more to the story? Did you leave something out?"

"No. Why?"

"Just wondering."

He nods his head with furrowed brows and moves over to his dresser. Mateo drops his towel on the floor, and I glance away to give him some privacy. My hands tighten around the fabric of the blanket, bringing it closer to my body as he slips into his sweatpants and T-shirt.

"Did we sleep together last night?" My knuckles turn white as I brace myself for the answer, clutching the comforter.

"Yep." A weight drops in my stomach. There's no way Hunter was right about this. "You slept right there, and I slept right next to you." Mateo points to his bed.

"No, I mean, did we have sex?" My heart beats so fast at the possibility that he took advantage of me.

"Of course not."

"Then why am I naked?"

"Because you refused to put on clothes last night, even though I tried a thousand times. You kept on complaining that you were freezing, but every time I put something on you, you'd take it off."

That sounds vaguely familiar.

"What's going on?" he asks.

I drop my head into my hands, wanting the pounding to stop. "Hunter."

"Hunter?"

"Yeah, he called when you were in the shower and said all this stuff."

"What kind of stuff?" Mateo's voice is controlled, but I can hear the tension rising in his words. I shake my head, not wanting to tell him the slew of offensive things that Hunter said about him. "Elle, what did he say? It's clearly something that bothered you."

"It was just a bunch of insults."

"Such as?" As he sits next to me, I lift my head up to look at him.

"He was going on about how you're some kind of ex-con and that you probably sexually assaulted me while I was drunk last night."

"He *what*?" His voice still isn't raised, but there is fury pulsing behind it.

"I'm sorry. He can be awful."

"I don't give a shit about what he says about me. I care that he said that to you. He's just trying to mess with your head. You have to know that I would never, ever do that." Mateo adjusts so that he's kneeling on the bed directly in front of me. He clasps his hand over mine and brings them near his heart. "Elena, I have done a lot of fucked-up shit, but I would never do that to any woman, especially to you."

"I know." There's no second-guessing Mateo's words. I trusted him the night of Halloween, and I trust him now. Hunter just fucks with my brain sometimes.

Every muscle in Mateo's body eases at my response. He grabs the first shirt within reach, tossing it to me, and I pull it over my head, covering up.

"What about the ex-con stuff?"

"I went to JDC when I was younger for stealing, so if that makes me an ex-con…" Mateo shrugs.

"What's JDC?"

"Juvenile detention center."

"Oh." Whoa. I never realized he was arrested before. "You were in prison?"

"Yeah."

Observing the twinge of nervousness that sparks at his fingers as he fidgets with his shirt collar, I debate asking my follow-up question. But my brain won't allow me to carry on with the day without knowing, so I do it anyway. "What happened?"

"The people I used to hang out with mugged some guy and got his credit card. Then they gave it to me to buy us stuff. I got busted the third day using it. The cops came, I was cuffed, and went to JDC," he states as if he's rattling off mundane facts.

"Did the other people get arrested too?"

"I'm not a snitch."

"So you took the fall for mugging the person?"

"Yep."

"Why?" Confusion pulls at my features. It's bizarre that he, of all people, would take responsibility for other people's actions.

"Trust me, extra time in JDC is nothing compared to what would've happened if I ratted them out."

"That's so messed up!"

"It is. But I'm happy that it happened."

My head spins, his statement throwing me off. "Why?"

"It's what got me into placement. After I got arrested, I spent a week in JDC waiting for my trial, and then the judge chose to send me to the residential program instead of making me finish my time in prison."

"I thought you went to your placement because you didn't go to school."

"That was part of it, but the arrest was the icing on the cake."

"How come you left that part out when you first told me?"

Mateo's gaze shifts around the room. "It's not something I'm exactly proud of." He looks back at me. "And I didn't think I'd be able to get you to be mine if you knew."

"I'm still not yours." I playfully remind him of our convoluted relationship.

"Technicality." He winks.

"So…that's it?"

"I've done a lot of other shit. I only went to JDC that one time and was arrested once more after that, but the charges were dropped."

"What were you arrested for?"

"Assault. I got into a bad fight."

My attention shifts to the scar on his arm. "The guy with the knife?"

"No."

"Oh." I hesitate, unsure if I should press him further. I don't know if I want to open that can of worms, and to be honest, he doesn't seem like that past version of himself. I believe him. I have no reason not to, aside from Hunter's paranoid phone call.

"I wonder how Hunter found out about me last night," I say aloud, but really to myself.

"Probably from his asshole frat brother."

My eyes widen. "I forgot Derek was there." A few memories from last night are coming back to me—Derek, dancing, Michelle and me acting like best friends, bits and pieces of the car ride. *Oh my god, the car ride!* I instantly gasp.

"What?"

"I'm starting to remember the drive home," I say in utter humiliation.

Mateo laughs. "Yeah, you were a little frisky."

"I am so, so sorry!"

"Don't be. I fucking loved it."

Another glimpse of the car ride pops up in my mind. "Did I give you a hand job while you were driving?"

He shakes his head. "I wouldn't let you do anything."

"Apparently, I can't drink around you because I turn into some sex-crazed maniac."

"No, that's the reason why you should drink around *only* me," he corrects, and I let out a little giggle. "There's that laugh I love," Mateo says.

A tendril of sadness weaves its way around my heart.

Don't say things like that, Mateo. Don't say you love something about me when we both know full well you won't actually ever love me.

Mateo kisses my forehead. "You want pancakes?"

"Pancakes sound amazing right now."

"Good, go make them," he teases. I playfully glare at him, and he chuckles. "Go shower, and I'll meet you downstairs with your breakfast."

Smiling, I watch Mateo drift out of his room, and my heart fills with appreciation for him. Mateo is so easy to talk to.

He's open and honest.

Nothing like what I'm used to.

Dropping my gaze, my thumb skims over the faded marks on my wrist as my mind floats elsewhere.

"Where have you been? You said to meet you at your house at seven," I confront Hunter. I've been sitting alone in his bedroom for over an hour. He wouldn't answer any of my calls or texts.

"I had to take care of something."

What a bullshit answer.

"Something like what?" My mind goes to all the endless possibilities that

could've caused him to be late and why he's not telling the truth. I glance down at his swollen, red hand. "Did you get into another fight?"

Hunter busies himself and moves things around in his room. "It wasn't a big deal, Ellie."

I spring to my feet. "Who did you fight?"

"Don't worry about it."

"Hunter, tell me who you fought right now!"

"It's not a big deal. Just let it go."

"It is a big deal! You can't keep going around fighting, Hunter!"

"No, it's not! Fucking drop it!"

"I'm not going to drop it. You need to stop being so violent and hurting innocent people!" I feed off his fury, drawing closer, my hands flying as I reprimand him.

"He wasn't fucking innocent!"

"Who was it?"

"You don't know him!"

"Tell me who you fought right now, or else I'll—"

"You'll what, Elena?" He towers over me.

"I'll…I'll…" I can't think of anything quickly enough, and he starts smirking. The condescending, smug look on Hunter's face is infuriating. I try to shove him.

Hunter moves faster than me, grabbing hold of each of my wrists. A wave of exhilaration flickers behind his eyes. He stalks forward, backing me into a wall.

He has me pinned.

In some fucked-up way, this turns both of us on. My brain immediately switches from my passion of anger to a passion of lust. He kisses me. Hard. Not letting my arms free. I'm constantly confused by how we always get here, but I kiss him back. The way he controls me is scary, but thrilling.

He moves his mouth to my neck, roughly sucking. My skin stings from the contact. He brings his lips to my ear. "When I let go of your wrists, you're not going to fight me. Got it?"

I nod in agreement, obliging to his command. Hunter frees my arms, and we start ripping each other's clothes off.

A chill runs down my spine, bringing me back into the present as I shudder at the memory.

Self-loathing weaves its way around my bones. A sour taste coats my tongue as I grow angry with myself for allowing my brain to think of Hunter.

If Mateo only knew how fucked-up things were between us—how fucked-up I am—he'd see me as a walking red flag and cut me loose.

And I wouldn't blame him for a second.

Later that night, as I go into the bathroom to brush my teeth before bed, my phone vibrates.

HUNTER

Ellie...

ME

I'm fine.

I press the send button, then drop my phone onto the vanity. Thankfully, he doesn't reply back. I wish I could ignore him, but if I do, he would most likely show up here ready to fight Mateo. I can suck up texting Hunter at night in order to save him and Mateo from each other.

As I gently pad back into Mateo's room, I find my spot next to him in his bed. Snuggling into his hold, my body relaxes. The aggravation from Hunter's text seeps away as I press my ear up against Mateo's chest, hearing the soft thud of his heartbeat.

As annoying as it might be to check in with Hunter every day, I'd rather do that than be the cause of any potential trouble for Mateo.

The way I see it, I'm protecting Mateo.

CHAPTER THIRTY-NINE

Ellie

Winter break is flying by. I've been spending my time bouncing between Mateo's place and the Cozy Nook. His managerial duties call for him to work more hours than I do, but I've been able to keep myself occupied during my alone time. However, today I find myself particularly restless. Mateo won't be home from work for another half hour, and I'm not sure what I should do with my time. Pacing around his bedroom, I let my fingers pluck a few strings on one of his guitars. Maybe I can kill my boredom by playing one of his instruments.

Glancing around at my options—guitar, drums, or keyboard—excitement simmers in my chest as I make my way to the stool behind his drum set.

The drumsticks tingle in my hands as I pick them up. Lightly tapping my foot on the pedal in front of the kick drum, I playfully pat on the cymbals, making a horrible concoction of sounds.

The door opens, and I jump. My attention swings to Mateo, who's grinning at me ear to ear.

"I'm sorry. I should've asked before I touched your stuff."

"I don't care. Keep going," he encourages, getting closer to me.

"Didn't you just hear me? I suck." I laugh at the obvious.

"Want me to teach you?"

My veins buzz with exhilaration as I nod my head. Mateo seems just as eager and pulls up another stool directly behind me. He opens his legs so that they are on the outside of both of my thighs and positions himself forward so that his chest is kissing my back. His long, tattooed arms cover mine, and he holds my hands in his.

My heart pounds, his warm body enveloping mine. An earthy scent from his cologne tickles my nose, and I almost get lost in his hold, but his deep voice snaps me back.

"This is the snare." Mateo controls my hand to hit the drum. "Loosen up." He shakes my wrist a little and tries again. "There you go." He guides my other arm to a cymbal. "This is the hi-hat." A loud crashing sound fills the room, and he has us repeat it a few times. "Good. Now we're gonna put the two together," he instructs, continuing to move my hands to beat on the snare and hi-hat. We do the same rhythm over and over again, then he lets go of my hands and has me do it alone. I'm able to keep it up for a few seconds, but eventually mess up.

"I told you I'm not good." I chuckle.

"It's all about practice and muscle memory. You're doing great for your first time."

Mateo takes my hands to continue playing. Without letting go, he pushes his hips against me and extends his leg toward the pedal on the floor. After a few seconds, he adds in the kick drum to our melody, and it sounds like an actual song. My heart erratically flutters as he teaches me while simultaneously holding me.

Mateo slowly releases my hands again, while keeping the beat with his foot. The two of us play together, and it actually sounds decent. After a few moments, his hand rubs my right hip, and I immediately lose the beat.

"You can't do that!"

"Do what?"

"Touch my hips. I can't focus."

"Oh, you mean like this?" Mateo clutches my hips with both hands, digging his fingers into my skin, causing me to laugh.

"Yes, like that! I'm trying to play!"

"Sorry, I didn't mean to mess you up. Keep going."

I try to restart what he taught me, but as soon as I do, he moves my hair to one side and runs his tongue down my neck. "Mateo," I complain, but also move my head to the side so he has more access.

"Keep going." He kisses my shoulder. "I'll be here enjoying the view."

Shifting my gaze, I spot his eyes looking down my shirt. "Hey!" I playfully give him a little nudge.

"Okay, okay, let's get back to your lesson." He repositions himself back to teaching me and continues to introduce me to new drums and rhythms.

He then has me experiment with the guitar and keyboard, both of which I'm terrible at playing. "I don't think any of these are my instrument," I state.

"It's okay. We'll find the right one for you."

"I'm pretty sure no matter what I try, I'll be bad at it."

"Well, if you have that kind of mindset, you will."

A soft smile tugs my lips upward. The way Mateo challenges me is different from Hunter. It's not in a confrontational way, but in a way that is urging me to be a better version of myself. It's a different type of experience. I like it. He makes me feel like I have something special to offer the world, even though I don't know what that is. I've never felt this way about myself. I like who I am around him.

Tonight is the last night I'll be staying at Mateo's. Bree gets back tomorrow morning, and I promised her I'd be back in the evening so we can catch up before school starts.

"What's on your mind?" Mateo asks me while we cuddle under his covers.

"Thinking about the new semester." It was amazing to stay in our little bubble for the past month, but I'm excited for what awaits me the second half of my freshman year.

"I got used to sleeping next to you. It's going to be weird without you here."

"I got used to it too." I smile, but the sound of my phone buzzing makes my stomach drop.

I know exactly who it is. I've been slyly texting Hunter on a nightly basis. "One sec," I tell Mateo as I reach for my phone and position myself so that he can't see it.

ME

I'm fine. I'm not doing this anymore, break is over tomorrow.

I flip over to face Mateo, and I hear my phone vibrate multiple times.

"You need to get that?" Mateo asks.

"Nope. The only person I want to talk to is right here."

Mateo sneaks his hand under my shirt and drags his fingertips up and down my spine. I lean in and kiss his soft lips, running my hands over his tattoos, savoring every inch of him. I'm going to miss spending my nights like this.

CHAPTER FORTY

Ellie

The cold air freezes me down to the bone, so I scurry as fast as possible to get to my classes in order to avoid turning into an icicle. When I make it to Critical Thinking, my first philosophy class of the semester, there's a twinge of sadness in my chest when I notice that someone claimed my old seat, as well as Mateo's. Rolling my shoulders back, I choose to change things up and sit directly in the middle of the room. People sit on either side of me, but there is no electric charge like there was with Mateo.

"Challenge your thoughts. Challenge the thoughts of those around you. Challenge the system. That's what we will be doing this semester," Professor Boland dramatically commands the room. He passes around the attendance sheet as well as the syllabus. Contrary to last semester, there's no partnering up with another student for the final.

"There's a lot more reading in this class than my intro class," Professor Boland informs us, and the majority of the class groans. I don't mind the reading, though. I actually find it interesting. As he continues speaking, my mind can't help but jump back to Professor Boland's email he sent me at the end of last semester. Truthfully, I've avoided thinking about the potential of studying abroad over the summer because I know the back and forth of pros and cons would cause an overwhelming anxiety and exhaust me, and I wanted to spend my winter break enjoying my time with Mateo rather than spiraling.

After Professor Boland wraps up the class, I walk past him, and he gives me a small grin. It's the tiniest action in the world, but I know what's behind it as the thoughts of running away to France for the summer take center stage in my brain. Still unsure if I'm even going to bother applying for the scholarship, I return the gesture and avoid a conversation with him by fleeing the classroom.

My brows jump up in a pleasant surprise when I see Mateo in the hallway, holding two coffee cups. "What are you doing here?"

Mateo hands me my drink. "I thought I'd surprise my girl and walk her back to her room so she can tell me all about her day."

Hearing him call me his girl makes me feel like I'm floating. But I'm quickly grounded as we approach the main doors to leave the building, and a girl with jet-black hair passes us.

"Hey, Mateo," she says in a sultry voice, with a knowing glint in her eyes.

I trip over my feet but quickly regain my composure. I hate that she's looking at him like she knows exactly what lies beneath his layers of clothes and wants more of it. Jealousy constricts my veins, and my shoulders tense.

"Uh…hey." He nods his chin toward her, then takes my hand and escorts us outside. The small contact calms me down.

"Who was that?" I inquire as the chilly air whips around us.

"Someone who I haven't spoken to since last year." He loops his arm around my waist, his embrace warming me up. "How were your classes?" He swiftly changes the subject, and I attempt to push away my envious thoughts.

We walk back to my dorm, filling each other in on our day. I ignore the giant neon sign in my head telling me to talk to Mateo about France. But I don't want to add another stressor into the mix if I'm not even sure about it.

The next day, I find a seat in my algebra class. My eyes drift around the room to see if there is anyone I recognize, but there isn't. Getting comfortable at my desk, I take out my laptop and open it up to double-check its charge.

"Hey, Ellie." Hunter's voice slices right through me.

My body freezes in shock. *How the hell did I completely forget that we planned on taking this class together?*

"H-hey," I stammer.

"How was your break?" he asks, as if he hasn't had me text him every day for over two weeks.

"Uh…good." I play into his casual behavior. "How was yours?"

"Good," he says, and redirects his attention to the professor.

It's nearing the end of class, and Hunter has barely looked my way, which surprisingly is irking me. He pressured me into texting him, and now acts like he hardly knows me. He's being too relaxed and cordial. It's off-putting.

I tap my nails on my desk, waiting for this class to end so I can get away from Hunter. My phone begins to vibrate, and when I glance down to see Mom calling, my stomach automatically coils with anxiety. I haven't spoken to her since Christmas, and as much as I feel horrible for admitting it, it was nice not to hear from her.

I silence the call and attempt to focus on the lecture.

A few moments later, my phone goes off again.

Worry starts to cloud my thoughts. *I haven't spoken to her in a month, and now she's repeatedly calling me. What if something's wrong? What if she got arrested again? What if she's hurt? What if something bad happened in Florida? What if…*

I jump out of my seat and dart into the empty hallway, answering the phone. "Mom?"

"Elena?"

"Yeah? What's going on?" My clammy palm clutches onto my phone.

"Where'd you go?" she slurs.

My shoulders slump. She's fucking drunk dialing me. "I'm away at school, remember?" She doesn't answer. "Where's Aunt Margaret? She's supposed to be helping you out." I make a mental note to flip out on Aunt Margaret later. She's supposed to look after Mom. That's the whole point of her being in Florida.

"She's been out for a while."

I sigh. "Are you okay? Are you in her home at least?" The last thing I need is for her to be out in public.

"Yep. Lying down on the couch."

"Get some sleep, Mom. We'll talk another day."

I hang up, then close my eyes for a brief moment and try to clear my head before entering the classroom.

My phone buzzes in my hand.

I guess it's going to be one of these days until she passes out.

"What, Mom?" I answer, massaging my temple.

She says something that I can't decipher, and I tell her for a second time to take a nap before hanging up.

My phone goes off again.

I hit the ignore button, but she keeps calling. I should shut off my phone, but I won't. I'm half waiting to one day get a terrifying phone call from a hospital telling me Mom is on her deathbed. It's a fucked-up thought, but if it can happen to one of my parents, it can happen to the other. I'd rather have her badger me until I know she's passed out at home than have her get in a car.

Leaning my body against the wall, I drop down onto the floor. She calls again, and I decide to answer. "Mom, I'm supposed to be in class."

The classroom door opens, and out walks Hunter, holding my belongings. He knows exactly what's going on because he's been through this with me before. He passes me my jacket and bag.

"Thanks," I say to him.

"No problem," Hunter says.

"Is that Hunter?" Mom chimes in.

I let out a loud puff of air and talk back into the phone. "Yes, that's Hunter." Hunter smiles as he stands over me. "I need to go, Mom. We'll talk when you're sober," I say, hanging up the phone. She won't remember any of this. She never does, which is why she's usually so charming when she's sober. She can't recall any of the pain she caused the night before. Or maybe she pretends not to remember.

My phone vibrates again.

"Oh my god!" I shout in the hallway, tugging at the roots of my hair.

"She's pretty persistent today, huh?" Hunter asks.

"Yeah." I look up at him. "She's been good for a while. I guess it's past due."

My phone stops and then starts again, and I sigh, exasperated.

"Why don't you go back to your dorm?" Hunter suggests. "She's going to call you until she falls asleep. There are only a few minutes of class left anyway. I'll let you know if you miss anything important."

I stare at him, confusion blurring my vision, wondering why he's being so kind to me.

This is always so confusing to me. People are nice to me one minute, and the next, I'm spinning in chaos. Everyone I'm close to is so hot and cold. Everyone except for Mateo.

"Okay," I say, gathering my things. "Thanks."

My phone continues to vibrate.

CHAPTER FORTY-ONE

Ellie

The rest of the week goes smoothly. Mom texted me a couple of times, acting completely fine. Hunter generously filled me in on what I missed during our next class. He was acting very cordial again, which was strange, but maybe this is our new normal. I haven't told Mateo that Hunter is in my class to avoid any issues that might come along with him knowing.

It's already the end of another philosophy class, and when Professor Boland ends his lecture, I slip my laptop into my bag and bundle up, bracing myself for the cold.

"Ms. Connor," Professor Boland calls me, and my head snaps up.

"Yes?"

"I'd like to talk to you for a second." He waves me up to his large desk. I quickly gather my things and make my way to him. The whole classroom has not emptied.

"Don't look so scared. You're not in trouble." He chuckles. "I want to talk to you about the abroad program."

"Oh."

"Your final paper last semester was one of the best ones I've read in years."

"Really?"

"Yes. I think that you should seriously consider joining us this summer. It would be a great opportunity for you, and we could definitely use someone with your inquisitive mindset."

"Thank you, Professor." I shift my weight back and forth. "I'm not sure if I can afford it, though."

Like magic, he pulls out a piece of paper. "Here's the information for the scholarship application. You can apply online."

I take the paper from him and put it in my bag.

"Elle?" Mateo pops his head into the room to see why I haven't walked into the hallway yet.

"Mr. Rivera." Professor Boland smiles.

"Hey, Boland," Mateo greets him as if they're friends.

Professor Boland focuses back on me. "Think about it. Applications are due in a few weeks."

I nod and exit the classroom toward Mateo, who has my coffee in his hand. Luckily, we don't bump into the same girl as last week as we walk out into the frigid air.

"What was that about?" Mateo asks.

"Oh, he was complimenting my final." I sniffle, the winter wind biting at the tip of my nose. "And then suggested I should do some summer program."

"That's awesome. What type of summer program is it?"

"I have a flyer about it in my bag. I didn't really look at it, so I don't know."

When we get into my room, we instinctively toss our winter gear onto my chair. My movements are quick as I sit on my bed, yanking on his shirt to pull him onto me.

My lips land on his, but he moves away after a few seconds. "Bree is going to walk in any second," he reminds me, as her class ends shortly after mine.

"Right." I tend to forget those sorts of things when I'm with Mateo.

"Why don't we look at the flyer?"

"Um…no, it's okay. I'm not going to do it anyway, so there's really no point." I move to kiss him again, in hopes of sidetracking him, but he stops me.

"You're trying to distract me." He squints. "Why don't you want me to look at the paper?"

Groaning, I reach for my bag and take out the crinkled flyer. "Because it's not going to happen, so I don't want to get my hopes up." I don't want to tell him that I already got accepted, and the last piece of the puzzle is getting the money to go. I pass the paper to him and watch his face change as he reads it.

"Elle, this is in France!"

"Yeah, I know," I say with a dismissive wave.

"This is perfect for you."

"Yeah, I know."

He stops reading the paper and glances up at me. "Why are you not excited about this?"

"Because I'm not going to go."

"Why not?"

I shrug. "Lots of reasons."

"Such as?"

My brain goes over all the reasons why I shouldn't do this trip—fear, Mom, money, and an extremely small part of me that doesn't want to go because of him—but there's no way that I'm letting him know that. "Well, for starters, the cost."

Mateo points to the flyer. "This is an application for a scholarship."

"It's also all the way across the world."

"And?"

"And…that's too big of a move for me."

"You're scared?"

I reflexively take offense. In an instant, my guard flies up. His question triggering me, I spring to my feet. "Do not tell me I'm being some fearful girl, incapable of doing this," I snap.

"Whoa!" He puts his hands up in innocence as bafflement paints his features. "Those words did not come out of my mouth."

"You were thinking it!"

"No, I wasn't." Hurt flashes in his eyes. "I was just asking a question."

I fixate on him, deciphering if he's being honest. *Was he simply asking if I was scared, or was he implying that I'm not capable enough to do this?*

"I wasn't suggesting that I don't think you can do this. I think you should go."

"You do?" Something about him saying that stings worse than two seconds ago, when I assumed he thought I was unfit to go. His telling me to go is like a thousand paper cuts to the heart.

"Yeah, it could be a great experience for you."

Air deflates from my lungs, my muscles slowly slouching.

I think I was hoping that he'd tell me not to go and stay with him. He burst my bubble by encouraging me to go. If he had loved me, he'd tell me to be with him, but instead, he's telling me to leave. I am crushed yet again. I was holding on to the hope that a tiny part of him would be capable of loving me.

Bree opens the door and picks up on the range of emotions written across my face. "Need me to come back?" She stands in the doorway, looking back and forth between Mateo and me.

I shake my head. "No, Mateo was just leaving," I inform both of them.

"What?" Mateo whips his attention back toward me.

A low rumble builds in my ribcage, and I want to cry, but I don't want to cry in front of Mateo for the billionth time. "We'll talk later," I dismiss him.

Mateo stays frozen for a brief second. "Okay," he mutters. He grabs his coat, then turns toward me to give him some type of goodbye, but I know if I look at him, the tears will start. I gaze down at the ground as he comes over to me and wraps his large arms around me, giving me a kiss on the top of my head. He exits the room, and I allow the tears to drip down my face.

"What happened?" Bree asks, concern wrapping around her soft voice.

"I think...no, I *know* that..." I sit down on my bed and stare at my feet. I take a deep breath, preparing myself to say my thoughts out loud. "I'm in love with Mateo."

Bree gasps. "You are?"

I nod. "But I know that he's not in love with me."

"What makes you think that?"

"You have to trust me on this one. He's not." I glance up at her. "I don't know what I'm doing with him. I'm just tormenting myself, but I want to be with him."

"Is that what you two were talking about? Him not loving you? Or you two not being together?"

"No, he found out about the abroad program. Not that I got accepted, just that it exists, and my professor suggested I apply for the scholarship. Mateo thinks I should go."

She hesitates. "I'm confused. Why is that a bad thing?"

"He was so quick to tell me to leave that...I don't know. It sounds stupid now that I'm saying it out loud. I just wanted him to want me to stay, I guess."

Bree smiles. "Well, either way, you shouldn't let a man dictate your life. If Mateo wasn't a thing and Hunter wasn't a thing, would you take the program?"

I contemplate her question but skirt around answering it. "I won't be able to go if I don't get a scholarship." There's no way in hell I'm asking Mom for thousands of dollars.

"Cross that bridge when you get there," she encourages me. "If you want to go, then apply for the scholarship and see what happens. Do whatever feels right for you."

Her words linger in my mind, and I let them sink in as I reflect on what she's saying.

I haven't heard from Mateo all evening, and I'm beginning to think that I scared him away. Pulling out my phone, I message him.

ME

I'm sorry. I don't know why I overreacted

Several minutes go by with no response. I bite my nails, worried that he's going to end things because I was an overdramatic bitch.

MATEO

It's ok. Let's talk in person—you free after class tomorrow?

That doesn't exactly ease my nerves. It sounds like he wants to end things with me in person rather than over text.

ME

Yeah

MATEO

Okay, I'll pick you up and we'll go back to my place to talk

Nope, I still don't feel any better with that text.

I place my phone to the side and open up my laptop. Still chewing away at my nails, I stare at the scholarship application on the screen.

Frustration boils under my skin the longer I fixate on my computer. For the majority of my life, I've let people have some type of input in my decisions. Even if their intentions are good-natured, like Professor Boland, Mateo, and sometimes even Hunter, I can't help but be annoyed with myself for not stepping up and taking hold of my choices.

Fear of what would happen to Mom if I were to leave for the entire summer comes to the forefront. She's one of the main reasons why I wouldn't want to go—her and Mateo.

I'm worried that if I leave for over three months, Mateo and I will really be over. He has no reason to wait for me, and it wouldn't be fair for me to make him pause his life just so I can live out a dream of mine.

But that's the thing. This program *is* a dream of mine. I've always done what others wanted me to in order to make them happy. I'm tired of being told what to do. I hate it. It's time for me to find some inner strength and break that pattern.

Taking a deep inhale, I start the application. My fingers tap on the keyboard, filling out all the necessary information and completing the extra writing assignment to qualify. I can only afford to go if I'm offered the scholarship, so that will be the deciding factor. I'll keep this to myself and won't tell Mateo about it until I find out.

CHAPTER FORTY-TWO

Ellie

The following day, Hunter sits next to me in algebra. I can't concentrate on anything the professor is teaching us. I've turned into a little ball of nerves, anticipating what's going to happen when Mateo picks me up later.

"What's wrong?" Hunter whispers.

Confusion paints my features as I glance at him, wondering how he knows something is up. His eyes drift down to my leg that's violently bouncing up and down.

"Oh." I place my hands on my leg to get it to stop. *Stupid nervous habit.*

"Anxious about something?"

Dammit, he knows me too well. I shake my head and focus on the front of the room, acting like everything's fine.

When class is over, Hunter speaks in the same caring tone he's used countless times. "You know, if something is the matter, you can always talk to me."

"Thanks." I walk out the door, but his hand on my shoulder stops me from getting too far.

"I'm serious. I know things haven't been great between us, but you know if you ever need anything at all, I'm always here for you."

I give him an appreciative nod. He probably thinks this has to do with Mom, which is why he's being so nice to me.

Turning around, it's as if I've instantly been sucker punched in the gut. Mateo is at the end of the hallway, looking back and forth between Hunter and me. Technically, it wasn't clarified if he'd be picking me up here or at my dorm, so I can't be upset that he showed up here. I glance back to see what Hunter will do or say, but he already left, which either means that he didn't see Mateo standing there or he really is opting to be a better person this semester.

I stroll up to Mateo, his head tilting to the side with a wary expression etched on his face.

"Still want to come over?" Mateo asks.

I nod.

We walk to his car in silence, and I brace myself for what's coming. I have no idea how he will react to this. All I can picture is how Hunter reacted when the situation was reversed last semester.

Once we're on the road, Mateo turns down the radio. "You didn't tell me he was in your class."

"I know," I respond. My stomach cramps, waiting for some sort of fury to ensue.

"Why not?"

"It didn't seem important."

Mateo's eyes fixate on the road as his head bobs up and down.

I grip the leather seat, anxiously waiting.

Waiting for him to scream at me.

Waiting for him to drive excessively fast.

Waiting for my panic attack.

It doesn't come.

My heart beats against my bones, nervousness spiraling down my body from unbearable anticipation.

Why is he being so calm? Yell at me already! Tell me I'm a piece of shit for keeping this from you! I know I am. Say it, Mateo!

When we get to Mateo's place, no one else is here. It's quiet, and I'm not sure what to do or say. His being so calm is making me more nervous. Standing in his bedroom, I watch Mateo make himself comfortable on his bed.

Tiptoeing closer, I make sure I'm as composed as I can be when I ask, "Are you mad at me?"

"I'm not mad," Mateo states. "I'm..." He pauses, collecting his thoughts. "I don't know what I am, but it feels like you were trying to hide from me that Hunter is in your class."

"I wasn't hiding it from you," I say on instinct. Mateo gives me a face to let me know that he can see right through my lie. "Okay, maybe I was."

"But why?"

"I wanted to avoid you getting angry and flipping out on me."

Mateo's eyebrows shoot up. "Elle, in all these months that you've known me, have I ever raised my voice at you?"

"No, but I don't think you've ever really been angry with me before."

"Oh, I have."

"You have?" I try to remember a time when I saw him angry toward me, but can't think of any. "But you've never yelled at me."

"That's because I control myself so that I don't."

"You're telling me that you purposely don't yell at me?"

"Yep."

I look at him like he has twelve heads. "Why?"

Mateo shrugs. "I try not to yell around women in general. But I especially don't want you to hear me yell."

I gaze at the gentle giant in front of me and join him on his bed. "I'm sorry I didn't tell you about Hunter."

His shoulders soften. "It's cool. Just don't hide stuff from me. Please?"

"Okay," I agree, even though I know I'll be hiding the fact that I'm head over heels in love with him. There's no way I'm letting that out, knowing he doesn't feel the same.

"Can we talk about yesterday?"

"That's the whole reason I'm here, right?" I've been waiting for him to bring up my tantrum.

"I thought you were here because you wanted to spend time together. I mean, that's why I invited you over."

I roll my eyes. "If you say so."

He looks at me and sits in silence. His quietness today causes annoyance to prickle inside me. "So…what do you want to talk about?"

He chuckles. "You wanna tell me what the fuck happened yesterday?"

"I…" I think for a few seconds about how best to approach this. "It sounded like you were telling me that I was too afraid to study abroad, and that pissed me off at first. Then you seemed a little too eager to throw me onto a plane and get me thousands of miles away from you, which also made me upset."

"I'm sorry if I came across like I didn't believe this is something you're capable of doing, because I absolutely do. And I certainly don't want you across the world for over three months. I was just trying to be supportive. I guess that came out wrong too. I'm sorry."

A lightness fills my chest, my anxiety subsiding the more I stare at this beautiful man. He's always so levelheaded, and I'm so hypersensitive and rash. I've never had an argument end this calmly, ever—not with my parents, not with Hunter, no one. My heart rapidly beats as I hear Bree's words of wisdom, "Do what feels right," ringing in my ears. Although I might end up regretting what I'm about to say, this is what I want in the present moment.

"I want to be your girlfriend," I blurt out.

Mateo's eyes widen in complete shock as I throw him off guard. "You do?"

"I do."

There's a long moment of silence. Mateo's attention shifts off me. "I…"

Oh my god. "You changed your mind. That's okay. Forget I said—"

"No!" Mateo reaches for my hand. "No, it's not that. I just don't know what I'm supposed to do now."

I laugh. "You don't have to do anything. Nothing's changed except that we're official now."

"So…you're mine," he says with a warm smile.

"And you're mine."

"I like the sound of that." Mateo works his way closer to me. He leans over and places a kiss on my lips, heat sparking in my body the second we make contact. He weaves his fingers through my hair, and my hands cup his stubbly jaw. With each movement of our mouths, the kiss deepens, our tongues dancing around each other's. My body and mind relax with every passing second.

This feels so right.

Mateo is stable and accepting, something I've never had before.

When I'm around him, it's as if the fog is temporarily lifted. I feel like I can fully be myself around him.

Not only am I falling in love with Mateo, but I'm also falling in love with myself.

CHAPTER FORTY-THREE

FEBRUARY

Sitting down at the kitchen table in my apartment, my stomach growls as I pour milk into my bowl of Cap'n Crunch.

"Why the hell are you smiling at your cereal?" Nick asks, walking toward the fridge.

I'm quick to school my features. "I don't know what you're talking about."

"I haven't seen you around much," he says, taking out the egg carton as he preps for his breakfast.

"I could say the same about you. You and Rosa are barely here, and if you are, you two are locked away in your bedroom." Sometimes I forget that others, aside from Michelle and me, live in this house.

He smirks. "Can you blame me?"

Shrugging my shoulders, I take a spoonful of my cereal. Nick struggles to get the stove on, the burner clicking a few times before it finally ignites.

"I haven't seen Jasmine around lately," he states.

"I haven't hooked up with her in months."

The skillet sizzles as Nick pours his whisked eggs onto it. "Been hooking up with that girl, Ellie, instead?"

My spoon hovers as I debate telling him the latest development in my life. "We're kind of…"

"Kind of what?" His face drops. "Fuck, dude. Did you knock her up?"

"What? No." I take a hefty bite of Cap'n Crunch so my mouth is full when I mumble, "We're official."

"I'm sorry. I must've misheard you. Did you say you're official?"

I nod.

"As in, she's your girlfriend, and you're her boyfriend?"

I nod again.

Nick lets out a lively laugh and takes the seat across from me at our kitchen table. "You—the guy who never wants to settle down and thinks relationships are pointless for him—have a girlfriend?"

"Yeah."

"Damn. I never thought I'd see the day. The sex must be amazing if she's got you wanting to be a boyfriend."

I give a halfhearted chuckle, my eyes falling off him and onto a piece of chipped wood at the edge of our table.

Nick picks up on the subtle shift in my energy, asking, "Have you guys not fucked yet?"

"She's a virgin."

"What!"

"We've done other shit but not…you know what, never mind." Picking up my bowl, I move to the sink to wash it.

Nick laughs at my evasiveness. "I never thought you'd actually catch feelings for a girl."

"Shut up." A pungent odor of over-crisp food overtakes the scent of dish soap, causing me to glance over at the skillet. "Your eggs are burning."

"Oh shit." Nick jumps up to take care of his breakfast, thankfully changing his focus off me.

Going to my room to continue getting ready for class, my mind replays Nick's reaction, and a shroud of doubt drapes over me.

I don't know where exactly I'm hoping things with Elle and me will go. The thought of being a boyfriend is barely enough for me to consume. The thought of falling in love and all the consequences that come after that is terrifying.

Glancing at myself in the mirror, my heart sinks into my stomach. The fear of falling for Elle intensifies as I stare at my reflection, the large scar on my arm forever reminding me of the anger I once housed inside me. I've crawled through my own personal hell to get to where I am today, but I still know there's a part of me that has my father's traits lingering in the background.

I don't want Elle to see me as violent.

I don't want her to see me as impulsive or wounded or spiteful.

I don't want any part of me to resemble my father.

I don't know if that's possible, but at least I'm trying.

CHAPTER FORTY-FOUR

Ellie

Settling down at my desk in algebra, my last class of the week, something catches my attention. It's Hunter, only not. He looks like shit. His hair is a mess, and his eyes are sunken in and bloodshot. He looks like he hasn't slept in weeks.

"Are you okay?" I whisper to him after he takes a seat next to me.

"I'm fine," he snaps without glancing at me.

The bitterness of his voice makes me jolt back in my seat. He's been nice to me for weeks, but I'm all too familiar with how he can switch to being hostile. My senses are on high alert, observing an angry fire building inside him. Nervousness bubbles in my stomach, and I do a mental recall of the past few weeks, wondering if this one-eighty has anything to do with me or if it'll be directed toward me.

Hunter is always concerned with his appearance. Even if he were having a difficult time, he would never show it. Considering how distraught and disheveled he looks right now, worrisome thoughts infiltrate me, coming up with a million possibilities of horrid scenarios happening in his life.

"Hunter—"

"Not now, Elena."

Anxiety takes over my mind.

I try to focus on the professor, but her voice is drowned out by my own thoughts. I try not to let my anxiety sink me, fighting with all my might to pay attention to the lesson. A whirling storm of paranoia takes over, worried that whatever is going on with him is going to spill onto me. Even though we're not even friends, I can't stop the growing fear that he'll take his anger out on me since he has no one else to.

He's always said that I'm the only one who understands him and that he needs me. What if he really does need my help right now but doesn't want to ask for it because I've been removing myself from him? What if he's going back to that dark place he was once in and now has no one to help him out of it?

When class ends, Hunter hurriedly packs up his things and heads for the door.

"Hunter!" I say to catch his attention. He turns around and gives me a few seconds to catch up to him. "What's going on?" I ask.

"Don't worry about it."

"Well, I want to make sure you're doing okay."

"Why don't you focus on someone else's problems. How's your mom doing, by the way?" He bites out the question in a vicious, sarcastic tone, causing me to flinch.

"I…I don't know what's going on with you, but I just wanted to let you know that I'm here if things get bad again and you need to talk."

Hunter studies me, debating which avenue to take in response. He settles on "Thanks," and walks off.

Before I'm able to overanalyze his response, my phone vibrates in my hand.

MATEO

I can't wait for our date tonight

Grinning, I allow my worries about Hunter to dissipate as I text Mateo back.

ME

me too 😊

The long silver chain with the green crystal pendant hits the center of my chest, sparkling beautifully against the black sweater I'm wearing. I wanted to make sure to wear the necklace Mateo gave me for Christmas for our date tonight. Mateo won't tell me where he's taking me, and we've been driving for about a half hour. I told him repeatedly that I didn't need him to be taking me out on dates, but Mateo insisted, now that we're in a relationship.

We pull up to a huge pool hall, and a wave of excitement crashes through me. "Have you ever played pool before?" Mateo asks as we get out of the car.

I pause for a moment, thinking of how best to answer this. Smirking, I decide that this could turn out really fun. "Not much," I lie. I haven't shared with him yet that my parents would take me into dive bars when I was a kid, where I was taught how to play pool by them and the local patrons. I loved playing pool when I was younger and got really good at it. Dad was always so proud of me and would brag about how I was going to win tournaments one day. Playing pool has always been a fun memory I have with my parents. Although it was usually clouded by liquor and beer, I remember a lot of laughter and joy. In a weird way, I feel like it's something that can connect Dad and me.

I haven't played since he passed, except for one night over the summer when I was at Cape Cod with Hunter and his family. I beat everyone except one of his uncles. My game is rusty, and I'm not sure how skilled Mateo is, so I want to watch him before I tell him I've spent years playing.

"You wanna break?" Mateo asks as he racks the balls.

"No, I suck at that." That's the truth. It's always been something I needed to work on.

Mateo bends down, and the light fixture overhead, that's perfectly measured to illuminate every inch of the table, beams down on his arms. He breaks, getting in one stripe, leaving me with solids strategically placed throughout the table. There are multiple shots that Mateo could get in, and he chooses the most obvious: a straight shot into the corner pocket. I watch as he sinks the ball and attempts to get in a third but misses because his aim was slightly off.

"Your turn," he says. Analyzing the layout in front of me, I spot a trick shot that I can attempt. But I don't want to blow my cover this soon, so I look at what else I can do. "You want me to help you?" Mateo asks as he watches my eyes travel around the balls.

The thought of his hands on me while trying to assist me makes me sizzle with lust. "Sure."

Mateo walks up behind me and tells me to aim for a solid that is impossible to get in because the angle is off, but looks doable to someone who isn't an advanced player. He lines me up and has me bend over the table to set up my shot. Leaning into me, he places his hand on my hip as he instructs me on what to do, his sexy, deep voice tickling my ear. Mateo's callused fingers sneak their way onto where my shirt and jeans part, and he slowly massages my skin. Sparks dance through my heart and down to my core as he touches me. Images of what could possibly happen on the pool table if we were alone pop into my mind.

My cheeks flush with my dirty thoughts, but I box them away for another time. "Are you going to let me shoot?" I nudge him with my hips.

"Sorry," he says in the least apologetic tone possible and moves to my side. "So you know what to do?"

"Yep, just hit the white ball into the purple one." I do as I say, and unsurprisingly miss the shot.

"That was close," he praises me and then gets in another stripe. His turn is over when he misses an easy shot. I have a nice lineup for my turn, so I get that one and then purposefully miss the next one. Mateo is excited that I was able to get one in and compliments me. He misses on his next round, which makes the perfect play for me.

I can't give up this flawless layout, so I blow my cover. Hitting the cue ball into the orange solid, I sink it, lining myself up where I intended to. I knock the cue ball across the table directly where the diamond is, which causes it to ricochet and hit into another solid, which goes into the side pocket. Finally, I hit the cue ball into my third solid, which diagonally goes into the corner pocket. There aren't any more opportunities for me, so I disperse a small cluster of solids and stripes.

Looking up at Mateo, his jaw hangs in disbelief. "You know how to play," he states.

"A little." I bite down on my lip to fight back my smile.

Mateo closes the gap. "You were trying to hustle me!"

My grin can no longer be hidden. "A little pro tip: when your girlfriend's parents are alcoholics, it usually means that somewhere in her childhood, there was a pool table involved," I tease.

He starts tickling me, and I giggle uncontrollably in his hold.

We play a few rounds. I win two, and Mateo wins the final round. He seems to be thoroughly impressed with my talent and not turned off in the slightest.

"I'm gonna have to work on my game during my free time in order to keep up with you," Mateo says as we drive back to campus.

"I haven't played in years. You should see me when I'm actually in my zone."

"'Scuse me," one of the workers interrupts, mumbling as he tries to maneuver around Mateo and me. "Don't mean to get in your way. I just need to put up some of these," he says, referring to the stack of flyers in his hands. Using his meaty fingers to rip a piece of Scotch tape, he then presses a flyer onto the wall that's covered in scuff marks from pool sticks and ambles off.

Coming into view, I give the flyer a quick glance. It's an advertisement for an extra half hour at a pool table on Valentine's Day.

"Fuck," Mateo mutters from behind me. When I spin to look at him, his face drops in disappointment. "I forgot all about Valentine's Day. I have to think of something good."

I chuckle. "No, you don't."

"We have to do something."

"No, we don't. I don't care at all."

He takes out his phone, checking his calendar, and groans. "I'm fucking working all day Saturday."

"So I'll study during the day and then come hang out at the coffee shop all night. I need to spend time studying anyway. I have a test in algebra, and I'm falling behind."

Mateo shakes his head. "No, I'm playing a gig at a bar at night."

"I'll come watch you!"

"I'll be there for hours. It'll be boring."

"No, it won't. I love watching you."

"I should do something more for you."

"No, you shouldn't." I snuggle into his chest, reveling in how warm he feels. "I'm perfectly content watching you play."

"But I want you to be more than just content. What would he do with you on Valentine's Day?"

Jerking my head up to see him, my jaw hangs open, baffled that he brought up Hunter. "No way. You are not doing that."

"Doing what?"

"Comparing yourself to Hunter. If I wanted another Valentine's Day with him, I would've stayed with him."

Mateo's attention goes off me. "I feel like a dick. I already messed up our first holiday together."

"Right, because Halloween, Thanksgiving, Christmas, and New Year's don't count," I say sarcastically.

"You know what I mean."

"Baby…" The word catches his attention, and he locks eyes with me. "I don't care about Valentine's Day. I'm going to come and watch you play all night, and I'll love it." I lean in and kiss him, parting his mouth open with my tongue.

He starts to give in, but suddenly pulls away. "You're falling behind in algebra?"

"What?"

"You said you're falling behind."

"Oh, well, not *behind* behind. I just haven't been paying enough attention, so I've been a little confused with the formulas. Nothing I can't figure out."

"Why aren't you paying attention?" he asks with slight suspicion in his voice, very aware of who is in the class with me.

"Not because of…" I avoid saying Hunter's name. "But because I've been too busy daydreaming about my amazing boyfriend."

"Seriously?"

"Yes, you're all I can think about sometimes. It's actually quite annoying," I joke.

"Don't fuck up any of your classes because of me."

"I'm not."

"If you need to focus on papers, tests, whatever—and if I'm distracting you—please tell me, and I'll leave you alone."

"Okay."

I press my lips against his before he can get another word in, but he stops us again. "What are you daydreaming about?"

"You."

"What about me?"

"I don't know…you…us."

"Dirty things?" Mateo asks as his voice gets huskier.

I can't help but smile. "Sometimes."

"Tell me."

"No!" I laugh. "Besides, it's not all dirty. Sometimes it's just normal everyday things. Don't you ever think about me?"

"Of course I do," he says. "I just like to hear that you do too, and that sometimes it's dirty."

I shake my head and bring my lips to his once again. Mateo talks in between our kisses. "You'll tell me one day?"

"One day."

CHAPTER FORTY-FIVE

Mateo

My wooden drumstick pounds down onto the snare, setting a bright, upbeat tempo for the rest of the band to follow.

Music has been my personal brand of therapy for years. As soon as I start playing, I'm in the zone. Nothing can distract me.

Not colorful lights that flicker overhead as we play.

Not the packed room filled with people, either loving or hating Valentine's Day.

Not the sweat forming at the rim of my backward hat.

But when I look into the crowd and spot Elle smiling at me through the crowd of heads, I falter for just a split second.

No one notices, aside from the band. The bassist, Johnny, whips his attention toward me, assuming something is wrong because I never, ever miss a beat. Ignoring him, I'm immediately back in sync, and no one else pays any mind to my minuscule blunder.

As our set moves on, my heart beats faster than the songs, and my line of sight has zeroed in on Elle. I wink at her, and she blows me a kiss. For a moment, it feels as if it's only her and me in here.

My body stirs when I get more of a glimpse of her. She's in a dark-green dress with black tights, and the necklace I gave her for Christmas falls perfectly above her cleavage. The harder I play, beads of sweat dripping down the tattoos on my arms, the more Elle's eyes light up with desire.

Triumph blasts through my veins, knowing she's turned on by me playing. Each time I crash down on a cymbal, my ego gets boosted by the look on her face. My grin stretches wide, and even though I might've messed up Valentine's Day plans, at the very least, I'm not going to mess up the climax of the holiday.

The band plays the last song before our break. Our singer, Max, announces that we'll be back soon, and then the DJ takes over. Grabbing my water bottle, I down it as fast as I can, then hop off the stage to get to Elle.

"You were so awesome!" She beams, then cups my cheeks to give me a kiss. I can taste the hint of lust on her lips, and I'm struck with the urgency to make the most of my break.

"Let's go outside," I shout over the DJ. Placing my hand on the small of her back, I lead her out the side door. We walk into an alleyway where there aren't any people. The cold February air is surprisingly refreshing compared to the hot, stuffy bar, and when I lean against the brick wall, the chill soothes my muscles. "You look beautiful," I state, leaning up against the brick wall. My eyes flicker all over her body, not hiding how much I'm mesmerized by her curves.

"Thank you." She gives me a coy smile, her small dimple making an indent on her left cheek. "You were amazing. I don't know how you can get in front of so many people and play. I love watching you."

"Oh, yeah?"

"Yeah."

She gets on her tippy toes to kiss me once more, only this time I decide to seize the moment. Threading my fingers through her hair, I linger in her silky strands, then cautiously inch my hand down until it's resting on her neck.

Unsure if Elle's going to be into this, I make sure to be gentle when the pads of my fingertips clutch her. I apply a light amount of pressure, and she moans into my mouth.

Heat shoots down my body. Incapable of suppressing my excitement, I spin her around so that her back is now against the cold bricks, pinning her against the wall. Her hands slide under my shirt, and I revel in the touch of her icy fingertips roaming around my body.

My hormones are wild, lust continuously building with each swipe of my tongue. Bending down slightly, I sneak my hand up her dress.

"Mateo! We're outside!"

My fingers crawl up her thigh. "Who cares?"

"Someone might see us."

I pause, looking directly into her sage eyes. "If you want me to stop, all you have to do is tell me, and I will."

She hesitates, but then a glint of passion ignites in her pupils. "Keep going," she whispers.

On her command, I begin rubbing her clit through her tights. Her tension releases as she lets me take over. It's so incredibly hot to watch her feel safe in my arms.

Her soft sighs drive me crazy. My cock rams up against the zipper of my jeans, aching with need.

Never in a million years did I think I'd get so fucking turned on by going slow with Elle. I like that I have to be gentle with her. I like that she gets to learn what she likes at the same time I do. I like that I'm forced to restrain myself from hiking up her dress and pounding her into the wall. It's a torturous form of edging, but it aches so good.

My other hand still wrapped around her neck, I apply a bit more pressure, and her lashes flutter close.

"Eyes on me," I rasp, circling her clit faster.

She does as I say, both of us getting high off each other the second our gazes lock. Her trust in me causes my cock to throb even more. She grips onto my shirt, pressing her lips together to prevent her moans from echoing off the alleyway walls.

Her limbs begin to tremble, and her eyelids shut.

"Eyes on me." My command is stronger this time, rushing her toward her climax.

Elle opens her eyes as my fingers continue to make fast and strong circular motions. She digs her nails into my torso, the pleasurable sting eliciting a deep groan from the back of my throat. Both of my hands apply more pressure, and her body melts into the bricks. It's impossible for her to keep quiet as she reaches her peak. My heart roars with satisfaction, never taking my eyes off her as we indulge in her orgasm.

With one last moan, her knees buckle, and she almost collapses, but I'm quick to react, catching her. "I got you, baby," I say.

Elle glances up at me, out of breath. "I didn't think I was into that."

A mischievous grin tugs at my lips. "Into what?"

"Any of it."

"Being outside? Or being choked?"

"I-I don't know."

"Don't be shy." My eyes rake over her body. "I'm just learning what you like so I can make it even better for you, baby."

The side door swings open, pulling our attention toward the noise. It's Johnny, the bassist. "There you are, man. We're going back on in ten." He pauses, glancing at Elle and then back over at me. "Sorry to interrupt."

"You're not!" Elle squeaks out, and I chuckle.

"I'll be right there," I tell Johnny, and he goes back inside. I help Elle smooth out her hair and adjust her dress. "Beautiful," I say, giving her a peck on her forehead.

By the time my band is finished playing, it's late, but I want to spend the last few minutes of Valentine's Day with Elle. We walk hand in hand toward my car, and when I open the door for her, she lets out a gasp.

"You got me flowers?"

Glancing down at the bouquet of roses I placed on the passenger seat, all I can notice is the browning on the tips of the red petals. "Don't get too excited. They're pretty shitty. Apparently, all the good ones sell out early on Valentine's Day."

"I love them."

I smile, making a mental note to buy flowers earlier next time. But regardless of some of them wilting, Elle still admires them as I go to sit in the driver's seat. My chest gets warm, watching her dote on the shitty roses.

"Do you…" I clear my throat of the sudden nerves that seemed to pop up. "Do you want to spend the night? Not in that kind of way. I mean, do you want to sleep over just to sleep?" My voice softens. "I miss holding you." We haven't had a night together since winter break, and I've missed falling asleep next to her.

The look of delight dances across her features. "I'd love that."

CHAPTER FORTY-SIX

Ellie

The rest of the week flies by, and I'm thankful for the weekend. Sandy had me come in to work early today to hang up new photographs and rearrange the display tables by the front of the store. Every few months, they cycle out the pictures and books as a way to support local artists. After putting the framed artwork on the brick walls throughout the entire bookshop, I plant myself at the head of the store to showcase the latest books of varying genres.

"You know," Edgar says as he strolls my way. "You're not half bad at this job."

I chuckle. "It only took you how many months to realize that?"

"Oh, I realized it after the first week. I just didn't want to inflate that big ego of yours."

"How thoughtful."

He shifts one of the books on the table a fraction of a hair. "See, as soon as I compliment you, you start getting sloppy."

I glare at him, and he breaks out in a boisterous laugh.

"What are you doing to Elle?" Mateo startles both Edgar and me as he hovers in the archway between both shops.

"What are you doing on our side of the store?" Edgar retorts.

"Checking in on my girl." Mateo moves into the room and toward me.

"Your girl?" Edgar looks at me in confirmation, and my cheeks get hot. He shakes his head and mutters something under his breath. "You better not mess with her." He points at Mateo. "She's the best one I got." He looks back over to me. "Pretend you didn't hear that. I don't want you to get overconfident and start slacking."

"My girl is a lot of things. A slacker is not one of them." Mateo gives me a tender kiss.

"Hey, hey, hey." Edgar waves his hand around. "I don't give a shit what you do in your personal time, but none of this in front of the customers."

"It's dead in here." Mateo motions around us.

"No one has been in all day," I add.

Edgar runs his hand over his stubble. "Yeah, I know. I was actually coming over to tell you that you can go home early, Ellie." He points at Mateo again. "Not you. You're stuck here until close."

Mateo brushes him off and focuses on me. "Can I stop by after my shift?"

"Of course." I get on my tippy toes to reach his lips.

"Hey!" Edgar shouts at us.

"I'm off the clock," I say in between kissing Mateo.

Once I'm back in my dorm, I decide to work on my world history paper that I've been procrastinating on. Luckily, I have the entire room to myself this weekend. Bree left yesterday to visit Amber in Manhattan.

Planting myself down at my desk, I force myself to focus on my laptop, free from distractions.

After a few hours of getting sucked into ancient Egypt, there's a rapid tap at my door, breaking my train of thought. I open it and see Mateo.

"What are you doing here? Aren't you supposed to be working until close?" I ask as I step aside, allowing him to enter.

"Edgar had me go early because of the snow. I'm coming to pick you up and bring you back to my place so you don't get snowed in alone for the weekend."

"Snow?" I peer out the window and see a dusting on the ground. "I didn't even know that was in the forecast."

"Yeah, me neither," Mateo says from behind me, looking out the window.

I turn toward him and notice him admiring my leggings and his black T-shirt on my body. He places his hands on my waist and brings his lips to my neck.

"Mateo." I give a halfhearted protest.

"Mmm?"

"Aren't we going back to your place?"

"Ten minutes." He slides his hands under my shirt.

"Ten minutes can make a big difference. It's scary driving in the snow."

"Then we can stay here tonight. I don't care." He takes one hand out from under my shirt and uses it to cup my face, drawing me in for a kiss. I almost unravel from the contact, but I can't fully relax knowing I'm so close to being done with my paper. I really need to finish it before he turns my brain into a puddle.

I create space between us. "If you're going to stay here, can I finish my paper first? And then we can do whatever you want."

"Whatever I want?"

"You know what I mean."

He smiles. "Sure." He lets go of me and takes his shoes off. "I'm gonna take a nap while you write. I'm so tired."

"Okay." I watch as he takes his jeans off and gets under my covers. *So much for being free from distractions.*

By the time I'm done writing, Mateo is sound asleep. I take a peek out the window and see the snow rapidly falling, covering the entire campus in a thick white blanket.

My eyes drift back to Mateo, who looks so tranquil. I should probably wake him up so his sleep schedule isn't thrown off for the night, but instead, I join him under the covers and snuggle up to him. My gaze goes toward the big scar on his arm, and my fingers gently trace it, wondering what that experience must've been like for him. Probably terrifying. I wish I had known him then and could've saved him from that situation.

"What are you doing?" Mateo's eyes flutter open.

"Sorry," I say, moving my fingers away from his arm.

"You finished your paper?"

"Yeah."

He nods, and like a switch went off, he immediately wakes up and kisses me. He's being extra tender and careful, filling my body with warmth and desire. I take my hands to his shirt, pulling it over his head.

Once he's shirtless, he brings his hands to his black T-shirt I'm wearing and glides it off me. Mateo's hands are delicate and slow-moving. Slower than I want, so I tug on his boxers and wiggle them off.

Mateo lays me back down, spreading me out on my mattress, and softly kisses my neck, working his way down. His tongue teases my nipples and then brushes over my stomach, causing me to clench my legs together. He isn't talking like he usually does. Instead, he's taking his time to idolize my body. His gradual, sensual movements are driving me mad.

He reaches my pants and hooks his fingers inside of my panties, leisurely dragging them down. I try to kick them off to help him, but he takes hold of my legs. He shakes his head, letting me know we're going slow, then he steadily peels my clothes off me.

His snail speed makes my heart erratic.

Mateo caresses my calves and gradually moves his hands up my legs. He teasingly draws his fingertips up and down my inner thighs.

"Baby," I sigh, pleading with him to do something.

Mateo smiles and brings his body next to me, lying on his side. He doesn't touch me. Instead, he lets his eyes wander up and down my bare body. Fully exposed, I ache with the need to be touched by him.

Catching me off guard, he lifts my left wrist, rubbing his thumb over my scars.

Oh my god. Panic seizes my chest. I never realized he noticed them before. *This is it. This is when he sees how fucking crazy I really am and walks out the door for good.*

"Um…" I try thinking of an excuse as to why they would be there. "That's…um…"

Mateo shakes his head. "You don't have to tell me about it." He studies my wrist for a moment before bringing it to his lips, carefully brushing over each scar. "Only when you're ready."

I watch him fully embrace what I am ashamed of. I never thought someone would accept my brokenness and flaws, yet here he is, trying to kiss my pain away. I know that he'll never love me, but I love him more than I've ever loved another person.

"I'm ready," I say.

Mateo stops and looks at me, waiting for me to tell him a story. He's so adorable. "No. I'm *ready,*" I say and reach for his face, luring him closer so I can kiss him.

His large arms embrace me, and a burst of heat explodes between us as our legs become tangled. I can tell he's trying not to show his eagerness too much, but his tongue around mine tells me how ready he is too.

"Are you sure?" he asks, our lips breaking contact ever so slightly.

"I'm sure."

Passion whirls through my bloodstream as he positions himself on top of me. Suddenly, he freezes. "I don't have a condom," he realizes as his face drops.

"What?" I ask in disbelief. "Why not?"

"They're at my place. I didn't think you were ready, so I—"

"I don't care." I kiss him harder. Everything I've ever learned in years of sex ed classes gets wiped from my mind.

Mateo moves his mouth away from mine. "What?"

"I said I don't care." I go back to kissing him.

"Elle," he says between our lips. "I don't think this is a good—"

I pull away from him and cut him off. "Mateo, have sex with me."

Mateo pauses, the desire evident in his eyes. Then, he nods his head and moves his body so that we're perfectly aligned. He pushes my legs open even wider with his knee. "If it hurts too much, just tell me to stop. Okay, baby?"

"Okay," I whisper.

Mateo starts slowly, only entering me a little bit. It's somewhat uncomfortable but doesn't hurt. He stops. "Keep going?"

Smiling, I nod. He pushes himself in a little more, and we both let out an audible exhale. He stays there for a few seconds so I can get used to the new feeling. "Keep going," I urge him, and he slowly pushes in more. I sharply inhale and wince. A shooting pain causes me to tense up.

Worry washes over Mateo's face. "Want me to stop?"

I close my eyes to try to relax into the pain. "No, just give me a second."

His chest rises and falls fast against mine, his breath skating on my skin.

I slowly inhale and exhale a few times until I feel ready. "Keep going." My lashes flutter back open, and our gazes lock. He does as I say, entering me completely. We both let out a moan, and an overwhelming sensation takes over.

Mateo cautiously studies me, his eyes divulging that he's also feeling extremely vulnerable right now too. Leaning down, he brushes his lips on mine. Then he brings his head back up to watch me as he very carefully rocks his hips.

Heat wrings my veins tight in the most intoxicating way. I let out strong moans as the sensation of him moving deep inside me strengthens with each thrust. Mateo's dark hair falls in front of his face, and I push it back for him so I can continue to gaze at my soulful man.

"You good, baby?" His voice strains.

"Yes." The answer comes out as a moan.

My pulse accelerates as Mateo's right hand grips my hip in an effort to control himself and not go any faster. Pushing himself up with his left arm, he admires my body under him. Lustful tingles run down my spine as I watch Mateo's eyes wander over every inch of me that he can possibly see in this moment. He bites down hard on his bottom lip as if to stop all the filthy words from tumbling out of his mouth.

I've never felt this beautiful in my entire life.

I've never felt this *alive*.

Shutting my eyes, I allow myself to relax as our bodies meld together in the most blissful way. "Mateo, I—" I instantly clamp my mouth shut.

Oh my god! I almost said I love you! What the hell is wrong with me?

Mateo freezes, and my eyes fling open. "Should I stop?"

"Don't stop," I say, out of breath.

He grins, leaning back down and continues to move. Our lips touch, but we don't kiss. We breathe each other in and out, our moans creating the most beautiful harmony.

I wrap my arms around his body, wanting even more of him. Mateo takes his hand from my hip and gracefully slides under my back, bringing my chest nearer to his. Both of us yearn to get even closer, although this is as close as we possibly can be. Intense sensations take over my body, and my sounds become louder.

An explosion of desire bursts from my heart, and my legs begin to shake.

My orgasm takes over, blinding me with pleasure as I tremble and moan and pant beneath Mateo.

Mateo's movements get sharper, and he buries his face into the crook of my neck. He lets out a deep sigh. "Elle, I—" He stops himself from saying more.

Was he just about to tell me that he loved me, like I was with him?

"I..." He struggles to get out his sentence. "I'm not gonna last long..." he pants. "I'm so sorry, baby. You're just so tight...and warm...and wet." His own words instantly make him pull out, and he comes on my stomach.

He reaches for his boxers and cleans me off. Then he pulls the covers over both of us, protecting our vulnerability. Our eyes are locked onto one another as we attempt to catch our breath.

"Are you okay?" he asks.

"Amazing." I plant my hand on his fast-moving chest. "Sore, but amazing."

Mateo kisses my forehead and plays with the ends of my hair. I cuddle up into his large frame and let the heat of his body keep me warm as the snow continues to fall outside.

CHAPTER FORTY-SEVEN

Ellie

Placing the Straylight Run record Mateo gave me onto my player, the vinyl begins to spin. I've listened to this album on repeat since Christmas, but for some reason, the lyrics to "The Tension and Terror" hit harder this time.

Gorgeous green eyes smiling…

I die trying just to keep myself from kissing you…

And it comes down to me and you,

And whether we're supposed to or not, we still will.

My cheeks sting from grinning so much. I've been replaying the scene from Saturday in my head nonstop, and I couldn't have pictured it going any better. I've never felt as empowered about making a choice for my body as I did in that moment. I've never felt closer to another human being than I do with Mateo. Even if he's not in love with me, he was so kind and gentle that I truly felt respected.

I get lost in the music and the sensations until Bree enters our room bundled up with at least five scarves on and carrying a small luggage bag. Due to the storm, Bree wasn't able to come back yesterday like she originally planned.

"Tell me again why I moved here instead of staying in sunny California?" she says, unraveling layer after layer of winter gear.

I laugh at her dramatic entrance. "How was your time with Amber?"

"Incredible! How was your weekend with Mateo?" Bree slings her coat on the back of her chair, then spins to face me.

"Probably equally as incredible."

Tilting her head, she studies me. "Something's different," she states, squinting, trying to figure out what's changed. Biting the inside of my cheek, I attempt to stifle my growing smile, but I must be doing a poor job of hiding it because a second later, she gasps with excitement.

"Oh my god! You slept with him!"

Nodding, I can't help chuckling at how thrilled she is for me.

"When? Where? How was it!"

"Saturday. It was amazing, Bree. It felt so right. Like, in that exact moment, I *knew* that it was supposed to be then and there and with him."

"I fucking love that! I want to hear every dirty detail—" The sound of the alarm on her phone interrupts. "Shit, that's my reminder to get ready for class."

Glancing at the time, I realize my algebra class is starting soon. "I gotta head out too."

"Okay. When we get back, promise you'll catch me up on your weekend?"

"Absolutely!"

In a delighted haze, I end up in my class, paying no mind to what the professor is lecturing. My thoughts are still twisted around bedsheets and tangled around the feel of Mateo's body on mine.

Time passes by as I continue to zone out, but the sound of the classroom door opening brings my attention back into the room.

Hunter skulks in, his hair unkempt and darkening circles around his eyes. As he walks closer, I do a double-take at the empty desk next to me. I was so invested in my post-sex daydream, I didn't realize he wasn't here.

But the moment he sinks down in the chair, I'm immediately grounded in the present.

The professor carries on, asking us to pull up our latest test on our laptops so we can go over some of it. Quite pleased with myself when I see the A-minus on the screen, a smile tugs at my lips, but it is quickly suppressed when I hear a huff of anger next to me. Peeking at Hunter's laptop, an F stands out, clear as day.

Something must be going on with him. I don't think he has ever failed anything in his entire life. Glancing at him, his eyelids are heavy as he stares at his screen. He looks exhausted, like he hasn't gotten sleep in weeks.

When class is over, my worried mind takes the initiative to check in. "Hunter?"

"Yeah?" He glares at me, lasers shooting out at me as if I'm the one who caused whatever's going on.

"Are you okay?"

"Elena, don't pretend like you give a shit about me."

What is that supposed to mean? Before I can get the words out, he leaves. I'm left standing in the middle of the hallway, my head spinning in confusion.

Hunter ignores my existence during our next class, so when I see his name pop up on my phone tonight, I hesitate to answer. *What could he possibly want from me?* I hit ignore and continue to get ready to meet Mateo at the coffee shop to hang out during his shift.

My phone vibrates again, and I hit ignore once more.

Nope. Not answering you, Hunter.

He calls for a third time.

What is he not understanding about my ignoring his phone calls?

Focusing back on prepping to see Mateo, I clasp my favorite necklace around my neck and smooth out my shirt before putting on my jacket. Suddenly, there's a loud banging at my door, making me jump out of my skin. *What the fuck?*

Opening it, there's a fiery redhead glowering at me. "I think this belongs to you?" She points down the hall at a plastered Hunter, trying to get into what I can only assume is her room.

"Ellie!" he shouts with gusto, stumbling over to me.

I turn back at the redhead. "Sorry."

"Next time, make sure your boyfriend knows which room is yours before he gets shit-faced." She storms off as Hunter pushes his way into my room.

"Come on in," I deadpan, closing the door.

"Where is he?" Hunter slurs.

Waves of nausea tumble in my stomach when I note how bloodshot and glassy his eyes are. "Where is who?"

Towering over me, the scent of alcohol expels from his pores. "Your new boyfriend." He gives me such a sinister smile that the tiny hairs on my arms rise.

In all the time I've known Hunter, I've *never* seen him drunk. Fear snakes up my spine, knowing how awful people can act when they're messed up. I don't know how he's going to be toward me.

"Well?" Hunter urges me to respond, but I cross my arms and refuse. He pokes around my room, moving papers on my desk. "I don't see any pictures of you two. It can't be that serious."

"Can you get your hands off my stuff?"

He smirks. "You never had a problem with my hands before."

"Hunter, I'm not doing this. Go back to wherever you were and leave me alone."

"Fine," he grumbles, taking his car keys out of his pocket.

"You *drove*?"

"How else was I gonna get here?"

"I can't let you drive like this. Get an Uber."

"I'm not getting a fucking Uber, Elena." He moves toward my door, but I run in front of it to stop him.

"Fine." I take out my phone. "I'll get an Uber for you then." Hunter snatches it out of my hand. "Give me my phone back!"

He slips it into his front pocket. "Here you go," he says, pointing his hands toward his crotch. "Come get it."

My jaw clenches. I'm not sure what the best move is here, but this is the only thing I can think of. "If you give my phone back, I'll let you stay here until you're sober enough to drive."

"You gonna babysit me?"

I click my tongue. "If that's what I have to do, then yes."

"Promise you won't leave me before I wake up?"

"I promise I won't leave you, Hunter," I say, knowing he needs to hear me say the words.

He scoffs. "You already broke that promise. I said, Promise you won't leave me *before I wake up*."

"Don't be a dick." I shove him aside, and he stumbles but catches himself on my desk. "Go lie down."

He does as I say, shutting his eyes. Sitting at my desk chair, I go to text Mateo that I'm going to be late but then pause. *Dammit. Hunter still has my phone.*

"Hunter, I need my phone back."

Without opening his eyes, he sticks his hand in his pocket and tosses my phone on the opposite end of the bed.

"Thanks," I say, reaching for it.

I zone out for a while. I had assumed Hunter had fallen asleep, but his voice brings me back. "I fucked up, Ellie," he mumbles into the pillow.

"Sleep it off. You'll be fine in a little bit."

"No. That's not what I mean."

"What do you mean?"

He groans and rubs his hands over his face. "Shit's so bad."

"What is?"

"Things at home. It's so fucking bad."

My face scrunches, wondering what he could possibly mean by that. Everything always seemed relatively calm at his house. Almost too calm. His parents uphold the image of a perfect family in front of others, but at home, they're distant toward each other. Hunter's not close with his parents, and he doesn't spend much time with them, but everyone appears to coexist.

"Do you want to talk about it?" I ask, getting up and tiptoeing over to him.

As he lifts his hands from his face, I see tears streaming down. My stomach drops. Whatever's going on has to be bad if he's crying like this. "Hunter," I whisper, sitting next to him on the bed.

"Do you think I'm a bad person, Ellie?"

"What? No. Why would you ask that?"

"Because I think I am, especially after what I did to you with Delilah."

That name makes me want to punch things. Specifically, Hunter's face. "Let's talk about this when you're sober." I go to stand, but he clasps my hand.

"I need you. I need you to help me through this." His voice breaks, and he cries—really cries. Like, uncontrollable sobbing, the not-able-to-catch-his-breath kind of crying. "I know I don't deserve you, but you're the only one who cares about me."

My chest breaks open, empathy drawing me to his tears. "That's not true. You have your parents—"

"I don't have them, Ellie."

Hunter pulls me into him, clutching on to me like I'm his only lifeline. Fear pounds through my heart, my breath getting shallower at the thought of him getting back into a dark mindset. He buries his head in the crook of my neck, hysterical. Anxiety fills my body. It almost becomes too much to keep inside. The compulsive urge to fix whatever is going on and help him takes hold of me. I wrap my arms around him and let him cry as I rub my hands over his back. He mumbles something, but between the alcohol and the tears, I can't make out what he's saying.

Only one word. *Kayla.*

His little sister, who died when he was seven. He's only talked about her twice, but clearly, something about her is weighing on him.

I don't know what to say, so I hug him tighter as my heart pours out to him. I never knew his grief was hurting him like this.

I guess there are a lot of things I don't know about him.

I thought I did.

The wetness from his tears coats my hair and shirt, and Hunter grips me tighter, as if he's never going to let go.

"Hunter, please talk to me." I need to know what's wrong. I need to know where this is coming from.

He backs away so we can see each other, his blue eyes drowning in agony. "I can't."

I nod. If there's one person who understands wanting to bottle up their pain, it's me.

Hunter wipes his face and catches his breath. "I can't lose you." His voice strains as he grasps my hand again.

"Hunter, I—"

"Just say that you'll answer my call if I need to talk? I promise not to bother you too much. I'll never show up like this again, I swear."

His eyes capture mine, and I'm unable to break the connection. He looks so defenseless. I can't let him sink to the bottom. If I'm the only one he's got, then I'll be there for him. "Okay."

CHAPTER FORTY-EIGHT

Ellie

MARCH

Mateo's tongue teases mine as we make out in one of the private study rooms in the university's library.

"We're supposed to be studying for midterms," I whisper into his mouth.

"We will," Mateo assures me while sneaking his fingers under my shirt. "Eventually."

Chuckling, I don't bother coming up with any logic because I'd much rather be doing this. Mateo kisses along my jawline, dragging his lips down to my neck. My lashes flutter close, giving in to the lust spiraling around my body.

Just as he starts to suck on my delicate skin, we're interrupted by my phone vibrating. I roll my eyes when I see it's Mom calling and try to bring Mateo's attention back to me.

"You should answer it," he says.

"I'll call her later." I move in to kiss him, but he leans back.

"Talk to her. I need to start studying anyway. You're distracting me," he teases, reaching for his laptop.

Holding my breath, I answer my phone. *Please be sober, please be sober, please be sober.* "Hey, Mom."

"Hi, Elena, I haven't heard from you in a while. How are you doing?" Mom's voice is upbeat and clear, so she most likely hasn't hit the bottle yet.

"I'm fine. How's it being back home?" I ask. Mom got back from visiting my aunt in Florida a few weeks ago, and I'm fully prepared for her to slip back into her reality.

"Things are good. When's your spring break?"

"Two weeks," I tell her. The realization of how close midterms are has me opening my laptop to actually study this time.

"Can I borrow your charger?" Mateo asks. The sound of his voice has me shooting him a shut-the-hell-up look.

"Who's that?" Mom inquires, clearly hearing him.

"Um…that's my friend," I say, digging my charger out of my bag.

"Oh? And what is your friend's name?"

"Mateo." Glancing at him, he's beaming over the fact that I'm mentioning him to Mom.

"Mateo?" She pauses. "So is Hunter out of the picture?"

"Um…" I try to think of an answer that will result in the fewest follow-up inquiries.

"Well, I hope to meet this Mateo someday if it gets serious."

If it *gets* serious? It's *been* serious. "Uh…okay."

"Are the two of you spending spring break together?"

"I don't know what his plans are yet."

"Okay. Well, keep me posted. You can always come home for break."

Yeah, okay, there's no way I'm taking her up on that offer. "Thanks." We keep the conversation short, saying a quick goodbye and then hanging up.

Mateo grins. "You told your mom about me."

"I told her you exist."

"You gonna tell her I'm your boyfriend?"

"Eventually," I tease, forcing my focus on my computer. "I'll tell her once I have the mental capacity to field all the questions. And for when I have the time to talk to her, because she'll want to know everything about you and what your plan is."

"My plan?"

"Yeah, like becoming a social worker and living in Queens. And she'll want to know if you want to get married, have kids…all that kind of stuff."

I didn't think anything of my flippant statement, but what I said was enough to change the energy in the room. Mateo's playfulness is erased as he quietly stares at his computer. A stoic expression paints his features, and I'm certain I struck a nerve.

"You…you do want that stuff, right?" I ask.

"I'm too young to think about marriage."

"Yeah, but is it something you'd ever see yourself wanting down the line?"

Mateo lets out a heavy sigh. "No," he answers. "All the people in my life who were married were fucking miserable—my parents, for one. Angela had to get a divorce from her shithead husband, and I don't think

Valentina actually wanted to get married. She just did after she got knocked up."

My heart plummets to the bottom of the library. Even though we *are* too young to be talking about weddings and families, he doesn't see that kind of future with me at all. There's zero chance of this going anywhere. I'll be his girlfriend until he either gets bored with me or tires of my antics. I've fallen in love with a man who prides himself on never loving a woman and who never wants to be married. *Way to pick them, Ellie.* The rational part of me is asking why I'm choosing to be with him, knowing all of this, but the lovestruck part is urging me to make this all work out.

"Elle…" His brows draw in with concern. I must've spaced out for too long.

"You're right." I bite on the cuticle of my thumb. "We're in college. We don't need to be having this serious conversation."

The two of us quietly go back to our work, the awkwardness still lingering in the empty space between us. I reread the same sentence four times, not able to absorb anything. The uncomfortable air in the small room puts me on edge.

I should've never brought anything up. Stupid, stupid, stupid.

I can fix this.

As I open my mouth to attempt to make a joke and laugh this whole thing off, my phone rings…again. Only this time, it's not Mom.

My gut clenches when I see Hunter's name. I never told Mateo about Hunter coming over since Hunter has been acting like it never happened. I don't know if he even remembers crying in my room, but we haven't spoken since, so I assumed not.

Mateo's eyes are glued to my phone, vibrating on the table. His features draw in tight. "Why's he calling you?"

"I don't know." I hit ignore, but the anxiety growing inside me intensifies. My leg bounces up and down. Jitters run up and down my body, and I impulsively spring to my feet and start pacing. "You know how you asked me not to hide anything from you?" I blurt out.

Mateo's shoulders tense. "Yeah?"

"Okay." I walk the length of the tiny, bland room and then back again, avoiding eye contact. "So Hunter showed up at my room drunk, and I let him sleep it off. He didn't spend the night or anything. He just slept for two hours and drove to his frat house. I couldn't let him drive until I knew he was sober enough."

"Did anything happen?"

My eyes flash over to him. "No, I swear! He didn't do anything, and I stayed at my desk. I was just helping him sober up."

He processes what I said and nods. "Anything else?"

"He's going through some stuff right now and asked if he could reach out to me if he needs to, and I said yes."

Mateo closes his eyes and sighs. "Okay," he manages to get out behind gritted teeth.

I cautiously walk over to him. "I'm sorry, I—"

"Elle, I don't need an apology. Just promise me that you'll be careful and you won't let him fuck with your mind. The second he puts some shit in your head, please tell me."

"I promise."

He chews on the inside of his cheek, as if he's debating saying more. Since he doesn't, I move in closer. As I wrap my hands around his neck, he lets his thoughts out. "You know it's not your responsibility to take care of anyone, right?"

I freeze, staring at him. His dark eyes are swirling with sincerity and worry as he reaches for my hands to hold them. He clutches me gently as he says, "It's not your responsibility to fix people."

My muscles become rigid. "I know. I'm just being a nice person."

"Okay. I just don't want you to feel like you *have* to do something."

"I don't," I snap.

Mateo nods, a small smile sweeping across his face, but it doesn't reach his eyes. He draws my arms back up, placing my hands around his neck. "I'm sorry. I didn't mean to upset you," he says in a deep, soft voice that causes goose bumps to rise on my skin. "I just want to make sure you're also taking care of yourself."

"I am," I promise in a peaceful whisper.

He goes in for a kiss, and any annoyance I had toward him is washed away the moment his tongue engages mine. When he sticks his fingers under my shirt, my brain hazes over with lust, but he pauses before it gets too hot and heavy.

"You're distracting me from studying," he teases.

"I could say the same about you." I smirk. "How about we study for an hour, and then we'll take a break and reward each other for working so hard?"

Mateo chuckles. "Sounds like a fair deal to me."

Checking the last of my notes before my algebra midterm starts, Hunter claims his seat next to me. "Why didn't you answer my call the other day?"

My face drops. I completely forgot to call him back. I'm a fucking asshole. "I'm so sorry, Hunter. I was studying. I meant to call you, but I got caught up with school stuff."

"Oh."

"Was everything okay?"

"Yeah, just wanted to talk." He tugs at the collar of his shirt.

"Sorry," I repeat. "We can talk after the test."

"No, it's fine. I'm good now." The way his blue eyes lock onto mine reminds me of our strong, yet complicated, bond. Guilt pushes its way through my bloodstream.

"I'm sorry. That was a sucky friend move."

"Friends?" Hunter raises his eyebrows. "Is that what we are?"

"I thought…I guess so? But if you don't want to be, we don't have to be."

"No, I want to. I didn't think *you'd* want to be friends."

"Oh." I didn't even consider what I wanted. I assumed that he wanted to be my friend, so I blindly agreed.

Before we can say more, the professor hands out the test, and we begin our exam.

CHAPTER FORTY-NINE

Mateo

Now that our midterms are over, the plan was to go out for dinner tonight and have some fun back at my place. However, we nixed that idea when Bree came back to Elle's dorm early from a party, completely trashed. She's pretty fucked up, and neither of us felt comfortable leaving her alone, so we decided to stay in and babysit her while watching movies.

Thankfully, the effects of whatever is in Bree's system are making her sleepy. She's finally lying down in her bed with heavy eyes as she rambles on.

"I'm so happy for you twoooo." Bree elongates her words. "Mateo," she says, but I don't reply right away. "Mateo…Mateo…"

Chucking, I answer. "Yes, Bree?"

"You're soooo good for Ellieeeee."

"Oh, boy." Elle rolls her eyes while changing into pajamas.

"No, seriously. She tells me, like, so much stuff. You're, like, so perfect for her," Bree slurs.

"Oh, yeah?" I perk up, my curiosity piqued. "What does she tell you?" Smirking, I glance over at Elle. Her face drops, nervousness crossing her features.

"I tried to have her get with you when she was with that asshole, and she was all like, 'No, I'm with this asshole…'" Bree sits partially upright to do an inebriated, dramatic reading of how Elle and I got together.

"Okay, Bree." Elle tries to blow off her comment, crawling into her bed with me.

"Shh! You're not even here!" Bree says to her. "Anyway, Mateo, Ellie is all like, 'Mateo's so fucking sexy…'"

"Oh my god." Elle hides her face with the covers.

"And she's all like, 'His dirty talk is so fucking hot…'"

"This is my worst nightmare," Elle mumbles into the blankets.

"'He's so fucking good at eat—'"

"That's enough, Bree!" Her head shoots up, and I can't help but break out into laughter. "I never said any of that."

"No?" My brow arches, tickled with amusement.

"Lies!" Bree exclaims. "She also told me a secret..."

"Bree!" Elle shrieks, practically jumping out of her own skin.

My eyes widen. Now I'm *extra* curious. "What kind of secret?" I ask both of them to see if either will spill.

"There's no secret. She's making shit up. She's drunk."

"And high!" Bree says with a giggle.

"And high," Elle repeats.

I nod, pleasantly entertained. "Okay, then."

"I feel the vibe," Bree says to us.

"I'm sure you do," I respond.

"No. Like between you two...I feel it. The energy. It's there." Bree closes her eyes and starts to nod off.

Once Bree's finally out for the night, Elle suggests rewatching the last half of our movie that Bree talked over. As our eyes are on the TV, Elle curls up by my side. The sweet scent of her shampoo tickles my nose while the warmth of her body lures me closer. The movie carries on, but my thoughts are stuck on what Bree shared. Or rather, what Elle shared about me with Bree.

Smirking to myself, the ego boost has me carefully slipping my hand under Elle's shirt. Caressing her waist, goose bumps pattern her skin as she relaxes into my hold. Peppering her with kisses, I slink my finger between the elastic band of her pajama pants and her soft body, gliding it back and forth, waiting for an okay to drop my hand lower.

"Mateo," Elle whispers. "Bree is right there."

"So? It's hot." I nibble on her earlobe.

"You and I have different definitions of the word hot."

"Right, since you apparently don't like my dirty talk," I rasp.

She playfully glares at me, but I don't say anything. Instead, I wait for her to give me the green light. Just when I go to draw my hand away, assuming it's a no for tonight, she parts her legs for me.

A burst of adrenaline flies through me, blood rushing to my cock. *Fuck, yes.* Dipping my hand further into her pants, I begin teasing her, slowly grazing her clit. A small moan escapes from her lips.

"Shh. You gotta be quiet this time, baby," I whisper into the shell of her ear.

She nods, her body melting into the mattress as my finger enters her. Watching her is intoxicating. The way her chest moves up and down at a fast pace, the way she bites down on her lip to keep quiet, her writhing at my touch. The way she feels safe with me and hands her trust over makes me harder than anything else ever has. It electrifies my veins. I want her to always trust me. I want her to know that she can tell me anything.

"I wanna know your secret." The words tumble out of my mouth before I can stop them. But I do want to know. I want to know what she told Bree. I want to know everything.

My fingers move at a quick pace, expertly going back and forth between circling her clit and gliding in and out of her pussy. She struggles to stay quiet as she gives over more and more.

"Tell me, baby." The desperation rings in my voice as I beg.

"No way," she tries to softly say, but it comes out as a moan.

"Please tell me." My mouth moves to her neck. "I don't want there to be any secrets between us." Licking her throat, dragging my lips down to her collarbone, she shudders.

"Tell me your secrets, and then I'll tell you mine."

Like a record scratching, her statement brings me back to reality. I'm not proud of my past, and I'd rather leave all those skeletons stuffed in a closet. Groaning, I slide my hand out from her pants, placing it on top of her hips.

Elle chuckles. "You thought you could seduce me into telling you my secret?"

"Maybe." I shrug, even though that wasn't my initial intention. "Was it working?"

"No." Her lips twitch, giving away her lie. "Tell me your secrets first."

"Who says I have any secrets?"

"Oh, please. You're telling me that you shared everything from before I met you?" She calls me out, and I have no comeback. My mouth twists, and I move onto my back. "Thought so," she says.

Staring up at the ceiling, hesitancy tenses my muscles, but I force myself through it, asking, "What do you want to know?"

"Everything."

"I don't think you want to know everything." I laugh.

"Oh, I do," Elle says, leaning over to kiss me.

Her lips caress mine, our bodies molding to each other, but my self-criticism lingers in the back of my mind.

I hold her tighter. With each teasing swipe of her tongue, I'm able to silence the voice that's telling me I'm not cut out for any of this. And soon enough, we're too distracted by each other's bodies to finish our conversation.

CHAPTER FIFTY

Ellie

I decided not to go home for spring break, which means I've been spending the week at Mateo's place. Similar to the last school break, I've been working here and there, but Mateo has more hours than I do. Today is one of the days he has a shift, and I don't. While he's out, I take the opportunity to do my laundry.

Putting music on to help me get through the mundane task, I sing along to the Straylight Run album that is now downloaded on my phone. I've never had singing lessons before, but somehow my voice naturally knows how to move through the songs. My voice weaves in and out of melodies and harmonies. There's no rhyme or reason to which part I sing. I do whatever feels right for me. As I fold my clothes, I find myself closing my eyes and getting lost in the lyrics to "Existentialism on Prom Night."

No one is home, so I allow my voice to loudly fill the room.

"Sing me something soft, sad, and delicate, or loud and out of key, sing me anything. We're glad for what we've got, done with what we've lost, our whole lives laid out right in front of us."

"You can sing," Mateo's voice comes from behind. I whirl around, startled, and immediately stop the music. "You can sing," he repeats, astonishment lighting up his features.

"No, I—"

"That's your instrument. Your voice."

I shake my head. "I can't sing."

"Yes, you can," Mateo insists. "Sing again."

Heat rises to my cheeks. "No, I don't like singing in front of people. Just by myself."

Mateo's dark eyes gaze at me with wonder, excited that he's discovered another new thing about me. I go back to folding, turning away from him. "I'm almost done with my laundry."

Mateo wraps his arms around my waist. "Your voice is beautiful, baby," he whispers.

"It's really not, Mateo."

His arms slink away, and his tone grows more serious. "Why are you so embarrassed about everything?"

"What are you talking about?"

He sits down on his bed so that he can face me as I fold the remaining clothes in the basket.

"You're ashamed of almost everything about yourself."

I furrow my eyebrows. "Like what?"

"Your voice, your body, your thoughts."

Am I?

My voice, yes. My body, obviously. My thoughts—no one needs to know those.

My shoulders drop at the realization. I'm full of shame about practically every part of me.

"I've never had someone point that out before. I don't know why I'm like that…" My voice trails off, and I put the laundry basket on the floor so I can sit next to him.

"I wish you could see yourself through my eyes. You wouldn't spend another second being embarrassed about anything."

"How do you see me?"

Mateo stares at me for several moments. He looks like he wants to say something, but he doesn't. Instead of using his lips to talk, he grazes them onto mine. A sudden flush of warmth spreads from my core, temporarily incinerating my insecurities. My body gives in, and he gently leans more weight on me so that I lie back on the bed.

I let him strip me down, his large hands attempting to be tender but becoming rough. "You're so incredible, Elle," Mateo tells me as his eyes and hands continue to grope me. His words make me enter a magical trance, even if they're only full of lust and not love.

I'm thirsting for him, wanting every last drop.

Once I get Mateo's clothes off, he lies on top of me, struggling to remain gentle. His teeth nip at the thin flesh on my neck as his arm reaches down my body. I part my legs so that his fingers have easier access. "Tell me what you want, baby," he rasps against my throat.

"Fuck me, Mateo."

Mateo hovers over my body, giving me a quick peck before taking his hand to help guide himself into me. Both of us let out a loud exhale. His hips lightly roll, mine naturally moving with his.

The quicker he moves, the louder I become. The mixture of pleasure and pain is overwhelming and makes me dig my nails into his back. "Elle," he sighs out.

Oh, I think he likes my nails on him. I scrape them down his skin, and he moans. *Yep, he's definitely into it.* I love that I just made him make that sound. I do it a second time and moan with him this time.

He brings his body upright so that one of his hands is holding on to his headboard.

His thrusts are becoming harder, more intense. He moves faster and faster, with less self-control. Watching him become less restrained, knowing I'm the one causing the pleasure on his face, lights my veins with pleasure.

Mateo smiles and picks up my hips so that my body is on a slant. He kneels and keeps himself inside me while rubbing my clit. "Oh my god," I gasp.

His thumb moves over me, back and forth, adding pressure, then quickly taking it away.

I clench around his length, causing him to curse under his breath. My body squirms in delight while he makes me come with one hand and tightly holds my hip with the other. My orgasm rolls through me, a wave of ecstasy making me scream out his name. Every single muscle seizes up, then relaxes as I sink into the bed, closing my eyes. I lie there with my chest heaving for a few moments, when Mateo begins rocking his hips into me.

I instantly moan again and look up to see him biting down on his lip. A lock of his hair falls into his face, but he's too busy to notice. He puts his hand back on the headboard and moves slower, yet deeper than before. "Fuck. I love being inside you, Elle," Mateo pants.

"You're the only one…who's ever been inside me."

A rumble erupts from the back of his throat. "What else?" Mateo pleads with me to talk dirty to him. His sexy voice and rolling hips lure me into feeling confident. His eyes are glued to me.

"You're the only one who's ever made me this wet…" I say, out of breath. "You're the only one who…" He keeps thrusting deeper and deeper, and I struggle to talk.

"Who what, Elle?" He's desperate for me to continue.

The sensations in my body don't allow me to keep talking. Fireworks are going off inside me. Sparks run up and down my veins, my body shuddering as my back arches off the bed.

"I'm the only one who has ever made you come like this?"

The only thing I can do is moan.

"Fuck, yeah, I am," he says. The pleasure lasts several seconds but feels like an eternity. "You look so fucking gorgeous when you come for me."

A surge of self-assurance courses through me as I come back down from my high. "Flip over," I demand. "I want to be on top."

"Goddamn, Elena, I'm not gonna last long with you riding me." He protests but twists our bodies so that he's lying down, and I'm the one in control.

My hips instinctively know what to do, rocking back and forth. Mateo has a look of sheer bliss etched across his face, and this newfound power ignited in me makes me move faster.

Taking my nails, I drag them down his chest with just enough pressure to make it sting. Mateo squeezes my hips as his legs tense up. I watch what I'm capable of doing to him as he fights to keep his eyes open.

"Elle," his hoarse voice calls out my name as he comes.

After a few seconds, his body slackens, and he reaches for me, pulling me down to rest on his chest. His arms heavily drape over me as he catches his breath, hot air blowing on my neck. I thread my fingers in his thick hair and kiss his shoulder.

We lie there in silence for a long time, neither of us wanting this moment to end. It's as if our world only exists inside this bedroom. The way he worships my body awakens a new side of me—confident, indulgent, lustful, powerful. I fucking love it. I love who I'm becoming.

CHAPTER FIFTY-ONE

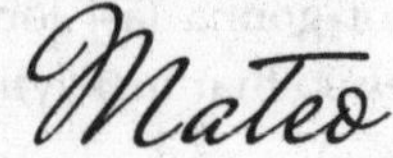

APRIL

Spraying cleaning solution onto the countertop at the Cozy Nook, I wipe it down while putting Steph on speakerphone. "What's up?" I ask her.

"So Valentina and I were just talking. You're going for your master's next semester, right?"

"Yep."

"Which means you're getting a bachelor's soon."

"That's usually how that works, Steph."

"So you're graduating next month."

I freeze, knowing that my sister's wheels are turning. "Yeah…"

"Why the hell didn't you tell us about your graduation, Mateo?"

Spraying down the display case, I vigorously circle the cloth as I speak to her. "I'm not going to my graduation. I'll have another one in two years. This one isn't a big deal."

"Yes, it is!"

"It's not."

"You have to go!"

"I don't have to do shit."

"Does Ellie know?" Steph asks, knowing that's the only way I'd even consider going.

"No." I toss the cloth to the side and lean on the counter, getting ready to argue with Steph. "I didn't tell anyone because I'm not going."

"Oh my god, you should invite Mr. Kevin from placement. I'm sure he'd love to come if he's free."

She's right. He would be here in a heartbeat. But this doesn't feel like any reason to celebrate since the actual degree I want is another two years away. I sigh into the phone, ready for this topic to be over. "I gotta go."

"Okay…but this conversation isn't over, Mateo!"

"Bye, Steph." Clicking the red button on my screen, I lock my phone and slide it into my pocket.

The bells above the front door chime, and several people enter. "Hey, stranger," a familiar voice resonates from the back of the group.

When I spot burgundy-colored hair, I smile. "Hey, Jas. How have you been?"

Jasmine saunters over to me while the people she's with stare at the drink menu. We haven't hooked up since Halloween, and a few weeks after I let her know that I want to give dating Elle an actual chance, so we've kept our distance ever since.

"Super busy. How about you? Are you still with that girl?"

"Ellie. Yeah, things are pretty serious."

She grins, studying me. "Look at you. You're all starry-eyed and smitten."

I laugh, heat forming around my shirt collar. "I guess."

"I'm so happy for you," she says. "We're all going to order and hang out here for a while. Can you fill me in on all about Ellie? I want to hear everything!"

"You got it."

After making their orders, I pop over to Jasmine so we can catch up before someone else comes in. I don't know if it's weird talking to my past fuck buddy about my current girlfriend, but Jasmine doesn't bat an eye when I go on about Ellie.

"I can't wait to meet her one day," Jasmine says. "Oh! Bring her to my end-of-the-year party!"

"All right, I'll see if she's down to go."

"I hope she is. I want to see the girl who's capable of taming you," she teases.

"Yeah." I glance past Jasmine and out the window. I speak more to myself than to her when I say, "I don't know how she did it, but I've changed since being with her. She allows me to be the type of person I always wished I could be."

CHAPTER FIFTY-TWO

Ellie

This morning, I woke up to birds chirping outside my window bright and early. A ray of sunlight spills into the dorm room, teasing me with the prospect of summer lingering in the air. Only a few more weeks to get through, and I'll have completed my freshman year of college.

Extending my arms out in a wide stretch, I finally get out of bed and check my computer. Opening my email, my breath gets caught in my throat when I see my inbox potentially holding the fate of my summer—and quite possibly my relationship with Mateo. The big, bold letters stating, "Congratulations," coil me with mixed emotions as I click to open the email.

I got the scholarship to France.

My jaw hangs open for a solid two minutes. I can't fucking believe it, but there it is. I stare at the blue box that reads, "Accept," in white letters, and then shift my gaze to the box that says, "Decline." All I have to do is click accept before the end of the semester, and one of my dreams will come true.

But my old friend, self-doubt, is quick to smother any hopeful thoughts.

This feels too good to be true and also feels like way too much. My frayed cuticles suffer the brunt of my anxiety as I pick at my nails, fixated on my screen.

I can't make this decision now. I still have to get through the rest of my classes and finals. I'll think about it closer to the deadline.

I slam my laptop shut and attempt to push away any thoughts of studying abroad for the summer out of my brain.

"Where are we going?" I ask for the millionth time as Mateo continues to drive.

"You'll see. We're almost there," Mateo responds, exactly the same for the millionth time. We've been driving on the parkway for at least fifteen minutes, and I still can't figure out where he's taking me. The car slows down as he exits off the highway and turns down a side street. There aren't a lot of houses where we are. The area is mostly consumed by nature.

Mateo pulls into a parking lot. "Where are we?" I ask.

"An arboretum," he says, parking his car.

"An arboretum?" This is the cutest thing ever.

"Yeah, I figured we could walk around and look at trees and shit."

"Trees and shit?" I snort.

"I don't want to do the boring dinner date crap." He frowns. "You hate it. I don't know what the fuck I'm doing, Elle—"

"Mateo—"

"I'm just making shit up as I go—"

"Mateo—"

"We can do something else. What do you want to do?"

"Mateo." I take his face in my hands and squish his cheeks together. "I love it." Mateo relaxes his shoulders. I pull his face toward mine and give him a quick kiss.

Our hands instinctively lock together, and the green crystal on my necklace sparkles in the sunlight. We walk and enjoy the beautiful landscape. The acres of trees and flowers are absolutely breathtaking.

"I've never been to an arboretum before," I share.

"Really?" Mateo asks, surprised. "You seem like the type of person who could spend all day looking at a leaf."

"And you seem like you'd never even want to step foot near a tree." I poke fun at his city roots. "If I hadn't met you under one, I'd assume you'd never even touched one before."

"Michelle told me about this place last year," he explains. "I've only been here once before, but it seemed like a nice place to take you."

"It is." I beam at him, and he happily glances down at me. "You're walking too fast, though."

"I'm walking my normal speed."

"Exactly. We're supposed to be strolling. You're so busy getting from point A to point B that you're not paying enough attention to all the beautiful things around you."

Mateo smiles and slows down his pace. "Better?"

"Much," I say as we aimlessly wander through the stunning scenery. I point out how unique and spectacular nature is, and Mateo seems to soak it in with me, observing the world around us.

"Bree and I are rooming together next year." I shift my attention off the landscape. "We confirmed it earlier."

"I'm assuming that means she doesn't mind me hanging around next year."

My stomach flutters at the thought of him thinking about our future, even if it's just one year ahead. "Of course not. She loves you."

And so do I.

Mateo grins as we continue to walk. The trail we're on takes us alongside a lake, and the way the sun is hitting the water seems to be out of some picturesque fairy tale.

"Wow," Mateo says as we drink in the scenery.

"It's so pretty," I agree with him. A few feet away, there is a small pier outstretched over the lake with a wooden gazebo. My body guides us in that direction.

When we walk into the gazebo, I hurry to the furthest end, getting as close as I can to the water. Mateo comes from behind and wraps his arms around me.

The water is calming for both of us. We don't speak much. Instead, we stay quiet in our embrace. My fingers trace over the vines and thorns that are tattooed on his forearms, and my touch seems to soothe him. Mateo holds me tighter and presses his cheek closer to mine. This would be the perfect moment to tell him that I love him if I weren't so scared of his rejection.

"What are your plans once the semester ends?" Mateo asks.

"Um..." My stomach contorts into a little knot at the mention of summer plans. I haven't said a word about France to Mateo since my freak-out. In all honesty, I'm scared that if I go, that will be it for us. Plus, I know Mom will need the extra support once I'm home. I should probably work over the summer instead of running off to a foreign country in order to help replenish her savings now that she's been spending Dad's life insurance.

I don't think I'm going to go to France.

"I don't have any plans," I say.

"I was thinking, maybe..." Mateo clears his throat. "Maybe you can spend some time here...with me?"

Warmth fills my heart. "I'd love that."

"Good." His tone brightens with joy. "I'll be here for most of the summer. I might go to Queens to see my family, but it's not going to be much."

"Okay."

"This is my last summer of freedom, so I want to have as much fun as possible, especially with my girl."

"What do you mean, this is your last summer of freedom?" I spin around to face him.

"Once grad school starts, I'll be crazy busy. I start my internship during the second semester, and it carries all the way through until I graduate. Not to mention that I need to work on top of everything."

"Oh, I didn't realize that."

"Yeah, we need to complete a bunch of clinical hours to graduate. And I'll have to write a lot of research papers and attend seminars. It's going to be a lot of work. I won't have as much free time as I do now."

"Okay." I gaze at him, smiling. "I'm really proud of you."

"*Proud* of me?" His brows shoot up, astonished that I uttered those words.

"Yes. You've been through a lot, and I'm proud that you've made it to this point and you want to keep going." He doesn't say anything. Instead, he looks past me, out at the water. His eyes widen with vulnerability. Then it dawns on me. "Has anyone ever told you that they're proud of you?"

Mateo still focuses on the water. "No." He threads his fingers through mine, guiding us back on the trail. "Well, Mr. Kevin probably did, but that's more of an obligation thing. I'll probably tell my pain-in-the-ass clients I'm proud of them when they're getting discharged too." He chuckles.

My heart breaks for the man in front of me who has never heard that someone was proud of him. Even though my parents were rarely clear-headed, they would still occasionally tell me that they were proud of me when I was younger, when I came home with a good grade or an ugly art project.

I look through Mateo's hardened outer shell and see a sad little boy who grew up too fast. Awareness strikes me, and I realize we're more alike than I originally thought. Although we haven't walked the same path, he hasn't felt like he was enough during times of his life either, just like me. I want to make him feel that he is more than enough for me.

"Well." My free hand loops around his arm so that we're even closer. "I'll have to tell you more often then."

I kiss his arm, which just so happens to be where his big scar is, and he watches me as I embrace his past. Even though we haven't outright said it, we are both committed to helping each other work through our individual issues. He's already helped me so much, and I don't think he realizes it. I'm a much better person around him—still fucked up, but a less crazy version of myself. I wonder if I have done the same for him.

"I was close to not getting into the social work program," he blurts out. His focus stays trained on the dirt path as he continues, "I almost got kicked out of UConn my freshman year."

"What?"

"I had some issues with my roommate," he states.

"What kinds of issues?"

The sound of the soles of our shoes padding along the dirt fills in the quiet gaps as I wait for him to divulge more. Sensing my eyes on him, he blows out a puff of air, prepping himself to talk.

"We didn't know each other beforehand, but for whatever fucking reason, he rationalized in his head that he wasn't happy he had to room with me. He made all these comments. At first, it was just stupid shit. It didn't bother me until one day he started claiming that I was stealing his shit, which I never stole after I got sent to JDC. I swear, Elle." Panic emerges in his eyes, as if I'm going to think less of him.

"I believe you."

Mateo focuses back on the trail. "Then, one day, he tried fighting me, and I won. And that was that."

My head tilts, trying to make sense of the last part, but there's something missing from his story. "Why did he fight you?"

He presses his lips together as if debating telling me the rest. "I got sick of the accusations and the rumors, so I got back at him the only way I knew how."

"How?"

He avoids eye contact at all costs. "I hooked up with his girlfriend."

"Oh."

"We were sleeping together for months until one day he caught us. He was livid and tried taking some swings. I dodged him, but then he started going after her, and I snapped. I lost it. I kicked the shit out of him. Bad. I was arrested, but even though he dropped the charges, the university said I was no longer allowed residency on campus. I was completely screwed, so Edgar said I could live at Michelle's place as long as I promised to stay out of trouble and pay rent."

I inhale and hold the air in my lungs for a few seconds before letting it out. "Oh."

"You wanted to know my secrets. That's one of them," Mateo says, still not looking at me. He pauses briefly to see if I'm going to talk, but I don't because my mind is too busy swirling with questions and comments. I know he has more stories like this, and I have a burning desire to dig deep into his soul and unearth every single one.

Mateo slows down his pace until we both stop walking. "Elle?"

I take a moment. "Thank you for telling me."

"That's it?"

"I mean, don't get me wrong. I have a lot of thoughts about what you just said, but I can't deny the fact that you seem like a completely evolved person now. We both have a lot of secrets, and the only way we can continue to have a trusting relationship is if we're honest with each other."

"You're…you're serious?"

I think over what I said, and although I'm not ready to share all of my secrets, I do believe that if the relationship is going to work, we can't both hide our pasts from one another. I don't think I'll ever tell him that I love him, but I can see myself warming up to the idea of me sharing several other secrets that are weighing me down.

"Yes," I state with a confirming nod of my head. "But I have a few questions."

"Go for it."

"How many times have you been arrested?"

"Only those two times I told you about."

My gaze flashes to the scar on his arm. "And you used to get into a lot of fights. Probably more than I realized?"

Mateo slowly nods his head, ashamed that it's his answer. "But I'm not like that anymore. I promise."

"I know." I reach for his hand to assure my belief in him. "Does any of this impact being a social worker, though? Don't you have to get licensed and stuff?"

"I'm on thin ice," he admits. "But I'll be okay, as long as I don't fuck up."

"You won't." Pressing onto my tippy toes, I kiss him, feeling his relief as the tension eases in his body. "Oh, one more question," I say, pulling away. "How many people have you slept with?" I know I've asked this before, but I never got an answer.

His mouth opens and shuts like a fish out of water. "I…I don't know."

"Like, more than ten?"

"Elle…" Mateo rocks on his heels. "I don't know the exact number, but it's a lot."

"Okay." Air gets trapped in my chest as I force my features to stay neutral. I knew that would be his answer, but I wasn't prepared to hear it.

As if he can read the thoughts in my head, he delicately caresses my cheek. "Elle." He draws my focus up to meet his eyes. "You're the only one I've truly cared about." Gazing at him, I'm met with pure honesty.

"Out of all the people I've had sex with, you're the only one I've cared about too," I say, making light.

Mateo chuckles, then brings me in for a gentle kiss.

CHAPTER FIFTY-THREE

Ellie

MAY

The refreshing spring weather surrounds Bree and me as we walk through the Great Lawn on our way to class. The trees and flowers are blooming, and the campus has a familiar feel to when I first moved in.

"We need to go shopping for some sexy spring clothes," Bree states.

I snort. "I don't know if the thirty bucks in my bank account will get me much."

"Okay, so we'll bargain shop. I'm so good at finding the best deals."

"Works for me." I shrug. "We can go later, after class."

"Perfect!" She blows me a kiss before parting ways, heading to the fine arts building.

I walk along in the sunshine when I hear someone call out my name.

"Ellie! Wait up!" Hunter jogs over to me.

I spin to face him. "Everything okay?"

"Yeah. I-I wanted to…" His eyes shift around, making sure we're talking in private. "I never apologized for busting into your room drunk. That was an asshole move."

"It was." Even though I'm still worried about him and what triggered the whole outburst. "I didn't think you remembered doing it. You haven't brought it up since."

"I know." He nods. "I didn't want to talk about it, but I've been thinking a lot about things lately. I'm sorry I bombarded you. Let me make it up to you."

"Hunter, I don't need you to make anything up to me. Just don't do it again." I turn to leave, and he walks alongside me.

"Let me at least buy you lunch as an apology," Hunter presses. He and his need for big apologies. "Or ice cream, even."

"It's okay, Hunter. It was no big deal."

"All right." He eases up on the topic but still treks next to me. "Oh, I keep forgetting to let you know that I came across some of your stuff in my room from before we broke up."

"You did?" My forehead crinkles, trying to recall what I left at his frat.

"Yeah. A pair of earrings, a black sweater, and I think a few other things."

"Are you sure they're mine?" I make sure to give him a pointed look when I ask the question.

"Yes, but if you don't want your stuff, I can just give it to another girl."

"No." My face scrunches in disgust at his gifting my belongings to one of his hookups.

"I'm kidding, Ellie." He laughs at his own joke. "I'm not going to pawn your things off. But if you want them, let me know when you want to come pick them up."

"Yeah, I guess."

"Tomorrow?"

"Sure."

I'm not sure if it's the sun or his mood, but his face brightens. "See you tomorrow. You know where to find me."

The next day, I do a little twirl in my full-length mirror, checking out my new black skirt that I picked up yesterday while I was bargain shopping with Bree. It turns out she was able to help me stretch my thirty dollars more than I imagined. She also convinced me to pick up colorful lace thongs to surprise Mateo with. I opted for the bright red one for today.

With some spare time, I decided to stroll into town. The *Welcome to Mahogany Ridge* sign has daffodils around it in full bloom. I'm going to stop by Hunter's in a little bit to pick up the last of my things, but I figured I'd pop into the Cozy Nook to surprise Mateo beforehand.

The scent of coffee grinds circles around me as I enter. Mateo is busy talking to a girl with burgundy-colored hair at the opposite end of the counter, so he doesn't notice me. She's laughing at whatever he's saying, and I pause, as my mind jumps back to earlier in the school year with Hunter and Delilah. The girl takes out some money and tries to hand it to Mateo.

"It's on the house," Mateo tells her, reminiscent of when he first told me that. My chest tightens, knotted with jealousy. Mateo's attention turns to the entrance where I stand frozen. "Hey, baby. Come here." He waves me over. Cautiously padding over, I sidle up next to him while staring at the taller, more mature-looking college student in front of me. "This is my girlfriend, Ellie," Mateo tells her. "Ellie, this is my friend, Jasmine."

"Hi," I say.

"Hey, Ellie. I've heard so much about you!" Jasmine gushes. "It's so nice to meet you."

My brows knit together in confusion as I glance up at Mateo. He has never mentioned this person to me before, but apparently, he talks to her about me. My attention goes back to Jasmine. "Nice to meet you too."

"I need to run, but let's catch up soon, Mateo." She turns to me. "I'm happy I finally got to put a face to the name. See you two later." Jasmine leaves, and it's just me, Mateo, and Lynn in the coffee shop.

"Who was that?" I ask Mateo as he walks back around the counter.

"That's Jasmine," he states, as if I missed out on our introduction from twenty seconds ago.

"Who is she?" The bite in my question has Lynn glancing up to gauge my reaction.

"A friend." Mateo picks up the edge in my voice. "Why don't you come in the back?" He waves me over, and I follow him into the office, shutting the door behind us. "What's going on?"

"Nothing." I cross my arms, leaning my weight against his desk. Mateo looks like he's fighting back a smile, which fuels my anger. "I just think it's funny that—"

Mateo starts chuckling.

"What the hell are you laughing at?"

"I didn't think girls actually said that." He composes himself, schooling his features. "Go on. Tell me what you think is funny."

"Don't be a dick."

"I'm not trying to be. I'm…"

"You're what?"

Mateo's lips twitch. "I'm amused that you're jealous."

"I am not jealous!"

"No?"

"Who is she, Mateo?"

"She's just an old friend. Nothing to worry about, baby." Mateo reaches for my hand and interlaces our fingers together.

Studying his eyes, my muscles relax little by little. He's not defensive or aggressive. He's Mateo—his calm, gentle self. "Well, I don't like it when you hang out alone with friends who are girls," I mumble my nonsensical, envious thoughts.

"Seems like a bit of a double standard."

"What do you mean?"

"I trust you enough to be alone with your ex-boyfriend, but you don't trust me enough to be alone with a friend."

"Okay, just to clarify, I'm not spending time alone with Hunter. I'm just going to pick up my stuff and leave," I remind Mateo. I told him about it yesterday after my run-in with Hunter. Mateo let out a strained "Okay," and we left it at that. "And it's not that I don't trust you to be alone with Jasmine."

"Then what is it?" He loops a strand of hair behind my ear.

Heat rises to my cheeks. "I don't want to say. It's stupid."

"Nothing in that beautiful head of yours is stupid."

My attention goes to his shirt instead of looking at him directly. "I get… insecure."

Mateo brings his hand to my chin so that my head tilts up and our eyes connect. "You are the most incredible woman I have ever met. I don't want anyone else but you." He brushes his thumb over my jawline. "I swear," he adds.

Sighing out a breath, the tension between my shoulder blades eases. "I believe you," I say. Because honestly, with the way he's looking at me, it's impossible for me to think that he's lying. "Sorry I had a mini freak-out. My mind went somewhere else."

"It's all good, baby."

"I don't want to be with anyone else either," I say.

"Good." He smiles. "It's settled then."

Mateo softly places his lips on mine and moves his hands down to my waist, gently embracing me. My hands wrap around his neck and play with the ends of his hair. He parts his lips from mine for a brief moment. "You're perfect, Elle." I push our lips back together and drag my hands down his chest and stomach.

His tongue swipes mine, and I play along with his teasing. As our kiss deepens, our hands get friskier. It's crazy how quickly this boy can light up my entire being with passion and lust. Without a second thought, I draw my fingers to his pants and unbutton them.

He's startled by my eagerness but sticks his hands under my shirt, gripping my waist. "You look so fucking good in this skirt," Mateo says before moving his mouth to my earlobe. A small sigh escapes my mouth. "What do you want to do?" Mateo asks, the thickness of his voice sending shock waves through me.

"You," I whisper, my breathing already becoming labored. Any annoyance I had vanishes, and I am completely consumed by desire.

Mateo stops and looks at me, tucking a piece of hair behind my ear. "You up for something a little different?"

The concept of different makes me a little bit nervous, but I know that whatever it is, I'll be safe with him. "Yeah," I say.

Mateo's eyes rake over my body. "You have to be quiet, though. Okay, baby?"

I nod, even though I know that's not possible when it comes to him. Mateo smiles and quickly spins me around. I stand there with my back facing him, hearing his pants unzip and the condom wrapper rip open.

Mateo's body gets close to mine. "If it's too much, tell me to stop," his alluring voice softly says in my ear. My heart is racing, not knowing what is about to happen. I nod again, and as soon as he sees that I agree, he pushes my body forward, bending it over his desk. My eyes widen with excitement.

Mateo flips up my skirt and lets out a little gasp. "This is new," he says, rubbing his hand along my red lace thong. "So sexy." I wait for him to pull it off, but instead, he just pushes it to the side and impatiently enters me. I draw in a sharp inhale and tense up. "Relax, baby," Mateo coaxes me while pushing on my lower back to create more of an arch.

His fingers sink into my hips as he cautiously moves me forward and back. *Holy shit. This is the deepest I've ever felt him inside of me.* I firmly press my lips together to smother my noises, but I don't know if it's doing any good.

"Can I go a little faster?" Mateo's voice strains.

I nod, keeping my mouth closed. He moves us at a faster pace, and I search for anything on his desk to hold on to. Sparks of pleasure mixed with pain ignite my nerve endings, but it feels so fucking good.

"Fuck, Elle," Mateo whispers. "I've been wanting to take you like this since the day I fucking met you." His movements are fast, and I need some type of release, so I grip on to my own hair. "I think about bending you over like this when I jerk off." Mateo clutches my hips tighter as he moves in and out of me even harder.

"Tell me more," I say in a sultry voice that I don't even recognize.

Mateo lets out a deep chuckle. "You want to know what else I think about when I jerk off?"

"Yes," I moan.

He's trying to catch his breath in between his words. "I think about…if you ever go on the pill…I can fill up every fucking inch of you…and watch my cum drip out of you."

His honest words make me blush, yet again. Mateo spanks me, causing me to jolt and let out a little squeal.

He slows down but pounds into me even harder, each moment hitting the spot that makes my toes curl. My knees weaken as my thighs shake. I grasp on to my shirt and put what little fabric I can into my mouth to cover up my sounds.

"I want to hear you," Mateo demands. "I don't give a fuck."

I open my jaw, and my moans are set free each time Mateo thrusts deeply into me. Pleasure floods my entire body, causing me to be even louder as I reach my orgasm. He starts to moan with me, and I feel his pace dramatically ease up until he finally stops. He stays inside me for a minute and catches his breath while he enjoys the view.

A few moments later, both of us adjust ourselves. Mateo zips up his pants and watches me comb my fingers through my hair. "How was that?"

"Incredible," I tell him. My curiosity from before is still lingering. "Do you…" I stop myself from asking the question.

"What?" Mateo crinkles his brows.

"Do you…think about me a lot?"

"Yep," he says as he helps fix my hair.

"Oh." I straighten my skirt. "Do you think about any other stuff with me?"

Mateo laughs. "Yep." I want to know all the filthy fantasies that have crossed his imagination, but I don't press it since he didn't offer up any more information. "You good?" Mateo asks as he approaches the door.

"I think so." I give myself a once-over, and everything seems to be in order. Mateo opens the door, and Lynn turns away from the counter and faces us with a wide grin. My face feels like it's turning the color of a tomato, and I focus on the floor.

"You didn't hear anything," Mateo tells Lynn, and she bursts out laughing. I glance around to see if there are any patrons, and luckily, no one else is here.

"I-I should probably get going," I stumble over my words.

Mateo smiles. "Okay." He comes to me and gives me a hug. "I have a gig tonight, so I'll see you tomorrow."

"Oh god, I completely forgot. I should go…"

Mateo shakes his head. "No, it's at some crappy bar way out of town. Stay here and hang out with Bree." Mateo puts his lips close to my ear. "I'll play a private show for you another time."

I giggle and give him a small kiss. I awkwardly wave goodbye to Lynn and then head toward Hunter's frat to reclaim my belongings.

CHAPTER FIFTY-FOUR

Ellie

An icky feeling crawls up my skin as I trek up the driveway to the gray frat house. I'm so thankful to have only been here a few times last semester. I don't know if I could've stomached more rowdy parties.

Tapping my knuckles against the front door, it takes a few moments for it to open. Rhett, the sleazeball of the frat, comes into my line of view. "Whoa. I never thought I'd see you here again." Rhett gives me a smug smirk.

A girl wearing a sorority tee and obnoxiously chewing gum pops up by his side. "Who's that?"

"That's Ellie," Rhett states. "Hunter's..." He wants me to finish the sentence.

"Ex." I glare.

"Cool," the girl says. "I'm Tammy, Rhett's girlfriend." She drapes her arms over Rhett's body, and I laugh to myself at the thought of Rhett being a decent boyfriend.

Hunter appears, shooing away the two of them. "Hey, Ellie." He gestures for me to come inside, and I follow him up the stairs.

Rhett's eyes are glued on us. "Where are you two going?" he baits.

"Hanging out," Hunter says, not turning around to look at Rhett.

"Have fun." Rhett snickers as he watches us enter Hunter's room.

Anxiety zips up my spine when I enter Hunter's room. He closes the door, and my eyes wander about as I stay glued to the wall. His room is slightly disorganized, but nothing horrible. He has a pile of dirty clothes sitting on his desk chair and a few textbooks on the floor.

"Sorry. He's still an asshole," Hunter says.

I shrug. "It's fine."

"I don't remember where I put your stuff," he says, opening a drawer and fishing around. After several moments of searching, he comes up empty-handed. "It's here somewhere, Ellie, don't worry," he assures me as he tries another drawer.

"Need help looking?" I offer.

"No, I'll find it. Why don't you sit and hang out while I look?"

Glancing over to his chair, I note that it's occupied by a mound of laundry. Peeling myself off the white-yellow wall, I slowly make my way to sit on his bed. "If it's no big deal if you can't find it."

"Nah, it's in here somewhere." Hunter moves toward his desk. "I wasn't sure if you were actually going to show up."

"Why?"

"I didn't know if he'd let you come, so I wasn't sure if I should expect you or not."

"Mateo doesn't control me. I do whatever I want." I make an obvious dig.

"That's a dangerous move with you." He smirks.

"Oh?" My brow arches. "And what do you mean by that?"

"Nothing."

He turns, going back to his task, and I take a few moments to observe him. He doesn't have the same distraught look that he did earlier in the semester, but I'm still bothered about the night he showed up at my dorm in distress. Rolling my lips together, I decided to ask the question that's been sitting at the tip of my tongue. "Is everything okay?" There's a beat of silence, so I continue, "I don't know what happened, or what's going on, but you really worried me that night."

"You're worried about me, Ellie?" There's a strum of pleasure rising in his voice as he glances to look at me.

"Don't play stupid. You know I'm worried about you. Just because we're not together doesn't mean I stopped caring."

Or wanting to know why you were hysterically crying out your dead sister's name.

"I'm okay."

"Do you want to—"

"No, I don't want to talk about it." His features draw in tight. "Things got pretty ugly at home." His mind seems to drift off to somewhere else, but he reins himself back in. "It's over now, though."

"Is that why you looked…" I try to think of a polite way to say that he looked awful.

"Like shit?" He chuckles. "Yeah."

"I'm sorry I wasn't there for you," I say, guilt intruding on my thoughts. I know his mind has gotten dark in the past, thinking about killing himself, and I knew he was suffering this time around, but I did the bare minimum. Drifting my attention off him, I shift in my seat, sensing his eyes on me.

Hunter clears his throat. "Ian has Mr. Turner this year," he informs me about his younger brother, changing the subject.

"Oh no. I feel so bad for him." I remember how horrible he was as an English teacher.

"You remember that time you cursed Mr. Turner out?"

"I did not curse him out. I just happened to let a few curse words slip when he gave me a bad grade on my paper," I correct him.

"That *was* some shit. Your paper was awesome."

"Thank you." I laugh, and Hunter laughs with me as we travel down memory lane, reminiscing on stupid high school stories. Stories that now seem like a lifetime away. "How does your brother like St. Anne's, besides Mr. Turner?"

Hunter's disposition goes back to how it originally was. "Fine, I guess. We don't really talk much. You know how he is." I think back on the several times I've tried to interact with Ian, and he was always so quiet. "Although," Hunter continues. "He did tell me a few months ago that he heard us in the shower once." He starts chuckling, and my face drops.

"Oh my god." My hand flies up to my mouth, mortified.

Still laughing, he tells me, "It's fine, Ellie. Seriously. No big deal."

"You always told me he was downstairs!"

"I thought he was."

My mind flashes back to the countless times Hunter's parents would leave us alone, and we would strip down and spend our time in either his bed or his shower, or both. Getting close—extremely close—but I would always draw the line at sex.

In those moments, he'd build me up. Make me feel on top of the world. I can still hear his whispers, his breath tickling the shell of my ear.

"You're so beautiful," Hunter says as he admires my naked body. He holds me as we lie in his bed, skin on skin. We lie over the blankets, choosing to keep each other warm by our body heat. "I love you, angel." He kisses my forehead, and I smile at my pet name.

My eyes flicker up to look at his. "I'm so glad I have you."

Hunter's fingers gently play with my hair. "I'm glad you do too. You needed someone in your life to protect you and take care of you. I'm always going to be here to save you, Elena."

My stomach twists in knots. I hate that one of those memories popped into my head. Tightly wringing my hand around my left wrist, my eyes shift around, looking for anything to change the subject.

I notice a few of his papers sitting on his bed marked with an A. "Look at you, killing it!" I say, picking them up, thankful to have found something else for us to focus on.

Hunter shifts to see what I'm talking about and smiles. "Are you snooping through my stuff?" He stops searching for my belongings and sits down across from me on the bed.

"Sorry. I didn't mean to. I just saw the A and got excited."

Hunter chuckles. "You've always been my little cheerleader."

"I'd make a pretty sucky cheerleader," I say, laughing at my own expense. "I can't even do a cartwheel, and I'd look horrible in the uniform."

"I don't know. You look pretty good in that skirt right now." Hunter's gaze drops down to my bare legs. Red flags go off in my head. "I'm having a really nice time spending time with you," he says. "Are you?"

"Um…yeah." My pulse picks up. I attempt to casually shuffle toward the edge of the bed.

"I've missed you, Ellie." Hunter's voice is husky. He shifts himself closer to me. "I missed everything about you, even the way you drive me crazy with that little attitude of yours," he teases. "I've missed your laugh…and how soft your hair feels." Hunter goes to push a strand of hair behind my ear, but I jerk my head away.

"Hunter—"

"I don't want to stay away from you anymore. I need you, Elena."

I go to stand, but Hunter grabs me by the arm and slams me back down onto his bed.

My heart pounds so hard it could break through my ribs.

I don't know what's happening.

Fight, flight, or freeze. Out of the three choices, my fucking brain chooses to freeze.

The weight of his body is on top of mine. I can't move.

My chest tightens.

I can't breathe.

I can feel Hunter's fingers run over the outside of my underwear. The same underwear Mateo had just seen and consensually touched. Hunter makes sure I can feel how hard he is, even through his gym shorts. He rubs himself up against my clit.

Again.

Again.

Again.

He puts pressure on my body. He doesn't enter me, but he pushes on top of me so that I know he has the power.

His body threatens mine.

I'm frozen.

My brain has accepted that whatever is going to happen will happen.

I can't move.

I can't fight.

I can't breathe.

I can't fucking breathe.

Hunter abruptly jumps off me.

I fling myself off the bed, gasping for air. My heart is thrashing as my chest compresses. My hands shake as I wind up, attempting to hit him, but before I can, Hunter catches my wrist and grabs the other one so that I can't try with that hand, either.

I try to yank free, but he pulls me closer, tightening his grip. My blood flow constricts, making my hands go numb. "You just…you just almost…" I stammer. No other words are coming out.

"No. *You* did, Ellie." Hunter's voice is deep and commanding. "*You're* the one who chose to come here wearing a skirt. *You're* the one who chose to sit on my bed. *You're* the one who was flirting with me."

Tears are welling up, and I violently shake my head at his comments.

"*You* wanted this, Elena."

"No!"

"Why else would you wear that when you knew you were seeing me?" His blue eyes are piercing through mine. "You know what turns me on. You know better than anyone else."

Tears are now gushing down my face. I try to catch my breath and wiggle out of his grip.

"You did this on purpose. You knew exactly what you were doing. You were trying to fucking tease me again. You wanted this."

"Stop!" I shout and finally tug my wrists out of his hands. I reach for my phone as quickly as possible and run out of his room, down the stairs, past Rhett and his girlfriend making out on the couch, and out the front door.

As soon as I'm met with the warm spring air, I take a deep inhale, attempting to get my lungs to fill up, but I break out into a sob. My eyes are so watery that it's making my eyesight blurry. It's difficult to see the sidewalk.

Millions of thoughts are racing through my head the faster I walk.

Did I cause this? I did know that Hunter likes me in skirts, since he'd always tell me in high school. I didn't wear it for him, though. I didn't even wear it for Mateo. I wore it for myself. Obviously, the skirt is a turn-on, though, because Mateo clearly liked it.

Fuck. I should've known. I should've worn something else. Why did I sit on Hunter's bed? Was I leading him on? I didn't think I was flirting, but sitting on a boy's bed sends a certain message, and I should've realized that. I'm so fucking stupid. I could've moved the clothes off his chair. I could've fucking stood up the whole time. I didn't need to sit, especially on Hunter's bed.

He had forcefully lain on top of me and touched me. He used his power to control me. He always does. Nothing happened, though. He didn't actually enter me.

A cyclone of confusion consumes me. My chest compresses, and my body trembles. I'm lightheaded. Black spots are flooding my vision. I'm only a few blocks away from school, but I need to sit. My body half collapses onto someone's lawn, and I close my eyes.

Inhale. Exhale.

Inhale. Exhale.

Inhale. Exhale.

CHAPTER FIFTY-FIVE

Ellie

"Sound good?" Mateo's voice slices through my thoughts as we cuddle on my bed after my philosophy class.

"I'm sorry, what?" I wasn't paying attention to anything he's said the past several minutes. Professor Boland gave me a knowing nod as I left class, prompting my memory of needing to respond to the scholarship email.

Mateo puts his hand on my head and playfully wiggles it around. "Where are you today?"

"Sorry. I just have a lot on my mind."

"Like what?"

I shrug. "School." It's partly true. However, I can't get what happened in Hunter's bedroom out of my head. I've felt sick to my stomach, riddled with guilt and shame. I don't want anyone to know what just happened, especially Mateo.

This secret will never get out.

"Anything I can help you with?"

I smile. "No, but thank you."

Mateo kisses me and wraps one arm around my body, drawing me into him. I think he enjoys the closeness as much as I do. His tongue parts my lips open as my legs coil around his.

"Where's Bree?" Mateo rasps.

"At her friend's," I say into his mouth. He smiles against my lips, and his hands travel under my shirt. His fingertips stroke my skin, giving me goose bumps.

"Did you have fun in my office the other day?" he asks, moving his mouth to my throat.

I tilt my chin upward so he can cover more area. "Yes," I sigh. My body is already hot, aching for more of him. The only person I ever want to control my body, aside from myself, is Mateo.

Mateo's phone rings, and he takes it out of his back pocket, tossing it on my desk without looking at it. My attention flickers over to it and sees his sister's name flashing.

"Stephanie is calling you," I tell him as he makes his way to my collarbone.

"Don't care."

"Mateo, answer it. It could be important."

He shifts his body over mine. "It's not."

"How do you know?"

Mateo pulls my shirt up slightly, exposing my stomach. "Because she's just calling to bitch about me not going to my graduation."

I abruptly push him off me and sit up. "What do you mean you're not going to your graduation?"

"I'm going to graduate again in two years. There's no point in going to this one."

"Mateo, you have to go. This is a huge deal for you."

He lets out a groan. "I shouldn't have said anything."

"Did you think I wouldn't notice you not showing up to your graduation?"

His eyes move off me to the ceiling. "They want to throw me a party," he mutters.

"Mateo! Why did you keep me out of the loop about this?"

"Because it's stupid. I don't want to make a big deal out of this."

"Well, too bad because I'm going to call up Stephanie and tell her that you're going to your graduation. *And* that she can throw you a party." I reach over him and snatch his phone.

"You better not!"

Mateo tries to get his phone from me, and we wrestle while laughing and grabbing at each other. I hop on top of him, pinning him to my bed. My arm raises up, holding on to his phone. "You think I can't flip you over and get that?" Mateo taunts.

"I know you can. But I don't think you want to." I grind my hips over his jeans, and a grin flashes across his face.

"Elena, are you trying to seduce me so that you get your way?"

"I might be." I move my hips again. "It seems like you need some persuasion."

"I could use *a lot* of persuasion."

My free hand runs over his stomach. "I'll give you whatever you want." My voice drips with lust, and I feel him getting hard underneath me. "As long as you give me what I want." I shake the phone in my hand.

His eyes narrow. "You're playing dirty."

"Very dirty."

My hips move faster, and he groans, "Fine." I stop my movements and hand him his phone. "Hell, no. If you're gonna make me do this, then we're fucking first." Mateo tosses his phone, then flips me over.

After much persuasion from me, he eventually calls Stephanie and agrees to the graduation and party. Once the call ends, he focuses his attention back on me. His hands run up and down my partially covered body. We comfortably lie in the stillness, our legs intertwined. My fingertips brush over the stubble on his face. "I'm happy you're going to your graduation."

"You made it incredibly difficult to say no." He smirks.

My fingers continue to explore him, outlining his tattoos as my mind roams through a myriad of questions. "What was your first impression of me?" I softly ask.

"Nice rack."

I glare at him. "That's not true."

"Of course it is," he states, as if it's obvious. "Then, as we talked, I saw that there was something else hiding behind your eyes, and I wanted to know more. The night that we accidentally fell asleep in your bed after staying up talking, that's when I *knew* I was in some deep shit because I was catching feelings. That's never happened before. I had no idea it would lead to this."

Yeah. You're telling me.

"What was your first impression of me?" Mateo asks.

I think back to when I first laid eyes on him. Most people would normally say that a physical feature lured them in, but I remember very distinctly my first impression of him. "It's going to sound weird."

"Oh boy."

"It's not bad."

"Okay, then what was it?" Mateo hesitantly inquires.

"When I first saw you, it felt like I knew you."

"I looked like someone you knew?"

I shake my head. "No, it didn't have anything to do with you physically. It was like there was something about you that *felt* familiar."

His features lift up in shock, as if I just read his mind. "I felt it too."

"You did?"

"Yeah." Mateo thinks for a brief second. "Maybe we know each other from a past life."

I smile. "You think that?"

"Yeah. I thought about it before." He interlocks his fingers with mine. "Maybe our souls already know each other. Maybe we traveled through different lifetimes together."

Joy swims through me at the thought of our two souls journeying together, learning from one another so that we can be better people. I adore the fact that he has thought about us like that. I didn't think it was possible for me to love him any more than I already did, but after hearing that, my feelings for him have quadrupled.

"My turn to ask you a question," Mateo says.

"Shoot."

"If it's too personal, you don't have to answer."

"Okay..."

"How come you don't like it when..." He clears his throat. "When I put my hand on your head?" My brow furrows, unsure of what he's referring to. He realizes that I don't understand what he's saying, so he clarifies. "When you're blowing me."

"Oh." I pull away from his embrace.

"You don't have to answer. I was curious if it was a personal preference, or maybe something you've never done before..."

I slink out of bed to change into clothes. "Um..." I say, grabbing his shirt and throwing it over my head. "I don't think you want to know the story."

"Story?" Mateo instantly sits up.

I find my yoga pants and pull them up. "Story is the wrong word," I say. "Either way, I don't think you'd want to hear it."

"I want to hear it if you want to tell it."

If I want to tell it.

The words echo in my head. I haven't told anyone before. Not that it's a big deal. It's just embarrassing.

"Promise you won't get mad?" I gently ask.

Mateo's body tenses. "I can't promise that, Elle."

"Well, can you promise me that if you do get angry, you won't act on it?" I offer another option.

Mateo stares into my eyes, trying to figure out what I'm about to tell him. He gives in. "I promise."

CHAPTER FIFTY-SIX

Ellie

"Ten days, Hunter. Ten fucking days!" I shout at him. The two of us stand across from each other in his bedroom, breathing heavily. We were having a screaming match, which escalated to us throwing things around his room. I broke a wooden picture frame that was holding an image of the two of us from a date we went on months ago. I might've also broken his remote.

"I thought we were done, Elena!" Hunter yells back.

"So you were celebrating your newfound freedom by getting with some girl you barely know?" I pick up a random book on his desk and aim it at his stomach, but it ends up slamming against the wall instead.

"I was upset." He tries to justify his behavior.

I wildly laugh. "You were so upset you got Katie to give you a blow job to make you feel better?" Katie is a few years older than him and works at the country club his parents are a part of. I always had a suspicion that she liked him, but now I have confirmation.

"Well, I sure as hell wasn't going to get it from you," he snaps at me, stopping my laughter. His words stab my heart, and I can feel the sting behind my eyes. I try with all my might to hold back my tears. I don't want him to see me cry. Hunter notices that I'm upset, and his tone changes back to normal. "I didn't mean it like that, Ellie."

"No? Please enlighten me and tell me what you really meant by that."

Hunter plops down in his desk chair, partially defeated. "I know you're not ready. I didn't mean to throw it in your face like that."

"Then why did you?" I cross my arms and stand over him. Hunter has been begging me to go down on him for months. He has a legitimate argument. He does it for me, so why don't I reciprocate? I've never had a rebuttal other than I wasn't ready. Maybe I'm a prude. I don't know. He has been patiently waiting—that is, until last week, apparently.

Hunter shrugs. "Because you make me crazy, and I say shit I don't mean when I'm mad." His defenses are dropped, and he seems sincere. "This was the first time you broke it off with me. I thought we were really done this time, Ellie. I thought you didn't want to put up with my shit anymore."

My energy shifts to match his. "You know I don't think of you like that." I glance down at my feet. "I just needed a break."

"Because I'm too much."

I lift my head to look at him. "No, you're not— "

"Yes, I am. I'm too much for you to deal with, and you don't trust me."

"I never said any of that."

"So you do trust me?"

"I..." He holds my gaze, waiting for an answer. Obviously, I trust him. He's the only one who has ever known the real me. "Yeah, I trust you."

"Then believe me when I say that I thought we were really done this time." His hands reach for mine, and he draws me closer. He wipes the last of my tears and cups my face in his hand. "I love you, Ellie."

"I love you too."

Hunter pulls me in for a kiss, and I am under his spell. He positions me so that I'm straddling him on his chair. "I've missed you so much," Hunter says between our mouths touching.

"I missed you too."

"Ten days is way too long," he says, sticking his hands under my shirt. I nod in agreement, and he pulls my shirt over my head. I can tell that he's getting hard as he quickly unclasps my bra. "I'm so sorry, Ellie. I never want to hurt you, ever," he says right before sucking on my nipple.

I lightly moan. Hunter takes my hand and puts it inside his sweatpants.

Insecurity twists inside me. What else did he and Katie do? Where were they when they did stuff? Why was she so willing to blow him, but it's such a big deal for me? Maybe it's really nothing, and I'm just making a mountain out of a molehill. If she can do it, then I certainly can. She doesn't even love him. Did he see her naked? Does she look better than I do? How do I make sure that he knows I'm the better choice? He loves me, and I love him. This shouldn't be a big deal.

Before I know it, I've convinced myself to get on my knees in front of him. Hunter lets out a sigh at the sight of me about to go down on him. I have a horrible feeling in my stomach. I don't want to do this, but I feel like I have to. He's my boyfriend who I love. It's long overdue, and if he doesn't get it from me, who knows if he'll try again with someone else.

I put him in my mouth, and the pit in my stomach grows. I don't like being on my knees. This doesn't seem sexy or fun. It feels degrading. I should've done this on the bed at least. My heart is pounding as I hear Hunter's deep moans. I don't like this. I want to stop. I slow down to lift my head up, and he puts his hands on the back of my head, not allowing me to stop. I try to force my head up, but he's stronger than me. He moves my head up and down so fast that I can barely process what is happening. My eyes are squeezed shut, with tears welling behind them. I try to stop, but I can't. He won't let me.

It all happens so quickly. His strong movements. His moans. My neck and shoulders tensing up. My palms pushing against his legs. My rapid heart rate. My chest tightening. Holding back my tears. The awful feeling rising in me. His cum filling up my mouth and making its way down my throat.

Hunter releases me with a smile. I feel disgusting. My hands are shaking as I wipe my mouth. "That was amazing, Ellie," Hunter happily states and relaxes back in his chair. He doesn't seem fazed by anything.

"Good," I say with a forced smile. "I'm going to go to the bathroom." I excuse myself and scoop up my shirt, throwing it on before exiting his room. I go into the bathroom and stare at the girl in the mirror. I allow myself to take long breaths, bringing down my heart rate.

CHAPTER FIFTY-SEVEN

Ellie

My heart pounds, analyzing Mateo's expression.

He looks livid, but also…sad? I can't get a read on him.

He hasn't said anything since I finished the story. Maybe this was a bad idea. I should've just kept this to myself. Maybe this isn't as big a moment as I remember it. Maybe what happened the other day in Hunter's room wasn't a big deal either. I'm stupid for acting like this was something significant. "That's it." I shrug.

"I should've never let you go to his frat," Mateo says.

"*Let me*?"

"Yeah."

My defenses shoot up. My face gets hot. Logic slips out of my brain, and my irrational emotions take over. "You don't control me. You don't have a say in who I can and cannot hang out with."

"When it's something potentially dangerous, I feel like I should have some input. Who the fuck knows what else he could do to you."

"It's not that big of a deal." But the bile shooting up my throat would disagree.

"Yes, it is. He assaulted you."

I shake my head. "No, it's not that simple."

"Yes, it is."

"No, it's not, Mateo."

"I don't know, Elle. I've had my dick sucked a lot of fucking times, and I've never had to forcibly hold down a girl." His words burn for multiple reasons. Mateo winces at what just came out of his mouth. "I'm sorry. That was really shitty of me to say." He stands up and begins to pace. "I'm just so fucking angry right now, and don't know how to deal with this."

"You promised me that you wouldn't do anything." My eyes pierce into his.

"That was before you told me he assaulted you."

"Stop saying that. That's not what happened."

"Why are you defending him?"

"Because it's not that cut and dry. I willingly started. I could've tried harder to get him to stop. Maybe he thought I was fine. Maybe he didn't even realize what he was doing. Maybe—"

"He knew what he was doing."

"How do *you* know?" I snap.

"Did he ever do that again?"

"No."

Mateo scoffs. "Because he knew that once he ripped off the Band-Aid and got you to do it, then you wouldn't put up a fight anymore. He could get you to do it whenever he wanted once you got past your first time."

"That's not true," I say, staring at the floor, realizing that what Mateo said actually makes sense.

"He fucked with your head, manipulated you into doing it, and then forced you to stay down."

Hearing Hunter's play laid out so simply turns my nausea violent. "It's not that black and white. It's complicated…and confusing. There's too much of a gray area."

"Elena—"

"Stop!" I cut him off before he can finish reasoning with me. I look up into his eyes, and he seems pained by my pain. "I don't want to talk about this anymore." My voice cracks, and I burst into tears.

Mateo walks over to me and wraps his strong arms around me, letting me cry into his bare chest. "We won't talk about it anymore. I'm sorry," he whispers into my hair, squeezing me tighter. He kisses the top of my head as I continue to release the tears I've been holding on to for years.

Dread devours me as I wait for Hunter to enter our final algebra class.

I made sure to wear concealing clothing. I even opted for a cardigan over my short-sleeved shirt, even though it's too warm for one. My eyes catch his as he walks into the room. I immediately look down at my laptop to avoid any misconstrued communication.

Hunter takes his usual seat next to me and shuns making any contact with me as well. But his strong presence fills the room. His power and control still hover over me, and he knows it. My breathing gets shallower as anxiety ripples through me. My tongue swells, making it difficult to inhale. The class drags. I'm not sure if it's because it's nearing the end of the semester or because I'm sitting next to Hunter. I occasionally glance up to see what the professor is talking about, but I spend most of the class with my head down. Every time I look up, it feels like people know what happened between Hunter and me at his frat house.

When class finally ends, Hunter manages to saunter out of the room without a care, leaving me in his dust.

CHAPTER FIFTY-EIGHT

Ellie

"It has been a pleasure imparting knowledge to you. I hope that as you move through your time at school and even beyond your academic studies, you continue to question and seek meaning in the world around you," Professor Boland says, ending our last philosophy class. He dismisses our final class with a reminder that we need to email him our paper by next week.

As the students happily exit with the excitement of summer break just within reach, Professor Browne calls me over. "Ms. Connor?"

My eyes nervously connect with his, and I walk over to his desk. "Yes?"

"I wanted to remind you that you have until next Friday to accept the scholarship," he says to me. I politely smile and nod, trying to leave the room. "I hope you give it some consideration. It's a fantastic opportunity." He grabs my attention again, and I turn my head to look back at him.

"I will," I say, even though I'm pretty positive I'm going to decline the offer.

"Hey, baby." Mateo enters the classroom. He sees Professor Boland and me facing each other. "Oh, sorry. Am I interrupting? I can come back."

Professor Boland shakes his head. "No, I was just talking to Ellie about…" His eyes flicker over to mine, and he sees me pleading with him not to say anything about the abroad program. He continues, "How she's one of the best students I've had in years."

"No surprise there." Mateo wraps his arms around me.

"Have a good summer, you two."

"Thanks, Browne. You too," Mateo says as the two of us walk out of the room. I glance over my shoulder at Professor Boland, who's no longer looking at me but smiling to himself.

"What are we doing next Thursday?" Bree asks Mateo and me while we eat Chinese food in our half-naked room. We started packing our belongings earlier today.

"What's Thursday?" I ask.

"Last day of finals," Bree and Mateo say at the same time.

"Oh," I say, not understanding her question.

"Do you know of any parties?" Bree asks Mateo, and now I catch on.

"A bunch."

Bree's enthusiasm dances across her face. "Oh! Which one should we go to?"

Mateo takes a bite of his egg roll and glances over at me to see if I'm interested in going to a party. I give him a look, letting him know I'd be fine if we went somewhere. Mateo takes a sip of his soda and then speaks. "Depends on if we want to go to a small party or a big one."

"Big!" Bree shouts.

Mateo chuckles. "My friend Jasmine lives in a huge house, a town over. She and her roommates always throw a big end-of-the-year party." He looks over at me at the mention of Jasmine's name, but I let it slide off my back. I'm not going to let an ounce of jealousy ruin my fun.

"Sounds good," I say.

"I know this probably isn't the best time to bring this up." Bree passes me lipstick as we get ready for the party at Jasmine's. "But did you ever accept the scholarship?"

"My mom needs my help this summer, so I'm going to stay home with her."

Technically, not a lie. But I don't want to admit to her that I'm also staying home so I can be with Mateo.

Bree nods. "Okay." I can tell she doesn't fully buy my story, but I'm fine with that as long as she doesn't press me for more information.

"All set?" I turn to her to get her final stamp of approval on the ensemble she put together.

"Perfect!" She beams. At the same time, there's a knock at our door. "Come in," Bree says.

Mateo enters the room, looking extremely handsome. He has on black jeans with a white T-shirt, the sleeves of his shirt tightly hugging his muscles. The stark white shirt contrasts against his tan skin and black tattoos. As my eyes check him out, his do the same to me. "You look amazing," Mateo says, embracing me.

"Ahem." Bree playfully clears her throat and swishes her dress.

Mateo loosens his grip on me and turns to Bree. "You look amazing too," he says, like the kind gentleman he is.

Bree laughs. "Thank you."

When we get to Jasmine's house, my jaw nearly drops to the floor at how spectacular it is. I don't know how Jasmine and her roommates are able to pay for a place like this as college students. I doubt I'll ever be able to afford something like this, even with a degree.

College students gather in every room, either drunk or stoned. Long tables take up the basement and backyard, where people play beer pong, flip cup, and some other games I never heard of. Fun pop music is playing through the surround sound speakers mounted on the walls. Bree sees someone she knows from across the room and runs over to say hello.

"Do you want to drink?" Mateo asks me.

I shake my head. "I don't think I'm going to drink tonight. I don't really feel like it."

"Do you want something other than alcohol?"

"Sure."

Mateo takes my hand, and we walk into the kitchen. There is a large granite island filled with cups and all types of drinks.

"You guys are here!" a voice screeches. I move my head to see who it is, and before I can fully recognize the face coming toward me, Jasmine is group hugging Mateo and me. "I'm so happy the both of you came!" Jasmine says with an extra pep in her step. "It's so good to see you, Ellie." She runs her hands through my hair. *Whoa, girl. I'm nice to you, but we are not friends like that.* I try to respectfully reposition myself away from her. "You and Mateo are so cute together!"

"Thanks," I say.

"Do you want some coke?" Jasmine asks me.

"Sure." I was planning on grabbing a soda anyway.

"No," Mateo says over me. *What the hell?*

"Molly?" Jasmine asks me.

"Ellie," I correct her. *She literally said my name fifteen seconds ago. How drunk is she?*

"We're good, Jas. Thanks," Mateo states.

"If you guys change your mind, you know where to find me." Jasmine winks at us and flitters off to another group of people.

I turn to Mateo, crossing my arms over my chest. "Why can't I have a Coke?"

Mateo grabs a cup from the sparkly gray island and opens a bottle of Coke. *Now I'm just fucking confused.* "She didn't say *a* Coke." Mateo pours the soda and hands it to me. I squint, unsure of what he's saying because she clearly asked me if I wanted coke. "She was offering you cocaine and ecstasy," Mateo says bluntly.

My eyes widen. I knew that people were drinking and smoking weed, but I didn't expect any other types of drugs. Have I been that naïve to think people at the parties I've been to haven't been doing those drugs the whole time? Did Mateo used to do those types of drugs? Did he do pills like my mother?

Mateo gives me a gentle smile, then links his arm around my shoulders. "Let's play some flip cup." He changes the subject and guides us to a table in the backyard.

When we get outside, I recognize several people from my classes. A few people say hello to me as if we're the best of friends, and I play along.

"Ready?" Mateo asks, prepping two cups with water. I nod my head and stand next to him in a row of people.

"Oh my god, you're in my algebra class!" A giddy, drunk girl next to me says. She looks vaguely familiar.

"Oh, yeah." I try to match her enthusiasm, but I honestly don't care.

"You sit next to that cute boy with the blue eyes," she slurs, and I can sense Mateo's body tense up. I never told him that Hunter and I sat next to each other in class.

"Um…yep."

"Oh shit. He's not your boyfriend or anything, is he?"

"No," Mateo interjects as he pretends to be distracted by the water bottle in front of him.

"Oh, good!" she says, relieved. "He's so adorable. Do you happen to have his number? I saw that you guys used to talk all the time."

Oh my god, this highly intoxicated girl needs to shut up. "No, sorry," I lie. It's for her own good, really.

"Are both sides even?" Some guy at the other end of the table shouts down to us. Everyone starts counting how many people are on each team. Our team is one person short, so the guy calls over one of his buddies, who just so happens to be Mike from Hunter's frat.

"Hey, man." Mike stands on the other side of Mateo and puts out his fist for Mateo to pound it.

"Hey." Mateo tilts his chin up but doesn't acknowledge Mike's fist.

We end up playing several games, winning all the rounds. Mateo and I are the only sober ones, so we have a clear advantage over the other team. I've lost track of what number game we're up to, but I know that I have chugged a good amount of water. "I have to pee," I say in Mateo's ear.

"I'll show you where the bathroom is."

"I can find it myself. I'm a big girl."

"I'll still walk you there." Mateo grows protective of me, and I roll my eyes as we make our way into the big house. "Use the upstairs one," he instructs.

"I can choose which bathroom to use, thank you very much." I purposefully strut past the stairs to find the bathroom on this floor.

Mateo stops me. "They're doing coke in this bathroom. Use the upstairs one."

"Oh." I should trust his intentions more. I've been so influenced by my time with Hunter that it's difficult for me to decipher control from helpful shielding.

The bathroom is around a corner, down a long hallway. Of course, there's a line. Now I wish Mateo had come upstairs with me so I could talk to him while I wait.

The line slowly dwindles down, and two people ahead of me enter the bathroom at the same time. I can only imagine what is happening in there.

By the time they're finished doing whatever it was, my bladder is about to burst.

After finally using the bathroom, I quickly check myself out in the mirror, fixing my hair and makeup. Walking down the hallway toward the stairs, I spot Mateo and Jasmine chatting by the kitchen island down below.

"You guys broke up?" Hunter's voice startles me, making my senses go on high alert. I wasn't expecting him to be here.

"What? No." I scowl and keep moving.

Hunter follows me. "I assumed since he's talking to his fuck buddy that it meant things were over between you two."

His comment stops me in my tracks right before I get to the stairs. I glance over at Mateo and Jasmine, animatedly talking about something. Are they really fuck buddies, or is Hunter trying to mess with me? My chest tightens.

"Oh, you didn't know?" Hunter says with an air of arrogance, letting me know he's enjoying every last second of the look of surprise on my face. "I thought everyone knew. Oops." He continues down the stairs.

I watch as Jasmine playfully swats Mateo's arm and, in an instant, I'm reminded of the dynamic between Hunter and Delilah. My heart pounds against my ribcage. I can't tell if I'm furious, jealous, or heartbroken.

I need to get out of here.

I race down the stairs, past Mateo and Jasmine, and out the side door.

"Elle?" I hear Mateo calling after me.

"Get away from me, Mateo."

"What's going on?" Mateo is right behind me. I spin to face him, my confrontational side stepping up to bat. We're on the side of the house. There are several people in the front smoking and drinking, but none of them are paying any attention to us.

"Who is she, Mateo?" I snap at him.

He looks baffled. "Who is who?"

"Jasmine!"

"She's a friend. I told you that. What's going on?"

"Friends with benefits?"

Mateo's shoulders drop. "It was a long time ago, Elle," he tries to calmly explain, but I'm not having any of it.

"How long ago, Mateo?"

"Before us. I swear—"

"When was the last time?"

"A while ago. I swear, baby." He goes to touch my arm, but I aggressively jerk it away from him.

"Give me a date."

"It was before us. I promise."

"Date."

He presses his lips together, and then he lets out a sigh. "A few hours before the Halloween party."

My eyes widen. "You mean a few hours before you took care of me, changed me, and had me sleep in your bed, you were fucking another girl?"

"We weren't anything yet, Elle."

"You told me you liked me already by that point. So…what? You lied to me? You didn't have any feelings for me? You were playing me?"

"No, I—"

Before Mateo can speak, I cut him off, ready to spew some hurtful words. "You thought I was some drunk girl that you could sleep with and then stopped because I threw up! You were trying to take advantage of me just a few hours after you fucked another girl in the same fucking bed—"

"You know that is absolutely not true, Elena." His voice is strong and stern, but not raised. "I didn't lie to you. I *did* have feelings for you then—"

"No, you fucking didn't!"

"Yes, I—"

"No, you didn't. Otherwise, you would never have done that!"

"I didn't think you and I could ever be a possibility. You kept going back to Hunter! For Christ's sake, I had to stand in your goddamn closet and watch him fucking finger you!"

"What?" Hunter's voice slices through, startling both Mateo and me. We snap our heads to see Hunter walking out the side door, making a beeline for us, his chest puffed out, ready to fight. "He was in your closet?"

"Yep, I was." Mateo smirks.

"Stop it," I command Mateo, and his face drops, only slightly.

Hunter starts laughing. "This is your thing, isn't it, Ellie?"

I stare at him as if he's deranged. "What are you talking about?"

"You're going to play the both of us. Go back and forth between him and me?" Hunter says with a leer.

"No."

"Come on, Ellie. You get with him while we're together, and then get with me while you're with him." Hunter's eyes flicker with a maniacal glower. The blood in my veins goes cold. He's not going to try to spin what happened in his bedroom as something consensual, is he?

Mateo takes a step closer to me. "What does he mean by that?"

"If you're not going to tell him, then I will," Hunter threatens.

"Tell me what?" Mateo asks just above a whisper.

"There's nothing to tell," I snap at Hunter.

"Oh, come on. You're not going to tell him about how you came over in your little black skirt?"

I glance over at Mateo, who looks like he's seconds away from losing it because he knows exactly which skirt Hunter is talking about and what we did together while I was wearing it. "Ignore him," I tell Mateo.

"And how you laid down on my bed?" Hunter taunts.

"Elle." The composure in Mateo's voice weakens, threatening to combust.

"It's nothing," I plead with Mateo to believe me. My eyes dart back and forth between the two men, trying to decipher which bomb will be the easiest to defuse. My hands are shaking, and my lungs won't fill up completely.

"And how you wore that red thong." Hunter smiles as if he's getting off on watching me panic.

"Elena." Mateo's tone is rough around the edges.

"It's not what it sounds like—" My voice reaches a higher pitch. If I can just talk to Mateo privately and explain everything, this will be fine.

"You laid down on my bed—"

"Stop it!"

"Got nice and wet for me too—"

"Hunter!"

"You let me lie right on top of you—"

"You pinned me down!"

In the blink of an eye, Mateo's fist connects with Hunter's jaw. Hunter stumbles a bit but takes a swing at Mateo. It takes me a few seconds to realize what's happening.

My heart sledgehammers against my rib cage, hard enough to snap each bone into a million pieces. I can't catch my breath.

The two of them reach the front lawn with a crowd of people swarming them. Then someone shouts loud enough for the heavens to hear, "Fight!"

CHAPTER FIFTY-NINE

Red.

All I see is red.

And I fucking lose it.

My knuckles crash against Hunter's bones.

I punch him harder and harder with each swing.

The screams around me do nothing but entice me more.

I want him to hurt.

I want to see him on the ground, in a puddle of his own blood, in pain.

I want him to fucking hurt as much as he hurt her.

I can't stop.

A blow to my face snaps my head to the side. He gets in another swing, but that only fuels me more. Adrenaline blasts through my bloodstream, electrifying me with rage.

My heart races at the speed of light, unable to slow the fuck down.

I picture him manipulating her. Controlling her. Assaulting her.

Hunter is knocked to the ground, and I jam my foot into his stomach. Jumping on top of Hunter, my fists repeatedly strike him.

Suddenly, the demons of my past surge into my brain, and as I kick Hunter's stomach, images of my dad infiltrate my mind, and I can't control myself.

I want him to hurt for hurting them.

For hurting us.

I don't know who I'm hitting right now.

I can't stop.

Someone's hands come around my biceps to stop me, but I throw them off me in one swift motion.

I go harder.

Blood everywhere.

Multiple hands wrap around both of my biceps, and I'm yanked off him.

Stumbling up, copper fills my mouth, and I spit out a wad of blood. Catching my breath, I push my hair out of my face, staring at a mauled Hunter. My gaze slowly travels up, and I lock eyes with Elle. In an instant, I'm brought back to reality. The sudden urge to puke all over the once green grass comes over me as I see the terrified expression that appears on her face.

It's haunting.

A chill comes over me. In all my life, no one has ever looked at *me* the way Elle is right now. Fear is etched on her beautiful face as she cowers away from me, striking me like a sword to the chest.

But I don't just see Elle standing there, seeing me as a monster. I see my mom looking at my dad. I see the faces of all my sisters. All the ghosts of my past stare at me through Elle's eyes.

I see a face that I *never* wanted to be the cause of.

CHAPTER SIXTY

Ellie

I run.

I run as fast as I can. Away from the crowd. Away from Mateo. Away from Hunter. Away from Jasmine and her house. I run past the endless line of parked cars and onto another block.

Terror causes my bones to rattle as I continue to aimlessly run, fighting off tears. Between the spurts of my shallow breaths, I can hear the quick scraping of sneakers pounding against the pavement. "Elle!" Mateo calls out. I ignore him and keep running. "Elle, wait!" Mateo is catching up to me. *Damn him and his long legs.*

A sharp pain in my side has me slowing down, my run turning into a fast-paced walk as I gulp for air.

I have no clue where I am. We're several blocks away from the party, and there are only a few streetlights, which makes it difficult to figure out where I'm going.

The sound of Mateo's shoes lets me know he's a couple of feet behind me, keeping his distance. "Make a left," he says as I approach the end of the block.

I make a right and hear him sigh out of frustration at my defiance.

We've been silent for a while, but his voice finally breaks the quiet. "Why didn't you tell me about what happened with Hunter?"

"I handled it on my own," I snap. My focus stays trained in front of me, refusing to turn around and look at him.

"Oh yeah? How?"

"I got him off me."

"And then what?"

And then nothing. Nothing. I planned on never speaking of what happened and burying it deep inside of me until the end of time.

"This isn't the first time he's done something like that to you," Mateo reminds me of a time that I don't need to be reminded of.

"I'm aware of that, Mateo."

"You let him get away with everything."

"No, I don't! It's complicated!" I shout, still facing forward.

I feel like what happened was mainly my fault. I was stupid and led Hunter on. It's not as clear as Mateo perceives it to be.

"No, it's not. He knows exactly what he's doing." Mateo quickens his pace, and I try to walk faster. "He tells you all these nice things, and then he gets into your head and starts fucking with you, but he does it in such a smart and cunning way that you don't even realize he's the one tearing you down." Desperation pours into Mateo's words, pleading with me to view things his way.

"That's not true."

"Yes, it is." Mateo is directly behind me. He could easily put his hands on my shoulders to stop me, but he doesn't. "He manipulates you, gaslights you, controls you…" Mateo trails off, waiting for me to respond, but I don't. "He emotionally abuses you, Elle."

My jaw stays locked shut. I keep marching ahead. Mateo has no idea what he's talking about. Hunter has never hit me or directly threatened me. Hunter is emotional and intense, but so am I.

I am just as guilty as Hunter.

"He abuses and assaults you," Mateo reiterates.

"No, he doesn't!" I yell. There's too much of a blurry area. It's not as simple as he puts it.

"See!" Mateo's frustration rises. "You're defending him because he conditioned you into thinking he's a good guy when really he's just spinning everything around. He's got you thinking that he's not capable of these horrible things because he does it in such a way where you think you have some part in it, so that he can blame *you*!"

"Stop it."

"You know it's true."

"You have no idea what you're talking about." My voice breaks.

"I know that whenever things are going well between us, you two always find your way back to each other. It's like you're fucking junkies, needing a quick hit of toxicity, and then you go your separate ways until you're both craving your next fix."

Mateo's venomous words make me spin to face him. My swift movement alarms him, and he takes a step back. "Did you just compare me to an addict?"

Regret flashes across his face, and he seems stunned by his own statement. But he doesn't answer me, which *is* the answer.

My veins ignite with boiling hot rage. I want to curse him out. I want to punch him in the face.

Mateo opens his mouth to speak, but before he can, a car pulls up next to me.

"Hey, Ellie," a voice says. Bending my knees, I peek in the passenger window and see Rhett driving. I didn't even know he was at the party.

"Oh. Hi, Rhett." A sinister smile tugs at my lips.

"You need a ride?" he asks. I glance back at Mateo.

"Elena, do not get in that car," Mateo demands, knowing exactly what I'm thinking.

Too late, Mateo. The spiteful bitch is coming out to play.

I turn back to Rhett. "I would love a ride."

"Elena." Mateo walks toward me, but I move faster than he does.

Rhett pulls away, and I can hear Mateo shouting my name.

CHAPTER SIXTY-ONE

Ellie

Rhett's engine roars. "Where do you want to go?"

"I don't care," I say, looking out the window. None of the streets or houses we pass are familiar.

"Want to go back to my room?"

"You have a girlfriend."

"And you have a boyfriend, yet here we are."

I shut off my phone and push my body into the black leather seat, hoping to dissolve into the fabric.

Rhett puts on rap music and rambles on about his car. I don't even pretend to be interested. Instead, my mind is on fire from Mateo's words and actions. I know he's probably trying to call or text me, but I can't handle talking to him right now.

"I was going to meet some people at a bar. Want to come?" Rhett asks.

I shrug. "Sure."

We drive several more minutes as Rhett continues to try to impress me with car jargon. He's so self-absorbed that he doesn't even realize his talk isn't making an impact on me.

His expensive car slows down, and we pull up to a small dive bar in the middle of nowhere. It's a brick building with a neon sign that says, *Dave's Sports Bar*.

When we enter, the stench of cigarette smoke and stale beer invades my nostrils. Rhett leads me over to the barstools where a bunch of men in their mid-twenties say hello to him and then look me over.

"Who's this?" a drunk man asks Rhett.

Rhett scoops his arm around my neck and pulls me into him. "This is Ellie," he announces to them. "You want a drink?" Rhett asks me.

I shake my head. "I'm good."

"Tony doesn't check IDs. You'll be fine."

"You're not twenty-one yet?" the drunk man inquires, seemingly turned on that I'm younger than the legal drinking age.

Before I can answer, Rhett is ordering two beers, one for him and one for me. He passes me a tall glass, and I debate drinking it. The men watch me as I stare at the amber-colored drink. Whatever I'm feeling inside, I hate it and don't want to feel it anymore. I bring the cold glass to my lips and start drinking as the men around me cheer.

A few rounds later, I'm feeling more relaxed. The pain is still lingering, so I do a shot with the men to numb myself. The sense of danger is rising, and in some twisted way, I'm getting a high from it. I spot a pool table toward the back, and the thought of hustling them makes my lips curl upward.

I jump off the stool. "Who's up for some pool?" I ask, twirling a strand of hair around my finger.

"I'm in." Rhett finishes off his beer, and a few of his friends agree to join us as we head over to the table.

I pretend to be an awful player as I scout out my opponents. They suck. Every single one of them. I'm not sure if it's because they're drunk or if they're actually horrible, but either way, they are going to be easy to play.

Boys are so easy to play.

Everything is just a game to them.

These men aren't actually attracted to me. They're attracted to the idea of me and what I represent to them—a broken girl, vulnerable enough for them to take advantage of. I could be any other girl in the world as long as those boxes were checked off. It's all a game of power and control with them.

"You're really good," I lie to Rhett after he accidentally sinks another ball. He happened to line me up perfectly to do a trick shot that I can't give up.

"Want me to show you how to play?" he asks. Memories of Mateo enter my mind, and I quickly ignore them. I could flirt even more with Rhett and let him wrap his hands around my body, but I don't want him like that.

"I think I got this," I decline, bending down to line up my shot. I sense multiple eyes on me, waiting for me to blow my turn. I do a four-in-one shot, hitting into a row of four balls, sinking two in the corner pocket and the other two in the side.

The men shout in amazement. I stand back up with pride, smiling as they compliment me and give me high fives. "That's it! I'm done!" A man puts down his cue stick and throws his hands in the air. I laugh at his reaction as he draws nearer.

"Damn, Ellie. That was fucking awesome!" Rhett says, closing in on me.

My body tenses as my personal bubble shrinks. I continue to giggle, but this time it's because I'm uncomfortable. However, the men assume that my girlish laughter is an invitation, and they inch closer. The sense of danger is no longer fun or enticing. My control is diminishing as fear hits my body. I don't know what any of them are expecting to happen, but each of them gets too close for comfort.

My internal alarm system goes off and tells me to leave immediately. I wish Mateo would walk through the door, but he has no clue where I am because I'm an asshole and shut off my phone. I'll have to save myself this time.

"I need to go," I say, pushing past them. Rhett grabs my arm and spins me toward his body.

"Go where?" he asks. My nose wrinkles when I get a whiff of the beer lingering on his breath. The scent has my mind flipping through bad memories of my parents.

"Somewhere else." I try to get out of his grip, but it doesn't work.

"Why?" Rhett steps in so our bodies are touching. My heart beats faster. Rhett's face gets close to mine, his eyes glance down to my lips, and I can tell that he's about to kiss me.

"I don't want to do this," I say before he can make his move.

Rhett pulls his head back but doesn't let go of my arm. "Then what do you want to do, Ellie?"

I stare at him long and hard, digesting his question.

What do I want to do?

What do I *want* to do?

What do *I* want to do?

"I want to go to France," I blurt out.

The blurred effects of the alcohol are somehow letting me see more clearly. The beer and liquor have become my truth serum, and my blinders are off. What I want to do—what I *truly* want to do—is live out my dream and discover myself in France.

I don't want to stay home and work endlessly to fix Mom.

I don't want to let a boy stop me—not that Mateo even would.

This whole time, I've been using them as an excuse to stop myself from going. I can't stop myself anymore. I've been letting too many people dictate my life. It's my turn to take control of how I want to live.

Rhett scoffs. "I can't help you with that."

His grip loosens, and I use that as my opportunity to move away from him and race out the door. Darkness greets me, and my gut tells me I'm not in a safe area of town. I take out my phone and turn it on. As soon as it lights up, I get an influx of texts from Mateo. I ignore them at first so that I can order an Uber.

Five minutes until it's here.

My finger almost clicks open his texts, but before I do, I go to my email. If I don't do this now, I'll stop myself from doing it later.

Without another thought, I click the Accept button on the scholarship email.

My hands shake with disbelief.

Before I can begin to process my decision, my eyes move over to Mateo's texts. I open them up and read them as I wait for my ride to come pick me up:

Elle, please answer me

I'm so sorry for everything

Where are you?

I'm really worried.

I'm sorry I called you an addict. That was fucked up of me. If you hate me—I get it. Just let me know you're safe and I'll leave you alone.

Elle?

My heart rips into shreds. *Why am I like this?* I love this man more than anything, and yet I purposefully ignored him to get back at him for what he said to me.

It was fucked up of him to call me an addict. But in a way, he's right.

I am like an addict.

I'm addicted to the highs and lows. I'm addicted to the instability. Not because I want any of those things, but because it's the only way I know how to live. There is comfort in pain. It's all I've ever known. I don't know how to survive in calmness. I'm searching for the next chaotic moment because, in a way, it eases my anxiety by confirming my fears. It's a fucked-up state of being, but I can't stop it. I crave the dysfunction. It's carved into my bones.

"Uh…Ellie." Rhett steps out of the bar. "I know you're having your come-to-Jesus moment, but I wanted to let you know your guy got arrested."

All the air gets yanked out of my lungs.

"What?"

"Yeah, someone called the cops, and they chased him down. All the brothers are talking about it." He holds up his phone, showing me a group text. "Hunter is hanging out at our frat house. Your dickhead boyfriend fucked him up pretty bad."

My entire body trembles to the beat of my erratic heart. This cannot be happening.

Mateo can't get arrested.

He *can't*.

This is going to ruin every single fucking thing he's worked toward. I don't know a lot about the criminal justice system, but I can only imagine that a judge will not go easy on him since this is his third time being arrested. He even told me himself—he's on thin ice.

The Uber pulls up next to me, and I jump in, changing the drop-off location. I know exactly where I have to go, and it's not back to my dorm.

CHAPTER SIXTY-TWO

Ellie

I see the light on in Hunter's bedroom as I run up to the front door of his frat house. Not bothering to knock, I open it and dart up the stairs toward his room.

"Hunter?" I crack open his door and see him sitting on his bed. Gasping at the sight in front of me, my hands cover my mouth in utter disbelief.

Bruises cover his face with dried blood crusted on his cheek. His lip is swollen and busted open.

Bile rises in my throat at the thought of Mateo being the one to cause the damage.

"What the fuck are you doing here?" Hunter snaps.

I pad closer to him. "Are you okay?"

"I'm fine."

"Do you need anything?" I approach him but still keep a distance.

"If you're not here to tell me that you dumped that asshole, then I need you to fucking leave."

I swallow. This is going to be harder than I thought.

"I..."

"What, Elena?"

"I have a favor to ask."

Hunter doesn't say anything, just stares at me with his ice-cold eyes.

This was poor planning, Ellie. Who the fuck asks someone for a favor mere hours after they got the shit kicked out of them?

"Maybe this wasn't a good time." I spin around to leave, but Hunter jolts up, grabbing my wrist.

"What's the favor?" His hold gets tighter, starting to cut off the circulation. He jerks me in toward him, and I'm getting dangerously close to the bed that I never wanted to be near ever again. "Tell me the fucking favor you need."

"You're hurting my arm." I do my best to hide the panic in my voice.

He lets go, and I take a step back. "Sorry. I had a *bit* of a rough night," he says, glaring at me.

"I'm really sorry about—"

"I don't want to hear it." Hunter crosses his arms. "Tell me what you came here for."

I nibble on my lip, debating saying the words that are burning on my tongue. "Do you remember when you came to my room drunk and asked if I thought you were a good person?"

I wait for a response, but he's as still as a stone, not letting any expression cross his face. He's unreadable.

"Well, you did…" I continue, "And I said I didn't think you were a bad person—and I still don't. I think that sometimes your emotions get the best of you." Still nothing on his face. "And I know there's a part of you that still cares about me, or at least I hope there is." I don't even think he's fucking blinking at this point. "I need…I need a really big favor." Taking a deep breath, I tell him what I came here for. "Please don't press charges against Mateo."

Hunter humorlessly laughs. "Not fucking happening, Ellie."

"Hunter, please." I clutch my hand to my heart. "Mateo has come so far. He has goals, dreams. He wants to be a social worker."

"Good luck becoming a social worker with a record."

"That's why you can't press charges. I know he shouldn't have done that to you, but just hear me out. He's worked so hard for this. I can't let him lose everything because of me."

Hunter shakes his head.

"Hunter, please. I'll never ask a single thing from you except this. I'm begging you." My body inches forward. "I-I…"

His eyes flash up to mine. "You what?"

"I love him."

My eyes sting, and I try to blink away the tears. I can't believe I just admitted that to Hunter before telling Mateo.

He takes a long pause, drinking in my confession. "You love him, huh?"

"Yes," I say, barely audible.

"Okay." He nods. "I won't press charges."

Relief rushes through my body as my shoulders relax. "Oh my god. Thank you so much, Hunter. You have no idea how much this means—"

"If you break up with him."

My heart stops.

I swear, for a solid minute, my heart stops beating.

Time stands still as I blankly look at Hunter.

"W-what?"

"If you break up with him, I won't press charges against him."

I study his face to see if this is some kind of sick joke he's playing on me. But there's nothing giving away that he's kidding. He's serious.

"Why would you do that to me?" I whisper.

Hunter stalks over to me, his body looming over mine. "Because you were never his, Elena. You're mine. Always have been and always will be."

I shake my head. "No. No, you can't do this."

"I can." He tenderly places his hand on my cheek and drags it down my jawline. "And I will."

I peer into the blue eyes that I've known for years, not knowing who this person is before me. This isn't him, or maybe it always has been, and I was blinded by my feelings toward him.

Everything inside me is telling me to run. Get the fuck out and never look back. But I won't. I have to do this for Mateo. He's had this ambition for years. I don't know what that's like. I've only had a plan to escape to France, nothing more. I need to do this for Mateo's future.

"Post his bail."

Hunter scoffs. "No fucking way."

"He needs to pay his bills. He can't afford bail."

"Not my problem. Should've thought about that before he started swinging."

"Pay for his bail, don't press charges, and I'll…" I clamp my eyes shut, despising the words that are about to come out of my mouth. "I'll break up with him."

Hunter considers my wager for a moment. "Fine." He takes a step back. "Pack your shit and be ready to leave by eleven tomorrow morning."

"What about graduation? That's not for another couple of days. Don't you have to attend for your fraternity?"

He smirks at me, knowing exactly why I want to stay until graduation. "Nope."

"Well, I was going to go."

"Not anymore, you're not. Not if you know what's good for your soon-to-be ex."

Is this how it's going to be from now on? I need to follow every command, and if I don't, he'll dangle the prospect of ruining Mateo's future in front of me?

Anger bellows inside me, but I swallow it down. "See you at eleven."

CHAPTER SIXTY-THREE

Mateo

"Mateo Rivera." The corrections officer calls my name, escorts me out of the cell, and gives me my stuff.

I spent the entire night sitting on a dirty floor, feeling like a douchebag for everything that went down. Elle is pissed as hell at me—and rightfully so. She had better not have posted my bail. I don't want her thinking she's responsible for any of this. This isn't her problem to take care of. It's mine.

Walking out of the precinct and into the blinding sun, I squint, looking around to see if anyone is here to pick me up, but there aren't any cars.

Someone posted my bail first thing in the morning but didn't stay to drive me home? What the fuck is up with that?

The release form crinkles in my hand, and I glance down at the small slip of paper. It barely has any information on it aside from my name, my upcoming court date, and that I was discharged on a cash bond. Nothing else.

Since whoever paid to get me out didn't stick around to give me a ride, I reach for my phone so I can tell Michelle to get my car and pick me up.

It's not turning on. Fucking great.

Going back inside, I ask one of the officers if I can make a phone call from their phone, explaining that mine is dead.

An old white guy with gray hair and a police uniform scoffs at me. "You wouldn't be stuck in this situation if you didn't assault that guy."

No shit, Sherlock.

"Well, *that guy* shouldn't have assaulted my girl." My molars grind together. "I was doing my civic duty since no one else holds him accountable for any of the shit he's done. God knows what else he's gotten away with."

He glowers at me, passing me the precinct phone. When I get ahold of Michelle, she had no idea what happened last night. I thought Elle would've gone to her first since she's family. Fuck, I hope she didn't go to

Tío Edgar. I'll never hear the end of it. That asshole probably posted bail and drove off just to teach me a lesson.

As soon as I get home, I plug my phone in and run my ass into the shower. I reek of piss and God knows what else that covered the floors and walls of the jail cell.

Shaking my hair and letting the water droplets fall onto my shoulders, I make my way back into my room and toward my phone. Nervousness juts through my veins. I thought Elle would've answered Michelle's phone when I tried calling her on the drive back, but she didn't. I thought Elle would be here, but she's not.

Checking my phone, the text that's glaring back at me makes my heart fall to the fucking ground.

ELLE

I can't do this anymore. We're done.

She's breaking up with me?

Over a motherfucking text?

Hell, no.

On reflex, I grab whatever clothes I can find and stumble into them. I search for my keys, then run to my car. My hands tremble as I put my key in the ignition.

There's no way this is happening. I know I said and did shit last night that was awful, but I'm going to make this right. I don't care if I have to get on my fucking knees and beg for her forgiveness for the rest of my goddamn life.

Zooming down the street, the trees and houses become blurry as I push down harder on the gas.

The only thing my mind can fixate on is her. My Elle.

I never thought I'd be one of those guys who would panic over a girl wanting to end things, but I also never thought I was able to have these feelings for someone. I thought those emotions deep down inside me could never be unearthed. But Elle somehow lured them out of me.

Who would've thought every fucked-up twist and turn of my life would lead me to her?

She's the only person I've ever let in, and when she looks at me, it's like she can see me for my fullest potential—the man I've always wanted to become but always felt was out of my reach. She found the light in my darkness. She sees me for more than my ugly and messy past.

She sees *me*.

And I sure as hell know that I see her for everything she hasn't yet discovered in herself.

My pulse spikes the closer I get to campus.

I won't let her go like this. Not without her knowing everything. My biggest secret of all.

That I've been in love with her for months, and I was just too much of a bitch to admit it.

CHAPTER SIXTY-FOUR

Ellie

Bree caught her plane early this morning. When she asked about Mateo, I told her that I covered his bail and that he'll be absolutely fine. I plastered a smile on my face and pretended like I'm not dying inside. I must've put on a good performance because even I'm-good-at-reading-people Bree didn't realize. When I told her I'm officially going to France, she jumped up and down in glee, and I played along, doing the same.

The thought of that next hurdle makes my head pound.

Picking up the clock on my desk, I notice there's only half an hour until Hunter gets here. I yank the cord out of the wall and toss it into a box.

I'm almost finished packing. Only a few things are left.

My eyes wander around my naked dorm room. So much has changed in ten months.

After stacking my record collection in a bin, I fish around under my bed, packing away the few things remaining. My hand pulls out the hideous quote board from my mom. One specific quote sticks out, haunting me.

You are the music while the music lasts. —T. S. Eliot.

The broken shards that my heart has turned into stab me even deeper.

I wrote in my philosophy paper that life is like a song, but it's much more than that. People are like symphonies. There are different instruments, notes, crescendos, and intensities that make up who we are. Only in life, we don't get to hear everyone's full song. We hear the bits and pieces that are exposed to us. Willfully or not. And most of the time, it doesn't sound like a brilliant masterpiece. It's a cacophony of sounds. The instruments are out of sync, remnants of the past bleeding into the present melody. If you were to look at the notes, they'd be overlapping. Blurred together. A mess.

That's what people are.

Blurry messes.

If there's anything that I'm going to take with me after this year, it's that.

A knock on the door pulls me out of my thoughts. *Come on, Hunter, I'm already indebted to you. Can you at least give me my last half hour in peace?* Or the last half hour that he assumes I have, since he doesn't know my plans for the summer. I'll be freed from him for three months. That's enough time to figure out an escape strategy for when I come back, right?

"Come in," I say as I shove the corkboard filled with quotes into a bin.

"Elena."

I whip my head around and see Mateo standing in my doorway.

No.

No. No. No. No.

This wasn't supposed to happen. I was supposed to send the text and leave with Hunter before Mateo had a chance to do this.

My mouth opens, but no words come out.

Mateo inches closer to me, and I back away. "I know you're mad at me, and it's totally justifiable. But I'm not going to let things end like this. We need to talk about everything."

I furiously shake my head, slamming my eyes shut so he can't see my agony. I can't let him know that I'm hurting. Otherwise, I'll cave.

"Elle, please look at me."

"I'm not doing this, Mateo." I spin toward my belongings. "Let's be realistic. We both knew this was going to end eventually. I'm me, and you're...*you*."

"What is *that* supposed to mean?"

Here we go. I'm going to have to break his heart in person.

"We're too different. We've led two very opposite lives. While I was studying and taking care of my mom, you were whoring around and committing crimes."

Silence.

I don't have it in me to turn around and look at him. I know it hurt. I don't need to see it stamped across his face.

"I need to finish packing."

"Pack later. I'm not taking you home for a couple more days."

"No. I'm leaving today."

"Who's taking you?" The edge in Mateo's voice makes my spine straighten.

"Don't worry about it."

"No, I'm gonna fucking worry about it because you're my girlfriend, and I wanna know if you're planning on having that piece of shit drive you."

I snap my head up to look at him. "I'm not your girlfriend anymore, Mateo. And yes, I am planning on having Hunter drive me back. You know me, just a fucking addict craving the toxicity that he gives me."

Mateo winces. "That was awful of me to say. I'm sorry. I didn't mean it like that."

"No, you meant it *exactly* like that." I let the anger bubble inside me. The angrier I am, the easier this will be.

"Elle, you have every right to be mad at me, but I'm not letting you go that easy." He reaches for my hand, and I quickly recoil, not wanting to be singed by his touch. "I have something really important to tell you, but I don't want to do it like this. Can we just take a few minutes to talk about everything?"

"No! I don't want to talk to you. I don't want to see you. I don't want to even think about you."

He nods and backs away. "Okay, I'll give you your space. We can talk another time."

"No, we can't." I muster up the courage to tell him what I've been holding on to. "I'm leaving for France at the end of the month and don't want you screwing with my head before I go."

Mateo looks beside himself. He takes several seconds to process what I just told him. "France?"

I turn away from him.

"You-you..." He lets out a puff of air. "How long have you known about this?"

"I got accepted into the program months ago."

"You've been hiding this from me for *months*?"

"I didn't hide it from you—"

"Bullshit. You could've told me at any fucking time. When were you planning on telling me? When you were boarding the motherfucking plane?"

Good, Mateo. Get mad at me. Hate me. Please fucking hate me.

"I didn't want to tell you!" I snap.

"Why?"

"I didn't want you to stop me!"

"I would have *never* stopped you from going."

"Yes, you would've!" I shout. "You would've convinced me not to go, and I would've stayed here the entire summer stuck at your shithole place instead of actually getting to do what I wanted to!"

Mateo's shoulders drop, and his voice softens. "Is that what you really think? That I would've stopped you and held you fucking captive so you couldn't do what makes you happy?"

"I don't know what to think anymore, Mateo. I don't even know the real you."

"Yes, you do. You know me better than anyone else in the fucking world."

My stomach clenches. He's not getting this. My ribcage cracks open as I go for the jugular.

"No, I don't. You almost killed Hunter—and probably would have if people didn't pry you off of him!" I take a deep inhale before I gouge out his heart. "You want to know what I thought while I was watching you act like that? That I'm next. That's my fucking future. I'll say the wrong thing or do something you don't approve of, and you'll beat me into the ground." I make sure to stare deep into his soul as I go for the final blow. "You're going to end up just like your fucking father."

There it is. The look on his face. I just broke him. Crushed him. Fucking annihilated him. I see the pain creeping behind his eyes as they begin to water. He swallows down his tears. "Is that what you really think of me?"

No, not for a fraction of a millisecond.

"Yes."

Mateo bobs his head up and down. "Okay," he whispers and walks backward toward my door. He pauses before leaving, and we stare at each other for a moment.

In that moment, I hope that I can express everything that I feel about him.

I love you, Mateo. I love you more than you will ever know. I love you more than any love song could ever convey. You were it for me. You are the one that my soul travels lifetimes with. You are who my soul will always long for. And since we couldn't have a happy ending in this lifetime, I pray that we'll have it in the next.

He leaves.

Minutes feel like hours.

I'm frozen in the same spot where Mateo left me.

I can't break down and cry like I want to. I don't have the time.

A numbness glosses over me.

With that, a knock on my door snaps me back to reality. It swings open, and Hunter leans on the doorframe, unaffected, as if he didn't just make me sell my soul to him. His dazzling white smile was once enough to light up the whole world, but now I can see right through it.

I know the part I have to play.

The role that I know all too well.

The one where I pretend I'm absolutely fine.

The only time I was truly happy was with Mateo. I never needed to pretend with him.

I stare into Hunter's eyes. My heart ices over, and coldness fills my veins.

"Hey, angel."

Year Two

CHAPTER SIXTY-FIVE

Mateo

AUGUST

Her plane landed ten minutes ago.

My fingers strum on my steering wheel as I watch the time pass on my clock. I don't know how long it'll take for her to get through customs and baggage claim, but I've been sitting in this parking spot at Bradley International Airport for what feels like an eternity.

Glancing over to my passenger seat, the worn leather upholstery looks extra shitty while a bouquet of multicolored roses rests on it. I'm not sure if I should've gotten her flowers. Hell, I don't even know if ambushing her at the airport is a good idea, but it's the only way I know she couldn't avoid me. The handful of texts sent over the beginning of the summer all came with no reply. She probably blocked me, not that I blame her. I fucking terrified her that night.

The night that ruined everything.

The night she saw me as the type of person I swore I'd never become. The expression on her face when I lost my cool and acted like the old me, a person she never knew until that moment, was shattering.

She used to look at me like I was the only one in the room. No girl had ever looked at me the way she did, and damn, did it feel good seeing my reflection shine in her eyes. The truth is, I'm not sure when or how it happened, but I fell in love with her. Little by little, she crept into my mind, and I found my curiosity for her expanding each day.

I never had feelings for anyone else like I do with Elle.

And that's terrifying.

Since getting my act together during my court-ordered residential placement back in high school, I was only focused on continuing to work on myself and becoming a social worker. Nothing else. I had no plans of being a boyfriend, falling in love, or having a future with someone.

But with Elle, I found a part of myself I never even knew I was missing.

I was becoming the person I had always hoped to be. It never felt attainable before, but for the first time, it seemed like that version of myself was within reach.

I loved.

My whole life, I kept myself protected from heartache. I experienced that soul-crushing, slashing-my-heart-into-shreds type of pain when Dad left, and I swore to myself never to willingly expose myself to that shit again, in any type of capacity or relationship.

Until one day, a spot in my chest began to soften at the sound of Elle's voice—at the questions she'd ask, the emotions she'd set free, the kindness she'd offer. The more she wanted to know about me, the more I wanted to find out about her. Each day was a new discovery with twists and turns. She's the only one who found her way in. I don't know how she did it, but she did.

And now, I'm fucked.

Even if she doesn't take me back, I want her to know everything. I want her to know that I love her more than any fucking human on this planet. I want her to know that she will always be safe in my arms. I want her to know that I'm sorry for scaring her. And I want her to know that I will never, ever turn out to be like the person she compared me to—my dad.

I admit I'm doing this for myself too. I need to prove to myself that I'm nothing like him.

I *need* that reassurance.

The past three months have been a giant mind fuck.

Have I gotten into bad fights before? Of course. Was I arrested for it? Yeah. But what's different about what happened in May was that all of this went down in front of someone I love, an unwanted action on her behalf, and it resulted in her being petrified of me—if not borderline traumatized by seeing what I'm capable of. I spent the whole summer ruminating over every little thing that I've done, trying to convince myself that I'm not like my dad. But the proof of Elle being scared of me, Hunter's fucked-up face, and spending the night in jail tells me something different. I've even been second-guessing if I'm on the right path.

My phone rattles against my car console, signaling a text. I'm quick to grab it, hoping that it's Elle but knowing it probably isn't. A smile crosses my face when I notice who it is.

MR. KEVIN

How many hours of community service do you have left before school starts?

Mr. Kevin, my social worker from placement, has been checking in on me throughout the summer when I reached out to him after getting arrested. Hunter might've dropped the assault charges, but I still had to go to an arraignment where the judge slapped me with two hundred hours of community service and a two-thousand-dollar fine.

ME

finished them yesterday

MR. KEVIN

Good job, Rivera. Any update on Ellie?

Seeing her name causes my left leg to bounce up and down.

Did I pathetically go to Mr. Kevin, asking him what to do with the whole situation between Elle and me? Yes, I did. Would he approve of my surprising her as soon as she steps off the plane? Probably not, which is why I won't answer until I have a legit answer to give him after talking to her.

I continue to watch the time on my phone drag out.

She's got to be at baggage claim by now.

I don't know what my plan is. I spent so much time thinking about what I would say to her when we finally came face-to-face that I don't know how to go about doing it. I should've thought of *something* instead of impulsively getting in my car and driving all the way here.

All right, maybe it wasn't completely impulsive, considering I called up the university a few days ago requesting the flight information from her summer abroad program. I promised myself I wasn't going to come here like some psycho ex stalker. I just went for a drive to clear my head, but apparently, my head is only thinking about one fucking thing since I drove all the way to the airport.

I shift my weight around in my seat.

Fuck this.

Grabbing the flowers, I jump out of my car. I'd rather stand by the terminal entrance for the next half hour than sit in my car and watch the minutes pass by. Luckily, I had the foresight to park in the parking garage because I had no idea how long it would take for her to get out, and I didn't want to circle the airport for God knows how long.

As I get closer and closer to seeing her, my heart knocks against my ribs.

Approaching the elevator, droplets of sweat on my palms make me grip the stems of the flowers tighter so they don't slip out of my hand. My free hand pushes the down button, and I rock back and forth on my heels while I wait.

Out of the corner of my eye, something at the other end of the parking garage catches my attention. I turn to see a bunch of people making their way down the staircase.

With little to no patience left, I dart in the direction of the stairs. That'll be quicker than waiting for this goddamn elevator as it hits every fucking floor.

With large strides, I aim for the opposite end of the garage, but something far away stops me dead in my tracks. Or rather, some*one.*

Her.

My Elle.

For the first time since May, I feel like I can breathe again.

I stay motionless, admiring her from across the space. Her golden hair is up in a ponytail, and her skin is sun-kissed. Her sage-colored eyes roam around the parking lot, searching for her ride.

Oh shit. That's supposed to be me.

Snapping out of my daze, I lift my foot to take a step toward her, but the second I do, the blood in my veins turns white hot.

Hunter steps into my line of vision, his back blocking my view of Elle. The world stops turning as I watch in slow motion as he wraps his arms around my girl.

And she wraps hers around him.

Bile jumps to my throat at the same time my heart drops into my gut. My chest concaves inward as if I'd been kicked in the lungs. My grasp on the flowers strengthens until my knuckles turn white and the thorns on the stems pierce through my flesh.

I try to force myself to turn back around, but my eyes are glued to them.

He takes her luggage, and she follows him to a car, where a woman—who I assume is her mom—gets out and hugs her. Elle is all smiles as the three of them get into the car.

They drive off, and I stay motionless.

CHAPTER SIXTY-SIX

Ellie

"Sing for me," Mateo attempts to coax me in his husky voice.

I chuckle at his plea for the millionth time. "Not happening," I say, then rest my head on his lap, looking up at the large green leaves above us. I've lost track of how long we've been sitting under this tree. The branches shade us from the sun as we relax ourselves into the earth.

It's peaceful here together. Calm. Just us.

My fingers trace the outline of his tattoos on his right arm, the roses, down to the vines with thorns on his hands and fingers.

Mateo leans his back against the sturdy trunk, mindlessly combing his long fingers through my hair with his free hand. "Why not? I've heard you sing before."

"You've heard me sing once, and that was an accident. No one was supposed to be home. I didn't think anyone would hear me. Besides, I'm lying down. I can't sing lying down."

Mateo moves his hands under my arms, pulling me into a seated position, and I squeal at the swift motion. "You're not lying down anymore," he says with a smart-ass expression on his face.

The way his soulful brown eyes light up when he looks at me almost makes me want to give in.

Almost.

"Still not happening," I reiterate and lie back down.

"I want to hear that beautiful voice of yours."

I press my lips together and shake my head in response.

"Oh, this means you're not talking too? Okay, I can settle for that. You haven't shut up all day."

My jaw drops open, and I spring back up. "Rude!" I start to tickle him, but he tickles back and ends up winning. He always wins our tickle fights.

Our breaths are labored from laughing and trying to squirm away from one another.

He goes back to resting against the tree, but this time, I straddle him.

My arms wrap around his neck, and my fingers twirl the ends of his dark, thick hair. Our lips draw together, and he clutches my hips. We both know exactly where this is headed, and we don't want to waste any time getting there.

"Elle," he whispers into my mouth.

"Yeah?"

"I want to hear your voice."

My body jolts awake.

These fucking dreams.

I run my hands over my face, coming back to the present. The here and now, where there is no Mateo. No flirty disagreements. No tranquility.

I thought these dreams would stop while I spent the summer abroad in France and tried to distract myself with every outlet possible, but they didn't. They continued and followed me back here. Back to America. Back to the University of Connecticut. Back to my dorm room.

The bare white walls of the dorm surround me, my belongings carelessly tossed on my side of the room. I didn't unpack as much as I would've liked yesterday because I was too excited to see Bree. We ended up staying awake half the night talking instead of arranging our room.

So now I have piles of clothes on my desk, a poster of the Eiffel Tower that I intend to hang up is lying on the floor, and my books are messily stacked in the corner. The few things I did manage to put away are the things I want hidden—the necklace Mateo gave me last year and my medications. The necklace I keep out of sight for obvious reasons, but I also don't want anyone knowing I'm taking medication. Not that Bree would even care, but it's my own insecurity that makes me conceal them in my desk drawer. One bottle of anti-anxiety meds and a packet of birth control.

I was a fucking disaster after last semester ended, and I knew I needed to be as clearheaded as possible in order to get the most out of the abroad program. So I reluctantly scheduled an appointment with my old psychiatrist before I left, and he prescribed me medicine and also suggested I see a gynecologist and go on birth control to regulate my periods. I squeezed in that appointment too, before jetting off to France to study philosophy for three months.

France was amazing. A nice break from reality.

But that's exactly what it was. A break. And as soon as I was greeted at the airport when I got back home, I knew the break was over.

I wheel my bag toward the parking garage, searching for Mom's car. The smile on my face is evident. This summer transformed me. I spent the past several months discovering myself and figuring out who I truly want to become. As my feet touched down on American ground, I felt a strong shift in my core. For one of the first times in my life, I have the sense that I can handle whatever life throws at me.

Hurrying through the parked cars as people hug their loved ones, I find the steps to go up to the next level, hoping she'll be up there.

As soon as I make it up the stairs, I round the corner.

My body stills.

I don't see Mom.

I see him.

"Hey, angel."

My blood runs cold at the sound of Hunter's voice. I knew I'd have to face him eventually. I just didn't think it would be the second I landed.

I should run.

I attempt to lift my foot and bolt down the stairs, but I can't. My feet are cemented to the ground. I can't move.

I'm frozen.

Again.

"I missed you," Hunter says, approaching me. He wraps his strong arms around me in a hug.

The contact zaps me into the role I need to play. I wrap my arms around him and force a smile.

"I missed you too," I say.

"Come on." He takes my luggage from me. "Your mom's waiting for us in the car. She seems to be doing really well."

"Oh, good."

I know I have to play nice with Hunter for the time being because if I don't, he'll press charges against Mateo.

That was the arrangement we made at the end of the semester, the night of the fight between Hunter and Mateo, because it would absolutely harm Mateo's name and career. Hunter agreed under one condition: that I break up with Mateo.

So I did. To protect him. Mateo could lose everything he's ever worked for, all because of me and my fucked-up issues—Hunter being one of them—and I sure as hell am not letting that happen.

While I was away, I googled the statute of limitations for a physical assault, and it's one year.

I have to play the part until May.

Then I can breathe easily.

Mateo will never want me back by that point, but at least I'll be out from under Hunter's thumb.

"Hi, sweetheart!" Mom exclaims, getting out of the car and embracing me. I give her a warm hug back, and she gives me an extra tight squeeze. "I can't wait to hear all about your summer."

"Me neither," Hunter chimes in. "Grace, why don't you let me drive home? That way you can rest, and Ellie can show you the billions of pictures I'm sure she took," he says.

"It was only millions," I joke as we get into the car.

Sitting in the passenger seat, I turn to look at Hunter behind the wheel. The shades of blue in his eyes swirl together just like the whirlwind of emotions that live behind them.

The reminder that I'm forced by Hunter's side in order to keep him from screwing with Mateo's future has me clutching the oversized black T-shirt I'm wearing. I bring it up to my nose and inhale. It doesn't smell like Mateo anymore, considering I wore it every night while I was abroad. It was risky for me to wear it last night, but I figured I was in the clear from any surprise visitors once it became two in the morning.

The sound of blankets shuffling in the bed across from me makes me shift my head. Bree gives me a sleepy smile, with her curly brown hair wildly sticking up every which way.

"Hey, roomie." Her voice croaks.

"Morning."

"You ready to make sophomore year our bitch?"

"You know it."

After a gigantic stretch, I finally sit up and plant my bare feet on the cool, tiled floor. My shoulders slump, weighed down by guilt as I watch Bree spring out of bed and grab a water bottle from her mini fridge. I lied to her yesterday, telling her that Mom was dropping me off. I told Bree I'd be here at a different time than I actually intended on, in hopes she'd be out with people instead of sitting in our room waiting for me. My plan worked, but now I need to somehow explain to her why Hunter might be occasionally popping by.

"So what's first on our agenda? Decorating our room or going into town?" she asks after wiping the water droplets from her lips with the back of her hand.

My mouth dries up at hearing her mention going into town. The thought of being anywhere near where Mateo might be hanging out or working makes my hands tense, gripping onto the edge of my mattress. "Let's focus on our room. I don't foresee myself going into town anytime soon."

"No way." She shakes her head, making her way toward me and plopping herself next to me. "I'm not letting you hide in our room for the entire year because you don't want to run into Mateo. You don't even know if he's still working at the Cozy Nook, and even if he is, we'll walk past it. We don't have to go in."

"How about I start by hanging out on campus first? That seems more manageable." Mainly because Mateo will be taking classes in the social work building, which is on the opposite side of where I'll be spending my time this year.

Bree empathetically tilts her head to the side. "Are you ever going to tell me what happened with you and Mateo? You were there for me all summer while I was heartbroken over Amber, and every time I tried asking you how you were doing, you'd always answer with, 'I don't want to talk about it.'"

It's true. Bree and I texted almost every day while I was away. Her girlfriend, Amber, broke up with her a few weeks after she got home from school. Bree was devastated, so I did my best to help from the other side of the world.

"I'm being real here, Ellie," she says. "You were my rock over the summer, and you somehow managed to do that all the way from France. The only thing my friends from home did was get me drunk and high whenever I started crying. No one ever just wanted to sit and listen to me, but you did. And I want to do the same for you. I know you have to be hurting from Mateo."

I nod. "I am. I just don't want—"

"Don't want to talk about it. All right, all right. I'll take a hint." She playfully throws her hands up in the air. "But if you ever do want to talk about it, I'm all ears."

"Thanks, Bree."

It's not that I don't want to talk to her. It's that I *can't*.

I can't tell her about the arrangement I made with Hunter. I have to keep everything under wraps. Otherwise, it has the potential to turn to hell.

My voice is locked away, trapped and buried beneath the endless layers of lies and fake smiles. All the words I wish I could say die inside me, causing a slow and painful suffocation of the truth.

"So…since you're still being tight-lipped on what happened last year, will you at the very least indulge my fuck relationships mindset this year?"

I snort. "I think I can get on board with that."

"Yes!" Bree bounces up onto her feet. "This year is going to be all about us! We're single and smart and hella hot. If we want to hook up with someone, then we will, and if we don't, then that's cool too. We're gonna do whatever the fuck we want, and we're not going to be tied down by anyone!"

"Amen!" I cross my fingers, silently hoping that someone out there heard the unorthodox prayer that was just let out into the universe, even though I know I'll be tied down to one person for the time being.

Let the countdown to May begin.

CHAPTER SIXTY-SEVEN

Mateo

The smell of coffee grounds soaks into my pores as the mad rush of students has me working behind the counter at the Cozy Nook for my whole shift. It's better than staying isolated in the back office making schedules or doing inventory, which is what I've been doing most as of late.

The coffee shop has brightly painted walls with eclectic art hanging up and mismatched furniture spread throughout. It's the complete opposite of the other side of the shop, the bookstore. That side has brick walls and vintage rugs covering the hardwood floors. There are also oversized chairs with side tables next to them so people can chill and read. A metal spiral staircase leads up to the loft area, where more bookshelves are and a hideous teal couch sits.

A large glass window is carved out in the wall between both shops so people can look through to the other side, and there's a hollowed-out archway letting patrons move back and forth.

The two juxtaposing sides somehow work together. I don't know how, but there's a cool vibe here, and I don't mind working in this place. Even if *Tío* Edgar wasn't the owner, I still think I'd like it.

I used to pick up a lot of girls here, but I'm not into doing that anymore. Earlier, a customer was overtly flirting with me and even not so subtly traced the V-neck outline of her shirt while she was ordering. If this were a year ago, I would've gotten her number and had her in bed later that night with a painfully detailed explanation that I'm only interested in fucking and could never offer her anything more.

But that's not who I am anymore, not after falling for Elle.

Never would I think I'd see the day when I was turning down meaningless, no-strings-attached sex.

"Iced vanilla latte," Lynn, our purple-haired barista, shouts to me as she takes orders behind the register.

I've been shooting back and forth, making drinks as quickly as possible to get the line to die down. Normally, I'm in a zone, but hearing that drink order makes me falter. My heart rate picks up as I turn around, hoping that Elle is standing on the other side of the counter, but when I do, it's not her.

I can't fucking escape the thought of her. She's everywhere, memories of her filling up every inch of my brain. I haven't been able to work a single shift since the day she dumped me without staring through the large glass window into the bookstore, hoping she'd appear from thin air and start working there again.

Instead, some redhead stands in Elle's place. *Tío* Edgar hired her the other day, but I have yet to walk my ass over there to say hello. I watch as the redhead attempts to carry a stack of books to her register but ends up dropping them.

"Dude," Lynn says to me. "I need an iced vanilla latte."

Nodding, I make the drink and slide it across the counter.

"Can I get one of those?" My cousin Michelle's voice cuts through the chatter and is aimed directly at me as she enters the coffee shop.

"Hey, there's a line!" some guy snaps at her.

Michelle twists her head so fast that the end of her tightly pulled ponytail whips the side of her cheek. "My dad owns this place, you f—"

"Michelle," I interrupt before she causes issues for Edgar. "Hang out over there, and I'll make it in a sec." I point toward the end of the counter. With zero fucks, she walks to where I suggested and pulls herself up onto the countertop, letting her feet swing.

Once the line eases up, I finally make my way over to her and hand her the drink in a to-go cup. She takes a long sip while I check the time on my phone.

A few minutes until I have to leave for my first class of the year.

"Who's the new girl?" Michelle motions toward the redhead across the way, who appears to be ending her shift.

"Haven't met her. Besides, when have you had any interest in who your dad hires?"

"Just wondering." She shrugs. "Want to go to a party tonight?"

"I'm good," I say, quickly cleaning up the area.

"How about this weekend, then?"

"Pass."

"Come the fuck on, Mateo. You haven't gone out all summer. Are you seriously going to hibernate all semester too?"

My features twist, my expression turning sour. I haven't been in the mood to go out and party or go out to do much of anything. And I especially don't want to go out now that school has started. I want to avoid running into Elle or Hunter. The breakup did enough damage. I don't need to see them together. I had some stupid vision that when I showed up at the airport, I'd whisk her away and everything would go back to normal. But that died the moment Hunter crossed into the picture. The fact that she would choose him over me—or choose him over being fucking alone or with some other guy—twists a knife around my organs.

"I don't feel like going out," I say, hoping Michelle will shut the fuck up.

"Whatever." She rolls her eyes and thankfully drops the subject. "How's your first day of classes?"

"Didn't start yet, but I'm leaving in ten minutes so I can get there early."

"Aw, that's cute. You're nervous for your first day of school."

"I'm not nervous. I wanna get there before it starts. It's grad school. I have to start acting like a fucking professional."

Michelle squints her eyes, assessing me. "Did you buy a new black T-shirt?"

"What?"

"I didn't get to see you before you left for work this morning, but you did. You totally bought a new shirt for your first day of school!" she teases. "What happened to your other ones? Not professional enough for you?"

I glare at her. I didn't buy new clothes for school. I'm behind on laundry, so it seemed easier to buy clothes than to do the mundane task. Plus, I'm down a black shirt.

"I'm gonna be late," I say, then head toward the back office to get my shit.

"You mean on time."

"Shut up." I grab my backpack, then lock the office door behind me. "See you later," I say, slipping my keys into my pocket.

"Wait." Michelle jumps down from the counter. "Can you drive me to work later? I picked up another shift."

"Why don't you just come work for your dad?"

"Because I like working at the restaurant. Plus, do you really want to deal with me and my dad bickering the entire shift?"

She has a point. I'd much rather help her out and give her a ride somewhere than deal with the two of them arguing all day long.

"Yeah, you're right. Text me what time you need a ride."

Over the summer, whenever I had downtime—which wasn't much—I'd chauffeur her ass around. Not that I minded. It gave me something to do and kept my mind occupied. When I wasn't playing taxi driver, I picked up shifts at the coffee shop whenever I wasn't drowning in community service hours. I ended up quitting my band because I wanted to complete all the hours before school started. On the rare occasion that I did have a spare moment of free time, I was acting as the handyman of our place. I repainted my room and the living room, got us better couches—ones without cigarette burns in them—rehung the kitchen cabinets, and worked on the landscaping. I kept myself busy. The busier I was, the less I was focused on the gaping hole in my chest.

Since May, all I did was attempt to distract myself from Elle. It didn't work much because, without realizing it, my thoughts would eventually drift off to thinking about her—the small dimple that pops out on one side of her cheek when she's being flirty, or the way she throws her head back when she laughs really hard, or her deep sighs when she's about to come.

I shift my stance.

Shit. Don't think about her coming.

"So what do I do?" Michelle's voice is like a fucking bomb exploding my thoughts.

"About what?"

"You weren't paying attention to anything I was saying, were you?"

"Nope."

She huffs. "Fine. I guess I'll figure it out myself then."

"Sounds good to me," I say, tugging on the strap of my backpack. "I'm out."

"Have a good first day of school!" Michelle obnoxiously waves.

Walking out of the Cozy Nook and into the hot, end-of-summer air, a twinge of nervousness spikes low in my gut. Making my way to the municipal parking lot, I hop into my used gold Toyota and take a short drive to campus.

Moving past the Great Lawn to get to my first class, I do my best not to pick out Elle in the crowd. To be honest, I am not sure what I'd do if I saw her. Do I say hi? Do we ignore each other?

When I approach the brick building, my neck cranes upward, looking at the giant, bronzed lettering that reads, *School of Social Work*.

Hesitancy stops me from entering.

I feel like a fucking fraud. I doubt anyone else here has gotten arrested, and even if they did, it most likely wasn't three months ago.

Swallowing down my uncertainty, I go inside and take a seat in the classroom. The syllabus is handed out as students enter the room. Sitting down at the desk, I look over the papers, and my eyes widen.

Goddamn, I knew grad school was going to be a lot of work, but this…

this is college on steroids. Classes, research papers, internships, seminars. How the fuck am I going to balance all of this while working?

My attention moves off the syllabus and onto the classroom. A lot of the people in my social work program are older than I am. They probably saved up so that they could stop working while getting their master's degree. I, on the other hand, am an asshole with a pipe dream, thinking I can make an actual difference in some kid's life. But I knew if I didn't go straight through from undergrad to grad school, I'd fall off track, fuck up, and never make it back.

"Wow. This is a lot of work," the girl next to me whispers.

I glance over at her and see a redhead smiling at me. The same redhead who replaced Elle's position at work.

"I'm Rebecca," she introduces herself.

"Mateo," I say, feeling like a dick for not meeting her when I had several opportunities over the past few days.

Her gaze sweeps over me, and I do the same to her. She's around my age, with wavy red hair, light-brown eyes, and a nice body.

"Welcome," a woman with short gray hair says with open arms. My focus goes straight to her, since I'm definitely not interested in starting something with Rebecca.

Had this been a year ago, my feelings might be different.

But this isn't a year ago. This is now. And now, I've been ruined by a woman who showed me what it's like to love someone who doesn't love you back.

Once class is over, I step out into the long hallway, only to hear someone calling my name.

"Mateo?" Rebecca says from behind me.

I turn to face her. "Hey. What's up?"

She gestures to a few people who are in our class. "We're thinking about going out for a bite to eat before our next class starts. You know, so we can all get to know each other and see what we're getting ourselves into for the next two years." She gives a small laugh. "Want to join?"

The social work program was a twenty-person cohort, meaning the same people would be in all of my classes until graduation. I should probably go out and socialize, but I have no desire to do that. They're going to ask me about myself and what I did this summer, and I don't want to say that I spent the past three months picking up trash from the side of the road, hating myself while being heartbroken over the woman who might as well have offed me.

"I gotta drive my cousin to work. I'll catch up with you guys later."

Not a complete lie. I do need to drive her, just not until later.

My fingers reach for my keys as I make my way toward my car, planning on sitting there listening to music for the next hour before needing to be back in the social work building. I pretend to casually look around the campus, through the blur of people striding back and forth. Elle is nowhere to be found.

This is going to be a long two years.

CHAPTER SIXTY-EIGHT

Ellie

Ava sits down next to me in my last class of the day, philosophy. "Hey!" she says, pulling out her laptop.

Ava was my roommate in France, and I lucked out with how well we got along. She helped take my mind off all the things I didn't want to be thinking about. Not that I told her any of the details of what went down before I left, except that I broke up with Mateo, but she was able to distract me from time to time.

"Long time no see." I smile at her.

Ava wears her mousy-brown hair in a loose braid over the front of her shoulder and small stud earrings in both ears. She goes on to tell me about the end of her summer and how she met a cute guy while she was moving in yesterday.

Someone takes a seat next to me, and when I shift to see who it is, my heart jumps into my throat. The person looking back at me seems just as unsure of how to react as I am.

"This was the last seat available," Michelle says, her eyes surveying the room to see if there are any other open chairs.

"T-that's okay," I respond as a sudden rush of light-headedness hits me.

She whips her attention to the front of the class, even though the professor has yet to walk in. My mouth opens and shuts multiple times. I have so much to say. So many questions to ask, but I can't seem to muster up the courage to do so.

"What about you?" Ava grabs my focus back to her. "Have you seen any cute guys you want to hook up with?"

"No!" I practically scream the answer. Clearing my throat, I continue, "Definitely not."

Michelle starts texting, and I pull a muscle attempting to inconspicuously get a glimpse at who she's talking to and if it has anything to do with me.

"Welcome back." Professor Boland commands the room with his loud voice. My focus goes to him, and he's wearing the same professor attire as last year—khaki pants and a tweed blazer. Although he opted for a more casual look during our summer abroad.

It's strange seeing your professors outside of the classroom. When I officially decided to declare philosophy as my major before we left France, we all celebrated, and even Professor Boland got a little tipsy from having one too many glasses of wine with us.

He goes on to discuss the syllabus while the attendance sheet floats around. I keep checking the phone facing up on Michelle's desk, my mind wandering to who she might've texted. I'm aware of the irrational thought that she'd be talking to Mateo about me, but that doesn't stop me from biting at my cuticles as my brain weaves together a story of all the possibilities of what that conversation would entail.

My concentration is shot to hell, and I'm only absorbing a few sentences at a time as Professor Boland lectures.

Michelle's phone lights up on her desk, and my gaze shoots to the screen to see if it's from Mateo, like the crazy ex I am. She's quick to pick up her phone, but I caught a glimpse of his name.

My pulse races, wanting to know what they're talking about and needing to know everything that happened over the summer after I left. I don't even know if Michelle will even tell me, but I at least have to try.

As soon as philosophy wraps up, I say goodbye to Ava and speed walk toward Michelle as she exits the old, ivy-covered building.

"Michelle," I call out after her.

She spins around and gives an eye roll when she realizes it's me, then keeps walking.

Not exactly the reaction I was hoping for.

"Michelle," I say again, and she stops so I can catch up to her.

"Yeah?" She crosses her arms over her chest.

Her brown eyes intimidatingly press into me, waiting for me to talk. I have everything, yet nothing to say. When the silence lingers a beat too long, she huffs and turns back around, going toward the parking lot.

"No, wait—"

"What do you want, Ellie?" She faces me once again.

"How…" The words get caught in my throat, but I manage to push them out. "How is he?"

"I don't know. Why don't you ask him yourself? He should be here any second."

My knees lock. "What?"

"He's driving me to work."

"Oh." I force myself to take steps backward. "Can you just..." I trip over my feet. "Just don't tell him you saw me, okay?"

I turn, darting away.

Real fucking smooth, Elle.

Once I convince myself I'm in a safe range away from seeing Mateo, I slow down my pace to a regular speed. Air fills my lungs as I catch my breath, walking back to my dorm room.

I can't believe I was that close to seeing him. I don't think my heart would be able to handle that right now. Or ever.

Stepping into my hallway, my steps falter when I see Hunter leaning against my door, scrolling on his phone. My mind jumps from one boy problem to the other. I roll back my shoulders, seemingly unaffected by his presence, although apprehension sparks inside me, wondering if he knows I'm in a class with Michelle, even though I'm pretty sure he doesn't even know who Michelle is.

"Hey," I say, approaching him.

"Hey, how were classes?" Hunter moves out of my way so I can unlock my door, and he follows in behind me.

"Good."

He nods his head, assessing my room. He hasn't made an appearance here since he dropped me off the other day.

"Do you need help hanging those?" Hunter points to my poster of the Eiffel Tower and a few framed pictures I took while in France, which are still sitting on the floor waiting for me to move them. Before I can answer, he's picking them up and examining the photos—one of the Louvre and one of Ava and me. "I'll come back with my stuff and hang them up for you. Next to your bed?"

"Sure. Thanks."

"Of course," he says, grinning.

When I saw him after coming home from France, I wasn't sure how this was going to go, but truthfully, he hasn't been any different from how he used to be. Although Hunter does look different. His dirty-blond hair is a little longer than usual, and he's more buff. He must've worked out all summer long. The muscle tank he wore when he moved me into my dorm the other day showcased how much time he's been putting in at the gym. It also showed off fresh black ink across his left pec. The name of his deceased sister, Kayla, is written in script across his heart.

As soon as I saw the tattoo, fury thrashed through me. Sure, when I said I wanted a tattoo to cover up the self-harm scars on my wrist, I was told not to and called trashy, but he goes ahead and does it, thinking he's hot shit.

Little does he know, I got a tiny tattoo in a secret spot while I was away. Euphoria swam through my veins as the needle punctured my flesh, knowing that I could never undo it.

"I was thinking we could go out to dinner tonight," he says, coming closer to me. I can see his arms reaching out to pull me into him. I sidestep, pretending to search papers on my desk.

"It's the first day of school."

"Exactly. You don't have any work to do, so I know you're free."

I bite the inside of my cheek, wanting to tell him no, but I decide not to as the image of Mateo pops into my head. *You can do this until May, Elle.*

"Okay." I sit at my desk and open up my laptop, hoping that Hunter will get the hint that I don't want to be around him until we go out.

Hunter makes himself comfortable on the edge of my bed, close to my chair. An awkward silence falls between us. "What's wrong?" he asks.

Gee, I don't know. Maybe you forced me to break up with the man of my dreams and now have me wrapped around your little finger?

"Just tired." I stare at the computer screen, mindlessly clicking tabs.

"Why don't you rest before we go out?"

"Yeah, I think that's a good idea." *That way, you can get the hell out of my room for a few hours.*

Hunter stands and grabs my hand, pulling me out of my chair and onto my bed. "Lie down for a bit."

I do as he suggests, but then he climbs onto the mattress, settling behind me.

My body becomes stiff as a board.

I don't want to be on this bed with him. I don't want him here while I'm sleeping.

Hunter moves my hair out of the way. His hands slide up my shoulder blades, slow and calculating. I focus on keeping my breathing leveled. He begins massaging my shoulder.

"Hunter." I attempt to shrug him off. "Hunter, stop."

He moves away from my shoulder and runs his fingers through my hair. I sit up, trying to avoid his touch.

"Don't do that."

"Why not?" He pushes himself up to sit.

"Because we're not a thing. This"—I move my index finger between the two of us—"is not part of the arrangement."

His back straightens, and an unreadable expression crosses his face.

Fear coils in my stomach as the realization that there might have been a misunderstanding comes crashing down. I hug my knees to my chest. We never agreed upon us getting back together, but maybe I was wrong in assuming that he thought we wouldn't be back in a relationship.

The blue hue in his irises sparks with unfavorable emotions behind them. "You're right," he says.

My arms slowly release the hold on my legs as I watch him stand up.

"I'll come back and pick you up for dinner, okay?"

I nod.

He goes to leave, but stops himself. "Oh shit, I forgot. I need your key."

My head tilts to the side. "My key?"

"Yeah, I'm going to make a copy. One of my brothers knows a guy who'll make duplicates."

I jump to my feet. "I'm sorry—*what*?"

"I'm making a copy of your key."

"Why the hell do you need a copy of my key?"

"For emergencies. It's for your protection, Elena. I want to make sure you're safe."

"You didn't need it last year."

Hunter takes a step in, closing the space between us. "Things are going to be a bit different this year, angel." His tone is gentle and soft, but the iciness behind it stings the blood in my veins.

I've never had the urge to drive before, but right about now, I'd love to hop in a car and drive across country without any traces of me left behind so I can escape this mess.

"You can't do that," I state. "I have a roommate. You can't walk in on her whenever you please."

His jaw clenches as he considers my point. "I'll let you know beforehand if I plan on coming. Does that make you feel better?"

"No, it doesn't make me feel better!" My arms fly up as my voice rises. "You're not making a fucking copy of my key!"

His body tenses as he puffs out his chest. "I think this is a pretty simple request, considering other things I can add to our *arrangement*." He glances to my bed behind me, and a lump forms in my throat.

The air thickens with animosity as I glower at him, choking down what I want to say.

Hunter opens his mouth to speak, but as soon as he does, my door swings open.

"Hey, roomie—oh." Bree stops in her tracks. My insides twist, realizing

I have yet to come up with some explanation as to why Hunter is back in my life.

My head spins with all the stories I need to keep up with and people I need to shield from one another.

"Hey, Bree." Hunter turns to look at her, deflating his intimidating stance and switching on his charming persona. "Did you have a nice summer?"

"Probably not as eventful as Ellie's," she says, arching an eyebrow.

"Well, who could top going to France for three months?" he replies with a smile.

"Right." She nods slowly, staring at both of us.

I do the same as Hunter and paste a grin on my face. "We were just talking about going to dinner. Want to join?" I ask her, and Hunter immediately shoots me a look.

"I'd love to, but I already made plans with Bianca," she answers.

"That's okay. I'm sure you can catch us next time. We'll be going out a lot," Hunter says to Bree before facing me again. "I'm going to go take care of that thing we were talking about, and I'll be back to pick you up for dinner." He holds out his hand, waiting for me to give him my key.

Mateo's face appears in my mind. *Remember that you're doing this for him, Elle.* I need to suck it up and deal with Hunter. Otherwise, he might go ahead and follow through with pressing charges. How long could Mateo be in prison for? One year? Two? Five? I have no idea. But what I do know is that this is Mateo's third offense, and Hunter comes from a lot of money—enough to swing any decision to go his way and make Mateo's life a living hell.

I glance over at Bree. She's focused on the things on her desk. Giving Hunter a curt nod, I swallow down my pride. Grabbing my keys, I twist the one to my dorm room off the ring and slam it into Hunter's palm.

"See you later, angel," he says right before brushing his lips against my forehead. "Bye, Bree." He closes the door behind him before she has the chance to respond.

Bree spins around. "Um…I think you left something out when we were talking all summer long."

"It's nothing," I say, plopping down on my bed.

She mirrors my movements and sits on hers. "Is that why you didn't want to tell me about your breakup with Mateo? Because you got back together with Hunter?"

I shake my head.

"Then how did this switch happen? How did you go from Mateo to Hunter?"

"I'm not with Hunter. And things with Mateo ended naturally. I was away for three months. I couldn't expect him to stay and wait for me."

"Hmm." She purses her lips together. "I know there's more of a story there, but if that's the one you're sticking to, I'll let it slide."

My cheeks rise. "Thank you."

"Of course. And any time you want to tell me the real story, I'll be ready."

I give her a playful scowl and slide under the covers. I'll need all the rest I can get if I have to keep juggling everything, all while wearing a mask.

Several hours later, Hunter walks me back to my dorm after getting dinner together. I thought he'd drop me off in the parking lot, but that doesn't seem to be the case. When we reach my door, I stop in front of it. "Um…I think Bree just wanted to have a girl's night tonight."

Hunter nods. "That's okay. I have to get back to the frat house anyway."

"Thanks for walking me back." I go to take out my key, but then realize I don't have it. Glancing up at Hunter, I notice his lips slightly twitch.

He takes my hand and flattens out my palm. Digging in his pocket, he pulls out my key and presses it against my skin.

"Bye, angel."

CHAPTER SIXTY-NINE

Mateo

SEPTEMBER

The fluorescent lights in the classroom occasionally flicker while I sit in my Foundations of Social Work class. It's only the second week of school, but I can already tell this one will be my favorite. Barbara, the professor, puts emphasis on expanding our self-awareness so we can be more competent clinicians.

"The more we learn about ourselves, the more we learn about what has clouded our perception. We need to acknowledge our own history and challenge ourselves to evolve in order to be effective professionals," Barbara states.

Oh, trust me. There has been a lot of "acknowledging my past" going on since the summer.

We go around the room, talking about what inspired us to become social workers. I listen to stories of wanting to work in veteran hospitals, others want to advocate for the homeless, while some want to work with geriatric patients.

Rebecca's turn comes, and she talks about her goal of becoming a school social worker, stating she loves kids and wants to help with their emotional growth. Rebecca and I haven't spoken much, but I always catch her smiling at me or wanting to start some type of conversation at work. As of late, the coffee shop has been ridiculously busy, so I don't have time to idly stand and talk to her even if I wanted to.

"What about you, Mateo? What made you choose social work?" Barbara asks.

I sit up a little straighter in my seat. "I'm hoping to work in a residential facility. You know, for teens who get sent there to get their shit together."

Fuck. I don't know if I should've said "shit." Everyone else sounds so educated, and my mouth can't go five minutes without letting a curse word slip.

"And what inspired you to want to work with that population?"

"I, uh…" I clear my throat. "I was court placed at a residential placement facility when I was in high school following an arrest. My social worker there, Mr. Kevin, changed my life around. I hope that one day I can be some kid's Mr. Kevin."

A few people nod with empathetic eyes, and I notice Rebecca placing her hand on her heart with a kind expression on her face.

Why the hell are people looking at me like that?

"Thank you for sharing, Mateo. I hope one day I'll have a student in my class telling me about how a Mr. Mateo made an impact on their lives." Barbara smiles, the lines around her eyes deepening.

The corners of my mouth turn upward.

I hope so too, Barbara.

The next person goes on to share their story, and I stare down at my desk. Mr. Kevin would keel over if he just heard the words that came out of my mouth. I chuckle to myself and let my mind wander, thinking of him and the beginning steps of what got me here.

"You've been refusing sessions for the past three weeks," Mr. Kevin says. He's a Black man in his mid-thirties with not a single hair on his head. I sit across from him in his small box of an office, with chipped, pale-painted walls, and a worn wooden desk.

"And?" I reply.

"And I need to send your judge a report of your progress every six weeks. It won't bode well for you if I put in your very first one that you've been refusing to meet with me."

"I don't give a fuck what that old man thinks of me."

"Well, you should, since he has the ability to send you back to JDC."

I roll my eyes. "We done here?"

"No, we're not done here. You just entered my office. How have you been adjusting?"

"I haven't had pussy in three weeks. How the fuck do you think I've been adjusting?"

"First off, we don't refer to women that way. Second, you're a teenager. You'll live."

That's what he thinks. He probably only gets laid twice a year, if he's lucky.

I check out his room—a bulletin board with a stupid emotions chart, a roster of all the shitty kids that are here, some handmade sign that says, "Thank you, Mr. Kevin." A little conceited, aren't we, Kevin? *I zero in on a small picture on his desk of him and a woman.*

"Is that your girl?" I gesture my chin toward the frame.

"Yes. That's my fiancée."

I scoff. "Fiancée?"

Yeah, this guy only gets laid twice a year.

"Something amusing about that?"

"I don't know why anyone would want to be with just one person at all, let alone pretend that they're going to be together forever."

"Monogamy not your thing?"

"Definitely fucking not."

"Why not?"

"It's all a lie. No two people can stay together forever. Marriage is just bullshit. People don't actually love each other."

"That's pretty jaded coming from someone so young. Parents didn't have a good marriage?"

"My dad's dead."

"It says in my records he's estranged."

"If that's some fancy way of saying he bailed on his family, then yeah. But I don't think of him as estranged." I lean in closer. "I think of him as dead."

Mr. Kevin nods, and I wait for him to ask some more intrusive questions, but they don't come.

"Now *are we done?" I ask. My jaw clenches, pissed he had me come to his office just to grill me on my dad.*

Mr. Kevin rests back in his chair and observes me. "Do you want to be like your dad?"

"Fuck no."

"Do you think you're going down that road?"

I tug at the collar of my shirt. I'm not answering that fucking question.

"What do you think is the point of working with me?" he asks.

"So you can rat me out to the judge and get a big ass paycheck every two weeks?"

"No, it's not. And if you can tell my supervisor of this nice-sized paycheck that I'm so deserving of, I'd appreciate it. I could use the extra income."

I stare at my fingers that are strumming a beat on my lap, waiting for this asshole to shut up.

"The point of you being here is to make the most out of it. This might be your one opportunity to change your life around. You either work hard on yourself while you're here or waste years of your life. You're here until you graduate. The choice is yours."

The fluorescent light flickers again as the memory drifts away, leaving nothing but the last few words echoing in my head.

The choice is mine.

Digging my phone out of my pocket once class ends, I shoot a text to Mr. Kevin, asking if he's free for a call. We've been talking every so often. He's been my anchor throughout these shitty months.

"Rivera." Mr. Kevin's voice flows through the speaker of my phone as I drive back to my place. "What's going on?"

"You would've had a heart attack if you heard me speak in class today," I say, holding back a laugh.

"Oh god. What'd you say?"

I fill him in on how highly I spoke of him and all the other shit that was said. He radiated pride, satisfying a void in my chest.

"Any plans for this weekend?" he asks.

"Nah." I pull into my driveway. "Don't want to make a thing out of it this year, so I'm keeping this weekend boring."

"Sometimes boring is what we need. It lets us slow down and process everything that's been going on."

"Yeah, yeah," I tease him, even though that's exactly what I plan on doing. Since I gave everyone strict instructions that I didn't want to do anything for my birthday, everyone made plans, and my roommates will be out for most of the weekend.

I get to be by myself and just *be*.

Mr. Kevin chuckles. "Happy early birthday."

"Thanks, man."

We hang up, and I get out of my car, headed for the front door. When I push it open, the smell of fried food whirls around me. Taking steps further inside, I pass the staircase and move into the living room, where I have a clear view of my sister, Stephanie, dancing around my kitchen while she fries something in the skillet.

"Hey!" Steph greets me.

"Hey." I cock my head to the side, confusion pulling at my brows. "What are you doing here? And how did you get here?" I give her a small embrace, then go to the fridge, grabbing a cold beer. *So much for being alone and processing all the shit in my brain.* I'm not upset to see her, but a heads-up would've been nice. This obviously wasn't an impulsive thing since she came here all the way from New York.

"I wanted to see you, so I took a train and then grabbed an Uber. I like what you did with the place." She quickly changes the subject as she waves the spatula around, gesturing at the kitchen cabinets I fixed up and the new coat of paint in the living room.

"Thanks." I take a peek over her shoulder to see what she's making. My eyes light up when I spot pork chops. "You're making *chuletas*?"

"I thought I'd make you your favorite."

I squint. "Why?"

"It's your birthday."

"Not yet."

"It's your birthday weekend."

"And?"

"And I wanted to do something nice for my baby brother. Fuck."

"Steph—"

"Mateo, I don't want to hear it. I haven't seen you in forever. Plus, Michelle tells me that you're becoming a hermit."

"Oh my god, I'm not—"

"I said I didn't want to hear it! I'm doing something nice for my brother's birthday, so deal with it."

I lean against the counter and fold my arms over my chest. "I swear I'm fine."

"Good. Then you'll be *fine* with hanging out and having a movie marathon with me tonight."

I guess there are worse things in the world that I could be doing. "Fine," I say, and she gives me a smug smile.

Later that night, we sit on the like-new tan couches I recently bought, watching an action movie Steph picked out.

"This movie blows," I complain.

"Shut up." Steph takes a sip of a wine cooler, and I cringe watching her drink that nasty shit.

"You know you're not fifteen anymore. You can have a big girl drink."

"I like these, asshole."

"You've always had questionable taste." I take a dig at her past relationships.

"Fuck off." She kicks my leg, and I can't help but laugh.

My eyes go back to focusing on this crappy movie, but I can sense Steph staring at me. "You gonna watch this or are you just gonna force me to sit through it?"

She reaches for the remote and hits pause.

Here it comes. I knew she's been waiting for her in to talk to me.

"I missed hanging out with you," she says. "You managed to drive your ass home once during the entire summer."

"I didn't feel like being home."

"Why not?"

"Did you forget about those community service hours I had to complete?"

"You weren't doing them twenty-four seven."

"I spent all my other time restoring this place and working. I wanted to keep busy and avoid conversations like this."

"Mateo." Her tone grows serious.

"Stephanie," I mock.

"Mom is worried about you."

"Mom is always worried about me."

"Yeah, but it's different this time."

"Tell her I'm fine."

"I'm worried about you too. All of us are."

I let out a humorless chuckle. "That's why you're here? They sent you because they thought you're the only one I'd actually talk to?" It's not that I'm not close to my other three older sisters. It's that I'm closest with Steph. Being a year and a half apart in age and dealing with an abusive father will do that to siblings. At least it did with us.

"We don't know what's going on with you. You barely speak to any of us."

"You all know what's going on with me."

"Actually, no, we don't. We know you and Ellie broke up, and that's it." Steph lets out a loud sigh. "You've never gotten like this when you've been upset before. You're usually raging, not shutting us out."

I raise my eyebrows. "You're saying you'd rather me be tearing shit up right now?"

"No. What I'm saying is that we don't know how to help you like this. We know how to deal with angry, rebellious Mateo. We don't know how to get through to sad, sulking Mateo."

My shoulders stiffen, and I grow defensive. To think I'm acting like this over a girl makes me seem like such a bitch. "I'm not sulking, Steph. I got my heart broken."

"Listen, I don't know what it's like to be in love, and I don't know what it's like to break up with someone I love, but I *do* know you'll get through it. You've gotten through everything else so far."

I nod.

I know I'll get through it. I know I'll get over her. I just don't want to.

My phone buzzes, and I get a spark of hope that it's Elle, but when I glance down, the feeling is immediately diffused when I see it's Jasmine.

JAS

Let me know when you're ready to party. xx

I'm surprised she's still talking to me. I tried hooking up with her the day I saw Elle with Hunter at the airport, but I had to stop. It was pathetically embarrassing, considering we used to bang like rabbits on a daily basis before Elle came into my life.

"I'm here for you, Mateo," Steph says.

"Enough with the sappy shit. Let's finish this horrible movie you picked out." I reach for the remote and hit play. She turns toward the TV, dropping our conversation. "Thanks, Steph." I catch her smiling without looking at me.

CHAPTER SEVENTY

Ellie

The third week of classes is almost over, and my professors are cracking down on the workload. Typing the due date of an upcoming paper into my phone, I leave my English class and navigate through the crowd to get outside. There are a number of centuries-old oak trees as I stroll past the Great Lawn. I fixate on the one tree that is different from all the rest. It's narrower, and the leaves hang low, creating a secluded, shady area over the grass. Memories of when I met Mateo dance around in my mind, and the pull to find respite under the tree's canopy is stronger than my desire to avoid thinking about him.

Planting myself on the grass, I press my back up against the bark. Shutting my eyes, I hope to hear a voice on the other side of the tree.

But I don't.

He's not here.

It was stupid of me to think that he'd magically appear, soothing the ache in my soul.

Another piece of my heart cracks, and water pools behind my eyes. I clamp them tighter, hoping the tears will seep back in.

His birthday was this past weekend, and it physically pained me to completely ignore it. I want so badly to go to his place, wrap my arms around his broad, tattooed body, and tell him how much I love him until I'm blue in the face.

"Ellie!"

My eyelids fly open.

Did someone just call me?

"Ellie!"

I turn my head and see Ava waving me to her from across the quad. "Come here!" she shouts.

Normally, I'd love to hang out with Ava. We're only in the one philosophy class together, but seeing who she's with makes me internally cringe. It's Derek, one of Hunter's frat brothers. Not that Derek is a bad guy. He's always been nice to me. I just know how the brothers work. If there's one of them lingering around, that means there'll be more of them coming over soon.

I force a smile on my face and join them.

"Hey, Ava. Derek."

"Hi, Ellie." Derek grins at me.

"You guys know each other?" Ava asks with a twinkle in her eye.

"Yeah, Ellie hangs out with one of my brothers." Derek's gaze shifts, and he looks behind me. "Here he is now. What's up, Hunter?"

Fantastic.

Hunter and Derek fist-bump, then Hunter turns his attention to me. "Hey, Ellie." He hooks his arm around my shoulder. "Who's your friend?"

"This is Ava," Derek speaks before I can, and she and Hunter exchange hellos.

"I was Ellie's roommate in France," she tells both of them.

Hunter's eyebrows rise. "Oh, really?"

"Yeah, Ellie and I go way back." Ava chuckles. "And I met Derek a few weeks ago when I was moving in. He was helping move in his friend." *Oh,* he *was the cute guy she was telling me about.* She looks at me. "Derek was just telling me about their party. You should totally come, it's on—"

"Saturday?" I interject.

"Yeah, how'd you know?"

"They're creatures of habit. I may have gone to some in the past." And last weekend, and the weekend before. I didn't really have the option to get out of them, all things considered. So I played nice and showed my face for a little bit, pretended I was exhausted, and got an Uber back. I have a pretty good system going until Hunter inevitably catches on, which I am hoping is after May.

"Oh my god, Ellie. You have to come this weekend!" Ava exclaims.

"This one isn't much of a partier," Hunter interjects. "You'll have to do some heavy convincing, Ava, but I trust you." He gives her a charming wink.

"Hmm…I don't know. Ellie seemed to party a lot when we were rooming together in France."

"Oh, did she? She must've left that part out when telling me about her summer." Hunter grips my shoulder a little tighter. It's not noticeable to anyone but me. "Sounds like we have some more chatting to do about your time abroad, Ellie." He glances down at me.

"As much as I'd love to stay and tell embarrassing stories about myself,

I have a class to get to." Moisture forms at my hairline as I let out yet another lie.

Ava checks her phone. "Oh shit. My class starts in five minutes."

"I'll walk you over," Derek says.

We say our goodbyes, and I change my position so I'm no longer under Hunter's arm. "Lying about a class so you don't have to relive your drunken stories?" he asks with a smirk.

"Possibly."

"Knew it." He abruptly shifts his focus off me and onto two girls walking by, his eyes moving up and down their bodies.

"Don't do that." I swat him.

"Do what?"

"Check those girls out right in front of me."

"Why? Jealous?"

Yes.

"No." *What the hell? Why am I jealous? I shouldn't be jealous. God, I'm so messed up.* "I'm standing right here. It's rude."

"Yeah, but we're not together. Unless you're saying that you want to get back together?"

"No, I'm not saying that."

"Then what's the issue?"

"I…" A couple of minutes in his presence, and he's making my head spin. "I don't know. Would you like it if I did that in front of you?"

"You wouldn't."

"I very well could. In fact…" I spin myself around, scouring for a hot guy. I spot someone walking between buildings, texting on his phone. "I'll be right back." My body lurches forward, attempting to catch this person and flirt with them. Hell, I'll even make out with them in front of Hunter just to spite him.

"Elena." There's a grasp on my wrist, halting me. It's not tight, but it's enough to let me know not to move forward with my plan. "I don't think you want to do that."

A knot contorts in my stomach. My head turns to look at Hunter. I say nothing.

"Come on. Let's grab some lunch, and I can tell you about our plans for the weekend." Hunter draws me close to him, and I fall into step.

Stepping over a puddle of God knows what type of liquid, I push my way past drunk frat boys to get some fresh air. Although standing in the backyard of the house isn't much better, considering it's littered with red Solo cups and people doing keg stands.

Another Saturday. Another frat party.

Nothing changes.

The big gray house is a disaster.

Everyone is trashed.

Rinse, repeat.

Loud bass music catches my ear, and I spot a DJ playing in the place where Mateo once performed with his band.

I wonder if he's still with them. Maybe I can find out when their next show is and just so happen to make a random appearance. I wouldn't mind staring at Mateo performing all night long, even if I'm hidden in the back of a dark room somewhere.

Hands grip my waist, and I jolt. "Why'd you run off?" Hunter asks.

"Needed a break from beer pong," I say, bringing my cup to my lips. I've been nursing the same beer for four hours, and now it's turned into a warm, bitter drink.

Hunter comes to my side, one hand still linked around me. "You up for a keg stand instead?" he teases.

"Pass." I fake a yawn. "I'm actually really tired. I think I'm going to get going."

"Why don't you just stay the night?"

Fear runs down my spine at the thought.

I've managed to avoid his room at the previous parties because Hunter let me leave early due to my dulling his fun by being a complete bore. But it seems like he's caught on to my trick.

As my brain searches for an excuse, I scan the yard and spot a shit-faced Ava. The strap of her dress is sliding down her shoulder, and her once-perfect beach-wave hair is now matted to her flushed cheek. A few guys who I've never seen before stand around her as she giggles. Intuition kicks in, and I know I'm not the only one who needs to get out of this party.

I point at Ava. "She's a mess. I need to get her back to her dorm," I tell Hunter.

He turns to assess her, and before he can come up with some type of reasoning as to why I should stay anyway, I'm off to go get Ava.

"Ellie!" Ava flings herself on me, wrapping her arms around my neck. We almost topple over, but one of the guys standing nearby helps us.

"I think it's time to get you back to campus," I say.

"No," she whines, her bottom lip jutting out. "I just met these really sweet guys. They're so funny!"

"I'm sure they are. Come on." I take her hand, dragging her to the front of the house, bypassing people who try to talk to us.

While we wait for an Uber, Ava's footing becomes wobbly as she begs me to go back inside. "I didn't get to say goodbye to Derek! He went to help his frat brother with something, and that's when those guys came up to me. He's going to think I'm a bitch for leaving without saying bye!"

"No, he won't. I'll have Hunter explain."

Ava goes in for a hug. "Thank you so much, Ellie. I love you, girl." During our time together in France, I had seen Ava drunk, but never to this level.

"Love you too," I say as our Uber pulls up.

Once we manage to get into the car, Ava asks the driver to change the destination location.

"What? Why?" I ask her.

"I'm starving. I need food. There's this amazing restaurant nearby that's open late, and their wings are so good." Before I can open my mouth to say something, she's already telling the driver to drop us off at some place called the Loft.

When we get there, Ava stumbles over to the wooden table, and I help her into the booth. The restaurant has dark walls and industrial-themed decor, with several string lights spanning the entire length.

"Oh my god, mozzarella sticks!" Ava beams while looking over the menu.

Laughing at her drunkenness, I flip through the food options to find something cheap enough that'll fill my growling stomach. As I look at my phone, checking my bank account to see how much I can afford to splurge on food, the waitress places black napkins down on the table.

"Welcome to the Loft, I'm—" She stops talking.

The abrupt action takes my attention away from my phone and up to the person standing in front of me. Michelle.

She clears her throat before continuing, "Can I start you off with something to drink?" Michelle barely blinks in my direction, which is the most acknowledgment she's given me since I awkwardly ran away from her after class, so I'll take what I can get.

"You look so familiar." Ava points to Michelle. "Why do I know her?" she asks me.

"I'm in your philosophy class. Drinks?" Michelle asks again.

"I think I want another beer," Ava slurs.

"Two waters are fine. Thanks," I tell Michelle, and she nods, walking away.

My hands wring together under the table, hidden from Ava as she babbles on about the party. Before long, she orders her late-night meal, but I no longer have an appetite.

As Ava takes a bite of her mozzarella sticks, I spy Michelle cleaning a table behind her. Michelle carefully puts the ketchup and salt back in their rightful place as Ava continues to speak to me. "I really like Derek," she says, wiping crumbs off her fingers.

I chuckle. "I know."

"He invited me to hang out at some bar on Thursday with him and his friends. Can you come with me?"

"Um…" I chew the inside of my cheek. I peek over to see if Michelle is paying attention, but she seems to be focused on spraying the empty table with cleaning solution. "I don't know if that's such a good idea."

"Please, please, please? I'm so nervous hanging around hot frat guys and could really use some female support. You already know most of them."

Unfortunately.

"I'm not below begging." Ava clasps her hands together and pouts. Just then, Michelle finishes cleaning and walks past us, moving behind me so I can no longer see where she is.

"Fine. But you owe me."

"I'll buy you drinks!" Ava exclaims, throwing her hands in the air. "And apparently, this place doesn't ID, so I'll get you as many as you want. It's called Dave's Sports Bar. Have you ever been there before? I haven't."

Nausea strikes, and I get the sudden urge to throw up my empty stomach as all the memories from the night when everything turned to shit come crashing back in.

"Once."

CHAPTER SEVENTY-ONE

Mateo

The coffee shop finally slows down after the midmorning rush, so I have time to check supplies behind the counter to see if I need to place an inventory order. As I'm checking the flavor bottles, I hear the faint sound of footsteps approaching me. When I turn around to see who it is, Rebecca smiles, looping a strand of hair behind her ear.

"Can I order something?" she asks. "I'm on my ten."

"Of course. What can I get you?"

"Just coffee with milk."

I nod and get to work. A weird feeling of guilt falls over me as I make her drink in silence. I've barely given her the time of day, in school or here, for no other reason than I wish she didn't take Elle's place. That's never been me. I've never been one to be a dick to someone who doesn't deserve it just because I can't put my own issues aside.

Placing her drink on the counter, I decide to strike up a conversation. "How are you liking working in the bookstore?"

"I enjoy it," Rebecca says before taking a sip. "It's only for this semester, though. I won't be able to squeeze this into my schedule once my internship starts next semester."

"Tell me about it. It's going to suck trying to balance everything."

"Are you planning on working while you intern?" she asks, leaning against the counter.

"Kinda have to. My uncle owns the place, and I'm sure he wouldn't be happy if I quit on him. Plus, I need money for rent and my car and, you know, regular everyday shit."

"Edgar is your uncle? I had no idea."

"Yep." I bend forward and rest my elbows on the counter, continuing to speak. "I'm sure he'd be cool if I needed to shift hours around for school, though."

"How are you liking the social work program so far?"

"It's a lot of work, but I like it. My favorite class so far is—"

"Foundations?"

"Yes! Barbara is awesome!"

"Oh my god, she's the best! I want to be her when I grow up." Rebecca laughs, and I chuckle along with her.

The bells over the front door chime, and in walks Michelle. She hesitates for a moment when she spots Rebecca and me laughing together.

"What's up?" I say to Michelle as I straighten my posture.

She walks over to the counter and shrugs. "Just came in to bother you since I have a long break in between classes." She glances at Rebecca. "You're the new girl at the bookstore, right?"

"Yep, I'm Rebecca."

"Michelle," she says while pulling out her phone to text someone. "Can you make me something?" she asks without looking at me.

"What do you want?"

"I don't know. Whatever you made me the last time I was here tasted good." She continues to text as I flip through my brain, trying to remember what I made her because it was weeks ago. "It was sweet. Vanilla-y."

"Iced vanilla latte."

"Yes, that was it!"

"All right. Give me a sec." I look over at Rebecca. "Sorry my rude cousin interrupted our conversation." Michelle gives me the finger, and Rebecca laughs.

"It's okay. We'll chat another time. I should head back over to the other side before my break is over anyway. How much do I owe you for the coffee?"

"Don't worry about it. It's on the house," I say.

"Oh. Thanks." Rebecca grins and goes to turn toward the bookstore but stops herself. "I almost forgot to tell you. A few of my friends and I are going barhopping tonight, if you want to join."

"I'm not sure…"

"Where are you going? I wanna go out." Michelle butts in as if she's part of the conversation.

"We're going to a bunch of different places. Our first stop is Dave's Sports Bar, then—"

"We'll be there," Michelle says.

"You weren't even invited," I tell her.

"Both of you are more than welcome to come," Rebecca assures us.

"Like I said, we'll be there," Michelle repeats and throws an icy look at me.

"I'm not sure if I'm free tonight," I say, glaring at her.

"What else do you have planned? You already repainted most of the house." Michelle gives me a fake smile and spins to Rebecca. "What time?"

"We'll be getting there around nine," Rebecca says, taking a step backward to go back to work.

"See you then!" Michelle says.

Once Rebecca is out of earshot, I snap at Michelle. "What the fuck was that about?"

"What?"

"Are you trying to set me up with her?"

"No, definitely not with her. Calm the fuck down. You're going barhopping, not ring shopping. And I think going out could be good for you."

"I don't want to go out," I say, making myself busy by continuing to check supplies.

"Come on, Mateo. You have to go out and have some fun eventually. You can't just sit around and sulk forever."

I press my lips together, piecing together why Michelle is being so incessant about this. "Did Steph talk to you?"

"Do I talk to my cousin? Yes, I do."

I mutter curses under my breath because I know Michelle won't give me a straight answer. "Fine, I'll go tonight. But you're buying me a beer."

"Deal."

We sit in the parking lot of the dive bar Rebecca told me the name of. The worn-down building has a sign that flashes *Dave's Sports Bar* in neon lights.

"This place is a shithole," I say.

"It is," Michelle agrees.

"Then what the hell are we doing here?"

"Hopefully having fun."

We get out of the car and enter the bar. As soon as I step foot inside, I'm slapped in the face by the stench of stale beer and cigarettes. Wood paneling covers the walls, and it looks like this place hasn't been upgraded since the seventies. But despite the horrendous atmosphere, the place is packed.

Michelle sticks her hands into the back of her jeans pockets, looking as if she's searching for someone as she scans the room.

"Expecting someone?"

"The girl from the bookstore," Michelle answers.

"Mateo!" Rebecca calls from the bar. She waves me over to her and her friends.

"Oh, look. There she is," Michelle points. "I'm gonna make a quick round and see who's here."

Before I can respond, she's off.

I walk over to Rebecca and lean my body weight on the bar since there's no place to sit. "Hey."

"I'm so happy you made it. I had a little bet going with myself on whether you'd actually show. I lost."

Wow. Am I that fucking boring these days?

"Yeah, it's been a while since I've gone out. But I'm happy I made it."

Rebecca studies me for a brief second and then bursts into laughter. "You do *not* seem happy to be here at all."

A smile cracks on my face. "All right, you got me. Maybe I've been in a weird place, and my cousin is forcing me to go out."

"Sounds like you need two things: a beer and someone to talk to." She signals the bartender and orders us beers. Once the cold drinks arrive, she holds up her glass. "Cheers to being in a weird place and not knowing what the fuck to do about it."

We clink glasses, and I take a swig. "You got shit going on too?"

She nods. "Not only did I break my parents' hearts by not going to med school like the both of them, but they recently learned that their only daughter is queer, and they are less than pleased about that."

"Oh god. I'm sorry, Rebecca. I'll never understand why parents would rather ruin their relationships with their kids than be supportive of their happiness."

"Tell me about it." She drinks some more. "Okay, I gave you the quick version of my shitty situation. You tell me yours," she says.

Suddenly, someone tugs at my arm. "We need to go," Michelle says, coming out of nowhere.

"I'm in the middle of a conversation," I tell her and turn back to Rebecca. I'm about to continue talking to her when some guy knocks into me, splashing his beer all over me.

"Sorry, man," he says before stumbling off.

Finding a half-dry napkin on the bar, I try to clean myself off, but it's a poor attempt. "I'm gonna grab some paper towels from the bathroom," I tell Rebecca before excusing myself.

"We should leave," Michelle grabs my arm again.

"Will you let me piss first?"

She chews on her bottom lip and nods, letting me go.

I head down a dark, narrow hallway where there's a sign for the restrooms. As I approach the men's door, the women's door opens, and I stop dead in my tracks.

And so does she.

Wide, sage-colored eyes stare directly back at me.

The ends of her golden hair kiss her shoulders.

My heart leaps into my throat, and I instantly feel like I'm in the middle of a heatwave.

"Hi," she says, so softly it's barely audible. But I heard it. I heard her voice, and it sends me into a trance. I haven't heard that sweet, high-pitched voice in months, and, fuck, it's better than I remember.

"Hey," I rasp.

Her chest quickly rises and falls, and I wonder if mine is doing the same. I take a step closer, and her body tenses up.

"I have to go." She scurries around me.

"Elle, wait—"

"I'm not doing this here, Mateo."

"Then where? Name a time and place, and I'll be there. I need to talk to you, Elle. I need to make this right. I have so much I want to tell you—"

"We can't."

Her eyes dart around the room as if she's nervous.

And then it hits me.

I've only ever seen her look like that around one person. The thought of her still being with Hunter makes me ball my fists. I thought by some miracle, over the past month, she'd be able to escape whatever spell he has her under. The reminder that they're still together makes me want to fucking explode.

Elle rapidly blinks, then spins around, blending in with the crowd.

I don't follow.

If she wanted me, she'd be with me. Not him.

After furiously cleaning beer off my shirt and arm while convincing myself not to punch a hole in the bathroom wall, I get back to the bar and another guy is cozied up next to Rebecca, buying her and Michelle a drink.

A loud cheer goes off in the far room, bringing my attention to a pool table. I zone in on Elle, holding a pool stick and giggling at the group of frat boys clapping for her. Her eyes skim the room but never connect with mine.

Grabbing my beer from earlier, I chug the rest of it down. I watch as she scours the table, lining up her next shot that she is no doubt going to make. She bends over the table, giving me a perfect view of her ass in those tight jeans she has on. Hunter inches his way closer to her. He looks bigger than the last time I've seen him, but I can still take him.

He has a smile smeared across his face right before he slaps her ass. Elle shoots up, her cheeks blotchy with embarrassment as she reprimands him. Once again, she checks around the room, probably for me, to see if I saw.

I fucking saw.

"I'm leaving," I tell Rebecca and Michelle, slamming my glass down on the bar.

"What? Why?" Rebecca furrows her brow.

I shake my head, letting her know I don't want to talk. "Need to go home, sorry. I'll see you in class."

Michelle follows me out as I push my way through people, not giving a fuck if I shove someone a little too hard.

Sitting in my car, I jam the key into the ignition.

"I'm sorry," Michelle says before I can put my foot on the gas.

"For what?"

"I knew she would be here, but I didn't know she would be with him."

I snap my focus in her direction. "You knew she would be here? How?"

"I overheard her talking at the restaurant with some annoying girl who's in our philosophy class."

"You guys are in the same class, and you wait until now to tell me?"

"I tried talking to you about it the first day of school at the coffee shop, saying that I need to take a philosophy class and what should I do if I run into her, but you weren't paying attention and didn't give me an answer. Plus, she didn't want me to tell you."

"You're talking to her?"

"Once. I spoke to her once. Trust me, I'm team Mateo in all of this. After what I just saw, that fucking bitch can—"

"Stop." I hold up my hand. "Don't go there."

Shifting my attention to look out the windshield, I pull out of the parking spot. We drive in silence as Michelle's comment plays on repeat in my mind. *She didn't want me to tell you.*

I need to stop fooling myself. Elle wants nothing to do with me. She made that loud and clear about a million times, and if I wasn't already sure of it, then Hunter's handprint on her ass sealed the deal.

Fuck this.

As soon as I park in my driveway, I reach for my pocket.

ME

you up?

JAS

be there in 20

CHAPTER SEVENTY-TWO

Ellie

The back room of Dave's Sports Bar spins.

He's here.

My entire body buzzes with pain and fear and need.

I thought I could handle running into Mateo if it happened, but after seeing his dark-brown eyes soften and the way he did that nervous lip bite—I can't. Hearing him plead with me to talk sent an arrow straight to my heart. And as I bleed out all over the floor, I pretend I'm perfectly fine.

I keep playing the part.

Ignoring my heart pounding against my bones, I lean over the pool table, lining up my shot. Steadying my breathing so that the cue stick doesn't tremble in my hands, I'm about to shoot my shot when Hunter spanks me in front of everyone.

"Hunter!" I spring upright, my cheeks flaming. I check the room to see if Mateo saw.

Please don't be here.

Please be far, far away from me.

"Sorry. Couldn't help myself," Hunter replies with a smirk.

"Ava, here." I shove the pool stick in her direction, blatantly interrupting whatever is going on between her and Derek. "I'm not playing anymore."

I start stepping away, but I have no idea where I can go. I can't use the excuse to pee again because I just did that. I can't go to the bar area or outside because I don't know if I'll run into Mateo, and I need to keep him away from Hunter.

I'm fucking trapped. Once again.

"Where are you going?" Hunter's voice comes from behind me.

"Nowhere. I just need a break." I massage my temples.

He wraps his arm around me and kisses the top of my head. "Sorry," he says in a low voice next to my ear. "I didn't mean to embarrass you."

I nod.

"We're still going to have a good night, right, angel? I promise I'll keep my hands to myself."

My mouth dries up so much that I can't talk. All I can do is nod for a second time.

"Good," he says, then releases me.

"Thanks for the ride back," I say to Hunter as he pulls into a parking spot in front of my dorm after spending hours at the bar, in which I was trembling with anxiety the entire time, even though I didn't see Mateo again.

"Of course," Hunter responds.

My hand goes to unbuckle my seat belt when my phone starts going off. Nerves wring my insides as my first thought goes to Mateo, but then I realize I still have him blocked. Checking the screen, I see it's Mom.

"Is she still sober?" Hunter asks, looking down at my screen.

"That's what she's claiming." I click the answer button. "Hey, Mom."

"Elena?" Her weak and muddled voice is like a weight dropping in my stomach. I shake my head at Hunter.

I had thought that she was doing well while I was in France.

Actually, no, that's a lie. I didn't think much of her at all—or anything I left behind. The moment the plane landed in Paris, I was free to be a different person for three months. I lived how I wanted, without pressure and expectations. I dreaded returning and came back ill-prepared for what I was walking into on all fronts. I didn't think I'd cross paths with Mateo again, especially because I've been avoiding all his usual spots.

The image of him standing right in front of me, looking so heartbroken, adds another layer of hurt while I talk to my drunken and depressed mother on the phone.

As I walk her through getting a glass of water, some aspirin, and lying down, Hunter runs his hand through my hair. The same hand that embarrassed me earlier is soothing me, and my brain rips down the middle in confusion.

Once I hang up, I let out a sigh and stare out into the darkness.

"Why don't I come upstairs and hang out with you for the night?" Hunter suggests as his hand gently drops to his side.

I shake my head. "Bree texted me before that she needs to go to bed early. I'm just going to go to sleep."

"Okay. I'll see you on Saturday for the party at our frat house."

"Yep."

After saying good night, I make it to my dorm room, taking a deep breath before entering.

"Hey, roomie!" Bree says, in the midst of changing outfits. "Where'd you go?"

I drop my purse on my desk. "I went to see a movie with my friend Ava."

"Was it good?" She shimmies into a denim skirt.

"It was okay," I answer. She stills, studying me. "What?"

"You seem off."

I internally groan. *Of course my roommate needs to be "good at reading people."*

"I have a headache. That's all."

"Okay." She moves to the full-length mirror behind the door to check her clothes, but then pivots to look back at me. "I was gonna go to a party, but I can hang here tonight, and we can talk."

"No way. Go to your party. I'll probably be passed out in a few minutes anyway."

"All right, but if you change your mind, text me, and I'll come back."

"You got it." I smile.

After Bree leaves, I change into my pj's, put on my Straylight Run record, and cozy myself under the covers. I let the weight of the loneliness sink in as my mind replays the ten-second hit of Mateo I received earlier. Letting myself get high off the quick memory, I spend the rest of the night thinking of him.

CHAPTER SEVENTY-THREE

Ellie

OCTOBER

My phone vibrates against my comforter for the twelfth time. I don't bother checking to see who it is because I know it's Mom. Her drinking has picked up over the past month, and today she has resorted to repeatedly drunk dialing me. Out of boredom or guilt, who knows? I tried getting her to take a nap over the phone for the past eleven phone calls. I think I'll sit this one out.

A knock on my door is a welcome interruption from the annoying sound of my phone.

"Come in," I say.

Hunter appears in my doorway with a calming energy about him. It's the same relaxing presence that he's had all month. Things between us have been absolutely fine. In fact, we even had some space from each other so we could focus on papers and tests.

"Hey, stranger." He sits down at the foot of my bed while I straighten my back up against the headboard.

"Hey."

"You going to answer her?" He motions toward my phone, ringing for the thirteenth time.

"She's in one of her moods."

"Got it." He nods. "You haven't said much about your mom. What's going on with her?"

"She's the same. Nothing's changed. Old habits die hard or some shit like that."

"They sure do." A familiar expression flickers across his face. I nudge his thigh with my foot, and he laughs. "I missed you at our party last weekend."

"Midterms." I shrug.

"Our Halloween party is this weekend."

"I don't have a costume. Too bad."

"We can go pick one out." Hunter puts his hand on my leg. "Come on. It'll be fun."

"My savings are getting low. I don't want to waste my money on a costume." I pick at my nails. "I need to start looking for a job." I sure as hell don't want to work at the Cozy Nook again and be faced with seeing Mateo every shift.

"You don't need a job. You have me."

"Hunter, I don't want your—"

"Focus on school this semester, and I'll help you get by."

I nod. If I keep myself on a tight budget, I'll have enough to make it through until next semester, barring my not having to help Mom out with any of her bills. Even then, I won't take a penny from Hunter. It's already an uncomfortable reminder that I had to ask him to post Mateo's bail last year—the final part of our arrangement. I'm assuming Mateo appeared in court because Hunter told me he got the money back minus a processing fee that the court keeps. When I tried to give Hunter what the court took out, he wouldn't take it from me.

Another debt hanging over my head.

Just then, Bree enters the room. "Hey," she says, her steps stuttering a beat when she notices Hunter.

"Hi, Bree." I pop up. "I hope you don't mind. Hunter stopped over."

"Hey," he says with a gentle smile.

"No, it's fine." She walks over to her side with an expression on her face that tells me it's definitely *not* fine.

Over the past few weeks, I've been making myself scarce or fielding any intrusive questions from her with the minimal time we do hang out here together. Thankfully, midterms took both of our attention away from what's going on in each other's personal lives.

Anytime Hunter wants to hang out, I make sure it's away from my dorm room. But the two of them being together right now has turned my stomach into a knot of nerves, knowing that neither of them is each other's biggest fan. I play with a frayed end of my blanket as anxiety weasels its way into my brain.

The anxiety medicine I've been taking helps to take the edge off, but it's not a miracle worker.

"Catch me up on what's going on," Bree says.

"Ellie needs a costume for my Halloween party, so we're going shopping."

"Cool." Bree bobs her head up and down. "Ellie, one of my friends in the fine arts grad program is having a Halloween party. Do you want to join?"

"She's already coming to my party," Hunter states.

"My question was directed at Ellie."

"And I gave you her answer."

"I think she can speak for herself." Bree throws a book down on her desk.

My muscles clench as the tension swiftly escalates. I jump in to defuse this as quickly as possible. "Thank you, Bree, but I already promised Hunter I'd go to his. I'll go to another one of your friends' parties. Promise."

She clicks her tongue. "Okay."

"Ready to go shopping for your costume?" Hunter asks me.

"Now?"

"Yeah, what else are you doing?"

My phone goes off again, and I silence it. "All right, let's go."

Slipping into my sneakers, I shoot Bree an apologetic look. I don't want this to cause any issues between us.

"Ellie, do you mind if we talk privately before you go?" Bree asks.

An immediate sinking feeling burdens me. "Uh…yeah, of course." I glance over at Hunter. "I'll meet you in the car."

His brows pinch. "Um…okay. Bye, Bree."

She gives him a wave and closes the door. Then she zeros in on me. "What's going on?"

"With what?" Sweat forms on my palms, and I casually brush them over my jeans, hoping she doesn't notice.

"I feel like we hardly even see each other. You're either studying or sleeping or out with Ava, and now all of a sudden Hunter is hanging out here?"

Guilt coils around my intestines because I've been using Ava as a cover-up so Bree doesn't think I'm spending all my time with Hunter.

"Are you two back together?" she asks.

"No."

"Okay, then what happened to us having our single ladies year? You barely talk to me anymore and haven't gone out with me once. Do you not want to be friends anymore or something?"

"No! Not at all! I think our schedules just aren't matching up. Plus, I've been busy and…" *And trying to avoid you so I don't have to admit what's going on.* "And Hunter just has a lot going on right now, so I'm trying to be there for him."

Her mouth scrunches to one side as she assesses what I just said. "Do you even want to go to his Halloween party?"

"I…" My fingers fiddle with the sleeves of my shirt. "Yeah."

"That was the least convincing yes I've ever heard." She finally cracks a smile. "Why don't you come to the party I'm going to?"

"I can't."

"Why not?"

"I already promised him."

"Who the fuck cares? He's a big boy. He'll get over it."

"It's not that simple."

"Ellie, what is going on?"

"What do you mean?"

"I can tell something's up," Bree states, folding her arms over her chest. I stay mute, and she continues. "Are you sure everything is okay between us? Did I do something wrong? Because it's feeling like you don't trust me anymore, and it's starting to really hurt."

My phone rings in my hand, and I groan, assuming it's Mom. I turn the screen upward to click the decline button, only to see Hunter's name on my screen. Bree glances down and sees who it is.

"Never mind. We'll talk later," she says.

"Bree, I do trust you. I'm sorry—"

"It's fine." She dismissively waves a hand and goes back to her desk.

Another seam in my heart rips open, and I try to blink away the tears forming behind my eyes. "You didn't do anything wrong, and I promise everything's the same between us, Bree."

"Okay."

Hunter calls again, and I grab my jacket, escaping the pain left lingering between me and the person I consider my closest friend.

"Damn, Ellie! Pool and flip cup?" Rhett praises my abilities.

"What can I say? I'm multi-talented." I chuckle to myself and finish off another red Solo cup. I've surpassed tipsy and am on the fast track to becoming wasted. I'm not supposed to be drinking while I'm on my medication, but I couldn't deal with being at another frat party sober—especially their Halloween one.

Hunter threads his fingers through my hair, and I lean my head into his palm. I've gotten good at pretending I'm perfectly fine.

So good that I'm even starting to fool myself.

"Are you feeling okay?" Hunter asks, taking a peek down my dress. We settled on a sexy flight attendant. It's a blue dress with an airline badge on the right side and only slightly dips at the cleavage. It's classy-sexy—or whatever the fuck Hunter deems acceptable for me to wear. I have to pick my battles with him. Arguing about a costume wasn't worth it.

"Just a little dizzy," I reply as the backyard of the house blurs together.

"Wanna go lie down?" Hunter trails his fingers down my back, softly caressing me.

"No, I'm good."

"Ellie, let's go. You're on my team this time," Derek says, and Ava sidles up next to him. Both of them are fawning all over each other. It's kind of cute to watch.

I need another fucking drink.

I down some jungle juice, no longer wincing at the harsh burn of the liquor. My body sways to the dance music playing through the speakers as I let the music flow through me. My eyelids are heavy, and I struggle to keep them open.

"Come on," a deep voice comes from behind me.

I'm helped up the stairs, stumbling with each step, and am ushered into a familiar room.

White walls with a yellowish tint surround me, and a chill runs down my body, causing my body to tremble. This is the first time I've seen it since last year. I've stayed sober at all his parties this semester and had my wits about me to know enough not to enter this room.

My pulse speeds up as my breathing becomes unsteady. "No." I spin to face the door, but Hunter steps in front of me.

"Just lie down and sleep it off." He shuffles me closer to his bed.

Panic rumbles in my chest as I'm moved backward. "I don't wanna lie in your bed."

"Then sleep on the floor. I don't care where you lie down, but you're shit-faced and need to go to sleep."

"I don't wanna be in your room, Hunter. I don't like being in here with you." I shove his arm.

"I'm not going to fuck you in your sleep, Elena. God, you make me sound like a horrible person."

Nausea twists around in my belly. "I don't know if you recall what happened in here last semester, but I sure do." As if I'm reliving the moment, the sensation of his body pushing down onto mine triggers panic to erupt throughout my nervous system.

My body shudders as I suddenly break out into a cold sweat, moisture dripping down my sides.

"I didn't think it was possible for you to be more overdramatic, but drunk you is ten times worse."

Crushed by his insult and the invisible weight of him, my eyes sting, and I fight with myself not to set my tears free. "Stop." I stumble, pacing back and forth across his room with my arms flailing around. "I hate when you say shit like that! I hate when you call me overdramatic!" My voice cracks. "I hate *you*!"

"Look at you. You're fucking crying right now over absolutely nothing. You're going to tell me that's not being overdramatic, Ellie?"

"I'm not crying!" I say sternly before my emotions betray me and I burst into tears.

Hunter lets out a long sigh while looking up at the ceiling. "Just lie down. You're too drunk for us to be doing this."

I shake my head while wiping the stream of tears flowing down my face. "I'm getting an Uber back to my dorm."

"Seriously?"

"Yes, seriously!"

He pinches the bridge of his nose, frustrated. Taking a step back, I hold my breath, waiting for an outburst from him. But there's a sudden shift in his energy, and he drops his hand. "Whatever. I'll see you tomorrow."

As soon as Hunter leaves, my fingers are quick to order an Uber even through my blurred vision. I race out of his room, almost tripping down the stairs on my way out of the house. I catch a glimpse of a bunch of sorority girls hanging over Hunter, and a range of emotions that I'm not ready to acknowledge make their way to the surface.

Slamming my head down on my pillow, my dorm room furiously spins. Bree isn't here, but I wasn't expecting her to be. She's spending Halloween with her other friends, while I'm kept on a short leash, not allowed to be with anyone else but Hunter.

Fuck. That realization hits me like a ton of bricks, and my body sinks into my mattress while I pray it swallows me whole.

I have no one.

Not a single soul.

I lie through my teeth on a daily basis, pretending I'm fine. No one has a fucking clue what's going on.

I'm completely alone.

My heart aches for the one person who never made me feel alone. The one person who saw me for me and was okay with it.

Pulling myself up from my bed, I stagger over to my desk and drop to my knees. Opening the bottom drawer, I take out Mateo's balled-up black T-shirt and bring it to my nose, sniffing it like a weirdo. My body slumps, clasping the fabric, hugging it, and imagining he's here. My gaze shifts to the green crystal necklace hiding next to the medicine in my drawer. I slap my hand around, trying to grasp it. Eventually, I connect with the silver chain and pull the necklace out to admire it. Holding it up, I see three of the same necklace, and I blink a few times, trying to make it come into focus.

The crystal shines, and even through my drunken state, I'm able to capture the multitude of shades of green that reflect in the streetlight coming through the window.

A sense of warmth just from holding the two items consumes my chest, but it's quickly stifled by my reality.

I hope this is all worth it.

He'd better be doing well in grad school. Otherwise, I'm gonna be pissed as hell.

Pushing myself off the floor, I crash onto my bed. I let go of the shirt and necklace and search for my phone. Before my brain can stop my fingers, I unblock Mateo's number and stare at the screen.

I really shouldn't do this.

I stare for one more second.

I'm gonna do it.

ME

yu bettr have good social workr gradess

There. Straight to the point.

I watch the screen, waiting for a response.

The room continues to rotate even though my eyes are heavy. I allow myself to shut them, knowing that at the very least, I'll see Mateo in my dreams.

CHAPTER SEVENTY-FOUR

Mateo

NOVEMBER

My textbook is propped up on the coffee shop counter, and I've been trying to read as much as possible in between customers. I don't know what's wrong with me. I've been working my ass off in school and acing all my assignments, but I still have this stirring feeling inside like I shouldn't really be there. Everyone else is deserving of it, but I feel like my hands are dirtied by my recent past.

Plus, the school workload is a lot more than I thought it would be. It's reading after reading and paper after paper. And today, in particular, I can't concentrate—not after the text I received two days ago.

"You good?" *Tío* Edgar asks, heading toward the back office.

My head snaps out of the book. "Yeah, just need to catch up on some reading."

He crosses over to me. "Listen, if you need to cut back on some hours, I'll have one of the managers in the bookstore cover for you."

"Who? Sandy? She tried working the espresso machine once, and it exploded." I laugh at the memory. She's a great person, but should stick to managing her side.

"Yeah, you're right." He scratches the scruff on the side of his face. "Well, I'd figure something out if you need—"

"Thanks, but I'm good. I can handle it."

Edgar nods and goes back to whatever it was he was doing.

I bury my head back in my textbook, skimming over the last few paragraphs before Rebecca comes this way after her shift. We're working on a class assignment together, assessing a case study and coming up with a treatment plan. We've gotten close over the past several weeks. That is, of course, after I apologized for up and leaving her at Dave's Sports Bar. I explained my ex was there, and I didn't want to see her, which Rebecca understood, and we never brought up Elle again.

Elle's been popping into my brain every damn day, but when it happens, it's more of a dull ache than an explosion of pain tearing my insides to scraps.

Up until two nights ago.

Her text threw me off-kilter, just when I thought I'd regained some balance.

"Ready?" Rebecca asks, and I spot her sitting at a large table with her books and laptop, waiting for me to join.

"Yep." I bring my belongings over to her, and we dive right into work. I watch out for any customers, but luckily, it's a slow day.

After spending a solid hour researching different therapeutic approaches to use for our case, we move on to talking about internships. As part of our program, we need to interview at several agencies, and my first one is coming up in a couple of days, adding to the mix of stress.

Rebecca groans. "I need a break from talking about all this." She pushes away her laptop. "What's going on in your life? Anything fun?"

"Nope. Same old shit. Work and school."

She chuckles. "Yeah, same, and parent drama."

"What now?"

"We're going to spend Thanksgiving with our family in Vermont, and apparently, my parents not only told them that I'm going to med school, but I also have a boyfriend."

"What!"

"Yeah, some next-level bullshit, right?"

"Want me to talk some sense into them?" I joke.

"If only that would work." She stretches in her chair. "I don't want to think about them anymore. How was your Halloween? What'd you do?"

I shrug. "Just hung out with my friend, Jasmine."

"And by hung out, you mean hooked up?"

"That's what hanging out has always been for us."

Nothing more and nothing less. It's a pretty good deal we've always had going on, only this time around, I feel like shit afterward. The night of Halloween, right after we got our clothes back on, my phone went off, and the second I saw Elle's text, I almost puked all over Jasmine's bed. It's like I'm cheating on Elle every time I'm with Jasmine. I don't know why I keep doing it. Maybe I'm waiting for it to feel good again, or maybe I'm just fucking horny.

"Does this mean you're over the ex?" Rebecca asks.

Her question is like a sucker punch to the gut. "Far from it." My fingers strum against the table. "She texted me on Halloween."

Rebecca's brows shoot up. "She did? What'd she say?"

Before I can fill her in, a customer makes an abrupt entrance, and my attention swings to the person standing in the doorway wearing maroon-colored pants and a giant winter coat as if it were blizzarding outside.

"Mateo," Bree says, making a beeline for me.

I jolt out of my seat, worry twisting around my chest. I haven't seen her since last school year. "Is everything okay?"

"No...yes, yes. Nobody's dying or anything. It's not like that." Bree takes a breath. "Sorry, I didn't mean to get you riled up. I just wanted to talk to you about something. You can go back to sitting down." She glances over at the table and notes Rebecca. "Actually, maybe I'll come back at another—"

"We're meeting for a class project." I clarify whatever Bree might have thought was going on.

"Oh."

"You can come join us," Rebecca chimes in. "We'll welcome the distraction."

Bree agrees, and we head to the table, taking a seat. Once Bree is out of her winter coat and unravels about twenty scarves from around her neck, she finally tells me what she came here for. "I need to talk to you about Ellie."

"What about her?" My heart rate quickens.

"She's off...really not herself this semester. I'm concerned about her. I think something might be going on."

"Like what?"

"I don't know. She won't talk to me. I know she's upset over what happened between you two, but she won't even tell me what happened."

"Is Ellie your ex?" Rebecca asks, already invested. Tugging at my shirt collar, I avoid looking at Rebecca and just nod. "The one who texted you on Halloween?"

"She texted you?" Bree's face brightens with surprise.

"Yeah," I answer.

"What'd she say?" Bree asks.

"It was a drunk text. I ignored it."

"You ignored it?" both of them say at the same time.

"I haven't heard a word from her in months. I wasn't going to respond to her drunk text, especially because I had a feeling where she was that night and who she was with."

"How'd you know she was with Hunter?" Bree asks.

For starters, you just confirmed it. "Wild guess," I say, putting my hands up, then slapping them back down on my lap.

"Mateo, I don't really know the situation," Rebecca says. "But it sounds like the both of you have some unresolved issues. Maybe you should actually talk to each other."

"Yep. I agree with everything she just said." Bree points at Rebecca. Smiling, Rebecca tucks a strand of hair behind her ear, and there's a look that crosses between both of them that suddenly makes me feel like I should leave the room. I clear my throat, and Bree brings her attention back to why she came here. "Like I was saying, I think Ellie is hurting a lot more than she's letting on. I think something's up. I just don't know what. And I think you'd do a better job than me at getting through to her."

My throat goes dry, and I shake my head. "She doesn't want anything to do with me, Bree."

"Then why'd she text you?" Rebecca challenges.

Leaning back in my chair, I consider what she's saying. But there's no way Elle wants me back in her life. Not after she made it very clear what type of person she views me as.

Still, Rebecca's comment gives me a sliver of hope that is getting me dangerously close to doing something idiotic.

"Just think about talking to her, okay?" Bree asks.

"Yeah. I'll think about it."

CHAPTER SEVENTY-FIVE

Ellie

My boots crunch against the multicolored fall leaves as I walk to Hunter's frat house. I haven't seen him since Halloween last week, but today is his birthday, and he asked for me to come over. I don't have enough money to get him a decent gift, so I hope he's okay with a shirt I found at Target. We've been texting all week, and naturally, we fell into our pattern of ignoring the issue after arguing with each other and getting close again. The erratic ups and downs are nothing new for us.

I could've had him pick me up, but I wanted to stroll through the autumn trees while listening to my music, hoping to clear my mind and process this mess I've found myself in.

Anxiety pricks at my fingertips as I check my phone for the thousandth time today. I've been glued to my phone for days, ever since I drunkenly texted Mateo, waiting for a reply, but I've gotten nothing but silence. Not that I blame him. I pulled out all the stops to make sure I stabbed him in the heart hard enough that he'd never want to come back to me.

And it worked.

Slipping my phone into my back pocket, I shove down the burning pain in my chest. I have no right to feel this way.

I have no one else to blame but myself.

And with each step, I accept my fate.

"Hey, angel," Hunter says when I enter his bedroom.

"Hey." I smile and outstretch the gift bag in my hand with the shirt in it. "Happy birthday."

"You didn't need to get me anything." He grins and pulls the shirt out of the bag. It's nothing special. A gray polo. "I love it."

"Good." I shuffle out of my jacket.

He places his gift and my jacket on his dresser, then goes in for a hug. "Did you walk here? You're freezing."

"Yeah, I needed some fresh air."

"Next time, just tell me you need a ride. You're going to get sick." He takes my hand and moves me toward his bed. "Come on. I'll warm you up."

"Hunter…" My chest tightens, and I draw my hand away.

"Ellie." For a moment, I think I see a flash of anger appear on his face, but instead, he gently brushes a strand of hair off my cheek. "I just want to hold you. I had a shitty day, and seeing you is the only good part."

"What's wrong?"

"Why don't we sit down, and I'll tell you." Glancing behind him at his bed, I nibble on my bottom lip. "Look at me," he says, and I do. "Do you think I'm *that* horrible of a person that I would try to make a move on you? You said you didn't want to be anything, so I'm trying my best to respect that." His blue eyes draw me in as I decipher the sincerity in his comment. "I really need my best friend right now. I need *you*."

His comment fills me with purpose, and my mind instantly puts any frustrations from last week on the back burner. "What's wrong?" I repeat.

"My parents."

I crinkle my brow. "Your parents?"

His gaze dips, and there is a slight hesitation before he starts speaking again. "You remember that embarrassing drunken meltdown I had in your dorm last year?"

The one where he sobbed and cried out his dead sister's name—yeah, no way I'm forgetting that. "It wasn't embarrassing," I assure him.

"It's okay, Ellie. You don't have to sugarcoat it. It was embarrassing as fuck." He lets out a small chuckle, and I sense myself loosening up.

"Compared to all my meltdowns, it was nothing," I joke.

He walks backward to his bed and sits down as he continues to talk. "Well, stuff has gotten pretty bad since then. Mom called me up a little while ago, hysterical, asking me to help her come up with a plan to leave Dad."

"What? Why?"

Hunter shakes his head. "I don't want to get into it. They hate each other. We'll leave it at that."

The image of Hunter's parents, Lisa and Dan, hating each other is bizarre. They're very put together, or at least they always appeared that way to me.

"I'm sorry," I say, wrapping my arms around him. I don't even know when I got into his bed, but we're already curled up in each other's embrace.

"Neither of them remembered it was my birthday," he says, his voice softened by the blow of being neglected. I squeeze him tighter, absorbing his sadness and pain while also letting him know that I didn't forget and I'm still here. "You're the only thing in my life that makes me happy, Ellie."

As I settle into his hold, my emotions battle with one another, as they run so hot and cold for him in the same breath.

Will I ever untangle myself from him? Even when May approaches, will it even be possible for us to sever this fucked-up connection we have?

Hunter rests his chin on my head, and I lean my cheek against his chest, hating myself every second I give in to the need for him. The need to feel desirable, like I can help him and make his life better, and I'm the only one who can do that for him.

And I hate how good it feels.

CHAPTER SEVENTY-SIX

Mateo

Dirty dollar bills fly past my fingers as I quickly count one of the register drawers while sitting in the back office of the coffee shop.

"Mateo." *Tío* Edgar enters, and I hold up my index finger, letting him know I need to finish my count before he interrupts. I pile the last of the twenties onto the stack and rubber band them together, then write down the total.

"What's up?" I ask.

"Need to talk to you for a second," he says, grabbing a stool to sit on.

"I don't like the sound of that." I rack my brain for something I could've done that would get me fired. Aside from bending Elle over my desk and fucking her from behind last semester, I haven't done anything wrong. Dear God, please tell me he doesn't have cameras in here.

"Relax. You're keeping your job. In fact, that's what I need to talk to you about."

I give him a quizzical look. "About me continuing to work for you?"

"When do you start your internship?"

"I start next semester. Why?" The reminder strikes a sudden surge of panic because I forgot to call Mr. Kevin to ask him to be a personal reference for one of the sites I interviewed for.

Edgar runs his hand through his salt-and-pepper hair. "I hate to ask you this because I know you're juggling a lot, but I need you to work more hours until the start of next semester."

"Okay…why?"

"I have to go to Puerto Rico and take care of your Great-Aunt Ester."

"Who?"

"You never met her. She's sick, and it's my turn to look after her and help get her things in order."

"Oh."

"They want me to fly down after Thanksgiving. Do you think you can help Sandy manage the bookstore while I'm gone?"

Sandy is the complete opposite of *Tío* Edgar. She has sunshine shooting out of her ass while Edgar huffs and puffs over the workload. I wouldn't mind working with her. I'd rather that than deal with Edgar. There's no way I'd say no. He's helped me out so much. I can figure out how to balance working extra hours on top of classes and writing papers.

"Yeah, that's no problem."

Edgar lets out a breath of relief. "Thank you." As he stands up to leave, he continues talking. "Oh, and if you know of anyone interested in working at the bookstore, we could use another pair of hands since Rebecca is quitting after this semester."

I nod, feeling like an asshole because if Elle and I didn't break up, she'd probably still be working here, and Edgar wouldn't need to keep looking for new hires. Going back to counting the rest of the cash, I try wiping my mind of her. Ignoring the fact that today is her birthday. Ignoring the fact that she's happier without me.

Pausing my count, I take out my phone and shoot Mr. Kevin a text. In minutes, he's calling me up to check in. I fill him in on needing a reference, and he gladly accepts.

"How's school going?" Mr. Kevin asks.

"Honestly?" I lean back in my chair. "It's a lot. The workload is insane. I don't even know if this is what I should be doing. I keep feeling like I'm going to get to my internship site and fall flat on my face."

"You might. Then you'll pick yourself up and try again."

"Yeah, but I'm tired of having to pick myself up. I just want to succeed at *something* in my life."

"And what makes you think you haven't succeeded so far? You've been running an uphill battle for a very long time, Rivera. You should be extremely proud of where you are today."

I absorb what he's saying and remember how much I've grown over the years, from who I was before I even first entered Mr. Kevin's office to right now, and he's right.

"I guess," I say into the phone.

"Why were you thinking that social work isn't what you should be doing?" he asks.

I blow out a puff of air. "Because social workers don't get arrested. They don't assault people. They don't have fucked-up pasts."

"I wouldn't be so sure. There's always more behind what people let on. We all have our stories, Mateo. We all come from somewhere. I'm sure you can think of someone who has a lot of chapters they don't like to read aloud," he says the last sentence in a knowing voice, and my mind immediately flashes to Elle. "You have enough battles to fight in life. Don't be at war with yourself too."

My cheeks rise. "You always know what to say. How do you do that?"

"Comes with the job," he jokes.

Just then, Lynn knocks on the door and pokes her head in. "A customer wants to talk to you."

Groaning, I give her a nod and end the call with Mr. Kevin.

If this is another customer complaining about paper straws, I'm gonna lose my shit.

When I get to the counter, I'm pleasantly surprised to see a curly-haired, pierced, and tattooed woman wearing an oversized winter jacket, smiling at me.

"What's up, Bree?"

"Oh, you know, just doing a coffee run and thought I'd say hi," she says, casually flipping her hair over her shoulder.

I chuckle. "I can't help but think you're here for more than just a hello."

"Okay, I might also be here to see if you've thought more about our conversation from last week."

Only every other second I'm awake. "A little."

"Cool." Her head bobs up and down as she waits for me to say more, but I won't. "Well, if you do decide to talk to Ellie so that the both of you can figure your shit out, this weekend's out. She's super sick. I've even been staying in my friend Bianca's room because I don't want to catch—"

"Elle's sick?"

"Yeah, might be the flu or something."

"Her birthday is this weekend," I say aloud, but really for myself as my gears start turning.

"I know. It's such a bummer. I wanted to take her out. That is, if she even wanted to go out with me." Bree continues talking, but I tune her out. Elle reached out to me a while ago. Maybe this is my opportunity to reach out to her. Extend a little olive branch, acknowledging her message, even if I hated that she sent it while she was shit-faced with Hunter.

I'll do something very, very small to let her know that I'm here.

And I'm ready to talk whenever she is.

CHAPTER SEVENTY-SEVEN

Ellie

A to-go cup with the words "The Cozy Nook" is cradled in my hands. I've been staring at it for the past hour. When I went to use the bathroom earlier, it was just sitting there in the hallway next to my door. There wasn't a note attached, but it's my drink order. Vanilla latte—hot, not iced, because it's cold outside.

As if my head wasn't pounding enough, this drink is causing a pulsating throb in my skull.

There's no way Mateo dropped this off, right? He doesn't even know which dorm room is mine this year, unless he and Bree are talking, which wouldn't happen.

But it's my drink. And it's my birthday.

Although he never texted me back after my drunken episode. So it's probably not him. God, I hope it's not poisoned because I downed that drink in a matter of minutes. The moment the sweet, comforting taste hit my lips, I couldn't stop. The warmth soothed my insides as it slid down my scratchy throat.

Now I sit here on my bed, surrounded by used tissues and boxes of cold medicine, staring at the empty cup, wondering who the hell left it for me.

The door handle jiggles, and I slip under my blankets and bring them up over my nose, hoping to shield Bree from my germs. She must have forgotten something to bring with her while she sleeps at Bianca's.

When the door opens, Hunter enters with a soft smile. Panic hits my lungs as I realize the Cozy Nook cup is still somewhere on my bed. Even if it wasn't from Mateo, Hunter wouldn't want me to have any connection with that place.

I'm quick to hide it under the covers, looking like I'm cleaning up the disgusting tissues around me.

"What are you doing here?" I ask, confused once again.

"Taking care of you." He showcases a container of chicken noodle soup before taking off his jacket.

"You're supposed to text me before you use the key," I say, reminding him of our agreement, even though he never used my key before this.

"I figured you were sleeping, so I didn't want to bother you. Besides, you told me that Bree is staying at her friend's, so I thought it'd be safe for me to come in and be with you."

My nose itches, and I sense another round of sneezes coming on. Reaching for the tissues, I let out a gross amount of mucus as my eyes water. Awareness of me not looking my best falls over me, and a sudden swell of self-consciousness strikes while Hunter watches me.

I once again pull the blankets up over my face. "Don't look at me."

Hunter chuckles. "I've seen you sick before."

"I look like crap."

"Not possible." He comes closer and draws my hands away from my face, pulling the blankets down. I look up at him and see him affectionately gazing at me. "See? Still beautiful, even with a runny nose and pale as a ghost."

I try to giggle, but it turns into a coughing fit. "You're going to get sick by being here."

He shrugs. "I don't care. Need anything?"

"I'm okay for now, thank you."

Hunter takes a seat in my desk chair and aims it to face the TV. I've been so consumed by the to-go cup that I don't even remember what I put on.

"You're staying?" I ask.

"Yeah. It's your birthday."

"Oh."

"Sucks you have to spend it this way."

"You're telling me." I blow my nose again.

"We'll make up for it on your twenty-first. We'll throw a big party."

"Wonderful," I say with obvious sarcasm. "That's exactly what I want."

Hunter smiles. "I hope you feel better by Thanksgiving. Are you still planning on coming over?"

"Yeah. I have to get through dinner with my mom first, and then I'll pop over."

"Good. We'll leave here Wednesday morning. Traffic is going to be awful."

"Okay." I plop my head back down on my pillow and watch Hunter make himself comfortable in my room. Shuffling under my covers, I clutch the Cozy Nook cup and hold on to a nearby tissue just in case, and my eyes start to close as I doze in and out.

Feeling healthier by the time Thanksgiving break gets here, Hunter and I head to see our families. "You were right," I say, tossing my sweatshirt into the back seat, no longer using it as a pillow.

"I'm always right, but what specifically are you referring to?" Hunter smirks.

I put my feet up on his dashboard. "That traffic sucks."

"At least we're almost home." His attention darts to my footrest. "And are you trying to give me an aneurysm? Get your feet off my dash. This is a nice car."

I reluctantly do what he says. Hunter turns down the exit ramp off the highway. Familiar buildings fill my vision. Anxious jitters skate under my skin the closer we get to my house. I hate walking through the door, never knowing what I'm in for. Will Mom be sober or a drunken disaster? The desire to escape before I even arrive takes hold of me.

"I think I want to get my license," I blurt out the sudden thought.

"You think you can handle it?"

"I don't know. I've only ever tried the one time, and it was like two years ago."

"Yeah, and you were a disaster."

"Things are different now."

"Ellie." Hunter gently reaches for my hand. I should probably move out of his hold, but the need to be cared for overtakes my need to pull away. "I'd be so worried about you out there on the road by yourself. It was so scary to watch you have a flashback when you got behind the wheel that one time. I really don't think it's a good idea."

He's right. It was scary. Two years ago, he tried giving me my first and only driving lesson. I didn't think that when I sat behind the steering wheel, I'd have a flashback to finding Dad unconscious in his car that was smashed into a telephone pole, but I did. And that one time was enough for me to swear off getting my license. But the recent urge to find my freedom, even if in the smallest way, such as driving, feels like a small ounce of independence. Like maybe life will become more bearable if I at least know I have the option of driving somewhere when things become too chaotic or overwhelming.

"I want to try again," I state, raising my chin up.

"I don't know, Ellie…"

Frustration tenses my joints. "Why are you so quick to tell me I can't do it? Maybe I need more than one attempt. Maybe I won't fail the second time. Or who knows, maybe I will, but I think I'm at least entitled to try."

Hunter sighs loudly, exhaling his annoyance. "Okay."

That ended faster than it started. Maybe we're getting better at this.

We sit in silence and drive up to my two-story ivory house. Nervousness bubbles in my belly, and I take a few deep breaths, readying myself for whatever is behind my front door. As I unbuckle my seat belt, Hunter begins speaking. "I'll text you what time to come over tomorrow. I think my mom wants to do Thanksgiving dinner around five, but I'll double-check."

"Sounds good. Thanks for the ride." I jump out of his Lexus and gather my small overnight bag.

Walking up to my house, I stand on my front porch for a couple of seconds. Even though unease flows through me, it feels natural. I'm used to being out with Hunter, him dropping me off at my house at the end of the day, and reluctantly going inside. I hate it, but this feeling is my default.

This is my normal.

Glancing over my shoulder, I see him still parked in my driveway, waiting for me to go inside. He gives me a small smile, knowing why I'm hesitant. I've stood here waiting to open the door time and time again. I smile back, and my gaze dips down, falling on my scarred wrist, which acts as a constant reminder that I truly can't escape much of anything.

My past *is* my present.

It'll always be there—on my wrist, behind the door, in the car.

I shake my head, hoping the depressive thoughts will fall out. Once I'm ready, I unlock the door and push it open.

"Hey, Mom," I say, entering our house. She doesn't answer, so I walk around, poking my head into each room. When I don't see her in the living room or kitchen, I make my way up the stairs to her bedroom.

"Mom?" I tap on her door and crack it open.

She's sitting on her bed with a photograph in her hand. "Oh, hi, sweetie." She wipes her eyes and puts the picture away in the drawer of her nightstand.

My insides contort. "Is everything okay?"

She comes over to me with a small grin on her face. "Yes, just looking at pictures of your dad."

"Oh."

We instinctively wrap our arms around each other, and she hugs me for a few seconds longer than I'd like, but I know she needs it, so I let her take from me what she wants. There isn't any alcohol on her breath, so I know her tears aren't liquor-induced.

When she releases me, any signs of distress are washed away. "Let's get you settled, and you can tell me about how your semester has been."

The next day, Mom and I fell into our routine of Thanksgiving food prep. I slice the vegetables, and she stuffs the turkey. Once that is done, we settle on the sofa to watch a movie. That's when the wine came out. "One glass," she assures me. I hold back my words, my teeth gritting hard, not wanting to get into a fight right now. As the credits roll, she ambles into the kitchen, and I follow.

"I burned the damn turkey." Mom slams the cooking sheet with the overdone carcass onto the kitchen counter. She takes a sip from her wineglass, then mumbles under her breath.

She's already tipsy, and we haven't even had dinner. I distracted her as much as possible last night to avoid her drinking, but she swore to me that she only has one nightcap and stuck to her word. Today's a different story, and she started with the wine early because "it's a holiday."

"Mom, it's fine. I don't even like turkey."

I sift through the pantry, searching for something else to eat. The shelves aren't as stocked as they usually are, and I have an awful thought clawing at my brain, telling me that she's running through Dad's life insurance much quicker than she should. I had hoped she'd have enough to get her by with that plus working her remote job. If she doesn't, I'll have to get a job and send her money.

I grab a box of pasta. "I'll make this for dinner. Go sit down."

She begrudgingly sinks into the kitchen chair with her glass in hand. Ignoring her pouting, I fill the pot up with water and place it on the stove. As I wait for the water to boil, I try to calm down the war that's going on inside my head. One part of me wants me to be as nonconfrontational as possible, get through Thanksgiving with her, and get out. The other wants me to yell at her and demand to know why she hasn't tried harder to do better.

My mind is made up. The first choice wins.

I go to clean up her mess.

"I wanted to do something nice for you," she says.

"You did. It just got burned. No big deal."

The voices from the TV in the living room fill the silence as she continues to sip, and I continue to clean.

"I'm going down to Florida to see Aunt Margaret again for Christmas. Do you want to come, or do you want to hang out at Hunter's like you did last year?"

I would love to do what I did last year, only it wasn't spending the holidays with Hunter. It was next to Mateo as he introduced me to his family, and they all welcomed me into their lives with open arms.

"I'll be with Hunter."

Speaking of, he has yet to text me what time I should head over.

"I'm glad you have him. He's such a sweet boy."

"He's all right." I pour the pasta into the boiling water and stir. I'm trying, but like the water, I'm struggling to keep my anger under the surface. I don't want to fight with her. I hate fighting with her.

Mom places her glass down on the table. "He's all right? You're usually singing his praises. Is something going on between you two?"

"I don't sing his praises."

"Okay, maybe not quite sing, although you do have a beautiful voice."

"Mom." I make a sharp turn in her direction and put my hand on my hip. "Why do you barely have any food?"

"What?"

"Are you blowing through Dad's life insurance?"

"Where is this coming from?"

"Just tell me if you are, because I need to know if I should find a job."

She takes a sip. "I still have some left. And I'm also working."

I spin back around to the stove and concentrate on stirring the pasta. Round and round. Over and over again.

"Why were you looking at the picture of Dad yesterday?" I ask.

She clears her throat. "I do that a lot."

"Oh." *Focus on the pasta, Elle.* "What was it like with him?"

"What do you mean?"

I put the spoon down but don't turn to face her. "Your relationship, what was it like?"

She lets out a drawn-out exhale. She's quiet for a few seconds, and I can't tell if she's thinking or drinking to avoid thinking.

"When things were good, they were great. When they were bad…well, you know what it was like when they were bad."

I nod.

"We both had a lot of demons we didn't know how to cope with."

I hear a sniffle and then the wine pouring into her glass. The sound lets me know that's all I'm going to get out of her. That's all I'll ever know about my parents' relationship, and all I've ever seen—the extremes. I'll never find out if it was ever more than that.

I rode my bike to Hunter's house for Thanksgiving dinner, even though he didn't text me today to tell me what time to come. I wanted to get away from Mom while she drinks herself into misery, and the only place of respite I have is Hunter's.

Walking up the driveway, I pass the extravagant shrubbery and make my way to the towering white house with columns holding up the overhang over the front door. I ring the doorbell and wait a few seconds, but no one appears. Taking the initiative, I open the door into the foyer and pad my way inside, but my body stills the moment I hear shouting.

The booming sound of Hunter's dad's voice echoes throughout the tall walls. I've never heard Dan yell. He's always very charismatic and controlled.

"Fuck you!" Hunter shouts and storms out from the back of the house where the dining room is located and toward the staircase across from the front door.

When he spots me, he freezes mid-step, his foot partly hovering above the shiny oak floor. Fear floods his being, and a weight drops in my stomach from the expression on his face. He rushes to me. "You need to leave," he says in a hushed tone, pushing me toward the door.

"What's going on?" I whisper.

"I didn't tell you to come here, Elena. You shouldn't have just shown up."

"I'm sorry, I figured—"

The sound of dishes shattering stops both of us, and Hunter bolts to the back of the house.

My heart pounds fast.

I know I should leave, but I can't without knowing no one's in danger.

Tiptoeing down the long hallway toward the dining room, the sound of screams and something slamming against the wall has my hands shaking. I round the corner, and it's as if the air has been punched out of me when I see the scene before me.

Glass litters the floor, and Hunter's mom sobs as she cleans up the broken plates in her expensive holiday dress, while Hunter's younger brother, Ian, recoils in a corner. My head turns to see Dan's arm pushing against Hunter's throat, trapping Hunter between himself and the wall.

My body rattles with fright, but I dash across the room to save Hunter.

Hunter's eyes widen as he watches me witness what's in front of me. Dan follows Hunter's gaze and focuses on me. His face is bright red, and his graying hair is disheveled.

"Welcome, Ellie," Dan says as he lets go of Hunter. Hunter coughs, catching his breath.

Taking a step back, I stutter a response, "I-I should go."

"No, stay. You're just in time. Someone here had the urge to take a trip down memory lane."

"Dan, don't," Hunter's mom, Lisa, begs him.

"Don't you think it's time for Ellie to know the truth about her boyfriend?"

"The truth?" My eyes dart to Hunter.

Dan slowly stalks over to me, and I back up, scared. I never realized he was capable of harming his son. My idea of his controlled persona crumbles beneath my feet as they crunch along the shards of glass. His posture grows intimidating, and the closer he gets, the more I shrink. The walls close in, and I struggle to stabilize my breathing.

"Did he ever tell you he had a sister?" Dan has a mocking smile on his face. It's an evil, malicious grin that causes a blanket of goose bumps to cover my skin.

"Kayla?" I look over again to Hunter, whose focus is on the ground.

"Oh, so he did man up and tell someone about her," he says to Lisa. "Did he ever tell you what happened to his sister, Kayla? My only daughter?"

I swallow around the lump in my throat and shake my head.

Dan scoffs. "Of course he didn't. He doesn't have the balls to tell you he killed her."

All the blood drains from my face, and my stomach plummets to the ground. My chest constricts, and I stare at Hunter, waiting for him to give me some type of acknowledgment that what I just heard wasn't true.

"He was just a kid!" Lisa yells at Dan.

"That son of a bitch let my daughter drown and refused to save her. I don't give a shit how old he was!"

My hands slam over my mouth, pushing the sound of my gasp back in. Tears fill my vision as I grow lightheaded.

This can't be true. There has to be more to this story. Hunter has his issues, but I would never in a million years believe that he'd intentionally let his sister die.

"Can we not talk about this in front of guests?" Lisa pleads.

"Hunter is the one who brought her up. I was perfectly content until he opened his big fucking mouth and dared to utter my daughter's name. So for that, I don't give a shit who knows."

The room falls silent as Dan storms out. The front door slams, and I jump at the loud noise.

I fixate on Hunter, who hasn't taken his attention off the floor. No one speaks or moves. Everyone is waiting for someone else to do something.

Hunter then clears his throat. "I'm going upstairs." He walks past me without giving me a glance.

My heart beats so hard, I'm certain it's about to break through my body and land on the opposite side of the room.

I know I need to give him a second to cool down. Hell, I need to give him a whole lifetime to cool down, but I need to know what the fuck just happened.

My legs shake as I make my way up the stairs toward his bedroom. His door is partially open, and he sits on the edge of his queen-size bed with his head hanging between his shoulders.

Taking a deep inhale, I enter, shutting the door behind me.

Stillness drapes over us. The only sound I hear is my staggered breathing and my pulse whirling in my ears. I open my mouth to speak, but I can't think of anything to say, so I close it shut.

Hunter sniffles. "It's not how my dad made it sound," he says, staring at his feet.

"Do-do you want to talk about it?" I cautiously take a seat next to him on his bed.

Hunter's shoulders tense up, and I can tell there's an internal battle going on in his head. "I never told anyone what happened."

"You can tell me," I say, my voice a gentle whisper.

His right leg bounces up and down. "I was seven. She was three." He pauses, the stretched-out silence twisting me with unease, and suddenly I'm not sure if I want him to finish.

He wets his lips and begins speaking again, "We were playing in the backyard while my dad was on a business call. Kayla had been following me around all day like my fucking shadow. She was begging me to teach her how to swim all summer, but I didn't want to. She was annoying me and wouldn't leave me alone. All I wanted to do was go inside and watch a movie by myself, so I told her that if she wanted to learn how to swim so badly, she should just jump in and figure it out herself."

Hunter's chest caves in, and he sucks in a breath. "I went inside, and a few minutes later I heard her shout my name, but I ignored it. Then…" His voice cracks. "Then I heard a lot of splashing and then suddenly nothing, and I knew something was wrong."

My trembling hand inadvertently clasps around his. My eyes burn with emotion.

"I ran outside as fast as I could," Hunter continues. "She was floating in the water. Silent. Unmoving. I tried to drag her out of the pool while yelling at the top of my lungs for Dad to come help, but it was no use. She was already dead. And it was my fault."

"You were seven, Hunter," I say, trying to lift some of the guilt off his shoulders.

His broken, blue eyes look over at me. "I should've never even brought up her name tonight. Otherwise, everything would've been fine. I ruined Thanksgiving. I ruined my entire family. Nothing was ever the same. My sister is dead, my dad hates me, my mom hates my dad for hating me."

I wrap my arms around his body, embracing him. "It wasn't your fault."

"No, Elena, it was my fault."

"No, it—"

"What aren't you getting about this?" He shoves me off him and rises to his feet. "You weren't even supposed to find out. You're not even supposed to be here. I didn't text you to come."

"I'm sorry I came over unannounced and found out things that you didn't want me to, but now that I know, I can help you—"

"I don't want your help. You can't fix this."

"I'm not trying to fix it. I'm trying to be supportive."

"I don't want your support! God, Ellie, can't you tell when you're not fucking wanted?"

The flip of his emotions makes me dizzy. I thought I was doing the right thing by being there for him, but clearly, I was wrong.

He stands over me, waiting for me to leave, so I do.

With my gaze on the shiny floor, I make my way out the door without seeing his mom or brother. Once I'm outside, I walk past the driveway where his dad's car is usually parked, and grab my bike. As the cold air brushes against my cheek, I turn back to look at Hunter's home.

No matter how many times I've walked inside that house, I have always been an outsider, their secrets kept behind locked doors and sealed lips. I've always assumed Hunter and I shared everything with each other, at least I did with him. But the more I think about it, there was always a level of him he kept at a distance, a part of him I always had a yearning to discover. The scarred, damaged version of himself that he never liked acknowledging.

Maybe that's why I was drawn to Hunter.

I saw a reflection of myself in him and wanted to save it.

When I get back to Mom's, she's passed out on the couch with the TV drowning out her snores in the background. I plop down on a nearby chair and stare at what surrounds me. My shoulders slump as the feeling of being unwanted at both places I was supposed to be at tonight sinks in. My eyes drift around the room and land on Mom's car keys dangling on the key hook by the front door. The urge to get out and overcome all of this dances around my mind.

On impulse, I grab the car keys and run out the door. I sit behind the driver's seat and put the key in the ignition.

You can do this. Start slow. Just try sitting in the seat for a few minutes.

My hands shake against the steering wheel as I grip it, my knuckles turning white.

Air moves in and out of me, quicker and quicker.

Intrusive images of my dad pop into my brain, but they're not overwhelming.

I sit and breathe.

Inhale. Exhale.

Being behind the steering wheel ignites a feeling of control, like I'm taking some of my power back. Power that I have given away so many times. Power that I thought was gone, but is now revolving around me.

And for a split second, I'm given the gift of hope that my strength will last more than this fleeting moment in time.

CHAPTER SEVENTY-EIGHT

Ellie

Since I haven't heard anything from Hunter since I left his house, I decided to take a bus back to school. I swallowed my pride and borrowed money from Mom to get back. Guilt crawls all over me for needing to ask her for the cash, but I fully intend on paying her back. I just need to get a job first. I don't want to depend on Hunter for income.

I'm folding laundry in my dorm room when there's a knock on my door. "Come in," I say, unsure why someone would be here since it's still Thanksgiving break.

The door pushes open, and Hunter stoically enters.

"You left this in my car." He tosses my sweatshirt on my desk.

"Oh." I stare at it. "How'd you know I came back?"

"Why'd you leave without me?" He counters.

"I thought…I-I don't know."

"You're not doing that next time."

I put a hand on my hip. "How did you find out, anyway?"

"I went to your house to pick you up and talked to your mom."

"Oh."

We stand there, silent.

The quietness is not a calm one. It's the kind of silence that has me sitting in apprehension, waiting for the noise to strike. I don't know if he's still mad at me for finding out about Kayla, or sad at the situation, or hurt by his dad. I have no clue what is going on in his head, but I can feel the tension radiating off him and permeating into my pores. Fearful of how he'll react, I focus on my breathing.

Inhale. Exhale.

He's still standing there, not moving.

Inhale. Exhale.

My fingers play with the end of the sleeve of my shirt for the thousandth time as his energy consumes the room. When I get bored of that, I trace the uneven skin on my wrist. In a sick way, the little lines make me unwind.

"I'm going to finish my laundry," I announce.

Grabbing my plaid pajama pants, I neatly fold them as he hovers over me. Getting increasingly uncomfortable, I speak again. "Do you want to talk—"

"No."

I stare at him, not knowing what he needs or wants, but I reflexively do what I think might help.

I hug him.

Hunter's body is like stone against mine, and I lean more weight into him, hoping to break down his walls.

He inhales deeply, and inch by inch, his arms come around my body. His head dips down, and his breath skates across my neck. I smile at my accomplishment, knowing that I got him to soften. Maybe I *can* help him.

Suddenly, his lips brush against my skin. The sensation sends a mixture of warmth and chills up and down my body, as confusion shadows my thoughts. It feels nice, even though I know it shouldn't. I try to back away, realizing this shouldn't be happening, but his hand goes to the back of my head, holding me still as he sucks on my neck.

The pressure of his mouth makes me become clearheaded, and I push him off. "Hunter." I wipe my neck with the back of my hand. "What was that?"

He lets out a dry chuckle. "We're not going through this shit again, are we, Ellie?"

"What are you talking about? You said that you were going to respect that I don't want anything more than whatever the hell we are."

"You want to talk about respect, Elena?" He moves closer, steam rolling off him. "Were you being *respectful* when you came into my room, telling me that you loved the guy who almost beat me to death?" He takes another step toward me. I take one back. "Were you being *respectful* when you fell asleep with another guy in your bed and hid him in your closet while we were still together?" My back hits my dresser. "Were you being *respectful* when you were meeting up with him for your fucking coffee dates?"

My breathing becomes shallow as his body looms over mine. His blue eyes turn dark with anger.

"You didn't think I knew about that, did you?" he asks. I sense myself retreating as my lungs struggle to take in more air. "You think I wouldn't find out that you were flirting like a whore with a fucking criminal?"

"Don't call him that," I manage to say, although my voice shakes.

"You don't tell me what to do. *You* listen to *me*."

"Fuck off." I shove his chest with all my might, but he pushes me against the dresser, the wooden lip slamming my lower back, causing me to yelp. A harsh pain radiates up my spine.

Hunter grips my jaw with his hand and forces my gaze up to his. "My family has enough money to make sure your ex gets locked up for a long fucking time. You wouldn't want that, would you?"

I stare him down, my chest moving rapidly, but he doesn't let up. So I shake my head, answering his question.

"Then it's understood. From now on, what I say goes."

He stares at me a beat longer, intimidation and control seeping out of him.

My mind whirls, unsure of how my hug led to him trying to seduce me and to him threatening me. His threat does the job he intended. I'm paying the price for my decision to ride home without him. As soon as Hunter releases me, my body sags. Without another word, he leaves my room, and I sink down onto the cold floor.

CHAPTER SEVENTY-NINE

Ellie

DECEMBER

A week has passed since the Hunter fiasco. He and Mateo dominate my thoughts, and I've been having angry internal conversations with myself about how all of this is playing out. In an attempt to shut up my thoughts, I've been trying to put all my energy into prepping for finals and assuring Bree that there's nothing wrong since she's been asking nonstop.

"You wanna go to a party with me on Saturday?" Bree asks as she types on her laptop. I'm glad she's still talking to me. I haven't been the greatest friend lately. She powers on, explaining, "It's my friend from the grad program. It's a totally different vibe than the parties you're used to. Everyone drinks boxed wine, smokes weed, and has intellectual conversations about life and art and shit."

"That sounds like a refreshing change of pace."

"It's decided then. Saturday night, you're my date."

A sense of joy swims through my veins. It'll be so amazing to go out with Bree and actually have some fun.

She starts to speak again, but a knock interrupts her. I tell the person on the other side of the door to enter, and there appears Hunter.

Air gets caught in my chest. I hate when he pops over and Bree's here. It hasn't happened often, maybe twice since Halloween. If they do happen to cross paths, I make sure it's extremely short. I've been adamant with Bree that nothing is going on between Hunter and me, and I'm just helping him as a friend because he's going through something. That's all I've said to her. I've been avoiding answering any more questions about him, but I have an itching feeling I'm going to be pressed for answers now that Hunter's standing in our doorway with a look of contempt stamped across his face.

The tension is immediately laid on thick as distress snakes up my neck. He's aimed straight for me. "Let's go," he commands.

"Go where?" I ask as my mouth dries up.

"Out."

I motion to the laptop next to me. "I'm working on my philosophy final."

Hunter steps up to my desk and flicks through the papers, looking for something. He finds the philosophy assignment sheet and drops it back on the desk.

"It's due next week. You'll be fine. Let's go."

"Where are we going?" I ask again.

"*Out*."

I roll my eyes and push my things to the side, standing up.

"You can have her tonight, but Saturday she's all mine," Bree says.

Hunter whips his head to look at her, a surprised expression on his face, not realizing she was here. "What are you talking about?" he asks her.

"She's my date to a party."

"Whose party?"

"You don't know them." She bats her eyelashes at him. Her antagonizing him has me rubbing a hand over my now queasy stomach.

"Whose party is it?" He faces me, demanding an answer.

"I don't know. One of Bree's friends."

His jaw tics, but he stays silent. I zip up my puffy black jacket and give him a nod that I'm ready.

When we're out of the building, Hunter grabs my wrist. "Why do you want to go to a party without me?"

"I don't. Bree invited me as her date, so I'm going with her." I twist my arm in his hold. "A *friend* date, not a *date* date." I chuckle, trying to make light. "Trust me, you don't have to worry about Bree and me."

"Is anyone going to be there who shouldn't be?"

"Meaning?" I ask, pretending not to understand the question. He tilts his head to the side and gives me a knowing look. "No, he won't be there."

"Good." Hunter releases my wrist, then loops his arms around my shoulders, pulling me closer as we walk to his car. We pass another couple on the way. They smile at us, and we smile at them as if we're blissfully in love.

When we get inside his car, Hunter locks the doors but doesn't put his car in drive. "Turn your location on."

"What?"

"The location on your phone. Turn it on. I want to know where you are."

My jaw drops open. "No."

"I need to know you're safe."

I scoff, knowing this has very little to do with my safety. "I'm going to be safe. I'll be with Bree."

"You're going to some strange house party with people neither of us knows, aside from a five-foot-five hippie."

"You never needed my location before."

"Yeah, well, shit's changed."

"Like what? Everything is exactly the same."

His fist punches the top of the steering wheel, and I jump in my seat. "I'm not going to ask you again, Ellie."

I scoot myself as close to the door as possible, getting farther from him even if it's only a few inches. "Fine, then I'll turn it on the day of."

"No. You'll turn it on now and leave it on."

I bite down on the inside of my cheek so hard that the taste of copper drenches my taste buds. I knew I shouldn't have left Mom's house without him. He's taken his control to the next level. With resentment stewing in my bones, I take out my phone and turn my location on. Hunter watches me, and when he sees that I did what he wanted, he grins.

CHAPTER EIGHTY

It's Saturday and open mic night at the coffee shop, which means it's packed. College students take up every available space. Lynn, a new guy named Greg, and I have been working nonstop for hours. The bottoms of my feet are stinging from standing for so long.

Just as the line dies down, another round comes in. I wipe down a spill while I hear Lynn talking to the group. She's trying to take their order, but they're being fucking obnoxious.

"What time does your shift end?" some guy asks her.

"How is that relevant to your drink order?" Lynn goes back at him.

He ignores the question. "You wanna come back to my place after work?"

"I'd rather light myself on fire."

"Yo, you ever hook up with a girl who has crazy-colored hair? They're fucking freaky in bed." I hear a guy say to the one who's hitting on Lynn loud enough so that not only can she hear but also everyone nearby.

Nope. Not fucking happening on my watch.

Spinning around to tell these assholes to fuck off, my face instantly gets hot with anger when I see who it is. A guy, who I think is named Rhett, is the one hitting on Lynn, while three of his frat brothers stand behind him —Mike, Derek, and Hunter.

"Leave," I tell them.

"What?" Rhett looks shocked for some fucking reason. "Why? I'm getting a drink."

"No, you're hitting on her, which you're failing miserably at, by the way, and you're embarrassing her. Leave."

"Oh shit. I didn't realize you guys were hooking up. I'm sorry, man," Rhett says.

Fury builds in my bloodstream, and my fists ball up, getting really close to knocking all of these dickheads out.

Before I can say something, Hunter snickers from behind Rhett. "You fuck all your employees or just the ones that are mine?"

My teeth grate together as I sense myself getting closer and closer to snapping.

You can't beat the shit out of him again, Mateo. Calm the fuck down.

"I don't know why you're so interested in my sex life. You need some pointers? Are you getting complaints because you can't finish the job?" I say casually to Hunter, as if he isn't the bane of my existence.

A resounding "Oh!" from his frat brothers has me grinning, although a surge of nausea rolls through my stomach at the thought of Elle sleeping with Hunter.

That's not happening.

She wouldn't.

Hunter broadens his chest and has a familiar look in his eye, like he's getting off on a potential fight.

The thought of last May slams into my brain, and I know that I can't react the same way. Not if I'm starting my internship next semester and being considered a professional. I can't add another assault to my list of shit that doesn't make me feel qualified for this career.

So I choke down my pride and ignore him. I shift my attention to Rhett. "Order or get out." Then I point at Lynn. "And leave her alone."

I step out from around the counter and go to clean up stray coffee mugs. The new hire, Greg, calls me over to a table across the way to ask me a question. Luckily, I'm out of earshot from Hunter, and by the time I turn back around, they're gone.

Once the coast is clear, I head back over to Lynn. "Um…one of the guys refused to pay," she says.

"What?"

"Yeah. Stupid of me to make him his drink beforehand. Sorry. I just wanted them to leave."

"Which one was it?" I ask, trying to tame my annoyance.

"The one who made the comment about Ellie. I tried to get him to pay, but he said that you owed him and then walked out."

"What the fuck?"

"I'm really sorry."

"Don't worry about it. It's four dollars. It's just the principle of the thing." *The only thing I owe that douchebag is another roundhouse to the face.*

"I hate men," Lynn says.

"I don't blame you."

"Thanks for sticking up for me."

"I got you."

She goes to stack to-go cups, and I slam my hands down on the counter, hanging my head between my shoulders. I blow out a loud gust of air, letting my anger diffuse.

"Dude, why are you more upset over this than me?" I hear Lynn asking, even though I'm looking down. I shake my head, not wanting to explain. "You should go blow off some steam," she suggests.

"Yeah." I push myself off the counter. "I'm going to later."

Jasmine pulls up her bra straps and throws her T-shirt over her head. "How have you been doing?" she asks as I rest my head on my pillow.

"Stressed as fuck. Edgar needs my help managing both stores, and something really fucking annoying happened there today. Plus, I have a shit ton of papers to write."

"At least the semester is almost over." She grabs her burgundy hair and puts it into a bun before stepping into her jeans.

"Yeah, I hand in my finals next week, and then I'm off until the end of January."

"You planning on working on finals tonight?"

"No, I need a fucking break from reading case studies."

"Wanna come to a party?"

I start to sit up. "I don't know, Jas."

"Oh, come on. When's the last time you've been to a party? You've been heartbroken and hurting for so long. But now that it appears you've moved on." She points to herself as the obvious example. "It's time for you to get out there and have a little fun."

Taking a long inhale, I consider her comment. I definitely haven't moved on, and I'm not sure if getting laid by someone who isn't Elle makes things hurt more or less.

"Come on, Mateo." She takes my hand and yanks me off the bed.

"Fine." I find my jeans and pull them up. "Whose party is it?"

"My friend, Tasha. She's a grad student in the art program."

My phone buzzes, and I glance down to a text from Rebecca. Lucky for her, she wasn't on the schedule to work today, so she was able to work on her finals.

REBECCA

My paper sucks. I need a break. What are you doing tonight?

"You mind if I invite my friend Rebecca?" I ask Jasmine.

"The more the merrier." She arches her eyebrow with a tickle of amusement.

"Thanks for letting me tag along. Staring at my computer screen all day was making me want to throw it across the room," Rebecca says, sipping on a glass of wine.

We sit next to each other on a couch in a room on the side of the house while chill indie music plays. There's weird art hanging on all the walls, and one painting that I swear is a vagina—even though people say it's "abstract"—is directly in front of me.

"I know the feeling," I say before taking a swig of my drink. I opted for a beer. Boxed wine is not my thing. It tastes exactly like it smells.

Jasmine saunters over to us, blitzed out of her mind. She plops down on my lap and drapes her body over me. Her fingers rub my neck and play with the ends of my hair. It's not the girl I want to be touching me, but it feels nice.

"You guys want?" Jas extends a joint to Rebecca and me.

"Hell, yes." Rebecca plucks it from Jasmine's finger and takes a hit, then passes it to me.

My features twist as I debate smoking.

"Come on, Mateo. You're supposed to be letting loose and having fun," Jas whines.

"This one is always so serious," Rebecca says, poking my arm.

"Let's change that." Jas takes the joint back and holds it up to my lips.

"All right, all right."

I close my eyes and inhale. As soon as I open them, I immediately begin coughing when I spot who's standing in the doorway. Through the cloud of smoke, I nearly burst out of my skin at the sight of Elle staring back at me.

Elle spins, running through the entrance she just came in through.

I shove my beer into Rebecca's hands, making her spill her own drink and shoot to my feet, causing Jasmine to fall. "Shit. Sorry," I say, but I don't stop to see if she's okay. Racing out of the room, I spot Bree. "Where's Elle?"

"Mateo?" Bree looks confused as fuck to see me.

"Where'd she go?" Before Bree can answer, I see golden hair walking out the front door. "Elle!" I go after her, running outside.

"I'm leaving," Elle says, walking onto the lawn.

"Why?" I step in front of her so I can see her face. My heart thrashes in my chest just from being in close proximity to her.

"Because I'd really rather not witness the threesome that was about to happen."

"What? I don't want a threesome with them."

"Well, I'm sure you can find two other girls. Take your pick." She gestures her arms toward the house.

"No, that's not what I meant. I don't want a threesome with anyone else but you."

Her eyes widen, appalled. "Me and *who*?"

"No…Shit. I'm fucking this up."

"It's fine, Mateo. Do your thing. I'm going back to campus." She starts to go toward the street, but I move with her, walking backward.

"You really don't want to be around me that badly that you can't stand to be in the same house as me?"

Her gaze is focused on the ground. "It's not that."

"Then what is it?"

"It's…" Elle stops walking and looks up at me. She chews on her bottom lip and blinks several times as she tries to come up with an answer. "Fine. Yes! I don't want to be around you. I'm leaving."

Another gash to the heart.

"No. I'll leave. You should stay and have fun." I take my keys out of my pocket, and her face drops. My brow furrows in misunderstanding. "What?"

"You're seriously going to drive?"

"Yeah?"

"You can't." Fear escalates in her voice, and now it registers for me. She thinks I'm drunk.

"I'll sit in my car and wait until I'm good," I assure her. I know she won't believe me if I tell her I'm completely sober since she saw me with a beer in one hand while I was taking a hit. She probably thinks I've been doing that all night.

Elle shakes her head. "I want to make sure you're okay to drive."

"I will be. I promise."

"No. I *need* to know," she presses as her eyes turn glassy. I can practically see the traumatic images she's witnessed flash in her eyes as she stares at me in distress. She takes a deep breath, and it trembles as she sighs it out. "I'll sit and wait with you."

CHAPTER EIGHTY-ONE

Ellie

I shouldn't have said that.

I shouldn't be walking to his car right now.

I shouldn't even be near him.

But I can't let him drive if he's under the influence of something. God forbid something were to happen. I'd *really* never be able to forgive myself.

Nearly breaking my neck, I make sure Hunter isn't here. I know he's not, but paranoia is creeping in at the thought of what could happen if he were to find out I'm alone with Mateo.

We sit in Mateo's car, and it looks exactly the same, with well-loved leather seats and the green pine tree air freshener swinging on the rearview mirror.

Feeling strangled by the heat, I unzip my jacket slightly to cool down my flushed neck. My tongue is like sandpaper in my mouth, and I try not to stare at Mateo too long. So instead, I keep my attention out the window as I pick at my nail polish.

Awkward silence encompasses the car, and I hear Mateo moving around in his seat. He clears his throat. "How was France?"

"Good," I say, checking the perimeter.

There's a long pause, and then Mateo speaks again. "Good?"

"Yeah."

"This was your biggest dream for your entire life, and I only get *good?*"

"What do you want me to say, Mateo? That it was the most magical place I've ever been to, and I had the most transformative summer of my life?"

"Yeah, something like that would suffice."

Despite my shattered heart, it was.

I shift to look at him. "I got a tattoo while I was there," I say, pride curling my lips upward.

He arches an eyebrow. "A tattoo?" A sly grin grows on his face. "Where?"

"Somewhere."

My teasing answer makes his eyes rake up and down my body as if he can see through my winter coat. In an instant, heat rushes to my cheeks. *God, I've missed the way he looks at me.*

I giggle. "Stop that."

"Stop what?"

"Trying to figure out where it is."

"If you won't tell me where it is, will you tell me *what* it is?"

"The coordinates of the Eiffel Tower. Stupid, I know, but everyone in the program did it our last week there."

He nods and subtly wets his lips. The small motion of his tongue sends sparks of desire to my core. I swear the air in here just thickened. If I thought I was hot before, I might as well be dying in the desert right now.

I swallow, fixating on his mouth. All I have to do is slightly lean my body, and our mouths will be molded together, forever fused and never letting go.

My pulse picks up, and the breath moving in and out of me shakes. I force myself to bring my gaze up to meet his eyes, and I see the same longing swirling around his dark irises.

Needing to pull myself out of my lust-fogged brain before I do something that'll potentially ruin both of our lives, I think of something to say. "How much longer until you're sober?" The words scrape against my throat.

"I've been sober."

"I saw you drinking and smoking."

"The beer was barely touched, and I didn't have a chance to fully inhale before I saw you."

I blink a few times and move back, annoyed that I put both of us in danger for nothing. "Well, then what the hell am I doing here?"

"I don't know. You're the one who didn't trust me when I said I'm good to drive."

"I trust you."

He scoffs. "Okay."

"What's that for?"

"You obviously don't trust me. Otherwise, we wouldn't be in this situation."

"I didn't know how much you had."

"No, I meant *this* situation." He points between him and me.

I press the back of my head into the seat, feeling like a pile of garbage. "I've always trusted you, Mateo."

"Don't bullshit me. Every single thing you said when you broke up with me fucking killed me, Elle."

The stinging in my eyes makes me turn to face the window. "I didn't mean it," I whisper.

"What?"

"I didn't mean what I said. Especially about you being like your dad. I never meant that."

"I-I..." he stammers, struggling for words. "What the fuck, Elena? You mean you took the one thing—the *one fucking thing* that I'm sensitive about—and purposefully chose to hurt me?"

A tear drips down my cheek, and I swipe it away.

"Say something," he demands. My body trembles the more I hold in the sobs that are building inside. "Tell me why you did it. Tell me why you said all those horrible things to me."

"I can't." My voice breaks.

"Then you need to leave my car."

My head whips around. "What?"

His lips press together, and he firmly grips the steering wheel. "If you have zero reasoning for how you ended things, then I can't be around you knowing that you wanted to break me."

My heart cracks open once again, but I nod, understanding why he's acting like this, and drag myself out of the car.

When I'm back out in the cold, my cries are finally set free. I gasp for air as I watch him drive off.

Shaking from anguish, I stare into the distance until I can no longer see his taillights. Tears stream down my face as I once again am forced to watch the love of my life leave. My vision blurs, each droplet of salty water rolling down my face mixed with so many different emotions.

"Ellie?" Bree's voice echoes from behind me. "Ellie, what's wrong? What happened?" She puts a hand on my shoulder, and I wipe my face before turning to look at her.

"Nothing," I say, choking down the remainder of my pain.

"This is clearly something."

"I don't want to talk about it."

"Why not?" she presses.

I snap, letting my emotions get the best of me. "You won't get it!"

"You're not giving me anything *to* get!" Her voice rises with mine.

"I told you a million times that I don't want to talk. What the hell aren't you getting about that, Bree? Why can't you just fucking drop it?"

"Because I know there's something going on, Ellie, and I know it has to do with Hunter. I just don't know what it is yet."

"You have no idea what you're talking about." I shove my hair out of my face as my body heats up with anger despite the low temperature outside.

"Listen, if you don't want to tell me, then that's fine. I'm over trying to help you. I even went as far as trying to get Mateo to talk to you, but obviously that was a stupid idea."

My eyes widen as I sense my brain slipping away from stability. "You *what*? I never asked you to do that!"

"I was looking out for you and trying to be a good fucking friend."

"No, a good friend would mind their own goddamn business! I'm trying to finish this school year without any issues, and that won't happen if you keep fucking meddling, Bree!"

Her body moves backward as if she's been wounded by my words. She studies me for a moment, her features drawn in tight. "You're not the same person from last year."

"Yes, I am!"

"No, you're not, and I'm tired of chasing you down to try to be friends with you. You're always with Ava, or busy with school, or never want to have an actual conversation. And don't even get me started on fucking Hunter appearing in our room."

"No, Bree." I inch closer to her, instigating. "Please, go ahead and get started."

"Fine," she bites out. "He's an entitled piece of shit, and I don't feel comfortable with him being in our room, but I've been sucking it up and dealing with it because of *you*."

"Then I'll make sure to spend all my time with him outside of our room. Is that better?"

"Don't fucking bother. I won't be hanging around the room that much anymore." She turns around, and that's when I notice all the people standing outside the house watching our shouting match, including Jasmine and the redhead Mateo was with.

It takes me a second, but I realize Bree is walking away from me. Instant regret zips down my spine and shoots through my veins. *Fuck.* "No, Bree. Wait."

"Not now, Ellie." She keeps moving toward the house, and people start going inside now that the show is over.

"I didn't mean to be a complete bitch. I'm sorry. I should've never been like that to you. You've been an amazing friend." The words come rushing out of my mouth as I try to stop her. "I just have a lot going on right now and don't—"

Bree spins to face me. "Don't want to talk about it?"

No. I *can't* talk about it.

The truth rattles in my chest, crawling its way to my mouth.

But I lock it away.

"Yeah," I answer.

She nods. "I get it. I won't push you anymore." She starts to move but pauses. "Maybe we should have some space from each other. I'll spend the next few days at Bianca's, and then I'm off to California for break. Maybe we can iron everything out when I come back."

"O-okay." My vision blurs again, and I watch her walk into the house.

I stand motionless. Numb. I'm not sure if it's from the cold or to avoid the self-hatred that is slowly tearing me down.

Each day, I've been digging myself deeper and deeper, and I'm finally swallowed whole by loneliness.

And I don't know if there's a way out.

CHAPTER EIGHTY-TWO

Ellie

Shuffling out of the cafeteria with my mac and cheese in hand, I briskly walk back to my dorm. The stockpile of food in our room has gotten down to a half-eaten box of cookies and a small bag of chips. Bree left yesterday for winter break, and even though it was an awkward goodbye with limited talking, she told me I have free range to anything in her fridge, which is a few bottles of soda.

Pushing open my door, I gasp when I find Hunter in my room, standing over my desk. Nervousness spins around my mind, and I pray that he didn't look in my bottom desk drawer. The one that holds my secrets—my medication, Mateo's shirt, the necklace he gave me, and now a to-go cup from the Cozy Nook, because yes, I'm that unhinged.

"What are you doing here?" I ask, catching my breath from being startled, forgetting he had a key to my room.

"How were your finals?" Hunter clearly doesn't plan on answering my question. My eyes are trained on the drawer with my medication. It looks untouched, but he could have checked before I came in.

I need to rein in my panic.

"Fine." I put my lunch down on my desk and take off my coat, trying to act like I don't care he's here. "I'm still finishing up my English paper, but after that, I'm done."

His head bobs up and down as he examines my belongings on my desk. "How was that party you went to over the weekend?"

I hesitate. *Shit.* "Also fine. What's with you?"

He pivots and focuses on me, the blue hue in his eyes both captivating and frightening. "I found out some information."

"Information about what?" I casually take my boots off, even though my hands tremble as terror spirals around my limbs.

"About who was at that party."

My lungs shrink. The tightening in my chest causes sharp stabs of pain.

I stay silent, trying to figure out the next best move.

Hunter slowly stalks over to me. "Did you see him?"

"No. Well, yes, but he was leaving just when I got there, so there wasn't a conversation or anything."

"Or anything."

"Nothing happened, Hunter."

His jaw clenches, and he continues to get closer, invading my space. "You know he's never going to love you, right?"

I tug at the sleeve of my shirt. "Yeah. I know."

"You know that *no one* has ever loved you, right?"

"Stop it."

"It's true. Daddy didn't even love his little girl enough to stop hitting the bottle. Hell, neither of your parents did."

My hand smacks him across the face before my brain can process the action. Hunter freezes for a split second, and then an arrogant grin appears on his face.

It happens fast.

He barrels toward me. My head smacks the wall, and pain radiates out. I struggle to push him away, but he's stronger. I'm pinned.

Gasping, my body tenses. He grasps my chin between his thumb and index finger, his hold strengthening.

"No one is ever going to love you, Elena. You're fucked up, just like me. That's why we're together, because no one else gives a shit about us. No one else loves us."

I'm heaving, my shoulders rapidly lifting and dropping.

"See?" he says. "You can't even deny it because you know it's true."

And I stay silent.

Because he's right.

Hunter's free hand grips my hip, and his fingers sneak their way under my shirt. My breath stutters as the feel of his fingertips snaking around my skin distorts any logic I once had.

"You're so fucked up that you're probably getting off on this right now like I am."

"Shut up," I say through gritted teeth, despising that he's once again right.

"Let me check and find out for myself."

Hunter's fingers trail the top of my leggings, and we have a stare-down as he dips his hand inside. He runs one finger between my slit, causing my body to shudder. He slowly circles my clit, and I close my eyes, letting the sensation surge through me. I haven't been touched by anyone in months. Giving in to him is vile, but my yearning for connection is taking over.

The smallest moan falls out of my mouth.

He yanks his hand out of my pants. "Just as I thought."

"Fuck you."

"No, Ellie. *I'm* going to fuck *you*."

And just like that, our mouths collide.

It's been over a year since we last kissed, but nothing about this feels like a homecoming. It's harsh and unforgiving as we rip each other's clothes off. Hands move so fast, I don't know whose is where.

It's a race to get to the bed as he pushes me down. His attention lands on my tattoo that is on the side of my ribs. He lets out a scoff and scratches the ink with his finger before making a condom appear from thin air. He tosses it on my chest. The weight of the tiny wrapper is crippling, granting me a split second to say no.

But I don't.

He rips it open with his teeth and rolls on the condom.

There is no foreplay.

Resentment is our foreplay.

Hunter slams into me, igniting a loud moan from me. He pulls out completely and pounds back in, even harder. His thrusts are strong and controlled as he revels in the sight of me coming undone beneath him. There's nothing sensual or intimate about this.

It's primal and animalistic.

I wrap my legs around him and start to push myself up, attempting to flip us over, but he shoves me back down. Hunter then grabs both of my wrists and tightly holds them over my head.

"Your piece of shit boyfriend might've let you be in control back then, but you're mine now, Ellie, and I'm in control." He thrusts harder and deeper.

"You'll never be half the man he is," I grit.

"We'll see if you're still saying that when you're coming on my cock." He slides his hand between us and rubs my clit.

I bring my hips up to meet his at our furious pace. Loathing every second of this, but craving it just the same. My fingernails violently burrow into his hand, and I hope when he lets go of me, I see blood trickling down his skin. My moans become stronger, and Hunter's smirk grows wider.

"You fucking love this," he claims, as he makes my body his.

Hunter has no fucking concept of the word love.

Let's call it what it is.

This is a hate fuck.

His fingers circle quicker, and fire within me builds just below the surface. I don't want to give him the satisfaction of finishing before he does. I press my lips together and clamp my eyes, trying with all my might not to come.

"Don't fucking fight it, Elena," he demands.

Sparks launch throughout my body, and I shake beneath him as my orgasm takes over. He lets go of my wrists and sinks down on top of me, grunting in my ear as he finishes.

Without missing a beat, he's off me.

Shame and regret instantly consume every fiber of my being. I cross my arms over my face, drenched in disgust.

By the time I muster up enough courage to open my eyes, Hunter is already dressed. I pull my blankets over my naked body, not wanting to expose myself to him for another second. I notice him putting on his jacket.

My brows draw in. "Where are you going?" I ask.

"Heading out."

"You're not, like, going to hang out or anything?"

"No. I'm good." He then fishes in his wallet and tosses a fifty onto my bed.

"What's this?" I grab the bill.

"You're short on cash, right?"

"Yeah, but I don't want your money, especially after we just fucked!"

Hunter shrugs. "You need it more than I do."

"I don't want it!" I crunch it up into a ball and toss it at him, but it falls to the floor. Wrapping the sheets around myself, I hop off the bed and go to my dresser. Grabbing my pajama pants and a T-shirt, I face away from Hunter and struggle to get dressed without showing any more of myself to him.

"I'll leave it on your desk just in case," he says, and I hear him moving some things around.

Once I'm dressed, I turn back around. Hunter is looking at his phone, already bored with me. "I told you I don't want your money," I say.

"I heard you." Hunter smirks, making me feel dirty as shivers run down my arms. He slips his phone into his pocket, then goes to my door and turns the knob. "Oh, and thanks for finally giving in. I knew you would eventually." He gives me a wink and shuts the door.

I'm frozen, watching him leave.

My heart clatters against my rib cage.

And my mind begins to spiral.

CHAPTER EIGHTY-THREE

Ellie

Nothing.

I feel nothing.

I am nothing.

I am a hollowed-out, empty shell.

My skin chafes from the number of times I harshly scrubbed my loofah over my body, wanting to rid any remnants of Hunter. But he's still there, sewn into my fibers, stuck to my soul.

While emptiness surrounds me, hatred consumes me.

I have no one.

And my hands are just as stained as Hunter's.

I tried reaching out to him before he left for break, and then again on Christmas Eve and Christmas Day. Multiple phone calls, multiple texts, and nothing in return. I even shut off my location, waiting for the angry demand to turn it back on, but he's been silent.

He discarded me.

I am nothing to no one, not even myself. I willfully let myself be used.

Mom thinks I'm with him right now because I lied and told her how fabulous my holiday was and how much I missed her and hope she's having a great time in Florida.

Curling up in my bed in my dorm, zoning out on the ceiling for hours on end, tears trickle down my face.

I hate myself.

I hate every choice I've ever made, every lie I've ever told, every step I've ever taken.

I want nothing more than to break free, but I can't. I thought France was my out. I came back so strong, so confident. But that was quickly washed away, and I am back to the old version of myself. The nothingness of a human that I am.

I have no out. I can't rectify or fix the situation. Any of them.

My gaze shifts off the ceiling and onto my desk to check the time, but I don't focus on the clock. I'm fixated on the medicine bottle sitting right next to it.

Now that no one is here to see them, I keep them out of my drawer. I'm supposed to take one pill every night, and I've been religiously doing so up until now.

My body sits up, and I extend my arm, reaching for the bottle. Untwisting the cap and pouring the contents onto my purple comforter, I pick one up, examining it.

Tiny, white, circular pill.

One.

I count how many I have.

Two.

Three.

Four.

This is a bad idea, Elle.

Five.

Six.

Seven.

You only need to take one.

Eight.

Nine.

Ten.

Eleven.

That's all I have. Eleven pills.

My breath shakes as I stare at the small circles spread out on my bedspread.

An avalanche of emotions barrels through me, and I break down into tears. My hands immediately go to my face as I cry into them, letting my loud sobs bounce off the walls.

I can't believe my mind just went there.

Kicking my blankets away from me, horrified by my own thoughts, the pills go flying and scatter on the floor. *Good.* I don't want them anywhere near me. I don't want my brain to get that dark ever again. It's only happened once before, and I didn't want to die then either. I just wanted the hurting to end.

"Dad," I cry out to the ghost of him in my empty room. "Dad, please help me." The waterfall of tears continues to flood my body as I uncontrollably weep. In between my gasps for air, I keep pleading for my dad to hear me—or anyone to hear me. Someone, some energy to wash away my pain.

"Please, Dad," I beg. "I don't want to live like this. I don't want to be like this. I need you. I need *something*. Dad, please."

My agony and pleas and tears and gasping take up the empty room until I'm too exhausted to cry any longer. Resting my head on my pillow in a puddle of my pain, my breathing slows down to a normal rate.

I lie in silence for a while. I'm not sure how long, but I know a significant amount of time has passed by the moonlight spilling in the window.

Clarity begins to poke through my mind as the fog of my heavy emotions starts to lift.

In my heart of hearts, I know this is not okay.

I'm not okay.

With the smallest particle of fight left in me, I reach for my phone and reluctantly do the thing that I've been avoiding for much too long. But if this wasn't enough of a wake-up call, then I don't know what will be.

Pulling up Google on my phone, I type in, "Therapist near me."

CHAPTER EIGHTY-FOUR

Mateo

It's New Year's Eve and the shops in town are dead. All the college kids are home on break, and only a few locals pop in here and there. No one else is working today except for me. I'm stuck doing book inventory in the front, while keeping an ear out for anyone who comes into the coffee shop. I gladly took tonight's shift, hoping to occupy my mind enough so that I don't think of last New Year's…or Elle in any capacity. But no amount of work can get my mind off her, or what she admitted to me the other night in my car.

As I scan another book and type the ISBN numbers into the computer, the front door opens. My heart nearly rips out of my chest as I see Elle entering. Her eyes are puffy, the tip of her nose is bright red, and her hair is windblown, golden strands sticking to her flushed face.

How long has she been outside in the cold? Wait. Why is she even here? She should be home for break.

In the one second that we stand here, a flicker of *What if I send her back out?* flashes through, but I know I can't do that judging by the way she looks right now, even if I'm pissed at her for confessing to purposefully hurting me.

She doesn't make a peep. She just continues to look at me through her wet lashes. Placing the book that's in my hand down on the glass countertop, I move from around the register so that I can be closer to her. "Elle?"

My voice breaks her frozen state, and she runs her fingers through her hair. "Um…is Edgar here?"

"No." My head cocks to the side, puzzled that she'd be asking for him.

"Sandy?" She fiddles with her gloves.

"She's off for the holidays."

"Is there another manager I can speak to then?"

"You're looking at him."

"No, I mean for the bookstore."

"So do I."

She cautiously approaches me, and I feel it—the pull to wrap my arms around her and hold her against my chest, never letting go. But I resist. "You're the manager of the bookstore now? What about the coffee shop?" she asks.

"I'm doing both for the time being."

"Oh."

I take a step closer. "What do you need to speak to a manager for?"

"I-I wanted to see if I could get my job back."

A surge of clashing emotions bubbles beneath the surface. As much as I want her back in my life, I don't think I could work with her on a daily basis, knowing what I know and feeling how I feel toward her. "Sorry, I think it'll be a conflict of interest."

Elle's shoulders drop. "Please, Mateo. I've gone into every store on this entire street. No one is hiring. I don't need a lot of hours. I just need some money for—"

She stops herself.

I wait for her to finish, but she doesn't. "For what?"

She focuses on the floor. "I need money for therapy. I found a therapist nearby, but I won't be able to afford to go for more than a few sessions. I just need to work a few hours so I can cover the copay."

Oh.

Well, fuck. I'm not going to deprive her of going to therapy because I'm stuck feeling like a bitch over how she broke up with me.

Besides, *Tío* Edgar would be through the roof if he finds out she's back.

"Therapy, huh?"

"I don't want to talk about it. Can you give me my job back, yes or no?"

Truth be told, I'm glad she's going to therapy. I don't know what got her to that point, but if she takes it seriously enough, it could be really good for her.

Going back to the register, I open it up, taking out a fifty-dollar bill. My arm outstretches, handing it to her.

She abruptly takes a step back with wide eyes. "What's that for?"

"An advance. So you can start going before you get your first paycheck."

"I'm not doing anything for it."

"Well, you're going to work for it."

"Excuse me?" She crosses her arms over her chest.

"What?"

"I'm not some fucking whore, Mateo. You can't just throw me a fifty and tell me to work for it."

My jaw hangs open as I stare at her in disbelief for several seconds. "I meant work at the bookstore, Elle."

I watch her take a deep breath and shake her head. "Yeah, that would make more sense."

"You seriously thought I was going to pay you to have sex?"

"No, I-I'm just in a weird place, and I misunderstood. That's all." Her head hangs down as she stares at her shoes.

"So do you want the advance or not?"

She nods.

"When can you work?"

"Whenever. I'm not going home during the break."

Tears well up in her eyes, and I can't bear to see her cry or know what is making her so upset, because I have this annoying feeling it has something to do with Hunter. "You good to start now?" I ask.

"Sure."

In an attempt to break the heavy moment, I toss a book at her.

She tries to catch it, but it slips out of her hands and ends up knocking over other books on the indie author display. I can't help but break out in laughter as I watch her fumble, and she joins in with that cute little giggle she has.

"Your first task is to fix that table." I point.

She unzips her coat, placing it on one of the oversized chairs. I try to turn my gaze back to the stack of random books in front of me, but I can't take my eyes off her. I'm hypnotized by the way her green sweater clings to her body, accentuating every single part that I've been aching to touch. She gathers all of her hair and sweeps it to one side, exposing a portion of her neck. My teeth inadvertently sink into my bottom lip as I stare at her, and I have to force myself to stop thinking about running my tongue up and down her skin and making her moan out my name in that breathy voice of hers.

Clearing my throat, I shift gears and focus on the books.

We work in silence for a long time. Awkwardness radiates off me because I'm not sure what to say to her or how to handle this situation. I'm not cut out for this ex-boyfriend shit. Hell, I wasn't even cut out for the boyfriend shit. I thought I got a good grasp of it, but it all went downhill in a matter of seconds.

"Are you going to act like this the whole time I'm working here?" she asks, sounding defeated.

My head springs up from the computer. "Like what?"

"Standoffish."

"I'm not being standoffish. I'm working."

"You were never like this when we worked together before."

I shrug. I don't really know what to say back.

"Mateo." She pads over to me. "I know you're upset with me because of all those awful things I said to you when we broke up."

I nod. "I am. If you wanted to end things that bad, I would've just left. You didn't have to stoop that low. I don't understand."

"I know." She draws in a deep inhale and then pushes it out. "And I know I can't give you a reason for why I said it, but...but what if I can, one day?"

My brows draw in. "What does that mean?"

"It means that when I'm ready to tell you everything, I will."

She gets even closer, and I get a whiff of the sweet scent of her shampoo as it tickles my nose.

"What if I told you that I am incredibly sorry and will never forgive myself for doing that to you? And what if I told you that I regret every word that came out of my mouth?" Her eyes begin to well up. "And what if I told you that I miss you more than you could ever imagine?" She blinks several times, trying to fight off tears.

I sense my armor cracking. My bitterness toward her no longer shields my heart. It's raw, battered, and bruised, and still only beats for her.

The one who has a piece of my soul and doesn't even know it.

"Then I'd say that I miss you too," I answer. "And that I'll wait until you're ready to tell me why you said it. And..." I mull over the words before I commit to saying them aloud. "And I'd say that I forgive you."

Forgiveness. It's a bitch, but it's something I've always prided myself on being capable of practicing, minus with Dad. I've learned that holding a grudge does more damage to me in the long run, so if a person is genuinely remorseful, why would I want to hold on to that sourness and have it drag me down? Resentment does nothing but eat away at a person until there's nothing left.

My statement causes immediate relief, and Elle's entire body relaxes. There's even a hint of a small smile on her beautiful face.

"Thank you." Her eyes glisten, and she seems like she's about to start crying again.

Before I can say anything else, she swiftly goes back to her station, cycling out books on the display tables.

My fingers strum a beat against the countertop, debating asking the question that is rolling around my brain.

Fuck it.

"You doing anything tonight for New Year's?"

"No. You?"

"Same."

Go ahead, Mateo. Ask the fucking follow-up question.

"You wanna hang out?" I clear my throat. "I mean, we can just do something here. We're gonna be closed anyway, so we can just chill in the coffee shop and watch the countdown or something."

She spins around. "I'd love that."

Once we finish our shift and tidy up the bookstore, we make our way through the brick archway and into the other side. Busying myself, I turn the TV on and wipe down the already clean counter, trying to mask any nervousness that is skating under my skin.

This was a stupid idea. Who the hell wants to hang out at an empty coffee shop with their ex?

My palms begin to sweat as I make her favorite drink.

"Do you need help with anything?" Elle asks, poking around.

"I'm good."

As I pour the latte into a large purple mug, I notice her go up to the small stage area where we have open mics. I swear to god, if she starts singing, I'm not going to make it through the night keeping things platonic.

She taps on the microphone but frowns when she realizes it's not on. I make my way toward her, placing the mug on a table, then go to plug the amp into the outlet. "There you go," I say.

"Oh, I didn't want it on. I was just messing around."

A small part of me is glad she's keeping her voice to herself. The smallest part imaginable, but still.

"Is this weird?" She twirls the ends of her hair.

"Is what weird?"

"Us. Doing this."

"It doesn't have to be."

Elle moves off the stage to take a sip of her drink, and all I can do is watch her like a lovesick puppy. Fucking pathetic.

My feet finally move, and I take a seat at the table, waiting for her to join me. Instead, she puts her mug back down and goes back to the stage.

"I found a place similar to this in France. It wasn't the same, obviously, but it reminded me of here." She paces the stage, and the microphone picks up her voice as she walks past it.

"You gonna tell me about France, or are you going to feed me more of that 'good' bullshit?" I crack a smile.

She smiles back, sighing.

"Go ahead," I urge her. "You have the floor."

Elle chuckles and steps up to the mic, taking it off the stand so that she can continue to pace. "It was incredible. Not only France, but also learning about philosophy. I declared that as my major, by the way," she states with pride. "I want a career at a nonprofit organization, one that really speaks to me. Or maybe I'll even create one myself one day. Who knows? But that's where I feel called to the most, and maybe working at one will be my small, positive contribution to the world."

Sitting back in my chair, I watch as more of her energy fills up the stage. The passion in her makes her noticeably more comfortable with owning her presence.

"Life is so much more than who we are and what we know," she continues. "We're conditioned to perceive the world through the lens in which we were taught, but the lens extends much wider than that. It's infinite."

I admire her as her entire being lights up with the yearning for knowledge and truth.

"I want to ask questions about everything. I love asking questions and challenging my beliefs. I never had that experience before I met y—"

She stops herself. A flash of pain appears on her face while she looks at me, but she's quick to mask it and continues to speak. "And France was just stunning. It was everything I always pictured and more. I felt at home there. Maybe it was my home in a past life." She grins at me. I smile back, knowing wherever her soul was, so was mine. I guess France was one of our stops. "I felt so strong while I was there. But when I came back..." Her voice trails off.

Curiosity pulls me to stand and walk over to her. "When you came back, what?"

She shrugs. "Things went back to normal. Nothing really changed. I'm stuck being me. I was different there."

I approach her, my steps measured as I inch closer and closer. "No." The mic picks up my voice. "You were you there. You just chose to embrace a different side of yourself." I take another step, and her breath hitches. "I know you know that feeling, of finding a new version of yourself and being blown away by it." I don't know a lot of shit, but this I would bet my life on. I knew she found a new version of herself with me, because I did with her. "It was always a part of you, Elle."

Both of our breathing grows shallow. The only space between us is the fucking microphone. My gaze goes down to her lips, and her tongue peeks out to wet them. My heart races. I don't know what the fuck to do here. Do I kiss her, or do I—

The piercing sound of the ringtone from her phone startles both of us, and we take a step back from one another.

"Sorry." She pulls out her phone, and I see her mom calling.

"How is she doing?" I gesture my chin toward her lit-up screen.

"The same." She passes me the mic to put back on the stand before pressing the answer button. "Hey, Mom."

I can clearly hear her mom as they exchange happy New Year's with each other.

"What are you and Hunter doing tonight?" The words from her mom were hard to miss. Elle must have felt the same, as she hurriedly spins away from me and moves to the table with our drinks.

"Um…just hanging out," she answers, taking a seat.

As they continue their conversation, a myriad of questions barrel into my brain.

Why is she lying to her mom?

Does this mean she's not with Hunter anymore?

Why the hell is she here alone?

Elle hangs up and fidgets with her sweater. "She didn't sound wasted, so that's good. She's been staying with my Aunt Margaret for the holidays. I hope that she keeps an eye on her since I'm not there."

"Why aren't you there?"

"I didn't really feel like being stuck in Florida with her and my aunt. Similar deal to last year."

"What did you do for Christmas?"

"Oh, um…" She focuses on the table. "Not much."

"It's okay. You can tell me." I hold up my hands in innocence. "I promise not to fight anyone."

She half-heartedly chuckles. "No, really, I didn't do much of anything. I stayed on campus."

All right, another question to add to my list: Why the fuck *wasn't* she with Hunter and would rather be alone for the holidays?

I'll just go off the assumption that she's no longer with him, because that's the only thing that would make sense.

"Only a minute left." She points to the countdown on the TV, and I force myself to play along with whatever facade she's putting on.

Memories of last New Year's pop into my head. Elle drunk and coming onto me. Her mouth sucking on my neck. Her hands groping me as we drove back to my place. Her cuddling up to me naked for the entire night, causing a massive hard-on that I wasn't able to take care of until I showered the next morning.

"Cheers to the new year." She raises her drink.

I internally groan. *I'd much rather be kissing you than cheersing you.*

Our mugs clink together. "To the new year."

CHAPTER EIGHTY-FIVE

Ellie

JANUARY

The walls are a light taupe color with neatly hung framed photos of a serene lake and garden. I sit on a small periwinkle sofa, repeatedly crossing, then uncrossing, my legs.

The woman sitting across from me smiles. She has dark, thick hair cascading down her shoulders and wears gold-rimmed glasses.

"What made you want to start therapy again?" Panavi asks. I've just spent a solid ten minutes complaining about how therapy has never worked for me in the past, yet here I am.

"Um..." My leg bounces up and down, and I catch her looking, so I immediately stop. "I sort of got caught in a downward spiral."

Panavi adjusts her glasses. She can't be more than ten years older than me. I've never had a therapist who was this close to me in age. All the clinicians I had were picked out by someone else. Maybe this time it'll actually work since I found her myself.

"What do you mean by that?" she asks.

"I'm not really sure where to start."

"Then let's start at the beginning. Why don't you tell me a little bit about your childhood?"

Oh, Jesus. Why did I voluntarily sign myself up for this?

The next thirty minutes are spent explaining what it was like growing up with two alcoholic parents, a brief overview of when I lost Dad, and leading right up to when I met Hunter.

"You've certainly been through a lot at such a young age," Panavi states.

I shrug. "I guess. There are people out there who have it worse than me, though."

"Just because other people have different stories than you, that doesn't take away the importance of yours. Comparing your pain to others won't heal your own wounds. In fact, comparison causes people to ignore their issues, which allows for the wounds to get deeper."

She has a point. I can't deny the fact that the more I avoid my problems, the bigger they become.

"So where do I go from here?" I ask.

She leans back in her chair. "We'll begin processing your trauma, focus on setting boundaries for yourself, and help you foster your self-worth."

"That sounds...like a lot of work." I chuckle.

Her mouth turns upward. "It is."

All throughout work, my mind bounces between the boy across the way and my first therapy session. I really hope it's successful this time. I have no other option.

"What a wonderful surprise to welcome in the new year!" Sandy says in regard to my working here again, interrupting my train of thought.

"I'm just thankful you had an open position." I glance over at Mateo, who is sweeping the coffee shop.

Sandy pulls her hairband out of her platinum-blonde hair and lets it fall down. "I think that boy will always find a space for you. Not that I know much of anything that happened, but I'm glad you two worked things out enough for you to come back."

I'm glad it seems that way. We haven't worked much of anything out aside from the fact that we can coexist.

"Want a ride back to campus?" she asks, zipping up her coat.

"I'm okay. I think I might run the vacuum through the store once more and then head out."

Sandy gives me a knowing smile. "Okay. Have a good night." She waves to Mateo, and he gives her a nod before she leaves.

I lock the door behind her, then return to adjusting the books on the display table. Not that they weren't perfectly set before. I just don't want to appear like I'm lingering around waiting to talk to Mateo...even though I am.

Circling the store, I pretend to put away stray books that were never even out. Then, I weave in and out of the aisles, reading the back covers of the books that I move.

"You gonna stay on that side forever?" Mateo's voice startles me. He's leaning against the brick archway with a hand in his front jeans pocket.

"Just finishing up cleaning." I shove a book back into its place.

"Come on." He motions over to the coffee shop, and we make our way over. He walks around the counter and passes me a mug that already has my drink in it.

"Thank you." I take it from him and sip on the comforting latte.

Mateo grabs his own drink before sitting down. I follow his lead and join him at the table. We both move around in our seats, trying to get comfortable with the unspoken, uncomfortable state of whatever type of relationship this is.

The New Year's Eve shift changed things. We ended our night with Mateo driving me back to my dorm. He stood in the hallway, watching me go into my room. I was half expecting him to invite me to stay with him at his place, but I can't blame him for not wanting to. We're nowhere near close to how things used to be between us.

I spent New Year's Day anticipating Hunter coming into my room to the point that I put my desk chair under the door. It was stupid, but it gave me a sense of protection from Hunter. I couldn't have been more pleased when Panavi had an opening so soon—another excuse to get out of the dorm room.

Just thinking about what would happen if Hunter found out causes a threat of panic, so I ask Mateo a question to focus on something else. "How is grad school going?"

"You mean how are my social worker grades?" He smirks, calling me out on my drunken text.

"Sorry about that." I stare at my fingers that are tracing the pieces of glass on the mosaic tabletop. "But really, is it going well?"

"It's fine," he says. My brow wrinkles. I definitely didn't expect his answer to come across so blasé. "I start my internship at the beginning of next semester," he states. "I'll be working at a foster agency."

Seriously? Foster kids? Just when I thought he couldn't get any more perfect.

"That sounds amazing, Mateo."

His fingers tap against the table as he nods again.

Silence comes over us, and I nibble on my bottom lip, trying to come up with something to say. "I started driving" is the only thing I can think of.

Mateo perks up in his chair, his face beaming. "You did?"

"Well…no, not technically. But I sat behind the wheel—for a while—and didn't have a meltdown."

Mateo's eyes quickly rake over me. So quick that if I blinked, I would've missed it. His cheeks rise as his lips curl up. "Come on." He stands.

"Where?"

He grabs his jacket and keys. "To the parking lot. I'm teaching you how to drive."

"What?"

I watch Mateo lock the front door as my heart races. A mixture of fear and exhilaration trickles down my spine. I don't know what is making me freak out more—the fact that I'm about to drive or the fact that Mateo is the one who's going to teach me.

After scurrying to get my jacket, we rush outside toward the municipal parking lot. The gold Toyota sits by itself.

I take a deep inhale, allowing the brisk air to swirl around my insides.

I can do this. I just have to listen to Mateo show me the gears and whatnot. Easy. I totally got this.

He tosses me the keys and gets into the passenger seat.

"What are you doing?" I ask, standing outside the car.

"You have to sit in the driver's seat if you're going to learn how to drive."

Right. Obviously.

My stomach muscles seize as I get into the car. Staring out the windshield, my body trembles with anxiety.

I had zero time to mentally prepare for this.

This is too much.

I totally don't *got this.*

"I don't think I can do this," I blurt.

"Yes, you can."

"What if I wreck your car?"

"It's a piece of shit anyway."

"Not funny," I say, despite my small laugh.

He ignores me and goes straight into instructor mode. "You're going to put your foot on the brake. You know which one that is?"

"Yes." I do as he says.

"Good. Now put the key in the ignition and turn it so that it starts." I continue to follow his directions. My hands shake faster as they grip the steering wheel.

"Relax, Elle." Mateo places his hand on one of mine, and my gaze shoots over to him. His touch sparks every deadened nerve that lies inside of me.

My breathing turns ragged. Not because of the car. Because he's leaning in to me, and I can see his dark eyes glance down to my mouth. I must be dreaming. He can't be looking at me in that way. Not that I'm even allowed to have him right now, even if he did. I don't want to chance it with the thought of Hunter's threats hanging in the back of my head.

Mateo slowly draws his hand away, running it along the sleeve of my jacket, and he sits back in his seat. "You're going to leave your foot on the brake and put the car in drive."

I swallow and blink a few times, remembering I'm about to drive and not make out with Mateo.

Holy shit! I'm about to drive!

I do as he says, focusing on the parking lot.

"Now, you're going to take your foot off the brake and lightly tap the gas."

I push on the gas, and the car lurches forward. Panic surges through me, and I immediately slam on the brakes. Our bodies jolt back and forth.

"It's okay," Mateo assures me. "This time, press on the gas lightly." I try again, and the car goes flying, and I slam on the brakes for a second time. "Goddamn, I'm lucky your hand isn't as strong as your foot."

"Mateo!"

"I'm kidding. Sort of." He goes on to continue to give me instructions, but I can't pay attention to what he's saying. My mind is gripping onto the innuendo that just flew from his lips. Did he want to kiss me before? Does he not hate me as much as I thought?

"Got it?" he asks.

I nod.

"You weren't paying attention to anything I just said, were you?"

"No." I laugh. He hangs his head down and shakes it as he laughs along with me. And for the first time, it feels normal. It feels like us.

CHAPTER EIGHTY-SIX

Ellie

Three loops around the empty lot were enough for my first time driving, and I'm now seated in the passenger side. "Thank you," I say to Mateo as we pull into the university parking lot.

"Anytime," he says as he parks.

We both know that he's going to make sure I get to my room safely, so there's no use in stopping him from getting out of the car. We walk in silence into the building and up the stairs. When we reach my hallway, he stops and watches me trail past other rooms until I reach mine. I approach my door and pause in front of it before putting my key in. I spin to look at him, dimly lit by the overhead hallway light.

I stare at him, and he does the same to me.

Mateo takes a step forward, and my breath stutters. He picks up speed until he's directly in front of me. Butterflies have free range of my body as I stand here, waiting for him to sweep me off my feet and hold me in his strong arms.

But he doesn't.

We look at each other, each waiting for the other to do something.

"Do…um…" I stammer. "Do you want to come inside?"

A flicker of his cocky side shines through when the right side of his lip lifts up. "I do."

I almost drop my keys trying to open the door quicker than I'm capable of, and I catch the faint sound of his chuckle.

His presence behind me fills me with nervousness and excitement, similar to the feeling I would get when he would enter my room at the beginning of last year.

We both take our jackets off, and he wanders around my small room, admiring the pictures hanging on my wall.

Mateo smiles. "It looks like you had a fun time in France." He points to a picture of Ava and me on a balcony with champagne flutes in our hands.

"Yeah, that was a good night."

"I'm glad you went."

"You are?"

"Of course. I'm not happy how I found out, but I think you would've regretted it if you didn't go. Maybe even resented me."

I shake my head. "There's no way I could resent you for anything."

A zing of desire surges through me when I watch his eyes drift over to my bed. He runs his large hand over the back of his neck and moves to sit in my desk chair, choosing the safer option of the two. Leaning his elbow on the desk, he shifts some papers, knocking over my medicine. "Shit, sorry." He bends down and picks up the bottle.

"That's for my anxiety," I announce, and immediately wince. I don't know why I just told him that. That was stupid. He doesn't need any more confirmation that I'm batshit crazy.

"Oh." He seems pleased. "They work well?"

"They take the edge off."

"Good." Mateo places it back on the desk, and his gaze shoots over to my other medication. This one is in a packet and is super obvious. His eyebrows rise when he realizes it's birth control.

"That's for—"

"You don't have to explain yourself, Elle." Mateo puts up a hand to stop me. "And honestly, I don't want to know." He avoids looking at me or the pills and focuses on Bree's side of the room.

"It's not what you think. It's to regulate my period."

Mateo glances back over to me, his shoulders dropping. "Oh. You still didn't need to explain. It's not like we're…" His voice trails off, and he adjusts the collar of his shirt.

It's not like we're a couple.

It's not like we're hooking up.

It's not like we're remotely close to being anything.

In a desperate attempt to distract myself from my thoughts, I click on the TV. Mateo probably needs a distraction too. I land on a reality show, and he groans. "Your taste in TV is still shit," he teases.

"I'm a creature of habit."

"I've noticed."

I don't know if that was supposed to be a dig or not, but I'll let it slide. He fixates on the TV, and I watch him pretend to be nauseated by the show, but I know he's engaged in some of the drama that's happening.

My phone vibrates, and I instinctively gasp, terrified it's Hunter, and he somehow knows Mateo's in my room.

"What's wrong?" Mateo's head whips to look at me.

Grabbing my phone, I see a text from Ava. Closing my eyes, I exhale a long breath of relief. "Nothing. I thought it was someone else."

"Who did you think it was?" There's a roughness around his words.

"No one."

My body begins to whir with the dread of Hunter finding out. I should tell Mateo to go home. It'll be better for him in the long run.

I yawn, hoping that Mateo gets the hint that I want to go to bed and that maybe he'll excuse himself so I won't have to kick him out.

He silently looks at me, although I can tell there's something he wants to say as his mouth slightly parts, then shuts. The longer he stares at me, the more I feel naked, like he knows something is off.

"I hate that you're here by yourself," he admits, a twinge of desperation in his voice.

I'm taken aback by his admission. "What?"

"I hate that you're spending the break here all by yourself. It's not safe, and it's creepy as fuck. What's going on? Why aren't you with anyone?"

Because I have no one.

"I-I just wanted to be alone."

His eyes bore into mine, waiting for me to divulge more, but I refuse to. "Elena."

"Mateo."

He stands up and slowly struts over to me. The simple action stirs my body in a way only he knows how to. He lowers himself to sit on my bed, and my pulse instantly spikes. Love and lust wind themselves around my bones as I sense myself wanting to be selfish and give in to my desires just this one time.

"If you're so concerned about me staying here alone, you could just stay over." My words come out like a seductive dare, and my cheeks burn with embarrassment. "Not like that." I tug at my sleeve. "I meant, like, you can sleep in Bree's bed—or something—if you want. But you don't have to."

His tongue peeks out from his lips, and the sensation of dread from earlier has switched to a heated desire vibrating inside me, canceling out any reasonable thoughts of why he shouldn't be here.

"If I'm staying over, we're not watching any of your crappy TV shows." He pushes off my bed and moves toward Bree's.

I smile. "Two episodes."

"One. And you get to deal with my commentary the entire time." Mateo takes his shoes off and sprawls out on the bed. I'm sure Bree won't mind when I tell her that he borrowed her bed for the night. At least I hope not.

He crosses his arms behind his head, and his black shirt lifts up, exposing part of his tattooed torso. The more I pay attention to the image of a sparrow inked on his tan skin, the more my body temperature rises. My hands tingle with the yearning to touch him, as thirstful energy pours out of my fingertips.

I scoot off my bed, but the second my feet hit the floor, I'm grounded and rethink going over to his side before I make the wrong move and fucking tackle him.

Instead, I go to my dresser and pull out my pajamas. My fingers clutch Mateo's black shirt that I've been wearing at night now that Hunter is nowhere to be seen. If I wear this, there's no way we're staying in separate beds tonight, and I need us to. I've already blurred too many lines. I don't know what Hunter is capable of if he finds out anything happened between Mateo and me.

Reluctantly, I grab my ugly plaid pajama pants and an old T-shirt. "I need to change," I inform Mateo.

"Okay." He sits up and goes to stand.

"Lie back down. You don't need to leave. Just close your eyes."

He does as I say and covers his face with his hands. It's unfair how adorable he is.

"You're good," I say after I've changed. Mateo faces me, his gaze traveling up and down me, causing my stomach to flutter. "I'm in baggy pj's," I call him out, even though I love it.

"And?"

"And there's nothing you can possibly see in this," I say, wiggling my clothes. He smirks, and I feel like I'm missing out on a joke. "What?"

"What's under your shirt?"

"What do you mean? Nothing."

"I know." His smile grows wider as my nipples harden, poking through the fabric.

Mateo and I have definitely crossed over into new territory. Or old territory? I don't fucking know, but the urge to rip off my pajamas and let him have his way with me is starting to outweigh any thoughts of Hunter.

"You're missing your show." He motions to the TV.

Okay, Mateo. Try playing it off all cool, like you weren't just thinking the same thing I was.

Slipping under my covers, I get comfortable in my bed. I force myself to pay attention to the TV, but I can't focus on anything that's happening. My hands twist my comforter as my eyes occasionally glance over to Mateo. He's as cool as a cucumber while I'm trying not to hyperventilate.

The sound of rustling sheets has me turning my head. As soon as I do, I see Mateo lying on his side, with his head resting on his fist while he looks at me.

"Yes?" I ask, fighting back a smile.

"Talk to me. This is lame. I didn't stay here to sit in silence."

"I thought you stayed here because you were concerned about me being by myself."

He shrugs. "Tell me something."

I scrunch my mouth to the side, wondering what to tell him. "I went to therapy today. The office is within walking distance of the Cozy Nook."

"Convenient."

"Very."

"How was it?"

"It was fine. My therapist, Panavi…she seems nice. She's pretty young, so that's cool." I twirl a loose thread from my comforter around my finger. "I really want to work on myself. I think I can do it this time."

"I know you can."

Mateo's confidence in me is a breath of fresh air compared to the harsh staleness I've been inhaling over the past several months.

"You tell me something now," I say.

"I—" He stops himself.

"You what?"

His attention shifts off me. "I don't know if I'm cut out to do this."

I roll onto my side to see him better. "Cut out for what?"

"Social work." His voice is soft at the admittance.

"What?" I jolt up. "Why on earth would you think that?"

Mateo shakes his head, not wanting to tell me.

"Mateo," I urge him to speak. He moves so that he's on his back again, looking up at the ceiling. He stays quiet, and I don't understand why he doesn't want to talk to me.

Until I do.

My hand goes over my heart, guilt bleeding through the cracks. It's my fucking fault. Here I am thinking I'm letting him follow his dreams, meanwhile, I'm the one who killed them.

"Please tell me," I say, needing to know if the thoughts in my head are accurate. "I pinky promise I won't get mad." I throw a wager his way, hoping he'll be honest and tell me.

"Pretty hard to make a pinky promise when your hand is all the way over there," he cheekily replies with a hint of a smile.

Taking the bait, I pad across the room, my body burning up with each step as I get closer to him. Unable to restrain myself, I sit down on the bed, and he immediately pops up. With our gazes locked, I lift up my fist, holding my pinky out. He brings his hand up to mine, and the second our fingers hook together, time freezes.

I forget how to breathe and blink and move.

Until he lets go and drops his hand. Then I'm back to reality, ready for him to tell me the truth.

His Adam's apple bobs as he swallows before speaking. "I've spent a lot of months second-guessing everything."

"Because of what I said to you when I broke up with you."

"No," Mateo says, surprising me. "Did you saying all those things hurt? Yes. But it's how everything went down that has been fucking with my head."

"You mean the fight with Hunter?"

"Sort of." His features pull together as a distraught expression appears on his face. "What's messing with me is not that you compared me to my dad. It's because you had the proof to back it up. I scared you."

He looks like he's seconds away from breaking, and the compulsive need to make him feel better comes over. "No, you didn't."

Mateo tilts his head to the side and gives me a look, letting me know he's not buying what I'm saying. "Be real with me, Elle."

My breath shakes as I admit to both of us what I've never acknowledged. "You did." A stinging sensation forms behind my eyes, but I push it back. "But that's not why…that's not…" Tempted to tell him everything, I press my lips together to stop any words from coming out. "Mateo, you're not your dad," I manage to say.

"I sure fucking felt like him in that moment. How am I supposed to be a social worker and help people when I assault someone in front of my girl and fucking traumatize her?" He sits up straighter. "How am I supposed to be a fucking professional when right before school started, I was sitting in a jail cell—not for the first time—and needed to complete community service hours all summer long?"

As he speaks, my eyes get drawn to the large scar on his upper arm, the one that starts under the sleeve of his T-shirt and twists down to his elbow crease, acting as a constant reminder for him of the road he once traveled down. A path of destruction, fights, stealing, drugs, and probably much more that I'm unaware of. To me, he always seemed to be able to separate his past from his present, but maybe he struggles more than I realized.

A memory pops into my brain. It's of last year when he took me on a date to the arboretum, and when it had clicked for me that he doesn't feel good enough at times either. It's a part of him that he hides from the world. A secret he keeps locked away under his tough outward appearance, yet kind and empathetic personality.

He's scared and insecure because of his past.

He has shame too. He just experiences it differently from me.

My hand slides across the silky bedsheets and reaches for his. His rough skin, covered in images of vines and thorns, feels like home. He opens up his palm, and our fingers naturally slip in between one another's.

"You are worthy of so much, Mateo," I say, tenderness outpouring. "You deserve this. You deserve to be here, at school, following your dreams. You deserve to be happy and to live a beautiful life." I watch as his line of sight drops down to our hands, and he bites the inside of his cheek, stifling whatever emotions are coming up. "Don't let your past mess up your future. You're nothing like your dad." Remorse contorts my stomach, feeling even worse knowing that he's been dealing with all of this. "You're more than enough."

Mateo nods, and after a few seconds, he draws his eyes up to find mine. "Thank you."

"Of course."

"Not just for this. For everything."

"What are you talking about?"

"You've helped me so much, and you didn't even realize it."

My head spins for a moment. "I did? How? Because I'm pretty sure *you* were the one who was picking up my broken pieces off the floor when I'd have one of my hot-mess breakdowns."

The corners of his mouth lightly tip upward at my comment. "Because of you, I was able to become the person I always wanted to be. You allowed me to do that, not only for you, but also for myself."

His words hit me right in the chest, breathing life into my heart. I had no idea I had done that. "Oh" is the only thing my brain can conjure up to say.

My arms are begging to wrap themselves around him and tenderly embrace him, but I know if that were to happen, my hormones wouldn't allow me to stop there.

So, regretfully, I draw my hand away. He scoots back, respecting my need for space. "Your one episode is up." He gestures to the TV, changing the subject.

I smile. "No fair. We talked through most of it."

"Too bad. We're watching what I want now."

"Nope. I have the remote!" Dashing over to my side of the room, I grab the remote from my bed and put on another episode.

"Fine," he groans and lies back down. "But only one more."

"We'll see about that." I climb under my covers and catch him grinning.

We both let the silence between us grow, and after some time, I have the extreme impulse to break it. "I miss talking with you."

"I miss it too, Elle."

CHAPTER EIGHTY-SEVEN

Mateo

"Mateo," she breathes out my name.

I rub my fists over my eyes before opening them and adjusting to the light. "Yeah?" My sleepy voice scratches against my throat.

Elle immediately shifts in her bed, sounding more awake. "You're here?"

I glance over at her. "Where else would I be?"

"I forgot you slept over." She combs her fingers through her hair. "I was having a dream. Sorry."

A fiery sensation sparks in my core. *She was dreaming about me. What kind of dream was it?*

I watch her toss the blankets off herself and sit up. I do the same, shaking off any thoughts of her possibly having a sex dream about me. God knows I've had plenty about her.

As I place my feet on the floor, a deep ache shoots to my lower back. "Fuck." I lean over to my left side, stretching the muscle. "I must've slept weird. My back hurts."

"That's what happens when you're old," she teases.

"Excuse me?"

"You're not a college kid anymore, Mateo. You're a grad student. That's borderline real adult."

"You'd better watch it."

"Or what?" She toys with me, leaning slightly over her thighs just enough so I can sneak a peek at her cleavage.

"Or…" My mind goes blank, distracted by her body. "I don't know. It's too fucking early, but when I'm more awake, I'll let you know."

She giggles and stands up, putting her hair into a ponytail. Her shirt rises just enough so I can catch a glimpse of her taut stomach.

"Thank you for staying with me last night," she says.

"No problem." I rise and adjust my jeans.

"I really am fine here, though. There's security on campus if I'm in any type of emergency. I don't need someone to stay with me."

"Oh. So…then tonight?"

"We can't." She turns away from me to hide her face as she busies herself with shit on her desk.

I don't know what exactly I was expecting here, but the sting of another rejection was not it, not after our talk last night and everything she said to me. It's moments like those that make me fall in love with her all over again.

But I need to give her space. She told me outright that she wants to focus on herself, and she can't do that if I'm in her face every day. Although I really do hate that she's in this big ass building all by herself.

Walking over to her chair, I grab my jacket, and my gaze drifts over to the medicine bottle and birth control on her desk. My heart almost stopped beating when I saw that shit. Not that she doesn't have the right to screw whoever she wants, but the thought of her doing so makes me want to rip any motherfucker who touches her in half. I can't even begin to explain the relief I felt when she told me it was just for her period.

"Don't forget your phone." She points to it on Bree's bed.

I grab it, then put on my jacket as slowly as possible, not wanting this to end. I want to spend each minute with her, awake or asleep. I miss every single thing about her—the way she fidgets with her shirt when she's nervous, how she looks first thing in the morning with her mascara under her eyes, her sweet giggle that makes my stomach do weird shit. But most of all, I miss being with her. Talking to her. Not only did I lose the only woman I've ever loved, but I lost my best friend.

I'm not sure if I should be kicking myself for opening up to her last night. The last thing I want to do is let my heart be wounded any more than it already has been. But it felt good to get it off my chest, and it felt good not only to have her listen but know she cares. Elle said words that no one has ever uttered to me, including myself.

I adjust my jacket one too many times, and now we awkwardly stare at each other. *What do I do now? Do I hug her?*

"I'm gonna head out," I announce as if she didn't fucking realize that with my jacket on and keys in hand.

"Okay. I'll see you at work."

"Okay."

I start to move but then stop. She looks at me with confusion behind her eyes, so I shut down any impulse to wrap my arms around her.

"See you later." I walk out.

Fuck this ex-boyfriend shit.

Two days.

It's been two days since I last saw her, but she's the only thing that's been on my brain. I even talked to Mr. Kevin about her reentrance into my life. Each night I lie in bed wondering what she's doing—if she's tossing and turning or texting someone else or thinking about me.

Now, we're in the parking lot after our shift at work once again. She's in the driver's seat. Her hands have a death grip on the wheel. Her grasp is so tight, as if we're about to topple over a cliff at any second. Her bones look like they're about to slice through her skin.

"You've got this," I assure her, and she does. She did absolutely fine driving in the lot, and there are only so many times she can drive in circles until she takes the next step.

Elle shakes her head. "I don't know."

"There's literally no one else on the road."

We idle in the car at the exit to the parking lot. I can hear the sounds of her deep inhales and drawn-out exhales. She's scared, but I wouldn't push her if I thought she wasn't ready.

"But…I don't even have my permit yet. Is this allowed?"

"You'll be fine."

"That's not an answer."

"You're not going to get pulled over, and even if you do, I'll explain that I'm teaching you. No big deal."

Panic builds in her eyes. "I don't want you to get in trouble."

Leaning in closer, we lock eyes. "I won't. I promise."

Her eyelashes flutter. One more deep inhale, and she finally sighs out, "Okay."

Cautiously, she pulls out onto the street. There's not a car in sight, but that doesn't stop her shoulders from rising so far up they practically touch her ears. Her lips move just the slightest, and I'm pretty sure she's giving herself some type of pep talk. I don't want to interrupt, so I keep letting her do her thing.

"Radio," she blurts out. "Music. I need music."

I crank the volume. Each station has fucking commercials. Finally, I land on a song. It's some shitty pop song with the singer's voice horribly auto-tuned.

We sit at a light, which is taking forever to change. Elle's body begins to relax as the abrasive red bulb glows. Soft giggles come from the driver's side, and I turn to look at her.

"This is the worst song in the world."

I chuckle along with her. "I'm sorry. It's the only one I could find."

"I like that it sucks. It makes it hard to concentrate on anything else."

The light turns green, and she gently taps on the gas. Thankfully, she got the hang of that.

She rounds the corner toward the parking lot we just came out of. The whiny voice on the radio sings about dancing on top of a bar in her bra. Elle continues to laugh as she shakes her head. "Whatever happened to poetic lyrics?"

I chuckle. "Or singers without overusing auto-tune?"

"Exactly!" She pulls into the lot, her hand moving away from the wheel as she speaks. She doesn't notice, but I do. "It makes them sound awful and unnatural." She parks in a spot and leans back in the seat.

She blinks a few times, gazing out the windshield. "Whoa."

"You did it." I beam.

Her head moves in my direction. "I did it."

"How does it feel?"

She lifts her hands to show me that they're still trembling. I clasp my own hands over hers, mine so large in comparison that they make hers disappear. Her tremors don't dissipate, but I'd be lying if I said I didn't take this opportunity purely for my benefit. Feeling her smooth skin connect with mine escalates my craving for her. The need to have my lips on hers skyrockets as mine tingle in anticipation. I've never been more desperate for anything in my entire life.

My thumb grazes over her hand, and I watch as it soothes her, causing her shoulders to soften. She blows out a puff of air. "I did it."

"Are you proud of yourself?"

Elle nods. "I am."

She draws her hands away, slowly and fucking painfully as her velvety fingertips graze against my callused palm.

And just like that, the moment is over.

The night ends early, with me driving her back to campus. I walk her up to her room, noticing the conflicting expression on her face on whether she should or shouldn't invite me in. I make the decision easy for her and back away once she unlocks the door.

"I'll see you at work," I say, taking another step backward.

"Thank you." She stands in the doorway. "For everything."

"Good night, Elle."

"Good night, Mateo."

CHAPTER EIGHTY-EIGHT

Ellie

Days move quickly, and I've gotten into the habit of working, driving lessons, and going to therapy. In my last session, I chewed Panavi's ear off about how shocked I am that I actually drove, considering I've been petrified for years on end.

Today, I get to tell her about my latest accomplishment. "Yesterday, I drove around the neighborhood for ten minutes," I state with a glimmer of pride at yet another successful drive with Mateo.

"That's wonderful." Panavi smiles.

"It is." I sit up a little straighter. "I'm tired of feeling stuck. I mean, I'm twenty years old. It's a little pathetic that I couldn't get my shit together and drive until now."

"It's not unreasonable that it took you a while. You were impacted by an extremely traumatic event."

"I guess." My eyes wander around the room and land on a small succulent that's placed on one of Panavi's floating shelves. Succulents don't need much to survive. Just a nice place to live. A decent environment. "It's also a nice feeling to gain some independence from Hunter," I say directly to the plant.

"You haven't spoken much about Hunter, aside from him being your ex."

"Hunter is..." I stop myself, checking over my shoulder.

What the fuck am I doing? He's not even here.

I've been scared ever since Mateo slept in my room, to say the least. I've been waiting for something to happen—Hunter to blow up my phone or him driving around and spotting me in Mateo's car, causing an explosive situation. But I've gotten nothing but silence. The unsettling calm has me checking his socials every day to see if he posts, which he does. And now that I know he's still at home and hours away from school, I find myself settling in more and getting to enjoy Mateo's company without feeling like an unpredictable hurricane is going to barrel through.

Panavi slants her head, waiting for me to open up about Hunter. This is maybe the first time ever that I don't feel like I have to defend him. I can choose to speak honestly about him and pray that Panavi doesn't judge me for still having him in my life—or sort of having him in my life, since I don't really know where we stand after he tossed money at me and walked out.

"Hunter is…complicated." I pick at my cuticles. "He was sort of the catalyst for me coming here."

"He wanted you to seek therapy?"

I humorlessly laugh. "No. What happened between us made me realize that things are more messed up than I originally thought."

She hums. "There's a lot we need to unpack there, I presume?"

"Oh yeah. I don't even know where to begin."

"Let's start simple. What's one of the first words that pops into your head when you think of him?"

"Controlling," I answer without missing a beat.

She does the signature therapist nod. "Would you say it was a healthy relationship?"

"Definitely not. I don't really know how to do 'healthy relationships.'"

"Have you ever had a healthy relationship modeled for you growing up?"

Immediately crossing my parents off the list, I rack my brain for any relationships I witnessed as a child that I would consider healthy. "No, I don't think so." I bring my feet up on the couch, sitting cross-legged. "I want to be in a healthy relationship, though. I want to be worthy enough of someone loving me. I think once I fix myself, then maybe someone will."

"Ah, that's the first thing we need to work on reframing."

"What is?"

"Your belief that you need to fix yourself in order to be worthy of love. Everyone is worthy of love, even on their worst days, including you."

The unexpected statement immediately makes my eyes go glassy. It's a similar sentiment to what I told Mateo about being worthy. But it's easy for me to see all the beauty in him and the bright light that his soul offers the world.

It's easy for me to find that glimmering part in everyone.

"Being in a relationship isn't going to take away your past, your emotions, your trauma, or your diagnoses," Panavi states. "If you really want a healthy partnership, you need to focus on the one you have with you first."

I sit in stillness, letting her words sink in, tears on the brink of being set free as a revelation blossoms in my mind.

My heart has loved everyone in my life, except for myself.

Although the task seems next to impossible, there is a lightness in my chest giving me the slightest bit of faith.

The vacuum drones down the aisles as I push it around the bookstore. Sandy went home several minutes ago, and Mateo is counting out the register. When I'm done cleaning, I lock the doors as he goes to make us a drink. It's become our evening ritual to hang out for a bit before my driving lesson.

"How's Edgar doing?" I ask, making my way to our table.

"Good. He'll be coming home soon." Mateo sits down in the chair across from me. "I'm sure he'll be happy to see you back."

"I'm happy to be back." A small smile draws across my face, and there is a spark in Mateo's eyes.

He rests his elbows against the tabletop, leaning his body closer to mine. He clears his throat. "Would you want to—"

The vibrating in his pants makes him pause. He takes out his phone and silences it before putting it down on the table. "Sorry. That was Steph."

"It's okay. What were you going to say?"

Mateo tugs at the collar of his shirt, appearing nervous. My emotions soar at the possibilities of what he might ask me. "Do you—"

The phone rings again with Steph flashing on the screen, and he presses the ignore button as quickly as possible. "Do you want—"

It rings again, and he groans, visibly annoyed as he answers, "What, Steph?"

I watch as the emotions on his face change. His shoulders knot with tension, and the color drains away from him. My heart thuds, knowing that this isn't a good phone call.

"Is she okay?" Panic rises in his tone. "Which hospital?"

My face drops as he rises to stand. "Okay. Bye."

As soon as he hangs up, he grabs our mugs and rushes to put them in the sink. "My mom," he explains in a hurry. "She…she had a heart attack. They're running tests now."

Jumping to my feet, my stomach coils into a million giant knots.

Thoughts swirl around my brain, not helping me think clearly as I help him close up shop. "Is she stable?" I ask, suddenly out of breath.

"Yeah. I think? I don't know."

Dread pushes through my bloodstream as my muscles shudder with fear. Both of us rush around, making sure everything is off. Mateo repeatedly runs his trembling hand through his hair. "I need to go to the hospital. Now." He walks in circles. "My keys. Where are my keys?" I stop him mid-step and reach into his pants pocket to pull them out.

"Thank you," he exhales.

"Let's go."

I pull Mateo closer to me and link my arm around his, guiding him to his car. To anyone outside, we look like a loved-up couple trying to keep warm in the chilly winter air.

We slide into the car, and he fumbles with the keys, slotting them into the ignition, yet he seamlessly manages to drive the car out in reverse before turning it to point out the exit of the lot.

Settling into unspoken words, the sound of Mateo's heavy breathing is the only thing my brain can focus on. I watch his chest moving, his shoulders dropping and rising. Reassuring words are on the tip of my tongue, but I don't want to say them. I don't want to tell him that everything is going to be fine because I don't know if that's true.

He zones in on the road, speeding past cars in order to get to New York as fast as possible. His pace makes my anxiety spike. I grasp onto the leather seat and focus on inhaling and exhaling. My eyes shut as I hear the cars whizzing around us.

A blaring horn makes my eyes pop open, and Mateo swerves to the side of the road, avoiding getting sideswiped. Shrieking, one of my arms grabs onto him while the other takes hold of the car door.

Mateo stops on the shoulder of the road and puts his car in park. He rests his head against the steering wheel. "Sorry. I just need a minute."

I rub my hand over his tense back.

"I can't breathe," he says. "Am I having a panic attack? Is this what a panic attack feels like? Because it fucking sucks."

I can't help but smile, even in the midst of the chaos. "Just focus on your breathing, Mateo," I instruct. "I'm right here."

He nods, and I continue to run my hand over his jacket.

Leaning in closer, I move my hand up so that I'm playing with the ends of his thick hair. I can only imagine the horrible thoughts going through his head. As much as I want to tell him his mom will be okay, I won't. I know better than anyone that when you think someone is going to pull through in the hospital, they don't.

"We don't know the extent of everything. Let's just get to the hospital and go from there," I say to help calm him.

Mateo nods again and slowly lifts his head. I sit back in my seat and watch as he shakily shifts into gear. He goes to pull out and almost immediately another car horn wails, and he jerks back into the shoulder.

"Fuck!" Mateo throws the car back into park and rubs his hands over his face.

"I'll drive," I announce, surprising both of us.

His hands fall away, and he looks at me. "No. You don't even have your permit."

"I'll only drive for a little bit, until you feel ready."

"No."

"Mateo."

"No. I'm not putting that on you."

My palms clasp his cheeks. "Mateo, I'm fucking driving."

Before he can utter another word, I'm out of the car and standing in front of the driver's door. "You going to switch seats with me or let me stand out here and get hit?" I say loud enough so he can hear me through the rolled-up window.

Mateo glares at me but hurries to the passenger side so neither of us gets in an accident.

"You sure?" he asks.

No, but I'm going to do it anyway. "Yes."

I'm not doing this because I feel like I have to. I'm doing it because I *want* to. He has held me up so many times when I was down. I want him to know that I can be strong enough to catch him when he falls.

My arms lock into place, and I hold on to the wheel so tightly my fingers cramp. It takes me a while to pull onto the street, making sure there's not a single car near me when I start driving.

Oh my god, oh my god, oh my god.

Why the fuck do these people have to drive so close to me? And so fast?

I'm pretty sure I'm going significantly less than the speed limit, but I'm too scared to let my eyes drop down to the speedometer to check. My attention is glued to the road while Mateo talks to people on the phone. I can't tell what's going on because it's all in Spanish, but he seems to be a bit more at ease.

I won't ask him to fill me in because I don't want to get him worked up while I'm driving. I need to focus on getting us to the hospital.

My stomach twists, remembering the last time I was in a hospital—the scent, the images, the trauma.

I hate hospitals.

Cars beep around me, and even though they're not because of me, it gives me jitters each time I hear the sound.

The beeping is the only thing I can hear.

I steady my breath and pay attention to what's in front of me, while my mind drifts elsewhere. And, for the first time ever, I'm able to create space from where my thoughts take me. This doesn't feel like a flashback. This feels like a memory.

The beeping is the only thing I can hear.

Everything else is drowned out.

The talking between my family members and doctors is nothing but low murmurs.

The bright lights are blinding, but not blinding enough. They don't erase the blood.

Red, red, red.

Beep, beep, beep.

He's hooked up to so many machines. I've lost count of how many wires are coming out of his body.

He looks helpless.

Hopeless.

"Dad," I whisper. "Dad, it's me. It's Ellie."

Nothing.

Not a single muscle moves.

All the nurses give me a sad smile. Why are they looking at me like that? Why are they treating me like I'm some broken little girl?

"Sweetie." My mom appears next to me and rubs her hand over my back. I turn to face her, her eyes bloodshot and watery. Her hair is pulled back, and she's no longer wearing her makeup. "Ellie, I think we need to have a talk. Dad's not doing well…"

"No." I furiously shake my head. "You can't talk like that, not around him. He can hear you. I learned in school that people in a coma can hear the people around them, and then when they come out of it, they tell everyone what they heard. You don't want Dad to hear you being negative. You'll upset him."

Her chin quivers, and she nods. She takes a step back and paces the room. Whatever voices I faintly heard before are no longer in the room. It's just my parents and me. The way it's always been—and always will be.

"How about I give you some alone time with Dad? I have a few phone calls to make."

"Okay."

Soon after she steps out, I pull up a chair to sit next to him. It screeches across the floor the entire way. I check to see if that bothered him, but he doesn't move.

He's still not moving.

"Hey, Dad," I say, taking his hand. "I know you can hear me. I know you can because I learned about it, and I know you'll tell me that you could hear me when you wake up." My eyes brim with tears. "You have to wake up, Dad." My voice breaks.

He's still.

Beep, beep, beep.

The fucking beeping. I don't want to hear it anymore. I need to hear something else.

I clear my throat. "I know you're listening, so I thought maybe I'd sing you a song, one of your favorites."

My eyes shut, and I softly sing out the first few lines of one of Dad's favorites. I keep singing, waiting for some miracle to happen, waiting for him to squeeze my hand or shift in the slightest way.

Something.

The more I carry on with the song, the more my hope fades.

I can't hold back the tears anymore, but I still continue the song. A cascade of tears drips down my face and onto my dad's arm. My once composed singing voice is broken and shattered, interrupted by sobs and sniffles. But I have to get to the last note. I have to finish the song.

I know he can hear me.

The night fades into day, which fades into night again until we reach the one-week mark since he's been here.

The machines change. The beeping continues.

He still doesn't move.

"Sweetie." My mom gently pats my shoulder.

"Yeah?" I've curled into a tight ball on one of the hospital chairs. It's been my bed for the past several days, even though I've barely slept. I can't sleep or eat.

"Let's go for a walk."

"A walk?"

"There's a nice chapel down the hall. We can sit and talk."

I don't feel like talking, but maybe the chairs there are comfier than this wooden block.

We head to the chapel. It's softly lit with a small, tranquil fountain placed off to the side. No one else is here, so I wander around the room, checking out the different pamphlets they have.

"Elena." The tone in my mom's voice tells me I should stop what I'm doing, so

I do, and I sit next to her. The seats are a tad more cushiony than the one in Dad's room.

"Elena," she says my name again, but this time takes my hands in hers. She inhales an unstable breath. "We're going to take Dad off life support."

I rip my hands from her hold. "No!"

"The doctors say—"

"Screw what the doctors say! He's still breathing!" I jump to my feet.

"Ellie, we're taking him off life support tonight."

The weight of the world comes crashing down on me.

Tonight?

It is *night.*

I race out of the chapel, down the long, sterile hallway toward Dad's room. When I reach where he is, the medical staff are quickly moving back and forth, getting ready.

They're getting ready.

It's like this is nothing to them. They pull the plug on some girl's dad, then go type it into their computer and move on to their next patient.

No one believes that he's going to be okay.

I'm the only one who can save him.

Rushing to his side, my arms grip his shoulders, jolting his lifeless body. "Dad! Dad, you have to wake up now!"

"Ellie," Mom's voice whimpers behind me.

"No!" I shout at her. "Dad! I know you can hear me. Dad, please! Please wake up!" I shake him harder.

Doctors and nurses swirl around me. They're saying words, but I can't hear them.

Why couldn't this be me? I would trade places with him in a heartbeat. God, take me instead. Kill me, please. I'm the one you want, not him. Not my dad.

"Please!" My voice becomes shrill.

I know he can hear me.

"Dad!"

CHAPTER EIGHTY-NINE

Mateo

Coming out of Mom's hospital room and into the hallway, I'm able to breathe easier now that I got to see her and talk with her. My shoulders loosen as I walk to where Elle is sitting in a nearby chair, picking at her nails. I sit down in the chair next to her.

"How's your mom doing?" Elle asks.

"She seems okay. Happy to see me." I shift in my seat. These hospital chairs are uncomfortable as hell. "Happy that you're here."

She smiles to herself, but her attention isn't on me. I watch as she thumbs over the scars on her wrist, lost in thought.

Shit. I didn't even realize how triggering all of this must be for her. Not only is she sitting in a hospital, but she drove most of the way because I was too busy being a bitch. Now that I know Mom is okay, I can think straight again. The doctors are keeping her here overnight to monitor her, but everyone seems to be in good spirits, including Mom. That woman is a fucking saint.

"Hey." Steph's voice brings both Elle and me back into the moment. My other sisters, Angela, Valentina, and Isabel, are trailing behind her. I've only seen Steph so far, and I'm surprised the other three are here at the same time.

Rising, I give my sisters a hug and kiss on the cheek, then they greet Elle in the same way.

"Did you see Mom yet?" Angela asks.

"Yeah, we've been here for a little while."

"Good." She places her hand on my arm. "She's going to be fine, Mateo."

I nod. I know she'll be okay, but it doesn't take away the fear that's still tumbling around in my gut.

Isabel and Steph take a few steps away from me and whisper to each other. Suspicion kicks in when I notice the look on their faces. They both are wearing serious expressions, so I know they're not gossiping about petty shit. There's something happening that they don't want me to overhear.

Valentina focuses on me. "I'm so glad you're here," she says. "How's your break going?"

"Don't you start your internship soon?" Angela chimes in.

My internal alarm system goes off. I know my sisters all too well, and they can't play me by trying to distract me from whatever the fuck Isabel and Steph are talking about.

"What's going on?" My voice booms, and all my sisters stare at me.

I sense Elle standing by my side, but I can't peel my eyes off my sisters. Something's going on, considering they're all looking at me like a deer in headlights.

Their lack of response stirs my irritation, and tension clogs the joints in my hands. "Any of you gonna speak?"

They all turn to Steph, who cautiously approaches me. "Why don't we go home, and we can talk about everything there?"

"Everything? What else is there to know? Mom had a heart attack, but she's going to be fine, right?"

She hesitates. "Yes, but there are some details that we can go over at home."

"I'm not making it home without knowing what else is happening."

All my sisters take a step in, and now I feel like a deer in headlights. My mind jumps to horrific thoughts as panic builds in my chest. The sound of my pulse thrashes around my ears, louder and louder for every second they're quiet.

Somebody had better tell me what the fuck is going on. Now.

"Mom…" Steph sighs and glances at the white speckled tiled floor. "Mom has something called atherosclerosis."

"What?"

"It's cardiovascular disease. It has to do with the narrowing of the arteries. It does have the potential to become serious, but she's been changing her diet and has been on medicine, which should be helping—"

"Hold up." I put my hand up to stop her. "She's *been* changing her diet, and she's *been* on medicine? Meaning she didn't just find out about this now?"

Steph swallows. "No."

My eyes widen, and I look to the rest of my sisters, waiting for them to speak and fucking fill me in on this common knowledge that apparently everyone else knew about aside from me.

She continues. "She's been experiencing some chest pain for a while, and we've been taking turns going to doctor's appointments with her. But with the medicine, she should be fine—"

"She's obviously not fine if she just had a motherfucking heart attack, Stephanie!" The veins in my neck pop out as I struggle not to scream. Flashes of when we were younger come into my brain when she told me I scare her when I yell, because it reminded her of Dad. I promised her I'd stop, but with everything in me in this moment, I wish I never made that promise because I want to flip the fuck out on her and all my sisters for keeping this hidden from me.

Elle's small hand connects with mine, stabilizing me but not completely. I bite down hard on my tongue, attempting to restrain my anger. "How long ago did she find out?" I ask, the muscles in my jaw tense.

"A few months ago."

"Months?"

"We wanted to tell you, but we were all worried about you. We didn't want to add to your stress."

"What stress?"

"You know, starting grad school and other stuff." Her eyes flicker over to Elle and then back to me.

The fire inside me grows bigger, embers burning my skin. How dare she claim I'm stressed, and how dare she use that as a lame-ass excuse to not tell me about Mom?

Stepping in closer, boiling with anger, I look back and forth between each sister, my gaze piercing theirs. "I don't give a fuck how stressed you *assume* I am. If there's anything going on with our mother, you tell me. I will not be the last to know, and I will not find out months later. Understood?"

They all nod in agreement.

I'm not sure when I flipped from baby brother to whatever the hell that just was, but the way I just spoke to them wouldn't have flown if I tried it a year ago.

"Mateo," Elle whispers. "I'm going to go to the lobby so you all can talk." She starts to step away, but I tug her hand back before she can get too far.

"No, don't go anywhere. We're leaving. Just let me say good night to my mom."

Mom is asleep when I go back in. Pausing my steps, I stare at her for a brief moment. A bout of nausea rolls through me when I glance at the IV in her arm and the machines surrounding her. Shoving down any unease, I give her a quick kiss on the forehead and hurry out of the room. Without acknowledging any of my sisters, I bring Elle close to me as we move down the hallway, away from my family.

When we get outside, I pat down my pockets, looking for the keys.

"Catch," Elle says.

"Don't want to do another drive?" I tease.

She gives me an are-you-fucking-serious expression, and I laugh. The tension is slightly broken as I unlock the car, and we both get in. It doesn't take long for my sullen mood to return while I drive the car toward Mom's apartment.

I'm angry. I'm sad. More than that, I'm fucking terrified.

"Christ," I mutter, putting the car into park outside Mom's apartment.

"Mateo, if you want to be alone with your family to talk things over, I can catch a bus back to school."

"No, definitely not. I don't want to be alone with any of them."

Anger doesn't even begin to describe how I feel toward my sisters. I can't be mad at Mom while she's lying in a hospital bed, but as soon as she's out, she's going to get a mouthful from me. Who the hell do they think they are to not tell me? Were they just planning on keeping her health problems a secret forever? I'm her fucking son.

Mom didn't look any different when I went to visit on Christmas. She seemed tired, but I figured that was from prepping for the holiday.

God, I'm such a dick. How did I not realize she wasn't okay?

A gentle prickle dances over my neck, and my attention goes to Elle's hands playing with the ends of my hair. I lean into her hand as she makes her way up my scalp, massaging the tension away. *Fuck, this feels good.*

Closing my eyes, my fuming thoughts dissipate as Elle's touch, which I've been so desperate for, sends a sudden flush of warmth through me. Her fingernails raking up and down my skin leaves a tingling sensation with each swipe. My back relaxes into my leather seat, and I widen the spread of my legs, craving for her to drop her hand down onto my lap.

I take my bottom lip between my teeth as she continues to lure me into a lust-filled haze. My eyes open, and I zero in on her. "Elle," I say in the huskiest voice I can conjure up right now because I know she likes it.

Her lashes flutter, her voice so delicate and soft when she says, "Mateo."

CHAPTER NINETY

Ellie

The deep rumble of his voice sends heat shooting straight between my thighs. My body heats up with desire, each passing millisecond getting me hotter until I'm burning. My cheeks and neck are reddened as I continue to run my fingers through his hair.

Mateo reaches and clutches my hand in his, stopping my motion. Without breaking eye contact, he gradually brings our hands down to rest on his jeans. My breathing picks up as I drop my gaze and notice that he's hard.

Butterflies swarm my insides when he gently touches my chin, bringing my attention back to his face. If my face wasn't on fire before, it sure is now after he just caught me staring at him.

Mateo's thumb tickles me as he trails it along my face. I swallow, knowing what's coming next. He adjusts himself even closer, and his body moves in, but something in my brain wants him to stop.

"Don't kiss me," I say, a breath away from his mouth.

Mateo pulls back with a shattered expression on his face.

As bad as I want to kiss him, I can't, not like this. Not when he's upset about his mom and pissed at his sisters. He'd just be using me to make himself feel better, and I don't want to be that to him, or anyone ever again. I want our reunion to be meaningful, not with pain leeching on.

"Not now," I say. His eyes soften as some sense of hope for the future hangs in the air. "Focus on yourself and your family right now."

He processes what I said, and after a beat, he says, "You're right."

After the air in the car shifts, we decide to make our way inside.

Camila's home looks relatively the same as when I was here last Christmas, beautifully taken care of with modern furniture and lovely, personalized embellishments throughout their home.

The sound of keys clamoring against the front door has me twisting to see who's there, my nerves jumping.

"It's Steph," Mateo tells me, as if he can read my mind. "Come on."

He leads me to his large bedroom with dark-green walls and goes straight toward his wooden dresser. "I don't really keep clothes here anymore." He shuffles through his nieces' and nephews' belongings that are in the drawers. Pulling out an old T-shirt, he examines it. It's brown with a few small holes in the sleeves and a bleach stain toward the bottom. "This is all I got."

I was fine with sleeping in what I have on, but the thought of wearing his clothes to bed makes my heart do a little happy dance.

"Works for me," I say, taking the shirt from him and clasping it to my chest.

There's a light tap on the door.

"Mateo?" Stephanie's voice is on the other side.

"Yeah?"

"Can we talk?"

Mateo's jaw clenches, and I watch as his internal struggle appears on his face.

"I'll be out in a sec." He takes my hands and holds them for a moment. The warmth from them seeps into me. It's hard not to miss the deep emotions coming from him. "Sorry. It shouldn't take long. Just hang out in here for a bit."

When he leaves his room to talk with his sister, I strip out of my clothes and throw his shirt over me. It doesn't smell like him, though. It has a musty scent to it, like it's been hibernating in that drawer for a long time. Regardless, I wrap my arms around myself, pretending that it's Mateo I'm hugging.

Other voices enter the apartment, and I can make out each one—Angela, Isabel, and Valentina. I tiptoe closer to the door to see if I can get a sense of how their conversation is going. Between their flipping from English to Spanish and the fact that they're down the hall, I can't make out most of what they're saying. There's no yelling, though, so that's a positive sign.

I back away from the door to give them privacy and scroll through my phone. My fingers tremble as I go to check Hunter's Instagram for what seems like the hundredth time since getting to New York. There's a quick clip of him and his brother playing a video game, and another layer of relief sinks into my muscles. *He's still at home, far away from you, Elle.*

My location has been shut off for weeks, and I know he can see that I'm watching his stories on social media, but he still hasn't tried to contact me.

Tossing my phone onto the bed and lying down next to it, I try to momentarily have a break from Hunter, but my mind naturally goes back there.

Does this mean all of this bullshit is officially over with? It has to be, right? Otherwise, he'd be harassing me nonstop or making some sort of appearance in my life.

My head cyclones into a dizzy spin of thoughts, and I rub my temples to lessen the ache. Checking the time, I groan when I realize I've been caught up in anxious thoughts of Hunter for over half an hour.

Distracting myself, I push off the bed and mindlessly pace around Mateo's childhood bedroom. Old concert tickets pinned to his mirror grab my interest, and I check out which shows he's been to. My gaze drifts down to a small stack of photographs on his dresser, and I take a peek at them, grinning. There's a picture of him, Stephanie, and Michelle from when they were younger, looking high out of their minds, a few pictures of him as a kid with his sisters, and toward the bottom of the stack, there's a photograph of him as a little boy with a man standing next to him. The man has his hand on Mateo's shoulder, and the smiles on their faces are very faint. Almost forced. The last photo is of Mateo as a teenager in an emerald graduation gown with his cap in hand. He's standing next to a man, and they both are smiling ear to ear. I study the picture, wondering if that could be Mr. Kevin.

A burst of laughter erupts from down the hall, startling me, and I nearly drop all the photographs. After placing them back in order on his dresser, I peer out the door to check on what's happening outside. The sight warms my heart as I spot Mateo and his sisters gathered in the living room, talking with one another. The air between them has definitely shifted compared to earlier in the evening.

I wonder what it would've been like if I had siblings to lean on when everything went down with my dad. I know not all siblings are like this, but it's so nice to watch the five of them together.

"Ellie! Get your ass out here. We've got to show you something!" Isabel shouts, unaware that I've been spying on them.

"No!" Mateo tries to rip a phone out of Isabel's hand.

With a smile on my face, I make my way out into the living room. Everyone freezes for half a second to glance at me. I pause my steps, second-guessing if I should've come out here. Confused, I look over at Mateo, who's holding back a grin. I notice his eyes dip down my body, and that's when I realize.

Pants. I forgot to put on pants.

"You want to see an embarrassing picture of Mateo?" Isabel dashes over to me. Clearly, we've all moved on from the fact that I'm only wearing their brother's shirt and nothing else.

"Always!" I answer.

"No, she fucking doesn't." Mateo jumps up and grabs Isabel, yanking the phone from her.

"Dickhead." She punches him in the back a few times, the deep thud sounding like she could really do some damage if Mateo wasn't strong enough. She turns back to me. "Don't worry, Ellie. I'll send it to you later."

We hang out with his sisters for a little bit longer, until the ones with kids state that they need to get back, which leaves Mateo, Stephanie, and me in the apartment. Stephanie is quick to tell us she's going to hang out in her room, leaving Mateo and me to have alone time.

Standing in the kitchen, Mateo pours us both a glass of water. "Everything went okay with your sisters?" I ask.

"Yeah." He sighs a breath of relief. "We had a long conversation, and once I was able to cool down, I was able to listen to them. My only options were to stay pissed at them and make this worse for everyone, or forgive them and move on." He passes me my glass. "I know why they didn't tell me. It doesn't make it right, but I get it. And I made it really fucking clear—again—I don't want that shit to happen anymore."

I admire his levelheadedness. I probably would've held a grudge until the end of eternity.

"Good." I take a sip, the cold water refreshing my mouth. "And what's the plan with your mom, if you don't mind me asking?"

"You pretty much heard everything. The hospital is going to put her on an additional medicine, and she'll have to go to doctor appointments regularly to monitor her symptoms. If things escalate, then she'll need surgery. But they're all telling me that everything should hopefully be okay." He wipes off the condensation on his glass. "Steph told me that it was my mom's idea not to tell me right away. She wanted to wait as long as possible so the news didn't throw me off track with school. Mom is always worried about me." He smiles down into his reflection in his drink. "Even though I told her a million times that there's nothing to worry about."

"Sometimes we can't stop worrying about the ones we love."

Mateo slowly shifts his attention back to me. "Yeah. I guess you're right."

Gazing into his dark eyes, I get sucked into a hypnotic trance. My pulse speeds up as I melt into Mateo's energy, feeling sedated and electrified all at once.

I blink, breaking my stare. "You should get some rest. You had a long day."

He nods. "I'll take the couch. Let me just grab my pillow from my room." He pushes himself off the counter and takes a few steps.

"No."

My response halts his movement.

"What do you mean?" Mateo asks.

"You had a rough day. I'm not going to let you sleep on the couch."

"It's fine. I don't care. I'd rather sleep there than you."

I tiptoe toward him. "Why can't we both sleep in your bed?"

He pivots his body to fully face me. "You'd be okay with that?" he asks, his voice dropping in pitch, causing goose bumps to rise on my skin.

"I think that'd be fine. Don't you?"

Mateo takes one step closer, shrinking the distance between us. My insides heat up, and I'm suddenly unsure of my last comment.

"I do."

CHAPTER NINETY-ONE

Ellie

We're in bed. Together. Half-naked.

Genius idea on my part. Suggest you two share a bed, watch him peel off his jeans, and awkwardly lie next to one another, ignoring the fact that you want to rip the rest of his clothes off. Great thinking!

We lie on our backs, staring up at the ceiling. The small space between us feels like the width of an ocean.

Mateo shuffles around on the bed. His foot accidentally skims my leg, causing sparks to fly up from my calf and straight to my heart. "Sorry." He adjusts his pillow. "Trying to get comfortable."

"It's okay." My fingers clutch the blanket.

He finally settles on his side, facing me. I turn my head to look at him. The gap between us suddenly doesn't feel as far, as our mouths are inches away from one another.

"Thanks for everything today," Mateo says.

"You don't have to thank me."

"I do. You fucking *drove*, Elle." A grin appears on his face.

"Yeah, I'm not so sure if I'm up to driving back." I let out a chuckle. "Once was enough for right now."

"You got it." He wets his lips, and my eyes follow the movement of his tongue.

My heart strums an erratic melody. Our gazes don't leave each other's as we breathe the same air. I move onto my side, facing him, getting even closer.

The heat from his body spurs mine with need.

"Can I tell you something?" he asks.

"Always."

"I've been trying to find your tattoo all night." He grins even wider, a smile so infectious that I'll gladly show him what he's searching for.

Without any hesitation, I silently shove the blankets down and roll up his T-shirt that I'm wearing. I make sure it's high enough on the side of my ribs so he can see the tattoo, but low enough in the front so my boobs don't pop out.

Mateo props himself up and leans over me to get a better look. His warm breath tingles against my skin. Taking his callused fingers, he traces over the coordinates inked onto my body. My head becomes woozy from the sensation of his touch, and my nipples noticeably stiffen under the shirt. I'm desperately trying to control my breathing, but the rapid fall and rise of my chest gives me away.

"They did a good job," he says.

"Mm-hmm" is the only sound I'm able to get out.

He slowly drags his fingers over me, and I suck in a breath as his fingertips graze the side of my stomach as he pulls away.

"Your first tattoo looks way better than mine," he says, looking directly at me as if he didn't stretch those few seconds his hand was on me to feel like it lasted hours.

"Which was your first one?" I try to act casual, even though the logic in my brain is trickling out, as the ache between my thighs intensifies.

Mateo lifts up his shirt a bit and exposes his sparrow tattoo. It's on his hip, with the tip of the bird's wing dipping down into the waistband of his boxers.

"I got it done in someone's apartment. It looks like shit," he says.

"No, it doesn't." I move myself closer to inspect the artwork and choose to do the same thing he did to me.

My fingers outline the uneven lines, which I never noticed before. I follow the beak of the bird, over to its body, and down to the wing, gently placing my finger inside the top of his boxers. His legs shift on reflex, and my gaze shoots downward, fixating on the giant bulge that's pressing against his underwear.

"Elle." His voice is thick.

I glance up at him and see the lust pouring out of his eyes as he struggles to keep it together, while I do the same.

I pull back and shift to lying on my side like I was before, even though I don't want to. I'm no longer the only one breathing heavy. The quick movement of his chest exposes his craving too.

My eyes drift over his body and back down to his boxers, unable to force my attention away, wanting to yank the fabric off him and let him claim me.

I sense his gaze on me.

"Are you wet?" His raspy voice lights a fire inside me that I don't ever want to put out.

I draw my awareness back to his face as a sly smile crosses mine. Dipping my hand into my panties, I check what I already know to be true. "Yep."

His eyebrows shoot up to his hairline as he becomes fixated on my hand.

I'm not sure what my next move is or if this is even a good idea to begin with. Embarrassment abruptly ruins the moment for me, my cheeks heating up. I take my hand out of my thong, but I am suddenly stopped by Mateo's large hand on my wrist.

"Keep going."

That's the only encouragement I need to temporarily wash away the shame that shrouds me on a daily basis. Slipping my hand back in, I actually start touching myself.

Mateo becomes enamored by the sight as he sits up, leaning his weight on his forearm. "Fuck," he says, unable to stop staring.

My fingers circle around my clit as I watch him watch me. Tension coils up inside me as my pulse quickens. Mateo bites down on his bottom lip, and I get the overwhelming urge to kiss him. Touch him.

But I shouldn't.

"I don't know if this is a good idea," I say, my hesitation building.

Mateo's eyes flash to mine. "Why not?"

"We're not supposed to be doing this together." My fingers have a mind of their own and keep circling. "We have so much of our own shit going on," I pant. "We should be focusing on ourselves."

"You *are* focusing on yourself." A devilish look appears on his face, and I giggle. "We're not doing anything together, so it doesn't count."

The half-assed reasoning is all I need to continue. "Okay. This doesn't count." I move my fingers up and down now, my hips moving to meet them.

"Let me see your tattoo one more time," he demands.

I know he doesn't just want to see my tattoo, so instead of rolling up the shirt, I pull my hand out of my panties and take the shirt off completely, tossing it to the side.

"You going to show me yours again?" I ask with sass tickling my tongue.

He's fast to pull his shirt over his head and throw it onto the floor. I take a second to memorize his shirtless body. First, the large, jagged, scarred line on his arm, but then the beautiful artwork inked on his skin. My gaze flickers to the sparrow, over to the large dead tree that is filled in with bars of music instead of shading, then to smaller, filler tattoos, and over to a phrase written in Latin across his chest.

"What's that say?" I motion to the lettering.

"Live again."

"Oh." As my eyes wander over him, I slowly let my fingers reenter my thong.

"You gonna show me what's going on under that lace?" He nods toward my hand.

"Depends."

"On?"

"If you're going to show me what you got going on under here." I use my free hand to tug at his boxers.

"You don't have to tell me twice." In the blink of an eye, his underwear is off him, and he's gripping onto his length.

I swallow hard as another spark of heat rushes through me and lands between my legs.

"Your turn." He snaps me out of my daze.

I hold up my end of the bargain and slip out of my panties. My fingers automatically go back to my clit, moving faster than before. Mateo becomes mesmerized by my actions, deep groans getting stuck in his throat.

"This still doesn't count," I say more to myself than to him.

"Definitely doesn't count," he assures me. His breathing becomes labored. His hand continues to move up and down from base to tip. "Finger yourself."

My brow furrows. "I am."

He shakes his head. "Inside."

I move my hand slightly lower and slide one of my fingers inside myself. Mateo stops his movements and glares at me. I freeze. "What?"

"I know you can handle more than one finger."

My jaw drops open. "Mateo!"

He lets out a deep chuckle and goes back to jerking himself off to me. I slip another finger inside, my wetness making them easily glide in and out. Our heavy pants are the only sound in the room while our gazes move back and forth between our faces and the motions of our hands.

We lie with our bare bodies close enough to touch, but we don't.

Our mouths are close enough to kiss, but we won't.

Heat ripples through me as my muscles seize up. I'm so close I can taste it. My lips press firmly together to suppress my moans. My legs shake, and I fight to keep my eyes open, but I don't win. Screwing my eyelids shut, my orgasm rushes through me.

"Mateo," I cry out.

He lets out one groan before warm liquid shoots onto my thigh, while I continue to tremble.

He slams his head on the pillow, and I open my eyes to look at him. Both of us are panting, content, but neither of us is completely satisfied.

"Doesn't count," he breathes out.

"Doesn't count."

CHAPTER NINETY-TWO

Ellie

"Well, that was an interesting turn of events," Panavi says.

My weight shifts back and forth on the periwinkle couch in her office. "Was it bad that we did that? I mean, I know I'm trying to focus on myself and learn how to be with myself and not depend on anyone else to make me feel whole, but I *really* wanted to do that with Mateo." I pick at my nails. "That was stupid, wasn't it?"

She shakes her head with a smile. "Ellie, I'm never going to shame you for having an intimate connection with someone."

Relief settles into my shoulders. "Okay, good. I needed to hear that because I wanted to do more than just…you know…" My face gets hot at the thought that I briefly explained to her what happened with Mateo two nights ago. "And I made sure that we were both in an okay place emotionally. I think that was a good choice."

It's so strange talking about my sex life to someone, but I need to get this off my chest. I've been thinking nonstop about it ever since it happened. I don't know why I'm putting off kissing him. For some reason, that act feels *too* real.

Panavi and I talk more about the events that led to that moment, and I explain about Mateo's mom, Camila, and what's going on with her health.

"She was discharged from the hospital yesterday," I tell Panavi. "We hung around for a while, and Mateo even cooked for her. It was cute." I grin, thinking about our day yesterday. "It was the three of us, plus his sister, Stephanie. We had a great time together. They treat me like I'm part of their family, even though it was only my second time being there. And Camila is just the most wonderful woman. She's so incredibly strong."

I continue gushing about Mateo's family when my phone begins to vibrate. I ignore it and try to move on to my next topic of interest—Bree. She's coming back tomorrow, and I want to ask Panavi how to go about making things right with Bree, but before I can, my phone goes off a second time and then a third. Rolling my eyes, I explain to Panavi that it's most likely Mom drunk dialing me. As it goes off for the fourth time, I reach down into my bag to click ignore, but the second I see the screen, my stomach falls out of my body.

"What's wrong?" Panavi asks.

"What?" My face snaps off my phone.

"You look terrified. Is everything okay?"

I swallow around the lump forming in my throat. "Yeah."

Panavi stares at me, waiting for the real answer. My phone goes off again, this time causing me to jump.

"What's going on?" Panavi asks, her tone serious.

"It's just Hunter calling."

My heart hammers so hard that it might rupture.

Sweat forms on my forehead.

I thought he was done with me. I had assumed after I slept with him and hadn't heard anything from him in an entire month that he was done. He won the game and got me to cave and have sex with him.

But I was wrong. Very, very wrong.

Waves of nausea crash in my belly.

If he finds out I've been spending time with Mateo over the break, this will get so bad. If he finds out what we did the other night, it'll get even worse.

The phone rings again. "I need to take this. Sorry."

I step out of Panavi's office before she can even respond. Going into the empty hallway, I take one deep breath to make sure my voice doesn't give away my fear.

"Hey," I say into the phone.

"Why weren't you answering?" Hunter asks.

"I'm at the dentist."

"Oh." Something rustles in the background, but I can't make out what it is. "I'll be back from break in a few days. There's an important alumni event for my frat on Saturday. I need you there."

"Okay," I automatically say without a second thought.

"Good. I'll see you then."

He hangs up the phone, leaving me dizzy. I go back into Panavi's office and collect my things. "I need to end today's session a little early," I tell her, avoiding eye contact.

"If there's anything you want to talk about before we end, you're more than welcome to."

"No, I'm okay. I need to head to work."

Shit.

Work.

Hunter's never going to allow me to work in the bookstore knowing that Mateo is in the other room.

Outside Panavi's office, another round of painful waves burst into my stomach, causing me to grip onto my abdomen.

My thoughts race a mile a minute, thinking of every way imaginable of how this can turn out. Wondering if anyone has seen me with Mateo. Trying to come up with some way to keep my job. My mind spins, coming up with different excuses, stories, and lies. I pick up my pace toward the bookstore, as if I could outrun the hysteria building up in me.

Inhale. Exhale.

It's January. I can keep everything at bay until May. May isn't that far away. I'll just tell Mateo I need space this semester, and he'll give it to me because he's a kind, respectful person, unlike the person I'll have to deal with in the meantime.

When I enter the bookstore of the Cozy Nook, I try to erase any signs of panic from my face, but it seems impossible.

Mateo waves to me from the coffee shop with a wide grin on his face. He's been all smiles yesterday and today when we drove back. We left his home early so I could get to my therapy appointment and he could get to work. Edgar returned today, so I know Mateo has that relief added to his happiness, since now he can concentrate on school and his internship, which is starting soon.

I give him a small smile, then go straight to the back room to drop off my coat and bag.

When I make my way to the front of the shop, there are a few customers browsing, which lets me focus on helping them instead of looking at Mateo.

After I ring them up, Edgar makes an appearance. "My least favorite employee is back," he teases as he drops a pile of books on the counter, his mood slightly lightening mine.

"Would it kill you to say you missed me?"

"I don't know, but I'm not willing to try."

"Fine. I'll just assume that you missed me terribly and were waiting for someone as good as me to set up the display tables every other week." I take a glimpse at the books laid out in front of me.

"Fair assumption."

"Everything okay with your aunt in Puerto Rico?" I ask.

"Man, that boyfriend of yours is a real blabbermouth, huh?" Edgar turns toward the glass window that's between both shops, watching Mateo as he pours a cup of coffee for someone.

Hearing Edgar refer to Mateo as my boyfriend tugs at my heartstrings, getting dangerously close to being pulled in every which way, leaving me a shattered mess.

"He's not my boyfriend. We're—"

Edgar puts up his hands to stop me. "I don't wanna know! Don't tell me any details."

I attempt to hold back my laughter, but can't. "It's not like that!"

Mateo's gaze shoots over to us, and after he gives his customer her drink, he makes his way through the hollowed-out brick archway.

"What are you two talking about?" Mateo asks, leaning against the red bricks.

"The parameters of your relationship." Edgar points between Mateo and me. Mateo's eyes slightly widen. "Aha! That look tells me everything I need to know, and I don't want to know any more." Edgar walks away from us, disgusted.

Mateo comes over to me and rests his elbows on the counter. "Please tell me you did not tell my uncle about what happened at my mom's."

"Of course not! He just put two and two together." I give a dismissive wave and put my attention on the pile in front of me.

"Something wrong?"

"No. Why?" I leave my spot and organize the display tables.

"Because you've barely looked at me since coming in here, and now you're avoiding me."

I shift my gaze up to him, proving my point even though he might be right. "I'm not avoiding you."

"It seems like you are." He takes a step in, and my whole body tenses up. "Listen, Elle, if you're regretting what happened the other night—"

"I'm not."

"Are you sure?"

I nod. "Positive."

"Okay." He reaches out his hand and places it on mine, pausing me from continuing to straighten out the books. Butterflies dance around in my belly at the contact. "I want you to know that you're calling the shots here. I don't want you to think you have to do anything."

"I know."

I've always known that whenever I'm with him. He's never made me feel like I was obligated to do anything with him. Quite the opposite. He lets me explore myself and what I like sexually.

"Good." He gives my hand a light squeeze. "I think we should talk about what's going on with us and—"

A loud group of people enters the coffee shop, forcing our attention to the cluster of college students. Panic sears my chest at the sight of Ava and Derek.

They must've come back from break early.

"Be right back." I run away from Mateo and down the bookstore, turning into an abandoned aisle, my heart thrashing in my rib cage.

Please don't see me. Please don't see me. Please don't see me.

If Derek spotted Mateo and me, I'm fucked. Technically, Mateo is fucked. I might as well go wave my white flag to Hunter now.

My vision suddenly gets spotty.

My lungs constrict. The air I suck in gets so sharp, it hurts to breathe.

Fuck, don't have a panic attack now. Get it together!

My head spins.

I shut my eyes and attempt to bring down my heart rate.

Inhale. Exhale.

Inhale. Exhale.

Sliding my body down the bookshelf, I sit on the floor.

I press my palms into the rug.

Ground yourself. You need to ground yourself.

I run my hands over the stiff material over and over again until it's all I can concentrate on. The rug becomes soft against my hands as I continue to comb it out.

Minutes go by, and the clamp around my chest loosens up. When I open my eyes, it takes a few seconds for the room to come into focus.

It's quiet. I no longer hear the crowd of people that walked in. I don't know how long I've been sitting on the floor, but it seemed to work.

I'm okay.

With shaky legs, I stand, my muscles slowly regaining strength.

"You good?" Mateo appears from thin air.

I spin to face him with a forced smile on my face. "Yeah, why wouldn't I be?"

"You ran away when we were in the middle of a conversation."

"I just forgot I left something over here and needed to get it."

"Did you find it?"

"Yes." There's a smirk tugging at his lips, and I wish I could seal with mine. "Don't give me that smart-ass look." I point a finger at him.

"Don't lie to me."

"Don't…don't…" Flustered, I run my hands over the ends of my hair.

Mateo chuckles and brings his fingertips to a stray strand, gently looping it behind my ear.

"Mateo!" Edgar's voice bellows through the store. "Get your ass back on your side!"

Mateo brushes his finger down my neck before slowly moving backward, breaking the magnetic pull between us. Then he gives me a wink that shoots desire between my thighs.

Damn him.

CHAPTER NINETY-THREE

Ellie

The next day, I clean, then reclean my side of the room, needing to get out some of my anxious energy over Hunter's impending arrival. I'm so freaked out that I texted Edgar telling him I can't work for the next two weeks. That should buy me some time to figure out how to balance work and Hunter. Maybe if I only take shifts during Hunter's classes, then he'll never find out.

My head pounds while I reach for my phone and send the next text that I'm going to hate myself even more for.

ME

I need some space to figure some stuff out. I'm going to keep focusing on myself for now and when I'm ready I'll let you know.

Throwing my phone onto my bed, not wanting to see Mateo's reply, I shift gears into getting ready for Bree to come back. We took some time apart from each other, like Bree suggested, and I've been praying for things to smooth over between us as soon as possible. I don't think I can bear another heartache—especially from her.

I washed Bree's bedding, made her bed, and straightened up her side of the room. And now I sit on my chair, swinging my feet back and forth, waiting for her to come back any second.

When I hear the doorknob twist, a rush of uncertainty takes hold of me. She enters with her large rolling luggage in tow.

"Hey." I jump up, tugging the end of my sweatshirt sleeve.

"Hey." She pulls the door closed.

We stare at each other for a beat, then both start talking at the same time.

"I fucked up."

"I'm really sorry."

"You go first," she says.

"How about you unpack, get settled, and then we talk?"

Bree nods, then shuffles over to her bed. She pauses. "Did you clean my side?"

"A little."

While she empties her clothes from her suitcase, I decided to go downstairs to the lounge area and make us both hot chocolate.

Once I'm back in the room, Bree is perched on her bed, and I hand her the drink. "Come sit." She moves her legs so that there's more room.

Sitting down on the stiff mattress, I take a sip of my drink and then get the courage to speak. "I'm really sorry for how I acted last semester and for everything that went down at the party."

"I'm sorry too. I shouldn't have gotten so pissed at you for not talking to me and said those things to you."

I shake my head. "No. You were right. I haven't been like myself lately. I know I haven't." Letting out a sigh, I tell her as much as I can. "I'm in a complicated spot, and I'm trying to figure it out and get out of it the most peaceful way I can."

"When you make it sound so elusive like that, I start to get worried."

"It's nothing I can't handle, I swear. And once I'm ready to, I'll fill you in on everything." *And hope that you don't judge me for being so weak and voiceless. Hell,* I *judge myself for being in this situation.*

"Okay..."

"I started seeing a therapist, so that's a plus." I give a smile to ease any of her concerns.

Bree sips on the hot chocolate. "Is Hunter still going to be hanging around?"

"That's one of the things I'm trying to figure out. If he does pop up, I'll make sure it's not when you're here."

"Okay." There's a drawn-out moment of silence. "So...can we be fine now because I really want to tell you about what happened on my break?"

"Please!"

She perks up, grinning, and the tension immediately washes away. "I hooked up with this extremely hot girl in Malibu, and now I'm in love."

My eyes bulge. "You are?"

"No, not even close to love. I don't even know her last name, but she's superhot. Wanna see?"

Bree grabs her phone and shows me pictures of this beautiful bikini model, then goes into way too much detail about their time together.

"God, I wish I could be one of those people who just goes to a random place and hooks up with someone," I say.

Bree playfully gasps. "Are you calling me a slut?"

"No! Not in the slightest! You're having fun and…free. I would kill to be free."

"So, then this semester, embody that, Ellie! Be free!" She throws her arms up in the air, and hot chocolate splashes onto her sheets.

"Girl, I just washed those."

"You washed my sheets too? You know you don't have to buy my friendship, right? We could've just had the conversation we did earlier, and things would still be fine."

"I wanted to wash them after Mateo slept in your bed."

She freezes. "Hold the fuck up. *Mateo slept over*?"

I chuckle and decide to give her a very brief synopsis of how we linked back together and where we stand now, which is something I'm not clear on.

"So you kinda sorta hooked up with Mateo?" Bree asks.

"Yes."

"But you're kinda sorta still talking to Hunter?"

"Yes."

"Damn. You got some TV drama, love-triangle shit going on."

I groan. "I know, and I fucking hate it."

"Let's consult the professionals on this." And with that, Bree grabs the remote, and we settle in, watching our favorite reality show, letting me dissociate from my own life.

The following day is Saturday, the night of Hunter's alumni dinner. He hasn't spoken to me since the phone call I received in Panavi's office, but when I came back to an empty room after getting lunch earlier, I found clothing and a shoebox sitting on my bed with a note attached saying he couldn't wait to see me tonight.

I stare at myself in the mirror behind the door of our room, shocked that *this* is what Hunter wants me to wear.

"Wow, Ellie!" Bree twirls her head around to get a better look. "You look fierce!" She's been out shopping with her friend all day. When I explained to her that I'm going out with Hunter tonight, a weird expression crossed her face, and I'm pretty certain it was from biting her tongue too hard.

"You don't think it's too…much?" I pull at the hem of the red dress so it's not as short, but as soon as I do that, my boobs pop out. Adjusting myself, I continue to fixate on my reflection.

The red dress is tight with skinny straps and a deep heart-shaped neckline exposing my cleavage. It hugs every curve of my hourglass figure that I'm uncomfortable owning. My shoes are designer, black with red bottoms. I've never worn anything designer in my life. I never had the desire to.

Bree sidles up next to me so I can see her in the mirror. "I don't think it's too much," she says. "I just don't think it's you."

"It's not."

"Then wear something else."

"I can't. Hunter bought this for me to wear."

"*Hunter* got that for you?"

"Yeah, why?"

She shrugs. "I don't know him very well, but I can't picture him voluntarily picking that out for you to wear in front of all his brothers."

Grabbing my phone, I text him.

ME

are you sure about this dress?

HUNTER

send me a picture

I snap a photo of myself in the mirror and send it to him. Nerves jump around my insides, thinking about what his response will be.

HUNTER

wow.

I stare at the screen, waiting for another text to pop up, but nothing else follows.

"If you want to hang out after your boring dinner, text me, and I'll let you know what bar I'm at," Bree says as she zips up her coat, getting ready to go out on another one of her adventures. Envy stirs inside me, wishing I could steal her freedom. I'd love to completely let go of all my inhibitions, even if it was just for a night.

Before long, she's off, and I continue to look at my phone, waiting for Hunter to tell me to change or that he's picking me up a new dress or something along those lines.

The silence from his end causes knots in my muscles.

Apprehension pumps through my veins.

My throat has an annoying itch the more my unease dries me up.

My fingers run over the ends of my hair over and over again, while I take some deep breaths.

A gentle knock causes my attention to go to the door.

"Come in," I say.

Hunter stands in the doorway in a black suit and his hair slicked back. His smile somewhat relaxes me. He wouldn't be smiling if he knew I've been seeing Mateo. He wraps his arms around me. "Hi, angel," he says into my hair.

The pet name summons more relief, uncoiling the fear in my stomach, considering he doesn't use it when he's angry.

"Hey, I'm just finishing getting ready." I move toward my purse, but he stops me, taking one of my hands in his. His eyes drop down my body, taking me in.

"You look stunning."

"Thanks," I say, taking my other hand and smoothing out the fabric of my dress.

"But," he says, fishing something out of his pocket. "I think you'd look even more beautiful wearing this."

Hunter showcases a black velvet jewelry box and opens it up. My mouth hangs open when I spot a gorgeous diamond bracelet. I stare at the gift, dumbfounded. *Why the hell is he buying me things?* This is wildly confusing. My eyes move up to look at his, and I notice them sparkle. The younger version of him peeks through, the one that I thought I once knew and loved. The one that somehow always hits a soft spot because he seems so genuine and innocent.

"I can't accept that," I tell him.

He ignores my comment and places it on my left wrist, conveniently hiding my scars. My head tilts, wondering if the bracelet was placed there on purpose.

His gaze catches mine, and his eyebrows crease together. "Do you want it on the other arm?"

"No, this is fine. I just didn't know if…I thought…never mind."

I glance back down to the shimmering jewelry hanging like a ball and chain on my arm. Hunter's thumb goes to my chin, and he gently moves my head up so I look at him.

"You can't see them unless you're close," he says about my scars. "Don't be self-conscious. You look absolutely incredible."

I nod. "Thank you for all of this." I wave a hand around myself.

"Anything for you."

My abdominal muscles tighten once again.

Anything except letting me go.

He leans in for a kiss, but I pull back. The sudden realization that he probably thinks we're going to sleep together again slaps me across the face.

"What's the matter?" he asks, puzzled.

"We're not doing this."

"Why wouldn't we?"

"Are you serious?" I stare at him, but he looks at me blankly, unsure why I wouldn't want to hook up. "Well, for starters, you *left* me, Hunter. I didn't even hear from you all fucking break."

He parts a crooked smile. "You missed me, angel?"

"I…you…" I brush the hair away from my face and gather my thoughts. "You dismissed me right after we fucked and then went home. I was stuck here the entire month. I spent Christmas alone, Hunter." My voice cracks, hating the reality that what he did still hurts me.

Confusion appears on his face. "Why did you spend Christmas alone?"

Tears prickle behind my eyes, but I pinch the bridge of my nose, pushing them back in. "Because my mom went to Florida."

"Well, I didn't know that, Ellie. You didn't tell me."

I open my mouth to defend myself, but he has a point. I never told him.

Hunter continues. "You were assuming you'd spend Christmas with *me*?"

"I…yeah, I guess I was."

"Did you really think you could come over after the shit that went down at Thanksgiving? And I didn't text you all during break because I was dealing with family drama for the entire month. You knew you wouldn't be able to come over, and I wouldn't be able to hang out during the break. You *knew* that."

My emotions betray me, and salty moisture hits my lips.

"I'm sorry you were alone for Christmas. You never told me," he says.

"It's okay." Another tear slides down my cheek. I'm not sure why I'm crying this hard. I guess admitting how used I felt and how lonely I was makes it all resurface.

Hunter hugs me, and I cry into his chest. I cry because I hate this situation I've found myself in. I cry because I don't want him to touch me, but I know that I need someone to. I cry because I'm stuck being taken care of by my captor. I cry because I'm confused about how nice he's being.

"Hey," Hunter whispers, running his hand over me in an attempt to be soothing. "You don't need to cry anymore. I'm here now. Things will go back to normal. I won't leave you again. I promise, Ellie."

I nod, knowing he'll keep his word on that, even though I wish he wouldn't.

He takes a step back to look at me. I manage to pull myself together, and he wipes away any evidence of pain on my face. "Let's have a nice time tonight. This is supposed to be fun. You think we can have some fun tonight?"

I take a deep breath and check my makeup in the mirror. "Yeah. Yeah, sorry. I'm fine now." I reach for my purse and jacket. "Come on. Let's go have some fun."

We enter a banquet hall with extravagant chandeliers hanging from the ceiling. Each table has beautiful, over-the-top floral centerpieces and a complimentary crystal glass of champagne in front of every seat.

"I didn't know it was this fancy," I whisper to Hunter.

Our arms are linked together, and he pulls me in tighter. "Don't worry. We don't have to stay for too long. I know it's not your thing."

Definitely not my thing. I couldn't even deal with being at my prom the entire time, so Hunter and I ended up hanging out at a local park while I was in my gown and he was in his tux.

"What's this dinner for anyway?"

"It's a special fiftieth anniversary."

"Fiftieth anniversary of what? The fraternity?"

"No. I zoned out when they were talking about it, so I actually don't have a clue. I felt too stupid to ask anyone, so I've just been pretending to know what the fuck everyone's been talking about for the past few weeks." A giggle slips out, and he chuckles with me. "Let's get a drink and act as if we know what's going on."

"Sounds like a plan."

My brain has gotten so used to how I'm supposed to act with Hunter out in public that it's become second nature to neglect every sane thought I have while we're together. And when he's being nice, it's even easier.

We spend the hour schmoozing and sipping on expensive drinks. Technically, Hunter does the schmoozing. I stand there and smile. I hate talking to random people and having surface conversations, so I'm grateful the alcohol is loosening up my nerves.

"This is Ellie," Hunter introduces me to yet another alumnus, only thankfully, this man doesn't feel the need to stare at my dress and give Hunter a nod of approval.

"Nice to meet you, Ellie. I'm Hank." He shakes my hand, and we talk for a bit about UConn and Hank's good ole days in the fraternity.

"What are you studying, Ellie?" Hank asks.

"I'm a philosophy major."

His eyebrow rises. "A philosophy major?"

I nod, unsure of his reaction.

"Are you liking it?" he inquires.

"I absolutely love it," I gush. "I even spent the summer abroad studying philosophy."

"Don't be modest, Ellie," Hunter interjects, then speaks to Hank. "My girl got a full scholarship to the abroad program in France and is at the top of her class." My cheeks redden at the bragging Hunter is doing on my behalf.

"Is that so?" Hank glances at me, and I nod again. "Well, if that's the case, I might have an interesting internship opportunity for you starting in the fall. My company will be taking over a local nonprofit soon, and we'll be looking to hire an intern to help with the ethics and policies. There'll be a lot of writing and potential opportunities for presentations, which I can guarantee will look wonderful on your resume." He reaches into his jacket pocket. "Here's my card. Reach out by the end of the semester if you're interested, and we can set up an interview."

I let out a small gasp as I take the card from him. "Thank you so much. You don't have to do this."

"Listen, if you're as good as he says you are…" Hank motions his head toward Hunter. "I want you on my team."

"She is. Trust me." Hunter places his arm around my waist, and I lean into him.

Hank excuses himself as another one of his college buddies comes up to greet him. I turn into Hunter. "I just got someone's business card!" I whisper with my excitement bubbling through as I slip it into my purse.

"I know," he whispers back.

"He doesn't even know me, and he offered me an interview."

"It's all about networking and connections. That's how all the important people got to where they are today." He pulls me in closer. "I'm proud of you, angel. And no more of this nice girl shit. When someone gives you their card, you say thank you, and that's it. You deserve every opportunity that comes your way. It's time for you to start believing that."

I'm struck by his words. The way he can so easily fill me up with confidence sends me off balance. I thought I was past this. I thought I would no longer be affected by his sentiments, yet here I am, soaking up the kind words he throws at me. How can I have such animosity for a person yet get a wave of adrenaline and happiness when they lift me up? The way he has me wrapped around his finger makes me feel brainwashed, and there's nothing I can do about it.

After dinner and more conversations with people I don't know, soft music plays through the speakers, and couples make their way to the dance floor. They're all ages, from young to old, but they all look genuinely happy.

Hunter rises to his feet and extends his hand. "Dance with me?"

"I don't dance."

"Liar. We slow danced at my prom *and* yours."

I roll my eyes. "Fine. One dance. That's it."

I place my hand in his, and he guides me to the dance floor. Bringing me closer to him, he rests his other hand on my lower back. We sway back and forth to the light strums of the guitar.

Hunter's eyes fixate on mine. There's a familiar flicker that appears in them right before he bends down to kiss me.

Hunter's lips against mine wring my insides tight as he adds another bar to my jail cell.

I make sure not to kiss him back, and I stand there motionless as he tries to take more from me. He's already taken so much. I'm not sure I'll have anything left to give by the time he's done with me. And a part of me thinks he wants it that way.

He pulls back, realizing I'm not willing to give him anything. "Ellie," he brushes a strand of hair away from my face.

"I'm not doing this." I move out of his grasp.

A flash of anger crosses his face, but then he looks around, realizing we're in front of a lot of important people. Backing away, I head back to our table, where I continue to play pretend.

The rest of the night, I can sense the explosion building inside of him with every glance, gesture, and word that comes out of his mouth.

I couldn't have been happier to find Ava a few tables away from us, sitting next to Derek. And when she asked Hunter and me for a ride back to campus because Derek's car broke down, I was elated.

I know Hunter won't do anything to me in front of her. I'll have to face his wrath another day. But tonight, I'm safe.

CHAPTER NINETY-FOUR

Ellie

Sitting in Panavi's office, I have yet to mention this tangled web I'm stuck in. It's always on the tip of my tongue, but my shame lets the words disintegrate.

"I had a panic attack at work last week." I fill her in on my episode at the Cozy Nook when I saw Derek and Ava.

"Do you know what prompted it?"

Yes. "No." I bite my nails. "I think I have to quit."

"Because work is triggering panic attacks?"

"Not exactly." My attention drifts to the small succulent collection on her floating shelves as I think of a way to shift this conversation. "It's annoying. I'm taking these stupid pills to make me feel better, and I still have panic attacks."

"The medication decreases your symptoms but doesn't always erase them altogether."

"I know." I lean back on the couch. "I wish they would, though. I've been on and off them since I was fourteen. I definitely feel better on them. I can't even lie about that. I just hate that I need them."

"How come?"

"I don't like the idea of being controlled by something."

"Perhaps you've been displacing your distaste of being controlled onto your medicine instead of where it really belongs."

My mind ping-pongs this thought back and forth and lands on the realization that Panavi is really fucking good at her job.

"Yeah, you might be right," I admit.

"Where else might this hatred of being controlled be stemming from?" she asks as if she doesn't already know the answer.

"I guess Hunter."

"Why don't you tell me more about your relationship instead of skating around the topic?"

So I do. I tell her what it was like when Hunter and I first started dating, and how we're both emotionally charged people, and that has brought out the best and worst in each other. I tell her about the roller coaster of being on again and off again, the highs and lows that make things feel so extreme, and how confused I felt during our relationship. I tell her how he has the ability to make me feel on top of the world and then lower than dirt. I leave out certain parts, like sleeping together and our *arrangement*, but I think she gets the gist.

"Sometimes I don't like it when he's nice to me. It makes it harder to hate him. It probably doesn't make any sense, but when he's kind, I get these glimpses of who I thought I once cared about."

Panavi uncrosses her legs. "Do you know what a trauma bond is?"

"No."

"It's common for those who are in emotionally abusive relationships."

Her comment catches me off guard. The only other person who ever used that term was Mateo the night he and Hunter got into the fight. "You think what I had with Hunter was emotional abuse?"

"Yes. Do you?"

"I'm not sure. I don't even know if I really understand what it is."

"Simply put, it's a pattern of behaviors that is intended to control another person. They use varying manipulation tactics, whether subtle or grand, and over time, these actions chip away at the abused person's perception and self-esteem, and can distort their reality, giving the abuser the power."

"Oh." I'm quiet for a moment as I absorb what she's telling me. "What are some of the tactics?"

"Gaslighting, isolating the person from others, shaming, emotional blackmail, intimidation, creating chaos—the list goes on and on. Do any of those resonate with you?"

"All of it." I rub my hand over my belly to soothe the queasiness. "I guess a part of me doesn't want to believe that, for multiple reasons. I feel like abuse is such a weighted word, and I don't want to think someone who I once loved is capable of that…and another reason being, I feel like a complete idiot for staying with him through all of that."

Panavi shakes her head. "You're not an idiot at all. You most likely stayed with him for so long because of the trauma bond you two formed."

"Can you explain that?"

"I don't like to speak in absolutes, but for many people it stems from their foundation during childhood, and considering I know your background, I'm pretty confident that's what has so strongly impacted your romantic relationships." She sits up straighter and continues, "Growing up like you did, your emotional needs were inconsistently met. You were raised in a household where you were taught that love was caring acts, but also conflict, verbal abuse, and emotional turbulence, which makes you more susceptible to being drawn to partners such as Hunter because that's the type of dynamic you normalized. Those intense ups and downs might actually feel like home to you. In fact, being in a calm, loving, romantic relationship might actually be scarier to you than a dysfunctional one."

The wind is knocked out of me. Everything starts clicking together.

I get a weird mixture of nausea and relief whirling around under my heart.

She studies my face. "Do you want me to continue? I know I just threw a lot of information out at you. We can talk about the rest another day."

"No. I need to know more about what a trauma bond is."

Panavi nods and speaks again, "For starters, your codependency combined with Hunter's own issues that he has failed to acknowledge, let alone process, has the makings of a trauma bond."

I cringe at being labeled as codependent, but deep down I know it's true. It's just another thing to add to my list of what I need to work on.

"It's an unhealthy emotional attachment that has a cycle of behaviors: abuse, devaluation, and positive reinforcement—and the positive reinforcement is one of the reasons that makes it difficult for many people to cut ties. During the abuse and devaluation stages, your stress hormones increase, but when the abuser shows affection and kindness, there is a quick release of the happy hormones. The more this pattern continues, the more your brain gets used to the fast intake of happiness, then withdrawal of those chemicals, then another burst, over and over again. One of the reasons why you excuse the lows is because your mind is craving the high moments, and you're conditioned to know that they're coming."

"So…it's like an addiction?" I ask.

"Similar. Many clinicians believe that the chemical release in the brain parallels an addiction."

In that exact moment, my world blows up into pieces.

I didn't know there was a logical reason behind why Hunter and I became so enmeshed with one another, but there it is. Our past and our behaviors made for the perfect storm. Everything makes perfect sense as to why it was so hard to leave him and why it was so hard to settle into a healthy relationship with Mateo, as much as I love him.

As if I'm watching a movie of my life in front of me, I can see how all these things connect—my parents, my codependency, the emotional abuse from Hunter, how I was uneasy being with Mateo because I kept waiting for him to fuck with my head and emotions. I fought so hard not to become my parents, only to end up being addicted to another substance: toxic love.

The urge to run out of this room and escape all the information that was thrown at me is taking over, but I fight it, knowing that if I want serious change, I can't avoid and ignore all my issues like my parents and Hunter have.

Another realization comes crashing in—I hurt people. I hurt people just like I've been hurt by others' inability to reflect and heal. The image of Mateo bombards my brain as I picture his devastated brown eyes.

My heart races.

Wave after wave of insights hit me.

The session with Panavi finishes, and I end up back in my dorm room. I'm not really sure how I got here, but the second I reach my desk, I sit down and let myself melt into the chair. My earbuds go in, and I listen to whatever song plays first, drowning out any outside noise and tuning in internally.

A blank paper stares at me, and I do something that I've never done before.

I write.

I write about my pain, my lack of knowledge until now, my regrets, my confusion. I let it all out on paper, unable to stop. My fingers cramp as they tightly curl around the pen, but I can't bring myself to take a break.

Music pours into my ears.

Words pour onto the paper.

My mind can't stop processing this earth-shattering breakthrough.

I may not know where I'm headed in life, but I know what path I *don't* want to go down, and it's the exact one I'm traveling on.

What has gotten me to this point in my life may not have been my doing, but the change I want to see in my life is up to me.

Without giving it a second thought, I drop the pen and pick up my phone.

ME

can we talk?

I spin my phone in circles on my desk. I sent that message an hour ago and haven't gotten a response yet.

I'm emotionally drained from my session with Panavi and writing all my thoughts out, but I know if I don't get this over with now, with confidence rushing through my bloodstream, I never will.

My black screen finally lights up.

HUNTER

be there in 10

My confidence is immediately smashed down by my anxiety.

Okay, maybe this was a bad idea.

My mind jumps to Mateo and what this might mean for him once I speak with Hunter.

And what this might mean for me.

I've been telling myself I'm in this situation for Mateo's sake, but there's more to it. It's fear that also has me staying compliant. The little things, that maybe aren't so little, are what keep me next to Hunter—the passive-aggressive threats, punching inanimate objects, his hands gripping me extra tight. They're all purposeful actions…to scare me, break me down, force me.

This runs deeper than blackmail over Mateo.

And I'm just now being honest with myself and realizing that.

The pit in my stomach expands until I'm nearly doubled over in pain by the time I get another text from Hunter letting me know he's coming up.

Before he can come inside my room, where it might be difficult to kick him out when the time comes, I grab my jacket and race down the stairs and out of the building.

"Whoa." Hunter holds on to my arm as I nearly run into him.

"Sorry," I say, out of breath.

We stand in the frigid air, a few feet away from the building. There are several lampposts and a metal bench nearby.

"I was just coming up." He starts to move, but I stand in front of him, blocking him.

"No."

"Didn't you say you wanted to talk?"

"Yeah, but not in my room."

"Okay, then let's go back to my place."

"No." I know I'm not going to be safe there once I say what I need to. "We'll talk over there." I point to the bench.

"It's freezing out."

"I know." With clattering teeth, I march over and plop myself down on the icy metal. I want to make sure there are witnesses in case things go south. I'd rather suffer from hypothermia than be alone with him.

Hunter follows my lead, sitting next to me. "You're acting weird. Is everything okay?"

That's a loaded question. My body starts trembling, and I'm not sure if it's from the cold or from the anticipation of having this conversation. The cramping in my stomach continues, so I place my arms around myself to help ease the pain.

Hunter stares at me, waiting for me to speak. My throat dries up, and there's a scratchy sensation when I try to swallow. I decide to start this off with a nice approach that might soften the blow. "I had a nice time with you at the alumni dinner."

Hunter's face brightens. He leans in and takes my hand in his. "Me too. It got me thinking about a lot of stuff."

"Like what?"

"Like I don't want to do this anymore."

I swear some type of divine white light beams down on me as I let out the biggest sigh of relief. A weight is lifted off my shoulders, and it instantly becomes easier to breathe. "Oh, thank God, because I don't either."

"I don't want to hold you hostage in whatever type of relationship this is. I want to forget all of that."

Tears well up with the immense amount of liberation that's pumping through my heart.

Hunter continues, "I want to do this for real, Ellie. I want to start over and get back to being us."

The air around me vanishes, taking the miracle with it.

Those were not the words I expected to come out of his mouth.

"Elena?" Hunter inches his body closer, awaiting a response. His hand still grasps mine, but it feels more like a chokehold than anything else. His eyebrow quirks, urging me to talk.

I stare at him, bracing myself for whatever will happen when I finally speak. And through dry lips, I have the bravery to say, "No."

"What do you mean, no?"

I slowly move my hand away. "We're not getting back together."

There is pain building behind his blue eyes, and my gaze darts away from his, so I'm less affected by it. "Why…why don't you want to get back together?"

"We're not healthy together, Hunter."

He shakes his head. "I'll forget about everything. We'll start over, I promise." He takes my hand back, this time squeezing. "I love you, Ellie."

"No, you don't. You love the hole I fill inside of you, and that's what I loved about you too. You were right when you said we're both fucked up. We loved each other's pain just as much as we did the pleasure."

"I'll work on myself. I promise. What do you want me to do? I'll do anything." His voice breaks, and when I look into his eyes to confirm what I just heard, they're filling up with water. Guilt for making him feel this way climbs up my throat and almost makes me say something I don't mean, but I swallow it back down. "You know I love you. You know I've never felt this way about anyone before."

"You've never felt this way about anyone before because I play into the twisted relationship we have." My eyes sting, not wanting to hurt yet another person, even if it is Hunter. "We're not getting back together."

He brings our hands to his heart in a silent plea as tears drip down his cheeks. My vision blurs with my own. "Don't do this, Elena," he whispers. "You're going to regret it."

"I don't think I am," I say, my voice matching his soft tone.

He releases my hand and focuses his attention elsewhere. The moment lingers as staleness fills the void between us. The longer we sit here, the more fearful I become as my brain lights up with thoughts of Mateo. Hunter didn't automatically retaliate against me, which I'm thankful for, but that doesn't mean Mateo is in the clear. I have to offer another bargaining chip.

"I did everything you asked of me," I say, referring to our initial deal. "I just can't do *this* anymore. I'll do anything else. Anything you want, tell me. I'll give you everything in my bank account. I'll—"

He scoffs. "I don't want your money, Elena."

"I'm sorry," I say, not really meaning it. "I really think this is the best for us. You'll be happier without me—no more dealing with crazy Ellie." I try to make light, but it doesn't seem to work.

Hunter stares off into the distance, looking like he's thinking hard. Almost as if he's calculating. Out of nowhere, he says, "We're done here," and gets up and leaves.

The sudden announcement is jarring, and I almost want to call him back to have some sort of *real* closure. But I think that was it.

I watch him until he reaches the parking lot, then he blends in with the darkness.

There have been a lot of times in my life when I needed to be strong, but I never realized it at the time. But right now, I know what I did was courageous. Willingly acknowledging the toxicity and stepping away from the pain that my fucked-up brain craves the most, *that* is strength.

A sense of freedom whirls around me.

Am I free?

Is this it?

I hesitantly step toward my dorm, unsure of each one I take.

CHAPTER NINETY-FIVE

Mateo

FEBRUARY

My professor, Barbara, stops me from leaving the classroom once she wraps up the lecture. "Mateo? Can I speak with you for a moment?" Even though she's smiling, I still get a sense of unease in my gut as if I'm a kid in high school again.

"What's up?" I make my way to her.

"You start your internship tomorrow, yes?" she confirms. All the students start at different times because we're all working at different sites.

"Yeah, at the foster agency."

"Do you remember what you said at the beginning of the year when I asked why you wanted to be a social worker?"

"More or less."

"You said you wanted to help children turn their lives around," Barbara says, and I nod, remembering exactly what flew out of my mouth that day. She continues, "I could tell last semester was a little stressful for you, but you wouldn't have been accepted into the program if you didn't have what it takes. Now you just need to believe it for yourself."

I laugh to myself. It seems so obvious and easy. This is the same shit I've said to Elle, but for whatever reason, I can't seem to take my own advice. "Thank you, Barbara," I say, sincerely meaning it.

Once I leave the classroom, I spot Rebecca waiting for me. We're grabbing lunch before our next class.

"What was that about?" Rebecca asks, checking behind her to make sure Barbara isn't walking behind us.

"She was just checking in to see if I'm all set to start my internship." We get outside, and I shove my hands into my coat pockets to keep them warm as we walk to one of the university cafeterias. It's shitty food, but it's all we have time for. As we stride past the dead trees with frost on them, my mouth moves before I can stop it. "Do you ever get worried about the future?" I ask Rebecca.

"What do you mean?" She rubs her gloved hands together.

I shrug. "I don't know. All last semester, I felt like I wasn't cut out for this."

"How come?"

"I kept thinking about my past and shit that didn't make me feel like I would be good at the job."

She hums. "So what you're really asking is if I ever had impostor syndrome?"

Fuck. Is that what this feeling is? How the hell did I not recognize that? God, my head has really been up my ass for the past several months.

"I didn't even realize that's what I've been experiencing until right now." I chuckle. "You know, Elle kind of mentioned something like that a few weeks ago."

"Wait. Elle, your ex?"

"Elle for me. Ellie for everyone else," I correct her. "But yeah."

"I didn't know you were talking to her again."

"Oh, she kinda took over your job during the break."

Kinda being the operative word. She told Edgar out of nowhere that she needs to cut back her hours for the time being. She said that to him the day after we got back from Mom's, which leads me to believe that I fucked up. *We* fucked up. She wasn't ready for us to mess around, and now she's regretting it. I've texted her a few times, but I've only been getting short replies, so I'm doing my best to give her space. She wants to work on herself, so I'll let her do that without blowing up her phone.

"Mateo!" Rebecca gives my arm a little shove. "We've been back to school for a week and a half, and I'm just finding out about this?"

I hold my arm, faking injury. "I should probably also tell you that my mom was in the hospital." Her face drops. "She's going to be fine, though," I assure her and myself.

"We have so much to discuss over lunch!" Rebecca urges me to pick up the pace, and I do, filling her in on what went down over break.

My first day of interning has been a whirlwind of information for the past several hours, but now my supervisor, Dominique, is throwing me right into the wolves: kids.

I thought about texting Elle or Mr. Kevin to amp me up and give me a little confidence boost, but I want to try getting through today all on my own.

Rebecca really opened up my eyes yesterday when she called it like it is—impostor syndrome. As soon as I got home, I googled that shit and how to cope with it because now that I know the name of this internal monster, there's no way I'm going to let it drag me down. Talking to people about it, separating fear from fact, challenging negative thoughts, and doing daily positive affirmations are all on the giant list of what I found online.

So as I stand outside the playroom in the foster agency, waiting to meet my first official client, I try doing some positive affirmations.

I'm not a failure.

I'm capable of doing this.

My past doesn't equal my future.

Entering, I step into a room filled with toys and art supplies. This is where the kids have supervised visits with their parents.

I meet my client, David, a five-year-old boy with an insane amount of energy. As soon as Dominique introduced me to him, he ran up to me and gave me a hug. He's here to become reacquainted with his mom. David has been out of her care for over two years while she's been getting clean. This is the longest she's been off heroin, so the courts allowed her to reenter David's life.

It's a sad story. They're all sad stories. There isn't one kid here who's had an easy life, and at the age of five, David has jumped around from one foster family to the next more than anyone should. According to his last family, he apparently "acts out" and has "behavioral problems." The poor kid just needs guidance and love.

I watch as David bounces around the room, his mom grinning ear to ear. They play with blocks and stuffed animals, giving each other hugs and high fives in between. Warmth fills my chest as thoughts of my mom and me pop into my head.

Then the dreaded thoughts of her heart disease come in, making my eyes burn.

"I'm going to get some water," I tell Dominique, excusing myself. Pacing the hallway, I compose myself, knowing that I'm going to have to man the fuck up if this is my career path. I'm going to get triggered—a lot—and I need to work through my own shit so I can handle helping others.

I take a sip of water at the fountain so that I'm not a complete liar and reenter the room. Dominique has now been roped into David's stuffed animal play, all three of them sitting on the floor.

David holds a plush rabbit up in the air and stretches his arm out toward me. "Come here, Mr. Mateo! You can be the dad!"

CHAPTER NINETY-SIX

Mateo

Self-care was also on the list of how to cope with impostor syndrome. So today, after a few days of class, work, interning, and papers, I decide to do something I haven't done in a while—play music. My own form of therapy that I've been neglecting for way too long.

My arms flail as I use the wooden sticks to beat down on the drums and cymbals, letting my frustration out. Letting go of any leftover anger toward my family as I crash down on the brass spheres. Getting out my stress and worry for my mom as my foot rapidly presses down on the pedal to the kick drum.

It's been way too long since I've been able to do this. I've been going at this for almost an hour. Sweat drips down my face, but I don't care enough to wipe it off. It's a freeing experience to get lost in the music and let my pent-up emotions release themselves into the air through the sound vibrating off the instrument.

I don't plan on stopping until the joints in my arms are screaming at me, begging for a break. Nothing can get me out of my zone. Nothing except my phone lighting up on my bed, signaling a text.

Tossing my drumsticks into their holder, I go to my bed to grab my phone. Hope builds inside of me with every step, wanting it to be Elle. I'm still trying not to suffocate her, but some conversation with substance would be nice.

Picking up my phone, the hope that Elle messaged me is gone in an instant.

REBECCA

the amount of reading for human behavior class is killing me! want to split it up and trade notes?

ME

definitely, there's no way I'm going to finish it all

Although it's not the woman who I want to hear from, my shoulders drop in relief knowing that Rebecca wants to partner up and tackle schoolwork together. Another form of self-care: divvying up reading assignments. I don't know if my professor will see it that way, but I sure fucking do.

Rebecca and I agree on who is reading which part and set a date to meet up tomorrow at the coffee shop.

Snow is slowly coating the street, causing the majority of the patrons to leave the Cozy Nook early tonight.

"See you later, Mateo." Tío Edgar waves before locking up the bookstore.

I wave back and hurry the rest of the customers out. "It's getting shitty out there," I say, walking up to Rebecca. Her nose has been in her laptop for the past hour.

"Yeah, I'm going to leave soon. I just want to email you these notes first," Rebecca says.

"All right. I'm gonna close out the register." I grab the cash drawer and head to the back office, but not before checking my phone to see if Elle texted. I haven't heard from her today, but I've been hoping for some sort of acknowledgment that she's still breathing.

Paying attention to the blank screen on my phone as I walk into the office, I accidentally bump into the stool, causing me to fumble and knock half of the change out of the cash drawer, coins spilling all over the floor.

"You okay in there?" Rebecca asks.

"Yeah. I'm just an asshole." I put the drawer on my desk and crouch down to pick up the change.

Rebecca laughs at my reply, the sound of her voice getting closer. "You need help?" she asks, standing in the doorway. Before I can answer, she's on her hands and knees searching for coins.

"Thanks."

The bell over the front door chimes. "Shit, I forgot to lock the door."

Rebecca and I pick up the last of the change, and I escort her out of the office. When I see who just walked in, the air gets stuck in my chest.

Elle's gaze flickers rapidly between Rebecca and me, standing still in the office doorway. Distress is written all over her face, and I can only imagine what type of images are racing through her head—images that probably look similar to us fucking in the same office last year.

"S-sorry," she stammers and spins around, bumping into a table.

"Elle, wait." Before I can explain that what she's seeing is not what she thinks, she dashes out of the coffee shop and back into the snow.

"Fuck." I turn to Rebecca. "If anyone comes in, tell them we're closed." I make my way toward the door and chase after Elle. She's speed walking, already three storefronts down. "Elena!"

I pick up my pace as the snow falls harder, blurring my vision and icing over the hairs on my arms. "Elle, it's not what it looks like," I say, catching up to her.

She stops marching forward and turns around. Her face contorts when she sees me. "Why don't you have a jacket on? It's snowing, Mateo!"

"I don't give a shit." I close the space between us and grab her hand. "I don't want you to think something happened between me and her that didn't."

Elle shakes her head. "You don't need to explain anything to me. We're not together."

That reminder sears a hole in my chest, but the pain only spurs me on. I might not ever win her back, but I won't let something as stupid as this be the deciding factor. "I dropped some change, and she came into the office to help me. Nothing else happened."

Elle's gaze drops to my shirt, and I can see the thoughts that are swirling around behind her eyes.

"I know it looks bad, and it looks like I did something that I only ever did with you, but that's not what happened." I take her hand and bring it up to my chest so she can feel my heart beating. Snow coats her hair and lashes, and my burst of adrenaline wears off, causing me to feel the same chill that she is.

"I believe you," she says.

Dropping her hand, I cup her face, bringing her closer. I press my forehead against hers, our breath mixing together as the desire to taste her on my lips continuously builds inside of me. But I won't kiss her. I told her flat out that she's the one calling the shots. It's up to her to choose whether or not to move her head the slightest amount.

My thumbs graze over her cheekbones, the softness of her skin making me want to give in to my temptation even more.

"Mateo," she whispers.

"Yeah?"

"You need to get a jacket on." I feel her cheeks rise beneath my palms, and I can't help but smile, too.

"Come back inside with me." I release her, and she immediately links her arms around one of mine, running her hands up and down in an attempt to keep me warm. It doesn't work at all, but I don't tell her that. She can keep doing this all night.

When we get inside, Rebecca greets us with a grin.

"Elle, this is Rebecca. She's in my grad program," I say. "Rebecca, this is her…Elle. This is Elle."

"It's nice to meet you," Rebecca beams.

"You too. Sorry about the dramatic moment. That can sometimes be my thing," Elle lets out a small chuckle.

"I was just heading out," Rebecca says, getting her coat and hat on. "I emailed you the notes, but don't worry about it if you don't have time to look at them tonight."

"Thanks."

"Have a good night, you two," she says before exiting the coffee shop.

It's just Elle and me. My brain fights with itself on if I should keep this a casual conversation or jump into talking through what happened at my mom's and where to go from here since she's been avoiding me ever since. I decide to tread lightly. "What's been going on? I've barely heard from you."

"I know." Elle shifts her weight onto her other foot. "I've been waiting."

"Waiting for what?"

"For shit to hit the fan." She nervously adjusts her scarf. "It hasn't yet, so I think we're safe…good. I think everything's good."

My brow furrows, confused as hell because I feel like I'm missing out on some info. "What are you talking about?"

She lets out a frustrated sigh. "I don't fucking know. Thoughts in my head are making me feel crazy. But I think everything's fine now, and I want it to be fine. I *need* it to be more than fine, Mateo. I don't want to be scared anymore."

"Scared of what?"

"I don't know. Everything…life. I want to take my life back, and that's why I came here."

Select words that she used swim around my brain—waiting, safe, scared, life. I want to ask her more, but she seems exhausted just from saying those few sentences.

Elle continues, "I came here to let Edgar know I can start working again."

"He went home."

"Oh."

"But you could've just texted him."

"I know." Her gaze falls off me. "I was just thinking about stuff and wanted to see you."

I take a step closer. "What kind of stuff?"

"The snow." She turns her attention to the window.

"The snow?"

She nods. "It reminds me of you."

Of me? Why the hell does snow remind her of me?

I notice her cheeks getting rosy, and I start connecting the dots. The first night we had sex…*Oh*. She was thinking about me in that way, so maybe she doesn't regret what happened a couple of weeks ago as much as I thought.

"I don't know why I came here. There was really no point," she says, taking small steps backward. "I'm sorry if I interrupted anything with Rebecca."

"There wasn't anything to interrupt." I move forward so we're the same distance as we were before. "And I think there is a point to you coming here."

Her pupils dilate as we naturally move closer, drawn to one another's energy. A sudden flush of warmth spreads through me as she fixates on my lips. She parts hers ever so slightly. The unintentional teasing gesture becomes torturous. My body fucking aches with the need to kiss her, and my muscles tense as it grows more difficult to restrain myself.

The bell above the door chimes, ripping us out of the moment. "We're closed," I snap at the person who is covered in snow.

"The sign says—"

"There's a snowstorm. We're closed."

The person leaves in a huff, and Elle helps me close up shop. I give her a ride back to campus and obviously make sure she gets to her dorm room safely. We stand outside her door, and I don't want her to feel pressured to invite me in, so I take a step back.

"Wait," she stops me. "Do you want to hang out?"

"As long as that's cool with you."

Elle nods, smiling. When she opens the door, a fully face-masked Bree gasps when she spots me behind Elle.

"Sorry I didn't give you a heads-up," Elle starts to apologize to Bree.

"Oh my god, I don't care. I missed hanging out with Mateo." Bree glances up at me and says, "You better be ready for some reality TV."

I groan. "Both of you need to start watching better shit."

Bree takes Elle to her side, and they whisper. I rock on my heels, trying not to listen to this obvious private conversation about me. They giggle about something and quickly go back to whispering.

"Mateo, do you want to sleep over?" Bree asks.

My eyes flicker to Elle, and she gives me the okay by grinning.

"I'll run down the hall to Bianca's room and ask to borrow her air mattress," Bree adds.

That must've been what they were murmuring about. "Sure."

"Amazing! Be right back." Bree dashes out of the room.

"You sure you're okay if I stay here?" I ask Elle now that we're alone.

"Yeah. It'll be fun, the three of us hanging out again. We can set the air mattress up over there." She points to the empty space next to her bed.

Air mattress. Got it.

That's her boundary, and I'm going to respect it.

She'll let me know when she's ready.

By the end of the night, we have eaten an enormous amount of junk food and watched an obscene amount of reality TV. Bree is passed out, lightly snoring, while Elle tosses and turns on her bed. And I'm on an air mattress that has a slow leak.

"Are you awake?" Elle whispers, poking her head over her mattress to check for herself.

"Yep," I answer.

There's a beat of silence, and she speaks again. "Did you leave a to-go cup outside my room on my birthday?"

My cheeks lift up. "Yeah."

"Thank you."

I don't respond. Instead, I watch her as she rests her head on her folded arm and looks out the window. "It's still snowing," she states.

"It is."

Her gaze is trained on the blanket of white, while mine is fixated on her. We stay this way until she eventually passes out. Sitting up, I drape her blanket over her shoulder to keep her warm, then go back to my half-inflated mattress.

CHAPTER NINETY-SEVEN

Ellie

Ava sits next to me before philosophy class starts, chewing my ear off about how she got snowed in at the frat house the other day. I've been more selective about what I tell her since the semester started because I don't want any possibility of what I say to get back to Hunter. I thought after I ended things with Hunter, he'd immediately press charges, and Mateo would be behind bars by now. My stomach has been in knots waiting…and waiting…and waiting. Until finally, the night of the snowstorm, I came to the conclusion that Hunter truly meant what he said when he uttered the words, "We're done here."

I'm tired of living my life assuming that a giant piano is going to fall from the sky and come crashing down on me. So, although I'm still nervous, I want to try to actually *live*.

"How come you stopped coming to the frat parties?" Ava asks.

"Hunter and I had a falling out," I say, biting back a grin.

She puts her hand up to her heart. "Oh my god! I didn't know that. Are you okay? Are you in need of some girl time?"

"Actually, I'm completely fine."

More than completely fine. I'm overjoyed!

I've also made sure not to rush into anything with Mateo. I picked up a few shifts at work, so I know I'll be seeing more of Mateo there, but I want to focus on me.

"I'm glad you're okay," she says. "But maybe one day—"

The professor enters the room, thankfully interrupting Ava. The class begins as a theological discussion, diving right into a debate of what is considered a "moral person" and what makes a "good life."

I often think about how Mateo views life, that we're all here to learn and grow so that our souls can evolve and be even better in our next life.

Clearly, my soul has some learning to do in this lifetime.

As the conversation in class continues to become more profound, determination flourishes within me. I am more than just a product of my environment. I am more than the shitty situations I found myself in—with or without realizing it.

I'd rather have all the doors open in front of me than be pushed through one I don't want to enter. Although I'm far from perfect, I'm going to make the best of whatever my life is right now instead of letting it pass me by.

The next few days speed by as I continue to make myself a priority. My new hobby of journaling has taken on a life of its own, and I make sure to set aside at least a half hour in the evening to write.

My earbuds are in, and I'm focused on my journal when Bree jumps on my bed with a wide grin on her face. I pop my earbuds out to hear what she's so excited about.

"What's up, Bree?"

"Remember when you told me you wanted to feel more free?"

"I do…"

"Well, I'm going somewhere super fun in a couple of days, and I want you to join."

"What kind of place is this?"

"Okay, I need you to keep an open mind…"

"Oh god."

"It's nothing scandalous or illegal, like you're probably thinking." She sits on her knees. "It's a ski resort."

I snort. "You want me to go skiing?"

"No. I want you to come hang out at the resort with us."

"Who's us?"

"My friends from class, who we went to Valentine's brunch with—Tamara, Liv, Jaxson, plus a few others."

Yes, I opted for spending all of Valentine's Day with Bree, because as much as I would've loved to be with Mateo, taking care of my friendship with Bree is also a priority of mine.

"I can't ski."

"Um…hi, me neither. I'm just going because there's a cool nightclub and a huge indoor pool and hot tub," she states, and I laugh at her reasoning. "I really think you'd have so much fun if you went!"

I scrunch my mouth to one side, debating her offer. "I don't know if I can afford it."

"It's not that much. We'll split the room, and you don't have to pay for any of the ski stuff, so you'll actually save."

"I'll save money by going on a trip?"

"Well, compared to everyone else, we'll be saving. Girl math."

I shake my head, chuckling, but then grab my phone to check my bank account. I've been able to save up in anticipation that Mom will eventually ask me for money. Is it selfish if I take that money and use it on myself?

"Come on, Ellie. Be a little wild!" Bree gives me a pouty face.

Selfish or not, I want to escape this place for a bit. I'm sure I could always pick up extra hours at the bookstore if Mom needs the financial support. The idea of stepping out of my element and relishing in my independence seems like the ideal medicine for what I'm needing right now.

I smile. "I think I can use a couple of days of being wild."

A short hour's drive from the college, we pull up to the ski resort in Bree's friend Tamara's car, wide-eyed at the acres of land before us. There's a huge main building, a few smaller ones scattered off to the side, and a glimpse of ski lifts in the far distance.

Inside, the resort is warm and comforting. The walls are designed with faux logs, giving the feel of being in a cozy cabin. There are huge fireplaces blazing, with chairs and couches nearby. The scent of hot chocolate swirls around us as we move toward the front desk to check in, then upstairs to our room.

The log walls continue into mine and Bree's hotel room, where there are two queen-size beds and a giant TV hanging up. After unpacking, we meet up with everyone by the pool area.

This sense of liberation from Hunter is still making me wary, but I find little ways to get comfortable with my newfound freedom. Like, for instance, this bikini I'm wearing. I didn't have a bathing suit with me at school, so I had to settle for one at the gift shop. It's a black string bikini that doesn't leave much to the imagination. Even though I'm feeling a bit self-conscious, I'm trying to allow myself to be more comfortable in my own skin.

Mateo and I have been texting on the regular, and sometimes my anxiety spikes up, worried that Hunter will somehow find out and retaliate, but that hasn't happened.

Hunter hasn't acknowledged you in weeks. You're safe, Elle.

I keep telling myself that, over and over again.

I'm safe.

I'm allowed to talk to Mateo. I'm allowed to text him every day. When I told him I was going for a mini getaway with Bree, he encouraged it.

That's the type of energy I need in my life.

"Here." Bree passes me my new favorite drink, a strawberry daiquiri, before she steps into the hot tub.

"Your fake ID works like a charm." I take the drink from her and begin gulping it down, easing any lingering trepidation I might be experiencing. My third one so far, and I'm feeling very relaxed, especially thanks to the scorching hot water that's soothing my muscles. I'm pretty sure my legs are going to feel like jelly when I eventually get out of here.

"Uh-oh, Ellie's got her thinking face on." Bree wiggles her finger in front of me.

"Thinking about how difficult it's gonna be getting out of here." Another sip of my drink.

"Sure, sure." She gives me a look, letting me know she knows there's more, before she downs her pink drink.

I groan. "Fine. You know how I told you I officially ended things with Hunter?" Several days ago, I gave her an extremely abridged version, but I did tell her I cut ties with Hunter. I wanted to give her an update, especially after I brought Mateo over during the snowstorm.

"Yep," she responds.

"Well, it still doesn't feel like it's over."

"Why's that?"

The alcohol lifts my filter a bit, and I let some of my thoughts out. "I don't know. He hasn't tried to contact me at all, but it still feels like he'll pop up at any moment. But if he's not reaching out, then he's over me, right?"

"Sounds like it to me. Are you upset about that?"

"No! Not at all! I don't wanna talk to him or see him ever, ever, ever again." My vision sways.

"Then why the long face?"

"I'm nervous he's gonna try to come back into my life." I splash my hand in the water. "And on top of that, I'm still stupidly in love with Mateo."

"That's no surprise." Bree chuckles.

"This whole situation sucks."

"Don't worry. Everything will work itself out. I can sense these things."

Her comment sends a tendril of ease straight to my heart. I sure hope she's on the money about that.

Bree and I shift the conversation while indulging in the daiquiris, and her friends rush over to tell us that they're headed to the nightclub.

"Do you wanna join?" Bree asks.

"Definitely! I'll meet you there. I wanna relax here for a little bit longer."

"Okay." She hurries out of the hot tub and chats with the others about which outfit she should wear as she goes to leave.

Time passes as I hit the bottom of my glass, slurping the very last drop from the straw. I pout when I realize my yummy drink is gone.

I need more of these.

Getting out of the hot tub is when it hits me. Not only am I lethargic from the heat of the water, but I'm definitely drunk. The room tilts, but I manage to grab my phone from next to the hot tub and make my way over to the bar to grab another daiquiri.

"Can I see your ID, please?" the cute bartender asks.

Damnit, I forgot about that part. "It's up in my room. I don't have any pockets." I giggle and showcase my barely there attire. His gaze follows exactly where I intended it to go. "I've been drinking all night in the hot tub with my friends," I tell him.

"Yeah, I noticed."

"You noticed?"

He takes out a glass and begins mixing a drink. "I need to keep an eye on the patrons to make sure they don't get out of hand."

"Oh, well, I never get out of hand. I can assure you that."

He pours the mixed drink into the tall glass and slides it over to me. "This is your last one. After this, I'm actually going to need to see your ID."

"Last one. I promise."

I take the drink from him and strut back over to the hot tub, sensing his eyes on me. Placing my phone back down on the ground before stepping into the water, I burst into a fit of laughter. *I can't believe I just got away with that.*

Amused with myself and needing to tell someone, I look around to see if there's anyone here I know. No one's in the hot tub with me, and I don't recognize anyone in the pool.

Wanting to talk to someone, I grab my phone and click the video chat button.

CHAPTER NINETY-EIGHT

Mateo

I lie down on my bed after my phone call with Mom. She swears she's doing fine and is adamant about my focusing on school. I told her about working at the foster agency, and I could sense the joy pouring out of her through the phone. Interning there has been going a lot better than I imagined it would, and I'm getting more comfortable with the fact that maybe I am qualified to do this, despite everything.

My attention goes to my laptop, and I groan, remembering the whole reason I locked myself in my room all day was to finish yet another paper.

Luckily, my phone vibrates, and I grab the chance to procrastinate. When I pick it up, my heart races as I realize it's Elle trying to video chat with me.

"Hey," I answer, and see an almost naked Elle in a hot tub. Not the image I expected to see when she's at a ski resort, but it's not like I mind.

"Hi." She covers her mouth to stifle her laughter.

My lips tug upward. "What's going on?"

"I have to tell you what just happened." She slurs her words as she attempts to whisper. She's fucking wasted, her cheeks bright pink and her eyes glossy.

"What happened?" I widen my legs on my bed.

"I somehow talked my way out of showing the bartender my ID, *and* I got a free drink. Well, I don't know if I talked my way out of it so much as *showed* my way out of it." A carefree attitude shines through her.

My muscles tense with jealousy because I know exactly what she means by that and exactly why the bartender gave her a pass. But I push my envy down and play dumb.

"Showed?"

"My bathing suit." She dips the phone down so I can get a better view, and my cock comes to life as I zone in on her cleavage. "Do you like it?"

"I do," I rasp.

"Do you like it as much as the bartender does?"

My jaw clenches as my envy baits me. I adjust myself, knowing that nothing positive will come from my jealousy if I let it become unleashed. "I can guarantee I love that bathing suit more than any man ever will."

Her cheeks turn a deeper shade of red, and she nibbles her bottom lip. "I think you'd like it off me more."

Goddamn, it's been way too long since I've seen her like this. "I sure would."

My cock strains against the zipper of my jeans, and I unbutton them, getting myself more comfortable. If there's one thing I know for sure about Elena, it's that she gets horny as fuck when she's drunk.

"If you were here, I'd let you take it off of me and do whatever you wanted to, right in this hot tub."

I clear my throat. "Why don't you go to your room, baby?" *Shit.* I wince, hoping she didn't pick up on the pet name.

"Why don't you come to my room with me?"

"Because I'm not at the ski resort."

"You should be." She gasps as if she just realized what she said. "You should come here, Mateo! Come!" She begins to hop up and down. The sound of water sloshing around becomes louder. "Come, come, come!"

"Elena, go walk to your room. We can keep talking." The last thing I want is that shithead bartender staring at her as her tits bounce up and down as she screams, "Come."

"Okay."

Elle puts the phone down so that I'm looking at the ceiling, and then suddenly I'm watching her feet as they walk toward her room. She has no clue that the camera is turned the wrong way.

After several minutes, she finally crashes down on her bed. "Mateo." I can see her now, her hair falling into her flushed face.

"Elle."

"You told me I call the shots, right?"

"That's right."

"Well, I'm *literally* calling you. Shots fucking fired, Mateo."

I swallow, unsure if this is the alcohol talking or what she really wants. "We can talk in the morning and see if you still want me to go there."

"I'm always gonna want you here with me, Mateo. No matter where I am in the world. I want you right next to me, forever."

Her words illuminate every dark speck inside of me. "You sure you want me to come there?"

"More than sure."

An hour drive later and several attempted texts to Elle, I've finally found her, thanks to Bree answering her phone. I find both of them laughing and drinking at the bar of the nightclub. No longer in a bikini, she wears a pink shirt with her skintight dark jeans. The flashing colored lights dance across Elle's face the moment her eyes lock with mine. My heart shoots off little sparks at the sight of her as she looks at me like I'm the only one in existence.

"Mateo!" She rushes off her barstool, nearly knocking it over, and links her arms around me. She squeezes me so tight, it's as if she hasn't seen me in decades.

"You feeling good, Elle?" I chuckle as I walk her back to the bar where Bree is.

"So good! I have a new favorite drink. You want some?" She holds up a glass with pinkish-red liquid in it, and I try it. Wincing at the sweetness, I put her drink back down. "It's delicious, right?"

"Something like that."

"I'm so happy you're here." She leans into me. "I just wanna be happy and have fun, Mateo. Can we have fun? Please?"

"Of course." I swipe a stray hair away from her face.

"Hey, Mateo," Bree interjects.

"Hey, Bree. I hope you don't mind me crashing your weekend."

"You're always welcome!"

I notice as Elle observes the room. She's fixating on the people dancing by the DJ. "You wanna dance?" I ask her.

She smiles, but shakes her head. "I can't—"

"You *just* told me you want to have fun, and don't give me that bullshit that you can't dance when I've seen you. I know what those hips can do."

She giggles. "I'm not as good of a dancer as you."

"You've never seen me dance. You're assuming I can, when in reality I could be horrible."

"A horrible dancer wouldn't ask someone to dance."

I bring my face closer to hers. "They would if they wanted to get close to the person they're asking."

Her eyes drop down to my mouth. "Okay," she breathes out.

I take her hand and guide us to the middle of the dance floor. We're surrounded by drunken people who move their bodies to the up-tempo song. Without missing a beat, I spin Elle around so that her back is against my front. My hands come down to her hips as I sneak my thumbs under her shirt so I can touch her skin. I sway her back and forth to the rhythm of the music and help her relax into it. I know what she likes when it comes to her body—me taking the lead until she feels confident enough to do so herself.

Which is exactly what happens as she begins to grind into me. My hands loosen up around her hips as I let her take over, each push of her ass into my jeans making me harder. My attention goes down to her shirt, where I have the perfect view of her sexy body. One of her arms reaches up and wraps around my neck. I take advantage and bring my hand up to feel hers and then drag it all the way down her extended arm, down her rib cage, over her stomach, and then back to her hip.

And for what feels like a lifetime, we allow ourselves to get lost—lost in the music and in each other, our bodies closer than they have been in months. The friction between us increases until I can't take it any longer.

I turn her around so we're facing one another. Her drunken eyes are wide and lustful. Her lips are open and parted, ready for me.

"Kiss me," she says. It's barely audible through the loud bass, but I know exactly what she says and what she wants.

Weaving my hand through her hair, I give a tug when I get to the base of her neck. She lets out a gasp, and I bring my lips to the shell of her ear.

"No."

"Why not?" Her plea is a mere whisper.

"Because when I kiss you, I'm going to make damn sure you remember it." I press my other hand against her lower back and fuse our bodies even closer. "You're going to remember the way I taste." I nibble on her earlobe. "How my lips feel against yours." I give her jaw a peck. "Every swipe of my tongue." I dip down and gently suck on her neck.

She holds on to my shirt for dear life and pushes her hips into mine. I release her hair and take a step back. Elle stares at me with lust exploding through every pore.

"Let's go back to my room," she says.

I smirk, knowing exactly why she wants to go back and knowing full well that instead of banging, I'm going to get her into bed so she can sleep.

CHAPTER NINETY-NINE

Ellie

My head throbs the moment I hear a chuckle coming from next to me. For a second, I'm paralyzed by the fact that I'm not alone, and the voice is male—and most certainly isn't Bree's. But the deep rumble next to me starts again, and I'm instantly aware of who it is. My head gives another pounding throb. "Shit. Too many daiquiris."

Flipping over, I see Mateo, looking freshly showered and shirtless. I rub my hands over my eyes, recalling the night and how we ended up here. I don't have to ask if anything happened between the two of us because I know the answer. Although I could use a refresher on why I'm wearing his shirt.

"How did I get this?" I tug at his shirt that smells like him.

"You were pretty persistent with me giving you something last night, so I settled on my shirt."

My brows crinkle together. "I wanted you to give me something?"

He bites down on his bottom lip to suppress a smile. "Yeah. Not so much an object as much as it was an *act*."

"Oh god." I cross my hands over my face. There goes drunk-and-horny Elle, begging for sex.

Mateo pulls my hands away and shifts the subject to avoid any prolonged embarrassment. "What do you want to do today?"

"Do you want to go skiing?" I ask.

"Do I seem like a skier?"

"No, but there are a lot of things I wouldn't have thought you were that you are."

"Like what?"

"Like…" I sense my body heating up as I struggle to find words.

"Like you're secretly into watching reality TV." Bree's voice comes from the other side of the room as she lies in her bed. I didn't even realize she was here.

Mateo glares at her. "I don't like that shit."

"Uh-huh, sure." She pushes off her blankets and plants her feet on the carpeted floor of our hotel room. "Anyway, *my* plan for today is to spend the first half in the lounge area by the fireplace and the second half in the hot tub."

I turn to Mateo. "Want to hang out in the hot tub all day?"

"I don't have a bathing suit with me."

"They sell some in the shop downstairs."

He nods and then gets himself out of bed. "All right." He leans down and places a soft kiss on my jaw. My pulse immediately picks up speed as I remember the events of last night. He could've seduced me into complete submission right there on the dance floor if he wanted to.

My fingers touch my jaw as if to keep the tingly sensation of his kiss there forever.

I press my lips together to hold back my laughter.

"Don't say anything." Mateo points his index finger at me.

"I really like it," I manage to say through my chuckles.

"I didn't bring a bathing suit. This is the only thing the store had." He looks down at his bright-orange Hawaiian print swimming trunks, a stark contrast to his tatted upper half. Still, he somehow makes the hideous bathing suit look sexy.

"I'm going to change, and then we can head down to the hot tub."

Once I'm in the bathroom, I tie the thin black straps around my neck and back for the bathing suit top, and then tie them on each hip for the bottom. "Ready." I step out into the room to face Mateo.

His eyes dance around the tiny scraps of fabric on my body. Heat bursts inside me as he fixates on me. He doesn't say anything, but his thoughts are written across his face. Adjusting his bathing suit, he clears his throat. "We should probably go. Bree is waiting for us."

I nod, leading the way with him next to me. The backs of our hands occasionally brush each other's, sending sparks from my hand straight up to my heart before dropping down to between my thighs in ecstasy. We're in the elevator, and Mateo stands next to me as a few people get in. His hands are planted by his side, but twitch every few seconds as if he's fighting with himself to put them somewhere else. I wouldn't mind. He could put his hands anywhere on my body.

The elevator doors open, and we enter the pool area. Bree is in the hot tub with Tamara and Liv, whom I've gotten on really good terms with. She waves us over, and we head that way, passing the bar.

I spot the bartender from yesterday and turn to Mateo. "Want a free drink? I can try to work my magic."

"That's the bartender from yesterday?"

"Yep. Want something?"

Mateo shakes his head as we get closer to Bree. "I'm good, and besides, I'm of age. I don't need you to work any magic."

The bartender and I exchange smiles, and Mateo wraps his arm around me, his hand landing on my hip. His fingers circle around my skin, dipping between the black strings of my bikini. It's oddly possessive of him, but I fucking love it. I lean into him, and his grip gets tighter.

Keeping his composure as he stakes his claim, Mateo enters the hot tub and extends his hand to help me in. My muscles tense at the heat, then start to relax. We chat it up with Bree and her friends for a while, but every so often, I notice Mateo's attention is over at the bar, and his jaw clenches.

"Are you sure you don't want a drink?" I ask.

"Yeah. Why?"

"You keep staring at the bartender."

"I'm not staring at him. I'm just looking around the room."

I flip my hair over my shoulder. "Okay. If you change your mind, let me know, and I'll get you something." Mateo grips my waist, pulling me into him. I'm tickled with amusement, and my lips tug upward. "Are you jealous?"

"No. I don't get jealous," he declares, and I arch my eyebrow. "Okay, fine. I get jealous sometimes. But I don't act on it." He clears his throat, adding, "Without reason."

"I know." I place my hand on his chest, and he sucks in a sharp inhale as if surprised that I would touch him.

Our bodies draw closer, and it's as if everyone else in the room melts away. Without a care of who's watching us, Mateo lets his fingertips wander around my skin, caressing every inch he can. Goose bumps rise up, and the heat of the water is nothing in comparison to the heat that is bubbling between us.

"Mateo." Bree's voice breaks our trance. "Can you help me carry some drinks for us back from the bar?" She uses her finger to indicate Tamara and Liv.

"Uh…sure," he says, still fixated on me.

"You want anything, Ellie?" Bree asks.

"I'm okay, thanks," I say, knowing that if Mateo thinks for even a split second that I'm drunk, he won't touch me more than this, and I want him to. I want him to erase the dirty feeling of Hunter off my body. I want Mateo to claim me. Every part of me is his for the taking.

To put it quite plainly, I'm fucking horny. And I want Mateo to be the one who takes care of that problem. I want him on top of me, in me, consuming every part of me.

I have this new freedom, so I might as well take advantage of it and do what Bree suggests and be a little wild. The burning need between my legs doesn't give my mind a chance to come up with reasons why I shouldn't.

This is an urge I'm absolutely not fighting off.

I watch as Mateo steps out of the hot tub, the weight of the water making his bathing suit drop lower on his hips. He and Bree head to the bar, and after they order the drinks, they seem to be having some type of meaningful conversation. Mateo chuckles at something Bree says, and he nods his head.

They make their way back with drinks in hand, and Mateo steps back in. He takes a seat and positions me so that I'm sitting on his lap. We engage in casual conversation with everyone, pretending not to notice the growing hardness under Mateo's swim trunks every time I wiggle my hips.

This time, I move them in slow circles around his crotch, making sure to tease him every second I can. I catch a small groan escape from behind his lips, and he slams his hand on my hips to stop me.

"If you keep doing that, I'm gonna need to take you back to the room," he says in a voice so low that only I can hear.

My heart rate skyrockets. "Then let's go."

"You sure?"

I nod. I've never been more sure of anything in my life.

Within seconds, we're racing to my room, laughing as we take the stairs instead of wasting time waiting for the elevator.

We enter the room, and the two of us stand frozen, staring at each other.

Both of our breathing is heavy as our eyes attempt to read one another's thoughts. We inch closer and closer, invisible sparks flying between us, lighting the entire resort on fire. He wets his lips eagerly, waiting, wanting me to make the first move. I'm the one who's supposed to be calling the shots here.

I take a step in and interlace my fingers between his.

"You're shaking," he says.

I didn't even realize I was until he pointed it out.

"I don't know why." That's not true. I know exactly why. Because the second our lips touch, I know everything will come flooding back, and I'm scared. Scared this is going to come back to bite me, and even if it doesn't, I'm scared I'll somehow mess things up with Mateo again.

"We don't have to do anything, Elle."

"I want to."

I release his hands and cup his face, bringing him closer to me. Getting on my tippy toes, our lips finally touch.

I'm gone, hypnotized by the sensation of him against me.

My soul has drifted up to the stars, never planning to come back down because right now, this is heaven.

My fears evaporate, and I finally feel completely free and buzzing with desire as all my reserves fall away from me, disappearing into thin air.

Fireworks ignite, and every particle that exists inside me awakens to new life. He tastes exactly the same. He *feels* exactly the same, with tenderness and passion spun together.

Mateo's tongue swipes against my lips, pleading for entry as his hands clutch my hips in desperation. I open my mouth, and his hungry tongue taunts mine. Each playful touch acts as a moment of conviction, reminding me I'm safe. I'm with him.

More. I need more of him. I need all of him.

The more his lips move against mine, the more I thirst for him. Our bodies press into one another's as our hands roam around, attempting to connect with every part—needing to cherish and worship every inch of skin.

Mateo tangles his fingers in my hair and breaks our kiss by tilting my head back. His eyes are needy and ravenous, his lips swollen and red. We pant into each other's mouths as I wait for him to do whatever he wants with me.

"Can I do something that I've been thinking about all day?" he asks.

I nod, excitement swirling through my veins.

Once granted permission, Mateo slides the hand that is tangled in my hair down to the back of my neck, his other hand comes to my back, and at the same time, he pulls on the black bikini strings, making the top of my bathing suit fall to the floor.

I gasp when the cool air hits my breasts, my nipples already hard.

Then I lose my breath again at the sight of Mateo dropping to his knees. He positions himself toward my right side, looking up at me as he takes the tiny string of my bikini between his teeth and pulls on it until it unties.

My whole body shakes, the desire becoming too much to bear.

Mateo lets his hands travel up my calf and thigh and grazes over my clit. My breath hitches as he teases me before he brings his hands onto my other leg. He yanks on the last string that is holding not only the bathing suit in place but also my composure.

"Fuck me."

CHAPTER ONE HUNDRED

Mateo

Those are the only words I need to hear until I'm on my feet, hoisting Elle up, wrapping her legs around my waist.

The bed is yards away, so instead, I slam her back against the wall. Her lips are glued to my neck, and her hands tug on my hair. I manage to pull this fucking horrendous bathing suit down just enough so that as soon as my cock is free, it's inside her. She lets out a loud moan as soon as I enter her, stretching her tight pussy.

"Goddamn, you feel so fucking good," I say, tossing my head back, reveling in her wetness.

She feels better than I remember.

My fingers sink into her hips, moving her back and forth as I thrust into her. I try to be gentle with her, but months of pent-up need for her is making this a fucking struggle.

Her nails claw my back, making me groan with each swipe, rousing me on. "More," she moans, hugging her legs tighter around my waist.

I do what she says and move faster, the tension already building up at the base of my spine.

Our lips find one another's, our kisses deep and messy—just like us.

"Harder," she says into my mouth.

She no longer has any hesitations, and neither do I.

I let myself go, just as she is.

Doing what my girl wants, I pound into her harder than ever before. Washing away the feeling of needing to be careful with her like I was in the past, my grip on her gets tighter as I get rougher. She moans so fucking loud, draping herself over my shoulder and yanking on my hair.

"Mateo!" she cries out my name over and over again, and it sounds like the most perfect fucking song that I've waited far too long to hear.

"That's it, baby," I say, panting. "Let the whole fucking resort know who's making you come."

Her pussy clenches around me as she gasps for air. She scratches my neck and shoulders. My body tenses, coiling with heat. I can't come this fucking soon. Pressure builds and builds, but I refuse to let this be over so fast.

I bite down on Elle's shoulder to relieve some of the tension, and she throws her head back in pleasure.

"Come inside me," she says.

"W-what?" I almost fucking drop her, but in no time, I regain my rhythm again, going just as hard as before.

We lock eyes.

"I'm on the pill."

My teeth sink into my lip so goddamn hard I'll be tasting copper soon if I don't ease up. Heat courses through me. I can't fight off my orgasm any longer. "Tell me again," I demand, digging my fingertips into her so hard they might leave a mark.

"Come inside me."

That's all I fucking need to unravel. My vision goes white as I press my lips against hers, allowing her to swallow my moans while I finish inside her.

Her body relaxes as soon as I stop moving. I press my forehead against hers, and we breathe each other in and out, our chests kissing as they rapidly move.

Elle begins to unwrap her legs from around me, but I press her harder into the wall and put her legs back around me. Back where they belong.

"I'm not finished with you yet," I say, then shuffle us to the bed and toss her down on the white plush comforter.

I step out of my bathing suit and join her on the bed. She looks up at me from under her lashes, her face rosy with a sheen of sweat. Her hair is wildly thrown across the pillows as she splays out her body for me.

I hover over her. "Beautiful," I say before giving her a kiss. Trailing my lips down to the column of her neck, which I know she likes, I suck the thin flesh. "Gorgeous." Then I go a bit lower and draw her nipple into my mouth while roughly twisting the other one between my fingers. I forcefully pull my mouth away, and she lets out a huge sigh. "Incredible." I move to the side of her rib cage and bite down on her inked skin. *I've been wanting to do this since the second I saw the tattoo on her.* The second my teeth bear down, she moans. I do it again, harder, and elicit another sound from her. My eyes light up, realizing something new she likes in bed. I give the tattoo one last nibble, then travel downward, dragging my lips and tongue over her stomach to her thigh and down to her knee.

Sitting up, I push her legs wider so I can see my cum dripping out of her.

"Sexy as hell," I rasp just before taking my two fingers and entering her. Her hips buck to meet my movements, and I watch as my cum moves in and out of her. Her muscles tense, then release with each motion we make together.

She moans again, and I notice a flash of something I've never seen before flicker in her eyes. It's different from her sensual side. It's…filthy and completely new territory for me when it comes to her.

With the blazing look of lust, Elle's fingers encircle my wrist, and she draws my hand out of her, then pulls me closer. She brings my two fingers up to her mouth, and she closes her eyes as she sucks them clean.

Holy. Fuck.

This is the hottest fucking thing I've ever seen in my entire life.

My brain and dick can't fully process what she's doing as she licks both of our cum off me, her tongue tickling as she slides it between my fingers. I let out a moan—a loud one.

Her eyes fly open, and she takes my hand away, giggling.

She's fucking giggling.

"You're bad," I tell her.

Her face drops as worry momentarily washes away her confidence. I smirk at the thought of her not knowing what I meant by that.

Bringing my body closer to hers, I press myself against her. "You make everyone think you're a good girl, but in reality, you're bad, Elle."

A smile appears on her lips. "Only for you," she says in a throaty, sultry voice.

"Damn right."

Elle lies naked next to me, her body on full display as the blankets only wrap around our legs and feet. I play with the ends of her golden hair, admiring my love. I don't know where the hell sweet, innocent Elle went, but last night she was completely gone. I did some serious damage. She's covered in hickeys and bite marks from her neck down to her thighs. The possessive fuck in me loves that I not only marked her on the outside but also the inside.

It's stupid as hell to come inside her, but that didn't stop me from doing it a second time while she rode me. Or a third when we woke up in the middle of the night, and I fucked her from behind.

The sound of a swipe card clanking against the door makes me swiftly pull up the sheets to cover Elle and me. Bree pops her head in, and her jaw opens at the sight of me trying to conceal the nakedness, but it's so fucking obvious.

Bree looks like she's about to burst into some awful musical theater song as her eyes light up. I press my index finger against my lips to motion to her to be quiet, although my lips can't help but turn upward in a sleepy smile.

Bree is the fucking best. She saw the flames between Elle and me in the hot tub and told me at the bar that she'd sleep in one of her friends' rooms so that Elle and I could have alone time. Ultimate wingwoman.

She quickly grabs whatever it is that she came in here for and gives me a wave goodbye as she shuts the door. The sounds make Elle stir, and she turns on her side to look at me.

"Hey, baby," I say.

A giant grin appears on her face, making the dimple on the side of her cheek pop out. It's a wide, genuine smile that I haven't seen in such a long time that I almost forgot the way it makes my heart skip a beat.

"Hi." Her voice is low and tired.

I place a tender kiss on her forehead. "How'd you sleep?"

"Best I have in months." She stretches her arms out and does a little yawn. She glances around the room and then moves her attention toward the sheets on her. "We probably shouldn't do that again."

My breathing stops.

If she regrets this and never wants to be with me again, I might as well rip out my fucking heart with my bare hands and leave it to bleed out on this white comforter. "Do what again?"

"You know…" She motions her hand to the lower part of her body. "You doing that…in me."

"Come inside you?"

"Yeah, that."

Relief and amusement fill my chest as I chuckle. There she is, the bashful Elle who gets bright red from hearing the word cock. "You had no problem saying it last night."

She pulls the covers closer to her chest. "I was swept up by the heat of the moment. Dirty Elle took over."

"I'll say."

She cringes. "Was that weird last night? I'm sorry. I don't even know where that came from."

I press my lips against hers to shut her up. "You don't ever need to apologize for letting those thoughts come out." I move back to give her some space. "But you are right. We probably shouldn't do that again. However, I'd be open to exploring any other options Dirty Elle might have."

She lightly slaps her hand against my chest and lets out a chuckle. Then she rests her head on me.

This right here is fucking bliss.

There's nowhere else I want to be, no other person I'd rather be with.

Just with her, doing this, until the end of time.

CHAPTER ONE HUNDRED ONE

Ellie

Mateo puts a new band he recently discovered on the radio as we drive back to campus. It was a no-brainer that I would be riding back with him and not Bree's friend after last night's events.

I keep replaying our night over and over again. It was more than I had been expecting and more than I even knew I wanted. The perfect reuniting.

I don't know what this means for us or where we stand.

I don't know if I can allow this to be more than what it was. The anxiety switch inside my brain has been flipped as the nagging thought of not being completely in the clear eats away at me. There are still a few months left for Hunter to move forward with pressing charges against Mateo.

Before this weekend, I was more at ease because there was no way for Hunter to find out where I was or who I was with, but now, my skin is marked with love bites, letting the whole world know Mateo and I are back on.

Glancing down at my phone, I triple-check that Hunter hasn't reached out. Thankfully, there's nothing from him. This feels too good to be true. I didn't think he'd let me off the hook that easily. It doesn't feel real. It feels like a trap.

I let out a sigh and flip my phone over so I don't continue to check it.

"You good?" Mateo asks.

"Yep." I take his free hand and hold on to it. He gives me a gentle squeeze, and the act has me wishing I could squeeze any thoughts of Hunter out of my mind.

Taking an extended inhale, I hold it in, allowing the fresh air to whirl around my lungs.

Forcing myself to focus on something else… "I have a plan on when to get my license," I state.

"What is it?"

"Over spring break, I'm going to get my permit. Then I'll practice driving once the semester's over, and hopefully by the end of the summer, I'll be confident enough to pass the road test. Then from there, I'll have to save up for a car, but that's a whole other issue."

Mateo smiles. "That sounds like a good plan."

"I thought so."

"Guess that means you're going home for spring break?"

"Yeah, for a day or two. Just to get my permit and spend some time with my mom."

"How is she doing?"

"She's…her. She claims to be doing fine, but when I was there during the Thanksgiving break, she was really low on food. I hope she's not blowing all her money on alcohol. It's going to be hard to help her get by, and also myself."

Mateo's thumb strokes the back of my hand, and I can practically see the words he doesn't say dance on his lips. The ones that are probably something along the lines of my mom isn't my responsibility and that giving her the money I worked for is just enabling her. But he stays silent and continues to caress me with his thumb.

I missed this. I missed our conversations while I sat in the passenger seat, and how much could go unsaid, but still, we listened.

"How's *your* mom doing?" I ask.

"She's doing okay. I make sure to check in on her every day. I still feel like a dick, though."

"How come?"

"Because of the way I reacted when I first found out. And also, for not noticing that something was wrong when I was there for Christmas. The fact that I was too lost in my own world to not have even picked up on that makes me angry with myself."

It also makes me angry with myself, because I'd bet my life that I had something to do with him not being fully present. I hurt him so badly by saying the vilest words that I could muster up the day I broke up with him that he was still fixated on it months later.

"I'm sorry," I say.

"For what?"

"Everything."

He doesn't say anything or look over at me, but he also doesn't pull his hand out of my grip. That has to count for something, right?

The following day, I still don't receive any messages from Hunter, so I assume I'm safe. Even though this all seems to be okay, I have difficulty ignoring the anxiety that coils around my veins, leaving my whole body to vibrate in fear as I exit the Cozy Nook and hop into Mateo's car. My head twists and turns, making sure Hunter's not lurking in the shadows.

"Everything okay?" Mateo asks.

"Yeah, I thought I saw someone I knew, but I didn't."

Mateo places his hand on my thigh. "I'm really excited for you to come over tonight."

My eyes widen. I've been so caught up in worrying if I'd get caught that I didn't even take the time to let it sink in that I'm going back to Mateo's place. I haven't been there in almost a year at this point.

"You still want to come over tonight, right?" Hesitation rises in his voice.

"Of course!" I put my hand over his to assure him.

When we pull up, it looks the same. However, the inside has changed. Gone are the days of overworn couches with cigarette burns and kitchen cabinets with the doors hanging on by a thread. The old furniture is replaced with gently used couches without any stains, and all the cabinet doors are hung perfectly in place.

"You spruced up the place," I say as we walk farther inside.

Mateo shrugs. "It was past due."

"Hey, Ellie," Nick, one of Mateo's roommates, says to me as he makes his way out of his bedroom.

"Ellie's here?" Rosa, Nick's girlfriend and Mateo's other roommate, is in tow behind Nick.

"Hey, guys." I smile, and Mateo takes my jacket from me.

"It's so great to see you." Rosa wraps her arms around me and gives me a big embrace. The two of them were always welcoming whenever I came to visit Mateo in the past. Both of them are slightly older than I am and are finishing up their last year of grad school.

"I missed the both of you," I say to them.

"We missed having you hang here with us," Nick says. "And I know Mateo missed you. I was worried he was going to start ripping up floorboards to get his mind off—"

Mateo shoots him a disapproving glare, and Nick immediately shuts up.

"Come on. Let's go upstairs." Mateo hurries me up toward his room.

As I walk down the familiar narrow hallway, my heart rate spikes knowing all the sacred memories that are held behind his bedroom door—

staying up late talking about life, moments of intimacy and pure ecstasy, tears shed, and laughter booming. All of this is going to open back up the second I turn the brass knob and push the wooden door open.

My fingers reach for the doorknob, and as I start to turn it, the door to the room next to us flies open.

Michelle stands frozen, with a stunned expression on her face when she sees me. Nerves rise in my chest, unsure of her reaction, considering she ignored me all last semester.

"About damn time," Michelle says to both of us before walking down the stairs.

It's not what I was expecting her to say, but I'm happy it was that compared to the hundreds of horrific scenarios my mind just created in a millisecond.

Mateo reaches from behind me and opens the door to his room.

The second I step inside, I smile. It's exactly the same, with the dark wooden furniture pressed up the perimeter and the middle overtaken by his instruments. Only…one of them is missing.

"Where's your keyboard?"

"I sold it." Mateo sits down on his bed and takes off his boots.

"Why?"

"I wanted to buy a couch, so I put the money toward that. I didn't use the keyboard much anyway."

I peruse his room, searching for anything new, but I don't find anything. "Why did you get a new couch?"

"I already told you. It was past due. I don't want the place that I live in to look like a shithole anymore."

His tone is genuine, without a hint of resentment toward me, but I feel it toward myself. I wonder if he even realized that his choice of words were originally *my* words. The ones I used to puncture his ego and slice his heart in half.

"Can we talk?" he asks.

"What do you want to talk about?"

Mateo shifts himself so that his back is against the headboard, and he pats the space beside him. After taking my shoes off, I crawl over to him, but instead of sitting next to him, I lie down, turning my body horizontally, placing my head on his lap. I curl myself into a tiny ball so that all of me is able to fit on the bed.

Mateo's fingers reflexively run through my hair, and I hum at how peaceful this feels. How right this is.

"I want to talk about what happened at the ski resort," he says.

"About what? We already decided no more…you know…"

Mateo chuckles. "Still embarrassed to say that I came inside you when it's not in the heat of the moment?"

"Yes, I am. Don't make fun."

"I would never make fun of you." He brushes his thumb down my cheek and drags it over my lips, parting them open. The simple action makes me lightheaded.

"Is that what you wanted to talk about?" I say into his finger.

Mateo shakes his head, and he pulls his hand away from my mouth, moving it back into my hair. "No. I want to talk about us."

"What about us?"

"What we're doing. Where we should go from here or…" He swallows before saying, "If this is the extent of us."

The thought of merely being each other's hookup as our line in the sand crushes me. The last thing I want is for this to be the extent of us. I want to be his and him to be mine forever. Hell, I'd marry him right now if he asked me to.

Okay, maybe not right now. I want to get my head on straight first. I need to if I'm going to give Mateo my all. Not only do I owe it to him, but I also owe it to myself. I deserve to be happy and not constantly sabotage myself. I'm not sure if I'll ever be able to do that, and it's not right of me to make Mateo my guinea pig.

My attention moves off him as I pick at my cuticles. "I'm not like you, Mateo."

His hand stills. "What do you mean?"

"I mean, I'm fucked up. I'm realizing a lot about myself in therapy, and it's wonderful, but it also made me aware that I don't necessarily know how to fix all my issues. I don't want to string you along, waiting for me to be a normal person."

"Look at me," he says. With shame carved across my face, I slowly let my eyes meet his. "I want you to listen to every word I say. Are you paying attention?"

I nod, surprised that a smile is creeping its way onto my lips.

"Everyone is fucked up. There is not a single person walking this planet who is normal. Throw the idea of normal out the window because not only is it subjective, it's bullshit. I don't want you to be what you think is normal. I want you to be you. There are times in everyone's life when they can choose to work on the fucked-up parts of themselves or ignore them and make things worse for themselves." He cups my face with his big hands. "You're not ignoring it, Elle. You're choosing to work on yourself. Why would I not want to be with you because of that?"

Silence fills the space between us. I don't have an answer for him, even though he's waiting for me to give him one. I give him a small shrug, and he grins.

"I think you have this idea of me in your head that's not entirely accurate. I'm pretty tame now, minus the one incident, but I wasn't always like this. It took a lot to force me into improving myself. I needed to have a major breaking point."

Intrigued, I sit up so I can see him better. "What was your breaking point?"

CHAPTER ONE HUNDRED TWO

Mateo

"Cocaine, Mateo?" Mr. Kevin shouts. "You tried sneaking in cocaine?"

My jaw clenches, trying to keep my entire body rigid as his eyes throw daggers at me. The size of Mr. Kevin's office is shrinking. I make a mental note of my two outs: the door behind him and the window to my left. I can easily jump out the window and fucking flee from the hurricane that is brewing inside Mr. Kevin.

The longer he looks at me like that, the more my stomach sinks. It's the look of disgust and disappointment—how Mom looks at me.

My leg furiously bounces up and down as I debate making a run for it. I don't have to sit here and take this shit. I don't give a fuck.

"Look at me." The tone of his voice sends a shiver down my spine, and I do as he says. "You look me in the eye and you tell me the reason why you decided to screw up everything we've been working on by bringing drugs into the program."

I break out into a sweat the longer he stares at me. He's waiting for an answer. I don't have one. My mouth opens and shuts. I've got nothing.

"Tell me," he demands.

"I-I don't know," I stammer.

"Where did you get it?"

"My friends."

My fucking "friends." I shouldn't have seen them on my home visit, but I did. One of them gave me the little baggy to help me get by before my next visit. I didn't intend to use it, but I also didn't get rid of it. I slipped it into my pocket, thinking I wouldn't get caught, but they did a high-risk check when I got back to the program a few minutes ago, meaning I had to hand everything over and change my clothes. I don't think I ever prayed before, but I prayed as hard as I could that they wouldn't find the tiny bag in my jeans pocket. They did.

"You know this can get you back into juvie, right?"

I nod my head.

"Do you want to go back to prison?"

I shake my head.

Mr. Kevin blows out a puff of air. "I don't know what to do with you, Rivera."

Suddenly, my eyes sting. It's an unfamiliar sensation that I attempt to blink away. There's a tremor building in my chest, and I don't like it.

Fuck this.

Jumping up from my seat, I dart to the door.

"Go ahead, Mateo. Keep running."

Mr. Kevin's words strike me, and before I can get my foot out the exit, I freeze. "What the fuck is that supposed to mean?"

"Exactly what it sounded like."

"I'm not fucking running." I slam the door shut and march farther into the office.

"I thought we were working toward your future, Mateo. I thought your progress over the past few months was real, not that you were bullshitting me during all your sessions."

"I wasn't."

"I can't make you want a better life for yourself, but the least you can do is respect me and not spew more lies at me."

My fists ball at my sides, and the temptation to get the fuck away from Mr. Kevin has taken a back seat to wanting to prove him wrong. I grab the chair I was just sitting in, pull it toward me, and plop down.

"Go ahead." I egg him on. "Tell me you're disappointed in me. Tell me I'm a piece of shit and deserve to live in prison. I really don't care."

Mr. Kevin shakes his head. "I'm not going to tell you any of that. Instead…" He leans in closer, but I refuse to sit back as he says, "You're the one who's going to do the talking."

"I already told you I got it from my cousin, and I don't know why I brought it with me."

"Did you want to get caught?"

"What kind of idiot wants to get caught?"

"Sometimes people do stupid shit to see if anyone out there actually cares enough to tell them not to."

There it is again, the fucking stinging in my eyes. I blink harder, but it only burns more. "Fuck you," I snap.

"What are you so angry about, Mateo?"

My nostrils flare as my shoulders stiffen. "I'm not fucking angry."

"I think we've been making really great progress. You're not getting into fights anymore, and you're not attempting to punch holes through the cement walls," he says, slightly smiling as he tries to crack a joke. "But it's still in there."

"What is?"

"Your sadness. And it's shielded behind all that anger."

I grind my teeth together, but it doesn't stop my vision from becoming blurry.

"You can tell me if I'm wrong, but I'll tell you what I've been witnessing. For years, I've watched young men come in and out of my office for all different reasons, but why you're here is quite simple. You've been rebelling and acting out because you want to avoid feeling the true depths of your emotions, because if you do, it might mean you have to acknowledge something else that you've been trying so hard to let go of. So you've been running to get away from all those thoughts and feelings. But it finally caught up with you."

Water pools in my eyes, and I know what is about to happen, but I fight it so goddamn hard.

"Let it out, Mateo."

That's all I fucking need. A loud sob comes from the back of my throat as my chest heaves in pain. Each rib feels like it's being cracked open by my heart, the bones puncturing holes in my lungs, making it harder to breathe. I cry into my hands, tears running down my wrists.

"You're not wrong," I manage to get out.

Mr. Kevin sits with me as I release years of hurt that has been rotting away my insides. I don't want to be the angry kid that everyone shoves to the side. I don't want my mom to hate me. I don't want to feel like this and act like this for the rest of my life. I don't want this to be it for me. I don't want to end up like him.

"My dad" is the only thing I'm able to get out in between sniffling.

"What about your dad?" Mr. Kevin asks.

"I'm angry at my dad."

"Why?"

"Because he left me."

Those words flying out of my mouth make me break down even more. Unable to stop, Mr. Kevin places his hand on my shoulder as it violently shakes. I gasp for air, trying to talk, but I can't. I want to tell him that I'm mad at myself for still wanting my dad around. I want him to know that being discarded by my dad was way fucking worse than any blow to the face. And I want him to know that I hate myself for being broken over this.

"You're a good kid, Mateo." He squeezes my shoulder. "But when you keep acting out of spite instead of being honest with yourself and allowing yourself to heal, you're not hurting your dad back. You're hurting yourself and your future."

I let his statement sink in, every cell in my body absorbing the realization.

My tears slow down but are still present. Taking my shirt, I wipe the snot off my face, then I look up at Mr. Kevin. "I don't want to be like him," I admit.

"You don't have to turn out anything like your father if you don't want to. What you've been feeling and experiencing doesn't have to be the end of your

story. You are much more than what led you here. You just have to believe it, then put the time and effort into working on yourself."

I wipe under my eyes with my thumbs.

"Now, I need you to be one hundred percent honest with me." Mr. Kevin squares off with me, his gaze so strong that it's impossible to glance anywhere else. "We're going to have to stand in front of the judge and explain this situation, and I'm going to be the one who's going to speak on your behalf. I want to know if you're worth me putting my ass on the line and pleading for you not to go back to JDC. And I'm only going to do that if you're going to take the rest of your time here seriously. Are you going to work on yourself while you're here, or are you trying to skate through? I need to know the truth."

I swallow, scared that I'm going to give the wrong answer. Or worse, give the right one and not follow through. I take a giant sigh and decide to go with what my gut is telling me. "I'm going to work on myself."

CHAPTER ONE HUNDRED THREE

Mateo

Nothing but compassion pours out of Elle once I finish telling her what really made my ass get into gear at placement. It wasn't just that I lucked out and got stuck there instead of spending the years in JDC. It was after my conversation with Mr. Kevin that I chose to make a change in my life. I never saw anything more for my life because I was too clouded by pain to realize the hole I was digging myself into until that moment of clarity.

"I'm guessing he vouched for you in front of the judge?" Elle asks.

"Yep. He pleaded with the judge, and after the judge reamed me out, he agreed to let me stay on the condition of weekly drug tests and that if he ever saw me in his courtroom for another offense, he would send me right to prison. Luckily, I never got that judge again." I crack a small smile.

Elle shifts herself to straddle me, and I place my hands on her waist. Her small fingers caress my jaw, my stubble prickling against her skin. "I can't picture you crying that much. Or ever, really."

"It doesn't happen often."

To be honest, the only other time after that was when she broke up with me. No matter how hard I tried to shove it down, I cried like a little baby.

The fact that not only am I willing but also *wanting* to put myself back into a situation where I could potentially feel that pain once again says something monumental about how I feel about Elle. I now realize I'd rather suffer the heartbreak a million times over than not have another chance at loving her.

"You see what I mean when I say I wasn't always like this? I had to get to this point, and I still need to do so much work on myself. Being in school makes me realize how much more I have to do. But I don't want you to think that just because you're not your version of perfect, that means you shouldn't be with me. I want to be with you and stand next to you while you work through all the heavy shit."

Her green irises glisten as tears begin to brim, but despite that, there's a smile on her face. That's when I know that even though she's hesitant, she wants to be with me too. My hands slide down to her hips, and I tug her closer.

"I want a second chance with you, Elena, if you'll give it to me."

"I'm scared I'm going to ruin it and hurt the both of us again," she admits.

"If we get hurt, it'll be on both of us, not just you." The longing to tell her how much I love her surges through me, but I don't want to freak her out and say it too early when she's still wavering to be with me. Instead, I'll tell her every way I can without letting the actual words come out.

"Elle, life is going to suck sometimes—that's a given. But when we were together, I experienced something I never have before. You gave me the opportunity to be a person that I never thought I could be. It felt right. I became alive in a whole different way. It was like I was living for the first time."

Her smile widens as a single tear drips down her cheek. She doesn't say anything, so I continue, "The only thing guaranteed in life is death. So, while I'm still breathing, I want to feel alive. *Live* with me, Elle."

She brings her lips to mine and wraps her hands around my neck, the way she always does. Her kiss is slow and careful, but I already know her answer before she pulls away and says, "Okay."

My heart lights up, radiating joy down my limbs. "If we're going to do this, I want to do it right."

"What does that mean?" She chuckles.

"I don't want to carry any of the drama that happened from last year into the present. I want a clean slate. If there's something or someone that's bothering us, both of us need to talk to each other instead of making assumptions. I'll be an open book. I'll tell you whatever you want to know, and I hope that you'll do the same."

Her shoulders go stiff, and it takes her a few seconds, but she nods in agreement.

"And I want to meet your mom."

Her face drops, and her eyes bulge. "What?"

"When you're ready. It doesn't have to be anytime soon, but I want to know your family, and I want you to know mine better. Let me do this the right way. Let me be that man for you."

"You always were that man. I'm sorry I made you second-guess that."

I shake my head. "We're leaving that in the past. Clean slate, remember?"

"Clean slate."

"And—"

"You have a lot of conditions before we commit to this," she teases.

"I do."

Elle smirks. "Continue."

"If you want out at any time, you tell me, and I won't put up a fight. I want you to be happy, and if that means I'm not a part of that, then I'll let you go. Just promise me you won't purposefully say something to hurt me so that I'll leave."

Her gaze goes off me and down to the collar of my shirt. "I promise."

"Okay." My hands shift so that I'm grabbing her ass. "Those were my stipulations. Do you have any?"

"No."

"Well, if you think of any, then let me know."

She innocently kisses my cheek. "I will." Her fingers play with the neckline of my shirt, and she zones out, lost in thought.

"What are you thinking about?" I ask.

"You remember when you told me about all that soul stuff?"

"Soul stuff?"

"Yeah, like how a group of souls travel through lifetimes together to help each other grow in different ways?" I nod and let her continue. "Do you think you and Mr. Kevin knew each other in a past life?"

Her question throws me off a bit. "Maybe. I never thought about that. Why?"

She shrugs. "I'm just wondering how many people out there my soul traveled with."

"Whether you knew them in a past life or not, you still got to this point, so they're all still important."

Her fingers stop moving, and she looks at me with admiration in her eyes.

I love when she looks at me like that. It's as if I'm the only one she truly cares for, and I'd be lying if it didn't gas up my ego.

"How many lifetimes do you think we traveled together?" Her voice is delicate and sincere.

I cup her face with my hand, and she leans into my touch. "All of them, baby."

CHAPTER ONE HUNDRED FOUR

Ellie

His long fingers run through my hair. My head is on his lap again. My vision is consumed by brown eyes and tattooed skin. I can lie here forever.

Until I can't anymore.

Someone grabs my arm and pulls me up. Icy-blue eyes freeze me. *His* hands are now in my hair. *His* hands are on my body. I try to move away, but he yanks me down. I search for the brown eyes but can't find them.

"Mateo," I call out.

No answer.

"Mateo," I say louder.

Silence.

"Mateo!"

"Yeah?"

My eyelids fling open, and I see Mateo staring back at me. It's dark in his room, but I can see his face from the moonlight that pours in from the slit in the curtain. My hand goes to his face to see if he's real. He is.

He's here. *I'm* here.

"It was just a dream," I tell him.

Mateo smiles. "You dreaming about me again, baby?"

"What do you mean again?"

"You were dreaming about me when I slept over in your dorm room, remember?"

"Oh, yeah." I shuffle under the covers. "Sorry. Go back to sleep."

Mateo rolls onto his stomach and rests his weight on his forearms. "I don't wanna now. I wanna know what you're dreaming about when I'm in them."

I giggle and move so I can see him better. I can't believe that we're back together. He wants a clean slate, but I don't want to hide everything that happened with Hunter from him. I don't want it to blow up in our faces down the line, so I've decided I'm going to tell him every single thing. I just need to do it when the timing is right and not chicken out like I did last night. I was so close to word vomiting all over the place, but after everything he shared with me, I just wanted to listen.

The more I listen, the more I learn, and I want to learn as much about Mateo as I possibly can.

Last night, not only did I find out more about his past, but I also realized that I don't have to let myself be consumed by him in our relationship. He's giving me my space to heal and grow, and I want to allow him the same.

"Was it a dirty dream?" Mateo asks with a huge grin.

"Oh my god, shut up and go back to sleep."

"I wanna know how dirty my girl gets in her dreams."

"It wasn't one of those dreams this time, but I can assure you that I can get very, very dirty." I lift my head up to give him a quick peck.

"Tell me."

I flip onto my side, chuckling to myself. "Good night, Mateo."

He throws his head on the pillow. "You'll tell me one day?"

"I'll tell you everything one day."

CHAPTER ONE HUNDRED FIVE

MARCH

It's been a couple of weeks since I spoke to Mr. Kevin, so I decided to call him up once I'm back home from working at the foster agency.

"How's the internship treating you?" he asks, his voice coming through my speakerphone as I sit on my bed, restringing my acoustic guitar.

"I'm feeling more settled. More confident."

"More like you know what the hell you're doing and you were made for this?"

I chuckle. "Still getting my footing, but I'm getting there."

"It'll take time. Don't pressure yourself. All you need to do is find compassion for your clients, and the rest will fall into place. I know just how compassionate you can be, Rivera."

"Yeah, I guess that's something I don't suck at," I joke.

"How are things going with Ellie?"

"Awesome. I'm taking her out on a date tonight. I've got something special planned that I think will *really* make her wanna—"

"Oh god, please don't tell me."

"No, not like that." I laugh, plucking a string. "Well, I got something like that planned too, but that's not what I was talking about."

Mr. Kevin sighs. "Do I even want to know?"

"I'll let you know how everything goes after."

"Have fun, just not too much."

I rest the guitar on my lap with a beaming grin on my face. "Can't make any promises."

After hanging up and finishing tuning the strings, I prep for the evening ahead.

Since we've decided to give a relationship another try, I wanted to show Elle how much I'm putting into this. So naturally, I had to take her out on an official date like the motherfucking gentleman I am.

BREE

where are you taking her?

ME

not telling you. I know how this shit works

BREE

as her wardrobe consultant, I need to know what type of outfit she should wear

ME

something I can easily take off of her

BREE

okay… but I don't think Ellie is going to be too crazy about you taking her to a sex club for a date.

Laughing, I make my way back into my room and change my clothes. My phone goes off a few more times, and I already know it's Bree begging me for clues. After it goes off again, I finally give her a response.

ME

tell her to wear whatever she feels comfortable in. We'll be sitting down and hanging out. She'll look beautiful no matter what she decides.

Once Bree replies with a thank you text, I grab my keys and head out to make a few pit stops before my date.

My knuckles tap against Elle's dorm door.

Bree answers. "One sec," she says, then closes the door in my face.

At least two minutes go by, and I knock again. This time, Elle answers, stealing my breath away. She's wearing her hair like I've never seen it before, with loose curls and the sides pinned back. Her dress is black with thick straps, and she has black lace tights on, which look unbelievably sexy on her. My eyes go to the top of her exposed cleavage, where the green crystal pendant from the necklace I gave her last year hits her.

Elle looks up from her long lashes, waiting for me to say something.

"You look incredible," I say.

"Thank you." Her gaze goes to my hand.

Oh shit. I forgot I was holding flowers.

"These are for you." I extend my arm to give her the purple and white flowers. I don't know what kind they are, but I didn't want to buy her the typical red roses.

Elle takes them from me and smells them. "They're beautiful." She places them on her desk, then grabs her jacket. "Where are we going?"

"You'll see."

"Keeping it a surprise?"

"The night is full of surprises, baby." I kiss her on the forehead before escorting her down the hall.

"Have fun, you two!" Bree pokes her head out the door.

Continuing to lead Elle toward the stairs with my hand resting on her lower back, I look over my shoulder and shoot Bree a wink. "Thanks, Bree."

CHAPTER ONE HUNDRED SIX

Ellie

Our hands are linked together as Mateo guides me into a small jazz restaurant. There's a long bar with black cushioned stools extending all the way to the back of the room, and different-sized tables with red tablecloths and flickering candles are arranged throughout. Posters and old photographs of musicians cover the walls. There's a small stage to our right, with one spotlight hitting it.

We slide into a small, rounded booth so we can sit next to one another. "This place is so cool," I say in awe of my surroundings.

"I was hoping you'd like it."

After ordering dinner, we listen to the musicians performing on the stage. People take turns coming up, playing their instruments without any vocalists. The types of music change from song to song, only adding to the music-themed atmosphere.

As I stare at the person performing, I sense Mateo's eyes on me. When I glance over, he doesn't break his gaze and leans in, giving me a peck on the cheek.

"What was that for?" I ask.

He shrugs. "I like kissing you."

Mateo's phone buzzes in his pocket, and he takes it out, checking to see who it is. Glancing down, I catch a glimpse of who's texting him. Jealousy bites down into my veins as he types back to the person before putting it away.

The waiter places our dinner on the table, but I can't concentrate on eating. I don't want to ruin this night that he planned, but I need to know what that conversation on his phone was about.

Clearing my throat, I pull Mateo's attention away from his plate. "What was that text about?"

Mateo drinks his soda before saying, "It was Jasmine."

That's all he says.

I know it was Jasmine. I saw her name. I need to know what the hell they were talking about.

"And?"

"And she wanted to know if I was free, and I told her I wasn't and I won't be anymore."

My envious thoughts are quick to shift to guilt-ridden ones. My shoulders slump. "What do you mean you won't be anymore? I don't want you two not to be friends because of me. I don't want to be that type of girlfriend."

He shakes his head and looks away from me. "I didn't mean in a friend way."

"Oh." My stomach sinks. I knew he would hook up with other people once we broke up, but the acknowledgment of it hitting me in the face during our date stings. Not that I have any right to feel this way, considering what I did with Hunter. It still sucks.

"I'm sorry, I don't want to talk about this now," he says.

"No, I think we should. I want to know about your relationship. We never had a chance to talk about it. Or her."

"You want to talk about this on our date?"

"Let's just air it out. I'm feeling like a jealous bitch, and I don't want to feel this way anymore."

He nods. "Okay. What do you want to know?"

"Everything."

"All right." He leans his back against the booth. "Jasmine and I started hooking up my freshman year. It's never been anything serious, and we've been able to be friends the whole time, even if she needed to stop because she was dating some guy, or I needed to end things because I was with you. We never got together while you and I were dating last year. I would never cheat on you—"

"I know you wouldn't."

Mateo twirls his fork between his fingers and glances down. "We got back together last semester. I hadn't seen her since, but she just texted me asking if I'm free, and I responded saying that you and I are a couple again. That's pretty much it."

I nod. That's all the information I need to know for tonight. I don't think I'm ready to hear about all the other girls he hooked up with while we were broken up.

Although guilt begins to tumble around my brain because I'm pretty sure this is the part where I'm supposed to say if I slept with anyone.

The words are bouncing around inside of my mouth, but I hold them in.

"I only did it because I was lonely," Mateo continues with regret washing over his face.

I bring my hand to the back of his neck, attempting to relax him as I gently rub my fingers over his muscles. "I get it, baby," I say, and Mateo's eyes flash over to me. "Let's talk about something else," I suggest.

"Please."

Mateo takes a bite of his dinner, and I do the same, the knot in my stomach releasing from his honesty.

"How's it been at the foster agency?" I ask.

"I really like it there," he says. "Don't get me wrong. It can be depressing as hell, but my supervisor told me some really good advice. She said to find the small moments of hope and hold on to them. The more I focus on hope, the more it'll expand in time."

"I like that."

"Me too. It's pretty much all I've been doing for the past several years. I've gotten up to this point by holding on to a string of hope." He looks over at me with sincerity, letting me know that he's been wishing for this moment with me. My body heats up as my heart pounds with the need to tell him my true feelings for him.

Don't overthink it. Just say it!

"Mateo—"

"Mateo Rivera," someone says into the microphone.

I swing my attention to the stage and then back to him.

Is there another person here with the same name or—

"Be right back," he says, then quickly brushes his lips on mine and heads to the stage.

Stunned, not able to speak, I watch him grab his guitar from the person who called his name and sit down on a black cushioned stool. Pushing his black sleeves up so that his sexy, tatted forearms are exposed, he gets himself into a comfortable position, and when he's ready, he plays.

It's a song I've never heard before, but three seconds in, I already know I love it.

My jaw hangs open as he continues to casually perform a solo piece as if it's no big deal.

He's playing for me, in front of everyone.

I watch as his big fingers press down on the bronze strings, moving from fret to fret. The rich vibration of the strings is captivating. Another song, another part of himself he's sharing with me. The delicate plucks remind me of his softer side, when he holds me and whispers in my ear. With each strum he makes, I become more drawn to him, feeling lighter and open.

The dim spotlight frames his face, but it does no justice to how his music illuminates our souls.

When he's done, everyone applauds, and he hops off the stage. He puts his guitar in its case and walks over to our table.

Mateo takes a bite of his dinner. "How's your food?"

"Are you kidding me?" I nudge him, and he laughs. Floored by what just happened, I stare at him as if he's the one who hangs the moon in my sky every night. "That was…that was…" I struggle to find the right words to describe how enamored I am with him.

"That bad, huh?"

"Fucking amazing."

He smiles. "I'm glad you liked it. I wrote it for you."

Butterflies flutter throughout my body. "You *wrote* it? For *me*?"

"Yeah. Around this time last year. I was just too embarrassed to play it for you."

"So you figured playing in front of a roomful of people would be easier?"

"No, but I thought it was about time I stopped being a bitch about it. And I thought this would be a good time to do it so I could see that face you're making."

"The face of shock because my boyfriend is fucking amazing?"

"That's the one."

CHAPTER ONE HUNDRED SEVEN

Mateo

We somehow made it up to my bedroom without fucking each other right on the staircase. Elle tears off my shirt and kisses my bare chest. Her hands fumble with my belt buckle, and I reach around her back, tugging at the zipper of her dress. I slide the black straps down her arms and watch the dark fabric drop to the floor. *Thank you, Bree, for making her go braless.* I step out of my pants and boxers as she stands there in lace stockings and a thong, looking like a fucking pinup model. Before I can stare any longer, she's pushing me toward my bed.

I would've played that song for her a lot sooner if I had known this is what it would get me.

The back of my legs hit my mattress, and I sit down. Elle drops to her knees.

"Fuck," I breathe out. I will never get enough of this sight.

Elle looks up at me through her lashes and wets her lips. Her small hand grips my cock and makes quick up-and-down movements. My heart thrashes in my chest, and my muscles throb with need as she continues to work me. "You seriously wrote that song for me?" she asks.

"I did."

"Why?"

Because I love you. "Because I—" She moves her hand faster, and I groan, tossing my head back.

"I asked you a question." She licks the underside of my cock, and my head springs forward to watch her. She fixates on me as she continues to tease me, twisting my insides into euphoric oblivion. "Well?" Her tongue circles the tip.

My legs tense. "Because…" I can't fucking think straight when she's doing that and looking like that. "Because you're you."

She chuckles, knowing that her tormenting is fucking with my head. But instead of pushing me for a legitimate answer, she takes me into her mouth and starts sucking.

Her movements are slow at first, but she begins to pick up the pace. I watch her, mesmerized by how someone so angelic can also be hot as sin. I press my lips into a thin line, struggling to keep my composure as her movements become faster.

I grip onto her hair, holding it out of her face so I can see her better. I want so badly to place my hand on her head and guide her down so that she can take more of me, but I don't.

Because I can't.

The realization of why I can't and who caused her to not want to comes slamming into my brain. And although Elle is sucking harder, the image of Hunter assaulting her kills the mood.

"Baby," I say. She hums, her mouth too busy to talk. "Hold on, baby," I gently push her shoulders back to get her to stop.

"What's wrong?" she asks with a confused expression and swollen lips.

"I wanna focus on you first." I help her to stand. My eyes rake up and down her body before saying, "Take this off." I snap the waistband of her stockings and thong against her skin.

As Elle strips bare, I slide back on my bed so that I'm leaning up against the headboard with my legs stretched out. Elle crawls over to me with a glimmer of excitement about her. She starts to straddle me, but I shake my head. "Turn around," I instruct.

Once again, she looks puzzled, but she does what I say. I adjust her to where I want her, sitting between my legs with her back to my chest. I drape my legs over hers and use my heels to spread her open.

My mouth finds her neck as my hands roam her beautiful body. Taking my time, I memorize every inch of her through touch. I trace her collarbones, slowly dragging my fingers across them. Her breaths get shallower. Dropping my hand down a little lower, goose bumps form on her soft skin. My fingers twist her hardened nipples, and she leans her head against me. My caress grows rougher, and I notice as her stomach tightens, then releases.

"You like that?" I say into her ear. She nods and grips my legs. "I bet you'll like this even more," I say, snaking my right hand down her belly, then resting it over her slit. *Fuck, it's so warm.* Her breathing quickens into short, quiet pants, excited by what's to come. Teasingly, I brush my fingertip over her clit, and she moans from behind her lips. I do it a few more times until her hips finally buck up toward my hand.

"Mateo," she whines.

Smiling, I add more pressure, giving her exactly what she wants. My left hand moves up to clutch her throat. Her pulse strums under my fingertips, getting faster with each tempting touch.

I glance across my room, where my mirror hangs over my dresser. I have the perfect view of Elle, and I watch as my two fingers enter her pussy, soaking me.

My hands in and on her look like pure corruption compared to her delicate frame.

An explosion of heat bursts through my veins.

She curses under her breath as her nails dig into my thighs. I take my fingers out of her and make hard, fast circles on her clit, causing her to loudly moan my name. Getting more and more worked up, she writhes against me, and my precum paints her lower back.

Her breathing picks up, and I continue to watch her come undone in the mirror. Her eyes are shut tight, her face and chest are turning red, her pussy is glistening, and her legs are shaking.

It's so fucking hot to watch. I don't want it to end.

So I stop rubbing her and run my fingers over her slit.

Her eyes fling open and connect with mine through the mirror. "Why'd you stop?" she pants.

I don't answer. Instead, I tilt her head to the side and suck on her ear before putting my fingers back on her clit. She automatically moans, shutting her eyes and arching her back off my chest. Her legs go back to trembling, and she tries to close them, but I use mine to stop her.

"Not yet, baby."

"O-okay." Her entire body is tensing up, and I know she's seconds away from coming.

So I stop and toy with her opening once again.

"What are you doing?" she asks, breathless.

I strengthen my grasp on her neck and bring my mouth to the shell of her ear. "Edging you."

"Why?"

I keep quiet because in a few minutes she'll know exactly why.

I go back to her clit, adding and taking away pressure, starting and stopping a few more times. Her entire body shudders with the need for relief, but I don't give it to her yet. My eyes are trained on the mirror, watching every breath that flows in and out of her heaving chest and every muscle that seizes up each time I tease her.

Her hands on my legs curl into fists, yanking at my hair, causing the most amazing sting. My cock is begging me to end this game, but watching her completely succumb to me is enough for me to keep this up for hours.

"You're doing so good, baby," I praise her, then press a chaste kiss on her temple. She moans at the sound of my compliment. I smirk as I realize yet another thing that she's into but won't dare admit aloud.

I keep edging her until neither of us can take it anymore. Adding pressure to her clit once again, her muscles freeze, and she draws in a sharp gasp.

"There it is." I encourage her. "Let go for me, Elle."

One last stroke of my finger and she screams over and over again. I release her legs and neck as she trembles, her pussy fluttering around my hand while she clamps her fingers into my thighs once more, sparking a burn that hurts so good.

"So fucking amazing, baby," I say, watching her dig her heels into the mattress as she rides out her high in my arms.

With one last loud sigh, she collapses her back onto my chest, then melts against me.

Elle lies there catching her breath, her body entirely sated.

"Wow," she says, sounding exhausted. "That was the strongest orgasm I've ever had."

I chuckle.

"You like torturing me."

"To be fair, I'm also torturing myself."

Her cheeks rise, and she gets a sudden burst of energy. Perking up, she turns to face me. "Two can play that game."

CHAPTER ONE HUNDRED EIGHT

Ellie

Ava and I meet up in the university cafeteria, getting something quick before heading over to our philosophy class.

"Do you know what you're doing next week?" she asks, paying for her overpriced salad.

I grab a wrap and a soda and meet her at the register. "What's next week?"

"Girl! It's spring break!"

"I'm probably just going to keep it low-key." A smile creeps onto my face as I'm reminded of my date with Mateo the other night and what we did afterward. I hope we have a lot of repeat *low-key* nights like that during spring break.

We find a nearby table and sit across from one another. "I wish you were coming with me and the boys."

"Where are all of you going again?"

"Cancun. It's going to be epic." She tosses her mousy-brown hair over her shoulder before digging into her lunch. "Do you want to join? It's not too late to book a flight."

"No, I'm good."

"I really wish you would. Screw Hunter. You don't have to even look in his direction. You can just hang with Derek and me."

"And when you and Derek are *just hanging,* what am I supposed to be doing?"

She laughs. "I don't know. It's Mexico. Get drunk on the beach and get a tan."

"As much as I could use some sun, I'll skip this one."

Ava pouts. "I miss hanging out like we did in France."

"Tell you what. Once the summer comes, you and I can book a trip somewhere and get drunk and do impressions of our professors."

"A girls-only trip!"

"Sounds perfect."

I sit cross-legged on the periwinkle couch in Panavi's office after my philosophy class. "I've been thinking about something that I can't get off my mind," I say.

"What is it?" she asks.

"A while ago, you said that our childhood acts as our foundation. And I get how I turned out to be how I am, and even how Hunter turned out to be who he is…but why is Mateo not as impacted by his upbringing?"

"He probably is, just in ways you're not necessarily aware of."

"Fair. But how come he is not as much of a disaster as I am?"

"First off, you're not a disaster. Secondly, people act differently in situations for a myriad of reasons. Genetics play a part, as well as what stage he was in his development when things were happening, his commitment to therapy, his support system."

His support system is definitely a big one. Just from the few interactions I've had with his family, I could tell he and his sisters lean on each other during their tough times. "I guess that all makes sense."

"The important thing is that the both of you are making healthy changes."

"You're right." I nod. "Speaking of changes, I'm going to stop home over spring break so I can take my permit test."

"That's exciting!"

"I know. I'm a little nervous, but I've been studying like crazy."

"How are things with your mom? You haven't mentioned her in a while."

"Things with her are okay." I shrug. "I've been trying to set boundaries, which is not my strong suit," I admit, and Panavi smiles at me. "We'll see how it goes over the break."

"If it becomes difficult when you're with her, try to remind yourself that your boundary is an act of self-love. You are taking care of yourself in those moments, and nothing about that is selfish."

I make a mental note to jot that down in my journal when I get back to my room later. "I'm still working on that part."

"It's a lifelong journey. Healing isn't linear. It's filled with obstacles and triggers, but it's how we address them and move forward that signifies our progress—even if there's only a slight difference."

I nod. "I can honestly say that even though it's in small amounts, I think I am making progress."

For the first time in what seems like forever, the sensation of pride swims through my bloodstream. I *am* making improvements, no matter how small.

Getting back to my room after the session, I grab my journal to write out my thoughts. I've been so focused on midterms this past week that I've barely had any time to write. Thankfully, break starts today, so I can ignore school for the time being.

"Wait!" Bree says as she zips up her luggage. She's leaving to catch a plane back home to California for break. "Before you get sucked into writing, give me a hug. My ride's here."

With a smile, I get up, and we wrap our arms around each other. "Have an awesome break with Mateo," she says.

"You have an awesome break doing God knows what."

She chuckles. "Promise I won't do anything that'll cause you to bail me out of jail." Her comment causes my breath to stick in my throat. "I'm sure you had your fill of that for one lifetime."

"I sure did," I joke back.

Only I never posted bail for Mateo the night everything went to hell. Hunter did. And I definitely don't want a reminder of him just as I'm starting to feel comfortable in my relationship with Mateo.

Once Bree is on her way, I sit down in my desk chair. In an effort to push Hunter out of my mind, I flip open to the last page I had written in my journal. It's about Mateo, and how when I'm around him, I feel like the better side of me steps into the light—not as overcome by emotions, more rational, less impulsive. Overall, more positive. I get to embrace this side of myself, and he's staying along for the ride.

A light tap on the door takes my attention away from what I've written. "Come in," I say. Mateo saunters in, and I slam the journal shut. His eyes immediately follow the action.

"What's that?" He motions with his chin to the book in my hand.

"Nothing." I pop up from my chair and move to give him a kiss.

"Seems like it's something," he says against my mouth. "Especially because I know you're trying to distract me right now." He shuffles our bodies closer to my desk, and I spin around to grab my journal.

"You can't read it." I clutch it to my chest.

"I don't even know what it is." Mateo gives me a smart-ass smile.

"It's my journal. I started it after one of my therapy sessions."

"Oh." He takes a step forward, and I take one back. "Don't worry, I won't read it. If there was anything you wanted me to know, I'm sure you'd already tell me." He gives me a kiss on my forehead and sits down on my bed.

If only he knew that there are so many things I want to tell him, all of which are literally in the palm of my hands.

"Maybe I'll show it to you one day," I say, placing it down on my desk.

"Only if you want to."

"I do. Just not yet." I sit next to him. "However, I've been thinking about something that I *am* ready for."

His eyebrow arches. "Anal?"

"No!" I burst into laughter and give him a nudge. "Where the hell did that come from?"

"Figured I might as well give it a shot."

"You're ridiculous."

He chuckles, then brings us back into the original conversation. "So what is it that you're ready for?"

"I want you to come home with me and meet my mom."

"Really?" Mateo's face lights up, grinning in surprise.

I nod. Mateo and I were planning to hang out at his place the majority of the break, and he would drive me to Mom's and stay at a hotel in Boston for the night, but I don't want him to have to do that. "I think it's about time."

"Does she know I'm coming?"

"No, I wanted to make sure you wanted to before I cross the bridge—"

"Yes, definitely."

"Okay." I smile. "I'll call her later and let her know."

My stomach suddenly twists as the reality of what I just said starts to sink in. Mateo is going to meet Mom in all her hot-mess glory. He's going to venture into another part of my world, one that I've always intended to keep hidden. But I don't want to keep hiding, not from him and not from myself.

I have no clue how Mom will handle Mateo being there. I've only mentioned his name once in passing.

I fixate on the tiled floor.

An immediate jolt of anxiety shoots into my lungs, making my breathing ragged. My mind spins and spins and spins, unable to stop the potentially horrific outcomes of the two of them meeting. What if she's drunk? What if she hates him? What if he decided this is the part of me that's too much baggage for him? What if—

"Elle?"

Mateo takes my hands.

I hear his voice again, but I can't make out what he's saying. The ringing in my ears is too loud.

He drops down to the floor in front of me, and my concentration is broken by looking into his dark eyes. His hands cup my face, and I follow his breaths. They're drawn-out inhales and exhales that I'm eventually able to keep up with.

My heart rate goes back to normal, and my shoulders slump. Mateo brings his hands to my thighs, his gaze never leaving mine.

"Baby," he says. "I don't have to meet your mom if you don't want—"

"I want you to. I'm just nervous," I reply.

"I understand. I'm nervous too."

"You are?"

"Probably not in the same way, but yeah."

Knowing that he's not as nonchalant about this as I thought he would be calms me down even more.

"We've been through a lot in the past year and a half," he says. "I doubt meeting your mom will be the worst of it."

I sure hope so.

"Would it take your mind off things if we go back to talking about anal?"

A weight is lifted, and I chuckle. "Shut up."

"Is that what I have to do to help you through your panic attacks? Because that's a sacrifice I'm willing to make."

"If you start saying anal in the middle of one of my attacks, I'll punch you."

Mateo laughs and sits back next to me while my breathing steadies.

"Wow," I say, blinking a few times, settling back into the room. "That panic attack only lasted like a minute."

"Progress."

"Major progress."

CHAPTER ONE HUNDRED NINE

Mateo

We stand on the front porch of Elle's two-story home. We've been here for several minutes, but I don't want to push Elle until she's ready. Truth be told, I'm glad we haven't gone inside yet. I wasn't lying the other day when I said I was nervous. I haven't been able to sleep since Elle told me she wanted me to meet her mom.

I want her mom to see me as more than a passing boyfriend. I want her to see me as part of Elle's future.

Elle seems to be talking to herself, calming herself down, and I notice Elle's thumb grazing over her left wrist.

"Ready?" Elle finally speaks.

"Whenever you are. I got your back if you got mine."

"What do you need me to have your back for?"

"Have you seen me?" I wave a hand up and down myself. "I'm not exactly the guy girls aim to bring home to meet their moms."

"You are for this girl." She gets up on her toes to kiss me on the cheek, and in an instant, I'm relieved knowing that whatever Elle's mom thinks of me won't change how Elle feels about me.

She reaches for her keys and unlocks the door.

"Mom, we're here," she shouts, walking inside with me tailing behind.

The living room has pictures of little Elle hanging on the beige walls. A photo of her and who I assume to be her parents is in the center.

"Hi, sweetie." Elle's mom rounds the corner and embraces her. Her eyes shift up to look at me. "You must be Mateo."

"Hi, Mrs. Connor. It's very nice to meet you." I extend my hand as her mom releases Elle.

"Call me Grace," she says, ignoring my hand, going right in for a hug.

Once we settle in, Elle gives me the grand tour of her home. It's not quite like I imagined. Nothing's new, and it all seems kind of…dull and dreary, like the life has been sucked out of it.

"Here's my room," Elle says once we're upstairs.

The second she pushes the door open, I sense myself smiling. Now *this* is what I envisioned as her room—lavender walls with a giant picture of the Eiffel Tower hanging up, fairy lights around her bookshelf, concert tickets sticking up on a small bulletin board next to her bed, and an old record player sitting on her white dresser. There is an air of innocence and youthfulness as I make my way farther inside.

"Sorry it's a little messy," she says, scurrying to put away some of her stray clothes and books.

"I love it," I say.

She turns her attention to her bed, where a big plastic bin sits with crap sticking out of the top. "Mom?" she shouts toward the door. "Why's there a bin on my bed?"

"I was cleaning out the basement and found a bunch of your stuff from high school," Grace says, walking up the stairs and into Elle's room. "I figured you could go through it while you're here, and whatever you don't want, you can throw out." She turns to me. "Mateo, you're welcome anywhere in the house. Just don't go in the basement because it's a disaster."

"I'll make sure to steer clear," I say.

"Speaking of steering, when are you going for your permit test?" Grace asks Elle.

Elle reaches for her phone in her back pocket and checks the time. "Three hours."

"Great. I can cook you a celebratory dinner afterward."

"Don't jinx me."

"You're gonna do great," I tell her. "You've been glued to your driver's manual for weeks. You even brought it with you into bed a few times," I tease.

Elle's eyes widen slightly at my comment, and a flash of worry crosses her face. The look she's wearing makes a tiny knot in my gut.

Grace clears her throat. "Well, I'm going to head out to the grocery store so I can make us dinner. Whether it's a celebratory one or not, we still need to eat. Are you okay with lasagna, Mateo?"

"I'm not picky. I'll eat just about anything."

"Glad to hear it. My lasagna is this one's favorite." She points to Elle.

"You don't need to do that, Mom. I'm fine with whatever's already here."

"Nonsense. If my daughter and her boyfriend are here visiting, then I'm cooking." Grace turns to leave, but Elle stops her.

"Wait." Elle digs into her purse and pulls out a twenty. "In case it's too expensive."

Grace arches an eyebrow and ignores the cash that Elle is waving in front of her. "See you two in a little bit."

Once we hear the front door shut, Elle swats my chest. "You told my mom that we're sleeping together."

"We are sleeping together."

"Well, if she thinks we're sleeping together, then she's going to think that we're *sleeping* together."

"What's the big deal?"

"It's a huge deal! I don't want her to know that I do anything." She takes the bin off her bed and tosses it down on the floor.

"Oh, come on. She's not that dumb. I'm sure when you had Hunter over, she was never assuming that you guys were just watching TV."

Those words tasted like acid on my tongue, but I had to say them. I don't want Elle upset the entire time we're here by thinking that her mom is having this new revelation that her daughter's sexually active.

"We *were* just watching TV!" Elle says, becoming more irritated. She sits down on her bed. The comforter is white with thin black flowers threaded into the fabric. She twists a frayed black piece of string around her finger tight enough to turn it reddish purple. "I've never been allowed to have a guy in my room, so when he came over, we'd be in the living room."

"And when your mom wasn't home?" I ask, sitting next to her.

She shakes her head. "I always felt too guilty to do anything here, so everything happened at his place."

As fucked up as it is, a wave of excitement rolls through me knowing that no one else has been in this bed with her.

A small smile appears on her lips. "What's the face for?" she asks.

Apparently, I'm not as good at keeping a poker face as I thought. Either that, or she knows me too well. She has a tendency to call me out at times like this.

"I'm just thinking about the fact that no one has ever touched you in this bed," I answer honestly. "Aside from yourself," I add as I imagine her fingering herself under the covers.

Elle chuckles. "That's never happened either."

"What do you mean?"

"I've never done that before."

"You mean you've never gotten yourself off in this bed or…"

"No. Like, ever."

"Never?"

"I mean, I tried a few times, but I felt weird, so I stopped. So technically, the first time I actually finished the job was at your mom's, when you were watching."

I study the woman in front of me, trying to make sense of her. This is the woman who licked our cum off my fingers like it was the last bite of her dessert that she wanted to savor, yet she's only ever touched herself once.

"Okay, now what is *that* face for?"

"Trying to figure you out." But I realize that I might never be able to do that, and maybe that's one of the reasons why I love her so much. The depths of her emotions and thoughts are endless, leaving me to uncover new layers with each twist and turn life throws at us.

Elle scrunches her face. "There's nothing to figure out."

"If you say so."

She jumps up from the bed, her demeanor suddenly shifting as if an alarm went off in her brain. "Shit, we only have a couple of minutes. Can you help me with something?"

Before I can answer, she's leading me out of her room and into her mom's. She flips on the light and points to her mom's wooden armoire. "Can you shimmy that out a little?"

"Uh…okay." I do what she asks, even though I have no clue why I'm moving this gigantic piece of furniture that feels like it weighs a few hundred pounds, as the muscles in my arms strain to move it.

Elle squeezes behind it and reaches for something. She pulls out a half-empty bottle of liquor.

"Thanks. You can push it back now."

I move it back to where it was and watch as Elle heads to the night-stand, searching through all her drawers. Nausea hits me as she crawls under the bed, pulling out another bottle.

I stand there horrified as she goes into the closet and starts opening up shoeboxes, searching for more alcohol. When she finds a small flask, she tosses it on the bed and carefully puts the boxes back in their original places.

Elle grabs all her findings and guides me downstairs to the kitchen. Putting the bottles on the table, she then pulls a chair over and hops up onto the counter.

"What are you doing?" I ask, troubled by her rehearsed actions.

"Keeping her sober."

"Elle…" I start to speak but stop myself. I don't have the heart to tell her that doing this isn't going to do the job. A person has to want to get sober. Cleaning out all the hiding spots isn't going to miraculously stop her mom from drinking.

"I didn't get to do this when I was here for Thanksgiving." Elle pats the top of the fridge. "Catch." She throws me tiny shooter bottles.

She climbs back down and heads over to the sink, twisting the caps of the bottles open and pouring them down the drain, the pungent smell burning my nostrils.

"Can you pause for a second?" I place my hand on her shoulder.

"Why?"

I take the bottle from her hand, getting her to turn and look at me. She doesn't seem fazed by what she's doing, but I'm sure as hell unsettled by everything I just witnessed.

"How did you know where all her hiding spots were?"

"I've been doing this since I was a kid, Mateo."

"A kid, as in, like, fifteen?"

"No, like eight or nine."

A ton of bricks drops in my gut as I picture her as a child cleaning up after her drunken parents and sneaking around to empty their bottles of alcohol in hopes that they would stop drinking. A shudder runs down my limbs, disturbed that this was her childhood—a kid trying to save her parents, a desperate attempt to ask for what she needed more of: love.

"I never realized," I admit.

"Realized what?" There's an edge of defensiveness in her voice, but I don't even entertain it. Instead, I stare at her with more compassion than I ever have before.

"I obviously know about your parents, but to see you come in here and…" My voice trails off for a second, getting lost in my thoughts, but I start up again. "I don't know. I see you differently."

"In a bad way?"

"Not at all," I say as gently as possible. "Let me help you." I pour the rest of the bottle down the drain while she opens up another.

CHAPTER ONE HUNDRED TEN

Mateo

"I knew we would be celebrating tonight," Grace says, placing a plate of lasagna in front of Elle and me. A strong whiff of meat sauce and cheese has my stomach growling, ready to devour the meal. I offered to help with whatever she needed, but she insisted that since I was a guest in her house that I relax.

"Thanks, Mom," Elle says. She's been all smiles since she walked out of the DMV with her permit. I've been beaming for hours, so proud of my girl.

"Can I offer you a drink, Mateo?" Grace asks as she pours herself a glass of wine from the fridge.

Elle told me all about her "system." She only gets rid of the alcohol that her mom hides because her mom doesn't catch on right away. Apparently, if she touches anything in the refrigerator or pantry, that incites anger because her mom is aware of what's in there. We hid all the bottles we found in a garbage bag and put it at the bottom of the recycling can. I'll take it out later tonight after Grace goes to sleep.

"I'm good with water. Thank you." I take a bite of the pasta dish, and my eyes widen as my taste buds explode. "This is so fucking good." *Shit.* I shouldn't be cursing in front of her mom. "Sorry."

Grace laughs. "No need to apologize. I'm glad you enjoy it as much as Elena does."

"It *is* really fucking good," Elle says, teasing me and relieving me at the same time.

While we eat, Grace drills me on all the normal shit—my family, where I grew up, what I plan to do after grad school. I ignored the nervousness beating in my heart as I answered her questions as honestly as I could.

I guess I passed the boyfriend test, because by the end of the night, after we watched a movie and had ice cream, Grace gave me an extra pillow to use in Elle's bed.

"She's letting you sleep in my room," Elle whispers, even though her mom's in her bedroom.

"You think she'd be cool if we had sex in there too?" I joke as I help her clean up the mess we made in the living room.

Elle playfully scowls, but before she can say something back, her mom's bedroom door swings open.

"Elena." Grace's tone of voice sends a chill in the air, and my back immediately straightens. Her tone is sharp and menacing, and nothing like the woman we spent the evening with. "Can I speak to you upstairs?"

"Um…sure." Elle wrings her hands together as she walks up the steps.

My heart rattles against my rib cage because I know exactly why she called her upstairs. I take a few steps to go up there, but I stop myself, unsure if I should get involved or not.

They speak in hushed tones, but their volume gradually gets louder. They begin to argue with each other about Elle taking the bottles. My body keeps lurching forward, but I fight the impulse to step in.

I won't go up there unless I have to.

"Don't you dare lie to me, Ellie," Grace snaps at her.

"I'm not lying! I had to go into your room for something, and I found a bottle, so I dumped it."

"You took *all* of my bottles."

"I'm trying to help you stay sober."

"I don't need you to help me stay sober. What I need is for you to not go through my belongings and then lie to me about it."

I peek my head up the stairs and see Elle marching out of her mom's room and going into hers.

"We're not finished speaking." Her mom follows her.

"Well, I am." Elle tries to slam her door, but her mom catches it before it shuts.

"You have no right to steal my things and then turn around and act like a bitch about it!"

And that's my cue.

I tread up the stairs. Elle and Grace are in a full-blown screaming match, but I figured Elle would snap as soon as her mom called her a bitch. Walking into the bedroom, I clear my throat to inform them that I'm there. Elle looks mortified, as if she completely forgot I was even in the house.

"Mrs. Connor," I say, and she spins in my direction. "I'm sorry, but I can't have you speaking to Elena that way." I make sure my tone is calm and nonthreatening, but I also let her know that I'm serious. "I know you're upset, and I understand why you would be. I wouldn't like it if someone touched my things either. But Elle's intentions were to be helpful and not harmful. And I think if you can take a moment to look at things from her point of view, we might be able to end this night on a good note."

Grace stares at me, her eyes piercing mine. My pulse picks up even more as I realize I might've just made this ten times worse. The longer the three of us stand in silence, the louder my heartbeat gets in my ears. I don't have it in me to glance over at Elle yet because I'm sure she's about to pass the fuck out.

"I apologize if I crossed a boundary," I say to Grace. "I'm just trying to do right by Elle."

Grace studies me a bit longer, then suddenly the fight exits her shoulders. She drops her crossed arms to the side, and she looks over to Elle. "I like him," she says and then exits the room without sparing either one of us another glance.

When I hear her bedroom door shut, I turn around to Elle. We stare at each other, unsure of the next move.

My head spins from the whirlwind of her mom's behavior. "Was that…" I point behind me to where Grace was. "Was that a good thing?"

"I…think?" Elle seems just as confused as I am. "I'm sorry you saw that." Her fingers clutch on to the necklace she's wearing—the one I gave her—and she twists the pendant around as a way to soothe herself.

"I want to be here for the real moments, Elle. I don't want you to hide anything from me, including the messy parts of your life."

She steps into me, melting against my body as my arms wrap around her. I kiss the top of her head and feel her press her lips against my chest.

I should tell her I love her, but I want to do it when the moment is right. I don't want it to be when something bad or upsetting has just happened. I'll set up a special day for us and make sure it's perfect for her. That's what she deserves.

Grace made us pancakes the next morning as if nothing had happened the night before, and now I'm aware of where Elle gets her avoidance from. She learned to plaster a smile on her face from her mom.

Grace has some errands to run and a doctor's appointment, so she's out for a few hours, but we promised not to leave until she's back. So, to kill time, we're in Elle's room, going through her bin of high school crap.

"Toss," Elle says when I hold up her old folder of science notes. I throw it in the garbage bag and continue to go through the box.

As Elle flips through a notebook, I come across some pictures. Most of them are people I don't know until I find one of her and Hunter. He's in a tux, and she's in a long black gown. "Prom?" I ask, flipping the photo over so she can see.

"Yeah. His." She grabs the stack from me and finds another picture. "This is what I wore to mine."

"Whoa!" I take a good look at her in a dark purple dress. "You grew up between those two proms. Look how big your boobs got."

"Shut up." She laughs and chucks the pictures into the trash. Satisfaction strikes me as I watch her get rid of memories of Hunter.

We go back to rummaging through her stuff, and I come across a handwritten note. "You guys passed notes to each other?"

"My school was super strict. If we had our phones out, we'd get suspended."

"Damn. I wonder what would've happened if they found out about Sammy copying your English homework during lunch." I showcase the letter in my hand.

"Thankfully, I never found out." She takes it from me and throws it out.

I come across another note, and as I start to read it, my fingers tighten around the paper, and the muscles in my shoulders stiffen.

Hunter,

You really scared me last night. I hate when you punch holes in your walls. It needs to stop. I'm sorry that I said all those horrible things to get you to that point. I didn't mean what I said. I can't control my mouth when I'm angry. I don't know why. I'm sorry. Please don't be mad at me anymore. I never want to cause you to get to that point again. I'll watch what I say.

I love you,
Ellie

Ellie,

It's fine. You have a bad temper, just like me. I'm sorry too, but when you start talking shit, you make me crazy. It's better I punch the wall than a person, right? At least I'm making some progress.

I love you. I'm not mad at you.

Cut 7th and meet me in the auditorium. We can put that smart-ass mouth of yours to good use.

Hunter

My teeth grind together. I attempt to swallow down my rage, but the fact that he passively threatened her and then manipulated her into sucking him off makes my body burn with fury. I want to tear him to fucking shreds. My hands shake as I crumble the note up into a ball and throw it into the garbage bag.

"What was that?" Elle asks.

"Nothing important."

She nods as if she knows that I came across something that had to do with that asshole.

I move around the rest of her shit in the box and spot Hunter's handwriting on another piece of paper. Being a fucking masochist, I decide to pick it up and read it.

Ellie,

We have to talk about what happened over the weekend. You can't keep avoiding my texts and calls. You need to go see someone, a doctor or a counselor. Someone. If I didn't happen to come to your house that night before you could take the rest of the pills, you would be dead right now. I can't fucking lose you, Ellie. You are the only person in my life that I truly love and care about. I can't leave for college in a couple of months knowing you're like this. I need to know you'll be okay for me. I swear I'll take care of you. I'll give you everything you've ever dreamed of. We'll get married as soon as you graduate and buy a house on the water. We'll have as many kids as you want and travel to France every summer.

I'm always going to be here to save you.

I love you,
Hunter.

I reread the sentence over and over again.

If I didn't happen to come to your house that night before you could take the rest of the pills, you would be dead right now.

My lungs shrivel up.

I have to be reading this incorrectly because there's no fucking way my life with Elena almost never existed.

My eyes scan over the entire letter once more.

Not only did Hunter promise her everything she wanted, but he also got it into her head that he was the only one who could save her.

Because at one time, he was.

More of the Elle and Hunter puzzle fuse together as I realize just how convoluted and fucked up their relationship was.

"What are you reading?"

CHAPTER ONE HUNDRED ELEVEN

Ellie

Mateo peers up at me, his eyes suddenly glassy, and an expression that I can't decipher appears on his face. My insides coil at the way he's looking at me. I snatch the paper out of his hand. As soon as my brain registers what it was that he read, my heart plummets.

He wasn't supposed to read that.

He wasn't supposed to know.

No one was supposed to know.

"Elle."

I shake my head. "That was a long time ago."

"Elena—"

"Relax. I had only taken one pill. It doesn't even count."

His brown eyes fill with water. "It counts."

"I don't want to talk about this, Mateo."

"I really think we should."

"It's in the past." I rip the paper to shreds. "It doesn't matter anymore."

Mateo's hands still mine. "Your past matters to me," he says, his words comforting me as much as his touch is. "Remember when we told each other we'd be open and honest if the other person has questions?"

I slowly nod, regretting that agreement.

"Well, I have questions, Elle."

He fights letting his tears spill over as he waits for me to tell him about my past. A part of me that I never wanted to own and never wanted to admit to. The ugly, troubled depths of my mind that I pretend don't exist.

"I didn't want to die," I tell him. "I wanted the situation I was in to end, and the only solution I could come up with was death."

He studies me for a moment, then tugs me over to him so he can wrap his arms around me as we lean against my lavender wall. "Tell me what the situation was like," he says into my hair.

"It was…" I swallow around the emotions swelling in my throat before continuing. "It's hard to describe."

"I'll make sense out of whatever you say."

"It was the feeling of emptiness and pain. It was numbness, but the numbness still hurt. I wanted something to change, but I didn't know what or how to make that happen."

"How long were you thinking about doing it?"

"I thought about it often after my dad died. It would come and go. But I didn't think about it seriously until that night, when there was a big blowup with Mom, and then shit happened at school with Hunter. And it was just me in this house, feeling so alone and tired of life and not wanting to feel that anymore. I had a stare-off with a bunch of medicine bottles for what seemed like hours. I texted Hunter something cryptic, but he obviously caught on, and the moment the first pill hit my tongue, Hunter was busting through my door."

Mateo holds me, and I rest my head against his chest, listening to his heartbeat, the gentle rhythm acting as a reminder of this new life I'm trying to forge.

"Did you ever try again after that?" he asks. Even though his voice is tender, the deep resonance of it causes his chest to vibrate against my ear.

"No."

"Ever thought about doing it again?"

I draw in a breath. "Yes."

"When was the last time?"

"December."

He angles himself so that we break apart enough for us to make eye contact. "December?"

I nod, not wanting to go into detail.

"That was a few months ago," he states with fear rising in his tone.

"I know."

"Elena." He pushes out his breath as the intensity in his eyes begins to build.

I run my hand down his arm, hoping to calm him enough to drop his shoulders that are rising toward his ears. "It was just a fleeting thought, and the second I realized I was going down that rabbit hole was when I found Panavi."

"Okay." That seems to ease him a bit. "But I need you to promise me that if you even feel remotely close to that"—he glances toward the shredded letter—"that you'll reach out to someone. Anyone. You don't have to be alone in this, ever."

"I will."

"No, promise me, baby." Mateo takes my hand in his. "Promise me you'll ask for help if you need it. Everyone needs extra support at different points in their lives, and there's nothing wrong with that. Sometimes we need someone to walk next to us through the tough times, to help remind us how strong we actually are."

"I promise," I say before leaning in to kiss him. His soft lips mold to mine, tender and careful as his hands draw me nearer.

As he embraces me, I choose to embrace a side of me that I never loved but always needed to be tended to. The dark, grim, low notes of the song that is my life, which I only play for myself, I finally let them be heard. And I'm not desperate to let them be drowned out by the high ones. I'm actually listening to them. They are what makes my song whole. They are what makes *me* whole.

Another step toward loving myself, a sense of vibrancy juts through my bloodstream, making me feel more alive. With the desire to shed this layer shadowed by trauma and shame, another experience of freedom lights up my energy field.

I shift onto Mateo's lap, parting my legs over his thighs. My mouth moves from his lips and over to his earlobe, where I gently suck. My hips begin to roll over his, and the seam of my jeans hits me in just the right spot.

"What are you doing?" Mateo clutches my hips to pause my movements.

"Trying to have sex with you?"

"Now?"

"Yes."

"But we were just talking about—"

"Me living."

My words spark something in Mateo, and he takes the initiative. He grabs me by the torso so he can look at me before taking my shirt up over my head. We both do our best to remove our pants as fast as possible. In seconds, I'm back to straddling him. Our gazes connect, and I think he's about to say something, but before he can, I lower myself onto him.

Mateo's jaw slackens as I slowly begin to ride him. His hands slide up and down my body, covering any part of my skin they possibly can. Then he roughly grips my hips and moves me faster. Our lips collide, and we sigh into each other's mouths as we try to kiss and moan at the same time.

He adjusts his back against the wall, and I gasp. The way our bodies are angled feels amazing against my clit, flames rushing through my veins.

"Don't move," I say, placing my hands on his shoulders so he doesn't change his position.

Mateo does as I say and stops rocking my hips, allowing me to take charge. "Why can't I move, baby?" he asks with a smirk.

"It feels so good." I grind against him. He tries to sneak his thumb down to meet my clit, but I push it away. "I said, don't move."

Biting down on his bottom lip, he rests the back of his head against the lavender wall, his arms falling to the sides. My hands drop down to his chest as I continue to get myself off, rubbing myself against his body, chasing the intensity of the friction.

"You look so unbelievably hot when you ride my cock."

Closing my eyes, I change up the pace.

Mateo continues to praise me. "You take me so good, baby."

Shivers and heat run through me at the same time. Mateo groans curse words, and suddenly, he thrusts upward.

A loud moan escapes my lips, and he pushes his palms down onto the bed as he lifts his hips up, hitting that divine spot inside of me.

"Fuck," I cry out as he does it again. This time, the strength causes my own movements to stutter. My forehead crashes down on his shoulder.

"Can I move now?" Mateo's stubble scratches against my face as he whispers in my ear.

The second I nod, his hands fly to my hips, pushing me down as he thrusts up. Sharp bursts of pleasure blended with pain consume my body.

He repeatedly slams me down while pushing up, and I moan with each motion he makes, unsure if I can take anymore.

Mateo brings his lips to my ear once more. "Touch yourself."

His gentle demand has me on the brink of ecstasy, and I crave to do what it takes to make me fall over the edge. I drag my fingers down Mateo's chest, and his muscles react to each drawn-out touch. When they eventually reach between where our bodies are connected, he pushes me up so I'm sitting straighter.

"I wanna watch you," he says.

With a smile, I connect with my clit, and his eyes shoot down to admire me. He pulls his bottom lip between his teeth once again as he continues to move in and out of me. My free hand grips his arm to steady myself as my body shudders.

"Baby," I say, attempting to let him know I'm close. His gaze snaps back to my face, and his brown irises soften as he leans in for a kiss. His lips swallow my moans as sparks ignite inside me. Mateo uses his body weight to reposition us, and my back lands on my white and black comforter.

As he climbs on top of me, the conversation we had in his room a few weeks ago rings in my ears. The sense of living fills me with hope and maybe even faith that I'll one day be able to fully live the way I want to.

His fingertips skim over the side of my body, touching each curve.

"Mateo," I sigh out.

"Hmm?"

"I like living. And I like it even more with you."

He pauses and smiles. "Me too, Elle."

CHAPTER ONE HUNDRED TWELVE

Ellie

We didn't have much time to lounge around after Mateo and I broke in my bed. We got dressed with seconds to spare as Mom pulled up to say goodbye to us before we left. It wasn't the worst time spent with her, but it sure was memorable. Having Mateo witness Mom and me go back and forth last night was something I never wanted him to see, but in a way, I'm sort of glad he did. We're getting to know each other on a different level, which is why we decided to take a day trip to New York to see his mom before spring break is over.

"I know you weren't big on going to see your mom, but thank you for letting me join you," Mateo says as he parallel parks in front of his mom's apartment.

"Eh, I just needed you for the ride," I tease.

He quickly turns the steering wheel, and I make a mental note to practice how to do that in the upcoming weeks. I'm going to need to know how to parallel park for my road test now that I have my permit.

It seems like a small feat to most, but to me, it's huge. And I did it.

Mateo takes my hand as we walk up the steps to the apartment, and when we step inside, we're greeted by Camila and Stephanie.

His mom looks tired and paler, but she still has a grin on her face when she wraps her arms around both of us and gives us a kiss on the cheek.

"I'm so happy you're here," Camila says, escorting us into the kitchen where Stephanie is cooking.

"Thank you for having me." I take a seat across from her at the kitchen table.

"You're always welcome here," Stephanie answers before Camila can. "We'll trade you for Mateo any day."

"Fuck you," Mateo says, and Camila whacks his arm, reprimanding him in Spanish.

Stephanie gets involved in the conversation, and I have no idea what they're saying, but it's comical to watch the two of them gang up on Mateo.

"What are you laughing at? You're supposed to be defending me," Mateo says to me.

"Sorry, you're out of luck. I don't know Spanish."

"Don't worry, we'll teach you," Stephanie says.

"You'll need to know some if you're going to marry into this family," Camila teases, but the look on Mateo's face implies nothing was funny about her comment. My stomach clenches at the reminder of our conversation last year when we realized our future goals never aligned. I want a husband and kids, and he doesn't want to even utter the word marriage.

"Christ, Mom. Don't start with that shit," he says, getting up to help Stephanie cook.

Camila says something to him again, but this time, whatever she's saying doesn't have a playful tone to it. The room falls silent, and I uncomfortably stare at the table in front of me, wishing I could evaporate into thin air and not have to sit in the room with everyone realizing that Mateo will never want me for more than this.

As the moment stretches out, I find myself feeling differently about all of this. Does it hurt that the man I love doesn't want more with me? Yes. It always has.

But this time, as the words come to the forefront again, I'm not letting it impact my self-worth. I'm not feeling like I'm not good enough or that I did something wrong, and that's why he doesn't want a future together. I know that what he believes about the topic of marriage has nothing to do with who I am as a person.

With confidence nipping at my nerve endings, I lift my head back up and choose to break the silence. "How have you been feeling, Camila?"

She smiles. "I'm feeling all right. My medication seems to be doing its job."

"Good, I'm glad. And if there's anything you ever need, please let me know. I don't know what I could possibly do to help, but I'll always be here for all of you." Behind Camila, Mateo's lips lift upward.

The four of us spend the rest of the afternoon together, and the entire time, I feel like a part of their world.

While Stephanie shows Mateo something in her room, Camila and I sit on the comfy leather couches in the living room.

"Mateo told me he met your mom," she says.

"Yeah, we took a trip there so he could finally meet her."

Camila chuckles. "I can't imagine what your mother must've thought when my son walked through that door."

"She really likes him," I assure Camila.

"And he really likes *you*. You bring out a different side of him. I spent years of my life praying he'd become the man he's turning out to be."

"He's doing that on his own."

"He is. But it helps to have you by his side to encourage him to grow."

"He's helped me too."

"I'm really proud of him."

"What?" Mateo asks, stepping out of Stephanie's room, looking stunned as his eyes bulge.

Camilla stills.

My brain flips to a conversation I had with Mateo last year when he told me no one ever said they were proud of him.

Mateo strides up to his mom, his hand rubbing the middle of his chest as Camilla repeats, "I'm proud of you, Mateo."

The energy in the room shifts as I witness a piece of Mateo's heart fuse back together, along with his mom's. My eyes brim with tears.

Stephanie pops out of her room, unaware of the conversation happening and changing up the feeling in the air once more. "You guys heading out?" she asks.

"Um…yeah," Mateo says, grounding himself back into the moment. "We have one more stop to hit up before going back to school, though," he says to me.

I tilt my head to the side. "We do? Where?"

"You'll see."

Mateo takes us to a nearby diner with sticky linoleum flooring and worn vinyl booths. I slide into the seat, and Mateo sits down next to me. I furrow my brow. "Why aren't you sitting on the other side of the table?"

"Because we're meeting someone," he responds.

"Who?"

Before Mateo can answer, the waitress comes over and takes our drink order. Once she's gone, Mateo still won't clue me in on who's joining us.

His face suddenly lights up when someone enters through the door. I follow his line of sight as the man looking back at Mateo has the same beaming expression.

Mateo jumps up from his seat, and I figure I should follow his lead. He hugs the man in front of him, the two of them patting each other on the back. They break apart from each other, and the man looks at me.

"This must be the infamous Ellie," he says.

Mateo turns to me. "Elle, this is Mr. Kevin."

"Oh!" My body expands with excitement. "Hi!" Before I realize what I'm doing, I'm giving this stranger a hug. But in a way, it feels like I already know him.

The three of us take our seats and jump right into conversation.

"I figured since we all have the time, you guys could finally meet," Mateo says.

"We can swap war stories about this one," Mr. Kevin jokes while pointing at Mateo.

"Oh, I'd love to hear what Mateo was like as a teenager!"

Mr. Kevin breaks out into a laugh. "How many hours do you have? I got plenty of stories."

"I have all night."

Mateo rests his arm on the top of the booth, chuckling. "Maybe this was a bad idea."

"Too late. You already committed, and now you have to sit here and listen to us talk about how awesome you are." I poke his cheek.

Mr. Kevin looks between both of us with a warm expression, and he gives Mateo a knowing nod. I'm not sure what that was for, but it seemed like a good thing.

Our time at the diner flies by, and we spend the evening talking about Mateo while Mr. Kevin and I get to know each other. By the time we're ready to say goodbye, we stand in the parking lot, ready to part in separate ways.

"You two work well together," Mr. Kevin says.

"I sure think so." I glance up at Mateo, who has happiness pouring out of him.

We say our farewells and get into the car. My heart flutters as my soul dances with glee. I just got to meet one of the most important people to Mateo. And I'm pretty sure Mr. Kevin feels the same.

CHAPTER ONE HUNDRED THIRTEEN

Ellie

APRIL

As I finish writing the last few thoughts about my revelations from the latest therapy session in my journal, Bree bursts into our room in a fit of giggles, stumbling. I'm quick to help her, tossing my journal to the side before shuffling her over to her bed.

"Ellie!" she squeals. "I'm sooo high. And maybe a tiny, tiny, tiny bit drunk."

"If you say so." I laugh as we fall on top of her mattress.

"I only had this much." She squeezes her index finger and thumb together. "Plus this much." She then opens her arms wide.

"However much you had, you need to sleep it off."

Bree takes her outstretched arms and wraps them around me in an aggressive hug that has both of us in hysterics. "I love you, Ellie."

"I love you too, Bree."

She gasps. "Have you told Mateo that you love him yet?"

"No."

"Oh my god, it's taking you forever!" she whines.

"Hush, you." I wiggle myself out of her hold and get off her bed. "Let me get you some water."

"You're the best!" Bree beams and continues to talk as I go to the fridge. "I didn't mean to get this wasted, but then we started celebrating, so I said fuck it."

"Celebrating what?" I twist the cap off the water bottle and help her drink it.

Once she's done, she answers, "My friend Tamara got an internship, and I applied for one on a whim." She gasps again. "It's nearby, so if I get it, we can hang out this summer whenever you're not rolling around in bed with Mateo."

I chuckle. "That sounds like the perfect summer."

"You should apply for an internship too. Then we can celebrate and smoke together."

"I don't smoke."

"Oh shit, I forgot. We can drink together!"

"I'm not really in the mood to drink."

"We can go streaking then—whatever!" She throws her arms up in the air. "Just do it!"

My laughter continues to build. "Bree, I don't have any internships to apply to, but we can celebrate something else another night."

"You don't know of *any* internships? Miss France philosophy girl doesn't have any internships to apply to?"

My mind flickers to the night with Hunter when we went to the alumni dinner, and that man, Hank, handed me his card. "Actually," I say, getting up and marching to my desk. I open up the bottom drawer and pull out the business card. "There is one."

"Do it!" Bree claps.

"Not now, it's late."

"Um…hi, Ellie, the internet exists in the nighttime too."

"You're sassy tonight," I joke.

"And you're celebrating with me tonight!"

I glance down at Hank's email address. I don't know if he'll offer it to me if I'm not connected to Hunter anymore, but there's no harm in trying. It would be an incredible opportunity if I did get it, and hopefully, I'll get my name out to other nonprofits in the area. It would be nice to forge a path for myself. As much as I love Mateo, I don't want my entire life to revolve around him. I want to go out and start doing things by myself, for myself.

"Come on, Ellie. What's stopping you?"

Independence strikes my core as I stand up straighter. "Absolutely nothing."

Within twenty-four hours of sending the email, I got a response from Hank setting up an interview.

ME

internship interview scheduled for the end of the month!

MATEO

fuck yeah, that's my girl!

A swirling sensation of nervous jitters swims through me.

What kind of questions will Hank ask me? What do I wear? Should I bring anything with me?

All these questions bombard my brain as I make my way to meet up with Ava for lunch. As I travel through campus, passing newly blossomed flowers, I spot her in a pastel dress and denim jacket right outside the doors of the university cafeteria. The second I see who she's talking with—Derek—I jump behind the nearest tree.

I'm sure I looked ridiculous to anyone who just witnessed me hide, but I know that the frat brothers tend to travel in packs, so when there's one, another one is bound to show up.

Poking my head out from around the trunk, bile rises to my throat when I spot Hunter walking up to Ava and Derek. He has his arms looped around the waists of two girls who are giggling at whatever the hell he's saying.

Realization hits me. That's why he hasn't bothered to drag me back into his life. He can't screw his way through campus if I'm glued to his side. He's also enjoying the freedom.

I've never been so happy to be so disgusted in my entire life.

My shoulders soften in relief as I watch them from afar, still hiding behind the budding green leaves. Even though I'm pretty certain Hunter is over keeping me captive and punishing Mateo, I still don't want to risk it with only a few more weeks left.

When they finally leave, Ava goes into the cafeteria, and I make sure the coast is clear before I enter. After grabbing my food, I head to the table she's sitting at and see her laughing at something on her phone.

"What's so funny?" I ask, taking a seat.

"Hunter just airdropped me a few pictures from spring break, and we all look horrendously shit-faced." Ava spins her phone toward me, and she's right. They do look disastrous.

She lets me scroll through, and I can't help but notice Hunter is with a different half-naked girl in every single picture.

Another round of relief lets my muscles ease.

"I really wish you would've gone to Cancun with us. It was amazing," Ava says, taking her phone back once I'm done looking.

"I had a great time staying here," I say, taking a bite of my panini.

"Really?" Her face scrunches. "What did you do that was better than being in Mexico?" A smile tugs at my lips, and she gasps. "You were with a guy!" I try to force my mouth into a straight line, but it doesn't work. "Oh my god! Who?"

I start to tell her about Mateo, but the words clog my throat, still scared there's going to be some type of repercussion from Hunter if he finds out. Ava is getting closer to all the brothers, and I can't chance her accidentally slipping up and saying something.

"Just…some guy," I say.

She leans across the table and wiggles my arm. "Come on. Tell me!"

"I'll tell you at the end of the semester."

Ava's brows draw in. "The end of the semester? Why?"

"Because that's when it'll be safe to tell you," I answer, and she tilts her head to the side. "I mean, if we're still together by then, then it feels like we're in the clear, and I can tell people about us."

"Oh, okay. You don't want people knowing until it's a sure thing?"

I nod. "Something like that."

She goes back to picking at her lackluster salad the university supplies and tells me about the parties with the frat boys. As she goes on to tell me stories about the past weeks, I grow more grateful for the fact that I left that life behind. I can't even bear to hear some of the things she's describing.

"But enough about me," Ava says, then shoves a piece of lettuce into her mouth. "What's going on in your life? You must be able to tell me something that doesn't involve mystery boy."

"Um…I applied for an internship." I shrug.

"No way. To where?"

"When I went to that alumni dinner with Hunter, I met this man—"

"Hank?"

I pause. "Yeah…"

"Oh." She places her fork down on the table. "Me too."

Fuck. The one downfall to befriending someone in the same program is that one day we'll be out in the real world competing for careers. Or in the case right now—internships.

"Maybe there'll be two positions open," I say.

Ava forces a smile that makes my stomach twist. "Maybe."

CHAPTER ONE HUNDRED FOURTEEN

Mateo

My supervisor, Dominique, is letting me leave a little early from the foster agency so I can drive Elle to her interview. I know she's nervous about it, so I offered to give her a ride instead of having her take the bus and adding that into the anxious mix.

Dominique was fine about me cutting out before my shift ended, encouraging me to take breaks whenever possible because this work can be so draining. She even went on to say that I'm doing a "wonderful job" and I am "gelling well with all the kids—including the tough ones."

Pride lit up my insides because I feel like I'm actually able to do this. It's all falling into place, just like Mr. Kevin said it would. The reflection of how much I've grown was right there earlier today when I got one of the "tough kids" to open up about what's really going on in his home. I know how to reach kids like him because I used to be labeled the same, and I know what they need the most. If there's one good thing from my past, it's that I'm able to use it to make an impact on others.

And no one can take that away from me, not even stupid fucking impostor syndrome. I can't even begin to describe what it was like hearing Mom tell me she was proud of me a few weeks ago. I know I wasn't the easiest kid to raise, and I don't blame her for keeping certain walls up. Thankfully, she's always been able to show me her love in other ways, but hearing those words come out of her was so fulfilling. And it's been further confirmation that I'm going down the right path.

Elle steps out of the office building where she just had her interview with some guy named Hank, looking beautiful in a colorful spring dress. She spots my car and dashes over to me. Her golden hair wisps around in the breeze, and the huge smile on her face lets me know the interview went well.

"Hi!" She beams as she sits down in the passenger seat.

"How'd it go?" I ask, already assuming the answer.

"Incredible! You know how I was freaking out before I went in?" she asks, and I nod. "Well, once the interview started, I loosened up and was able to have a real conversation about what I'm passionate about. Don't get me wrong. I was still super nervous, but I didn't mess this up. I sounded intelligent and like I knew what the hell I was talking about."

"Because you do."

"I know! As I was talking to Hank, it was like I popped out of my body for a second and listened to what I was saying, and I sounded legit."

I laugh at her sudden realization about herself that I've known for over a year.

"He wants me to email him a writing sample by the end of the week. He said any of my past papers will work. Could you look over some of them and help me pick the best one to give him?"

"Of course." I clasp my hand around hers. "I'm proud of you, baby."

She lifts her chin. "I'm proud of me too."

Leaning over, I place a delicate kiss on her soft lips, and she gently hums against mine. When I pull back, the sun reflects the varying shades of green in her eyes, and I notice specs of gold that I've never seen before.

I should spit it out already and tell her that I'm in love with her, but I'm holding out for the plan I have in my head. I'll take her out for dinner after she gets the news that she got the internship—because she *will* get it—then we'll go for a drive down to the arboretum I took her to last year. We won't be able to get in that late at night, but we can sit on the hood of my car and watch the stars. And when the perfect moment strikes, I'll tell her.

If she doesn't feel the same, then it is what it is. I've waited long enough. I don't want to keep this inside anymore.

"Where to now?" she asks.

"You tell me."

"Food. I'm starving. I've been a nervous wreck all day and couldn't eat anything."

"Let's go." I turn my key in the ignition.

"But," she says, stopping me. "Can I drive? I want to start practicing for my road test."

My cheeks rise as I smile at her. "You got it."

We hang out at the restaurant for a while after we finish our meal. We're in no rush to go anywhere, so we stayed and talked. Once night hits, we decide to head back to her dorm.

"Are you sleeping over?" Elle asks.

"I wish I could, but I have a paper I need to work on," I tell her from the driver's seat. I chose to drive back since the restaurant we went to was almost a half hour away.

"Are you sure?" She pouts.

I chuckle. "Yes, I'm sure. Unless you want to take it up with my professor."

"Do you think she'll give you an extension if I tell her you were too busy fucking me all night?"

My eyebrows shoot up, and I glance over to her, the little dimple on the side of her cheek popping out. "Is that the only reason you wanted me to sleep over?"

"Yep. I'm only using you for rides and sex."

"Well, then I'm glad to be of service." I place my hand on her bare thigh, giving it a squeeze. Sliding my hand up her leg, I gently massage her while my other hand grips the steering wheel. Her skin is silky smooth against my rough palm as I continue upward. I'm waiting for her to swat me away, but she doesn't. My pulse quickens, wondering how far she'll let me go. Eager for the challenge, my fingertips carefully push her dress out of the way.

Elle leans her back against the seat of the car and slowly parts her legs open.

Blood instantly rushes to my cock, and I lose all concentration on the road in front of me.

I run a finger over her thong, grazing over a damp spot. "Oh."

"What?" she asks.

"Didn't realize how serious you were when you said you wanted me to fuck you all night," I say, rubbing over the fabric. "You've been thinking about that for a while?" I glance over at her, and she nods. "How long?"

"All throughout dinner," she replies, her breath getting shallower.

"Huh." I take my hand away, placing it on her thigh as a way to tease her, and she groans in frustration. My dick is doing all the thinking now, and it's a miracle I'm not swerving all over the road. "Tell me what you were imagining at dinner."

"Just you, doing stuff…" Elle shifts her attention out the passenger seat window.

"No way. You're not playing shy with me. I know how fucking dirty you are."

She giggles, and I know I'm getting somewhere, even if she won't tell me her filthiest fantasies, which I know she has.

"I was thinking about that one time in your office," she says, her voice getting raspy, the sound sending sparks of heat down my spine.

I work my fingers up her dress once more, keeping my eyes on the cars around me. "You mean the first time I ever bent you over and fucked you from behind?" I see another nod out of my peripheral.

Twisting my arm, I sneak my fingers into her panties, shoving the lace out of the way. She gasps as soon as I connect with her, as if she wasn't expecting me to go this far.

"Is that what you were hoping for tonight, Elena?" A moan slips from her gorgeous lips. "You didn't answer my question," I press.

"Yes," she answers, widening her legs for me.

Sitting forward to touch her at a better angle, my hand tightens around the wheel while the other makes circles around her clit.

"Mateo." She says my name in a whisper, and I catch a glimpse of her grabbing hold of the seat as her body begins to tense up.

I speed down the parkway, needing to get her in a bed immediately. I don't care who's fucking bed at this point, as long as I'm burying myself inside her.

One of her hands wraps around my arm that I'm practically snapping in half in order to get her off. I move my fingers over her faster and faster until I hear her sweet sighs drip from her mouth.

Glancing over at her, I see the straps of her dress slipping down her shoulders, exposing her bra. My cock throbs against the zipper of my jeans, and I bite down on my lip, mesmerized by how sexy Elle looks. My eyes move back and forth between her and the road.

The amount of trust this woman has in me is insane.

"Oh my god," she cries out while pressing her nails into my inked skin.

"Fuck this," I say, pulling my hand out of her thong. I turn off at the nearest exit, only a few stops away from school.

"What's wrong?" she asks, puzzled.

"You're about to make me come in my pants," I say, and hear her chuckle.

I make a few quick turns, and if I remember correctly, there should be a park at the end of the block on the next left.

As soon as I make the turn, I spot the dimly lit park and travel down the road as quickly as possible. Pulling into the empty parking lot, I find a spot far away from the lights and the soccer field, just in case there are any random stragglers hanging out.

"What are we doing?" Elle gives me a look of confusion as I take the key out of the ignition.

"Get out of the car," I say, my voice dropping in pitch.

Rounding my car to the passenger side, I greet her as she shuts her door. My heart is about to jump out of my chest as I push her up against the cool metal. Her breath hitches, and her eyes grow wide, right before she grabs my face and pulls me into her, her tongue already in my mouth before I can blink.

My hands run down her body, hiking her dress up higher. I move my mouth away from hers and kiss along her jawline until I reach her ear. "Take off your thong."

I take a step back, and our eyes lock as she reaches under the fabric of her dress and exposes the purple lace panties. Taking her thumb, she pulls them off her hips. They hug her thighs, and she shimmies her legs until they drop past her calves, landing on the dirty blacktop.

Her eyes don't leave mine as she carefully steps out of them. I wet my lips and kneel down in front of her, picking her panties up and stuffing them into my pocket.

"Tell me what you want," I say, lifting her right leg over my shoulder.

"You," she answers, her voice breathy.

"What do you want from me?" I kiss the inside of her thigh and notice the blanket of goose bumps rising on her flesh.

"Your mouth."

"Where? Here?" I kiss her thigh again, and she groans. I chuckle, knowing that she'd rather be tortured than say the words "lick my pussy." Unless she's drunk, then all bets are off. Because I'm about to explode, I do us both the favor and choose not to drag this out any longer.

Leaning forward, I swipe my tongue along her clit. Elle's hand clutches a lock of my hair as she pushes me closer to her. Her breathing is ragged, and I can sense that I found a good rhythm for her.

I slip two fingers inside her, and she lets out a loud moan. My eyes dart up to look at her.

"Shit," Elle tries to whisper. "I'm not good at being quiet."

She presses her lips together as I continue to move my fingers in and out of her. Pulling my mouth away, I watch her reaction to make sure she's okay as I push in a third. Her hands slam against the car door, causing it to echo in the empty lot.

"You like when I stretch you like this, baby?"

Elle nods, unable to answer because if she were to loosen her jaw, she'd let the whole neighborhood know she's about to come.

Curling my three fingers inside her, I move at a harsh pace, the sound of her arousal only making me work her harder. She moves her hips with me, her chest heaving as she gets closer. The straps of her dress fall down to her shoulder once more, and if it was possible for me to fall in love with her all over again, I think I just did from the sight of her being on the brink of pure ecstasy.

"You're so fucking good at being dirty for me, Elle."

A high-pitched noise comes from behind her lips at the sound of my praise, and she brings her hands to my head, shoving my mouth back to where it was.

Chuckling, I do what she asks for and begin sucking on her clit, my fingers still moving inside her. Her legs shake, and I know she's seconds away. So am I.

Her pussy spasms around me, and her whimpers get faster and louder. Heat spirals around my bones as I work her harder. Sharper. Stronger.

Elle's entire body shudders like it never has before, and a burst of liquid rushes down my hand and onto my wrist while she gasps.

Fuck. Yes.

"What was that?" Elle asks as I move her leg off my shoulder and place it back on the ground.

"You squirted," I say, rising and wiping my face.

She looks horrified. "I *what*?"

Without answering, I shuffle her over to the front of my car because if I'm not inside her right now, my cock is gonna combust. I do a quick scan of the parking lot before turning her away from me, bending her over the hood, and flipping up her dress.

My heart rate skyrockets as I get the perfect view of her from behind. "Fuck, I want you so bad," I say, fumbling with the button and zipper of my jeans.

Elle glances over her shoulder. "Then what's taking you so long?"

I give her ass a slap, and she lets out a thick, sultry sound. I do it again, this time hard enough that she'll be riding back to campus with my handprint on her ass cheek.

Without any warning, I push myself into her warm pussy. My hands immediately grip her hips, and I thrust in and out of her while she tries to keep quiet.

Elle pushes back into me, and my eyebrow arches. "You want more?"

She nods, and I do what she asks, pounding into her faster, my dick slamming up against her walls. With one hand on her hip, my other reaches forward, taking a fistful of her golden hair, long strands knotting around my knuckles. Loud moans fall from her lips, and neither of us gives a shit about getting caught as we get lost in the most mind-blowing sex.

I thrust even harder, and she moves her body in sync with mine. Fire radiates from the base of my spine. My muscles seize up, and pleasure ignites in my veins.

With one last movement, I release my grasp on her and pull out just in time.

We're both still for a moment, catching our breath.

While I zip my jeans back up, Elle lazily stands and spins to face me. "I think that'll suffice for the night."

"Glad I could hold you over." I give her a peck and walk her over to the car door, opening it for her.

She holds out her hand. "Aren't you forgetting something?"

"What?"

"I need my underwear."

I wink. "No, you don't."

CHAPTER ONE HUNDRED FIFTEEN

Ellie

MAY

It's May.

I've made it to May!

If I could do cartwheels, I'd be doing them all over the fucking campus! I have mere days left until I'm free from the fear of Hunter.

It's all I can think about as I sit in my last philosophy class of the year, excitement and pure joy fluttering in my heart.

I barely realize class has ended, if it wasn't for Ava talking to me while she stands up. "Do you know what's up with Hunter?"

I do an internal eye roll at the mention of his name. "No, why?"

"Derek was telling me he had to go back home for a couple of days because some shit went down at his house. I thought you might have the inside scoop."

"No, I don't. Sorry." Worry prickles under my skin at what might have happened in the house that I had once assumed sheltered the picture-perfect family. But Hunter is no longer my problem.

Ava shrugs. "I heard he came back today, so I guess everything's fine." She closes her bag and changes the subject. "How did your interview with Hank go?"

"It went really well," I say, slipping my laptop into my bag. "How about yours?"

"Mine is tomorrow."

The two of us walk out of the building, squinting when we step into the sun. The warm air is a reminder that the end of the year is right around the corner, and I can almost taste the sense of final liberation from the thoughts of Hunter retaliating on my lips.

"I'm meeting up with Derek for lunch. Want to join?" Ava asks.

Just as I open my mouth to answer, Mateo steps into my line of vision.

"Hey, baby." The sound of his voice and his overall presence usually excite me, but I can't risk Ava saying anything about him when she goes to the frat house later.

"Baby?" Ava lifts her eyebrow at me.

"Hi…hey…what are you doing here?" I ask him.

"I met up with Rebecca to go over something for our final, and I didn't need to go into the foster agency today, so I figured I'd surprise you."

"Oh."

Confusion crosses his face. "Is that okay?"

"Yes, of course." I look at Ava. "We'll have to rain check."

"If you have plans, I can come back later tonight," Mateo offers.

"We were going to meet up with my boyfriend for lunch. You can come with. I'm Ava, by the way." She extends her hand, and he shakes it.

"Mateo."

"Mateo?" Ava looks at me, probably piecing together that this was the guy I cried to her about while we lived together in France.

"Is something wrong?" He glances at me, then back to her.

"No, I just heard your name a lot over the summer," she assures him before turning to me. "So *this* is your mystery man."

My cheeks get hot, and I rack my brain for something to say so it doesn't get back to Hunter but also doesn't fuck things up with Mateo.

"Ava was my roommate in France," is the best I can come up with, hoping that it shifts gears a little.

Mateo smiles. "Nice to meet you."

Ava starts to speak, but I interject, "I actually have to go back to my room and email Hank something. We'll go out another day."

"Okay. All four of us!" Ava says.

"Sure."

Picking up my pace, Mateo and I speed walk to my dorm. Fear runs down my limbs, suddenly concerned that we'll cross paths with Hunter.

"Ava seems cool," Mateo says when we finally get into my room.

"Yeah, she is."

"I should've recognized her from the picture." He points to the one of her and me with our champagne flutes, hanging on my wall. "But to be honest, I was always paying attention to the other girl." He winks, stepping out of his sneakers and sitting on my bed.

The second I see him getting comfortable on my mattress, my mind flips to somewhere else. Checking the clock on the desk, I calculate how much time we have before Bree comes back from her class. We've got hours.

I move to the door and lock it, just in case she comes back early.

"Want me to look at your papers so I can help you pick one to send to Hank?"

Oh shit, I forgot all about that the moment Mateo touched my sheets. I'm still on a sex high from what happened in the parking lot the other night.

"Yes, please." I take my laptop out of my bag and open up three papers for Mateo to look at, one of them being my final from last year—the one I wrote about him. "Read this one first." I hand him my computer, and he places it on his lap.

"Intro to Philosophy Final," he states with a smile.

Looking away so I don't stare at him while he critiques my work, I try to focus on something else to do. Deciding to write in my journal since I haven't had a chance to do that after my last session with Panavi, I open up my drawer and grab it.

I take the pen to paper and let my latest thoughts out while Mateo continues to read my work. The words easily fall onto the paper, and my web of messy thoughts slowly untangles with each strike of my pen.

This has become my secondary form of therapy these past several months. Nothing feels as relieving as when I can get everything out on paper. Even if it doesn't make sense, it takes up less space in my head and allows me to breathe every now and again.

"Wow." Mateo's voice startles me, causing me to jolt.

"What?"

"'Can our songs harmoniously intertwine, as if our souls already know which part to play?'" he recites a line from my final.

I place my pen down, unsure of his reaction. "Yeah?"

"Elle, you can write."

"I enjoy it sometimes."

"No, I mean you can *write*." He puts the laptop to the side. "This is one of the best things I've ever read, and it's a fucking final."

"You're just saying that because you're my boyfriend."

"I'm not obligated to say shit." Mateo leans across my bed and reaches for my hand, tugging me toward him.

I get up off my chair and move to straddle him. "You sure you're not saying nice stuff just so you can get lucky?"

"I already am lucky." He brushes my hair away from my face.

As he drags his fingertips over my cheekbones, I notice his breath shaking. "You okay?" I ask, paying attention to how his pupils dilate as they study me.

"I..." He wets his dry lips. If I didn't know better, I'd say that he's nervous—*really* nervous. "I wanted to tell you something, but I was going to wait until..."

"What is it?" My back straightens.

His mouth parts, but nothing comes out.

My stomach drops.

Oh god. He cheated. Or he's dying. Or he—

My focus suddenly goes to the opposite end of the room as the door handle jiggles, and the sound of Bree pushing her key into the knob has me adjusting my position.

The door flies open, and all the blood drains from my face.

I jump to my feet. "Hunter?"

Those blue eyes puncture a hole straight through me as he stares at me and then glances over to Mateo, who's now standing next to me.

My heart sledgehammers against my chest.

My toes and fingers instantly go numb as my vision gets spotty.

He has my fucking key. How could I forget he still has my key!

Anxiety builds inside me until I'm vibrating with panic.

They both look at each other and then to me, waiting for an answer as to why the other is here.

My brain freezes. It's completely fucking blank as I scramble for words.

"Um..." The only sound that comes from my mouth.

Hunter lets out a malicious laugh. "I should've known," he says to me. "You can thank your little friend Ava for the heads-up." Then he faces Mateo. "Just so you know, I fucked her on those sheets you were sitting on."

"Hunter!" My voice gets shrill as air is forced out of my lungs. He backs out of my room, and I chase after him. "Hunter, wait!"

"Elena," Mateo strains to say, following behind me.

"Mateo, stay here." I put my hands up to stop him from moving any farther, then spin back around to run after Hunter as he makes his way down the stairs. "Don't come after me, please. I'll be right back, I swear," I shout over my shoulder to Mateo.

Rushing out of the building, I spot Hunter striding toward the parking lot. "Hunter!" I call after him, but he ignores me. "You can't do that. You can't just barge into my room like that." My feet move faster as I catch up to him, getting right behind him. "I'll fucking report you for having my key!"

Hunter messes with his key ring, then looks over his shoulder and says, "Take it. I got everything I needed." He flings the key in my direction, and it skids against the blacktop.

I'm quick to snatch it up, shoving it in my pocket, then pick up my pace as he gets closer to his car. "Hunter!" I latch on to his arm. "Hunter, please," I say, out of breath. "I thought our agreement was over back in February, when we talked outside on the bench."

"Oh, we're far from over, Ellie."

Knives are stabbing my stomach over and over again. "What does that mean?" I ask. He doesn't respond and keeps moving forward. I follow him until we reach his Lexus. "Please don't do anything to Mateo."

Hunter opens his car door but hesitates before getting in. He pivots to look at me. "He's not the one you have to worry about anymore, Elena."

"I…what?"

"I told you that you'd regret leaving me." Hunter gets in his car as I stand there, confused. He backs out and drives off.

His words, mimicking the night I thought I ended things with him, sends a shiver throughout my body.

"Don't do this, Elena. You're going to regret it."

It wasn't a plea to get me back.

It was a threat.

My lungs twist, and my legs wobble as I dash upstairs to my dorm room. When I enter, Mateo is furiously pacing back and forth with his fists balled and jaw set. He snaps his head in my direction at the sound of my footsteps.

"What's going on?" he asks. The anger shooting out of him is enough to slice through my bones.

"It's not what it seems like. I can explain everything." I inch closer. "I just need to talk to Hunter first."

"Talk to him about what?"

"He said something outside that confused me, and I need to figure out what he means before I—"

"You promised me you'd be honest with me."

"I will. I am." I grip his shirt. "I swear I am—"

"Did you sleep with him?"

I stare up at him, unable to find it in me to answer his question. Through the tears that are forming in my eyes, I'm able to see the crushed expression on his face.

"Christ," Mateo says, backing away from me. He runs his hands over his face. "When?"

"December." I notice his shoulders soften as he nods, realizing it was before he and I got together. "It was one time," I continue to speak even though my voice cracks and salty tears trickle down to my neck. "And I've regretted it ever since. I'm sorry."

"I don't need an apology." He takes a deep breath, struggling to regain his composure. "We weren't even together then. It's not like I was a saint."

His blunt honesty makes more tears bubble to the surface, but I do my best to wipe them away as quickly as possible. Feeling nauseous at the thought of how many people he slept with after we broke up, I wrap my arms around my stomach.

"But I told you about my hookups. You conveniently left this out," Mateo adds.

"You only told me about Jasmine."

"Because that's all there was," he says, and I give him a look of disbelief. "What?"

"I'm not stupid, Mateo. I know there was more than just her. I saw you about to get with that girl."

"What girl?"

"The one from your class. With the red hair."

"Rebecca?"

"I think that was her name."

"I was never fucking Rebecca! I never got with her or anyone else aside from Jasmine. Why don't you believe me?"

"Because!" I throw my arms up. "I'm used to being lied to and getting hurt!"

"Then why the *hell* did you choose to get back with the person who kept fucking with you?"

"It's complicated."

"No." Mateo shakes his head. "That's a fucking cop-out. I need an answer. I need to know why he was here. There's something you're not telling me, Elena."

"There is. And I promise that once I figure everything out, I'll tell you."

"I'm not putting my heart on the line again if he's going to be in the way. I told you if you wanted out to just tell me, and I'll leave."

"That's the last thing I want!" Desperate, I run up and hug him, my tears staining his shirt as I cry into his chest. He wraps his arms around me, but it's not a soft and tender hold like he normally does.

We stay like this for several minutes. The sound of my sobs is muffled against his body until my crying finally slows down.

Mateo moves his arms to his back and unlinks my hands from around him. "I need to go to work."

I sniffle, trying to steady my breathing. "Okay."

His brown eyes fixate on me, a wave of uncertainty behind them. The urge to wash away any of the awful emotions he's experiencing builds inside me. But I know that they might never go away after I tell him everything.

Mateo glances at my bed and then back over to me. Without saying a word, he places a kiss on my forehead and goes to leave.

"Mateo," I say, halting him. "What was it you wanted to say to me earlier?" I ask, praying that maybe it's on the same level of what I have to tell him, and maybe we can call our past offenses even.

"It was nothing."

The door closes, and even though a million emotions are swirling around my head and heart, I move right into action. Calling Hunter over and over again only to get his voicemail every single time. My fingers shake as I go to text him.

ME

answer me

what did you mean that we're far from over?

we ARE over. This is done with. I made that clear months ago

you can't keep threatening me

you don't fucking scare me, Hunter.

The tightness claiming my chest and the sea of anxiety in my stomach tell me something different from the last text I sent him.

Still being ignored, I throw my phone onto my bed. My hands grip the roots of my hair, pulling, wanting to yank out all the horrible thoughts. All the what-ifs are slamming into every surface of my brain. I don't care what Hunter does to me, but I can't have him hurting Mateo.

Think of something, Elle. Think!

After walking across the length of my dorm about a hundred times, an idea sparks. Rushing to my phone, I scroll through every single text Hunter and I have, screenshotting anything that could possibly come across as abusive or threatening. Then I move to my journal and take pictures of every dated entry that might showcase the same. After that, I write down a massive list of every single thing I can think of that Hunter has done to me.

This is the best thing I can come up with. If Hunter presses charges against Mateo, I'll stand right next to Mateo's side and show the judge what has been going on, and maybe, *maybe* that'll be enough.

Now I just need to tell Mateo everything and hope he doesn't hate me for it.

CHAPTER ONE HUNDRED SIXTEEN

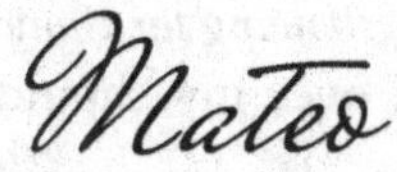

Tío Edgar comes into the back office of the Cozy Nook. I've been sitting in here for most of my shift, needing to cool the fuck off from what just went down in Elle's dorm. "You got the schedule out for next week?" he asks.

"Working on it," I answer, looking at the computer screen and not him.

"All right. Well, hurry up. I needed it an hour ago."

"Sorry. Just have a lot on my mind."

"Ah." He takes a seat on the nearby stool. "Does any of it happen to be about a pretty blonde who works in the bookstore?"

"And her douchebag ex."

"Who's her ex?"

"Some white frat boy."

Edgar breaks out into a boisterous laugh. "I guess she doesn't have a type, considering you were her next pick."

I scowl at him, then go back to staring at the computer screen.

"Listen, I'm not the one to talk to about relationships, but I *will* tell you not to do something stupid to fuck it up with her. The girl is the best thing that's ever happened to you, Mateo."

"Yeah. I know."

He stands up and starts to make his way out of the office, but then stops in the doorway. "But also, don't let anyone mess with her."

Yeah. I know that too. And I can't suppress this nagging feeling telling me that she is, in fact, being messed with. If she won't tell me the details, then I'll just have to figure it out myself and take matters into my own hands.

We had a mad rush, and Lynn ended up needing me up front for the past hour. It's finally calming down, so I'm able to refill some of the flavor bottles. With my back to the door, I switch out the giant containers of sweeteners while Lynn stands by the register waiting for the next person to walk in, which someone does a second later.

"How can I help you?" Lynn asks.

"Americano," a voice says, causing me to freeze.

There's no way this fucker is showing up at my job.

I cautiously turn to look over my shoulder to see if I'm hearing the voice correctly.

"That'll be four dollars," Lynn says.

"Your manager's got it. He owes me," Hunter says, his eyes drifting over to mine with a smug ass look on his face.

Lynn glances at me and then goes to make the asshole's drink.

"What the fuck are you talking about?" I ask, approaching the counter and silently thanking the universe for the extra distance between us.

Hunter doesn't answer me. He just smirks while he waits for his drink. We have a stare-off as I wait for some sort of response to come out of his mouth.

"Um..." Lynn appears next to me with the coffee in her hand, looking unsure if she should give it to him or not.

I hold up a hand, informing her to hold off. "I asked you what you meant by that," I say to him.

"Ellie didn't tell you?" Hunter baits me, and I fucking take it.

"Tell me what?"

"The court takes out fees when you post bail for someone."

My stomach drops.

Hunter motions at Lynn with two fingers for his drink, and she glances to me again, but I can't give her an answer on what to do because I'm fucking paralyzed. *He* posted my bail?

Lynn slides the drink across the counter. He picks it up and sips on it. "Thanks," he says, obviously pleased by my reaction.

The moment the door closes behind him, I get my ass into gear.

"I gotta go," I tell Lynn.

"What? You have to close."

I shake my head and take my work keys off my key ring and toss them to her. "You know how to lock up. I need to take care of something."

I continuously knock on her door. "Elena?"

She opens it with her brow furrowed. "Aren't you supposed to be at work for another—"

"I need to talk to you." I burst into her room.

"Is everything okay?"

My breathing picks up, not wanting to ask the question that I know I have to. "Who posted my bail?"

Her face turns white. Well, whiter than it usually is.

"Elena," I press.

"W-why are you asking that question?"

Shit. My head drops down. The avoidance of the answer *is* the answer.

After staring at the floor to calm my reaction to whatever else is about to fly out of her mouth, I force myself to look up at her. She's anxiously twirling the necklace she's wearing around her fingers, and her eyes are glassy. I step in closer, and her shoulders become rigid.

"Who posted my bail?"

She swallows. "He did."

Every cell in my body tenses. "Why?"

"Because I asked him to."

"Why?"

"I didn't want it to ruin your chance to pursue your dreams, so we made an arrangement, and he posted bail and dropped the charges."

"What type of arrangement?"

"What?"

"You just said you made an arrangement. What was your end of the deal?"

Tears spill over and cascade down her face. Her gorgeous eyes look at me, devastated and regretful.

And that's when everything clicks.

"No," I choke out, not willing to believe what she's silently telling me.

She lets out a sob. "I told you I never meant any of those horrible things I said to you when I broke it off."

"Holy shit." I back away, needing some space…or air because I suddenly can't fucking breathe.

She stands there, shaking and taking short inhales. I'm sure she's on the verge of a panic attack, but the white-hot anger pumping out of my heart is making it difficult to think of anything aside from the question, "Why the *fuck* would you do that?"

"I was protecting you."

"I don't need your protection!" My voice strains, struggling not to yell. I sense the veins in my neck popping out the more I suppress the inferno fueled by rage that is blazing inside me.

Her face twists, automatically on the defensive. "Well, I didn't need yours the night you beat the shit out of Hunter!"

"Do not start with that."

"Start with what?" She zeros in on me, and even looking utterly hopeless with a stream of sadness running down her cheeks, she gets in my face. "Huh? Tell me! What shouldn't I start with?"

"Comparing what we did. It was completely different."

"How?" She throws her arms up.

"The intention behind protecting each other isn't the same."

"No, I think it was pretty clear to everyone what your intention was that night."

"That's not what I mean."

"No? Then what do you mean?" she asks with the biggest fucking attitude.

"Nothing." I attempt to take a step back, but she's in my face again.

"No, tell me."

"No."

"We were both protecting each other. Why is yours different? Because you're a guy?"

"No, it's not because I'm a—"

"I never thought of you as the misogynist type."

"I'm not—"

"Yet here you are saying that you can protect me because you've got a dick, and I can't protect you because—"

"That's not what I'm saying at all."

"What are you saying?" She tries to catch my line of sight, but I look away. What I want to say is burning the tip of my tongue as my heart starts a riot in my chest.

"Mateo!" Her fury is becoming dangerously close to pushing me over the edge.

"Tell me!" It builds inside me, physically hurting my bones and joints to keep it inside. Ready to explode into a billion pieces. "What makes our protection different?"

"Because I love you!"

Fuck.

All the air drains out of my lungs as she steps back, her eyes wide.

"You…" She studies me before wetting her lips. "You love me?"

"Yeah." I shut my eyes.

I fucked this up. This is not how it was supposed to go. This was not the reaction she was supposed to have…the one that I was scared of.

"I love you too."

My eyes pop open. "What?"

"I love you," Elle repeats.

We stand a foot apart from each other, staring at one another, the air between us shifting, thickening, and becoming lighter all at once. Something I've never felt roots in my body, a tingling sensation bursting out of my nerves. A warmth in my chest expands until I'm flooded by an overwhelming awareness of being loved by her.

Elle smiles through her tears, and she glows. She literally fucking glows as if the sun is radiating through her.

She closes the gap between us.

There's a prickle in my eyes, and I attempt to blink away the wetness, but she catches it, bringing her thumb up to my cheek. I finally am able to move, and I thread my fingers through her soft, golden hair, leaning down to give her the most meaningful kiss of my life. Giving her my all and taking in the same.

"I didn't think you could ever love me," she admits against my lips.

I draw my face back. "Why not?"

"Because I'm a mess."

"We're all messes."

"But I didn't think you could love *my* mess."

"I love every fucking thing about you, Elena."

"I love every fucking thing about you, Mateo."

CHAPTER ONE HUNDRED SEVENTEEN

Ellie

I'm dreaming.

I have to be.

This isn't real.

But Mateo's lips tell me otherwise, because he just told me that he loves me—twice.

Every fucking thing about me.

Our mouths meld together, and our tongues tangle around each other's. Our arms embrace our bodies, never wanting to let go, as our happy tears mix and run down into our kiss.

My heart expands in size, so much so that if it gets any bigger, it might just pop out of my body. It keeps growing as it fills with love. Not just any love, Mateo's.

A sudden strike of panic makes me abruptly pull back as I remember what brought us to this place to begin with. "What about Hunter? What if he—"

Mateo shakes his head. "We'll deal with him later. Please don't let him ruin this for us, Elle."

That's all I need to hear to get sucked back into the moment. I won't dare let Hunter take this away from me. He's already taken so much.

My lips land back on Mateo's. He runs his hands down my back until he plants them on my hips, and he gives me a squeeze. Without breaking our connection, his feet move forward, and mine move backward until I hit my bed.

Mateo gently pushes me back until I'm lying down. He moves his lips to my neck, moaning as he makes contact with my skin as if he hasn't kissed it a thousand times before.

The heat building in my core makes me run my fingers down to my pants, trying to shuffle out of them. Mateo takes my hands and holds them down on the bed.

"We don't need to rush. We have our whole lives, baby," he says as his fingertips sneak under my sweatshirt and shirt. He mindlessly traces lines on my stomach, letting goose bumps form under his touch.

My whole life with Mateo.

The thought of that relaxes my back into the mattress, and he picks up on my ease. "There you go," he responds to my body.

His callused fingers glide around me, and my hand glides through his thick hair. We kiss for what seems like hours, never wanting this moment to end.

Mateo slowly pushes my sweatshirt and shirt up over my head, and I toss them over to the side. He smiles before dipping his head and running his tongue next to the seam of the cup of my bra. I suck in a breath, pushing my chest farther into him. He moves over slightly so he can give my other breast the same teasing attention.

His large hand grazes against my side and sneaks its way under me. I arch my back so he can unclasp my bra. Mateo drags the straps down my arms, slow and steady, the thin fabric scraping against my skin. He takes his time while my hormones go haywire.

"Can I take my pants off now?" I ask out of desperation.

He chuckles. "No. I'm doing that."

And he does.

In the most torturous way.

Carefully. Tenderly. Leisurely.

What feels like a year later, I'm finally down to my panties, and he runs his big hand across the band. His eyes lazily look over every inch of me.

My cheeks heat up with how he's gazing at me, and of course, he notices.

"Why are you blushing, Elena?"

"Because you're looking at me like that." I nibble on my bottom lip.

"Like I love every part of you?"

Butterflies take flight, and my breath shakes as I nod my head.

Mateo doesn't respond back. Instead, he hooks his fingers into my lace underwear and delicately pulls it down until it hits my feet. Then he stands up and finishes the job by throwing it on the floor. He steps out of his shoes and unbuttons his pants.

"No." I push up onto my elbows. He freezes, and confusion appears on his face. "You don't get to do all of that to me without me being able to do it to you," I say, and he grins, settling onto the bed next to me.

I climb on top of him, straddling his hips, and his breathing accelerates while his eyes are all over my body, unsure of where to look first.

Taking my hands under his shirt, I sweep my nails over his chest as he takes in a sharp inhale. He presses the back of his head against the pillow and groans as I do it over and over again. Finally, I take the hem of his shirt up, and he helps me as I lift it over his head.

My fingertips dance around the images tattooed on his body, then over to the large, jagged scar on his upper arm. I bend down, bringing my lips to his uneven skin, acknowledging the stories of his past while honoring the man he is now.

Scooting down his body, he involuntarily jerks when I graze over his erection. I work his zipper quickly, because as much as I enjoy teasing him, I would enjoy him being inside of me a lot more.

In an attempt to be as smooth as him, I try to drag his jeans off him, but they're too stiff to move in a swift motion. "I'm not good at this part." I laugh, and so does he as he helps me take his pants off.

When I get him down to his boxers, I palm him through the fabric, and he curses under his breath. I eagerly pull them down and hover above him, ready to sink onto him.

But before I can, he flips me over. "Not yet." His cheeks rise.

"Just fuck me already!"

"I'm not going to fuck you, baby." His tongue flicks over my nipple, and my breath hitches. "I'm going to make love to you." He moves his lips down to my stomach, then to my hips.

"Mateo," I plead with him.

His brown eyes glance up at me. "Let me love you, Elena."

His words and tone of voice strike the center of my chest with affection and desire. I want nothing more than to let him love me—my body, my mind, my past, my soul. All the broken and ugly parts of myself that I hated for so long but am learning to embrace.

I want him to love me through my healing. And I'll love him through his.

I nod, allowing him to worship my body as he has so many times before. Only this time, it's different because now we're completely naked. There is no veil of fear or doubt stopping us from baring our hearts to each other.

Mateo parts my legs as he settles between them. His fingers easily slide inside me. He lets a small smile slip, and I know why. It's because he likes how ready I am for him.

He moves his head lower, and his mouth works with his fingers, coiling my insides. I tug at the roots of his hair, and that spurs him on, lapping up my desire for him.

Getting closer and closer to the edge, my legs tremble.

I cry out his name as my back arches off the bed, and the rest of me convulses under his tongue.

He lifts his head up to look at me, panting and boneless on my mattress.

"I love you," he whispers, climbing on top of me.

Opening my legs back up for him, Mateo pushes into me, and we both let out a moan.

"I love you," I reply.

Mateo brushes his lips against mine. Our breaths blend together as we sigh into each other's mouths. One of his hands slides down my body until he reaches my knee, and he hooks it around his back. I do the same with the other leg until we're fully wrapped around one another.

He thrusts slowly and deliberately. I move my hips to his motion, and we work together, in harmony, loving each other. Pushing himself slightly upward to look at me better, his gaze peers into mine, seeing my soul for all that it ever was and what it's capable of becoming one day.

The tiny hairs on my arms rise the more I allow myself to be taken over by him.

Mateo smiles as if he knows what's going on in my mind. He's quiet, though, not making those sexy comments like he normally does. This time is like our first time.

I suddenly gasp at the realization.

"What?" Mateo freezes.

"You were making love to me," I tell him. His brow furrows. "The first time we had sex…you were making love to me."

Mateo gives me a beautiful grin. "I've loved you for a long time, Elena." He dips down to kiss me.

I want to ask him for how long, and when he knew, and a million other questions, but I'm too lost in the sensations taking over.

Our bodies move faster, chasing the high towering inside of us. Mateo places kisses all over my face and neck as the two of us moan, creating the most perfect symphony.

His shoulders tense, and he slows down his pace until he finally stills.

Dropping his head into the crook of my neck, we both relax and embrace one another. His heart beats so hard I can feel it against my chest.

Our fingers interlock, and his thumb grazes over the back of my hand. No words are spoken, but we know what we're thinking.

We *know*.

CHAPTER ONE HUNDRED EIGHTEEN

Ellie

I'm floating. I must be, since I have no recollection of getting to Pavani's office. I've been going on and on about my magical night with Mateo yesterday as if she's one of my best friends. After all these months of working together, she might as well be.

I leave out the Hunter part because we haven't talked about him in quite some time. Mateo promised me that if anything does happen with him, we'll figure it out. Since there wasn't immediate retaliation on Hunter's part, I'm feeling more confident with Mateo's assurance.

Mateo's words from yesterday are still at the forefront of my mind. *"Don't let him ruin this for us."* So I refuse to give Hunter more power and have him take away the happiest feeling I've ever felt.

Ignoring the glaring issue, I continue to beam about the man of my dreams. "I can't believe I waited this long to tell him I love him. I would've told him a year ago if I knew this is how awesome it would feel."

Panavi grins. "Maybe the timing worked out how it should be. Who knows if you would've gone to therapy and done all this work on yourself if things panned out differently."

"You're so right." I nod. "I'm glad I've been coming here and was able to focus on myself before diving into this new level of our relationship."

"I'm so happy for you."

"Me too. And I'm not trying to sabotage my happiness. I'm allowing myself to feel this and be in this."

"And how is that for you?"

I draw in a big breath. "Scary. But so worth it."

Once my session is over, I walk outside, heading toward the Cozy Nook, still feeling like I'm traveling on clouds.

I catch Ava stepping out of one of the shops in town, and I give her a wave. "Hey!"

She gives me a halfhearted smile. "Hey, Ellie." She makes a curtain with her hair. My steps slow down.

"Everything okay?"

"I just got a phone call from Hank." Oh shit. I know what she's about to say. "I didn't get the internship."

I knew she didn't because Hank called me about two minutes ago, letting me know that I was accepted for the position. My day has been getting better and better. That is, until now, when my feet feel like they're landing on the ground, realizing that my friend is definitely not on my wavelength.

"I'm sorry, Ava. I'm sure you'll get another one."

"Yeah, probably. But that was the best one."

I search my brain for something comforting to say without blowing my cover that I took the position she's coveting.

"It's whatever," she says, shrugging it off. "I'll see you later. I have to head back to my room."

"Okay. I'll check in with you later."

Ava puts her hand up to her heart in appreciation, and then we part ways.

As I walk down the block, I push away any feelings of guilt for being offered the position. I hate that the guilt always makes an appearance, even when I receive something I'm deserving of. That's something I definitely need to continue to work on with Panavi.

Checking the time on my phone, I have some time before my shift, so I step into the coffee shop. My eyes go straight to the tall, tattooed man behind the counter, chatting it up with Lynn.

When he sees me, his entire face lights up. "Hi, my love," Mateo says as I approach the counter.

"Hi!" I get on my tippy toes and lean forward to give him a quick kiss before Edgar sees. "I have exciting news that I wanted to tell you in person."

"I have a feeling I know what it is."

"What is it then?" My hands go to my hips, playfully challenging him.

"You got the internship."

My jaw drops. "How did you know?"

"Because I know my girl, and I know you're good enough to get offered it."

Warmth bursts out of my heart. I am good enough, and it feels so amazing to believe that for maybe the first time in my entire life.

Mateo rounds the counter to embrace me. "I'm taking you out this weekend to celebrate," he says.

My cheeks lift up, the motion hurting my muscles because I've been smiling so much over the past twenty-four hours.

"Deal." My hands cup his face to kiss him, but we're interrupted.

"Ellie!" Edgar shouts from the bookstore.

"Guess my shift started," I say to Mateo, stepping out of his hold.

"Get to work." Mateo gives me a wink and smacks my ass as I walk past him.

"Mateo!" Edgar reprimands him, and I giggle.

I've been caught between daydream land and helping customers, neither of which gets my full attention because I keep staring at Mateo through the glass window. He should probably be in his office. I have a feeling he's been staying by the counter on purpose, just so we can steal glimpses of each other.

Resting my elbow on a book that's on the counter and placing my chin on the palm of my hand, my mind drifts off to thinking of my future. This internship could be a huge stepping-stone in my career. Maybe I'll stay in Connecticut after college. Or maybe I'll go slightly south and wind up in New York with a certain someone.

I hear someone enter, but my brain is too busy creating the endless possibilities that lie ahead of me to focus on the person walking in.

Until my vision is consumed by him.

My spine automatically straightens the second his blue eyes connect with mine.

Waves of anxiety crash into my stomach.

Hunter's smirk sends an icy sensation down my arms and legs.

He strolls past me without a word and goes down one of the aisles. My head immediately jerks to see if Mateo noticed Hunter walk in.

Yep, he did.

Mateo's eyes darken as he stares in the direction of where Hunter walked off.

My mouth gets dry as dread contaminates my once optimistic thoughts.

The thirty seconds it takes for Hunter to step out of the aisle drags out as I wait for something to happen. I watch as he carries a book in his hand, thinking he's going to come up to me and make a purchase with some type of snide remark. But he doesn't. He plops down on one of the chairs, crossing his ankle over his knee, and cracks open the book.

He's…reading?

Why?

My gaze drifts back over to Mateo, and his attention darts back and forth between Hunter and me.

Minutes tick by. Minutes of silence. Of nothingness.

Except for Hunter's presence, letting me know—letting *us* know—that he holds the power. The one thing he's always needed was control, even when life was spiraling and slipping through his fingers. He aimed for control in any way that he could. Namely, with me. Like what he's doing right now.

Swallowing down bile, I march up to him. "What are you doing here?"

Hunter slowly lifts his head. "Reading." He motions to the book in his hands.

"Why?"

"Is this not a bookstore? Is this not a chair for people to sit and read?"

"What do you want, Hunter?"

"I want to read."

"Read somewhere else!" I gesture at the exit.

"Are you kicking me out?"

"No, I—"

"Are you allowed to do that?"

"That's not what—"

"Should I call your boss—"

"Ellie?" Sandy thankfully makes an appearance before I begin yelling like a lunatic. "Can I have your help in the stockroom for a sec?"

"Sure," I say to her, scowling at Hunter as I pass by. His chuckle makes me ball my fists, but I keep walking.

"This way." Sandy puts her arm on my shoulder and nudges me in the direction of the coffee shop, nowhere in the direction of the storage room.

My brows wrinkle as she continues to hurry me into the corner, next to a tucked-away table and out of sight from Hunter. Mateo meets us there, and now I realize why I'm here and not in the back.

CHAPTER ONE HUNDRED NINETEEN

Mateo

I texted Sandy to tell her to get Elle over to this side because I knew shit was going to escalate if Hunter was in her presence for another second. Sandy brings her over to the back corner and walks off once she spots me heading toward Elle.

"What did he say?" I ask with my voice lowered.

"He's *reading.*" Elle rolls her eyes.

I check to see if he can see us from where he's sitting, but he can't. "Go back to your dorm."

"I still have another hour—"

"Just go back, please. He's going to be fucking with you the whole time, and I don't know why."

"Yes, you do. We both do. This is his way of letting us know that he's still capable of screwing everything up for you."

"I don't care. I just want to keep you safe." *And preferably my ass out of jail again.*

"I'm safe. He's sitting there with his nose in a book."

I bring my face closer to hers. "You were never safe with him."

Elle blinks a few times, and I think with just that one sentence, she's reminded of all the times she was in danger. I'm sure it's a lot more than I'm aware of, and one day I hope she tells me…years from now, because right now I can't manage hearing another story about him. Especially because he's close enough for me to beat into the fucking ground.

"What if he presses charges? He still can. The statute of limitations isn't up until tomorrow."

"Then I'll figure it out," I promise her, but then my mind goes to her last sentence. "Wait. Did you do research on how long he could press charges?"

"Yeah." Elle's gaze goes off me. "I figured it would be a year under his thumb, and then I could tell you everything." She looks back up at me. "I didn't think you'd want me back after I told you."

A storm of emotions brews inside me, mainly anger that Elle was forced into this position. I school my features and give her a small, reassuring smile. "I'll always want you." I inch my way even closer. "I also want you to go back to your dorm. Now."

"Do you think Edgar will be mad if I—"

"No."

"I should at least go find him and—"

"No. I'll tell him. He'll be cool with it. Trust me."

And she does because she nods, agreeing with me. "Don't do anything stupid."

I hold my hands up in innocence. "I swear I'll behave."

"I love you." She gives me a peck and turns to leave.

"Hey." I reach for her hand.

"What?"

"I love you too."

God, I'm never going to get tired of saying that to her or hearing those words fall from her perfect lips.

Elle gives me a smile, and I watch as she leaves the coffee shop. Once she's gone, I take a deep inhale and focus on the fucker in the other room.

He really is reading.

Asshole.

I get back to work, making sure I stay stationed at the counter so I can keep tabs on Hunter. Noticing when he glances around for what I assume to be Elle, I get the satisfaction of watching him look like an idiot.

Finally giving up, Hunter places the book on the table without the courtesy of putting it back on the shelf.

It's nearing close, and the entire place is emptying out. The last of the patrons exits, and I'm about to close out the register when Hunter approaches the counter.

"Americano," he says.

"We're closed."

"Not for another minute." He flashes me the time on his phone.

Clenching my jaw, I swallow my pride. "Lynn, can you please make an Americano?"

With a nod of her purple hair, she does as I ask.

"Four dollars," I tell Hunter.

He ignores me, texting on his phone until Lynn slides his drink across the counter. He picks it up and aims for the door.

"I said it was four dollars." My volume getting louder.

"I heard you." He pushes open the door and walks out.

My shoulders hike up to my ears as my muscles stiffen. Is this what it's all about? Money? Fuck it. I'll give him whatever he wants, so long as he leaves Elle and me alone.

"Dude." Lynn wipes down the counter. "What's with you and that guy?"

"Hopefully nothing after I talk to him." I stride toward the door. "Be right back."

Stepping outside, I catch sight of Hunter turning the corner toward the parking lot. I pick up my pace, following him until he reaches his fancy car.

"How much do you want?" I ask, my voice making him pause. He glances over his shoulder and shifts to look at me. Taking my wallet out of my back pocket, I grab a wad of cash. "Here, take it, and leave us the fuck alone."

Hunter's gaze drops down to my hand, and a look of disgust crosses his face as if I'm holding a pile of shit out for him to take. "I'll have to check how much your bill is and get back to you." He takes a step toward his car door. "It's minus a couple bucks, though, so that must be a relief for you." He gestures at the coffee in his hand.

"Whatever, man. Just let me know how much, and we'll call it even." I start to walk away.

"That's what you think," he mutters under his breath, and I immediately spin back around.

"What did you say?"

There's a moment of hesitation, and I know I got him scared. I use the second of intimidation to my advantage and stalk toward him. My heart pumps faster, pushing out all the reasoning in my head telling me this is a bad idea.

"Let's get one thing straight." I invade his space. "If you fuck with my girl—"

"I already did fuck her."

Rage explodes through my veins, and I grip onto his shirt, slamming him up against his car door. I'm quick to press my forearm into his throat. "You will leave Elena alone, or I will end you. Got it?" I grit, using every ounce of self-control not to pound his face in.

The dickhead smirks at me.

"Mateo." *Tío* Edgar's voice is like a bucket of ice water over my head. I come to my senses, loosening the pressure on Hunter's neck, but still not removing my arm. "You good?" Edgar asks.

"Yep." My eyes don't go off Hunter. "Just clearing something up. But I think we came to an understanding."

I let go of Hunter, and he coughs.

"You dropped your drink," I say, pointing to his coffee that I must've slapped out of his hand when I grabbed him.

Walking over to Edgar, I don't bother to glance behind me because I know Hunter's not going to try anything.

"What the hell was that about?" Edgar asks as I get closer to him and out of earshot of Hunter.

"Elle's ex."

"Ah." He grips my shoulder, and I expect him to start reprimanding me. But he surprises me when he says, "You need backup next time, let me know."

"I think I got my point across."

At least I fucking hope so.

CHAPTER ONE HUNDRED TWENTY

Ellie

Last night, after I got home early from work, I balled myself up on my bed waiting for the chaos to ensue. But when Mateo walked through my door with no bruises and no sign of Hunter's blood on him, my anxiety eased a tad.

Today is the last day Hunter can move forward with anything legal, and since I doubt he'd wait until he's down to the wire, I'm beginning to think that his coming to my place of work yesterday was just to scare me. It was some sick thrill for him, and in a few hours, it'll all be over.

I decided I'm going to let Bree know everything that has gone down, now that it's all out in the open with Mateo. She stayed at a friend's place yesterday, so I figured we could go out to brunch today and hang out and talk since I have about five hours' worth of stories to tell her. It works out perfectly since I only have one final left to write, and Mateo is at his end-of-the-year review with his advisor—because apparently that's a thing in his program.

While Bree is in the shower, I finish putting on my mascara, getting ready to go out. My attention gets pulled from my eyelashes to my phone vibrating on my desk.

A sinking feeling drags me down when I see Hunter's name on my screen. There's a video attachment without any text to go with it.

Aggravated with myself for even entertaining his message, I slide open the notification and click on the video.

My entire body gets struck with horror.

With shaking hands, I watch the video before me…of me. The night I lost all common sense and let him fuck me…he filmed it.

Gasping for air, I continue to look at the perfectly cropped video of me moaning and coming. His phone was angled so you can't see his face. Just mine.

He set me up.

My insides contort until I'm made up of a thousand knots filled with terror. My stomach nosedives, and I run to my trash can, vomiting. My throat burns just as my eyes do as I continue to watch until the end.

The video is edited so that the next clip is a fifty-dollar bill getting tossed on my bed and me grabbing it.

Then it stops.

Oh my god.

He made it look like I was getting paid.

Another round of nausea hits me, and I continue to puke. I tremble on the floor, feeling disgusted, horrified, and fearful of what he's planning to do with that video.

My thoughts spin. I sense myself spiraling, but I can't stop it. They twist and turn until I'm in a puddle of tears and bile.

My lungs squeeze as my chest caves in.

I try to breathe.

Pins and needles prick my tongue.

Then my entire face.

I'm lightheaded.

I can't get air.

I need air.

Air.

"Ellie?"

Someone says my name. I hear it. I know I heard them. I'm not crazy. I swear I'm not crazy.

But before I can make out who it is, my head slams into the tile floor.

Droplets of water sprinkle my face, and I hear my name again. I slowly flutter my eyes open, my vision taking several seconds to focus.

Bree is hovering over me, her hair wet from the shower, repeatedly saying my name.

"I'm okay," I scrape out the words as I sense oxygen flowing through me.

"Should I call medical?" Bree's voice quakes with distress.

I shake my head. "It was just a panic attack."

Bree sits back on her heels and gives me space to push myself up into a sitting position. "I still think I should call medical."

"I'm fine, I promise." Regaining some of my strength back despite the pounding headache behind my eyes, I start to rise. "I have to go."

"Go where?" She helps me stand.

"I need to go take care of something. I'll be right back."

"Take care of what? Ellie, what happened to give you a panic attack?"

I shake my head again and grab my phone. "It's nothing." I quickly change out of my clothes into something that's not covered in vomit as she tries to convince me to have a nurse check on me. The sound of her voice gets tuned out by the intensity of my heart racing. I might be scared shitless, but my anger is what is fueling me to make my next move.

I start to walk out of our room but turn back to Bree. "This won't take long."

CHAPTER ONE HUNDRED TWENTY-ONE

ME

how's my love?

I sent that text a while ago and have yet to get a response. I focus my attention on the black screen as I wait for a reply. It's been calming my nerves while I wait for my yearly review from Barbara.

We all have a scheduled appointment with her where she tells us about our progress in the social work program and what our supervisors from our internships reported to her. This semester at the foster agency was eye-opening and heartbreaking at the same time. If anything, it escalated my passion to help kids and teens in shitty situations.

A twinge of worry jumps under my flesh, concerned that someone saw me in the parking lot with Hunter last night. I might be doing well in school, but clearly I still have to work on some of my shit if I threatened to off the guy. Which is why when I was on my way to Elle's dorm last night, I decided that I'm going back into therapy this summer. At the very least, it'll help me be a better clinician.

Barbara's door opens, and Rebecca walks out with a smile on her face.

"How'd it go?" I inquire.

"It went very well." Rebecca glances down at the notes in her hands. "Barbara gave me constructive feedback and some helpful pointers. But all in all, it looks like I'm stuck in the social worker field because it's the only thing I'm good at." She chuckles.

"Better tell those parents of yours to suck it up." I smile.

"Mateo?" Barbara stands in the doorway, waving me in.

"Good luck. I'm sure you'll be fine," Rebecca says.

"Thanks," I say before entering the office.

"Come, sit down." Barbara gestures to the chair across from her desk.

Her office is small but welcoming. The walls are an off-white color with pictures of her family hanging from them.

A little bit of nervous energy swims through me, and I take a seat. A grin appears on my face when I sit across from Barbara, the tiniest action bringing me right back to a very familiar office.

"Hey." I stand in the doorway of Mr. Kevin's office in my green graduation gown. I refused to wear the cap because that shit looks fucking ridiculous.

Mr. Kevin glances up from his desk, surprised to see me. "Shouldn't you be on your way back home by now?"

Home. This place has been my home for the past couple of years, not where I grew up. "Yeah. My family's waiting for me. I told them I needed a few minutes."

They all came here to see my graduation. Well, all except for one. But nevertheless, it was nice to have my mom and sisters here. I know they all had their doubts about me ever making it to the finish line and graduating from high school.

The token problem child got his shit together.

Mostly.

Mr. Kevin clears his throat. "Anything specific you needed to take a minute for?" He smirks, knowing why I'm here.

"I don't know."

"Come, sit down." He gestures to the chair across from him.

I make myself comfortable in the seat as I normally do. Any downtime Mr. Kevin had, I would pop into his office. Sometimes it was to shoot the shit. Other times, it was because I was going through something, but both were equally as meaningful.

"You're going to be just fine," he says as if he can read my mind. Fuck, at this point, he might as well. He knows me like a book.

"Yeah." I stare at my shoes.

Mr. Kevin leans back in his chair. "You remember that punk kid who refused to meet with me for weeks and who had a smart mouth and an iron fist?"

I chuckle. "Kinda."

"He should be proud of the man he's turning into."

My eyes do that stinging thing that I hate. "I don't want to leave," I admit.

"That makes sense. But a part of growing is letting go. It's time for you to start your next chapter."

I nod, not wanting to say anything else.

"You excited for college in the fall?"

"Yeah. My mom talked to my uncle up in Connecticut, who's going to hook me up with a job. I don't know him that well, though."

"So then this is your chance to connect with another family member. Maybe he'll even become a father figure for you."

"I doubt he'll be anything like—" I stop myself before saying you.

Mr. Kevin smiles and reaches into a drawer in his desk. He pulls out a busi-

ness card and hands it to me. "Now that you graduated, I can give you this." I look at the card with his contact info on it. "I'll always be a phone call away if you need anything."

"Thank you."

"You're capable of big things, Mateo. Continue to believe in yourself, and you'll see your world change."

"Thanks for everything."

I stand up, and so does he. Clasping a hand on my shoulder, he gives it a firm squeeze. His eyes become glassy, and I sense mine doing the same. "See you later, Rivera."

"Your supervisor gave you a glowing review," Barbara says, snapping me out of the memory. "I think you might have a niche for that population."

"Thank you." I grin.

As she goes on to talk about my professionalism and competency, happiness rolls around my heart. If someone would've told me in high school that I'd be going for a master's degree in social work, I would've laughed in their face. If they also would've told me I'd be in love and thinking about the future with the most incredible woman, I would've knocked them out.

Barbara continues, and all I can think of is telling Elle all the awesome shit she's saying because I know Elle is going to be elated and probably jump around the room.

Once I'm out of Barbara's office, I reach for my phone to text Elle, but it lights up with a message from someone I wasn't expecting.

BREE

call me

CHAPTER ONE HUNDRED TWENTY-TWO

Ellie

I thought my wrath would subside if I walked.

I was wrong.

With each step I take, a raging storm brews inside me, lightning bolts of fury striking through my veins.

Stomping onto the property of Hunter's frat house, there are people crowded on the lawn, and when I push my way into the house, there's some type of drinking game going on in the living room.

I catch a glimpse of Ava sitting on Derek's lap, but I need to get this over with before talking to anyone else, before I lose my nerve.

Running upstairs and down the hall, I try to open Hunter's door, but it's locked. I jiggle the handle and continuously knock.

"Open the door," I say in the most demanding voice I can conjure.

No response.

I hit the door harder, anger hardening my fists. "Hunter!"

Still nothing.

My hands sting from the force. Switching to my legs, I kick the door louder and louder. "Open your fucking door, Hunter!"

I hear people emerging out of other rooms to see what the commotion is about, but I don't give a fuck.

I strengthen the blow of my kick.

Again.

Again.

Again.

"You piece of shit! Open your goddamn door!"

The door opens, and I almost fly forward, but Hunter is quick to close it enough so that I can only see a sliver of him and a girl behind him, both shirtless.

"What the fuck, Ellie?" he snaps.

"You *know* what the fuck!"

"Who is that?" the girl asks, getting on her bra.

"Just my crazy ex."

Fire. A blazing, violent firestorm ignites from the very depths of my soul. "You wanna see fucking crazy?" I shove my arm into the small opening of the door. "You haven't seen anything yet, you fucking bastard!" I scratch his neck, and he attempts to push me out with one hand while trying to shut the door with the other. Jumping up, I yank a lock of his hair.

"Fuck!" His hands go up to his head, and I force myself into the room.

"Out!" I shout at the half-naked girl.

"You can't just walk into his room and—" she starts to say, but Hunter cuts her off.

"Why don't you go downstairs, baby girl," he says to her, and I nearly puke from his faux sweetness. "I'll take care of this. It shouldn't take long. Then we can get back to what we were doing." He gives her a wink, and she leaves, slamming the door behind her.

"You have impeccable timing," Hunter says to me.

"Oh, I'm sorry. Why don't we call her back in, and while she's giving you head, I can tell her what you did to me?"

He scoffs. "What I did to you? If I remember correctly, you were pretty quick to rip your clothes off that night."

"I'm not talking about the sex part. I'm talking about the fucking video you took without my permission or knowledge!" I shove him, and he doesn't budge. His dark laughter vibrates through my bones, and I slap him repeatedly on the chest. "Why? Why the hell would you do that?" Water forms behind my eyes, but I don't want to give him the satisfaction of my tears.

My hand crashes against his skin as he remains standing there mute. He doesn't answer my plea, begging to know why. Why does he need to continue to hurt me? Why does he need to keep me at his mercy? Why can't he let me go?

I lash another blow to his chest, a red handprint forming over the black ink that honors his dead sister.

And that's when I stop.

Taking a step backward, I stare at the mark I left. Becoming fixated on the script tattooed on his body, that's when it starts making sense. The name isn't just to pay homage to her. It's so he can hide his pain behind it. The pain that he refuses to let anyone see, including himself. The pain that is etched into his heart and dimming his soul.

He hides his scars from the world, just like I do. The only difference is that I internalize and personalize everything, whereas he ricochets his ugliness onto the weakest person he can find.

Me.

He uses me as a dumping ground for the issues he won't dare face himself.

And I let him.

And that's why he wants to keep me close. He was never going to press charges against Mateo. He just used that blackmail, so he had a solid reason to keep me near. He knows his time is running out with that, so he needed to find something else to hold over my head. And he had been holding out until now.

But why?

My eyes follow the line of the cursive on his skin. The way it twists and turns, the highs and lows. Then I remember all my conversations with Panavi, how she said he and I have the perfect makings of a trauma bond. My empathy and his projection.

Then I hear Ava ringing in my ear the day Hunter found Mateo and me. She said Hunter was going through something at home.

His trauma that he refused to deal with. His pain that he refused to feel.

I always dealt with and felt it for him.

I'm sure Hunter was feeling on top of the world these past few months as he screwed anything that breathes. But he knew. He knew he'd feel like shit again, so he kept this video in his back pocket, waiting to use it. Keeping me close so I can absorb all his self-hatred.

"Why are you looking at me like that?" Hunter's cautious tone draws my eyes up to look at his.

I'm terrified of what he plans to do with that video, but I refuse to continue to let him use and abuse me.

There's a tightness around my lungs. I take a deep inhale, pulling in as much air as possible because I will *not* have a panic attack in front of him.

"I hope you get the help you need one day," I say, like the strong person I know I'm capable of being.

"What the fuck is that supposed to mean?"

I fight the urge to give him an explanation. The longer I stay in this room, the more I'll get sucked into a cycle I've been so actively trying to break. So with my last piece of dignity hanging on by a thread, I lift my chin and leave his room.

The moment I step into the hallway, tears fill my vision, and I hear him calling after me as I dart down the stairs. Trying to get out of the house as fast as possible, I bump into someone.

"Ellie?" Ava narrows her eyes at me.

I wipe my cheeks, trying to keep it together. My mouth opens to tell her everything that Hunter is putting me through because I need to get this off my chest and figure out what the fuck to do about it.

"Ava, I need your help. Can we go talk somewhere?"

She takes a step back and shakes her head. My brow crinkles in confusion.

"Um…okay. Maybe later?"

"No," she says.

"Oh." A surge of unease tumbles around my insides. "W-why?"

"Because I know how you got the internship with Hank, and honestly, I don't want to be seen hanging around those types of people."

I stop breathing.

No. There's no way she's insinuating that she saw the video. Hunter wouldn't do that. It was just a threat.

It was just a threat.

Please God, let it just be a threat.

"I…What do you mean?" I stammer.

"I know you're sleeping around to get what you want. I saw what went down with you and Hunter."

"How…how…Who showed you?"

"Hunter showed me and Derek on his phone earlier, so don't try denying it."

The last thread of my dignity snaps right there.

Glancing up at the stairs, I see Hunter looking down at me with a smug grin tugging on his lips. Fuck him. I turn back to Ava, who I thought was my friend, and animosity floods my being. Fuck her too.

Pushing past her, I run outside.

With each step back to the university, I cry harder and harder. My negative thoughts downpour in my mind, dragging me down until my pace becomes lethargic.

What if my internship gets taken away because of this? What if I lose my scholarship? I'll never finish college. I can't afford it. I'll never have a career. What if no one believes that the video was edited? What if they all have Ava's reaction?

I'm done for, just like he wants. So he can keep me close. So he can abuse me to feel better about himself.

Clasping my shaky hand over my mouth, a loud sob comes out.

Feeling utterly hopeless, I take my phone out of my pocket and call Panavi, praying she answers.

"Hello? Ellie?" She picks up. I let out another cry, but this time out of gratitude because she answered. "Are you okay?"

"Not really," I manage to say between my sniffles.

"What's going on?"

Without knowing where to begin, I sit down on the curb of a street a few blocks away from campus. Taking a huge sigh, I decide that I need to tell her everything. All the pieces of my past with Hunter that I left out, I spill, connecting all the dots for her.

Once I'm done explaining, I take a breath, winded from talking so much. My tears have slowed down as I listen to the sound of her voice.

I tell her how he has trapped me this time, and after she lets some unprofessional language slip, she speaks. "You have two options here. Do nothing or do everything."

CHAPTER ONE HUNDRED TWENTY-THREE

Mateo

Worry brims behind Bree's hazel eyes. "I've never seen her that bad, Mateo. She didn't want to tell me what's wrong and refused to go to the medical center to get checked out."

"She's not answering her phone." I press the end button on my screen and toss it on Elle's bed.

"Where the hell would she have run off to?"

There's a pit in my stomach telling me exactly where she ran off to without letting anyone know where she went. Three minutes. She gets three minutes to answer either Bree or me before I go to that frat house and bust down the door looking for her.

"You don't think she went to…" Bree doesn't finish her sentence.

I blow out a sigh. "I don't know, but if she doesn't answer one of us soon, that's where I'm searching first." My hand connects with the back of my neck as I rub my tense muscles, trying to piece things together. "Was she acting strange before you went into the shower?"

"No, she was totally fine. We were getting ready to go out for—"

"Brunch."

"Yeah."

"Try her again." I motion my chin toward Bree's phone in her hand. "Maybe she's pissed at me about something."

"Like what?"

"I don't know."

"Oh, please." Bree rolls her eyes. "Ellie gushes about you nonstop. I doubt you'd do something that bad to make her ignore you. She's insanely in love with you." She gasps and slams her hands over her mouth.

"It's okay, Bree. I know." I chuckle.

Her hands drop. "You do? Since when?"

"Last night."

"And did you finally tell her?"

"Yes. And what do you mean by *finally*?"

"Mateo, anyone within a fifty-foot radius could tell you worship the ground the girl walks on. I'm just glad the both of you finally got the guts to say it before I had to stage an intervention. It's been going on for a fucking year!"

"You knew I loved her this whole time?"

"Obviously. I'm good at reading people, remember?"

"Then can you use your psychic powers to tell me what's going on with my girlfriend?"

"I'm not a psychic. I'm intuitive. It basically means that I pick up on—"

"Bree." My eyes glance down to her phone. "Just call her. Please."

"Oh, right." She taps on her phone and presses it against her ear. I can hear the sound of Elle's voicemail, and Bree shakes her head.

"Fuck." Grinding my teeth, I yank my keys out of my pocket. "All right, I'll be back."

Just as I move toward the door, it pushes open. Elle's standing in the doorway, looking like shit. Still beautiful. But…like shit. Her face is stained with mascara, her nose red from crying. Her shoulders lift and fall with her shaky breath.

She stares at me. The green in her eyes radiates with her never-ending depth of emotions. I've seen her look like this countless times before, but there's something else mixed in with her pain. A spark of ferocity that causes an unsettling sensation to roll through me.

Elle parts her lips to speak. "Hi."

CHAPTER ONE HUNDRED TWENTY-FOUR

Ellie

I stand in the doorway with my unsteady panting. I knew Mateo would be here due to the back-and-forth phone calls between him and Bree, but I needed to figure out a plan before I spoke to either of them. A plan that would stick this time and not temporarily get me out of hell, only to get sucked in by something worse.

Mateo cautiously watches me, waiting. Waiting for answers. Waiting for me to speak.

I part my lips. "Hi."

Mateo and Bree share a glance, then he brings his attention back to me. "Hi."

Closing the door behind me, I check my face in the mirror. I grab a tissue to clean myself up, needing to look as presentable as possible.

Mateo's gaze follows me around the room as I fix myself, running a brush through my tangled hair next.

"You gonna tell me what's up?" There's a bite to his tone, but I can't blame him for that.

"I need to go to the bathroom," Bree announces before exiting.

The negative, intrusive thoughts attempt to slither their way into any seam within my brain that they can find. But I push them out, knowing what needs to be done.

You can do this, Elle. You have *to do this.*

My hands tremble at the same rate as my breathing while I reach for another tissue. Mateo's hand covers mine, pausing me.

"Elena."

Forcing myself to look up at him, I round my shoulders and get ready to tell him something he doesn't want to hear. "Yes, I will tell you what's going on. Yes, it has to do with Hunter. But no, I won't tell you about it now."

His body becomes rigid. "I'm not doing this shit again. Tell me what he's doing to you."

"No."

"What do you mean, no? He obviously did something bad enough to get Bree involved and calling me up, telling me to come here right away because you were in the midst of crying and vomiting."

"He did," I say. Mateo's mouth opens, then shuts, incapable of letting his thoughts out as I render him speechless. I move closer to him. "I want to handle it on my own, Mateo."

"Why?"

I reach up, wrapping my arms around his neck. His muscles slightly loosen to my touch. "Because I know I can. I'm just scared."

"Then let me handle it for you." His voice softens as his hands go to my waist.

I shake my head, and he goes to talk, but I stop him by giving him a kiss. Slowly drawing back, I cup his face in my hands. "You remember what you said to me that time I was crying on the floor?"

His lips twitch. "I don't mean to offend you, Elle, but you've done that on more than one occasion."

I lightly chuckle. "Yeah, I guess I have."

"But which time were you referring to?"

"It was last year, at your place. I freaked out when you put your hand on the back of my head while I was blowing you because it reminded me of stuff with Hunter." Mateo's jaw clenches, letting me know he remembers. I continue, "I ended up crying on the bathroom floor, and we talked, and I thanked you for always coming in to save me. Do you remember what you said after that?" He gently shakes his head while my palms still hold his face. "You said that you didn't want to save me. That I'm going to save myself, and you're going to stand by my side while I do." There's a flicker in his eyes. "Well, this is me saving myself, Mateo. Let me do this."

He pulls out of my grip and straightens his posture, letting out a sigh. "Okay."

"Thank you."

We stand in silence, looking at each other for another moment, but my attention goes to the clock on my desk, letting me know it's almost time.

Spinning back around to the mirror, I adjust my shirt and give myself one last check.

I stare at the woman before me. The one who was always too scared to use her voice is finally making some noise. Even though I'm terrified, I'm proud of her. Of me.

Mateo comes into the reflection as he steps behind me, also admiring the person in the mirror.

"I have to go," I say.

"Can I ask where?"

"I made an emergency appointment with the president of the university."

Mateo's eyebrows shoot to his hairline, but he's quick to regain his composure. "Okay. Let's go."

I turn around to face him. "You're coming?"

"Yeah, that's the deal, isn't it? You save yourself, and I'm by your side while it happens."

I smile and nod. He threads his long fingers between mine and brings my hand up to his lips, placing a gentle kiss on my knuckles.

Without a word, we walk hand in hand into the sunlight. Mateo's presence sends me short seconds of ease, but I'm unable to calm my hands from shaking.

The knot in my stomach intensifies as a rising and dropping sensation continuously happens. Sweat drips down my sides as another round of nausea hits.

I pause. "I think I'm gonna puke." I lift the back of my hair off my neck and let the breeze cool me down while taking deep breaths.

The thoughts get louder, drowning out the rational ones.

The thoughts of me making a bigger deal out of this than it is. The thoughts of me ruining Hunter's life because of this. The thoughts that make me feel like the guilty one—the one who's doing something wrong and hurting someone.

His parents are going to be devastated.

My mind brings me back to Thanksgiving at Hunter's house. His dad pinning him up against the wall, ready to choke him out. Hunter trying to protect me from seeing that side of his life. The sorrow in his eyes.

I'm going to make him go through something similar if I go through with this.

What if his dad hurts him? What if something really bad happens, and it's because of me? Am I starting more problems by doing this?

"No." A girl's voice grabs my focus. I spot her in the parking lot with a guy. I've never seen either of them before, but I know the tone she's using.

"Get in the car," a guy says as they walk up to a Jeep.

"I don't want to."

Ignoring her response, the guy jumps in, slamming the door. The girl sighs, and we make eye contact. She gives me a small smile, completely washing away any signs of distress. The car horn blares, and she snaps her attention to where she's told to go. She gets in the car, and the door shuts.

My body moves forward, wanting to help her.

"You okay?" Mateo asks, unaware of the couple.

I nod and let my gaze travel over the campus as we continue to walk. My eyes float around the couples we pass. All different genders, all different people, but all wearing a smile. A smile that seems genuine, but so did mine.

I wonder how many of them are happy or how many are trapped, and not a single soul knows. How many of them are hiding behind glowing grins and white lies? How many of them are internally screaming, wanting, *needing* to tell someone about their suffering, but are too afraid?

My feet hit the pavement faster, and suddenly I'm seeing clearer. I'm not doing this just for myself.

I'm doing it for the girl in the car.

I'm doing it for one of the strangers who holds their partner's hand, smiling, but is dying on the inside.

I'm doing it for the ones whose stories were never told, and we'll never hear.

I'm doing it for the ones whose partners have blurred the lines of right and wrong.

I'm doing it for all the *me*s—the voiceless, the confused, the scared, the desperately seeking love from an external source because they're so ashamed to love the messy parts of themselves.

I'm doing it for us.

Approaching the towering brick building, I glance up, taking it all in. I wish I could say that this feels like an empowering, life-changing turning point in my life, but it doesn't. It feels horrifying.

In the blink of an eye, Mateo and I are sitting down in the waiting area of the president's office. The brown leather chairs swallow me whole as my veins buzz with fear. Mateo rubs his thumb across the back of my hand as I shut my eyes.

I try to push the thoughts away, but they grow louder and bigger, transforming into distorted monsters trying to rip me of all sanity.

What if I share my story, and it falls on deaf ears? What if I tell the president everything, and there's an investigation, and nothing happens? Will Hunter find another way to decimate me? What if I drag both of us through hell and back for nothing, and it turns out to be even worse for me? What if the president doesn't believe me?

"Elena Connor?" A woman with graying hair hangs up the phone on her desk. "Mr. Walcott is ready for you." She gestures toward the door down the hall with a large plaque with his name across it.

I look at Mateo, and a small smile appears on his face. "Time to go save yourself, baby." He kisses my cheek and brings his mouth to my ear. "Go use that beautiful voice of yours."

With trembling legs, I rise and walk to the office.

"Welcome, Ms. Connor. I'm Mr. Walcott." He extends his hand, and I shake it.

"Nice to meet you." I take a seat in front of his large desk with a sizable Mac computer sitting on top of it.

"My secretary tells me that you were quite persistent in speaking with me today, and that there's something urgent you needed to tell me."

"That's correct." My leg bounces up and down, and I push my palm against it to get it to stop.

"Okay." He nods. "What's going on?"

My mouth dries up the moment I open it to speak. The image of the girl in the car, the strangers on campus, and the reflection of myself in the mirror all surface in my mind.

I clear my throat and start at the beginning, leaving nothing out. I explain how my relationship with Hunter started in high school and followed me here, getting increasingly worse. I tell Mr. Walcott about the incident in Hunter's room last year when he assaulted me. The arrangement I was forced into in order to protect Mateo's safety comes out. I explain how I was at Hunter's beck and call last semester, and how I felt pressured into giving him a copy of the key to my room. Then, I tell him about us sleeping together.

"Hunter took a video of it without my consent and edited it to look like I was getting paid to sleep with him. He's already shown it to a couple of people, and he's threatening to share it with others in order to keep me close. I honestly don't know what his full plan is. I didn't wait that long to find out."

Mr. Walcott leans back in his chair with a frown on his face as he studies me. The only thing my brain can focus on is the ticking of the clock hanging on the wall. The monotonous tone becomes the soundtrack for this long, drawn-out moment as Mr. Walcott deciphers his next move.

Breaking his gaze, he shifts his posture to face his computer. "What's this young man's full name?"

"Hunter Callaghan."

He types on his keyboard, and I watch as he reads whatever is popping up on this screen. "Junior?" he confirms, and I nod. He keeps focusing on his computer. "His father is an alumnus."

Fuck. I forgot about that and the giant donation Hunter's family makes to the university every year. Hunter is a straight-A student with a rich family that has ties to the school.

I should've realized money and status would play a part in this.

Out of desperation, I fish my phone out of my bag. "I swear everything I'm saying is real. Here, you can watch the video if you want."

Mr. Walcott furiously shakes his hand, motioning me to put my phone away. "I don't need to watch that, Ms. Connor."

"Oh. Okay."

I can't believe I almost let some old guy watch a sex video of me. I must be out of my fucking mind if this is what I'm resorting to.

Mr. Walcott clasps his hands and places them on top of his desk. "Are you aware of the gravity of the statement you just disclosed to me?"

I nod, my heart pounding faster. My old friend, guilt, weaves its way around my bones, and for some reason, I feel like I'm the one getting in trouble.

"His parents are probably going to try to fight this if you don't have enough proof."

Who has proof of invisible scars?

But then I remember the screenshots and list I made if Hunter were to take legal action against Mateo.

"Is that enough proof?" I ask after informing him of what I have.

"I'll take a look at everything. Email it as soon as you can." He jots something down on a Post-it. "Do you have any witnesses to Hunter's behavior?" he asks.

"Yes, my boyfriend and roommate. And probably a few others if I could get some time to think about it."

"Think hard. I'm going to need to speak with as many people as possible." Mr. Walcott reaches for the phone on his desk, and after a moment, he speaks into it. "Please send an email to a Mr. Hunter Callaghan requesting his presence in my office immediately."

Wait. He's on my side?

Hope flourishes at the same time disbelief hits me.

After he hangs up, he levels with me. "Ms. Connor, I do not tolerate any of this type of behavior on my campus, and I am extremely apologetic that this is what you've been dealing with for your two years here. I will take care of it."

My lungs fill with air, and when I push it back out, I break down in tears. Covering my face with my hands, I try to do my best to talk. "I'm sorry. I don't know why I'm crying." I force myself to calm down and look up at Mr. Walcott. "Please make him stop," I plead softly.

Mr. Walcott nods. "I'll be in touch regarding your witnesses and the disciplinary hearing."

My body stills. "Disciplinary hearing?"

"Yes. It's the university's policy."

Fuck.

CHAPTER ONE HUNDRED TWENTY-FIVE

Ellie

"Why don't you try to work on your philosophy final for a little bit?" Mateo suggests after I spent the past two hours freaking out once I filled him and Bree in on everything.

"I can't, Mateo!" I snap at him while pacing my dorm room. "I have twenty-four hours to come up with as many witnesses as possible and beg them to give a statement to the president. Who the fuck am I even going to ask?"

"Don't worry about that. I got that part handled."

"I'm going to need more than just you and Bree." I spot Bree sitting on her bed with an empathetic look on her face. "They can easily claim that you two are just agreeing with me because you have a close relationship with me." The clamp around my chest tightens. "Oh god, this whole thing is going to blow up. He's going to find out I made all these claims against him and tried to ruin his life, and he's going to retaliate against me. I should've shut my fucking mouth. Why did I do this? Why am I so fucking stupid?"

Mateo stands up and plants his hands on my shoulders, grounding me. "First of all, you're not ruining his life. He's the one who chose to treat you the way he did. You're doing nothing wrong in this. You're holding him accountable."

"Yeah, well, no one told me that holding people accountable sucks ass!"

He presses his lips together, fighting a smile while I'm on the verge of a breakdown. I glare at him, and he continues talking. "Don't worry about finding witnesses. I already reached out to other people," he states.

"Who? Who could've possibly known what was going on when I kept everything a secret?"

"Michelle is currently in Mr. Walcott's office making a statement. And I got Edgar, Sandy, and Lynn vouching for you. I've been texting everyone for the past hour."

"They're…they're all doing that?"

"Yep." Bree hops off her bed and walks toward Mateo and me. "Face it, Ellie. People like you for some strange reason," she teases.

"It's your word, plus six witnesses, against his," Mateo says to me.

Warmth expands throughout my body, realizing that people would take time out of their lives to support me and be there for me.

"How does my outfit look?" Bree smooths out her red shirt. "Does it say I hate the patriarchy and that we should have a woman president at this university, but I'll suck it up and deal with an old dude so I can stand up for my soul sister?"

"You're going there now?" I ask.

"Yeah, my appointment's in ten. I sent Mr. Walcott an email as soon as you told me what's going down." She stares at us. "I wasn't kidding about my outfit. How does it look?"

I smile. "It's perfect." Before she can leave, I pull her in for a hug. "Thank you," I say into her curly hair.

"Of course. I'd burn his motherfucking frat house down for you."

"I wouldn't say that too loud." I laugh.

Once she leaves, Mateo's arms take her place. "At least it's officially past the one-year mark, and he can't press charges," I say to him. I expected Hunter to pull the trigger at zero hour yesterday, but he must've left Mr. Walcott's office too late in the day to make the move. "I just need to get through this part, and it'll all be over," I assure myself aloud.

"And you *will* make it through this," Mateo says. "This is just going to be a small part of your story one day."

"In *our* story," I correct him.

The day of the disciplinary hearing is here. I didn't get a wink of sleep, and I spent more time in the bathroom with an upset stomach than I did getting dressed. I debated calling my mom and letting her in on everything that's happening, but I decided to wait until this is over with, because I don't want to add her reaction to my stress.

Mateo grips on to my hand as we walk into the same building we did a couple of days ago. The hearing is on a different floor than Mr. Walcott's office. When we reach the elevator, I let out a huge sigh, realizing we're alone.

"I might throw up."

"Make sure you aim it at Hunter," Mateo jokes.

The elevator dings, and the doors slide open. As soon as I step out, I spot Hunter at the end of the hall speaking to a man in a navy suit. He nods his head as he attentively listens to the man.

"Let's hang back here." Mateo takes my hand and sticks me in an alcove, his body keeping me hidden.

"Can you hear them?" I whisper.

Mateo nods as he tries to listen to the conversation at the end of the hallway. "It's his attorney."

My eyes bulge. "He hired a lawyer?"

"You'll be fine, baby. He doesn't stand a chance, even if his parents chose to blow their money on some prick attorney."

Just as he finishes speaking, the elevator chimes. I peek over Mateo's shoulder and see Hunter's parents walk out.

My insides contort.

"Oh my god, his parents are here."

"Good. They should know what a fuckhead their son is." Mateo's gaze follows them down the hall as I cower away behind his large frame. "They all went inside."

I grip his shirt. "Mateo, I don't know if I can do this."

"You can."

"No, I really don't think I can. Why do I have to sit in the same room as him and listen to everything? How messed up is that?"

"Listen, the system is fucked. We can fight that another day. But today, we need to go inside and fight Hunter."

"I don't think you'll be allowed to go in."

"I don't give a shit. I'm by your side for this." He brushes a strand of hair away from my face. "I'll be by your side for everything."

"And I'll always be by yours."

Mateo bends down and delicately kisses me. Pulling back, he takes hold of my hand. "You ready?"

"No. But I'll go anyway."

Breaking out in a cold sweat, I open the door. Sensing multiple eyes on me, I hang my head and make sure not to look directly at anyone.

"Ms. Connor," Mr. Walcott says. My attention snaps to him, and he smiles at me, giving me a small glimmer of hope. "Have a seat over here." He motions to a chair next to him.

The room is long and narrow, with a table spanning most of the length. Chairs are sporadically lined along the table. Several faculty members are seated throughout, and luckily, Hunter and his clan sit at the opposite end from me. Mateo grabs a free chair and places it next to the one next to me.

Mr. Walcott gives him a nod as if there's some nonverbal agreement going on.

"Now that everyone is here, we can begin," Mr. Walcott states. "I've asked several members of the university to be here today, including the dean of admissions. We will begin by addressing Ms. Connor's claims against Mr. Callaghan."

Shrinking into my seat, I listen as he shares my statement. I glance down, noticing Mateo's feet fidgeting. In a weird way, it makes me feel better to know that he's nervous. It makes me feel less alone.

Once Mr. Walcott is finished, Hunter's attorney, Ronald, begins speaking. "My client states that all of these claims against him are false. Ms. Connor has years' worth of history with my client, in which she has been very open about her mental health instability. According to my client, she confided in him, asking for help multiple times, and she even needs to be medicated."

My jaw springs open. Heat blasts down my limbs as anger bellows through me. Mateo sits up straight in his seat, and he grabs my hand, giving it a firm squeeze. I squeeze his back, and he lets me dig my nails into his skin.

Ronald goes on to claim that I'm unhinged, and everything I stated was a lie, and the entire hearing should be wiped.

Instead of avoiding Hunter, I try to make eye contact with him, needing to see how pathetic he is that he could stoop so low. My eyes burn holes into him, but he refuses to spare me a flicker of acknowledgment.

"I see," Mr. Walcott says when Ronald is finished speaking. He then picks up several papers in front of him. "Moving on, we have several witness statements, which I will read aloud."

Sitting back in my chair, I listen to the words of my loved ones on my behalf. Lynn's is first, followed by Sandy's and Edgar's. Next are Michelle's and Bree's. Mateo's is saved for last, in which he must have conveniently left out the fight from last year, or Mr. Walcott chose not to state it.

"Mr. Callaghan, based on Ms. Connor's claim and the witness statements, you are hereby expelled from the University of Connecticut on multiple counts of misconduct."

Hunter's mom gasps and breaks out into a sob, while his dad starts screaming.

Mr. Walcott turns to me. "You have the right to move further with legal action. If you decide to, know that we will comply with the authorities and let them know of our findings."

"That fucking bitch!" Hunter's dad points at me, yelling.

"Let's go." Mateo pulls me up and rushes me toward the door.

A whirlwind of shouting and crying infiltrates my ears. The administration stands up, gathering their things, while the attorney pleads with the president. Hunter's dad jumps up from his chair, throwing insults my way, and his mom tugs on his sleeve. Chaos unravels as Mateo tries to drag me out of the room.

Before I step out, the entire room moves in slow motion. I turn my head, looking behind me one last time. My gaze catches Hunter's blue eyes.

A final goodbye.

CHAPTER ONE HUNDRED TWENTY-SIX

Ellie

Mateo and I walk across campus back to my dorm once we've scrambled out of the building to avoid being stopped by Hunter or his family. My mind is still catching up with everything that just happened, but for the first time in quite possibly my entire life, I feel free. Free from Hunter. Free from my shame. Free from everything that weighs me down.

A sense of rebirth flutters all around me.

"How are you feeling?" Mateo asks.

"Like I can finally fucking breathe!" I exclaim with my arms wide open and my head tilted back, inhaling the warm spring air.

He laughs. "It's about damn time."

"I can't believe he tried to say I made everything up because I was mentally unfit! What a dick!"

"I knew he'd try to pull something out of his ass to gain some leverage on you." Mateo takes one of my hands in his. "But it's finally over now. Let's go do something fun. You need a break from all this shit."

"I desperately could use a break from thinking about everything. We'll process all that another day. Right now, I just want to breathe."

"Breathe away," he says, taking a nice, deep inhale.

We keep walking, getting closer to my dorm hall. "So what should we do?" I ask. "We have the whole day ahead of us."

"We have our whole lives ahead of us. We can do anything we want."

"I think you mean lifetimes," I correct him, and he smiles.

"That's right."

"Only in our next lifetime can we agree to less drama?"

"Oh, baby, we won't be dealing with any petty shit in our next life. We'll be motherfucking royalty."

"And we'll live in France!"

"Obviously."

"French royalty. I like the sound of that."

Mateo moves to loop his hand around my waist, and he kisses the top of my head as we continue moving forward. We pass by the Great Lawn with luscious grass and large oak trees. A familiar tree, different from all the rest, with a narrow trunk and low-hanging leaves, sparks my memory of when I first met Mateo.

"If you think about it, if one of us chose not to sit under that tree…" I point to the one I'm talking about. "We might've never met."

"Nah," Mateo protests. "We would've met somehow or another. We were always meant to."

My lips curl upward. "You know, I had a dream about us under that tree once."

He arches an eyebrow. "Did I get you wanting to explore the outdoors a little more? Because I'm so down with that."

"No, perv." I give him a playful shoulder check. "We were just hanging out."

"God, your dreams sound boring. You should hang out in mine. We're a lot less clothed."

"Well, we were also talking."

"Naked?"

I giggle. "No."

His thumb connects with where my shirt and pants part, and he softly grazes it over me. "What were we talking about?"

"You were trying to get me to sing."

"That sounds pretty accurate," he says. "So are you ever going to give me the privilege of hearing your voice?"

Our pace slows down as we approach my building. I stop walking and turn to look at him. "I think so," I say. "And I think you already have, just not through singing. But you've heard my voice more than I've let anyone else hear."

Mateo's brown eyes light up while he gazes at me. "I love you, Elena."

"I love you, Mateo." A breeze moves past us, clearing away any old energy and making room for a new, refreshed version of ourselves. "Let's not go upstairs yet. I feel like I have the whole world at my fingertips. Let's go somewhere."

"Okay. Like where?"

I smile when an idea hits me. "Let's go for a drive and see where the road takes us."

"Exploring life together?"

"Always by each other's side."

"Sounds good to me." Mateo takes his keys out of his pocket.

"One condition, though," I say, taking the keys from him. "I'm driving."

ELLE

ELEVEN YEARS LATER

Warm water pours out of the showerhead, dripping down my hair and body. Shutting my eyes, I let myself relax despite the buzz of nervous energy running through my veins. *Only a few more hours until showtime.* The heat calms my muscles as I continue to stand in the shower doing nothing, much longer than I probably should.

My lashes, heavy from the water, flutter open, and I begin to wash my hair.

Our bathroom isn't updated yet—another project to add to our homeowners' to-do list. But I'm not bothered by the faded-pink tiles and '90s deco lights above the rounded mirror that hangs over the sink. Mateo and I have done a lot of work on our small house over the past two years, and we're in no rush to drain the rest of our savings on a bathroom.

After living in tiny apartments, it just feels nice to finally have a space that's ours. A safe haven.

We live in New York, about twenty minutes outside of Queens, where Mateo's family is, and we've both adjusted to living in the suburbs of the city quite well. It feels like we've always belonged here. Another corner of the world to make ours.

Letting water spray down my hair and back, I rinse out the conditioner and move on to lathering up my loofah with my peony-scented soap. The doorknob clicks open, and I hear Mateo entering.

"How's your mom?" I ask him.

"Feeling much better now that she's with Cadence."

I smile, thinking about our daughter. Well, technically, our soon-to-be daughter. We're in the process of adopting her, which feels like forever, but we've considered her our daughter ever since we began fostering her last year.

Mateo is the lead clinical supervisor at a foster agency, a population with which he loves working. There are a lot of difficult aspects to his job, but the part that makes it worthwhile for him is when he gets to connect with the kids and help families build a healthy bond.

When Cadence came into foster care at only a few days old, Mateo immediately rushed home to tell me about her. After a bunch of paperwork and a lot of red tape, she eventually came home to us and became a part of our family. And in a couple of short months, she'll officially be Cadence Alina Rivera.

I'm not exaggerating when I say Mateo is the world's greatest father. It's like he was born for this role. Watching him and Cadence together makes me fall more and more in love with him. He protects her fiercely while letting her explore and become her own little person. There's nothing more beautiful in this world than witnessing the two of them together.

"Oh no. I forgot to pack her elephant blanket!" I say, washing the soap off my arms.

"Got it covered. My mom had a backup one at her place."

"She's amazing."

And she truly is. Her health has been rocky over the years, and there have been more trips to the hospital, but having a new grandchild seemed to add a jolt of energy inside her. She helps babysit twice a week, but this week there's an extra day added because of what's going on tonight.

The shower curtain pushes open, and a naked Mateo gives me a sexy grin before stepping in next to me.

"Mommy and Daddy's time to play," he says before gripping my ass and pulling me closer.

I chuckle. "I can't! I'm going to be late," I protest, even though my hands are running over his now wet body. He's gotten more tattoos over the years, and he now has a close-shaved beard and shorter hair.

"You have plenty of time."

"I need to leave in two hours."

"Perfect amount of time to get ready *and* for me to get you off." Mateo reaches behind me and takes the showerhead down. "I want you nice and relaxed for tonight."

"Hmm. That does sound like it could be beneficial." I back myself up against the tiled wall.

"Extremely."

I widen my stance, and Mateo lowers the showerhead so it's lined up with my clit. He takes his other hand and twists my nipple, causing me to shudder.

"Have I told you how proud I am of you?" he asks, continuing to work me.

"Not since you entered the bathroom." I smirk, moving my hips along with the water.

"So fucking proud." He leans down to give me a kiss. "And after tonight, I'm going to keep showing you how proud I am of you until you can't fucking walk and you're passed out on our bed."

"Promise?" I moan.

"Swear." He pushes the showerhead closer, and I gasp. "I love you, baby," he says.

"I love you."

"Now be good for me and let me make you come so you can be calm for later."

Nodding, I shut my eyes and open my legs even more, letting him take over.

"Fifteen minutes." My manager, Nora, pokes her head into my dressing room.

"Thank you." I smile at her through the mirror, and she tells me to let her know if I need anything before she exits.

Pinning my loose curls back on either side of my head, I take deep breaths to ease my jitters.

The day has finally come.

I've been working toward this for months—hell, my entire lifetime.

It's the first day of my tour. A small tour around the tristate area, but a tour nonetheless. Twelve shows are sold out. Everyone in the audience is there to see *me*.

Never in my wildest dreams did I think all of life's turbulence would land me here: a motivational speaker.

My degree in philosophy bounced me around to a couple of different nonprofits until I found one I really clicked with. It was a nonprofit that offered support to teenage girls who had experienced dating violence. I worked there for some time, and then three years ago, I got an idea for a book. It morphed into a self-help type of book with copies of my journal entries over time to show how much I evolved and to show how much change *is* possible with the right type of environment and support. After self-publishing, it gained some traction and landed in the hands of a well-known publisher. Together, we revamped it and rolled it out as multiple self-help books focused on relationships and healing. From there, I started going on interviews and doing podcasts. Apparently, there are a lot of people in the world who resonate with my story and like what I have to say.

So my team came together, and we created a small tour where I speak with people and help them along their own journeys. After months of creating a script, performance lessons, and rehearsals, tonight is my night to shine.

"Damn." I spot Mateo in the mirror. Leaning against the doorframe, his eyes roam all over my body as if he didn't just see me naked a few hours ago. "My wife is hot."

A rush of butterflies dances around my stomach, even after all these years. I don't think I'll ever get tired of him claiming me as his wife. As soon as he felt settled in his full-time job, he got down on one knee and proposed. I got married at the ripe age of twenty-three with barely any money to my name but zero doubts in my mind. We worked long, tiresome hours just to afford rent and food, but somehow we pulled through and got to where we are today.

Mateo sidles up next to me, and we look at each other's reflections, him with a black polo and dark pants, and me with high heels, jeans, and a coral T-shirt that says, "Empowered Women Empower Women," in bold, black lettering. Nora wanted me to wear something fancier, but I opted for authenticity over what people think I should be wearing.

"Imagine if someone told us back when we first met that this is where we'd end up," Mateo says.

"I would've never believed them," I respond.

"Me neither."

He leans in, wrapping his hand around my waist. "Our life is beautiful, Elle."

"It sure is." Grinning, I place my head against his body.

We continue to stare at our reflections. A memory from years ago, back in college, jumps into my head. Knowing how desperately that girl from the past needed to be seen and heard makes me even more excited for tonight, because I know there will be a version of her sitting in the audience. No longer ashamed of who I used to be, I honor that part of myself and share her with others in hopes it'll offer someone the extra strength they need to get by.

"You need anything before you go out there?" Mateo asks.

"Nope. I'm going to take a few minutes to myself and then hang out in the wings."

"All right, I'll see you out there." Mateo kisses the top of my head. "Break a leg."

"Thanks, love."

Watching him leave, I twirl the necklace I'm wearing around my finger. The green crystal still shines as brightly as ever. He gives me a wink before closing the door. A sense of gratitude flourishes inside my heart. To think of who we used to be and where we are today is incredible. We're each other's biggest support system. We grow stronger as individuals as we stand by one another's side.

Taking a refreshing breath to ground myself, I then check my phone before going on stage.

MOM

I'm proud of you! Can't wait to hear all about it afterward

ME

thanks Mom, I love you

MOM

I love you too, sweetheart

Smiling, I place my phone down. We've had our constant ups and downs over the years, and while that's still something I struggle with, our relationship is getting better. So are my boundaries. She's currently in rehab. Otherwise, I know she would've been here tonight. I'm fine with it, though. I know I have a few familiar faces waiting for me in the front of the house.

After doing the quickest meditation to get as Zen as possible, I say a thank you to Dad, hoping he hears my whispers through the universe. Then, I'm up on my feet.

Pacing backstage, I peek through the curtain to see the audience. My pulse picks up when I notice it's packed. Every single person here is waiting to hear what I have to say. *That's* something I never saw coming.

"Are you ready?" Nora comes up from behind me, wearing a headset.

Am I ready? I have no fucking idea, but I'm going to do it anyway.

"Yeah." I smile.

"We're a go for the intro," Nora speaks into the headset. The lights of the theater go down, and the overhead announcement comes on.

I've rehearsed this about a billion times, but I still try to run through my lines and blocking in the thirty seconds I have.

My heart pounds. I feel like I'm at the top of a roller coaster, slowly inching my way closer to the edge.

"Without any further introduction, here is Elle Rivera."

Stepping out onto the stage, I free-fall.

Applause and cheering make me beam. My cheeks hurt from grinning.

As I make my way to center stage, under the spotlight, I'm quick to scan the audience. I can't see many people, but I know there's a special stranger out there who needs to hear my message. My story of brokenness turned into a tale of strength and empowerment. The greatest love story of not only me and Mateo, but me and myself.

My eyes drop down to the front row. Bree is taking a video on her phone, Stephanie and Michelle are calling my name, and Mateo is biting down on his fist, holding back his happy tears.

I shoot him a wink, and he chuckles.

Then I step up to the microphone.

Take a deep breath.

And I use my voice.

A Look At: Anything Rae Touches

A GOLDEN BAY BEACH ROMANCE

They met on the worst day of their lives. One kiss. One goodbye. And then, ten years of silence.

Now fresh out of rehab and desperate for a clean slate, Rae lands in Golden Bay Beach with two goals: stay sober and outrun the ghosts of her past. With a sharp tongue and a guarded heart, she's not looking for connection—especially not with *him*.

But fate has other plans.

Miles, with his golden-boy charm and relentless optimism, is the last person Rae expects to see again. He's everything she's not—and everything she doesn't want to need. But when their paths collide, old wounds resurface, and long-buried feelings begin to stir.

As they navigate the wreckage of their pasts, Miles is determined to show Rae that maybe—just maybe—they were always meant to find each other again. But healing isn't linear, and love doesn't come easy.

Can Rae risk her heart for a second chance, or will she choose the pain she knows over the future she deserves?

AVAILABLE NOW

A GOLDEN DAY BEACH ROMANCE

Afterword & Acknowledgments

First and foremost, if you have made it this far, thank you!

Scarred Hearts has been a wild ride for me, which started almost seven years ago. Or, really, an entire lifetime. Ellie is a dramatized younger me, and this novel first began as my private journal entries. It morphed into me putting those experiences into a fictional world while I was bored during the pandemic. When the world reopened, I had two books' worth of Ellie and Mateo's story. I'd never written a book before nor had an intention of becoming an author, but the more I tapped into the character Ellie, the more I remembered how ashamed and distraught I used to feel, and I began wondering how many "Ellies" are out there experiencing something similar. I decided to publish in hopes that the story would resonate with someone and, hopefully, they would feel validated and know they are not alone.

Ellie and Mateo's story was first self-published as a duet: *Blurry Messes* and *Messy Love*. Those two books opened the floodgates for me, and I've been writing books ever since, falling in love with each unique story my mind creates.

The past few years, I reflected on the duet and decided to combine it to be one thick book, strengthening the characters and storyline.

Thank you to everyone who helped me along the different versions of this novel: my beta readers, sensitivity readers, developmental editor, and PR teams. And thank you to my lovely PA, Corinne. You have helped me so much, and I'm so appreciative to be working together.

Thank you to Ellie, Kayla, and the whole Love N. Books Press team! I'm beyond grateful that you wanted to publish this story and for your ongoing support behind the scenes.

Lastly, thank you to my "Mateo." All the words in this novel are still not enough to convey how much I love you. The moment we met, I felt like I knew you from another lifetime, and I'm now fully convinced that we've traveled through all of time and space together. You changed me for the better. I would've never had the courage to write what was in my heart if you weren't by my side.

My parting words to anyone who's still reading: Your story doesn't end here. Keep healing, growing, and loving.

Until the next book,

Holly

Holly is a new adult & contemporary romance author. Lover of all things steamy and angsty— you're sure to get your fill of these in her books! She also likes to have an underlying message in all of her stories, bringing awareness to bigger issues that are close to her heart.

When she's not reading or writing, you can find her eating an unhealthy amount of bread and cheese, rocking out to emo music, or cherishing wife/mom life

www.hollycasteauthor.com

www.ingramcontent.com/pod-product-compliance
Lightning Source LLC
La Vergne TN
LVHW040213110826
845146LV00005B/1273

9798895676578